# THREE WOMEN

# ANNE McCAFFREY

**TOR**

A TOM DOHERTY ASSOCIATES BOOK
NEW YORK

This is a work of fiction. All the characters and events portrayed in this book are fictitious, and any resemblance to real people or events is purely coincidental.

THREE WOMEN

Copyright © 1990 by Anne McCaffrey

Reprinted by arrangement with Underwood-Miller

A Tor Book
Published by Tom Doherty Associates, Inc.
49 West 24th Street
New York, N.Y. 10010

Tor® is a registered trademark of Tom Doherty Associates, Inc.

Cover art by Eric Peterson

ISBN: 0-812-50587-5

First Tor edition: January 1992

Printed in the United States of America

0  9  8  7  6  5  4  3  2  1

# CONTENTS

# RING
## OF FEAR

**1**

I DON'T KNOW whether it was the June sun's heat or sheer blinding fury that made me sweat so. Sweat, not the "glow" that ladies are said to show. Like that heavy-handed, brass-haired, buck-toothed society *lady* on her flashy, hammerheaded black horse in the line in front of me, cool in her crisp yellow linen jacket and clinging pipe-stem hopsacking pants. (She must be either bowlegged or calfless.) Could the Sunbury County Fair judges see that the black gelding's gaits jarred every bone in her body? (How did she keep that smile on her face?) My mare, Phi Bete, had floated so easily through her paces in this Ladies' Hack Class, and simply hadn't been noticed. Not with the black pulling stunt after stunt, being "expertly" controlled! (He hadn't half the wits Phi Bete had.)

It wasn't fair, I thought bitterly, the sweat dripping down my nose now, my hands swimming in the heavy leather gloves. The white shirt was plastered to my back, because the wool jacket, suitable for winter riding, was the only one *I* had. (I'd seen Mrs. Flashy-Black in three other outfits so far, and the show was only two days old.) She didn't need the prize money, and she was taking hay from my horses and peanut butter from me.

Hay bills and Skippy notwithstanding, I had to admit that she was a good rider . . . even if Phi Bete was the better horse. Certainly as far as confirmation went. Would the judges consider that in the final totaling of points? And Phi Bete's gaits were as smooth as glass.

The judges signaled all contestants into the center now, and the black cavorted, snorting. Oh, the judges wandered about, appropriately frowning in deep thought. They nodded sagely to each other. I wondered which was the local

1

banker . . . there always is one asked to officiate if he knows which end of a horse wears the bridle. The thin man with the sad eyes looked like a coroner, but it was the character in the puttees (and he wasn't ancient enough to have worn them in the First World War, so *where* did he find them?) who was to be reckoned with. The thin man made a show of considering his verdict, but he finally nodded, and then, of course, the third one — his silvery hair denoted senility, not sense — made the decision unanimous.

Couldn't they see that the red ribbon of second was going to clash with the sorrel coat of Phi Bete? Not that she cared. But I did. The blue ribbon looked well against the black's cheek, but the $150 prize money would have looked better in my bank account than second's $75. Ho-hum, pull the girths in again, Nialla Dunn. You've been done in. I grimaced, unappreciative of my own feeble attempts to improve my humor. I managed to turn the grimace into a grin, for the thin judge was congratulating me. It's very difficult to give the proper picture of good sportsmanship when you're biting your lower lip to keep from crying. The rangy gray got the yellow, and the bay had the green fluttering from his bridle.

We winners trotted smartly around, and there was great applause for Mrs. Flashy-Black. I couldn't help myself. I kept trying to see Dad's face somewhere in the crowd as I circled. It was silly. But sometimes, I'd see someone whose shoulders also tilted to the right, or the set of a head of curly gray hair, or his way of standing, hipshot, or a chin jutting in the same belligerent way. But Dad was dead . . . horribly dead . . . would I always see the pitchfork swaying, its tines soaked red?

Suddenly a face did stand out from that anonymous mass of mouths and bodiless heads. A short man, in a brilliant blue-ribbon blue body shirt, standing up on the empty end of the bleachers, his legs spread slightly, hands in the slot pockets of his tight black breeches. I'd an impression of delighted amazement, blue eyes, black wavy hair under the white-grass Stetson . . . and his delight was for my mare! Then we had trotted past.

I was wondering why that one face should catch my attention . . . probably the color of his shirt . . . when Phi Bete snorted, tossed her head back at me, and slid to an abrupt halt. I shook my head and realized that the single file had slowed to go out the gate. Phi Bete had her mind on her work, at least. Mrs. Flashy-Black's friends were complimenting her in droves, crowding around her as she held her horse's bridle, smiling toothily for her picture. Someone, as Phi Bete and I trotted smartly past her, was stupid enough to approach the black's rear. Naturally he lashed out, and there were shrieks and oaths and scurryings.

I had to rein in, but I didn't dismount. It was eminently satisfying to look *down* on the lesser breeds, gawking and ah-ing at the exhibits and us Olympian creatures. I could feel safe and superior on Phi Bete's back.

It was disconcerting enough to have to go back to the stifling reality of G-Barn. I should have expected inferior quarters, of course. An unknown with a two-horse string, a battered trailer and station wagon, no money to grease the fairground steward's favor for better accommodations. And yet I'd been given D-Barn at first. Did *d* really sound that much like *g*?

G-Barn faced south, its T-shape backed against an old granary's concrete shell. It caught the sun all day long, with nary a tree to shade the sprawling roof. In the back stalls where I'd place Phi Bete and Orfeo—we had the barn to ourselves— the darkness deceived you into thinking cool.

There were still empty stalls in D-Barn. But once Budnell, the steward, had seen Orfeo, and worse, remembered him . . . Orfeo couldn't help that. For one thing, I'd made such a point of unloading him so that his docility would be noted. Noted, yes, but not trusted. I'd even heard the mutter of astonishment when the noble beast followed me, leadless, his long full tail switching placidly at the June flies, toward the reassigned G-Barn. I'd heard all the tales of Orfeo's viciousness from the Poiriers, and from astounded hostlers all the way from Florida. The jaws that bit, the claws that snatched—that description applied to the old abused Juggernaut, not to my mild, loving Orfeo.

Well, we were alone, and the small practice ring was right handy to G-Barn. I off-saddled Phi Bete. She was barely damp, though she'd worked hard in that ring for her lousy red. Gratefully I removed my jacket and hard top hat; both were soaked. I pulled my shirt from my pants to let the wind loosen the wet hold on my back. I slipped the bit from Phi Bete's mouth but left the bridle on, the measly red rayon flapping at her cheek. The bit tinkled pleasantly as I walked her. By the time she was dry, I was somewhat drier myself. Phi Bete drank deeply at the trough, slobbering affectionately down my breeches. Oh, well, I'd have to sponge them anyway before this afternoon, and she was a sweet-tempered dear.

*All* our horses were good-tempered, because Dad didn't . . . I stopped that line of thinking, but it was hard. Hard not to be able to remember him, even after a full year, without bitter, bitter hurt. One day I'd find his murderer. One day I'd make him pay for that death . . . and the little death in me. Marchmount's smug face . . . No, not that memory, too!

"C'mon, useless nuisance," I said to Phi Bete, and her ears wigwagged at the sound of her name. I jammed the red ribbon in my pocket and gathered up the tack. It was a hot walk in the full sun all the way to the front of the barn, so I led the sorrel to the rear door. As I passed my ancient station wagon, Eurydice sprang alert, all twenty-pounds of raccoon-marked Maine cat, subsiding with mock incivility. He'd known who was approaching all along.

"Catch any good meeces?" I asked him.

He told me all about his morning's labors with well-chosen phrases and flirts of his eloquent tail. Then he jumped out of the back of the car on some errand of his own. Nialla Dunn was back in charge. Dice was off duty.

I was looking over my shoulder, amused by the undulating curve of his insolent tail, so that I didn't even see the man until I crashed into him. Phi Bete's hooves clattered on the cobbled floor, because she was startled, too. Orfeo's head came up, ears forward, and he farruped softly before resuming his private meditation.

"I beg your pardon, miss. I was just admiring the transformation in old Juggernaut."

"His name is Orfeo!" I said with more annoyance than

was necessary, and then I saw who it was. The short, dapper man from the stands. And he stood head-even with mine.

"And you were his Eurydice?" he asked with a grin of such charisma that I stared at him a moment.

"Nnnnooo." I slipped past him as fast as I could. He looked the type who pinches. Short men do take odd ways of manifesting masculinity, most of them offensive.

By leading Phi Bete past, I forced him up against the box stall. I saw his apprehensive backward glance at Orfeo.

"He certainly has changed, ma'am," Shorty said with commendable aplomb. "Last time I saw him, he was trying to sample a hostler's hand for breakfast."

"There's nothing hungry about him now." I slipped the bridle from Phi Bete and held sugar to her lips, reassured by the velvet caress as she daintily nibbled her reward. She had plenty of good timothy hay. At least I got my money's worth on that. You had to be careful about hay. Dad used to bring his with him whenever he did the track circuit.

"Seeing's believing, but I had to see it once I'd heard he was here," the man admitted, lifting his hat to scratch his wavy hair, the picture of bucolic incredulity.

He grinned again, his blue eyes twinkling in the friendliest way. "Can I spot you a cup of coffee and learn the secret of your success?"

I was suddenly very conscious of my sticky clothes, of my bra showing through the damp shirt, my sweat-dried hair, although he wasn't looking at me *that* way. He was looking me square in the eye, and we *were* eye-level, though the stall separated us. I wondered if he found such parity as unusual as I did.

"You should have taken the blue, you know," he went on, "but Bess Tomlinson has to win her quota to hold her head up at the country club. And with her string, if she doesn't get 'em early in the season, she's out of luck!"

"Which of the judges is she married to?"

He laughed at my cynicism, and it was a real laugh, not one of those social whinnies. He laughed with his head back, his mouth wide open, so I could see he had very few fillings in his even white teeth. If I'd been buying a pony stud, he'd've been a bargain.

"I don't think she sleeps with the Colonel," he said, his eyes gleaming with pure malice for a moment, "but . . . "

I couldn't go on standing there in Phi Bete's stall, but I really didn't know what to do. I certainly didn't want to get chummy with any circuit riders. Dad had warned me against that long, long ago. You made your appearances in the show ring, not the bars and the fancy night spots near the shows. And you took care of your stock, not your libido, or you became fair game for everyone. I couldn't suppress my involuntary shudder, and Eager Blue-eyes caught it.

"You haven't had any trouble with the Colonel, have you?"

"No. No." But I would glance toward Orfeo, for I knew that the Colonel had been in the steward's office when I checked in. And it was apparent that the Colonel had been judging shows long enough on the East Coast to recognize that "fence-swallowing, man-eating" black gelding Juggernaut.

"Give you any trouble with Jug—Orfeo? Sorry, habit."

I'm not the kind to jump to conclusions and point fingers, but I was so sure that the steward had originally told me D-Barn. Then he'd come out of his office in an awful hurry to correct me, and the Colonel had been in there.

"Yes," Shorty said sourly, "he did." Then he jerked his head toward Orfeo's cocked hip. "He *is* reformed?"

I took my opportunity, left Phi Bete's stall, and slipped into Orfeo's, crooning to him as I always did, though, Lord knows, he was smart enough to know that I was the only person who ever entered his stall.

Orfeo arched his neck and ducked his head around, his deep eyes warm and loving, his scarred lips pouting out with old lesions nothing would heal. My hand, running up the gleaming black hide, slid across old spur and whip scars, up the curved muscular neck that gelding hadn't thinned. I always felt smaller—and bigger—next to Orfeo. Small because he was a giant of a beast, like those in medieval days who could carry a knight in full armor all day; and big because I, Nialla Donnel . . . Dunn (one day I'd stumble over that name aloud) had tamed the volcanic fury of the poor benighted creature.

Then Shorty was in the stall beside me, and his voice seemed to have dropped two full notes, to a deep affectionate murmur. He ran his hand fearlessly along Orfeo's rump. It was a short-fingered, wide-palmed hand, a strong hand; the fingers were well-shaped, the tips sensitive, the nails pared neatly; an odd hand for a man like him, somehow, a contradiction. A man like him? I scarcely knew him. But I wanted to.

He talked to horses the right way. I stood at Orfeo's head now, and he nudged me out of the way to look back, with idle curiosity, at this brave mortal. Orfeo farruped softly . . . acknowledgment? welcome? approval? And then, displaying massive equine indifference, Orfeo bent his head to lip up hay. As he began to munch, his eyelids drooped contemplatively.

"Yes, ma'am, I never would have believed it," Shorty said, the grin on his lips echoed by his eyes.

Dad always said to trust a man whose eyes smile when he does. I suddenly realized that I hadn't seen any smiling men for a long time. Shorty backed respectfully out of the stall and looked at me expectantly through the upper bars.

"Coffee? Or, in this weather, iced coffee? Coke? Right out in public, too!" The grin was crooked, and the smile didn't light up his eyes as much. In fact, Shorty suddenly looked as wary as I felt. "God in heaven, what's this?" he cried, jumping back and glancing down.

Dice announced his presence with a loud satisfied "br-row" and leaped effortlessly to Orfeo's rump.

"Don't tell me," the visitor begged. "That . . . that mountain lion . . . is Eurydice, which, I might add, is a misnomer," for he glared at me, aware of the cat's maleness.

I giggled. I couldn't help it. He was funny. He was even . . . cute. Though that's a word I hate, and highly inappropriate for this short blue-eyed man who could *not* be described by a single convenient adjective.

Now he cocked his head to one side as if he, in turn, found me cute . . . and funny. Then I realized something else. He spoke in various twists of accent, but he *knew* what good speech was, and he had pronounced "Eurydice" correctly. Not

"Ur-dis" or "Err-you-dice," but "You-ri-*di*-che" in the proper Italianate fashion. The man was a contradiction. An intelligent, educated circuit rider?

"Who led whom out of hell? and which hell?" he asked then in a complete change of tone. He had jammed his fists against the elegant hand-stitched belt that held up those body-clinging peg-legged breeches on his no-hipped frame. I noticed something else about him at that level and quickly looked up, anywhere but at the telltale and extraordinary bulge.

A sudden flood of curses, horse squealings and thudding hooves, the slap of a crop against flesh, and a chorus of suggestions distracted us both. Someone was using the practice ring outside G-Barn. Phi Bete snorted a soft question, her ears working back and forth, but old Orfeo took no notice of the ruckus.

"Hey," exclaimed Shorty, his eyes glinting oddly, "can *anyone* manage him now? I mean, I know I could step inside the stall, but you were at his head . . . "

"He's perfectly manageable and trustworthy."

That grin again, disarming me of my caustic mood.

"Even with me?"

"Yes!"

Without seeming to move with any speed, he was in the stall, telling Dice to get down, untying the halter rope, pressing against Orfeo's chest to angle him into the far corner of the box so he could lead him out head first.

"No, you watch," he told me, pointing to the window at the end of the cross-aisle. "It'll be more fun to solo." There was no answering twinkle of amusement in his eyes. He was dead serious and strangely grim.

Stepping jauntily, he led my gelding up the deserted corridor between the hot and empty stalls. As soon as he turned to the main door, I hurried to a dust-fogged window and rubbed a clear space. He must have recognized the voices, or the brand of curses, for the anger made the voices anonymous. But there was the putteed Colonel and Mrs. Flashy-Black up on an equally raw-boned hunter who was clearly dissatisfied with the exercise. Two other men leaned over the railings of the small ring, and an assorted number of fringe observers lounged in the shade of the oaks by F-Barn. Then, even the hunter seemed to freeze.

The Colonel, sensing that he'd a rival for everyone's attention, cut off his directions and turned. The shock on his face quickly turned to tight-lipped anger. With puttees, how else would he reflect anger manfully? Mrs. Flashy-Black's mouth dropped open, and she let up the savage hold on the hunter's mouth. He took the opportunity to pull her half down his neck as he got the bit between his teeth. Of course, he wasn't upset by Orfeo's leisurely stroll to the watering trough, but every other witness was.

No one said a word as Shorty stood while Orfeo snuffed over the water. The horse wasn't thirsty, but he stood, politely, switching at importunate flies with his beautiful full tail. You always knew what Orfeo was thinking by his tail movements. They were as good a gauge of his temper as Dice's. Shorty looked nonchalantly around and then shrugged a "you-can-lead-a-horse-to-water-but . . . " and led Orfeo back in.

I could hear him suppressing his laughter all the way down the aisle. In fact, I wonder he didn't choke on it, for his eyes were tearing when he slapped Orfeo's rump affectionately as the gelding plodded back into his stall and resumed his chewing.

"Could you see their faces?" He was doubled up with an excess of mirth. "I'll stand you a drink . . . Scotch, whiskey, champagne. Worth it. Worth it! Shut Colonel Melvin T. Kingsley up in the middle of Lecture Number Forty-two. And you did it . . . " Then he stopped, stared at me. "I don't know your name. I haven't picked up a program yet."

"Nialla . . . Nialla Dunn." I'd almost goofed.

"Nialla? A good tinker name for a horse-handling witch! C'mon."

He clipped one warm, strong-fingered hand under my elbow, and I have never been more conscious of a square inch of my own flesh than that moment. As if he sensed my reaction, he removed his hand and gave me a quick searching look.

"It's a cup of coffee, Miss Dunn, not an invitation to rape!" And though he spoke flippantly, there was a hint of defensiveness in his tone. "The name's Rafe Clery . . . a fellow mick and horse-coper." Evidently he could turn on the charisma—as he did now—instantly, and the flicker of deeper emotions was gone.

"*I* am thirsty," I admitted, covering my embarrassment by nodding toward the gelding. Then I walked quickly up the aisle so he wouldn't have an excuse to touch me again.

The main refreshment tent was scarcely conducive to any refreshment, for the canvas trapped the heat, and the heat trapped the people there in a sort of trance as they waited for watery franks, dry sandwiches, lukewarm beer, tepid soft drinks, and limp potato chips. Two cubes of ice withered in my container of coffee as I looked at them. The cardboard was hot in my hand. Before I could get it to my lips, Rafe had it out of my hand and was grinning at a harried counter girl. In moments it was back, crammed to the brim with ice. A turkey sandwich appeared before me, too, and because I was starving for something besides peanut butter, I didn't mention that he'd suggested only a beverage.

"You're brave, you know."

"Hmmm?" The dry bread threatened to go down the wrong way.

"Brave to go the circuit alone. I assume you've just the two horses." He looked somewhere over my head, concentrating. "That means, to make ends meet," and suddenly that impish grin lurked in his eyes as he glanced at the turkey hanging out the end of the sandwich. He meant to pun "meet" for "meat" " . . . You've got to place in all the competitions here, in every show, including the Jump Trophy at the Garden."

I nearly choked. He reached across the table and casually thudded me between the shoulderblades with such expertise that the bread descended.

"I left the crystal ball at home, but you'd be a fool not to try, with a leaper like Jug—ooops, sorry—Orfeo. If I had one who could clear anything in sight, and I've seen him go over pickup trucks, I'd try for the big prize, too. Only I haven't got an Orfeo, and I'd be three kinds of a fool to pit any horse in my stable against him. He does still jump like he used to, doesn't he? Or did that go?"

My eyes were watering from coughing and choking, and I still couldn't speak.

"Take a couple of deep breaths," he suggested amiably.

I did. "Thank you."

"Don't mention it. Well?"

"He'll jump anything." And my voice was patchy. He handed me the coffee, and obediently I took a big swallow. The icy stuff was soothing. "You know, he's awful fast, too."

Rafe grinned sardonically. "I don't think anyone ever bothered to find out. It was usually a question of staying up and holding back rather than urging him on." He paused, his eyes unfocusing. "Though there's a look of speed about him, for all that bulk." Then he looked at me, blinked, and seemed to be measuring me against some unknown gauge. "No! *You* haven't breezed him, have you?" And his eyes dropped to my hands. He covered his face with mock dismay. "Goddamn, you know," and he was suddenly eager, "with his speed and stamina, he'd make one helluva steeplechaser." He caught my look and began to shake his head emphatically. "Miss Dunn, you'd never get a man up on him, not with his reputation."

"He's changed!"

Rafe Clery gave a derisive guffaw. "I have to admit to witnessing a minor modern miracle, but his angelic disposition is going to take a lot of publicity before anyone else believes it. How did you do it?"

"I didn't. Dice did."

"That mountain lion?" He gave me a sideways look of pure skepticism. "Ah, c'mon. No feline could mesmerize that black piece of unadulterated—sorry—could make him as gentle as a kitten. Even one sired by that lion of yours."

"Dice helped, but it was a case of winning his trust."

Rafe snorted. "What'd you do? Hold his hoof to keep the ghosties away?"

That was far too close, but the ghosties had been mine, not Orfeo's. "You should have seen his mouth. And his poor tongue. I don't know what they crammed into his jaw, but it must have been something from an inquisition. And his head..." I shuddered.

"I don't need the details. I've got a vivid imagination,

and remember, I knew him 'when.' Oh, don't glare at me, Miss Dunn. And don't demand why I didn't try to stop it. I did. But you ought to know that the ASPCA has only just started slapping wrists for 'blistering' walking horses. Some of these small-town judges don't know when a horse has been 'treated.' " His face was grim and bleak. He had altered again. I'd hate to get on the wrong side of this small man. As abruptly, he was grinning again. "It restores my faith in humanity to see a good horse in good hands. Where'd you acquire the mare? She's well bred."

"Phi Bete's been mine since she was foaled."

"Yes, I thought she looked misused."

"Fer chrissake, boss, I been looking all over . . . " said a voice behind me. Rafe Clery looked up, his face assuming the mask of another role.

"And now you've found me."

"Hell's bells . . . ah, excuse me, ma'am," and a look from his employer made the lanky rawboned hostler touch his hat in the almost lost gesture of courtesy.

"Miss Dunn, my head stableman, Jerry MacCrate."

"How do, miss. Bartells is at the steward's office, boss. I know you wanted to see him. I've been combing the barns for you. And you know who I saw in G-Barn?"

"Yes, a black jumper named Orfeo."

"Huh? That wasn't . . . " The man was so astonished that I almost laughed outright.

"That was Orfeo, Jerry, no matter whom he resembles." Rafe Clery's voice was not raised one decibel, but his order was received, loud and clear. He rose, shoving silver under his sandwich plate. "You're jumping the mare in Ladies' Hunter Hack?"

I nodded.

"And Orfeo tomorrow?" He grinned a little absently. "See you."

Then he strode away, the lanky groom following, obscuring his employer's slighter figure. I watched as the two went across the paper-carton-littered grass toward the steward's field office. No, Rafe Clery didn't swagger or strut. He walked in quick strides, and Jerry MacCrate matched his step to his boss's.

"You finished, miss?"

I was startled from my observations by a party of five hot and tired people, hopefully glancing at my table. Hastily I rose. If they hadn't come, I'd've scooped up the unfinished sandwich from my host's plate. Dice could have had turkey for dinner. He must be tired of mice. But I couldn't with ten eyes watching me, so I regretfully departed. If you're hungry, you shouldn't be so proud, I told myself. But I was. And that's all there is to it.

 2

I DIDN'T MEAN TO, but I kept thinking about Mr. Rafe (Ralph? Surely not Rafael?) Clery for the rest of the morning, even while I was grooming and saddling Phi Bete for the afternoon class. I didn't see him in the stands when I went to observe some of the other classes. My jaundice toward the judges changed, for I had to admit that they weren't all that wrong in their other decisions. In fact, they chose my candidates with the one exception of the Roman-nosed bay in the Five-Gaited Class. It was obvious, to me, that the horse had been treated. He was sweating heavily as he lifted his legs with pain-driven height, and his nostrils flared redly. The other mounts were sweating, too, and they were working for those precise artificial gaits, but if you know the signs, you can tell the difference. And his rider? I don't trust people who can keep a smile plastered on their faces round after round, but then, I don't trust people who doctor horses.

I remember Dad the day Mrs. du Maurier (no relation to the writers) acquired the five-gaited bay gelding who had won out over her own entry in the Garden back in the early fifties. I was too young then to realize that people would deliberately mistreat an animal to win anything as paltry as a blue ribbon. (I was *very* young, for I didn't know that money and prestige accompanied the blue ribbons and silver trophies. I honestly thought the horses wanted to win. The ones Daddy trained always looked so pleased with themselves in the winner's circles.)

Mrs. du Maurier had had a house full of guests, but Dad marched up to the house and insisted that she come down to the paddock where he'd put the "pore crayture." I was weeping, I remember, for the salt of my tears is indelibly linked with that memory. Children see past sham, and I knew she was as shocked as Daddy by the bay's condition.

"My God," she'd said in her funny rough voice, so distracting to issue from a soft feminine face, "I'd no idea when I bought him, Russell. I've known Charlie Hackett for years."

"May be, ma'am, but what'll I do with this poor wreck, for I'm telling you flat out, I'll not show him for you, fire me if you wish, but I'll ride no crippled, blistered crayture."

Regardless of her elegant dress, Mrs. du Maurier bent to lift the trembling, scarred fetlocks, traced the black calluses of recent lacerations plainly visible.

"Jesus God!" she muttered, her face grim. "Ease the poor brute if you can, Russell. Turn him out to pasture. I'll take this up with Hackett. Don't you just know I will. And I'll get my price back, too."

"You'll not be giving the bay back to him, ma'am?"

Mrs. du Maurier gave father one of her famous stares.

"I should think you'd know me well enough not to have to ask, Russell." And she'd gone back to her party.

I used to ride the bay later on, but never in a show. By then he no longer snapped his feet high because they hurt but because he felt good.

Mrs. du Maurier had been no such enigma as Rafe Clery, and yet there was some subtle resemblance of manners between them. A certain assurance, knowledgeability, an almost detached confidence of bearing and charm. And Mrs. du Maurier had smiled a lot with her eyes, too. She'd been a good, kind woman who had her share of troubles (even I knew about Mr. du Maurier's drinking and wenching, although I don't think he'd ever have forced an employee's daughter . . . I *mustn't* think about that), and Agnes du Maurier had kept her humor and her perspective despite all the sordid incidents, and come out on top. Yes, she and Rafe Clery were curiously alike . . . and there was no reason to it. Because he certainly wasn't a Kentuckian, though there was a hint of softened vowels, the occasional slurred consonant.

I wondered what accounted for those odd touches of bitterness, the shadow of defensiveness about that young man. Only . . . he wasn't all that young. Now that I thought back, I realized there'd been lines around his eyes. His face was so mobile, they didn't show often. Korea? No, that would make him almost forty. Somehow I didn't want Rafe Clery to be forty. Then I chided myself sternly. He *looked* boyish, but that was partly due to his size . . . or lack of it. I'm wrong there, too. *He* didn't give the slightest impression of a lack of anything.

I heard the PA system calling the Ladies' Hunter Hack, and hastily led Phi Bete out of the sweltering stable. My other shirt was soaked already, and I didn't have the jacket on yet. Oh, Lord, what a way to make a living.

I could mount Phi Bete without a block, though she's a good sixteen hands in the shoulder. The saddle seemed a little loose as I settled myself and flicked out the off-side stirrup iron. Everything was stretching in this heat. Well, I'd let the saddle "sit" on our way to the ring, and then tighten the girth just before the class filed in.

There was almost a full brigade of entries for this class. It's always popular, because the jumps are nominal, and anyone with any pretention to the title of equestrienne must have one hunter hack. There were, however, some damned improbable beasts, all shined up and mounted by all types, from teen-agers to beefy matrons. Under the regulation hard-top hat, they were indistinguishable except for body size.

Some of the horses were fidgeting, backing, filing, tails switching, ears back as the entries crowded the gate. I kept Phi Bete back. I couldn't risk her being kicked. Nevertheless, even though I was wary, the sudden fracas boiled over on us before I could react. Phi Bete reared to avoid the flashing hooves of a short-coupled chestnut who bucked and kicked out of the melee, rider hanging gamely about its neck. Phi Bete reared again, somehow backing up on her hind legs and swerving to the right. I could feel the saddle go, and on reflex action, got my feet free of the stirrups. As the mare came down, I let her momentum throw me onto her neck as the saddle slid to one side, to be trampled by the other horses surging around.

I sat there on Phi Bete's bare back, looking numbly at the saddle. I could see that the girth had parted. And heavy-duty girth webbing doesn't snap like that. It can't. Not when you don't have a spare. The class was moving in now. And all I could do was stare at the useless saddle in the dust.

A gnarled old man, someone's hostler, picked the saddle up and shuffled over to where I sat, motionless, on the mare's warm back.

"Someone cut the girth, looks like to me," the old man said, squinting up at me. He hadn't a tooth in his head, and his lips were stained by tobacco juice. His eyes had the milky quality of the incipient cataract, although his gaze was steady and concerned. "Got a spare? Won't take a minute to fix."

I swallowed and shook my head.

"Here, buckle this one on, Pete." And Rafe Clery had appeared out of nowhere, a girth dangling from his hand. He grinned up at me. "I told them to hold the class a few minutes until you're ready," he said, taking Phi Bete's bridle and holding up a hand to me to dismount.

Obediently I slid down her velvet shoulder, and found myself holding her reins. Rafe was busy unbuckling the one side of the girth as Pete's stubby fingers moved deliberately on the other.

"Someone's real scared of the competition you provide, Miss Dunn," Rafe said in a sociable voice as he fitted the two parts of the girth together. The cut was obvious. Only a few threads had held the saddle on. "One, maybe two fences, and the first two are both stone, and you'd've bit the dust, badly."

I swallowed, unable to meet his eyes, and I was scared. Who in this small New York State Fair could possibly know who I was? I hadn't seen a familiar name on the list of exhibitors. Who had followed me from the West Coast? I'd hidden for almost a whole year since Dad's murder.

"C'mon. I'll give you a leg up. Mustn't keep the class waiting in that hot sun. Hard on the horses." He grinned, but his eyes didn't. He looked worried. He'd shoved the deliberately severed girth under one arm as he laced his fingers for my knee.

I started to protest, but his effortless assist nearly sent me over Phi Bete's back. He shoved my leg forward, checking the girth buckles carefully.

"Borrowed this from Bess Tomlinson. Wear it to victory." Then he stepped back, and I didn't even have time to thank either him or old Pete. I turned to wave, but Rafe was walking away, and Pete had turned his head to expectorate in the dust.

Such a close shave with disaster is no way to start a class. I managed to smile at the judges, who nodded solemnly as the gates swung shut behind me.

We were to jump the course in order of registration number. That put me at the end of a long, long line, but Phi Bete would stand quietly for hours. She would, but the others wouldn't, for the nervousness of the riders was being communicated to their mounts, and there was much nonsense. The officials ought to have put a limit on this class. Or made a novice classification or something. The judges didn't like the prospect of a long dusty session either. And issued additional instructions. Referees were summoned for each of the ten jumps. Eight faults disqualified. Refusal disqualified.

Well, that would pare the field down, I thought, and it did, although many of the riders as well as spectators muttered over the decision. By the time Phi Bete had faultlessly completed the round, there were only seven contenders, and much disgruntled argumentation beyond the gate, where the disqualified assembled to protest judicial prejudice.

The jumps were raised, and it was announced that this second round would finish the class. "Since we are running behind schedule, ladies and gentlemen, and it's unseasonably warm for June, I'm sure you understand."

Not very professional, certainly, but I was in sympathy with the decision. The wool of my jacket was steaming me, and it smelled. I longed to wipe the hatband. The damn hard-top would swim off my head at the next jump.

As I looked at the altered obstacles, I could see that the added second layer of the artificial brush was a bilious show-window green, guaranteed to frighten a nervous jumper. Had they done that on purpose? And the second course of bricks were now a poisonous fluorescent red. My competition consisted of two old tried and true hunters, totally bored with the affair; two obvious novices, riders and horses, kids all; and two high-strung beauties, including the horse Mrs. Tomlinson had been schooling and cursing. Only she wasn't up. Presumably it was her daughter. Maybe even her granddaughter, said I uncharitably to myself, but I had to consider every angle of my competition. And if she, the older Mrs. Tomlinson, did sleep with the Colonel, did his favor extend to the second and third generations? Somehow the detachment I could achieve on the bleachers failed me in the ring. I could not be objective.

I was now next to last to jump. Three faults disqualified one entry; a complete refusal to go over that horrid brush struck out another. One good round to Mrs. Tomlinson's offspring, who did tend to rush her fences, making both horse and rider appear more awkward than necessary. One fault; a fault and a refusal. Then my turn. Phi Bete was contemptuous of the course, flicking her tail in that annoying way of hers, as if brushing off her passage. There was a murmur of amusement for this trait by the end of our round, but no faults against her nimble feet. And a good public image.

The last contestant was one of the old tried-and-trues, but a slow round, as if the horse considered every step before taking it. In fact, I was unconsciously tense, helping the old dear over every jump.

So that left four in the running. The damned judges made us show gaits. Tomlinson's entry proved fractious, and the rider a poor horsewoman, so unless local sentiment prevailed, Phi Bete had taken the blue.

She had. The Colonel attached the ribbon with a wary eye toward her heels, as if he expected her to have acquired bad habits from her stable mate. It was the other way around, but why explain?

"What's this about your girth being deliberately sabotaged, Miss … ah …?"

"Dunn," I supplied my name. "Sorry to delay the class."

He harumphed, frowning, as if my answer were the wrong one. I smiled sweetly and kneed Phi Bete out of line to take my duty circuit. The announcer, hard up for material to fill in pauses, came out with some garble about my having overcome a bad start due to a faulty girth and triumphed in the good ol' Amurrican fashion. "Give the little lady a big hand, folks!" Irritating man, with a nasal twang that would get on your nerves even if you didn't have to listen to it amplified, whine, wow, and all.

Well, the applause didn't mean anything. It got heavier when old tried-and-true took his circuit with the red fluttering from his headstall. I took no satisfaction that Mrs. Tomlinson's progeny was third. Especially when she appeared out of the crowd, a wide grin on her freckled face, just as I dismounted. (Somehow I hadn't put freckles in my unkind mental image of her.)

"Damned good ride, Miss Dunn. Sorry about that girth business. Rafe showed it to me, and it was deliberately cut. No question of it." She held out a thin, sinewy hand with many charm bracelets jangling on her wrist. She was Mrs. Tailored-Lady and elegant-in-silk, but her smile was genuine, and so was her concern. "We've all been suffering from vandalism this year. I hope none of them think of glue in the saddles."

"It was kind of you to be generous with your tack . . ."

"Nonsense. Sportsmanship and all that best-man crap. Hate to see your mare scratched for lack of a girth. You made me ride up to the mark, I can tell you."

She meant it, too. And drifted away before I could repeat my expression of gratitude. Her offspring — and it was a girl her very image, freckles, and braced teeth showing in a rather sullen pout — came on the scene.

Mrs. Tomlinson stepped right up to her, her thin fingers spreading to pat the curved neck of the hunter. Whatever she said was soft enough to reach only the girl's ears, but the pout was erased instantly, and the eyes reflected the reprimand.

"Good riding, Susan," her mother said in a medium-loud voice. "Majority will crowd his fences when he's excited. And that godawful brush jump. However, a third for your first adult competition is ver-ree good. Very good."

Damnation. It was awful to be under any obligation, but she was so damned likable, teeth, bangles, freckles, and all.

And whatever was I going to do about another girth, I wondered as I led Phi Bete away. The money for the blue ribbon would just about buy grain and grazing privileges until the next show . . . if I could find a bargain on peanut butter and learned to fish better.

"Could only have been 'vandalism.'" Hmmm. Orfeo had to win, because that meant entrance money for the Taunton Do. And I ought not really to count on it until he'd won, only I was so sure he had to win . . .

"Hi there, Miss Dunn." And when I turned, who was catching up with me but Rafe Clery, a whole girth dangling from his arm. "Sorry to miss the class, but it was a cinch you'd win. Ooops, sorry about that."

I couldn't help but giggle, which seemed to delight him for some reason. I thought men hated girls who giggled.

"Sorry about the word choice. Happens all the time to me. Anyway, here's the damned girth. Pete ran it up on the machine at the harness shop. He's buddies with the owner."

"But I don't have any mon—"

"Pete chaws Red Devil. He did the work." And Rafe Clery dared me to protest as he handed me the mended girth. "A piece of chamois or sheepskin, and that'll prevent rubbing until you can get the kind of replacement you prefer."

First Mrs. Flashy-Black Tomlinson, and now him. I turned away, ostensibly to remove the blue ribbon for his approval.

"That calls for celebration. I'll pick you up at seven. I know a place that serves the best steaks this side of the Hudson." And he was off, calling to some acquaintance in the crowd before I could open my mouth.

I couldn't stand there gaping, girth in my hand, my horse in need of walking. And he had said "steak."

I reached the barn before I realized he wouldn't know where to pick me up, unless he automatically assumed the motel where most of the exhibitors from out of town stayed.

"No," I told Phi Bete, "that one will know to meet me at G-Barn. Just as he knew I didn't have a spare girth, or money enough for a replacement or anything. How does it happen he knows so much about me, and I don't know a damn thing about him?" Phi Bete butted me sympathetically, and we walked on.

When we reached the cross-aisle, there was a tiny breeze feeling its way in the back door. Dice spoke from Orfeo's stall, jumping neatly to the black's rump to continue his report. He yawned halfway through, but his tone was casual, so nothing had happened.

The heat of the stable was suddenly oppressive. I let myself out of the box, stripping off the heavy jacket as I did. My toes felt baked in the boots, and I reeked of horse and human sweat. And he asked me to dinner! For a steak! Maybe there'd be enough for a doggie bag, and Dice could join the feast? I'd go for Dice's sake.

I couldn't stand my clothes, but I took time to gather up all the gear. Maybe it had been vandalism. I'd been out of the barn. There'd been opportunity for malicious mischief. God knows, the papers reported enough bizarre incidents. So, I'd lock the small tack box in the trailer, and at least prevent the saddle and bridles from being sabotaged.

It was while I was bathing from a horse bucket in the cramped quarters of a john stall in the ladies' that I realized that I'd have to forgo that steak. Whoever had slit the girth had done it too expertly—just enough to hold through mounting, but not enough to endure the strain of jumping. My horses might be next. I couldn't leave them with just Dice on guard.

A woman came stomping into the "comfort" station. There were only two booths, and the other toilet was over-flowing.

"Can you hurry up in there?"

"I'm not feeling well," I said in a weak voice, and dunked my face cloth suggestively in the pail.

"Oh, dear." And the woman started out, then hesitated. "D'you want me to call the first-aid people?"

"No." I felt awfully guilty. People are always being *nice* when you don't need it. "The sun, I think. I'm sorry."

"Oh, that's all right," was the polite rejoinder, and the outer door banged to.

I hurried though my sponging then, and although the atmosphere in the ladies' was only slightly cooler than G-Barn,

*I* knew I was clean. My one luxury was the remnants of a bottle of good cologne, and I used it, for its morale-building value, so that, clean, sweet-smelling, in a cool shift and sandals, I could even face the loss of that evening's steak. I'd do my errands and then have my own "dinner."

This being a farm community, chewing tobacco was obtainable, though I got a quick stare when I asked for it at the cigarette counter. I could also afford it. Then I had to find Pete. I looked first among the groups of handlers awaiting the end of the class that had followed the jumpers. Great Percherons and Clydesdales were cavorting, causing the earth to vibrate with their thunder-hoofed maneuvers. I paused to watch respectfully, for their magnificence is part of the passing scene.

"That's what I said," repeated a man to my right, a little in front of me. "Juggernaut's here, and the girl who took the blue in Hunter Hacks is going to ride him for the trophy."

His companion cursed. "Thought he went to the knackers when he savaged a man a year or so back."

"Go down to G-Barn. He's there, large as life."

"No use spending entrance money in the Trophy Class, then." The second man was plainly disgruntled.

"He's changed. Colonel Kingsley said Clery walked him to water like he was leading a lamb."

"Clery? That bastard here? Looking for stock?"

"Going to sell him that tendon-sprung gray of yours?"

"Hah?"

The gray was evidently a source of much amusement to the first man and some irritation to the second.

"If he's looking, he's usually selling. And he trains a good jumper. He inherited his old man's eyes for horseflesh, even if he didn't get much else."

"Got a good eye for mares, too." There was a poke in the ribs and a leer.

"Oh?" The other man perked up. "Who's he after now? Thought he'd covered about anything that'd stand still for it."

"That sorrel hunter's rider. Saw him, feeding her in the snack tent. He's after a two-legged ride, if I know Clery."

"She looked like a nice kid, too. Heard her girth was cut clean through."

I ducked away for fear they might turn. I refused to credit the conversation.

I finally had to ask in the barns for Pete.

"Look in D-Barn, miss," I was told by the spokesman for the loungers in A.

"Does he work for one of the showers?"

"Only long enough to get a chow stake. But he's good with horses. Reliable, too, miss. Doesn't drink. Just chews."

Hat brims were fingered, a courtesy that gave me a needed lift. But did they think I was looking for a handler? Or a guard?

"Gossip doesn't fly among circuit riders, Nialla," Dad had told me four years ago when I first started riding shows in California. "It oozes through the ground like electricity, and suddenly everyone at a show knows what's happened. Watch your step and you'll be all right. Don't slight anyone. The guy in the patched pants may own the whole string. Pay your debts on time, and don't ever neglect your horses. Gives you a bad name that you'll never shake."

The two men hadn't implied that Clery's name was bad. On the contrary, they'd said he knew horses so well they were willing to buy his rejects. A two-legged ride, huh? And I looked like a nice girl? If they but knew!

D-Barn was cool, shaded as it was by the Exhibition Hall from the worst of the afternoon sun, and surrounded by big oaks. What is there about New York that cherishes enormous, long-lived oaks?

"Is Pete about?"

"Try the loft," one man said over his shoulder.

"Wait a minute, miss. I'll call him," said another, pushing himself off the red-and-black-striped tack box. "Nice ride in Hunter Hack, miss. Too bad about that girth."

He climbed the ladder, craning his neck, which corded when he yelled for Pete. I could see the old man's head fill the opening.

"Lady to see you."

Well, I had acquired that distinction, at least.

"Me?" Old Pete scurried down the ladder so fast he nearly trod on the other man's hands.

"I wanted to thank you for sewing the girth, Pete."

He wasn't much taller than I, and he seemed reluctant to take the tobacco. He kept not looking directly at me.

"Don't want nothing, miss. Shame to put you off just before a class. Heard you won anyway. Fine mare, that sorrel."

"Please, Pete," I whispered, and shoved the tobacco at him. I ended up stuffing it in his torn shift pocket. "Haying's dusty work," I said in a louder voice.

He snorted, and turned his head a fraction to one side, spitting neatly and accurately into a coffee-can spittoon, scratching at his ribs with a stained hand.

"Finished haying."

"Ah, would you know where Mrs. Tomlinson is stabling?" I asked him, holding up the girth I'd been lent.

"Here," Pete replied, taking the girth from me and tossing it to the man on the tack box. He seized it neatly out of the air and touched his cap at me, grinning.

"Is Mrs. Tomlinson around? I'd like to tell her . . ."

"No need, miss. I'll tell her."

I suppose it was naïve of me to think that she'd be back in the barn in that silk dress when she had all these men on tap.

"I'm ready now, ma'am," Pete said abruptly.

"Ready?"

"Yep. Said I'd keep an eye on your stock tonight. I can sleep one place's good as another."

I stared at him, puzzled. He jerked his head at me to go out and gestured with one hand. He was so emphatic that I nodded again at the other men and went out with him.

"Mr. Clery asked could I keep on eye on G-Barn," he said in a low voice as soon as we were in the yard. "Said he was taking you to feed. You need it. Don't know as I want to fool with that black bastard . . . begging your pardon . . . " And he reached for the brim of a nonexistent hat. "Girths cut'n all that. Don't like it. Said I could sleep there same as anywhere else. G-Barn's warm." He gave me a toothless grin. "Old bones like warmth."

"Pete, I can't . . . "

Pete had been someone once, for a trace of an old dignity returned with the offended stare he gave me.

"A little girl like you can turn old Jug into a lamb like I seen him this afternoon, and ride like she was hide of her horse—I can sleep in G-Barn same's anywhere else. And I got something to chaw, too."

And that was to be the end of the matter, according to the Word of Pete. We continued in silence to G-Barn.

"Known Mr. Clery long?" I heard myself asking.

"Yep."

A man of few words. But he had called him "Mr. Clery." Horsemen are as quick as any other subsociety to attach disrespectful nicknames to people they don't like or respect.

The afternoon's crowd was noticeably thinning, though the grounds officially stayed open until nine, when the exhibits in the hall closed. It was slightly cooler, I thought, as we turned into the barn. Pete's broken-seamed army-surplus boots made a shuffling sound on the cobbles. My sandals slip-slopped. A hoof stamped. The flies were bad, but I didn't like aerosol bombs around hay that horses would eat or wood that they might gnaw.

"Don't believe half what you hear about Mr. Clery," Pete said unexpectedly, and frowned at me a moment before he looked away.

Much as I'd've liked to have him qualify that commendation, I knew I would lower myself in Pete's estimation if I did.

We'd reached the lone occupants of G-Barn now. Pete peered rheumily at Orfeo as if to satisfy some doubt.

"He's watered and grained and the straw's down for both," I told Pete. "The mare may need watering later, but I left a pail for Orfeo."

"No sweat," Pete said on the end of a grunt, and swung open the box stall directly opposite my horses. "Be comfortable here." He took the pitchfork and had a cube of straw on the end of it before I could blink. "Be just fine." He separated the straw with neat, quick strokes.

"Here's a blanket." I handed him the clean one.

"Why, that's right thoughtful, ma'am, but I can see it's been washed recent, and I ain't. Won't need . . ."

As we heard the click of leather heels on the cobbles, we

both stood still. But the quick steps were easily identified by Pete, who grunted and went on making his straw bed.

Just as Rafe Clery reached us, Dice appeared. The cat startled Pete so much that he had hefted the pitchfork defensively.

"That's only Dice, your associate guardian, Pete," Rafe said, so amused by Pete's reaction to the cat that he, mercifully, did not see mine to the pitchfork's menacing angle. (I had thought I'd got over that reflex.) "Has that cat caught any foreign cars lately?"

"That's no cat," Pete said in a liquid growl. "That's a cougar. Ain't seen one of them since I crossed the Rockies."

"Back in fifty-two, wasn't that, Pete?" Rafe suggested, all too helpfully. "Eighteen-fifty-two, I mean." And winked broadly at me.

As Pete wheezed appreciatively, I gathered this must be an old joke between them. Then the old man noticed that Dice was eyeing him warily. He leaned forward on the pitchfork.

"Well, puss? Do I pass?"

Dice "spoke" in his throat and wandered over to me, to strop my legs and weave over to Rafe Clery, stepping on the high shine of the man's polished Weejuns with the utter disregard only a cat of high degree can assume.

"No scratching, cat, or it's back to the nether regions on the tip of my toe," Rafe abjured him sternly.

"Gawd!" Pete cried out in surprise, as Dice was suddenly on top of the bars surrounding Orfeo's stall. "You don't need *me* here." He sounded disgusted as he fussed with his straw.

Rafe took my arm, bidding him a cheerful good night, and led me out.

"That was very kind of you—"

"Horseshit, I'm never kind," he interrupted me. "Knew damned well you'd probably chicken out if you got to thinking about that slit girth. Besides"—and he grinned at me—"Pete can sleep in G-Barn same's anywhere else." His mimicry of the old man was perfect. I giggled. "You've got the goddamnedest giggle I ever heard."

I covered my mouth, but he dragged my hand down, his eyes looking directly into mine.

"I like it. Say, any idea who did slice that cinch?"

I shook my head. He favored me with another long look, somewhat quizzical.

"I could understand if it'd been Orfeo. But the mare?"

"A mistake?" I suggested.

He made a derisive noise. "The only two horses in that barn? The only saddle in the barn?" He stared out over the grounds, where some people were still wandering around. "Hoods? Out to make trouble for funsies?" He shrugged. "Bess Tomlinson doesn't play that kind of game. Well, here's the chariot."

He gestured toward the gun-metal-gray Austin-Healey of old but good vintage, and striding forward, opened the door with a flourish of his free hand. I giggled, because he didn't seem the type to make courtly motions.

"God, I like that silly chuckle of yours."

"So I giggle for my goodies, do I?"

I meant to be facetious, but he straightened, a cold austere light in his eyes. He turned his chin slightly, his eyes never leaving mine, as if he were a boxer, guarding a glass jaw.

"You've been warned about Rafael Clery?"

His sudden change startled me almost as much as his pronunciation of his first name. Then I coped with the fact that he knew there was something I shouldn't hear, or something he didn't want me to hear.

"Forewarned is forearmed," I said as gaily as I could, giving him my best grin. No matter what I'd overheard about "two-legged rides," I wanted to erase that awful wariness about Rafe Clery. I stepped into the car, and he closed the door.

He got in on his side and had his hand on the key when he paused. From the depths of the glove compartment he flicked out a gauzy yellow scarf. It harmonized with the background of my shift.

"Keep your hair in place. This is a breezy riding car."

He laid it across my hand, when I realized that there had been a nest of scarves in that compartment, all colors, as well as the round ends of lipstick cases and the edge of a compact. The leather seat whispered as he suddenly turned, while I sat stiffly, the filmy scarf dangling from my hand.

"Look, Nialla Dunn," he said in a very hard voice, his eyes narrowed. "I'm not out for a fast lay. I can get willing cooperation anytime I need it without having to spend time and effort broaching the Iron Maiden. Believe it or not, occasionally I can look at a woman without wondering how she strips. My invitation to dinner comes from what there is left of camaraderie in my evil heart, and was prompted solely by admiration for a horsewoman. Now, accept me on those terms, such as they are, as I have accepted you, or just get out and we'll part friendly."

"I'm sorry. I didn't mean to be . . ."

"Hostile?"

I started to protest, although how I'd explain myself, I didn't know.

"Yes, hostile." His voice was neutral.

"I didn't know who you were when you came into G-Barn."

"There're half a dozen people who would enjoy giving you all the vital statistics on Rafael Clery."

"But . . ."

He was wound up and wouldn't stop. "I *have* been in jail. I *have* gambled heavily. I have a violent temper, and I'm a dirty infighter. Small guys have to be. No reach. And I confess to having done any number of wild, unpredictable, irresponsible stunts. However, most of those incidents, colorful though they were, took place in my misspent youth." And he gave me a terribly bitter smile. "I'm thirty-eight. I've been married and divorced two times. Did they remember that? But I'm a horse-man. I'm sure I was allowed one virtue. I'm a good capable trainer and a decent rider. And this invitation to dinner is just that, and no more, between two horsemen."

"A two-legged ride"—that phrase was determined to haunt me. I always thought it was tunes you couldn't forget.

"Now," he was saying, "shall we enjoy a good dinner and some professional rapping, or will you return to a solitary peanut-butter-and-jelly sandwich in the sanctum of your trailer?"

Had he looked in my trailer, too?

"I've run out of peanut butter," I said as contritely as I could, and spoiled the apology by giggling.

Only it was the smartest thing I could have done, because all the tension disappeared from his face, and his eyes began to thaw. He flicked the scarf from my hand, twitched it over my head, and tied it deftly under my chin. I caught his hand, a little astonished at myself even as I did it. His fingers closed lightly on mine. "And," I went on truthfully, "the only person who said anything to me about you was Pete. *He* said I wasn't to believe the half I heard about Mr. Clery."

The smile reached the blue eyes first. The expressive lips curved up.

"Of course," I added flippantly, "he didn't say which half."

He chuckled and eased the car into first to pass the pedestrians also using the exhibitors' gate. A rather seedy man leaned against the fencepost on my side, the golf cap shading eyes that flicked over everyone. It was the golf cap that did it, and I suddenly felt everything falling in on me, as if the bottom of the Austin had dropped out onto the cattle grating.

Caps Galvano! There couldn't be two men in the world with the same S-shaped posture, chicken-breasted, adenoidal, raven-nosed, with wisps of stringy black hair, like a bird's crest, darting out all ways under the cap edge. It couldn't be Caps Galvano! That man wore nothing but houndstooth checks — pants, jacket, socks, tie, and always the same filthy spotted snagged-thread cap.

This man had on a gray cap. It couldn't be Galvano. How could he know where I was? How could he have followed me? And why? During my cross-country flight, I'd figured out what an absolute fool I'd been to listen to his whining assurances that he could help me clear my father's name. Yet it had seemed logical at the time: Caps Galvano knew everyone at the racetracks. He also knew just how straight Dad was, because Dad had shown him the door when he'd come around the house with a deal. Hindsight had shown me how very foolish I'd been, but at the time, Caps Galvano had been the only person to show an active interest in helping me prove to the police that Dad couldn't've been involved in anything shady.

And if Caps had had to have money to gather that evidence, well, after what the police had been suggesting, I'd've hired the Devil himself to vindicate my father's reputation. So another sucker was born, and I had given Caps every cent I had in my checking account. Dad's assets were frozen (as they say), pending probate and the investigation. So when Caps had come to me for more money, hinting that he was on to something very hot, it hadn't seemed the least bit wrong for me to approach Louis Marchmount. He had plenty of money. He was Dad's employer. He should be just as interested in clearing his employee's name as I was.

Louis Marchmount—racehorse owner, bon vivant, yacht captain, dressed by Cardin, received by society, fleeced by a series of voluptuous blondes who seemed to spring from the same mold. Louis Marchmount, whose lavish promises to my father had never materialized; Louis Marchmount, who had been perfectly willing to lend me any amount of money my heart desired, if . . . *if I "submitted" to Louis Marchmount, rapist.*

With an effort, I controlled myself. I couldn't have seen Caps Galvano. And the man had looked directly at me as we passed and hadn't registered any sign of recognition. Ergo, he couldn't be Caps Galvano. Besides which, Galvano was undoubtedly still on the West Coast, running despicable errands for Louis Marchmount. And Louis Marchmount had all he'd wanted of me, and from me. He'd done the worst. That hideous old man, his artificially tanned skin mocking the healthy young bodies that had wanted mine, so staunchly virgin. But it was Marchmount's bony frame that had covered mine, once he had punished himself enough to raise the man in him. I'd never forget his awful imprecations and the curses he'd used, blaming me for his impotency, screaming directions as he forced me to assist at my own rape.

"Too cool?" another voice inquired in the here and now.

I must have shuddered.

"No. Just one of those convulsive shakes you get."

He had to keep his eyes on the road, but he was so unusually sensitive . . . had he somehow been aware of my painful reflections? Oh, I hoped not. Surely I'd be allowed to enjoy his company for one evening. Because he *was* good company. Four-legged friends have limited conversational topics.

He took me to a quiet steak house, not, as I'd first feared, to the posh place across from the big motel complex on the highway. The restaurant was back from the county road, set among pines, where detached tourist cabins were unobtrusively, if unimaginatively, settled. The food turned out to be good, even if the decor was modern mother-in-law, down to the heavy crockery and the checkered plastic tablecloths.

Local high-school students, hired for this show weekend, served with enthusiasm, if not efficiency. Rafe ignored the waiter's suggestion of a cocktail, though I'd somehow thought he was a drinker. Maybe he still had trouble getting service? No, besides the lines on his face, he had much too much easy assurance to be mistaken for a callow youth, of any age.

"Rare, medium, or destroyed?" Rafe asked. "Remember, I did promise steak."

"Medium, please."

"The minestrone here is first-rate."

That suited me. I could go without lunch with such a full dinner in me.

"Tell Brown that Mr. Clery is here and doesn't want the tough steaks he's been saving for his wayward cousin."

The boy looked startled but grinned as he hurried off.

We got such astonishingly good service, judging by what the other tables didn't get, that Mr. Brown must know Mr. Clery very well. The fillets were definitely well aged, and tender enough to be cut with a fork. I was used to Daddy's silence at meals, but Rafe Clery liked to talk anytime. Which was fine by me. I could concentrate on the first meat I'd had in several weeks. He had a thousand and one anecdotes about circuit shows. He must know everyone. He certainly could sketch out characters, raising images in my mind that would let me identify everyone I'd be likely to meet.

By the time coffee and a very good rumcake had arrived, I realized that Rafe Clery had adroitly handed me years of experience in capsulated form. He had given me pointers about every fairground and show meet I'd be likely to enter this summer. I only hoped that I could remember the half of what he'd said when I needed it.

"I'm talking too much," he said abruptly, with a self-deprecating smile.

"I've listened to every word. So help me! You promised we'd rap professionally . . ."

"Rap, not bludgeon." And he grinned. "You need some fresh air."

The night was sweet and rich with the summer and the sun-baked woods beyond the restaurant. He took a deep, appreciative lungful, and I did too. The restaurant had been smoky.

"Did you ever have the feeling that you were smelling the same scent on the air as you did somewhere else . . . totally different?" I asked him.

"Indeed."

"Memory isn't supposed to be smell-oriented."

"Who says?"

"Well, colors are hard to remember, and smells are infinitely variable."

He held the door for me, and again I was intensely curious about him. Hold it, Nialla. He's not for you, girl.

"What does the air tonight remind you of?" he asked as he settled himself, checking the car's many dials by the dashboard light. I could see there was plenty of gas in the tank. He grinned as if he'd seen the line of my glance.

"Oh, a May night, as warm as this," I replied with as much poise as I could muster. "The night Phi Bete was born."

"Don't tell me you named a wee tiny wobble-legged filly Phi Bete? How in hell did you know she'd have brain one in her skull?"

"I'd picked the name, whatever the foal. Her dam was Smart Set, and her sire Professor D."

"Professor D? He's a West Coast stud. Doesn't Lou Marchmount still own him?"

"Yes."

"'Yes,'" he mimicked me. "Cold flat 'yes,' just like that, huh?"

"I'm sorry."

"Don't be." And that was said in as flat and cold a voice as he used in my company. "You apologized, and I'll clue you," he went on in a kinder tone; "I don't get them very often." He flashed me that grin. "I don't often deserve them, come to think of it."

When we approached the fairgrounds, I found myself in still another quandary. He probably would insist on escorting me to my "room"—only I didn't have one.

"Could you turn in at the barns?"

"Tuck your babies in bed, huh? I'll tag along, in that case."

Well, you can't win 'em all.

He pulled into the main exhibitors' parking lot and guided me over the cattle grate.

"Some enterprising locals were charging ten cents a shoe to fish 'em out of the stream or prize the heels out of the gratings," he said as we crossed it, his heels ringing. I was glad of my sandals, flat and safe.

"Shouldn't wonder. Worse than subway grates."

Pete was snoring magnificently when we reached the horses. He rolled over the next moment, looked at us, hawked, and spat deftly in the gutter. Then he turned over and fell right back to snoring again. In the cool dark barn I could barely make out the horses' bulks, but Dice, ensconced on Orfeo's rump, turned his white-accented face to us, and his eyes gleamed, blinked, and were obscured.

"Except that he doesn't chaw, do you notice a slight resemblance between watchmen?"

I giggled, but muffled it, because Pete's snoring rhythm halted and then resumed. I moved away from the sleepers, into the center of the barn's aisles, and extended my hand to Rafe.

"Thank you for a *lovely* evening," I said, hoping it didn't sound ungracious as well as stilted. "That steak was heavenly."

"The pleasure was mine," he replied automatically, taking my hand. Then he brought it to his lips, clicking his heels in stalwart Prussian style. "All mine, modom," he added in a guttural voice.

He did a precise about-face and goose-stepped down the aisle.

I stood for a long time, reviewing that departing figure, half-wishing many impossibilities, all of them involving Mr. Rafael Clery. The bubble of illusion was shattered by a raucous snore from Pete.

Well, I couldn't bed in the barn tonight. I'd never get to sleep with that cacophony. And I did have an air mattress to cushion me against the load bed of the station wagon.

 3

SOME PEOPLE DON'T REALIZE that show exhibitors have usually been up six or seven hours before the fairgrounds open or the first class has been announced.

At five-thirty I was wide-eyed and dressed. Old Pete had left his straw and gone about whatever duties earned him bread and coffee. Dice had successfully concluded a hunt, for he was cleaning his paws fastidiously, an operation that always fascinates me. (I'd save the doggie bag of steak remnants for later.) I often wondered how he kept from snagging his tongue on his claws when he laved so carefully between them.

I curried Phi Bete and grained both animals, because I planned to work Orfeo out on the development roads beyond the fairgrounds. The roads were all laid out; the level dirt surfaces were perfect for breezing a horse. There were even some oddments of old foundations for jumping. I'd inspected carefully when exercising Phi Bete the previous morning. There'd be few to observe us, and none to spook at the sight of Orfeo.

Somewhere someone had brewed coffee, and my belly rumbled hungrily at the smell. The steak dinner had primed the pump, so to speak, and I was far too hungry to be sated by another mouthful of peanut butter. Womanfully I ignored my inner rumblings and vain cravings; there couldn't be a stand open at this hour, could there?

By the time Orfeo had munched down all his grain, I had to find that coffee source. The aroma was too pervasive to have issued from a cup of instant or a fireside pot. Loop-

ing the hackamore reins over my arm, I led Orfeo and followed my nose.

One of those snack trucks you see everywhere nowadays
had drawn into the main barn parking lot. Exercise boys were
taking advantage of it, their mounts tied to the hitching rails,
heads down, hips cocked under their summer sheeting.

As always, Orfeo's massive black bulk attracted attention. This time, at least, it proved to my advantage, for when it
was apparent I wasn't tying him anywhere, way cleared magically right up to the surprised vendor. I got coffee, a Danish
fresh and still warm from its bakery oven, and a banana. A
gentle sufficiency, as Mrs. du Maurier's cook would have said.

I moved away, and the mob surged back.

"Orfeo, you extract certain perquisites I could never
obtain without you."

And to show that I loved him for his own sake, I let him
have a segment of the Danish.

When I'd finished and felt three times more alert, I
checked his girth, side to side. Examined the stirrup leathers
and the hackamore. Then I was faced with the problem of
mounting my mountain without a leg up nor a block in sight.

"Alley-oop," said a cheerful voice, and my left knee was
grabbed. Up I went, to stare down at Rafe Clery's impish grin.
Behind him loomed a rangy, deep-breasted mare; her
headstall's red and black stripes marked her as belonging to the
Tomlinson stables, or I missed my bet.

"Thought you'd be warming him up about now," Rafe
said, and was suddenly atop the tall mare, gathering in the
reins. Then he gawked at Orfeo's hackamore and pointed to it
in dumb show.

"You cannot," he said with measured incredulity, "be
serious. You do not ride that behemoth with a hackamore? On
an open road? When anything might happen?"

I didn't dignify the inane question with an answer. I
pressed my right knee, and Orfeo moved forward, his wither
twitching as it always did, some unconscious reflexive action
against years of crop and spur.

I didn't look back, and I knew the mare followed. I led
the way past G-Barn, through the narrow break in the old

cyclone fencing, clip-clopping over the cracked concrete loading apron, let Orfeo pick his way over the old railroad track until we reached the hard-packed dirt road. At my signal, he lifted into a dignified rocking canter, as slow and steady as any circus horse. We had a little stretch to go before the road ended in a mound of bulldozed raw, stony dirt. Beyond were the hard-packed but leveled streets of the embryo development.

Orfeo saw the impediment. His ears cocked forward, head lifted.

"You jump to level ground," I told him, and his ears twitched. I could feel the increase in his canter, could feel power surging through his frame. Sometimes I think that Orfeo is really alive only under a rider on a jump course. He's a born leaper, and it's my private notion that Orfeo was nothing worse than a jump-school dropout, a training-ring delinquent. He was born knowing more than any human trainer could impart to him, and because they were forcing him against his natural inclinations and talent, he contended their right to direct him. I'd never admit it to anyone but Orfeo, but I was in the saddle only to lend countenance to his presence in a competition.

Jumping Orfeo—or rather, sitting on, when Orfeo jumped—is an experience. He doesn't seem to leap. He just gets beyond the perpendicular obstacle in front of him smoothly, effortlessly. I could hear the rasping snort of the mare behind me, the plunging beat of her hooves, and then Rafe Clery was pulling her in beside the placidly cantering Orfeo. Before us stretched the inviting flat, curving roadbeds. The mare was excited, rolling her snaffle, trying to get her head away from Rafe Clery's strong, steady hands.

The mare was the same height in the shoulder as Orfeo, but she looked less substantial. Rafe grinned over at me with pure creature delight for the morning, the exercise, the prospect in sight.

He gave me a mischievous nod, which I returned, and we were off at a fast canter. The mare worked for her speed, but Orfeo seemed merely to sink and glide forward, just fast enough. I kneed Orfeo toward the slope that would lead to an old stone fence, decoratively left to separate two lots. Orfeo stepped over it—all four feet at once. Beyond was a stream bed, wide, sandy, good footing on either bank, and no harm done if you took a tumble. Down a ridge, over the wide storm gutters, up a long slope, across another ex-pasture to a gaggle of flat-topped stones, requiring neat, short hops. For someone supposedly running an unknown course, Rafe Clery was handling the fractious mare superbly. Then I remembered that he'd been touring the circuit for many years and perhaps the natural barriers I was taking were well-known landmarks to him. No matter, he rode superbly.

There was a high stone wall at the edge of the tract, a wide but empty meadow on the other side. We could go back and forth over the obstacle for height, and in one place, for breadth.

We jumped, until I noticed that the mare's approaches and landings were smoother, as if she'd decided that she could trust this rider and was letting him decide. When we finally eased up, even Orfeo had worked up a sweat. We walked them back to the little stream. Here the bulldozer had missed a few young willows and bushes. The sweat on Orfeo's neck had dried, and his breathing was easy. He pulled at the reins for water, and the mare was snorting for a taste of it.

"Oh, it's not polluted yet," Rafe said. "Runs through farmland back to forever." He released the reins, and the mare buried her nose in the clear water, slurping happily.

Orfeo drank with the dignity of an old veteran, his eyes marking his surroundings, and he quietly sucked in water. The mare finished, a long stream of saliva drooling from her muzzle. Alert, eyes up, neck arched, she gazed at some distant object, snorted, pawed, and pulled to get to the enticing grass on the far slope.

"Well, I'll tell Bess not to waste her entry money, but she will. 'Isn't sporting to withdraw,'" he drawled in a Westchester boarding-school accent. That wasn't how Mrs. Tomlinson sounded; she wasn't that artificial.

"She was jumping well for you."

"Yes, but I won't be riding her this afternoon. I'm just lick and a promise."

"A promise in return for the loan of that girth?"

"Lord love you, no." And his blue eyes twinkled. "I *took* that."

I discarded every rejoinder that occurred to me, because they would be provocative or saucy or bawdy and all wrong. Instead I gave Orfeo a signal, and he moved forward obediently.

"By the way," he said in an all too casual tone of voice, "I had a few nightcaps with some of the other exhibitors and Budnell. They are upset about that girth-slitting. A case of honor. I told them you hadn't for a moment believed it was anyone connected with the fair."

"Of course not."

"But Budnell says that there've been some funny incidents around here—oh, a missing blanket, a wallet or two stolen, bales of hay broken open for no reason, tack boxes ransacked, glue poured on a new saddle, a sheepskin cut up, and things have been lifted from the exhibitors' hall. In short, evidence of malicious mischief not directed at you or Orfeo."

I murmured politely. But Caps Galvano was here. He may not have recognized me, but he could have recognized Phi Bete. "You being alone in G-Barn would make it easier for a vandal to work," Rafe was saying.

"I never did think it could be another rider," I said. I wished he hadn't brought the subject up, because it had been such a lovely ride. He gave me a friendly wave as he turned the mare toward D-Barn. It had been such a nice morning.

By the time I had curried Orfeo to within a feather of his skin, wiping him till he shone, and was standing back to admire my handiwork, Rafe Clery was looking in on us with approval.

"It is now eight of the clock. You got a swimsuit?"

I was so surprised that I nodded.

"Get it."

"That stream is scarcely—"

"Stream?" Utter contempt for my outrageous notion. "There's that beautiful Olympic-style pool at my motel, complete with high dive for idiots, low board for cowards like me, even a water shoot, and it's all pining for some bodies to break its crystal chlorine clarity and justify its existence. Get your suit."

He grabbed my hand, outstretched in protest, and pulled me out of the stall, secured the door, whistled a call he evidently thought would bring Dice . . . and it did. He pulled a greasy bag from his pocket, and brushing hay dust from a patch of cobblestone, emptied meat scraps.

"Your salary, sir."

I was marched to the trailer, passing Pete on his way into G-Barn, and Rafe stood, glaring at me, until I found my bathing suit. We were off in the waiting Austin-Healey with a hearty "hiyo, Silver."

But he was right. There weren't any bodies in the pool, which was magnificent. He pointed officiously to a bank of louvered doors at one end of the pool. "Change!"

Unfortunately there was a full length mirror in the bathhouse, and the reflection of me in its crystal-clear surface was disheartening. My old suit was really old. In fact, it was two-piece because I'd had to cut it in half when the middle of me elongated. I'd seamed the rough edges around elastic. It had been a good suit eight years ago when Mrs. du Maurier had handed me a whole stack of clothes her younger daughter had briefly worn and discarded. The suit was mended and darned, and it covered as much as most suits these days, but candidly speaking, all it covered was bones. I didn't have much bust — a flat horsewoman's figure, boyish, with too much muscle in the arms and shoulders, hard thighs, and not too much calf. I had small ankles, yes, and my toes were well shaped from the roominess of riding boots and the exercise of sandals, but who rhapsodizes over toes?

I checked my hairline. The dye had been guaranteed insoluble in water, and the hair didn't seem to have grown much since the last coloring. Whom did I think I was fooling if Caps were here, and my saddle had been cut? The idea of teen-age hoods having funsies didn't quite answer my circumstances.

"Hey!" Rafe Clery was back.

I peered around the door, and then, disgusted with myself, flung it wide. I guess I stood there a longer time than was polite, but if I'd been a sculptor, I'd've wanted him to model for me. He was a man with a perfectly beautiful, superbly conformed body, in miniature, the most elegant example of "after" of a Body Beautiful ad, Steve Reeves with no coarse knots of muscle. Blow Rafe Clery up to six feet, and, well . . . I could sort of see why he'd attracted two wives. Why he'd *dis*tracted them could only print out "insufficient data."

Then he grinned as if he were aware of his effect on womankind and I hadn't disappointed him. At least, with my reaction to *him*. He padded across the green concrete skirting of the pool, and taking both my hands, held them out from my sides.

"You're neat, you know. Neat. Not gaudy." His expression was almost . . . proprietary? His hands slid up my arms to my shoulders.

I was close enough now to see the light dusting of black hair on his tanned arms and across the muscular plane of his chest, making a thin line down the ridge of the diaphragm muscles, disappearing into the excuse for a bikini he was wearing, which barely covered nature's compensation for his lack of stature.

There was a satisfied expression in his eyes when I jerked mine back from where propriety decreed a well-bred miss ought not to look. He looked suddenly so knowing, so smug, that he was no longer an *objet d'art*, but man, male, masculine . . .

"Neat, not gaudy, compact and . . ." His expression became avid. I'd seen that peculiar look once before. It revolted me. "... and sexy!"

I tried to wrench free, but his hands tightened, and our bare bodies touched. I struggled, remembering another bare hard body. Then I was free, staggering backward. He caught my elbow, steadying me, his eyes concerned, startled at my reaction.

"Hey, hey, gently," he murmured, his voice deepening to the tone he'd used with Orfeo. "Easy, girl."

"I'm not a mare." I thought, "Two-legged ride."

"Indeed you aren't. Last one in is a rotten egg." And he had swiveled around, launching his body flat out over the water in a long shallow dive. "Hey, it's great!" he called to me, surfacing, shaking wet hair out of his face.

I saw the scar then. With a hat on, with wavy black hair worn long, the hairless scar that went from the back of his neck up the side of his head to one temple wasn't noticeable.

I dived in, landing badly, and the contact with the water surface made my side smart as I came up.

"Tsck, tsck." He trod water, shaking his head.

I splashed him and ducked before he could retaliate. He hadn't done anything, and certainly he had released me quickly enough when he saw his attentions bothered me. And I liked him. I liked him. I liked looking at him. We began to swim about, the easy companionship of the morning's ride infecting us again.

"Hey, miss. Miss!" A stern summons floated to us. A mahogany lifeguard in trunks the same bright blue used as a decorative motif by the motel was gesturing to me. "You have to have a cap. Hair clogs the filter."

"I don't have one." Obediently I swam to the edge of the pool. Rafe's short fingers closed around my forearm and pulled me back into the water.

"Find the lady a cap, please, George."

"Sure, Mr. Clery."

Holding onto the gutter, I turned. " 'Sure, Mr. Clery.' Do you always get that response from people?"

The pleasure was wiped from his face as if he'd been douched in cold water. He regarded me with no expression at all. The water dripped from his hair, and some strands leaped up at odd angles but did not cover the heavy white keloid of that scar. The lines in his face were unrelieved by any touch of humor, and he looked weary as well as much, much older.

"Who turned you off, Nialla Dunn?"

I tried to pull myself away from him, but his arms caged me against the side of the pool. His chest pressed water against me, his legs dangled against mine, and the weightlessness of water brought our hips together.

"Here you are, Mr. Clery. It'll fit any size head, miss."

A disembodied hand thrust a white cap between us. Rafe took it, his eyes never leaving mine. Treading water, he stretched it and fitted it deftly over my head, tucking my hair up under the edges.

"Silly, actually. Your hair's sopping."

"It'll keep long hair out of the filter," George said above us, and then I could hear, above my roaring desolation, the slap of his feet moving away from us.

Rafe's body drifted against mine again.

"Who turned you off sex, Nialla Dunn?"

I wanted very much to cry. My head felt tight, my eyes smarted, and I desired more than anything else to put my head down on his shoulder. Which was a ridiculous notion.

"I'll rephrase that," he said in the deep gentle voice that was unnerving me. "Did someone turn you off sex, Nialla Dunn?"

I managed a short nod.

"Rape?"

It was almost a relief to admit it.

He began to curse softly, our bodies drifting apart from intimate contact. Only then did I realize how impersonal that contact had been. For him, at any rate. I shivered. The water was a good temperature when you were swimming, but cold, cold, when you stayed in one place.

With a rush of water, he had erupted from the pool.

"Hands up!" And his voice was light again.

I looked up, and he had extended his arms to me, crossed at the wrists. Puzzled, I obediently lifted mine, and the next thing, he had neatly extracted me from the water, twisted me around so that I was sitting on the edge. I was getting to my feet when a huge towel enveloped me and strong fingers massaged the back of my neck.

"George, would you ask Renzo to bring out two of those hearty executive breakfasts he's been touting?"

"Sure, Mr. Clery."

Only I heard an odd echo of that cheerful affirmative in my ear and realized, when I saw Rafe Clery's mischievous grin, that he'd chimed in. He gestured toward one of the double lounges at the pool terrace, scooped up a second towel, and began drying himself briskly, scattering his hair every which way, oblivious to the scar that showed so horribly. He smoothed his hair back, without even checking to be sure the scar was covered. He'd know it was, Rafe Clery would.

"Sure, Mr. Clery"—and yet I couldn't resent him. Couldn't even resent the admission that he had forced out of me. Water torture. New variety. "Who turned you off?" That was what Marchmount had done, wasn't it? He'd turned me off sex. Well?

Rafe pushed his arms into a thick toweling pullover, which, to my unsurprised notice, bore an intricate RC on the breast pocket in red embroidery floss.

"You warm enough, Nialla?" he asked courteously as he sat down on the glider.

I guess I'd been tense with anticipation of that beautiful body near mine, but he had evidently turned off that considerable sensuality of his. I might have been seated next to my father. The man was centaur, sybarite, roué . . . a chameleon. I gave up then, but he didn't know it. Nor did I.

"Yes, thank you," I replied with the same degree of courtesy. The sun was slanting in over the top of the motel now and warming me.

"'Yes, thank you,'" he mimicked. "Take off that bloody stupid cap." Only he reached over and flipped it off.

"'Sure, Mr. Clery.'" And I giggled.

"That's right. Giggle for your breakfast."

Oh, Mr. Clery, could the impossible be remotely probable? Even passing-fancy probable?

I assumed that no one else was awake and eating in that motel complex, to judge by the speed with which breakfast appeared for us by the pool. I was wagging my head from side to side with silent facetious "Sure, Mr. Clery" and "Thank you, Mr. Clery," while the waiter, Renzo, duck-toed around the pool and out of sight.

Then I tucked into that hearty executive breakfast with an appetite not a bit curbed by my six-o'clock snack. Before the first pool-monopolizing family of kids could invade the area, we had eaten, dressed, and were on our way back to the grounds.

Pete emerged from the dark shadows of G-Barn, nodded to Rafe Clery and me, and ambled off, marking his passage with neat squirts of tobacco juice. Did or did not Rafe Clery believe that glib tale of kid vandals?

"I'll be cheering in the bleachers at one, Nialla. Thanks for the company."

"Sure, Mr. Clery."

When I was safely in the barn, I let out an exasperated sigh, part tears, part frustration, but mostly anger, with myself.

By eleven I'd washed and ironed both shirts, sponged my breeches, shined my boots, brushed my hard-top, groomed both horses again, straightened my trailer and the wagon, saddle-soaped the saddle and Orfeo's bridle, locked away all unused tack, and developed a bad case of jitters.

So much depended on winning the jump prize money. I *knew* that Rafe Clery had been honest about the Tomlinson entry. But was there other strong competition that he didn't know about? And why, if not for nefarious purposes, was he making such an effort to be kindly, but scarcely avuncular, to Nialla Donnelly—Dunn.

I'd gone over every word we'd exchanged, conjured back every expression in his repertoire, felt his body against mine and absorbed the shock again, the delight that I had then suppressed. His beautiful, beautiful body—so unlike that bony hard filth that had stolen from me what I could never give again and wished so much I could still bestow. Oh, impossibility!

Marchmount punishing himself! The revulsion of his flabby thin flesh pressing against me. The pain; the sound of his hoarse, piteous exhortations, the slaps, the curses and promises, the demands for compliance. For *me*, to help *him*! Those ghastly sobs when he fell to one side of me, mouth agape, eyes closed, sunken into his head. I'd escaped him then. Gathered my clothes up, dressed hastily in the dark hallway, wanting to kill him! Wanting to die so I could forget the shame, the degradation.

And I was the girl who'd always been thrilled to see a stallion mount a mare, thrilled and stirred by his bugling, amused by the mare's coquetry and surrender. There'd been a dignity about such couplings that had been totally absent in my experience.

If that was what it was for humans, I didn't want any part of it. I'd crept away from Marchmount's so deceivingly elegant house. I'd packed as much of my belongings as I could cram into two bags. I'd've had to vacate the cottage anyway as soon as the new trainer came. The horse trailer and sedan were Dad's. The tack was his and mine, and so was Phi Bete. And the price of my virginity? Now both Donnellys had sullied reputations!

I'd considered going to some of Dad's friends south of the border. But Marchmount could find me too easily there, and so could Galvano. So I turned north, crossed the Rockies at the Donner Pass, and headed east.

The sedan died in Kansas, and I picked up the battered station wagon. I'd stayed at a farm long enough to get a Kansas driver's license and let Phi Bete rest her legs after the constant swaying of the small trailer. The farmer offered to buy her from me.

By the time I'd crossed the Mississippi, I knew I couldn't go back to the Lexington area either. Marchmount would be likely to turn up there, looking for yearlings. About then I remembered that one of Mrs. du Maurier's stockmen, whom Dad had always liked, had taken a position in Pennsylvania for a Dupont stable. The Poiriers took me in, no questions asked. I paid my own way, helping exercise and train the stock, helping Jean Poirier in the house. Jack had been very helpful in suggesting which shows would be best for me, and in February I'd turned myself, Dice, Phi Bete, and Orfeo south toward Florida and the first of the horse shows, and here I was. And where was I?

The PA system blared out the call for the Jumpers' Class. Pete appeared in the yard to give me a leg up. He made the victory sign, a toothy grin, then shuffled off, spitting.

Twelve horses were competing, most of them veterans of show rings, judging by their manner. A little fidgeting, bridle-shaking, anticipatory bad temper. They were in this for the money; $350 was a good prize for such a small fair. There were some riders I hadn't seen before, so I guessed that they had come in for this class alone. I saw the Tomlinson mare, too, Mrs. T. up, and she smiled at me. Funny how her freckles didn't show when she wore a hard-top.

The bleachers were nearly full. Well, one o'clock of a fine

June Sunday. With church over, there were no guilty consciences, and people were still pouring in.

As we filed into the ring, the announcer was twanging out all the vital statistics about horses, riders, owners, and trainers; and finally he got around to the rules of the jump course. Twelve jumps, one for each of us, I thought to myself, eyeing the angle of the nasty water gate, the course laid out in a rough figure eight. We could inspect the jumps, on foot; then we were to retire from the field, return on call, position decided by our competition number. There was a time limit for the run, with one fault for every two seconds over the limit. Lowest score determined the winner. In case of ties, there would be a shorter course run with a stricter time limit. We were dismissed to wait our turn.

I'd had a look at the jumps as they were setting them up, because I jolly well had no one to hold Orfeo. We sat in the hot sun and waited while the others had their look-see.

Just before the first contestant was called, the announcer abjured the audience to remain silent until the rider had completed the round. Anyone disobeying would be removed from the bleachers by the stewards. He meant it. There were a lot of kids in the audience, and hoody types. A sudden noise during a jump could put a nervous horse off his stride.

From where I waited with Orfeo, I couldn't see too well. But three horses racked up enough faults to be disqualified completely. Orfeo jumped as if he were on a Sunday amble in a park, completing the circuit exactly within the time limit.

As I waited for the others to go, sometimes a gasp of dismay or appreciation would indicate success or failure. I could also hear the rider of the leggy gray cursing his mount over the jumps. Mrs. Tomlinson employed a vocabulary of assorted monosyllables in praise, silence for under-performance.

The PA announced the winners of the first round and the time limit of the jump-off, over jumps 3, 5, 7, 9, 10, 11, 12. I wondered if they'd decreased the time limit so drastically to eliminate the "slow" horse, me. But then I decided that was foolish. I was being unnecessarily paranoid.

We were down to seven contestants now, three clear

rounds, and the others two faults apiece. Best score should win in this round.

I could see better this time. The rangy gray went first and fought for his head between seven and nine, which slowed him badly. He knocked off the top bar of the third in the triple-barred fence, which gave him two faults, and he picked up a time fault. Mrs. T. on her mare slid at the water gate, but it was the penultimate fence. The mare managed the final one, but knocked off the top row of bricks, and by the time she wheeled out of the ring, she was favoring her off-front leg.

Then it was my turn. The suspense was palpable as we came onto the course as the time clock began to turn. Those things make me nervous anyhow. I had him well in hand (or vice versa), and he took the first three jumps neatly. From nine on, the jumps were trickier, and his ears came forward as we swung toward the broad gate. He aimed himself squarely, flew over, and then was in position from the triple gate, which you can't rush. Just as he gathered himself for the third of that trio, a car horn blasted right beside the ring. The audience reacted with an indrawn gasp of horror, but old Orfeo soared effortlessly over, his hooves tucked up. Over the double sixes, away to the water jump, and out. Right on time. There was a spontaneous cheer for us, and as we came cantering out of the ring, people in the end seats leaned toward me to shout their congratulations and heap fury on the inconsiderate lout who had leaned on the car horn.

I? I was trembling with reaction, and I wanted very badly to get to a john. Who had touched that horn? At just that precise moment? That close to a horse at a difficult takeoff. That couldn't have been an accident. No hood, unless he was very knowledgeable about horses, could have timed that blast. But someone who knew Orfeo's reputation, knew how tense the second round could be, how dangerous that turn and jump could be, might try to spook my mount. I'd've lost the competition at the least, more likely been hurt.

But Orfeo was impervious to such distractions. There were no faults against him, and he won the blue.

Respectful admirers crowded around us, extolling my intrepid horsemanship. Someone took a photo with a big flash, but I ducked my head and, I hoped, spoiled the picture. Finally, pleading Orfeo's needs, I got away. As we passed D-Barn, Mrs. Tomlinson was deep in conversation with her trainer as he inspected the mare's off-front leg.

"Strain or pull?" I asked.

"Not to worry, Miss Dunn," Mrs. T. shouted, straightening and waving at me. "Beautiful ride. Beautiful ride. Absolutely faultless!"

That horn blowing had come from the south side of the field. She couldn't possibly have touched it off. Nor would she. She'd already had two faults before the mare went into the second round.

I was suddenly very tired. The fairground clock registered two-fifty, and while it seemed incredible that two hours had passed, I felt their passage in every muscle. Now was when I could have used that swim. And the heartening of Rafe Clery's cheerful presence. I'd looked for him again when we exited triumphant, but no short man had barged through the mob to congratulate me.

I'd fouled up that relationship, if there'd been a chance of one. He'd only wanted company for dinner last night, a companion to jump against this morning, and a little funsies with a neat not gaudy girl at breakfast.

Oh, gawd, would George think I'd spent the night with Rafe Clery? How many guests went swimming at eight o'clock in a motel, if they hadn't been badgered to it by their kids?

I dragged the saddle from Orfeo's high back and stuck it on the top rail of the little practice ring. I shrugged out of my hot coat. I would really have to get it cleaned before the next show. It was like being incased in an unaired gym locker. The hard-top had left a rim around my head, and I pulled off the ribbon, shaking out my damp hair, wishing I could also shake the elephant parade of Marchmount-Clery-Marchmount-Clery out of my mind.

Orfeo butted me with his head, and I realized he wanted a rub where the headband had sweated his forehead. I'd have to wash the shirt anyway.

Could I pick up my prize money this afternoon? Or would I have to wait until evening, when the steward tallied his accounts? The stalls were mine until tomorrow morning. I could pack up and get out this afternoon and disappear into the . . .

"Grand ride, gal." There he was, propping up the gate post, hat back on his head, figured silk scarf at the throat of the strawberry-pink body shirt. How could I have missed him in the stands? "Gave the crowd some real exhibition jumping. They loved you!" He fell in step by me.

"They loved me . . . indeed! Blew their horns to tell me so."

He scratched the side of his neck. "Well, now . . ."

"The south side of the field. If I knew . . ."

"Black Chevy country wagon, with simulated-oak panels, late model." He rattled off the description. "License number DN-1352, New York."

"Oh, thank you. I'll report it to the steward."

"Already did, and the owner was in the stands at the time. He was a bit put out that someone had used his car for such shenanigans."

Orfeo butted me with his head. I ignored him, staring at Rafe.

"That wasn't hoods or troublemakers, Rafe. I'm going to . . ."

". . . Pack up your tent like an A-rab and silently steal away? Fair doesn't close until eight," he pointed out. "You'll have to eat. And you ought to celebrate. So we will. Taking all sensible precautions for your stock. Pick you up at six. The lousy restaurants close early on Sundays in this burg."

He ducked under the rails and left.

I wasn't alone the rest of the afternoon, though the "sensible precautions" were subtle—a man soaping a saddle draped on the practice-ring bar, someone airing blankets, another fellow washing a car. Two breeders came in, offering a good price for Phi Bete, talking horse with me unaffectedly for almost half an hour. Some kids, impressed by Orfeo's size, came wandering in (they were genuine, I think); they asked all kinds of things that self-conscious horse-struck kids ask. Pete wandered over to congratulate me in an inarticulate manner, muttering imprecations about the horn-blowing. But he also inspected the barn, peering into every stall and up in the loft. I fretted about not being able to *leave*. That was silly, when I thought on it later, because at least at the fair there were many people close by — protection. On the road, by myself, in an old car with a slightly shaky trailer, I'd be so vulnerable. But I had to collect the prize money first. So I might as well have one last good dinner in the pleasurable company of Shorty Clery.

I passed time by inspecting the station wagon and trailer, and moving them from the rear of G-Barn to the shade by the ring. They'd be in clear view of people at F- and E-barns. I washed out my shirt and did eenie-meenie over my three dresses. The black linen looked more sophisticated, so there wasn't any real choice.

Then all of a sudden it was six. The moment I heard the crisp staccato sound of heels on the cobbles, my pulses began to hammer and my cheeks flushed with more than heat. Rafe was talking to someone, his words clear, the answers muffled. But it could only be Pete with him, and it was. He had a white Chicken Delight sack in his hand, and he was grinning. But how could he manage fried chicken without teeth? Then I saw Rafe.

He was a stranger. The white silk turtleneck emphasized his tan, the elegant dark red pongee jacket had been built for him, and the gray pants flared in swinging bells over the darker gray leather boots. I'd seen him in a different outfit every time we'd met this weekend. I wanted to hide, so I held my head up.

"Evening, Nialla. Heard you won't sell the mare for any price," he said, eyes dancing.

Dice smelled the chicken and began to make up to Pete, who'd settled himself on an upturned pail.

"When I've finished, cat, when I've finished," Pete said, and as Rafe guided me out, I saw Dice obediently sitting down to wait.

Rafe chuckled. "Between that damned lion and Orfeo's reputation, Pete's redundant. No, now, don't start hedging." He handed me into the car. "It wasn't a kid who blew that horn. A couple of people saw a seedy guy in a golf cap hanging around cars in that area."

Caps Galvano!

"Rafe, really. I don't think I'd better . . ."

I stopped talking because Rafe Clery leaned toward me, his face blank, his eyes . . . not angry . . . clouded.

"That's why Pete is not redundant, Nialla. You have to eat, and Budnell isn't on hand till around eight. That's two hours to stew yourself into a real swivet when you could be packing in a steak. I promise to have you back here. Scout's honor!"

I nodded, unconvinced. He shrugged and got in.

The Charcoal Grill across from the motel was like many others of the same name all across the country. This one was determinedly picturesque, with wagonwheels and ox yokes, but the management had had the sense to branch out with a bar wing that looked onto an agreeable patio, complete, of course, with the omnipresent charcoal fireplace, white-gowned, mushroom-hatted chef making appropriate passes with a long-handled fork over the broiling beef.

The maître d' ushered us immediately, and with deferential cordiality, to a corner-window table, although there were a good number of people waiting for seats. That's the first time *that's* happened to me. Chalk up another one for Shorty.

It was obvious to me that this place was many cuts above last night's — real linen, good silver, and the glassware was not restaurant-standard. Judging by the prices of appetizers, the originality was going to be amortized there for many years. A dollar and a quarter for a baked potato?

"Very good potato, grown for this place special. The cows who make the sour cream are bullied night and day. The chives are grown by itty-bitty green men . . ."

I stared at Rafe before I realized I must have muttered out loud. I giggled, and he gave his head a little shake.

"You have the goddamnedest nice giggle."

"I thought men didn't like giggling girls."

"Yours is an uncommon one, dear heart."

"Hi there, Clery, thought I saw you buzzing around the fair," said an overhearty voice. I looked up at a man whom I immediately recognized as one of the two I'd heard gossiping.

"Miss Dunn, may I present Jim Field."

Jim Field rested his hands on the back of Rafe's captain's

chair. Now he stared at me with slightly narrowed eyes, his glance flicking over my dress, my bosom, my left hand.

"Damn fine ride, Miss Dunn. And I want you to know that I don't believe for an instant that the gelding had been tranquilized. Just your fine riding."

"Tranquilized?" I was overwhelmed with a white-hot fury.

"Nialla . . ."

"Oh, no." And pushed at the table to make Rafe let me out.

"Nialla!" His voice was still low, but the reprimand was cutting. I was forced to remain seated, seething. "You're a ring-tailed bastard, Field," he said very pleasantly, turning his head toward the man but not bothering to look the man in the face.

"What's this all about?" I demanded, and although I tried to keep my voice down, my rage was being communicated to the people at the next table. "Don't *I* have a right to know? He's my horse!"

"Sorry, Miss Dunn. Thought you'd . . ."

"You never have thought, Field," Rafe cut in in a flat voice. "Why start now? It's nice to have seen you." And he turned away from the man with complete dismissal of his presence.

When Field had drifted off, I leaned across the table. "Tell me, Rafael Clery, who had the—"

"Goddamned bastard," Rafe muttered, but he looked only mildly annoyed, which inflamed me further. "Sure there was some babble. Too many people remember Orfeo, but it was *only* idle speculation. Because you damned well can't tranquilize a horse and have him jump a stiff course so flawlessly." He put his hand on mine, his eyes dark with sincerity. "Don't let anger obscure logic, Nialla. Tranquilizers put a horse off his stride, slow his reflexes. By the time Orfeo had completed the first round—you should have seen him in the old bad days charging his fences, wild-eyed, frothing—there was no question in anyone's mind that he could be drugged. Goddamn Jim Field. Sheer sour grapes. That rangy gray was his. What really

shook the audience was your riding Orfeo with a hackamore!"
And his grin was malicious, and proud.

The waiter was suddenly at Rafe's elbow.

"You like shellfish? Two appetizers with the house sauce.
Two fillets, one medium, one rare, and I mean rare. Baked
potatoes, plenty of butter on the side, green salads. And ask
Jack if he put aside the Chateau Mouton Rothschild fifty-nine
for me? Cork it now, please. It'll need to breathe. Don't rush
the steaks."

"Sure, Mr. Clery." And the waiter went off, hurriedly
scribbling.

"'Sure, Mr. Clery,'" muttered Mr. Clery, grinning impishly at me, and began to talk of other things with an unforced
cheerfulness that was impossible for me to resist.

While he talked, I had to concede that it was ridiculous
to fret over snide assumptions. However, I fumed all through
the shrimp cocktail, which I really didn't taste until I was nearly
finished.

The wine was presented to Rafe, and he really checked
it, label and cork. When the waiter drew the cork and placed it
on the table, Rafe picked it up and sniffed it, then nodded to
the waiter, who placed the accepted bottle on the table.

"Why does wine need to breathe?" I asked, then
wondered if I should display such naïveté. Rafe launched into
a gentle lecture with such pleasure in his subject that I forgot
to be self-conscious.

He knew so much about too many things. It was just as
well I would be leaving that night. In two weeks, between this
show and the next one I planned to make, I'd get back my
perspective on the impossibilities of horses casually passing
midstream in the night.

The waiter didn't rush the steaks, and I forgot the time.
The wine was marvelous to sip, and it was so wonderful to be
with Rafe. Dessert and coffee were naturally followed by an
after-dinner liqueur. So it was long past eight o'clock when we
finally rose from the table.

"What does the air remind you of tonight?" Rafe Clery
asked as we stepped out into full dark of a cooling summer eve.

I took a deep breath. "Smells like fall. Burning leaves."

We both heard the fire sirens, wailing down the road, the road toward the fairgrounds.

"Goddamnit," Rafe cried, pointing to the baleful yellow glow above the trees.

It was too bright to be the lights of the town. He and I made for the Austin with single-minded haste, scrambling over the doors. The roadster zoomed out of the parking lot and onto the main road with only inches to spare from the honking Mustang. When Rafe saw the stack-up of traffic ahead, he ducked down a side lane that paralleled the wide parking field on the south side of the show grounds. Risking more than he ought with such a low-slung car, he turned the Austin-Healey into the pasture, gunning it up the slope regardless of rocks we both knew littered the field.

It was a barn burning! And I knew it was G-Barn. When Rafe had come as far as he could, he jammed on the brakes. I was out of the car and running toward the deserted ring. I'd forgotten the snow fencing that separated the parking lot from the grounds, and I bounced off the paling. Rafe landed with both feet on the fence, and it splintered and flopped free of its stanchions and onto the grass. I skipped over and toward the bleachers.

"Oh, please, Pete," I heard myself gasping as I ran. "Please get Orfeo out. Please get Orfeo out."

The barn yards were crowded with screaming horses being led away, heads blanketed, with people rushing back for others from F- and E-barns, carrying tack, impeding the firemen, who struggled to position their hoses.

I was trying to get past a knot of wardens when Rafe grabbed me.

"Pete was *there*, Nialla. He'll have got the horses out."

"Not Orfeo. Not Orfeo!"

The stillness of his face, illuminated by the roaring fire that was consuming the loft of G-Barn, reflected the truth. And his moment's hesitation allowed me to break free and squeeze past the fire wardens.

"Hey, miss! Miss! Come back here, you damn fool!"

The firemen were not trying to put out the conflagration in G-Barn. They were doing everything they could to keep the fire from jumping to F- and E-barns. I could hear the screaming horse. One horse. Orfeo! Then I spotted my station wagon, where I'd left it, up against the ring fence. I dashed, fumbling for the keys in my bag. The motor started right way, bless it. Before anyone realized what I intended, I backed it around, pointed it toward the flaming barn door, and jack-rabbited right down the main aisle. Burning timbers fell around me, into the stalls, over the corridor. The tires bumped over one huge rafter. At the cross of the T, I looked right. Orfeo was rearing in his stall, striking futilely at the bars, his gallant head and neck outlined against the fiery debris crashing down around him.

I drove through the back door.

"The blanket, the blanket," I told myself, fumbling for it, grasping it, falling out of the car, slipping on the muddy ground. Someone came tearing around the barn, shouting at me. I ran for the door, jumping somehow over the burning timbers and bales.

"Orfeo! Orfeo!"

He couldn't hear me over his shrieks of terror. But when I flung the stall door wide, I had just time to flip the blanket at his head as he lunged through. He pushed me back against the metal post of the next stall. Something seared my side, and the pain thrust me forward against Orfeo. I grabbed the blanket ends. His hooves skidded on the cobbles and gave me just enough time to secure my grip as Orfeo's hysterical lunge pulled us both free of the box stall.

Then someone threw himself bodily at Orfeo's head, and hung on to the frayed halter rope. Between us we got Orfeo aimed at the back door.

I tripped and got pulled over the threshold, but the man was practically riding the horse's head. Orfeo was so fire-crazed that he plunged on in spite of the double impediments.

We got him clear of the barn. He crashed blindly into the practice-ring fence, snapping off the rails like sticks, pulling me, pushing the man at his head, on his head.

Men came to our aid now. Someone threw another blanket at Orfeo, someone else flipped a rope around his neck. Another man sloshed a bucket of water across his rump to put out the cinders. Sheer weight of numbers and lack of sight slowed the poor mad beast. He reared, shrieking, though, at the noise when G-Barn collapsed, showering us all with more sparks and debris.

"Take him to A-Barn," someone bellowed right in my ear.

"He'll respond to your weight, Nialla. Up you go!" It was Rafe, and then I was on Orfeo's trembling wet back. I circled his neck with my arms, calling encouragements to him. A rough halter was fastened over the blankets. The horse was breathing in gasps, half-suffocated, exhausted with terror and pain. Two men were at his head, holding it down; three more paced alongside, ready to assist. Thus he was led through the firemen, the troopers, the noise, the fire heat, and up to the relative calm of A-Barn. Into the blessed confines of a stall.

By the time the cocoon of blankets was unwound from his head, all the fight and fear had left him a quivering, heaving wreck. I went to his head, holding it down, talking to him, comforting him. His forelock was singed, bloody burn marks pocked his face, his eyes were rolling and wild, and all I could do was talk, talk, talk.

"Where's that vet? This horse is singed meat, and he's favoring the left rear," Rafe was bellowing nearby.

"Vet's coming, Mr. Clery," someone hollered, and then I saw a gray-haired man fumbling with the stall fastening.

"Then lemme in. Lemme in. Gawd, he's a mess!" The vet had his bag open, sorting through for a jar. "Here, you take the off-side," he ordered Rafe, shoving the jar at him. "This is what he needs. God in heaven, why'd they wait so long to pull him out?"

"That's Juggernaut, Doc," a spectator said.

The doctor jerked away from Orfeo, glanced at the whole horse.

"Can't be!" He went back to his medicating while Orfeo gave gasping snorts of pain, dancing halfheartedly when the longer, bleeding wounds were treated.

"Take a look at that off-rear, doctor," Rafe said.

"In a minute. In a minute. I can see he's favoring it. I can smell scorched hoof."

He got the brown goo on all the wounds before he tipped

back the hoof. "Yeah, must have stepped on a hot coal. Burned the frog slightly. Not too bad. Oops, easy now, fella." Orfeo squealed in pain, trying to pull his foot free. "Get this piece out . . . there!"

He jumped back from Orfeo as the horse instinctively lashed out with the sore hoof, put it down, lifted it quickly, trying to pull his head up. The next time the hoof went down, it stayed down, but it bore no weight.

"Did they get the mare out?" Rafe asked of the watchers.

"Yeah, she's down the aisle. Pete Sankey got her and turned in the alarm. The damned barn was going up so fast — "

"Thanks!" Rafe replied with acid ingratitude.

"He'll be all right?" I asked the doctor as he started a second go-round with the burn salve.

As if only then aware of my presence, the vet looked at me curiously.

"God in heaven, the horse doesn't need a doctor as much as you do."

He held out his hand to me, and I remember reaching for it, but the man seemed to be moving away from me rapidly, down a darkening tunnel.

 4

I CAME PARTIALLY OUT of the faint when the very cool air hit the burns on my arm.

"You're hurting me," someone whimpered. My side, where Orfeo had shoved me against the metal post, was on fire. Whoever carried me had his hot, hard hand over the sorest place.

"We're almost there, dear heart."

Mercifully I was laid on a soft bed, but my own body's pressure on a burn made me pass out briefly again.

"Shock is the most of it, Mr. Clery," a baritone voice was saying. "The dress saved her from a more severe burn. These cinder blisters look worse than they are, but this anesthetic salve will make her comfortable. They'll soon heal. It'll take longer for her hair to grow back, but I'm told singeing is good for hair. That was a brave and foolish stunt, but she should be all right in a few days. Looks a little rundown. You show people don't take care of yourselves in the summer."

"Rafe? Rafe?"

The room was so bright, and I was sore, stiff, and sticky. My toes hurt. The sheet was too tight.

"Yes, Nialla?" His face was a blur above me.

"My feet. The covers . . ."

The pressure was abruptly eased, with the fringe benefit of a cool draft of air over the burns. I thought cool was bad for burns, but it felt so good.

"Call me if you need me." That must be the people doctor. "Make an appointment with my secretary for tomorrow. Office opens at nine." A door slammed, so the doctor must have left.

I felt awfully sleepy, and limp too, and I wanted to stay awake. I had to tell Rafe. I had to get my money from Budnell tonight. I had to get my horses away from here.

"You're staying where you are, young lady, and that's that!"

Then I remembered. "Dice? Did anyone see Dice?"

I couldn't get my eyes to focus.

"The doctor gave you a shot, Nialla. Don't fight it."

A hand stroked my cheek gently, and I rubbed against it, the way Dice rubs against legs.

"Where's Dice?"

"Pete said he left before the fire, growling, prowling."

"I've got to find . . ."

As I woke up, I was almost instantly conscious of being stiff. What on earth could I have been doing? My side felt as if it were puckered from armpit to waist. My shoulders smarted in a dozen places. And when I yawned, my face hurt with stiff painful patches. I opened my eyes on a darkened room. Then my fingers touched the singed stubbly hair around my face, and I couldn't help crying out.

"Nialla?"

"My hair, oh, dear"—and that was because I couldn't even sit up.

Rafe was there, on the edge of an obscenely huge double bed.

"Do you really want to sit up? Dice came back in the night. Mac phoned to say he was curled up on Orfeo's rump. The gelding's groggy with shock, but the vet looked in again this morning and said he's doing fine. Fair steward says you're not to think of moving him."

"Is it night?" I kept my hands around my hair, somehow not wanting him to see me in such a state.

"God, no. It's nearly ten."

"Ohhhh." The tears sprang to my eyes, and I turned my head away.

"Has the salve worn off? I've got more to put on. Where does it hurt worst?"

I batted at his hands in a feeble, half-witted fashion, the tears spilling down my cheeks, the salt stinging in the burns.

"Nialla! Dear heart, don't cry," said Rafe in such an inexpressibly moving, deep voice that I cried all the harder.

Very gentle hands lifted me, limp and useless as I was. Then my face was pressed against a soft silk shirt. With exceeding care an arm encircled my shoulders, missing the sores. My singed hair was smoothed back, and I tried to shake his hand off, but I could only cry helplessly.

"That's good, just cry, honey. It's reaction. You need to get it out of your system. And stop worrying about your goddamn hair. It can get trimmed in one of those feathery cuts as soon as you can sit up . . . hey! Why, Nialla Dunn, you lousy fink. You *are* a redhead!"

That made me weep harder and struggle to get free. His other arm wrapped over my thighs, securing me to his lap as if I were a child. So I cried myself out. He gave me tissues to blot my eyes and blow my nose, until I finally just lay against his chest, mildly fascinated by the slubs of the silk shirt, the comforting bulge of the biceps in his left arm, the low table with the ghastly china birdbath monstrosity the motel thought a bedside lamp, the brilliant blue rug that went up to the floor-to-ceiling thermopane window, curtained in a rather attractive splashy floral. Moving my head slightly, I could see the opposite wall and the partially open closet where his clothes hung neatly on hangers. I counted five pairs of boots, heels out. A jacket had been dropped on the green velvet boudoir chair, the sleeve dangling to the rug.

"This is your room."

"I slept in the adjoining one," he said. Then added in a meek voice, "I told them we'd just got engaged."

I pushed myself away from him as if he'd been on fire, lost my balance, and slid off his knees to the bed, stinging all over as my exertion opened barely scabbed burns.

His hand connected with my bare buttock, one of the few portions of me unscathed. It was a disciplinary slap, and stung, as he meant it to, for he grabbed me around the waist and shook me. Then, not releasing me, he bent, his face right above mine, stern and angry.

"Behave yourself, Nialla. You're hurt, you're vulnerable. I want to be able to protect you."

Impossible. Impossible. Impossible.

"What's impossible, dear heart?" His voice was kind, but his face was so very stern. "Saving that black behemoth of yours? God, I was so proud of you, you goddamn fool. You scared me shitless. I thought we'd never be able to hold him. Do you realize I was riding his head?" He chuckled, awed.

Two-legged ride? Two-legged ride? Oh, God, I didn't say that out loud, too, did I?

"You did tell me Orfeo would be all right?" And I mustn't have babbled the other, because now I could *hear* my voice asking about Orfeo.

"Yes, and I told the truth. I wouldn't lie about your horses."

He had straightened, and looked awfully tall from where I lay in the bed. When he leaned down and twitched the sheet over me, I realized that I had been lying there half-naked; the nightgown (sizes too large anyhow) was wrapped around my waist.

As if there were absolutely nothing wrong or awkward, Rafe Clery sat down on the bed, a tube in his hand, and began to spread salve over the pinpoint burns on my arms and shoulder. He might have been back in the stall tending Orfeo, he was so impersonal. He worked in silence for a few moments, his face blank. Then he let out a long sigh and looked me in the eyes. He was about to say something, something very important, from his expression, when the phone rang.

He swore under his breath as he reached for it. He went very taut as he listened, his eyes still. I could hear the mumble of a man's voice on the other end, but not what was said.

"Orfeo?" I asked, grabbing Rafe's arm.

He gave a curt shake of his head and then covered the receiver.

"The police are here, and Haworth of the State Fire Insurance Company. They handle the fair indemnity." He just kept looking at me, waiting with a sort of odd patience for my answer. I knew I'd have to talk about the accident sooner or later. Sooner suited me, because he was here. And this motel room was costing money, money I didn't have to spare. I nodded.

Rafe gave them my consent, hung up, and strode to the bureau at the far end of the large room. There was evidently a kitchen and dinette behind the louvered paneling. The door to the adjoining room, his, was in the wall against which the bed stood.

He came back, unbuttoning a clean white shirt, which he then put around my shoulders, helping me get my arms through.

"Don't struggle. That nightgown is not only up to your waist, it's down to it."

A startled glance at myself confirmed this, and I buttoned the shirt right up to my throat. It was soft against the burns and exuded that comforting clean, ironed laundry smell.

"Oh, my hair. My face."

"Vanity, vanity." He extracted a comb from a hip pocket and ran it carefully through my tangled hair, gentle with the snags. Distressingly huge clumps came free. He studied the result of his handiwork with a smile that unnerved me more than he knew.

"Dear heart, your face could be covered with mud, and you'd still be worth a second glance."

There was a knock on the door.

The policeman was identifiable because he wasn't carrying an attaché case. He was a rough-hewn type in his mid-thirties, and he looked tired. His suit looked tired, and he walked with that beyond-tired, odd, broken-kneed gait that infantrymen develop. Korea? The insurance man, Haworth, looked more the picture of the hayseed county cop, except that policemen rarely look so worried. Stern, disgusted, annoyed, impervious, tired, but not anxious-worried.

"Jim Michaels, County, Fourth District. Sorry to trouble you, Miss Dunn." He flipped open an identity wallet and let Rafe get a long look.

"Nigel Haworth, representative of State Fire Insurance Company, Miss Dunn. We handle the fair." Haworth had a habit of hesitating between pauses, until you could almost hear the silent "ah" between them.

"We've about the same questions right now," Michaels said, glancing at Haworth, who nodded nervously. "Get it over with and leave you alone."

Haworth drew up a chair so he could open his case and bring out the necessary forms. He closed the case prissily and used the lid as a writing surface.

The questions were routine. Pete could have answered them, and probably had. Yes, my horses were the only ones stabled in G-Barn. I'd gone with Mr. Clery for dinner at six, leaving Pete Sankey in the stable. We had become aware of the fire only when we left the restaurant. No, I didn't remember the time.

"Full dark. I'd say nine," Rafe replied.

No, I didn't smoke, and Pete chewed. An expression of annoyance crossed Haworth's face, as if he were sorry he couldn't find us negligent.

Yes, the barn had been very hot all weekend. No, I had not gone into the loft for any reason. I'd kept my hay and straw in an unused box stall across the aisle for convenience. Yes, I'd've seen anyone who'd entered the barn, but I'd been in and out all afternoon.

Haworth cleared his throat. "Now, about your equipment. What was in the barn at the time of the fire?"

"Not much. Most of my tack, saddle, bridles, sheets were in the trailer."

Haworth grimaced, and I knew that the trailer and all my tack were gone. But, with insurance, I could even get a new girth for Phi Bete.

"I suppose the car is a complete wreck. You can't . . .'"

Rafe's hand came down on my shoulder warningly.

"Barn wall collapsed on it, honey. It's a total wreck. Even the peanut butter."

How could he? I giggled weakly.

"Miss Dunn's tired, gentlemen . . . "

"About that automobile? Do you have your registration?"

"Oh, Lord, I don't know if I do." My mind spun, for that car registration was in my real name.

"Do you happen to remember the license number?" asked Mr. Haworth with that patient forbearance prissy men often exhibit for the frailties of the opposite sex.

I rattled that off. No use to hide it, because they'd find out soon enough. "The car is registered under the name Irene Nialla Donnelly." I had to say it.

Haworth looked up from his writing, puzzled. I could feel Michaels' alert attention.

"Nialla's father was Russell Donnelly," Rafe said unexpectedly. From the calmness of his voice, he sounded as if he'd known all along. But how could he? "A well-known racehorse trainer. 'Dunn' is her *nom de cheval*, you might say."

He was mean. A wicked, mean, dirty infighter.

"Know any reason why someone might have deliberately started that fire, Miss Dunn?"

I closed my eyes and felt Rafe's fingers press lightly into my arm.

"I have to ask that," Michaels went on, "since your father's murder is still open."

Rafe's fingers tightened unbearably, but I couldn't move.

"I'm a horse fancier myself, Miss Dunn," Michaels continued. "I was so sorry to hear of his death, but I know it's still an open case."

"That's enough for now," Rafe said smoothly.

"Sorry, Mr. Clery, I need an answer."

"No reason, Mr. Michaels," I said. Anything to get them out of the room. "I've nothing anyone wants."

Rafe made them leave somehow. He told Haworth he'd find out what I'd had in the car and the trailer later, when I'd rested. We'd want replacements as soon as possible, of course. Haworth nodded glumly. Rafe told Michaels that G-Barn should have been condemned and torn down years ago, that they'd probably find the fire had been caused by spontaneous combustion. Nothing sinister. No need to harass Miss Dunn anymore today.

"Harass" is a marvelous word. Only it wasn't the policeman and the insurance agent who were harassing me. It was Rafe Clery.

I felt like crying again, and didn't have any tears left. I just lay in the bed, unable to open my eyes, unwilling to look Rafe Clery in the face. Not now.

The bed sagged. I could feel his body just beyond my hips.

"Shall I get the doctor over?"

"No."

"If anyone tells Haworth that you drove the car through the barn," he said in a very noncommittal voice, "he may hedge a total claim."

I couldn't say a thing. A hard splat made me open my eyes. He was driving one fist into the other palm, his expression ferocious.

"Aw, for God's sake, Nialla. I *want* to help you. And I can't if I don't know what the hell is going on."

"Nothing's going on." My voice was high and shrill.

"Nothing? Hell, you're scared. Your saddle girth is cut. There's a deliberate attempt to spook your horse, the barn is burned around your stock, and now I learn Russ Donnelly's murder was never cleared up. No reason? Why have you changed your name? Dyed your hair? Why are you on the East Coast? Russ went to California five years ago after Agnes du Maurier died."

"I don't know."

"Well, I know something. Someone's out to get you. Dear heart, you're in trouble. And right now, you're in no condition to run, hide, or dodge. Let me protect you?" Then, because he was a rough infighter, he added, "'Sure, Mr. Clery!'"

"Oh, Rafe!"

My hand went out to him, and I was folded in his arms, gently but so securely. His heart was pounding under my cheek, and that surprised me, because he seemed too cool, so confident. I looked up at him. With a groan I could hear reverberating in his chest, he bent his head and covered my lips with his. His hands lifted me against him, somehow getting under the shirt so that his wrists lay along my bare breasts. His lips weren't gentle. His lips were hard, forcing my mouth open. His tongue flicked mine as if he had to invade me.

I'd been kissed before. I'd petted. I'd enjoyed it. But I'd held out, wanting to be virgin for the man I married. His kisses, his hands on my nipples, seemed to touch invisible strings that sent hot fires to my loins, to that part of me I'd been trying to deny ever since Marchmount . . .

Somehow I broke free and scrambled away from him, crouching against the headboard.

"You liked that, Nialla!" He spoke in a rough voice, and his breathing was fast. "Whoever raped you didn't ruin you completely. But I won't force you. Although" — and his voice steadied with a funny laugh — "you'd better get under the covers. Fast."

I grabbed the sheet to my chin and huddled under it.

"Don't look so scared, sweetheart. See? I'm staying put. But —" and he paused for emphasis — "I'm not leaving until I get a few answers. You know" — now he grinned at me — "I'd wondered why you seemed familiar. I used to jockey for Agnes du Maurier. And I remember you as a redheaded tomboy, riding a show horse bareback in the pasture. I admired your father, and I was damned sorry when I read his obit. Wasn't he training for Louis Marchmount? Any idea why your father would be murdered?"

I shook my head.

"But how was he killed? Gun, car, what?"

"A pitchfork in his chest."

"Oh, God, Nialla."

"He'd been at Caliente. I was at college. He phoned me to meet him at home right away. He was furious about something. When I got home, he wasn't at the house, so I went to the barn and found him . . . the pitchfork was still going up and down. The cops said the murderer had wiped his fingerprints off. But Rafe, Dad didn't have an enemy in the world."

"I know, Nialla. I know. He was a decent guy."

"The police weren't. They were . . . like something in a bad movie. They kept suggesting the most horrible things. That Dad doctored horses to make them win because the Marchmount colors had been losing steadily. That he'd lost money betting and couldn't pay up. Awful things."

"About Russ Donnelly they were lies."

"Then . . . a man I knew called to say he thought he could help me clear Dad's name."

Rafe's expression altered, as I knew it would when he heard this part of my stupidities.

"And he needed some money to carry on the investigations?" he asked. I nodded. "A predictable confidence approach."

"I'm really not that stupid," I protested, irritated. "I knew the man. And he did know everything there was to know about racetracks and the people connected with them. It was also entirely likely that he could get people to talk who'd clam up in front of the police."

"Who?"

"Caps Galvano."

Rafe closed his eyes and gritted his teeth, shaking his head slowly, a kind of tired wisdom in his eyes when he looked at me again.

"You must have been hard up to trust that slimy excuse for a human."

"He said he knew!"

"All right, all right. So you paid him, and it wasn't enough, right? And he was back for more. So what did you do?"

I didn't want to go on, but there was an expression on Rafe's face that told me he'd find out if he had to sit there all day. He was worse than the police, this one.

"Galvano thought Louis Marchmount might help me."

Rafe's hand came down on his knee with a resounding crack.

"That figures. Galvano's been running Lou's errands for

him for years. So it was Marchmount who raped you." And Rafe began to swear with coarser words and phrases than I'd heard from the foulest-mouthed hostlers. Coarse but inventive, displaying such a knowledge of Louis Marchmount's erotic habits that I was appalled. How could Rafe Clery possibly know such things? Then he cut off the invective and looked at me pityingly, shaking his head slowly.

"You poor silly clunch of a kid. What a shitty thing to happen. And that bastard knew just how to put the squeeze on you. If you'd been one of his usual blonde broads, he couldn't have worked it. You'd've told him off and got the money anyhow. The nice girls, the good girls, they get screwed every time. Oh, Jesus!" And he threw up his hands and rolled his eyes in apology at his choice of words.

But the idiom was so appropriate, and I was so tired, that I began to giggle, and then kind of folded up again. He must think me such a despicable, stupid . . .

"No, dear heart, I don't. From where I stand, you were foolish, yes. But mighty inexperienced and innocent, and in a damned rough bind. How do I know what I'd've done if I'd been you?"

He stroked my head. Then his fingers rubbed my jaw gently, where I wasn't burned. It had the effect of a benediction. His weight shifted, and I felt his fingers on my back, lightly applying the salve. He began to talk in that deep wonderful voice of his, so comforting, so soothing.

"You aren't the first girl to be subjected to that old routine. 'Your virtue for my money, fair beauty.' You won't be the last."

"I can't ever get married," I heard myself murmuring wistfully. "I'm not a virgin."

He chuckled, tipped up my chin, daubing my right check with salve.

"How many wives d'you think are nowadays," he asked with a soft laughing tenderness. "None of mine were."

"But you divorced them."

"Not because they weren't virgins. Lie flat." When I had, he slipped the shoulder strap down to anoint my chest.

"You shouldn't've said we were engaged just to get a room next to me."

He paused, giving me a very level look.

"That wasn't exactly why. I'm well known in this town and in the business. I thought"—and his unsaid comment chided me for his lack of knowledge—"that some sour character was just giving you a hard time. If he knew I was interested in you, he'd bug off. A pretty girl with two fine horses, a championship rider, *but* with no obvious sponsor, is fair game. Now . . . "

"Because Mr. Clery is interested, I'm safe?"

"Don't get snotty. How'n'll was I to know murder was involved?" He lowered the other strap and dabbed at a cluster of blisters. "I suppose the police cleared Marchmount?"

"He was in Caliente when . . . it happened."

"And Galvano? Though I don't fashion that little worm as a murderer."

"He was in Caliente, too."

"Hmmm. Over you go." He deftly flipped me to my stomach, and I buried my face wearily into the pillow. It was so nice to be taken care of. And I did feel safe with this crazy little man.

"Come to think of it, Marchmount's colors haven't been winning much lately. Was he bearing down on your father at all?"

"Not that I knew. He always told Dad he had implicit confidence in him."

"He'd have to say that. Your father's reputation was high. Lift up. This gown's a mess." He was working on my legs now. "But to use you like that. Christ. Move your left leg a little. I can get most the burns this way. No. Over you go again."

I turned, carefully and languidly, but the stiff pains were easing off now that the salve was taking effect. He flipped the sheet over me, and it settled down with a cool sigh around my body.

"God, you look like a freaked-out case of measles. Lie still a minute."

Enjoying the respite from the myriad discomforts of the flesh, I heard him rustling around.

"Let's see, it's your right side that's got the bad burn, isn't it?"

I nodded dreamily, unconcerned even when I felt the sheet lift again, with a rush of cool air over my body. When I felt his bare foot touch mine, it was too late.

He had me pinned against the length of his warm strong body and had placed his hands just so, avoiding the worst of the burns. My head was caught in the crook of his right arm, and I couldn't move.

"This won't be rape, Nialla, because you'll want me as much as I want you. There won't be any nonsense about helping *me*. You ought to realize that right now."

He was pressed against my hip, firm and hard.

"Please, Rafe. Please don't." I was scared.

"Oh, no, Nialla," he said with gentle firmness, his eyes a brilliant blue. "You've built that incident all out of proportion. Happened over a year ago, didn't it? Yet when I touched you at the pool, you went rigid. It's ruining you for any normal relationship with men. And you're too damned fine a girl to be crippled like that. So *I'm* going to make *love* to you. And you're not going to resist me, because, dear heart, you can't."

He threw one leg across my thighs. Inched his body slightly to pin my left arm down. He already had my right hand captured at the elbow. Bending his head, he began to kiss my breast, teasing it with his tongue, stroking it with his free hand. Then his fingers lightly drifted down to my belly, to the soft part of my inner thighs. Between kisses, he kept talking to me, ignoring my pleas, my protests, my curses. He switched his attentions to my other breast, gently at first, then suddenly rough. And the pressure on my nipple hurt; it hurt in a different way, too, in my belly, and deep, deep inside me.

"I like a strong body. You're not soft, Nialla, or gaudy. You're neat and smooth," he told me. I'd stopped ranting and was whimpering softly because I couldn't resist him. And I hated him, more than I'd hated Marchmount, because Rafe knew exactly what he was doing, and that sick old man hadn't been able to help himself. Rafe didn't need to blackmail women into sleeping with him . . .

His lips were traveling around my body now, teasing, nibbling, arousing me, robbing me of my hatred with sensations that left me no room for anything but the touch of his fingers, his lips. I began to shiver, wondering where he would caress me next. Closer those prowling fingers came to the ultimate goal, and suddenly his hand gripped me there. Released me. And began to trace a delicate random pattern, until I was almost wild.

Surprisingly, he stopped, shifting back to my breasts and beginning the incredible sequence all over again, until I was trembling. Until I wanted more of him. By the time his fingers had returned to that throbbing portion of me, my legs separated of their own volition. My body arched, seeking his, reacting with a knowledge beyond my consciousness.

"That's my girl," he murmured encouragingly. My arm was free now, free to encircle his smooth muscled back, to pull closer to me.

His hands were gentle again. Why was he waiting? I knew what was coming next; why was he putting it off? His lips moved back to my breast, and I cried out with disappointment. He fastened fiercely on my nipple, and I strained toward him, my back arching.

"Nialla? May I, Nialla? May I show you what it's like?"

"Oh, Rafe, please. Please!"

A pillow was thrust under my hips, and his smooth silky body was no longer warm against me. His hands gently held my legs apart. I became aware of a gentle pressure against me, a slow, gradual filling of that aching emptiness. A filling that was a pain-pleasure so intense I cried out for the joy of it.

"Did I hurt you?"

"Oh, no. No!" I grabbed at his legs to hold him within me, trying to impale myself more deeply. He filled all of me, it seemed, with a throbbing warmth.

He shifted again, and I tightened my legs. When he chuckled, I opened my eyes and saw he was stretching out above me, his legs carefully placed to the sides of mine, where I'd not been burn-marked. His weight lay lightly, warmly along me, and he kissed my lips softly, almost gaily, all that time that glorious strength filled me.

He began to move so gently I wasn't first aware of the rhythmic sliding. And I began to move, imitating him, sensing approval in the way his kiss deepened. The pulse of his rhythm began to increase. Like Orfeo, the thought occurred to me, when he is facing a jump. His body began to tremble, too, as I clung to him, heedless of sores now, aware only of that thrusting, pulsing rhythm, again and again. Unbearably increasing to a tempo that threatened to split me. And it did, into a bursting, shivering height, totally unconnected with anything but Rafael Clery within me. Somewhere in the blaze, I heard his triumphant, "Oh, my God. My God!"

I came languidly out of nowhere into a reality where sensation was again possible, and he had not left my body. I was glad. He had bent his head to my breast so that his hair fell across my shoulder. I kissed his head, my lips falling against that awful scar.

"Thank you, Rafe."

"Nialla, don't." But his "don't" was gratitude.

Slowly he raised his head and looked at me, his eyes dark with emotion and a plea.

"I don't want to be engaged to you anymore, Nialla Donnelly."

"I'd no intention of holding you . . ."

He consigned my intentions elsewhere with an expletive and put a hand over my mouth. "I want to be married to you. Then I can really make love to you; I want to teach *you* how to make love. I want to get you well so I'm not inhibited by burns and scrapes and scars. Because you were made to be loved, often and well, and I want exclusive rights. God!" And he threw his head back, grinning with a sort of savagery. "I could almost thank Marchmount. Don't you dare tense up, Nialla Donnelly. He's past history. I'm your present and your future."

"Sure, Mr. Clery."

He looked at me with a gladness in his eyes and face that my heart leap. Then he kissed me, a kiss as different from any I'd been given as . . . as my two horses. His mouth was tender on mine, almost reverent. Which is ridiculous, because you can't combine passion with reverence . . . no, not passion . . . sensuality . . . no! Neither. The kiss was a total commitment, the spectrum of the shades of loving, exacting an unreserved response from me. Later, I'd look back on that moment and

remember that I became Nialla Clery then, signed, sealed, and
delivered by that kiss.

It was such an incredible luxury to be cosseted and comforted that I protested volubly when Rafe left me. He was so
beautiful as he stood by the side of the bed, so unself-con-
sciously male, grinning possessively down at me.

"Dear heart, there're things to do . . . a doctor's appointment" — he ticked them off on his short, sensitive fingers — "so
we can get Wassermanns" — this said with a comically lascivious
smirk — "I want to call the vet about Orfeo . . . and feed us." He
bent over, one hand gently cupping my breast. "You may not
be aware of it, but it's nearly one of the clock, and you haven't
had anything since that steak last night." He gave me
a squeeze. "I want to feed you up a little. You look positively
transparent, love."

He picked up the phone and ordered, mentioning items
and glancing at me for confirmation. I was too quiescent to
argue. I felt so light, lazy, and languid.

"Start thinking about what was in the car, Nialla," he said
as he walked with quick steps to the bathroom. "I'm ready to
eat insurance men who displease me. However, in the interest
of the devious underwriter mind, itemized lists, down to the
peanut-butter jars" — and he swung around the door to grin at
me — "always impress. Looks good when they run up statistics.
I wonder what the death rate on peanut-butter jars will print
out next year."

The shower came on hard, depriving me of his conversation. I squinched down under the sheet and saw the bloody
spots. Looked at my arms where the cinder burns were enlarged with smears of drying blood. I sat up, but there was no
sign of my clothes. Surely my bra and pants had survived. I
couldn't . . .

"I've got to get you some clothes, too. My bride comes to
me as she is . . . stark naked. And" — he paused in his toweling
to point a stern finger at me — "no nonsense."

"I can't be nonsensical, Rafe," I said meekly, covered to
my chin with sheet. "All my clothes were in the station wagon."

"I thought as much." He scrubbed at his hair as he
walked to the bureau, opening drawers to pull out various

items. He threw me another shirt, then pulled on shorts. I hated to see him covered when I was just getting used to him. "You take a size eight? Thirty-two bra? Padded? About six-and-half shoe?"

I stared. He'd only seduced me, not measured me. Or did those sensitive hands have inbuilt calibrators? Probably.

"No big thing. I've been married twice, love, and bedded many more—" He broke off. "Does that worry you?"

"I haven't had time to worry about it," I replied truthfully. "Should I?"

He gave me one of those charismatic grins. "No, love. *You* shouldn't. But you will, because it's in the same category as remembering not to think about the camel's left knee."

"You read Isak Dinesen?"

"Worry about that, then. It's more constructive."

He was shaving when room service knocked on the door. He stepped into his pants on the way to the door, grinning at me. Although I was decently covered, he kept the man out of the room, wheeling in the cart himself.

The moment I caught a whiff of the coffee and grilled ham, I realized that I was famished. To think I might never have to open another jar of peanut butter! Rafe finished shaving before he joined me—in three minutes—and quickly consumed the omelet he'd ordered for himself.

"I hate to leave you, Nialla," he said as he shrugged on an elegant white linen jacket, checking his pockets for wallet, keys, and such miscellany. "You're not to answer the phone or the door while I'm gone. Promise?"

All the ugliness that had been dispersed by Rafe's lovemaking and his presence crowded in on me. It undoubtedly showed in my expression, for he came striding across the floor and held me in his arms.

"Promise?"

I'd've promised anything with Rafe Clery's arms around me, his smooth lemony-expensive-smelling cheek against mine.

"Sure, Mr. Clery."

Warmth and security left the room when the door closed on him. I heard him try the knob.

"It's locked, all right, Nialla. Keep it that way!"

The phone didn't ring, and no one knocked. The chambermaid didn't even scratch to enter either room. I ate slowly to make time pass, and when I couldn't swallow another sip of coffee, I had to find something else to occupy me.

When I got up to go to the bathroom, however, I was awfully wobbly. My legs were a sight, my arms, my chest, and when I angled the medicine-cabinet mirror, so were my shoulders. Sitting on the toilet, I managed to sponge off the worst. I finger-brushed my teeth with his toothpaste. (For a bride, I was a bust as far as dowry, but my teeth were good.) There was a small bottle of shampoo in his kit, so I could get rid of the singe-stink in my hair. How could Rafe have stood it? Clean, my hair also showed the various lengths more. I groaned. Over my ears I could see the red roots showing. I was a mess!

And Rafe Clery had made love to *me*. Said he was going to marry *me*. Dispassionately I surveyed myself in the full-length door mirror. From knee to breast I was unmarred, unless I made a quarter-turn and you saw the vertical red streak. Though my body looked the same, boyish, I looked at it differently. A man had loved it, caressed it, possessed it.

I sighed for that man's absence, as I put on his shirt. And then my weakness betrayed me. I kind of crept back to bed, bloodstained sheets and all.

I must have dozed off, because suddenly the sound of the key in the lock had me bolt upright, scared stiff. Rafe entered, package-laden, grin-wreathed.

"Orfeo's okay. I got the check from the State Fire right here, but you're not to sign a release yet. This is for the car and the trailer, top prices, too. Haworth didn't give me any jazz. Dice's been stuffed with lamb kidneys, and Jerry—you remember him?—is bringing up our trailer because the vet says we can move Orfeo. That hoof's sore, but he can stand a trip. You've a hairdresser's appointment in twenty minutes, a doctor's in an hour, and I've lined up a minister—"

He broke off his monologue to look at me questioningly.

"Sure, Mr. Clery." What else could I say?

So I dressed in the clothes he'd bought and took pleasure

in the way the green silk molded itself to my hips. He put other
pretties away in the drawers and closet, allowing me a passing
glimpse at pants, dresses, a lightweight coat, sandals, Weejuns
that matched his, pale green Capezio slippers that were the
same shade as the dress.

"There's a good saddle-and-boot man in East Norwich,"
he was saying, and stopped. "You'll be living on a horse farm in
Syosset, did you realize that? Gawd, girl, you don't know much
about me, do you?"

"Yes, I do. You've been married twice, divorced twice, in
jail, been a jockey, in a war, you fight dirty, have a bad temper,
did crazy irresponsible things in your misspent youth—and
you're doing them still—but you've a good reputation on the
show circuit, and you're a fine rider, besides which I find you to
be kind, sensitive, intelligent, well educated, well bred . . ."

"Hey, you'll ruin my carefully built public image!"

He put his hands lightly around my waist, squeezing as he
grinned at me, a little sheepishly.

"I know more about you than you do about me," I went
on, worried.

He gave me a little pull, tilting his head to one side so that
our mouths met and my body rested against his. I could feel the
pulsing of him and kind of sagged, wanting him urgently. He
set me back on my feet quickly, his eyes wide and kind of
surprised.

"Enough of that now. We've got other things to do . . .
first."

Then he took my left hand and slipped a ring on the third
finger. I gasped in astonishment, for the stone was an emerald.

"You wouldn't expect a small-town jeweler to have such
good taste," he said in a sort of deprecating way. "However, if
you prefer diamonds . . ."

"I hate diamonds. They're so cold. Oh, Rafe, this ring is
just perfect." The setting was old-fashioned, and the stone, that
deep rich green that only a good emerald has, was bracketed by
two smaller chips.

"We could have the stone reset."

"No!" And I clutched my hand and ring away from him.

He grinned, sure he had pleased me, slipping his fingers under my chin to kiss me lightly.

"Come on," he said then with mock impatience. "I want you clipped around the edges, my proud beauty."

He supervised. The poor beautician was both nervous and amused. The net result was a hair style that looked deliberate. Pixie feathers about my face, the back layered, fire damage completely erased.

The doctor checked me over far too thoroughly, prescribed therapeutic vitamins, tranquilizers, the pill, told me my hemoglobin was too damned low, and promised to rush the Wassermanns. His final advice, which he delivered caustically, looking squarely at Rafe, was for me to get rest, undisturbed rest. I liked him.

The clerk at the license bureau had ridden in the Ladies' Hunter Hack Class, or so she told me as she filled out the forms, alternating between beams and clucks of sympathy over my losses. When Rafe left me in the Austin-Healey to take the prescriptions into the drugstore, weariness began to overwhelm me again.

"That junk'll be sent to the motel, dear heart. Now," Rafe said as he returned, "for a very brief look at the beasts, and then back to bed with you. For some of that undisturbed rest."

Orfeo looked about the way I felt, limp. But he brought his head up and wickered as I stepped in beside him. Dice uncurled himself from his nest in the straw, talking quietly in his throat, respecting the sick-stall atmosphere.

I heard Phi Bete's demand for attention. She'd been moved to the stall opposite. She pawed, tossing her head. The moment I spoke her name, she stopped her noise, blowing softly through her nostrils, as if reassured.

Someone came charging down the loft ladder. "Who's there? What's going on? Oh, Mr. Clery. I was just getting down some hay, Mr. Clery."

It was one of the men I'd seen with the Tomlinson stock. He looked at me, nodding embarrassedly as he continued more slowly down the ladder. His glance took in my scabby burns, my hair, dress, shoes, and lingered on the ring. His hand went to the hat brim.

"Hope you're better, ma'am? Scared us, passing out like that last night."

"Thank you. I'll be fine."

"The black's better. Took some mash this morning, but he wasn't interested in the hay. He's drunk plenty, and I keep his pail full and cool. Mare's been shedding, and she's a mite off her feed, too. And I ain't left them alone a minute." He pointed to the loft. "I heard you right away."

I looked at Rafe, feeling all the more apprehension at such vigilance. Then it was all too much.

"Jerry'll be here in about an hour, Mac. He'll spell you. Feed the cat?"

"He's been eating all day, Mr. Clery." Mac was disgusted.

"Seen Pete?"

"Come to think of it, I haven't. He'll turn up soon. Always does."

"Ask him to call me at the motel, would you please?"

"Sure thing."

Rafe guided me out, settled me in the car, companionably silent all the way back to the motel. He didn't talk all the time, after all. As we entered the lobby, the desk clerk beckoned. He handed over to Rafe a white drugstore sack, which clanked.

"You haven't seen us," Rafe said sternly, one hand passing over the clerk's. Judging by the motion of the man's fingers, our privacy premium had been paid.

The bed had been made up, the room-service table was gone, and there were flowers around—white flowers and a bouquet of sweetheart roses with silver-dyed spikes of something or other accenting the pink.

Rafe grunted when he saw the offerings and gave me a gentle shove toward the bed.

"Sacktime, Nialla." He took a negligee set from the drawer. Evidently he preferred me in green? He gestured at my dress, and I obediently took it off. He'd said "sacktime," and he meant it, for his hands were impersonal as he helped me into the soft silk gown. Gown? It barely reached my thighs. He threw back the bed covers and yanked out the tuck at the bottom so the sheet wouldn't drag against my sore feet. When he had covered me, he drew the blinds.

"I'll be right next door, Nialla."

I was almost disappointed that he left me so, but a weariness overcame me that I couldn't fight.

 5

BY RIGHTS I should have had nightmares of fires and things. I didn't. But suddenly a dream pivoted around someone shaking me, and I did wake, scared and trembling.

"It's Rafe, Nialla."

And the touch of hands was familiar. He was dressed, tonight in a gray turtleneck silk jersey, white jacket, and dark pants.

"You need to eat as much as you need to rest. It's past eight now, so eating is in order."

I didn't have to decide what I'd wear; he had it laid out on the end of the bed. I ought to have resented such management, but after months and months of decisions (right, wrong, and painful), I didn't demur. I only hoped that it didn't presage the tone of our relationship. I don't like clinging, dependent females at all.

"Dark green?" was what I said out loud.

"Dark green," he said with a laugh. "Size eights didn't go for green this year. Which is just as well. It's a good color for you . . . now and when your hair grows back."

The fact that I'd dyed my hair apparently rankled him. It bothered me, too, but it had seemed a sensible measure. Red hair is so damned conspicuous. No automatic second looks are cast at mouse-brown-haired girls.

"You'll have a wider selection when we get home. There are some good specialty shops in Locust Valley, and branches of the big New York City stores," he went on, sitting down to watch me dress, that slightly proprietary grin on his face.

He'd probably watched hundreds of women dressing, so he wasn't self-conscious. The strange thing was, I wasn't either. Good thing, I didn't have to fool with stockings, though. Gartering isn't a graceful operation.

Lipstick, a bottle of Replique cologne, and a silver-backed brush and comb had appeared on the cabinet shelf, along with the prescription bottles. I looked at the pill and wondered if I'd got them too late.

"Thank you, Mr. Clery, for" — something in his face stopped me — "for the cologne. I like it."

"Suits you," he said, and tucking my hand under his arm, headed us out the door.

I supposed that the other restaurant wasn't open on Mondays, but going to the Charcoal Grill was a mistake. I tried not to react when the maître d' approached. A fleeting smirk crossed his face as his too-knowing glance swept over the quality of the dress I now wore, the saucy cut of my hair, the ring on my finger. Had it been only last night?

Then I hoped that Rafe hadn't seen that look. But the man's face was absolutely correct when he smiled warmly at Mr. Clery and ushered us — to make matters worse — to the same table we'd had last night. If only I'd not gone to dinner here last night . . . What kind of an idiot was I?

"Goddamnit," Rafe swore, throwing down the napkin he'd been about to spread. "I should've thought twice, Nialla. We don't have to stay here."

"It's all right, Rafe. Even if potatoes at one-twenty-five outrage my Irish sense of fitness . . . after all, the restaurant's not to blame for the fire . . ." Unaccountably I shuddered. His hand covered mine. And he didn't remove it when the waiter appeared for our order, the same fellow as last night, of course.

To vary at least the diet, Rafe ordered roast beef au jus with Yorkshire pudding, and champagne, with the house pâté (which he said was very good) as an appetizer.

He didn't try to jolly me, just talked about news items he'd heard that afternoon, told me who the flowers were from, and that he'd called to thank Bess Tomlinson and the fair committee.

We were companionably silent when the roast beef arrived, and because it was excellent, we ate in silent appreciation. A noisy party sweeping in from the cocktail lounge made me glance up. I saw the back of his head first, and stared, my fork halfway to my mouth, willing him to turn and *be* someone else. But the sudden whinny of a laugh only confirmed that there was Louis Marchmount.

"A hasty retreat, Nialla, would be conspicuous," said Rafe in a low voice, as he kept carving his meat with neat strokes. "For that matter, would he be looking for Irene Donnelly in the Charcoal Grill?"

Of course not, I told myself, releasing my breath.

"Show people are clannish," he said. "He wasn't in town last night, or someone would have mentioned it."

Almost incuriously Rafe turned his head toward the loud cluster of people.

"He's with the Colonel and the Hammond groups, and . . ."

Louis Marchmount swayed to one side just then, revealing the blonde bubble hairdo and classic profile of a handsome older woman. She was laughing too, and the sound, slightly malicious, drifted to us.

". . . and Wendy Madison." Rafe's voice was cold and hard. His attention was riveted to the party as the maître d' waltzed up to them, all bright smiles, bowing, nodding, gesturing them . . . away from us. Only when they had disappeared beyond the room divider did Rafe turn back to his meal.

Neither of us finished the beef, but Rafe, apparently able to forget the unfortunate coincidence, made me join him in a rich pastry (you need the calories, Nialla) and coffee. Made me wait for a doggie bag (Dice would object, I know, to the terminology, but not the beef).

Rafe refused, too, to let me hurry out. At that moment, however, I didn't want to go to the stables. That would be pushing my luck. Caps Galvano might be about — he was always somewhere in Marchmount's vicinity. I should have left the area the moment I saw that cap and that fox face. At the latest, when Caps had been identified as the man who blew the horn. He'd obviously remembered the mare and informed Marchmount. So they knew that I was "Nialla Dunn" here, because Caps would have told him.

Rafe escorted me back to the motel without comment.

"So he's here. So what?" he demanded when we were back in our room.

I fumbled with the ring.

"What does that gesture signify?" He wouldn't take the ring I held out.

"I can't marry you now."

"Why not?" And Rafe was angry with me.

"Because ... because ..."

"Because you saw Marchmount? I thought I'd exorcised that. If I didn't ..." And he had whirled me around, unzipped the dress, and pulled it over my head before I could try to explain that I was afraid for *him*, if he married me.

"Rafe, it isn't ..."

He had unhooked my bra and spun me around again, his mouth fastening on one breast, his hand roughly flicking the other nipple.

"Rafe, please. Listen ..."

He jammed his mouth over mine then, his lips hard, hurtful. He was pushing me backward, and the bed came up under me, with Rafe's body pressing me down.

Somehow I twisted my mouth free.

"Not like this. Please, Rafe ..."

He got my head in the crook of his elbow again, covered my lips while his free hand tore my pants off and loosened his pants' zipper. Then his fingers were making sharp invasion of my body, to which I felt myself responding. Responding even as I tried to deny the deft seeking of those fingers, the searching of his tongue. He had somehow caught one nipple between his arm and body, and that was another fiery summons. He knew, too, when I was caught up by those responses, for he suddenly left me, gasping and writhing at the interruption. My legs were held up and spread, and he was as hard and firm and wonderful as before. He seemed to test himself against me, and when I moaned, he went in, all the way, like the invader he was. Then he withdrew while I cried out. The tentative insertion, the sharp intrusion and withdrawal. I clutched wildly for his arms, his legs, anything to keep him from leaving me.

"Don't leave me. Don't leave me!"

"You mean that?" His voice was almost a snarl.

"Oh, yes, yes. Don't leave me, Rafe. Come to me!"

"No. You come to me!"

My legs were lowered as he went in again, his body covering mine. His hands made a frame around my face, his thumbs stroking my cheeks gently as if apologizing for his cavalier treatment. But tenderness was not what I wanted now. I wanted the surging rhythm, and my hips began to move as if I could move him. His muted laugh was one of sheer triumph as he slowed the tempo. I trembled and twisted under him, trying to get him to increase the pace. He was adamant. I felt I could not endure his leisurely method. I felt I would burst. And then, suddenly, when I was all but certain I should explode, he began to thrust with unbelievable force, lifting me, higher and higher, until I did explode—within, without, all over. But he didn't stop, and before the first fantastic sensation had quite died from my loins, there was another, and then a third before he arched his back with an inarticulate cry.

How long we lay locked together, I don't know. His body was a beloved weight against mine, his hands warm on my shoulder and hip, his head beside mine on the pillow, his breathing quiet.

"Marchmount doesn't count, Nialla. *I* had you first, because you have *given* yourself to me, haven't you?"

His eyes were clear. I could see the fine lines at his eyes, the deep grooves from nose to mouth, the damp, black lock falling to his forehead.

"Sure, Mr. Clery."

We were married the next morning. Rafe tried to find Pete Sankey to be one of the witnesses. I thought Pete'd like that, and I felt that he was the nearest thing to family I could present. In his absence, Jerry MacCrate obliged, embarrassed and nervous, turning apoplectic when Bess Tomlinson put in an unexpected appearance.

"You've no kin, m'dear," she said as she walked in, two white boxes under her arm. "And you are young enough to be my daughter, Gawd knows I hate to admit it. Of course, if you'd rather . . . "

"How'd you hear, Bess?" Rafe asked when I'd reassured her.

She grinned. "Mac, of course. Can't keep a thing to himself. Nor can Jerry, for that matter. Good men with horses, though. Actually, I called A-Barn to find out how your gelding was doing, Miss Dunn. Frankly, Rafe, I didn't think you had this much sense left. Or is it her horses you're after?"

That hadn't occurred to me. Rafe threw back his head and howled.

"Nialla's Russ Donnelly's daughter, Bess. I've been waiting for her to grow up."

Bess eyed me closely, then chuckled. "You obviously resemble your mother's side of the family, child. However, since she's obviously grown up . . ." And she put down the boxes, opening the longer, flatter one first. From it she lifted a beautiful white lace veil, attached to a white velvet bandeau. Her eyes met mine, saw my hands lift and reach for the lovely thing, and suddenly her face lit with a warm, happy smile. "A bride must have something bridal. And borrowed. I may be a trial to him, but Gus Tomlinson and I have been married twenty-seven years, my parents fifty-five, and I'm told my grandparents lasted forty-two. We brides all wore this veil. I sincerely trust it'll work its charm for you two!" Though she spoke in a light voice, she deeply felt what she said.

She clipped the veil to my head and fluffed the fragile white lace over my shoulders, then drew the front veil over my face. She turned away abruptly and fumbled with the second box.

"These help, too, I fancy." And she presented me with a white orchid, its stem wrapped with streamers of white ribbon, to which were attached the blossoming twigs of a curious white flower. "It's stephanotis, dear, which the Greeks insist must be part of a wedding bouquet. I've a Greek gardener. Their marriages tend to last, too."

"Going to make sure this time, huh, Bess?" Rafe asked, raising his eyebrows.

"Ha!" She started to make a sharp remark, her eyes darted to me, and she said instead, "You've a suitably accoutered bride, witnesses, and I've got a meeting at twelve. Let's ask Reverend Norse to proceed."

I don't think that the minister approved of her gruff levity, but he was evidently too well acquainted with Mrs. Tomlinson to give any sign of dismay. He cleared his throat and began the marriage service in a sonorous voice.

And so Irene Nialla Donnelly married Rafael Stephen Timothy Rodríguez Clery, with Greek flowers and a Venetian heirloom veil lent by her matron of honor.

"I ought to stand you to a champagne lunch, but I can't," Bess said, hugging me and kissing Rafe. "You always take fences fast, you . . . " She ended her sentence in a sudden cough, flicking a glance at Mr. Norse's disapproving face.

"I'll . . . *We'll*" — Rafe squeezed my arm — "accept the thought for the deed, Bess. I want to be back on the Island by evening, and we'll have to drive slowly for the gelding's sake."

"Then the hoof is healing, isn't it?"

"Looks to be."

"Well, then, good-bye, good luck. He's a good man, m'dear. And such an experienced rider," she added with the kind of twinkle in her eye that left no doubt of her allusion. Then she was off, veil box tucked under her arm.

Fortunately the minister was busy with the marriage certificate and didn't hear her parting quip. He still looked slightly troubled, despite the appearance of such a well-known personage to give countenance to a rushed wedding. Rafe never did tell me how he'd persuaded him to officiate in the first place.

Rafe grinned impishly as he placed my marriage "lines" in my hand. Jerry had driven over a custom ranch wagon with "Clery Stables" in gold leaf on the green paint of the driver's door.

"Meet you back at the stable, boss?"

"Follow us."

We'd packed after breakfast, and our luggage was in the

Austin-Healey. Including the new suitcase that held my new clothes. My trousseau. We left the heavy station wagon behind as the Austin zipped down the quiet streets and onto the highway. When we reach A-Barn, I saw Mac leading Phi Bete, her legs bandaged, her body sheeted by Clery Stables' green and gold, up the ramp to an almost new two-horse trailer with heavy padded sides and heavy springs showing underneath.

"The vet and me bandaged the gelding, Mr. Clery," Mac said. He appeared to be surprised that he'd survived the experience. "Congratulations, Mrs. Clery. Did Mrs. Tomlinson get there in time?"

"Veil, stephanotis, and all, thank you, Mac," Rafe said, embracing me, to my embarrassment.

"Is my cat about?" I asked.

"He damned near—begging pardon—wrapped himself up in the bandages," Mac said, disgusted. "He was on top of us all the time. He's there, sitting on the black's rump and growling."

"Oh, dear." I broke free of Rafe's possessive grasp and hurried into the stable. At the sound of my footsteps, Dice started to complain garrulously, walking up and down Orfeo's backbone as if on sentry duty.

I ignored Rafe's chuckle as I hastily scratched Dice's ears and throat in reassuring approval.

"I've the bag of goodies for that mountain lion, Nialla. If we put him and the beef in the back of the wagon, it ought to be cat paradise enow. Or would he stay put in the trailer with the horses?"

"Well, yours is big enough so he wouldn't be stepped on, but it's strange to him."

So Dice was captured and put in the station wagon. He had plenty of space in spite of the suitcases, which Jerry had transferred from the Austin. When Dice discovered that there wasn't an open window and his protests were going unheard (he did look funny, mouth opening and closing and no sound reaching us), he stalked over to the roast beef.

"Orfeo better get used to me, Nialla," Rafe said when I made to lead the black to the trailer. "Hell, girl, I've got a reputation to uphold," he said in a low hiss that I alone heard.

I couldn't help thinking of what Bess Tomlinson had said — about his marrying me for the horses — but . . . that didn't make any sense, although Rafe had never said he loved me. Not once, despite the ardent moments we had shared. He'd said some pretty exciting things about me being made for love, had insisted on marrying me, but never a word that he loved me.

Orfeo had no such reservations, and followed him as docilely as Phi Bete had gone with Mac. Jerry stood by, shaking his head in disbelief. Just then the fair steward, Budnell, came striding into the yard, the anxious expression on his face changing to plain worry.

"I'd thought you'd left, Miss . . ."

"Mrs. Clery," Rafe corrected him.

Budnell paused in pulling an envelope from one pocket and a sheaf of papers from another. Then he grinned nervously.

"Your prize money, Mrs. Clery, and Haworth says you haven't signed the release yet."

"Nor will she," Rafe told him. "Not until she's been checked thoroughly by my doctor, and not until we know that the gelding has completely recovered from the fire."

"Now, Mr. Clery," Budnell began.

"Budnell" — and Rafe's attitude was of slight exasperation — "I'm no fool, so don't give me that jazz about the fair is not responsible for accidents and you're only doing this because at heart you're a sportsman. You know goddamn well exhibitors have been after you for seven years to condemn G-Barn and build a modern facility. Christ, that barn was put up by the farmers who used to race their mares on the flats."

"But . . . but . . ."

"We'll be in touch. By the end of next week. Good-bye and thank you!"

Rafe took the envelope and handed it to me, closed the window of the wagon, ignored Budnell's continued exhortations, as he gave the tow bar a knowing kick, checked the tires of the trailer and the fastening of the ramp. He got in, and left Budnell standing, mouthing words like a worried clown.

Rafe waved cheerily at all in the barnyard and drove off. We got to the cattle gate before Rafe eased on the brakes, swearing.

"Forgot Pete." He was out the door and running back to the Austin-Healey, which Jerry was driving home. They conferred briefly, but Rafe was cussing when he got back into the station wagon.

"No one's seen Pete since yesterday morning. I left tobacco money with Mac, but . . . " And Rafe shrugged.

"Doesn't he work for one of the exhibitors?"

Rafe shook his head. "He drifts from show to show in the summer. Used to train harness horses until he was in a bad crash on the Goshen track. Spokes of a sulky wheel caught him in the gut. Someone took him on as a caretaker when he finally got out of the hospital. He wasn't much good for anything else. He couldn't stay away from horses, but I suppose it was too much for him to go back to the trotting tracks, so he drifted to the shows. Wish I knew half of what he remembers about horses."

"Where do you suppose he got to?"

"He'll turn up," Rafe assured me. He reached over to pat my leg. "Hey, for chrissake, move *over*!"

Obediently I slid across the leather seat until our shoulders and thighs touched. He spared me a grin, flexing his hands on the steering wheel, then concentrated on driving.

He was a good driver, even with the erratic tug of the trailer. He kept in the right lane at a steady speed, slowing well in advance of lights and intersections so that there'd be no jerk and bounce for the horses in the trailer. There wasn't that much traffic on the road on a Tuesday anyhow.

He turned the radio on to a pleasant background level, increasing the volume slightly for the news broadcasts, in which he listened with far more interest than I.

Our wedding luncheon consisted of hamburgers, french fries, and chocolate shakes, eaten at a roadside stand. It was more fun than the most elaborate and appropriate banquet. Rafe was in a high good humor, and everything we said struck us as either funny or bawdy with double meaning. I couldn't be embarrassed or uneasy with him, although I was very conscious of the rings on my left hand, of my new status, of him. How could brides stand so many people around them, all thinking the same thing, their eyes knowing, staring at you?

Once we'd finished the last of the french fries, we disposed of the paperware, checked the horses, and were on our way—no rice, no leers, no weeping farewells. Shortly after lunch we hit the bigger highways and the concentration of traffic heading into the city of New York. It stayed with us to the approach to Throg's Neck Bridge (what on earth is a "throg's neck"?) where traffic thinned out. A few miles due south, and then east on the Long Island Expressway.

This didn't look like the Long Island I'd heard of, vast estates and potato farms, or desolate dunes and windswept grasses with sailboats prettily hovering in the distance. Developments were smack up against the six lanes of highway, all ticky-tacky, garish, hot, and treeless. Yet Rafe said he had a farm. Was it, too, surrounded by multiple dwellings in serried ranks, identical in design, differing only in the paint of the trim?

If he was aware of my growing apprehension, he gave no sign, but we'd both been silent since we crossed that Throg's Neck, the radio chattering into the hiatus.

There was some kind of problem that stacked cars down a long hill by a shopping center and up the other side. Traffic inched forward. When we finally reached the other hill crest, cars were stretching out again, with no sign of any impediment.

"Long Island Distressway," Rafe said, with an understanding grin. "Curvitis. Everyone slows down to take the curve, and it multiplies." He'd displayed no impatience with what was evidently a common hazard of this particular route.

To my intense relief, the ticky-tacky houses were abruptly left behind. Broad expanses of golf course could be seen through a comforting screen of huge old trees. One or two elegant homes came in view, well back from the highway, in lofty dignity among oaks. When we finally turned off the "distressway," there were actually crop-growing fields on either side, cultivated dark earth under the new green of healthy plants. Many trees overlapped the road, and it curved and turned like any respectable, little-used farming lane. Massive rhododendrons flanked an imposing gate of wrought iron and brick and here and there a long six-foot-high brick-and-ivy wall blocked off the curiosity of transients. We were obviously in estate territory. Signposts indicated that Syosset was in one direction, Locust Valley in another, and we were entering the village of Upper Brookville. I began to feel easier. There was a familiarity about this countryside, although, to my knowledge, I'd never been on Long Island before.

Mailboxes and signposts (elegant black, with gold lettering) announced homesites. Rafe carefully eased the car and trailer up a narrow blacktopped road, one which ought to bear the legend "hidden entrance," the turning was so abrupt. A Cyclone gate barred our way, and Cyclone fencing high with twelve inches of barbed wire slanting atop it went off in both directions into the woods.

Rafe pressed a control on the dashboard that I hadn't noticed before, and the gate clanged open. When we'd driven past it, it shut.

"I'm impressed."

"It sure beats getting wet or cold opening gates."

To the left, the trees gave way suddenly to a view of lawns sweeping up to the front terrace of a mansion in the Spanish style that had been so popular on the East Coast in the early part of the century—red-tiled roofs, creamy-pink stucco, square towers, grilled windows, all that, and probably a fountain in the central courtyard. A handsome wrought-iron gate between two stuccoed pillars led to the low garages behind the house as we swept obliquely away from it, down a narrow wooded road. Then the woods petered out, and we drove past a complex of paddocks, a jump ring, a fenced orchard with gnarled apple and pear trees under which grazed a bay yearling, just beginning to fill out. He came trotting inquisitively up to the fence and followed us as far as he could. Then he flicked up his heels and went back to his grazing.

"I've hopes for that youngster," Rafe said. "Bred him myself. You'll see his dam later on."

We drove straight into a wide flagged yard, through an arched passageway into the inner stable yard. On three sides were box stalls; the fourth, pierced by the arch, was broader, and held, I learned, twelve straight stalls for lesser breeds of horse, a hayloft on one side, and the tack room, garages with grooms' quarters above, on the other.

Everything was fresh paint and sparkle, the yard well

raked and concrete hosed down, with a sense of order and prosperity that ought to soothe but suddenly distressed me.

I had no time to wonder why I was upset. This was the kind of stable, barring a slight difference in style, in which I'd grown up in Lexington. I ought to be reassured. But Rafe had swung out of the car, and Dice was anxious to leave too. I just got the door closed in time to keep him in. Somewhere dogs barked fiercely.

As we let down the ramp of the trailer, a bowlegged man in the tightest pants I've ever seen on an adult male of fifty came rocking through the arch. He was clean-shaven, and his gray hair bristled from his scalp in a month-old crew-cut, but he looked permanently stained. He gave Rafe a dour nod, looked through me, but his face lit up when he saw Rafe backing out Phi Bete. He hurried to take the lead, stroking the mare's nose and crooning to her lovingly as only a misogynistic horseman can. Her restless prancing ceased, and she snorted at him, butting his shoulder, twisting her neck for his flat-handed caresses. Shameless hussy.

"A beauty, a beauty! Where'd you steal her, boy?"

"She's my wife's. Out of Smart Set by Professor D."

The hostler was impressed, but he still hadn't acknowledged my existence. Rafe took me by the arm and led me right up to him.

"Albert, this is Nialla Donnelly Clery. We were married today."

"Meetcha, ma'am . . . " he mumbled, touching his forehead with a purple-gentian-stained finger of a badly scarred hand. Some horse had teethed on him, from the look of it. Then he did a double-take and his watery brown eyes gave me a keen raking. "No relation to Russ Donnelly?"

"His daughter," said Rafe with almost as much pride as he'd announced Phi Bete's lineage. He shot me a wicked sidelong glance that intimated I must respond suitably.

"*Pleased* ta meetcha ma'am." And he was. Then he turned to Rafe. "Good blood. Good bones. She ride?"

Rafe's smile was pure malice as he turned toward the sheeted rump from which Orfeo's full tail emerged.

"You'd better do the honors, Nialla." He motioned Albert to move aside as I backed Orfeo carefully down the ramp.

"Juggernaut?" The old man's eyes widened, and the hand that had been stroking Phi Bete's nose was motionless.

"Orfeo is what Nialla calls him, and she jumped him two rounds without a fault on those nightmares Sunbury assembled for the trophy this year."

Albert was not to back down from his position. He gave a grunt. " 'S what I'd expect of any foal of Donnelly's. Put the mare in six?" he asked, turning to lead Phi Bete toward the east side of the stable.

"Yes, and we'll put Orfeo in seven."

"I moved the gray like Jerry said I should," Albert mumbled as he stumped off.

Rafe was feeling Orfeo's legs with a practiced hand. He tipped up the injured hoof and inspected the frog.

"I'll give MacNeil a call. We'll have him fixed up in next to no time, Nialla."

We watered and stabled Orfeo in a huge corner box, knee-deep in clean straw, the hay basket heaped lightly with fresh timothy.

"Now, about that lion of yours," Rafe said as we viewed Orfeo over the lower hatch of the stall door. "There's half a dozen beagle hounds, a few barn cats, and the guard dogs. Each is jealous and insists on his territorial prerogatives."

"Guard dogs?"

There was a muscle twitch in the corner of Rafe's mouth, and no amusement in his eyes.

"Against unauthorized entry," he said succinctly. "I'll introduce you to the dogs later. They're out at night, but they won't bother anyone to whom they've been properly introduced." He placed his hand on the flat of my back, pushing me toward a break in the hitching rail that ran the three sides, under the roof's overhang.

Dice was quite glad to be released from durance vile and made a low-haunched run around the yard, stopping to sniff at selected spots. Then he headed straight for Phi Bete's stall, jumped to the top of the open hatch, teetered, landed on the ground, and trotted to Orfeo's. He angled his rear legs and leaped up and over. I had to giggle at his muffled "yowie" of surprise. He'd've been submerged in the straw. I heard Orfeo wicker.

"Not that I wouldn't bet on Dice against any animal in the place."

"Boss, whatin'ell was that just now?" Albert demanded, appearing at Phi Bete's door.

"Mrs. Clery's coon cat. He stays with the gelding."

"Goddamnedest thing I ever saw," Albert muttered, and turned back into the dimness of the stall.

"Dice's not aggressive."

"He doesn't need to be," Rafe said with a snort.

He pulled the ramp up, telling me this'd take only a minute, but could I open the second garage door from the end. He backed the trailer into its slot with the ease of long practice, and I know how easy that maneuver is *not*. He unhitched the tow bar and motioned me to get into the car.

"Albert has obviously fallen in love with Phi Bete, and if Dice takes care of the gelding, they'll feel at home by morning."

When we rolled out of the stable yard, Rafe turned right, up a short drive flanked by heavy rhododendron and myrtle plantings, edged with ivy. Slightly hidden by three massive copper beeches was a hip-roofed, dusty-gray-shingled house, looking settled and pleased with itself. And welcoming.

The double-hatched front door was green and welcoming, too. With strap hinges of a trefoil pattern. Before I could take the first step from the car, Rafe swooped me up into his arms and carried me up the short flight to the porch. How he managed the door, I don't know, but it pushed in.

"Welcome home, Mrs. Clery," he said in a low voice, his eyes dark with feeling. I buried my face against his neck, against the pounding of his pulse. He let me slowly to my feet, his hands pressing me against him. "Never was able to do that before. Always married Amazons." Then his hands tightened on my shoulders. "None of them wanted to live here, Nialla. None of them ever came here. *You* belong here . . . with me."

There was an aching hunger in his kiss that effectively erased all thought of my predecessors. He broke the embrace abruptly, standing away and turning me toward the big living room, which ran across the entire front of the house, leading into a dining ell. It was a fireplace-leather-chintz room, with two huge soft Persian rugs. A dignified grandfather clock presided by the staircase opposite the door, by the cloak closet. I suspect there had been alterations on the original floor plan, because the house looked like the front-parlor type. It would likely have a huge kitchen, where most of the living had been done until recently, for the house was old, with broad-planked floors. And while it was not exactly the type of house I'd've thought Rafe would live in, it was exactly right for him now that I saw him here. It reflected tried comfort and taste, scrupulously clean and shining. Rafe Clery might affect "mod" sartorial elegance, but he demanded warm serenity, not modern sterility or passing fancy, in his home.

"I'll get the luggage," he said, leaving me to wander about the living room. I stepped onto the thick Persian, admired the flowers, and wondered who kept the place so spotless. Two men in the stables, a housekeeper here (live-in?). People who rode the circuit might put on a show of prosperity in public, but Rafe's was no sham.

"Mrs. Garrison usually leaves around three when I'm not home." He pointed one suitcase toward the stairs. "C'mon, I'll show you our room."

There was a reassuring emphasis on "our." Three steps led to the first, wide landing, where the steps turned at right angles for the longer portion of the rise, before branching left and right. Instinctively I turned right, toward the front of the house. The door to the master bedroom was invitingly open, and sun shone onto the dark-stained floor from the dormer windows. There was a huge, dynasty-founding bed with carved cherry posts and a hand-loomed cotton spread whose whiteness was accented by the muted tones of an old patchwork quilt. The room was masculine, from the heavy dark furniture to the comfortable leather chairs by the fireplace. Two doors in the right wall must lead to a dressing room and a bathroom, for the bedroom proper was not as long as the living room under it.

As Rafe opened the inner of the two doors, lights came up, revealing sliding closet panels, built-in cabinets, luggage racks on which he deposited the suitcases.

I was suddenly very nervous, oddly tense. I walked with stiff legs to the open window, gazing at the copper beeches, at the lawn beyond, the stable complex hidden by mature evergreens.

He was standing behind me, waiting, and I knew what he was waiting for, because I could feel myself ready. What had come over me, Nialla Donnelly, who had forsworn love? Who was this short man who, by his mere presence, could stir the juices in my loins, make rubber of my knees, and stir wanton lusts I'd never imagined I was capable of?

"Mr. Clery?"

As he unzipped my dress, he kissed the nape of my neck lightly, sensuously, and then progressed with kisses down my backbone, unfastening the bra in the journey. The dress slithered to my feet as his hands flipped the bra straps over my shoulders. As I wriggled out of them, his hands fondled my breasts, traced patterns down my hips to my belly, which drew in at the touch of his fingers. With both hands he pressed against the mound between my legs, pressed and pressed until he was against my buttocks, firm and hard. He released me to slip my pants down far enough so that they dropped the rest of the way to join my dress. As I stepped over them, I heard him undress, and turned to face him, my arms open.

He straightened up, his eyes on me with such an intense expression, hungry, lustful, possessive, and . . . wary . . . that it stopped my breath.

Then his arms closed around me, hard, and the next minute we were flat on the bed. He entered me and filled me. Incredibly, he had thrust only a few times before my body responded to his, arching against him. As we merged in a long, long, unbelievable release, I was dimly aware of two voices crying out at the same instant.

The warm blaze of the sun in my face roused me from a sleep as deep and restful as a cat's. The quilt was tucked up under my chin, a pillow under my head, but we were lying across the width of the bed, instead of the length. Rafe's hands were clasped behind his head, and his eyes were open, idly following the patterns of the sun-splotched leaf shadows on the white ceiling. His profile was somehow younger than full-face, the straight short nose, the sensitive lips, the sharp dip to the square chin. His beard was apparent. I could see the pulse in his throat, toc, toc, toc. The plateau of his chest with the fine edging of black hair. He smelled male, with overtones of anti-perspirant and after-shave, an enticingly sensual combination. I was suddenly conscious that my breasts ached and smarted and that my nether regions were sore, but I was too languidly relaxed to care at all.

He turned his head to grin at me, his eyes warm, and so loving that I felt my body inclining eagerly toward him. He gathered me gently, not passionately, to him, and cradled my head on his chest.

"For God's sake, I find I'm married to a sexpot." Then deliberate he passed his hand over one breast, and I flinched at the soreness. "I didn't intend to rough you up so much, dear heart," he said seriously, "but you're a powerful temptation to the beast in me, and so, so lovable." He gave me an affectionate squeeze and then touched the tip of my nose with one finger. "But you're not used to this sport of kings. I'm not about to override you . . . yet!" And his expression hinted of excesses to come, excesses I knew now I'd welcome at his hands, in his arms.

We both heard the faint engine throb and recognized the Austin-Healey's motor.

"Can't say I'm sorry Jerry took so long, but I was wondering what had happened to him."

With a sigh, Rafe threw back the quilt and padded to the mound of discarded clothes.

"No need to disturb yourself, Nialla. I'll be back."

I was only too glad to remain warm and lazy under the quilt, although I'd've preferred him alongside me. The Austin-Healey came throatily up the short drive from the stable, and then I heard Rafe's steps on the porch below.

"Car give you trouble, Jerry?" Rafe asked. "Or the cops?"

"Cops, but not with the car, boss."

"Oh?"

"That detective stopped me in Sunbury. Thought I was

you." Jerry gave a snort, and Rafe chuckled. "He was real pissed off because he'd been told you and Miss—Mrs. Clery had checked out of the motel Monday morning. And he had some questions."

At the tone of Jerry's voice, I sat bolt upright, clutching the quilt around me.

"What sort of questions?"

"Seems like they found Pete Sankey—dead!"

"Dead?"

"Head bashed in, lying in a culvert the other side of the parking lot."

I didn't want to listen, but I had to. I huddled under the quilt, trying to pretend the voices were from a radio program or something else absolutely unconnected with me and a Pete Sankey with his head bashed in.

"Poor old Pete. Who'd want to hurt him?"

"According to Mac—I checked with him after the cop finished with me—Pete was very upset about that fire. You know how he was about horses, boss. And Mac got the impression that Pete knew something about how that fire started. Last thing he said to Mac was he wanted to talk to someone about a horse. No one saw him after that on Monday."

"You got this last from Mac? Or did Michaels tell you?"

Jerry made a noise. "That Michaels doesn't say much, but he can ask some real sharp questions."

"For instance?"

"Oh, take it easy, boss," Jerry said, for Rafe's question had been sharp. "Nothing about *you.*"

A phone rang, the echoing jangle startlingly close to me. I hadn't noticed that there was an extension by the bed.

"Yes?" Rafe answered it downstairs. "Oh. No, madam, I didn't *sneak* in." The coldness in his voice was so marked that he was almost a different person. "I've been here several hours. No. MacCrate was driving the Austin. Yes, I was in Sunbury over the weekend. No. I understood you were in the Laurentians." His tone, if possible, got colder and . . . not insolently polite . . . but that terribly precise courtesy that's accorded someone hated and unavoidable. "What's his number? Thank you. I'll call immediately. No, Mother, sorry to disappoint you. I didn't murder anyone."

*Yet.* The word hung unsaid in the silence. Then the extension beside the bed gave a startled "twing" as the downstairs receiver was slammed into its cradle.

"I had to give Michaels this number, boss," Jerry said in a subdued apologetic voice.

"Not to worry, Jerry. I hadn't switched the line back to the Dower House, yet." Rafe sounded grim still, but he wasn't addressing Jerry in that stilted, almost-Englishy-affected way. "Albert can't be trusted to answer a phone, you know, so Garry always switches our line back to the big house."

"Shall I put the Austin up, or will you be needing it?"

"No, I won't be needing it. And please let the dogs out this evening before you go."

"I always do when madam's at home," Jerry said, sounding disgusted. "Will you be working the string tomorrow, boss?"

"Naturally."

"I thought being newlywed . . ."

"This time I married a horsewoman, Jerry. Good evening."

And Rafe had called that woman "Mother"? It must be his stepmother, I thought, trying to explain his astounding reaction to her. It had to be his stepmother, I decided when he came in, his face bleakly expressionless.

"I heard . . ." I said, gesturing to the open window.

"Yes, you would have heard it all," he said, shoving his hands into his pockets as he slowly walked across the room to me. He stood, for a moment, looking down at me where I huddled under the quilt, and then his expression softened, he became Rafe Clery—"Sure, Mr. Clery"—again.

"Shall we get the fuzz off our necks?" he asked with a rueful grin.

I swallowed my surprise, because the emotional tension of the phone call had caused me to forget completely the previous conversation.

I nodded, because, honestly, I didn't want to. Michaels had been polite and deferential, but he'd only been querying me about a fire, not a murder. A second murder, because Pete Sankey was dead because he had tried to help me. His murder was almost as senseless as my father's. Had the man who killed Pete killed my father too? And why? Why?

Rafe was dialing the number stolidly, frowning as the very brusque, bored voice of the sergeant-operator identified precinct, town, and himself. Rafe held the phone slightly tilted from his left ear so that I could hear perfectly.

"Michaels there?"

"Detective Michaels? I'll check."

Michaels answered after a very short pause.

"Rafe Clery here. I understand you've been trying to reach us."

"Yes, I have, Mr. Clery, and I've had some funny answers."

"I paid the desk clerk, because my wife had been bothered enough, and she needed rest more than rapping. Check with the doctor—Prentice, his name was, I think, if you like."

"You cleared out in a hurry today, too."

"I cleared out because I got married this morning, and show-circuit people have some pretty obstreperous notions of how to celebrate nuptials if they know about them."

Michaels mumbled something, then said, "I'd heard you and Miss Dunn were engaged. My congratulations." He sounded as if he meant it. "However, I have some questions about the fire, and . . . "

"Pete Sankey's death?"

"Yes," Michaels said after a brief pause. "I gather Mac-Crate got back. Where were you and Miss Dunn Monday night?"

To my astonishment, Rafe began to chuckle. "Michaels, man to man, I'd rather not answer that question. The desk clerk was paid twenty to say we'd checked out. We hadn't. But there's no alibi, because I gave Nialla a sleeping pill and took one myself."

I thought I heard a sigh. "Is Mrs. Clery able to come to the phone?"

"She's here, listening in, as I am." Rafe stressed the last three words. "A conference call, you might say."

I had no choice. Rafe tipped the phone toward me.

"Yes, Mr. Michaels?"

"I do apologize for disturbing you, Mrs. Clery, but I'd rather not have to make you come back here today."

"Not a chance of that, Michaels. Doctor's orders," Rafe cut in.

"I do have some questions that I'm certain you can answer right now, and we can get a statement later if necessary," Michaels went on, as if Rafe hadn't interrupted. "I understand that Pete Sankey worked for you over the weekend."

"Well, not exactly worked, Lieutenant. He was kind enough to stay with my horses while I was at dinner."

"I see. He was watching your stock the night of the fire?"

"Yes. He got the mare out and gave the alarm."

"Have you seen him since the fire?"

"No. I haven't, but they said he'd been into A-Barn on Monday. We wanted to thank him and couldn't find him anywhere."

"Then he never mentioned to you that he'd seen someone or something suspicious around G-Barn the night of the fire?"

"No, not to me, but then I wasn't . . . "

"Michaels" — Rafe had the phone again — "she passed out in A-Barn. And Pete said nothing to me when I saw him on Monday. He wasn't much of a conversationalist at best."

"Mr. Clery" — and Michaels' voice lost a little of its courtesy — "I'm trying to help your wife, not harass her. Her father was murdered, Pete Sankey is dead, and there have been three attempts to harm her. I'm frankly worried for her safety."

"Why the hell do you think I got her out of that town?"

Michaels sighed again. "Unfortunately, everyone knows where you live. I'm informing the local authorities . . ."

"My farm is fenced, Michaels, and I run guard dogs at night. Let Bob Erskine alone."

Michaels said nothing for a long moment, then asked to speak to me again.

"Please try, Mrs. Clery, to think back to the time of your father's death. Try to remember the most minute, unimportant details."

"It's no use, Mr. Michaels. I told the police everything then."

"You may know something, Mrs. Clery, you don't think you do. Give the matter some thought, please, for your own sake."

"There is something, though."

"Yes?"

"About this last weekend. I saw a man I used to know on the West Coast, Caps Galvano. He was at the Sunbury Fair."

"And that's a helluva funny place"—Rafe had grabbed the phone back—"for Galvano, Michaels, because he's a racetrack tout from California. And a guy answering his general description was seen leaving the car that blared a horn while Nialla was jumping the black." Rafe gave a quick description of Galvano. "He used to run a certain kind of errand for Lou Marchmount, and Lou Marchmount was in Sunbury Monday night."

"Russ Donnelly trained for Marchmount, didn't he?" Michaels' voice had quickened with interest.

"Yes, he did."

"Thank you, Mr. Clery. Thank you very much. And please stay put. I'll try not to bother you any more than necessary."

"That would be appreciated," Rafe said, and hung up. "We'll let him worry about it. Goddamn, why can't I *once* have a peaceful, uninterrupted honeymoon?" he demanded, slapping his hands on his knees in two loud cracks.

It wasn't a rebuke; it was an utterly exasperated complaint about conspiracy, which, combined with the long-suffering expression on his face, struck me as so ludicrous, under the circumstances, that I collapsed into giggles. His hard strong arms came around me, his laughter was in my ear as we rolled on the bed together. His eyes were merry, and he was not the frightening cold man who had stood in the doorway a few moments before. Suddenly he stripped the quilt from me, grabbed my wrist, and pulled me off the bed with such force that I was propelled toward the closet at a run, when he let go. As I passed him, I was sped on by a smart slap on my bare rump.

"Get some clothes on, woman. I'm starving. And if I don't feed you up, I'll chop off my hand on your bony arse."

The new dressing gown was at the top of the suitcase, and I was mightily relieved that he didn't suggest dining out. I wanted to be alone with him. Alone and safe with the high fence and the guard dogs on the prowl.

"There'd better be steak in the freezer, or Garry gets fired."

"Garry?"

"Garry. Mrs. Garrison. You don't think a bachelor keeps a house looking like this, do you? As far as I know," he said, clipping me about the waist and pulling me toward the stairs, "Garry doesn't eat brides."

"I guess you ought to know by now."

"That's a snide remark," he said, with no rancor, and turned me to the right at the bottom step.

It was a grand kitchen, and, as I suspected, had probably been the center of the house's daily life in other eras. A huge fireplace dominated one wall, but the kitchen fittings had been moved from the hearth to the east wall. A harvest table with rush-bottomed chairs was set in front of the fireplace now, with an electrified big-welled kerosene lamp hanging from the ceiling, its shade a rose color. Separated from the breakfasting area and the kitchen were closets and cupboards and obviously a freezer unit as well as a washing machine and a clothes dryer.

"What a marvelous kitchen!"

"Efficient, too. Had it redone to Garry's specifications — she drove the builder nuts — when I took the house over. She's not as young as she used to be . . . hey," and he hugged me, sensing my sudden anxiety about measuring up to someone he obviously cared for. "God, she's been after me to marry some 'nice girl.' She'll take care of you, too, and put flesh on your bones, so you'll be up to circuit riding."

"Rafe, do you think there's any chance of Orfeo showing . . ."

"With any luck," Rafe assured me smoothly, peering into the freezer. He came up with a freezer-wrapped square package. "Hey, how about meatloaf! With baked potatoes, the *cheap* kind. If you can find salad makings . . . you do know how to cook, don't you?"

"Of course I know how to cook!" I was indignant.

"None of my other wives could," he replied imperturbably.

I found silence the best reproof, and began to fix a salad. There were fresh strawberries, all hulled and washed, under a Saran sheet. They'd be marvelous for dessert.

"But if that hoof doesn't heal . . ."

"That hoof'll heal," Rafe assured me again, his eyes suddenly focused beyond me in a determined stare.

Almost as if Orfeo had to jump for a purpose beyond mine. Then Rafe told me where to find condiments and bowls as he started the oven, and we were pleasantly busy.

Sometime during the night, I heard dogs barking. At least, I was sure I heard the dogs, but Rafe's reassuring murmur, his hands clasping mine warmly, made the incident scant concern of mine.

 6

WHEN I WOKE UP, I was lying on my stomach, my head at the edge of the bed, so the first thing I saw were the dappled splotches of sunlight on the wide-planked floor. Along my left side was the comfortable warmth of a . . . husband. Rafe. I wanted to turn and look at him, catch him unawares, and satisfy a nagging uncertainty within me. And I also wanted to remain so comfortably content.

Unfortunately, I've got this habit, and once awake, I can't stay still. My back muscles were crying to be stretched. At my first tentative move, I felt Rafe stir.

"I didn't mean to wake you." I turned, penitent, to find him watching me, the slightest smile on his lips, and a dark, odd warmth in his eyes.

He slid one arm under my body, as if to pull me to him; in fact, I could feel myself leaning compliantly. Instead he stroked my face with his fingertips (lovingly, I told myself), as the smile deepened.

"I've been awake a while."

Neither of us had a watch on, but I could tell from the slant of the sunlight that it must be early hours.

"And, no, Nialla, you haven't kept me abed with your sloth," he went on teasingly, still stroking my face. Then his fingers trailed down my neck, tracing the outline of my shoulder before transferring, ever so delicately, to my breast. As he did finally pull me against him, my head on his chest, he sighed. "I was enjoying the sight of you, curled up in my bed like a trusting Eurydice." And his chuckle echoed rustily in his rib cage under my ears. (I had the fleeting notion that Rafe, for all his self-assurance, didn't quite trust me: surprising under the circumstances. I wondered how I compared to his other wives in bed. If they couldn't cook and didn't like his way of living, why had he married them?)

I felt his lips on my forehead.

"A daunting sight, I assure you," he added in an inconsequential tone.

I was desperate to stretch, but I could scarcely offend him by breaking his affectionate embrace.

"Do you wake up fast or slow, Nialla?"

"I'm one of those awful ones, up with the sun, and usually to bed with it." I'd better be candid and get us both off the hook.

"Thank God." And he released me, swinging himself off the other side of the bed, to stand and stretch until every muscle in his back was fully extended and his joints began to pop. I'd the incredible urge to run my hands freely over his body, for the touch of his skin on mine, to test the firmness of that musculature.

"Shower or bath? Milady has first choice." And he made a courtly bow toward the bathroom, destroying the image by a boyish smirk. "I'll use the john down the hall."

The speed with which I untangled myself from the sheet made him burst out laughing, head back, fists rammed against his narrow waist.

"You're no slugabed, I see, not with your background," and he was definitely pleased. But as he snagged a seersucker bathrobe from a hook of the dressing-room door, again I was reminded of Bess Tomlinson's flippant remark. Had he really married me for the horses? And because I was a horsewoman?

Well, if that *were* the case, I thought as I closed the stall-shower door, there would be many compensations, and I could make the most of them, while I could. For if he'd divorced two women already for cause unknown, I might not last long either. After all, he could marry someone better than a horse trainer's daughter. I turned the water on full force; the shower head, for once, was the right height for me, fringe benefit number one. I soaped myself thoroughly, aware that my breasts were sore — fringe benefits numbers two, three, four, five, ad infinitum.

Rafe had included a pair of Levis in his purchases for me, and a thin cotton sleeveless shirt. The day promised to be fair, and probably hot. The new Levis were stiff, but the slight flair in the leg kept pressure off my healing burns.

When I emerged from the bathroom, Rafe was just fastening the belt of his Levis — they must have been tailored for him, they fit so well — and his torso showed to advantage in the cotton knit pullover. He was a fast dresser, for he'd also shaved in the time it had taken me just to shower, dress, and stare at my reflection in the full-length bathroom mirror.

He grinned at me and took my hand, tucking it under his arm as we went downstairs.

"Levis aren't too tight on those leg burns, are they?"

I shook my head, because somehow he was too much for me. He was my husband, yes. He'd married despite my objections, my past, the knowledge that I was in trouble; he'd made passionate love to me, given me jewelry and clothes, shown me favor and approval in many small ways; if he *had* married me for my two horses — and he did have money enough to buy any beast he fancied without necessarily marrying the owner — then I should be glad I'd a dowry to bestow on him.

If Rafe noticed my withdrawal, my watery eyes, he paid no attention, cheerfully outlining his plans for our morning.

"I'd like to show you the place and my string after breakfast. I'll put in a call for MacNeil, the vet, to check Orfeo over. Then we can get to the shops and see what the local places might have for you to wear." He pushed open the door between the dining-room ell and the kitchen. "Hi, Garry," he greeted the woman in a neat nonuniform cotton dress and apron who was standing by the table, coffee pot poised over the cup of the single place setting. "This is my wife, Nialla Donnelly Clery. Nialla, this is Mrs. Barbara Garrison."

"Mr. Rafe!" Her eyes went wide, but there was nothing but surprise and pleasure in her broad smile. Or was she used to Rafe introducing new wives? "And no one telling me you got yourself married while you were away! You could have left me a note for the morning, you bad boy," she said in a good-natured scold. "Then I could at least have set two places and made Mrs. Clery feel to home here in her own house!" She was quickly remedying this negligence as she spoke.

Rafe, however, handed me into the place originally set for him, giving Mrs. Garrison an affectionate kiss on the cheek as she arranged silver for him.

"Oh, get on with you, Mr. Rafe. What will Mrs. Clery think?"

"That I'm smart to keep on good terms with the best cook in Nassau County."

"Oh, Mr. Rafe!" She poured coffee for both of us, smiling warmly at me as she filled mine. "Just wait till I see that Jerry. I'll tell him a thing or two, not tipping me off. Do you favor a big breakfast like Mr. Rafe, ma'am?" And her scrutiny was a little close.

"Yes, she does," Rafe answered me. "She likes a big breakfast, and she needs feeding up. Look at her, Garry. No better than a rail. We've got to get her back in form. She's a rider, Garry, and she's going to ride with me." I'd never heard that particular ring in his voice, and evidently, neither had Garry, for she looked at him with surprise. "You remember when I was jockeying . . ."

Her expression turned to one of disapproval, although I sensed it was not the occupation she disapproved.

"I used to ride for Agnes du Maurier, and Russ Donnelly was her trainer. Well, Nialla's his daughter. I've been waiting for her to grow up."

His hand tightened on mine, and I wondered why he felt

obliged to perpetuate that fiction with Mrs. Garrison, who so obviously adored him.

"Well, I never! Though I expect it's a good thing around here that you do ride, Mrs. Clery. Never hear anything else except horses, horses, horses. Would you prefer grapefruit instead of orange juice, Mrs. Clery? Someone"—and her tone underscored the pronoun which that meant she knew the culprit—"ate all the strawberries last night."

"We did," I said, like a penitent child. Then we grinned at each other. "Grapefruit will be just fine."

"Two eggs? Ham or bacon? Toast or muffins?"

She was sectioning the grapefruit as she queried me, and in a remarkably short time, I thought, had prepared and served beautifully cooked platters of eggs and bacon, with a pile of buttered toast.

"Where's your cup, Garry?" Rafe demanded as she started to leave.

"Well, I . . ."

"Nonsense, sit down. Got to catch up on my gossip." And Rafe leaned over, pulling out the chair opposite me and giving her no alternative.

Still reluctant, for she nodded apologetically at me, she picked up an outsize mug from the sideboard.

"Garry always has her ninetieth cup of coffee with me," Rafe explained. I could only nod to indicate I had no wish to change the custom.

She settled herself then; she wasn't a heavy woman, but old enough to be deliberate in her movements. She gave me a second apologetic glance as she filled her cup.

"Well, now," she said, clearing her throat as she spooned sugar into her cup and stirred vigorously, shedding the last of her scruples, "there's been some to-dos in the big house with Madam back way ahead of when she told staff. Does she know you're here, or do I . . ."

"She knows I'm here." I'd hate to have that flat tone directed at me.

"Does she have this place wired for sound?" Mrs. Garrison asked. "Well, there's been quite a bit of partying—I've been helping Mrs. Palchi, of course —but no publicity!" She pursed her lips and nodded her head to indicate the novelty of that. "You know how she likes to have her picture in the paper, Mrs. Wendy Madison entertaining the chairman of the board of this and the so and so of that, and how many of the jet set came. First I thought maybe she's ashamed of this new man of hers, but no, he's society. And horses, too, come to think of it. Then I understood he wasn't feeling well, but all those parties? Mrs. Palchi says he hails from the West Coast. Maybe you know him? Fella by the name of Marchmount." Her recital broke off as she saw the sudden stillness of Rafe's face.

"Is he at the house now?"

"Well, no, come to think of it, he isn't. Though they all went off together this past weekend to see the Marshalls upstate. Took the Hammonds with them, Mrs. Palchi said."

"Is he expected back?"

"I can't rightly say, but do you want I should find out?"

"Yes, I do."

"You don't like him none either, do you, Mr. Rafe?"

"You don't miss much, do you, Garry?"

"Not much," she assured him cheerfully, and I wondered if she'd noticed my reaction to the mention of Marchmount. "He's no gentleman, either, for all his pleases and thank-yous. You'd think a man his age would know how to behave in someone's house. Pinched that nice Marrone girl on the you-know-where, and she didn't know what to do about him. So Mrs. Palchi's been keeping her in the kitchen and lets Sam do the upstairs work. By the way, Albert did not want to let him into the stables, but Madam was along, and Albert didn't dare refuse with her staring at him that way."

"How long was Marchmount here?"

"Now, let's see. You've been gone since two weeks Tuesday, and Madam came back unexpected from the Laurentians then with him and that friend of his in tow. And then not near as much entertaining as you'd expect."

"And no photographers? Maybe her last face job is weakening," Rafe said, and his laugh was nasty.

Mrs. Garrison shook her head slowly. "I don't know, Mr. Rafe."

"What don't you know, Garry?"

"Can't say. A feeling I have. A trouble feeling. My right hand has been so itchy, I'd swear I'd touched poison ivy."

Rafe laughed tolerantly and turned to me.

"Garry's often troubled by 'feelings.'" And he patted my hand encouragingly.

"'Feelings' are what you trust when logic isn't worth a hoot," I said glumly, because I could feel "trouble" too. Just knowing Marchmount had been here depressed me. Because Galvano was usually his shadow.

Mrs. Garrison gave me a sharp approving nod and rose to clear away our empty dishes. "More coffee?" And she filled our cups without waiting for an answer. "If you could spare me a few minutes this morning, Mrs. Clery, I'd appreciate going over household matters."

I looked at her, startled. "I . . ."

Rafe leaned toward me, grinning. "All you have to do is listen, nod your head, and agree completely. Garry will do what she's always done anyhow."

"Now, Mr. Rafe, I'll do no such thing. I just want to know what Mrs. Clery prefers."

"Like no broccoli or French dressing, and starch in your shirts, and untucked bedsheets."

I nodded dumbly, feeling horribly inadequate, until I remembered Agnes du Maurier and snatches of conversations overheard.

"First let me go along with your routine, Mrs. Garrison, before I make any suggestions."

"Well, I don't know as what as few *sensible* ones wouldn't be welcome, Mrs. Clery," the housekeeper said, glaring at Rafe before she rose. "I'll just see to the beds while you finish your coffee."

"Madam entertaining Marchmount on the quiet, huh?" Rafe murmured as the door swung after her. His tone was pure distilled hatred. "What a pair!" I couldn't look at him, not when he sounded that way.

"Dear heart!" His fingers lightly but firmly turned my face so I had to look at him, but he was himself again. "Forget Marchmount. He was *here* before we came. He's probably still with the Hammonds in Sunbury. He couldn't possibly know I was going to marry you and bring you home with me. He needn't know you're here now, even if he should reappear. Although that seems unlikely, if she's back alone." He sounded very positive about that.

The realization that Marchmount had been here — where I'd thought I'd be safe, where Rafe had told me I'd be safe — was unnerving.

"Nialla, knock it off." And his voice was sharp. "We've got other things to worry about. Worth worrying about, like Orfeo." He pushed back his chair, tipped it until he could lift the one-piece phone from its wall hook. "Damn thing fascinates me." And he screwed his face up a la mad scientist as he punched buttons deftly. "Hello, Glen? Haven't you paid your answering service this month? Yes. Yes, I did. Got a gelding I want you to check over. Burned sole and frog. Yes, I've been soaking it, you bastard. Got it in a barn fire. No, not here, thank God. But I want him jumping in two weeks. Yeah, I know, but you're the local miracle worker, and I believe in giving my trade in the neighborhood. Yes, like what else is new? Around ten? Fine. No, nothing sensational *in* the ring, but just wait till you see what I brought home."

He hung up, beaming impishly at me. "Gives me a hard time, and always ends up doing what I want. You'll see. C'mon, time's a-wasting."

He knocked his chair back, catching it expertly before it reached the point of overbalancing. I rose hastily and reached for the coffee cups.

"And that's the biggest no-no, Nialla. No dishes for you." And he led me to the side door. "Although you may wish you were back with just dishes when I've finished with you." His voice was so dark and direful that I glanced back at him, and he was smirking like an old-time villain. "I've been trying to find a rider good enough to ride with *me* in a Jump Pairs Class, and you might just qualify."

He was so outrageous that I laughed.

"Wait'll you see 'em, Nialla." And his teasing turned into enthusiasm. "A pair of matched grays, half-sisters, not a bit of difference in height and conformation, might as well be twins. Broke and trained 'em myself, though Starrett in Lexington

bred 'em. But I haven't been able to use 'em in competition."
He put his arm around my waist and absently matched step
with me. "You can do it. Knew it the moment I watched you
riding Phi Bete at Sunbury."

He went on, though I listened with half an ear, telling me
about the nervy five-gaited bay mare who only needed a really
sure rider to show her properly, about his plans for the bay colt.
I was seeing much more that I ought to have realized before —
the prosperity of the well-kept lawn, the gardens, a
housekeeper, two men in the stable, all of which added up to
money. And suddenly I realized why I had unconsciously compared his manner to Agnes du Maurier's — it was the same
self-confidence of several generations of wealth and position;
the knowledge of family and background, of enough money to
satisfy need and afford luxuries. It explained his English and his
classical references; his handling of people and . . . What was
he doing marrying a trainer's daughter? Certainly not for her
horses. I could set my mind at ease on that score.

We had reached the stables, and I saw Jerry grooming a
long-legged bay mare who was cross-haltered and dancing
nervously as he brushed her. She must be the five-gaited that
Rafe meant. Beyond her, a rawboned youngster in very tight
jeans and a tie-dyed jersey was carefully wiping Orfeo down
under the close inspection of Dice. Someone else was forking
manure out of a stall, and I saw Albert coming out of the tack
room, a bridle on each shoulder and balancing two jumping
saddles precariously.

I managed to answer Jerry's cheerful greeting, his assurances that Phi Bete had already been attended, and he was
making sure Denny did a good job on the gelding.

I acknowledged that, realizing Jerry meant that no one
had told this Dennis of Orfeo's reputation. He was whistling as
he ran the cloth over the black's pockmarked hide.

"He sure is big and black," Denny said, glancing from me
to Rafe for approval.

"MacNeil'll be over to check this hoof," Rafe said, lifting
it. Orfeo glanced around with mild curiosity.

"He's taking notice today," I said, chirping to him.

"Over the worst of the affair then. Albert? Saddling the grays?"

"You told me to." Albert's reply was more an accusation than an affirmative, but evidently that was his way, for Rafe only grinned after the figure stumping to the far side of the stable quadrangle.

Then, instead of showing me the other horses, Rafe took me by the hand and led me through the low passageway to the pastures, out of sight and hearing of the stable yards.

"Now what's the matter, Nialla?" he asked in a level, impersonal voice.

I stared at him, unable to answer, because it wasn't one matter, it was a psychedelic composite of impressions and pressures, of a nebulous fear not even his presence and flip assurances could disperse.

"The house, the horses, Mrs. Garrison, Jerry and Albert and . . . and . . . all this. I'm . . . it's too much for me. I don't belong here."

"That, dear heart, is for me to say!" Rafe put his hands on my waist to draw me to him. I tried to lean away, but his hands flattened on my buttocks, pressing our hips together. I could feel him against me. He *didn't* fight fair. "I think you'll find you do belong here, Nialla. There's no question in my mind that your life is horses." His eyes compelled me to give some sign, and I nodded. "And you're certainly a horsewoman. The way you ride that black!" There was no escape from those searching blue eyes, from that strong will. (Was this how he trained his horses—sheer strength of will?) "You evidently want to make a go of it in the show business. So why not do it with me instead of eking out a peanut-butter-and-jelly existence on the fringe?" Still no leavening by the tolerant amusement that had forced me to concede folly before. "I admit I took an ungentlemanly advantage of your situation at Sunbury to forge a legal tie between us, but that, too, can be altered as circumstances warrant."

Only because we were touching so intimately was I aware of the sudden tenseness of the warm body against me and the fleeting shadow in those steady blue eyes. It wasn't regret; it was . . . I couldn't put a tag on it, but again I caught a glimpse of a crack in this man's apparently invulnerable self-assurance. I didn't want him ever to be vulnerable. My hands tightened unconsciously on his arms, and with my response, his eyes began to lose their impersonality.

"It's just that I didn't realize you were so . . . rich," I blurted out.

His eyebrows shot up, and his eyes began to gleam with an amusement that faded into a sardonic glance across the meadows.

"Rich? Well, I've money enough to run the place the way I like to, but the acres are, in effect, mortgaged, my dear, and the interest is high, very high." He kept one arm around my waist and turned me toward those mortgaged fields. His expression was bleak and unsettling. I hated that look and felt guilty. I should have suppressed my dismay and coped. After all, I had been raised in such an environment; I knew pretty much what would be expected of the wife of a horse breeder, and trainer, and I could learn to manage the graces required. Anything to keep that horrible emptiness out of his eyes, his face.

Suddenly a horse squealed, high and piercing. It snapped him out of the mood, and his head came around to the stables, his body taut with another kind of tension.

"That goddamned mare!" He looked to me, all trace of the strangeness gone. "She needs to be *worked*. She needs a good rider on her back."

"Well, what are we waiting for?" I demanded.

"She's a rough one, Nialla. Are you up to a real tussle today?" He glanced at my legs, and I remembered the burns.

"I wasn't burned where I grip a saddle—any kind of saddle."

"God love the girl." And he wrapped me in a hard embrace.

So I was atop Rocking Lady in a matter of moments, and she took my mind off anything else. That was all to the good, because fighting a fractious mare was something I could do. I made her sweat, and I made her obey me, my hands and my knees. I rode her right up to the bridle, and we were both sweating freely when I finally pulled her to a halt.

On Rafe's face was the same delighted smile he'd had in the bleachers at Sunbury the first day I'd seen him. As I wiped the sweat from my face, I saw Albert watching from the shadow of the stables, and I knew from his stillness that I'd done better than he'd expected.

"Mrs. Clery, you sure can ride," Jerry said, shaking his head respectfully as he took the weary mare's bridle and led her away.

Rafe grinned at me. "Not bad for a first session. Not bad."

"Not bad? I like that!" I rotated my shoulderblades to ease the strain across my back. "Why, she's been allowed to get away with murder."

Rafe chuckled, turning me slightly and kneading the muscles at the base of my neck. Did the man know people as well as he knew horses?

"You want the grays now?" Albert's words were not exactly a question, and not really a statement.

Rafe caught my eye. "Game?"

"I'm not ready for the dishes yet."

Albert came trotting up with the two mares.

Rafe had every right to be proud of them, for they were perfectly matched—probably right down to the position of each dapple on their sleek hides. They were dainty fillies, about 15.2 hands high, with good clean lines.

"Maisie and Sadie, born and bred here," Rafe said. "That's short for Masochist and Sadist, of course," he added with a reprehensible grin. "You'll find out why." He nodded to the left-hand mare and took the right-hand reins from Albert.

"How can you tell them apart?"

"You'll know, miz," Albert said as he gave me a knee up, "soon's he's up."

The words were scarcely out of his mouth when Rafe had mounted his mare, and she began to back, head tossing, hooves striking sparks on the cobbles. Rafe had her in hand and spurred her abreast of Sadie, who regarded her sister's display of temper with calm forbearance. Maisie resisted the maneuver with an ill-tempered fit of bucking, which Rafe sat out. Then, with a snort for her failure, Maisie agreed to move back to her sister, and Rafe led me toward the jumping ring.

Their opprobrious names made sense during that session, for time and again Masochist would attempt to get away with some maneuver to be hauled up, and patient Sadist would compensate. I got so I could anticipate Maisie's lunges and attempts to balk, and at the last we managed to take four of the six fences simultaneously. I didn't envy Rafe his jarring ride on Maisie at all, but sitting Sadie was a pure joy.

"Shall we switch?" I asked as we drew the horses to a walk.

"Switch?" Rafe was astonished. "No, we'll quit. We've had a good session on the twins. No sense souring Sadie, and I'm worried about opening those burns."

"Hey, boss, the doc's here," Jerry called from the ringside, gesturing to a tall figure standing in the shade cast by the stable.

"About time," Rafe muttered, and signaled Jerry to open the ring gate.

As if she had despaired of her freedom, Maisie made a dash and was pulled up sharply by Rafe. She squealed in bad temper and reared, coming down in a series of stiff-legged bucks. I'd not've thought she had the energy left. Evidently that was her final effort, for her head hung down in weariness, and she made no more fuss as Rafe trotted her out of the ring and around to the stable yard, Sadie following sedately. She was just beginning to sweat.

Glen MacNeil was the long bony type, with the "angry" face with which some Scotsmen are endowed. Actually he rarely lost his temper, but his features were clustered in the middle of a narrow face with so little space that his deep-set eyes appeared to frown, his brow was perpetually wrinkled where his sharp nose jutted out from his forehead. There were deep lines from his nostrils to the corners of his wide mouth, and between that and the cleft of his strong chin, one did have an overall impression of "anger" except when, as now, his face was wreathed by a broad smile.

"Show me the beastie I've got to miracle-ize."

"Nialla, come meet the MacNeil," said Rafe, gesturing me forward on the gray mare.

"Nialla, is it?" And Dr. MacNeil's smile threatened to break his face apart as he shook my hand. "That's not a common name."

"Russ Donnelly's daughter, Glen . . . and my wife." There was such a ring in his voice that I wondered if he was used to the notion of having a wife again.

"Wife, is it now?" Glen MacNeil boomed out, his eyes almost popping at me from under his heavy brows. "Wife, is it?" He rolled his eyes sympathetically. "Well, now, I wish you luck with him. Or is it Rafe I must console when he's wed to a girl who looks as if she can outride him?"

"Oh, Rafe's some hampered by his effect on the female of the species," I said very sweetly, and slid down the mare's side. Then I had to crick my neck to look up at the Scot.

"My charm was effective with you, at any rate, m'girl." And Rafe slipped a possessive arm around my waist as he shook hands with the veterinarian. "Heard about the barn fire at Sunbury?"

Glen drew in his breath and then stared at us. "You had horses in that? I thought they got all the stock out?"

"Nialla's dowry is two leapers, and one of them got a frog singed and enough hide gone to make him look like an Appaloosa. Give me your opinion."

"Of what? The wife or the horse?"

He had the lower half of the stall door part open when he got a good look at Orfeo. He backed hastily out and closed the hatch. "Are you kidding, Rafe Clery? That's . . . "

"That's *Orfeo*," I said, more sharply than I meant to, and brushed past the vet into the stall.

"Orfeo, is it? Orfeo!"

"Orfeo!" Rafe's eyes danced at the man's confusion and hesitation.

Glen took a deep breath and cautiously entered. Orfeo slowly regarded the newcomer.

"Christ, what's that now?" Glen demanded as Dice suddenly uncoiled himself from the shadows of the corner.

"The cat is Eurydice," Rafe said, his face straight.

Dice wove his way through Orfeo's legs and sniffed at the doctor, backing off as he smelled the antiseptics and aromatics clinging to the man's Levis. However, he did not raise his hackles, although he voiced a mild complaint about the disturbance. Orfeo swung his head down, whiffling at Dice, who made one further cryptic comment before retiring to his corner, where he observed the proceedings quietly.

"Coon cat, huh? Well, it oughn't to surprise me this black devil has an uncommon familiar."

MacNeil had mastered his reluctance, and crooning softly to the gelding, hoisted the damaged hoof, tapping at it carefully and then angling it so he wasn't standing in the shadow of the stall light.

"Another week might just heal it," he remarked, checking the hoof itself, mumbling approval that someone had stripped off the shoe. He ran gentle fingers over the other evidences of the fire. "You'd've thought fire wouldn't mark one of its own."

"Orfeo was horribly mistreated," I said, stung to speech.

"Never seen him look better or calmer, Mrs. Clery. How'd you tame him?" Glen glowered at me, but there was a glint of humor in his eyes that disclaimed his appearance.

Rafe cleared his throat as if he didn't want the conversation to take that turn. "Soaks, Glen?"

"You bet. What was the Sunbury man giving him by way of tranquilizers and medication? And, by the way, put the quietus on any brush or refuse fires for a bit. We don't need to stir up unpleasant memories in this boy, do we?"

The two men exchanged a glance of past experience which I knew neither would explain to me. I'd seen my father look that way at another man—a closed, men-only, questions-unsolicited look.

The vet gave Orfeo a thorough check, grunting occasionally as the horse submitted without resistance. He was shaking his head as he signaled us out of the stall.

"I know it's the same horse, Mrs. Clery, but I'd swear it wasn't." Then he snorted, rather like a restive horse himself, as he eyed Rafe's arm around my waist. "Seems your soothing influence extends to more than horses and cats!" His perpetual frown lifted in another of his beamish grins. "You brought him *two* horses?" he asked pointedly.

Rafe laughed and gestured toward Phi Bete's stall. She, coquette that she is, put her head out and farruped at her visitors. She looked inordinately pleased with herself, her hide shining like dark amber, her eyes rolling as she tossed her head against MacNeil's caress.

"Fine mare. Fine girl! Going to breed her?"

"Not with that crowbait stallion of yours, Mac," Rafe replied.

"I was talking to your wife, Clery. She's got a mind of her own as well as an eye for horseflesh."

"I bred her myself, but I want to jump her for a while." I glanced at Rafe, not really sure what my plans were for Phi Bete.

"Don't mind him, Mrs. Clery, he's just miffed because I bought Galliard right out from under his nose at an auction. What's her blood?"

"Professor D out of Smart Set."

"Say, you know Marchmount's been staying at the big house. You aren't going back to jockeying to give him a hand, are you? Seems his colors haven't been doing so well lately."

"I'm out of racing."

"Except steeple racing," MacNeil said in a sour tone of disapproval. "Well, I'll send over some more tranquilizers for the black." And he left.

"You'd like to steeplechase Orfeo?"

"The notion has certainly entered my mind since I won your hand in marriage, ma'am." And Rafe's accent was pure Kaintuck. "That is, if you really need an ulterior motive or two." His eyes dared me to challenge him.

"Boss?" Jerry leaned out of a nearby box stall. "You going to ride the bay?"

Rafe gave me a squeeze. "Your turn to watch me work . . . and marvel."

He gave the bay gelding a bruising workout in the jump ring, the big animal fighting him at every jump approach, standing off his jumps occasionally in an effort to thwart Rafe. Jerry and the two boys drifted to the ringside and off again, watching the fray, Jerry occasionally using body English along with Rafe's efforts to curb the bay's tendency to run out of the jump. (The gelding had a particular dislike for the brush fences.) The young Dennis blew only two bubbles on his gum, and then forgot to chew as he watched, and the other boy never dragged on the cigarette he was smoking. For when Rafe said he was a horseman, he had every right to capitalize the *H*. He was. The bay jumper stood seventeen hands in the shoulder or I'd lost my ability to judge; the gelding was nearly as broad in the chest as Orfeo, and certainly as well sprung, but the bay was rebellious. If he'd been Rafe's previous candidate for any steeplechasing, no wonder the man had hesitated. You couldn't expect to win on a horse that fought every direction of hand or knee; you needed one that would swerve pile-ups, take off-center jumps without shenanigans about when or how. Though the bay obviously had bottom enough for the arduous jump racing. No, Orfeo was the horse for Rafe. With my blessing now I'd seen him handle the bay. In spite of the amount of frustration, Rafe had rarely used his spurs, relying more on the crack of his riding bat to dissuade the gelding's notions. His hands on the bridle were firm, not rough, and despite the swearing phrases in which he addressed the horse, there was no hint of anger or impatience; sound but no fury.

Both horse and rider were wringing wet at the end of the session, but I felt better. Rafe had no sooner given the lathered bay to Jerry to walk than a gong sounded mellowly from the direction of the house.

"Good, I'm starved. Damned gelding pulls like a dredger," he added, slapping the flank of the bay in a "well-done." "We've time to shower. That was the warning gong. I hate to sit down sweaty if I'm not riding again, and *we're* going shopping this afternoon."

Actually we showered together, which was a unique experience for me, Rafe barking like a seal and making like a porpoise. I'd never thought showering could be sexy, too. Then he suddenly "turned off" and began kneading the muscles along my shoulders. With a slap on my fanny, he pushed me toward my clothes and strode off to get dressed.

I wondered how he'd learned to departmentalize the various facets of his personality. It must be a gift. Would I ever learn every side of the man? Much less know the appropriate response to each of his moods. Please God I never hear him address me as he had his mother . . . his mother? It must be his stepmother. I naturally dressed in green, a sheath that unfortunately showed the splotchy burns, but I couldn't stand anything over the ones that had opened during the morning.

Rafe came out of the dressing room, his heavy hair still shining wetly, but neatly combed and parted. He had on another of his elegant pairs of pants and an electric-blue Italian knit pullover which enhanced his tan as well as his eyes. He looked disgustingly vigorous considering his exertions.

He tucked my arm under his. It had come to my notice that Rafe always kept in touch with me. And he wasn't being possessive, exactly. Hadn't one of the therapy groups stressed the point that tactile communications were as important as verbal ones? I'd rather thought we'd established communication on several levels rather satisfactorily. The habit, however, was nice, a sort of "Hey, here I am!"

Succulent aromas dominated the hot-water/soap/clean-clothes odors in the room, and I felt downright starved. We were halfway down the stairs when the second gong rang.

Mrs. Garrison served us a tasty casserole of vegetables and sausages, hearty food for hard-working people, with a salad and a lemon meringue pie that stood six inches from the pan. Peanut butter and jelly, fare thee well! We talked of horses and MacNeil, of how to school Maisie, and we decided I'd ride her next, as horses respond differently to each rider. I told Rafe I'd like him to exercise Phi Bete. I didn't want to make her a one-rider horse.

We took off for the shopping tour in the Austin-Healey. The stores were grouped around the railway-station plaza in Locust Valley, which was not much of a town—actually a village, in the way western settlements never are. The architecture was consistent, just missing the cutesie, and the merchandise appropriately priced for the clientele—high. So were the antique stores and the specialty shops. Unused to being able to buy something that wasn't absolutely essential, it took Rafe's good-natured prodding, and sometimes high-handed manner, to get me to make up my mind. And then he'd add the gaudy sandals I'd hesitated over or the medallioned belt I'd fingered. The Austin-Healey's back was jammed with packages by the time we'd finished. I had not only the under- clothes I'd really needed, but five nightgowns and three wild muu-muus (for "schlepping around in" — Rafe had grinned lewdly), enough sandals and shoes for a different pair every day, four bathing suits (no caps, because Rafe didn't care if my hair got into his pool's filters). I didn't remember seeing a pool, but I also didn't cavil. Wonderful what unlimited funds will do to a gal's notions of shopping. There were five shirtwaist dres- ses, Villager and Norwich — Rafe said they suited the country image of me.

"There's a pretty good tailor nearby at Le Shack; he'll do some things for you in good fabric," Rafe said, "but that can wait a day or so."

The very idea of having clothes tailor-made for me was utterly fascinating.

"Right now, I want to get over to the saddlemaker in East Norwich and get you some proper boots, a couple of pair of breeks, and a jumping saddle."

We were pulling out of the parking space when a deep blue Cadillac convertible came within an ace of removing the rear half of the Austin. I'd been half-turned in that direction, as one does in a passenger seat when one's used to being the driver, and out of the corner of my eye I saw the Caddy's wide front just as the brakes shrieked.

Before the Austin had stopped bucking, Rafe had jumped out and was striding angrily toward the Caddy, mouth- ing oaths.

"Only you would pull such a half-assed trick, Madam. If you're high again, I swear I'll take steps."

Even before I had had a chance to twist around, I knew by the tone of his voice who the driver was.

I did not expect to see the bubble-haired blonde woman from the Charcoal Grill, and I certainly didn't expect to see Louis Marchmount sitting beside her, swallowing nervously and pale beneath his cultivated tan.

Equally evident was the fact that the woman was Rafe's mother, not his stepmother, for the facial resemblance was marked: the same set of the same blue eyes, the same straight nose and squared chin. But with the similarity of feature the resemblance ended. She looked young enough to be his sister. I'd've been happier if she were: a mother isn't supposed to hate a son that way.

"Well, Ralph, is that the new wife I understand you married out of hand in Sunbury? You might at least have had the courtesy to forewarn me. Particularly with Bess Tomlinson as matron of honor. The Hammonds must be enjoying a good laugh at my expense." Her voice carried clearly. She meant it to. "Present her to me." She turned her head to Louis Marchmount and added, "I shall have to have a reception for the girl, and I only hope she's at least presentable this time."

There was no expression on Rafe's face as he handed me out of the car.

"Madam, may I present my wife, Nialla?"

She raked me with a searching stare, stripping me of any confidence, as she perceptibly sneered at the marks on my arms and legs. Then her eyes narrowed angrily. "Well?" she demanded, rattling her fingers on the steering wheel in a peremptory fashion. "Surely you see Lou and remember how to make formal introductions."

"My wife already knows Lou."

"I do?" and to my utter astonishment, Louis Marchmount stared at me without a trace of recognition. He recovered himself and elevated his body a few inches from the car seat. Always the gentleman. "I apologize, m'dear. Can't think where we could have met."

"Nialla's father was your trainer for five years, Lou. Russ Donnelly."

Oh—why did Rafe have to say that? But for the steely grip of his hand around my elbow, I think I would have slid to the ground.

Louis Marchmount's hand went to his forehead, his eyes blinked rapidly. He was plainly disconcerted with this information, and peered at me again, frowning, trying to correlate fact with memory.

"I'm terribly sorry, m'dear. Haven't been well, you know. Awfully embarrassing. Really. Wendy?" There was a plaintive note in his voice.

"How could you, Ralph? I won't have Lou upset. He's not well." She stepped on the gas, and the Cadillac took off like a drag-racer, one tire scraping against the high curbing of the exit, leaving a touch of burned rubber in the air.

"It's to be hoped she'll drive herself to death one day," Rafe remarked as the car vanished.

I leaned against the Austin, taking a deep breath, trying to assimilate the impacts of that encounter. Wendy Madison hated her son: she loathed and despised him, and evidently took any and every opportunity to belittle and humiliate him. And Louis Marchmount did not remember a girl he'd raped less than a year ago. He couldn't have been feigning it; he actually didn't remember me.

"Well, will wonders never cease?"

I stared at Rafe, amazed at his reaction, at the laughter in his eyes. He laughed outright, for I guess I looked my astonishment.

"Marchmount didn't recognize *you*, and she was remarkably polite. You know, I wonder if Garry isn't right, and she's after Lou. 'I won't have Lou upset.'" His mimicry was appallingly accurate. He had seated me back in the Austin, and as he closed the door, planted a kiss on my head. "Otherwise, I can assure you, Nialla, she would have tried to reduce the pair of us to sniveling, groveling impotence. Which is one of her favorite pastimes. But if she's bemused by Marchmount . . ."

I caught his hand as he reached for the ignition switch.

"But don't you see, Rafe, if Marchmount doesn't recognize me, then *who* . . . ?"

"Who what?" He'd been following his own line of thinking while I was off on the tangent most vital to me. "Hmmm. We need a drink, and home's too far. Caminari's is close by."

Caminari's turned out to be a large Tudorish restaurant, complete with ivy, on the corner of the main intersection (if you could call it that) of Locust Valley. But the maître d' was obviously well acquainted with Rafe Clery, and we were ushered to a small table by the wide windows that overlooked an attractively landscaped parking lot.

I certainly wasn't the least bit interested in the damned parking lot, but the speed with which the daiquiris appeared at

Rafe's command was therapeutic. And he was in command again. For one brief moment there, with his mother, I had felt insecure in his presence. Silly, on reflection. He was wary of his mother, not cowed or awed. Though why he felt obligated to return courtesy for brickbats, I don't know.

"I had hoped," Rafe began after the waiter had retired, "that we could avoid an engagement with Madam, my mother, for a while."

"She doesn't look old enough to be your mother," I blurted out, startled that that was the dominant impression.

Rafe gave a snort. "Madam can afford the best surgeons, m'dear."

Face-lifting, of course. But her figure . . .

"She can also afford a masseuse and anything else her heart desires, up to and including Louis Marchmount." There was a world of disgust in his voice now, and his eyes, gazing past my left shoulder, reflected a cynicism I hated to see in him.

"I hate to see the way she affects you."

Rafe looked at me in surprise. "She doesn't affect me."

"You've never heard your voice when you're talking to her."

He gave me a very level look, apparently digesting a novel thought. "I guess she does affect me . . . up to a certain point. I let her strictly alone, but she doesn't always return the courtesy. She's big on courtesy!"

He was off again, in some . . . some purgatory of her making. Then his eyes snapped back to mine, as if he'd arrived at a decision. He leaned toward me and began to speak in that cold emotionless tone he always used when discussing anything connected with his mother.

"Sordid biography, Chapter Two. Wendy Herrington has been, in order of their appearance, Mrs. Michael Clery, Countess Milanesi, Lady Branegg, Mrs. Horvath, and Mrs. Madison. Widowed honorably twice, Mexico three times. I have a full younger brother, Michael, half-brothers John Milanesi and Presby Branegg. Mick is a partner in a good corporation law firm. He and his wife—they've five kids—rarely come to the island. Pres has just finished Yale and is 'looking for a job,' and

Giovanni has some position with the American branch of his father's textile firm. Mother always married more money.

"Strangely enough, I think my mother really loved Michael Clery. If he'd lived, she'd be a much different person. But he didn't. And she isn't. I was rising six when he died, and I've only a few memories of him. Unfortunately." The dead light in his eyes altered slightly. "I keep to the Dower House because I found you can't combine her sort of 'fun'"—his opprobrium was scathing—"with serious riding. I put up the Cyclone fence to limit social intercourse." He looked at me again. "She's mucked up my life too often, so that I limit the association to those occasions which are unavoidable in view of our unfortunate blood relationship. You need only accord her such civility as convention requires. And if she ever singles you out for her attentions, any attention, I want to know if I'm not present. Do I make our position clear in regard to Mrs. Wendy Madison?"

I nodded, because my tongue was very dry. Even the way he outlined his relations with his mother upset me.

"Good!" He raised his glass, and I hurriedly sipped mine to wet my throat. "Now," he went on, "about Marchmount's failure to recognize you. Had he seen much of you when your father worked for him?"

I thought that was an odd question. After all, the man . . . "No, actually, he hadn't seen that much of me. Dad usually went up to the house if he had anything to discuss with Mr. Marchmount. He rarely came to the stables the way Mrs. du Maurier had."

"Hmmm. And with your hair that stupid shade"—he gave me a look of affectionate disgust—"he'd not be as likely to recognize you . . . particularly in his condition."

Louis Marchmount hadn't seemed drunk to me. He was the kind of man who was a very boisterous drunk: I used to hear his whinny of a laugh when he gave pool parties. No, he'd seemed . . . sort of dissociated.

Rafe drummed his fingers on the table, just the way his mother had tapped the steering wheel.

"But, Rafe, he . . ."

There was just a shade of amused condescension in Rafe's grin.

"I think you have been refining too much upon that unfortunate incident, Nialla. I can't remember the face of every girl I've slept with, and Lou Marchmount is way ahead of me. Only because he's been around longer."

Shock battled with outraged humor, and I ended up giggling.

"It's not a trifling matter, Rafe."

He pretended remorse. "For him, it was." He grabbed my hands. "Honest, dear heart" — and his expression became serious — "I'm not being heartless: I'm realistic. I couldn't care less that your virginity was gone when I married you. I only regret you lost it under such circumstances and that it affected you so adversely. But if you thought you were branded, Lou Marchmount's lack of recognition ought to ease your mind."

"It doesn't, because now he *knows* who I am. And he'll surely remember that he raped Russ Donnelly's daughter because she needed money to clear her father's name."

"As I gather you were a scared virgin. I'd say with confidence he's not likely to want to remember that attempt under any circumstances. Particularly if he's courting my mother . . . Did you ever get the money? You never told me."

"Oh, you're impossible!"

"Well, did you take your ill-gotten gains?"

"No. I'd never touch it in a million years."

Rafe frowned. "Then you never saw Caps Galvano again?"

"I left that night, bag, baggage, and mare."

"Curiouser and curiouser. But you're sure you saw Caps Galvano at Sunbury?"

"Yes."

"Exactly when?"

"The first night you took me out. He was standing by the exhibitor's entrance to the grounds. He didn't look at me."

"But you passed close enough to him so that there's no doubt in your mind that you saw Caps Galvano?"

"Have you met him? Well, then you know that no two

people could *stand* like that. Sort of S-shaped. And he was wearing a cap."

Rafe grinned sourly. "Not that same houndstooth monstrosity?"

"No, it was gray, but the same style. I've never seen him without a cap."

"Are you *sure* that Galvano didn't recognize you?"

"Positive. His eyes sort of slid across my face and immediately away like . . . he couldn't care less. I should have been warned then."

Rafe turned the daiquiri glass around and around. "That complicates things, doesn't it? Actually, Galvano always had a memory for money owed him and horses. Did he ever see your mare?"

"He must have. He was always hanging around the stables when Dad wasn't there. He knew every horse Marchmount owned, and Phi Bete was stabled with them."

"He's one helluva long way from the West Coast, and there isn't a racetrack near Sunbury. Unless he's still running Marchmount's errands for him." Rafe sighed. "And while I don't put it past Galvano to slit the girth or honk the horn, why the fire? Unless it's *not* Galvano behind it. I certainly don't see him as a murderer. He's a sneak, a pimp, a bet-welcher, and a stoolie—but a murderer? For what motive? Your father never had anything to do with him?"

"Of course not."

He patted my hand reassuringly. "Michaels may be right, then—that you know something you don't think you know."

"And Marchmount is the murderer?"

Rafe brushed that notion aside with an impatient gesture. "Their appearance at Sunbury may just be a coincidence. Marchmount hasn't had enough grip on reality to murder a fly; lechery is his style. Sorry. Now, look, Nialla, take a swig of your drink and let's do some objective reviewing. Forget it was your father who was killed. Pretend you're describing a TV play, one of those fraught with symbolism and allegory, so that every bit of the scenery is relevant to the script."

I wanted to say that I'd been over every detail of that day with the police; I'd relived its horror a hundred sleepless nights, but I had no more chance of refusing Rafe's request than the bay had of refusing a fence with him riding.

"Dad had been down at Tijuana with the racers. I was at college . . ."

"Marchmount hadn't been winning much, had he?"

"No, but I know he wasn't dissatisfied with Dad. He knew his previous man hadn't been all that good. I don't mean to say that Dad was so fabulous . . . "

"Russ Donnelly knew his flat racers, Nialla, and better still, he knew who to put on 'em to win."

"Honestly, he hadn't much winner material in Mr. Marchmount's stables when we got there. But there were four very promising three-year-olds, and Mr. Marchmount certainly acted pleased. I mean, I know he was backing his own colors heavily."

"Hmmm. Too heavily?"

"Oh, I don't know, Rafe. You know, Dad never talked much about the betting end of racing. You weren't thinking that maybe it was a quarrel between Mr. Marchmount and Dad? It couldn't've been, because Mr. Marchmount didn't come back from Tijuana until the next afternoon. He couldn't get a flight out."

"And Galvano?"

"I don't know when he got back. I didn't see him until that night . . . that night I fell for his con game."

"We digress. Let's go back to your father returning from Tijuana."

"Well, he called me just after I got back from my eleven-o'clock class and told me to come home. He wanted to talk to me right away."

"You said he was furious."

"He was absolutely seething with anger."

"And Russ had a very high boiling point. But when he did get mad . . . What did he say?"

"That he wanted to talk to me and to come right home."

"Nothing more?"

I shook my head. "There didn't seem to be any need for more. I thought I'd be seeing him . . . in an hour, tops."

"Of course, dear heart. Take a drink and go on. You drove home. How long did it take you?"

"At that time of day, just under an hour."

"Then?"

"I got to the house."

"How'd your father get from Tijuana? Train? Plane? Car?"

"He had the stable station wagon. He usually took that with him."

"He'd driven that home? Where was it?"

"Pardon?"

"Where was it when you got home? In the driveway?"

"No, it was down by the stable. That's why I went there when I realized Dad wasn't in the house."

"Notice anything about it?"

"Should I have?"

"That's what we're trying to find out. I gather the police never uncovered a motive?"

I shook my head. "Not for lack of trying, though."

"And now three attempts to injure you suggest that someone thinks you know something you don't know you know."

"They've had over a year to kill me."

"But you hightailed it out of San Fernando, my dear, dyed your hair, and changed your name. It would take time to find you . . . and recognize you. And"—he pointed a short stubby forefinger at me—"neither Louis nor Galvano did at Sunbury. Ergo, I don't think they were after you. Now, you've discovered the station wagon. Describe it."

I tried to picture that scene in my mind. It wasn't easy, because I had so deliberately blotted out that whole period. Rafe let me think, not even touching me, though I was conscious of him, a bulwark against the terror and insecurity of those awful days.

"The station wagon was parked by his office. And the tailgate was down."

"Anything in the load bed?"

"Nothing except some loose hay. Dad always took his

own hay to Tijuana, you know. He got sold some moldy timothy once."

"Then why was he bringing hay back to San Fernando?"

"It was just loose stuff."

"Go on."

"I looked into his office."

"Anything out of place?"

I shook my head. The office had looked undisturbed. I'd been sure of that, because the police had questioned me over and over about his files. Was something missing? Would I know? Where had Dad kept records of his bets? Did he had an off-track bookie? They simply hadn't believed at first that Dad did not bet on horses. He didn't believe in it. Superstition. Once in a great while he'd place a carefully considered fiver on a promising yearling if he'd no horses in the race. Or he'd tell me to if I liked, but according to Dad, you just didn't bet on your own entries."

"The police questioned you about it, I gather?"

"Endlessly. They were sure that was the motive for Dad's murder, and, Rafe, they said the most awful things. They insisted he must be fingered by the Mafia. They tried insisting that Dad had doctored the Marchmount entry to win."

"That would have made your father seethe."

"If you think for one moment my father . . ."

"Christ, Nialla, I'm not even remotely suggesting he did. Remember, I rode for Donnelly. Don't waste your bristle on me. But you said that your father was livid with rage. If someone suggested he'd fixed a horse, he would be, and rightly so. Now, did a Marchmount entry win at Tijuana about then?"

"Yes, the one three-year-old Dad had ready. But he hadn't been doctored!"

"Don't overreact, dear heart. Only a fool would try that stunt, particularly so close to the Dr. Fagin nonsense. But something must have prompted that line of inquiry? Anyone strange hanging around the stables?"

"Honest, Rafe, I don't know. I lived at college during the week, and came home weekends only if Dad was there."

He patted my hands and then signaled the hovering waiter for another round. Abruptly I remembered that we were, after all, in a public place, however deserted it might be at this unfashionable hour.

"Okay, now let's abandon that tangent and go back. You looked into the office, and nothing was amiss. So then what did you do?"

"I went into the stables."

"And . . . ?" I could no more escape Rafe's insistent questioning than I could now escape total recall of that strangely distorted hour.

The stable had been cold and dark after the blazing California sun in the yard. The stable had smelled of sweat, grass, and horses. I'd called Dad. I'd called again, louder, when I didn't get an immediate answer. I'd even gone to the pasture door, to see if he was out there. It was then I'd heard the scuffling above, in the hayloft.

"I couldn't imagine what Dad was doing up there."

"But there was hay in the wagon bed?"

"Oh, you mean, someone had sold him bad hay at home?"

Rafe shrugged.

"That wouldn't have made him leave racers at Tijuana."

"So?"

"Then I climbed the ladder to the loft."

"More than one way up?"

"Yes." And I grimaced, because if I'd kept my wits about me instead of having hysterics when I discovered Dad was dead, I might have seen and identified his killer leaving by one of the other exits. "It's a big loft. Three ladders up, and the main loft door."

"Go on."

This was the hard part. I swallowed. "The loft door was open: I remember that. And there was hay scattered all over. And Dad was spread across three bales, the pitchfork going up and down . . ."

Rafe's grip hurt me, but I needed the pain. Just then the waiter set two more drinks in front of us. I drank almost half of mine.

"So," Rafe said in a quiet voice, "whoever had killed your father had managed to wipe his fingerprints from the handle and leave by any one of three ways, eliminating the ladder you'd used."

Rafe shook his head angrily, as if he was annoyed with himself. He frowned deeply again, his eyes dark with shifting thought.

"Now, a slit girth wouldn't necessarily have resulted in a fatal accident," he said at last. "A horn might have put your horse off, possibly resulting in your falling and injuring yourself."

"And a barn burning around my head?" I instantly regretted my sarcasm.

"Meant to frighten you, Nialla, not kill you."

"The difference is slight."

"True, but vital. And blackmail is not outside Caps Galvano's talents."

"I don't understand."

Rafe's expression was patient. "He extorted money from you the first time . . ."

"But, Rafe, I was down to peanut-butter sandwiches."

"That's true." Then he glanced severely at me. "You mean Russ didn't have any insurance?"

"Yes, but . . ." I felt so foolish I wanted to sink into the ground. "I never thought about it when I left. They'd told me something about probate."

"Russ did have a will?"

"Yes. It was in the safe-deposit box, but that was all sealed and things because of the murder."

"And you've never written to the lawyer or bank, claiming your inheritance?"

I flushed and mumbled that I hadn't. I couldn't bear Rafe grinning like that.

"We'll get on to that first thing. I rather think you'd feel more comfortable if you did have some money of your own, Nialla, though God know you're welcome to all I have, dear heart."

His fingers stroked my palms gently until I finally could look him in the face. Oh, God, how I loved him.

"And Caps knew there was money?" I asked instead.

"I wouldn't put it past him. The theory makes more sense

than a murderer seeking you out, particularly when none of those incidents could have proved fatal."

"One did. Pete Sankey's dead."

"And if that *is* Caps Galvano's work, we still don't have to worry. It's in the capable hands of Lieutenant Michaels now." He drained his glass and motioned me to do likewise.

"It's all so sordid, Rafe. So vile. Louis Marchmount and Caps Galvano are alive, and good, decent men like my father and Pete Sankey, who was only doing me a favor . . . "

"Easy, Nialla. Let's go home now."

"And you." I resisted his attempt to pull me from the chair. "You've done me a favor, too, Rafe Clery. What's going to be your reward?"

He raised his eyebrows in that sardonic way of his when he's amused with the antics of someone.

"Dear heart, Rafe Clery does *favors* for no one. And I can take care of myself . . . and you!"

He set his jaw, and bowing, offered his hand to me again.

"Sure, Mr. Clery," echoed, unsaid, in my ears.

 7

HE REFERRED ONCE to that conversation on the way home, to inform me that he'd call Michaels and tell him that Galvano had tried a con game on me in California and was obviously setting me up again. He appeared to have a great deal more confidence in Lieutenant Detective Michaels than I did, but then, I'd had a disastrous confrontation with certain law-and-order elements, and my judgment was a trifle prejudiced.

Rafe drove into the stable yard instead of up to the house.

"First I'm going to take you to the dogs, dear heart," he said. " 'Bout time, too."

As if they knew they were about to be visited, the deep canine voices raised a greeting. Rafe ushered me out of the stable yard, to the right, where a large enclosed run was partly sheltered by huge long-needled pines and the side of the stable.

The dogs were hysterically barking and leaping frantically up the ten-foot fence, but it was not our arrival that had excited them.

Calmly, with great precision of step, Dice was touring their pen on the upper bar. He seemed completely unconcerned by the efforts of the two large silver shepherds, oblivious to the snapping jaws that came rather close to his daintily placed feet. It was as arrant a display of confidence as I've ever seen, though I didn't in the least doubt that Dice could have tangled with both dogs and emerged alive. Quick as shepherds are, they're no match for the agility of an old campaigning tom.

"Dice! That's taking an unfair advantage. Get down here, you tease."

Dice regarded me with some surprise on his white-masked face, and flicked his tail saucily.

"Dice!" Rafe said. "No nice roast-beef scraps! No more chicken hearts."

He halted the insolent tail mid-arc, as if he believed the threat. He didn't seem to gather himself, but the next moment there was the flash of white belly fur over our heads. The thick evergreen branch whipped up and down from such an assault. Dice's complaints faded as he used the upper route to less parlous pursuits.

Rafe chuckled with delighted malice, and his eyes were dancing with mischief as he turned to me. "He's a dirty infighter, too, isn't he? But I won't peach on you and tell the dogs you're his." He pulled me close enough to kiss my cheek.

I had to laugh.

The dogs, beautifully marked silvery shepherds, weighing a good hundred and twenty pounds apiece from the look of them, were respectively Dame and Demon. They came readily to Rafe on command, tails wagging, their irritation over Dice completely forgotten. I was introduced, duly inspected with slightly damp whuffles, and then ignored as the two vied for Rafe's caresses. They all but knocked him over in an attempt to get his favor. He laughed and braced his legs against their enthusiasm, cuffing them playfully. They growled happily as they mouthed his arms and made to nip his ankles. After several passes he ordered them down, and they backed off, with much sheepish running of tongue around their chops. They'd been well trained.

As we left, they were already seeking the sun-warmed corner, circling the chosen spot before they dropped, to recline in Germanic dignity.

"Did you ever have a barn fire?" I asked as we walked back to the house.

"No." But Rafe's expression was grim. "But almost. And that's the kind of miss I'd rather keep a mile away. A couple of Madam's cronies elected to take a toss in my hay a few years back. Albert happened to be up with a sick mare and went to investigate the noises in the loft. The goddamned fools were smoking, and one of 'em tossed a lighted butt into the hay just as Albert got there. He smothered it before it could do more than light some chaff. I put the dogs in a year ago when there was a rash of vandalism and petty looting. Hard-liners will scale ten-foot fences to keep in their habit, but dogs make this farm very inhospitable. Let's get your loot organized before dinner. I want to see you in something besides green, love."

After Rafe had brought up all the packages, he muttered something about speaking to Garry and left me. It ought to have been fun for me to put away all the pretty things we'd bought together. Instead I found my pleasure soured by the disquieting scene with Rafe's mother and Marchmount. I was enervated by reaction. I could not dismiss the Sunbury accidents as easily as Rafe could, to the capabilities of Lieutenant Michaels. Nothing was that simple these days. And I had that awful "thing" about compensation. I'd the gift of Rafe's protection, the prospect of the kind of life I'd always wanted, and for such riches I'd have to pay. Somebody's Law of Equity.

But I'd better take my clues from Rafe. A glum superstition-prone wife would not win his affections. And it was reassuring to think I had some money of my own, even if it was, in effect, blood money.

I put such thoughts out of my mind and dressed for dinner in one of the elegant new gowns. I could scarcely call anything at those prices "dresses." I put on fancy sandals and a pretty necklace and earrings of dainty shells. I experienced a surge of pure feminine vanity as I looked at myself in the long mirror: by God, I looked like someone!

Mrs. Garrison served Someone and her husband a simple but elegant meal, starting with an excellent muttony broth, a flounder that was as tender and delicate as sole (she knew the man who'd caught it that morning off Lloyd's Neck, where the flounders were running), and a whipped concoction guaranteed to put flesh on anyone's ribs.

As she poured second cups of coffee, Rafe gave her a stern look. With a sigh and a slightly apologetic nod to me, she found her cup and joined us.

"Well, Mr. Rafe, Mr. Marchmount's back. Came in on the afternoon train, and that friend of his arrived by car a little later on. Of course, I told Mrs. Palchi I couldn't help out right now, but she said there was just them two more."

"That friend of Marchmount's doesn't wear a greasy gray cap, does he?"

"A greasy cap? Lands no, Mr. Rafe. He's a foreign gentleman and dresses very well, Sam says, though he does favor wild California shirts and those indecent tight pants that flare out." She seemed unaware that Rafe wore extremely close-fitting pants that flared out.

"No caps in sight?"

"None."

"Can you find out if there has been such a type—racetrack-tout type?" Rafe asked.

"Now, you know perfectly well that kind wouldn't get in Madam's house, Mr. Rafe."

"True enough," he agreed amiably, "but I still want to know if such a type has been seen there since Madam took up with Marchmount."

"That I can do easy enough," she said, and finishing the last of her coffee, arose. "Of course, Mr. Marchmount gave Sam strict orders that he wasn't seeing anybody."

"Oh?"

"That's right. Sam's to say that Mr. Marchmount isn't there. Orders from Madam and Mr. Marchmount. Sam said he was slipped a twenty."

Rafe made a grimace of surprise at me.

"Any indication why?"

"Well, it seems as if Mr. Marchmount's health isn't too good. And that's a fact, for Madam took him into a specialist Dr. Baumann recommended. All the way into New York. You ask me, it's all that drinking and late hours for a man of his age. Can't burn a candle at both ends, you know. Must say I never thought Madam'd waste so much time on a *sick* man. Would you be wanting any likkers?" (That's the way she pronounced it, at any rate.)

"Good brandy'll settle all that rich food, come to think of it."

"Rafe!"

My outraged exclamation came on top of Mrs. Garrison's, and Rafe ducked, utterly unabashed.

We took the brandies out to the veranda, watching evening close in until the big trees blended with the dark sky. Lights came up in the stable yard suddenly, underlighting the foliage dramatically. We strolled down to the stable to check on the horses. Dice sprang from a straw-filled corner of Orfeo's stall, prrrowwing softly with the inner contentment of a full stomach. I wondered how much flounder he'd had.

"You're a naughty boy, bothering the dogs." But I softened the scold by scratching his chin vigorously.

He pulled his head away, eyed me balefully, and jumped down. Rafe chuckled.

"Can't tell that one a thing, can you?"

"Well, he's been warned."

Rafe's arm around my waist tightened. "'I told you so,'" he chanted in a nasal nag.

"Dice's not foolish."

"I didn't imply he was."

"And he takes his job as stable cat to Orfeo very seriously."

"I've noticed." And Rafe was beginning to nibble my face with kisses.

The gong sounded, startling us both.

"Phone call."

Mrs. Garrison was on the veranda when we turned the curve of the drive.

"There's a phone call for Miss Nialla," she said, sounding surprised and a little troubled.

"For me?"

"Probably Michaels," Rafe muttered, his fingers closing around my arm reassuringly as we walked up the steps.

"Nialla Dunn Donnelly?" asked a man who was not Detective Lieutenant Michaels.

I glanced frantically at Rafe even as I stammered out a reply. Rafe mouthed something to Garry and then went up the stairs three at a time, but I didn't hear the click of the upstairs extension.

"Heard you've been having some real uncomfortable accidents lately, Miss Dunn Donnelly. You need some protection."

"Protection? I'm afraid you've got the wrong person."

"Oh, no I don't," the man said in a snarl. Did he sound like Caps Galvano? I couldn't remember having heard Galvano over the phone. "I've got the right party, all right, sister. Had your saddle girth cut, didn't you? Your gelding spooked? Yeah, sister, I'd say you needed protection bad."

"I have protection. I've got fences and guard dogs and a husband to protect me from con artists like you."

From his end I heard a sort of surprised snarl and felt that I was handling him and his threats properly.

"High and mighty all of a sudden, ain't you?" The vicious taunt was too confident. "Feel safe with fences and guard dogs. But how long will that fancy husband of yours protect you when he sees what I have to show him?"

"You're wasting your time."

"I don't think so. Not with the photos I've got in front of me."

"Photos?"

"Yeah, some pretty, pretty pictures of you and someone else. In a pretty compromising position. In fact . . ."

"You couldn't have any such photos."

"Oh, couldn't I?" The angry snarl was back in his voice. "You got a short memory, sister. The night of June eighteenth? . . ."

I slammed the phone down. He had to be lying. He had

to be. I'd've seen a flashbulb go off. And the candles that Marchmount had insisted on couldn't have given off enough light for a picture. I was trembling so badly I had to hold on to the phone table, and it wobbled. Mrs. Garrison came bustling in from the kitchen, and I wanted to run from her, but I couldn't move. Oh, God, what did I do now?

"The nerve of some people!" Mrs. Garrison's eyes were sparkling with indignation. She enfolded me in her arms, patting me on the back with comforting gestures. "How can they think of such filthy things? The very notion . . . I'd heard of such people, peddling faked-up photographs, just to get money from nice people who don't want their names ruined. But I never really believed such tales. How could anyone . . ."

"What do you mean, you couldn't trace that call?" Rafe was bellowing. "You had enough time. No, I don't need police authorization when I get crank calls. But, by God, the next time I ask you to trace a call, you better do it, my good woman, or you'll be damned sorry you didn't. Threaten you? I don't threaten! As you'll find out."

He was still damning the operator as he stamped downstairs, his eyes a brilliant blue. Then he caught sight of me, and his expression altered. He was down the last of the stairs and had me in his arms before the sob in my throat could be born. Mrs. Garrison's comfort had been strangely debilitating; his embrace was bracing. I swallowed my fear.

And nearly choked on it as the phone rang again, shrilly, viciously. But Rafe grabbed it. From the violent look on his face I knew that it was the blackmailer. He listened for just a moment.

"No, buster," he said in a deadly calm voice, "my wife is not coming to the phone. You've got me to deal with. What?" This time Rafe held the phone where I couldn't hear. "No. No, bud, that won't work. Send those photos to me if you feel inclined, send 'em to *The Daily News*, wherever you want. But I tell you this, loud and clear, not one red cent would you get from me, and all you'll get from the editors is a get-lost. So get lost. Shove it, boobie!"

He jammed the phone down on the cradle only long enough to disconnect that call, then began dialing again so hard the base jumped half across the table, until Mrs. Garrison steadied it.

"We can dispense with this kind of nonsense right now. Threaten my wife in my house, will he? He's made another mistake."

"You're not calling the police?"

He paused, stared at me incredulously, and then dialed the last two digits. "You're damned right I'm calling the police."

"But Rafe, if he . . ."

"There're no 'ifs' in dealing with a blackmailer, Nialla. You give them one bloody cent, and you'll be paying for the rest of your life." The fury in his face faded a little, and he pressed my head against his neck. "I *know* what I'm doing, Nialla. Believe me, I do. Hello? This is Rafe Clery. I want to speak to Detective Michaels. No? Then have him call me back as soon as you locate him. How's that?" The cords of his neck stood out against my forehead, and he didn't seem to breathe for a moment. When he spoke again it was in that dead, cold expressionless voice, the soft kind that no one ignores. "I'll repeat my message. Loud and clear, Sergeant Cartland. This is Rafael Clery in Syosset. I expect to hear from Lieutenant Detective James Michaels within the next half-hour, because if I don't, I know who to report."

He put the phone down so deliberately there was only a faint click when the plastic met the cradle.

I struggled away from him, bitter at such a betrayal. He caught me by the shoulders and held me, his eyes still blazing, his face grim.

"Nialla, you got sucked into paying off before, and what happened? Running didn't do any good. It never does."

"But he said he had pictures . . . Rafe how could he?"

Rafe's eyes darted, warning me that Mrs. Garrison was there. I gasped and burst out crying.

"Exactly, Nialla. How could he?" He scooped me up in his arms, carried me to the sofa. "We need some brandy, Mrs. Garrison."

"Rafe, there wasn't any flash," I cried when she'd left. "There wasn't."

"Whether there was or wasn't isn't the point, Nialla. Get a grip on yourself. I know what to do."

"But if he does send the photos . . ."

"Nialla"—and he shook me, his hands hard and hurting on my arms—"can't you get it through your head? Those shots aren't worth anything to anyone but you. Your fear is his currency. D'you honestly think that one more pornographic photo is going to make any dent in what pours in to most rag newspapers? Well, if you were bedding Richard Burton, possibly."

He held me more gently now, because even the notion of me in the same bed as Richard Burton was ridiculous. Just then Mrs. Garrison returned. She bore the brandy decanter and two crystal snifters on a silver tray, linen-lined. Somehow Richard Burton's face was superimposed on hers, and I burst out giggling.

"That's my girl," Rafe said. He splashed a healthy jolt in one goblet and told me to take a good snort. I did, and it burned all the way down.

"Mr. Rafe"—and Mrs. Garrison's lips were still thin with anger—"I'd be glad to stay the night."

"Garry, I don't think much of that character's threats."

"You certainly let him know where we stand, Mr. Rafe, but I'd rest a lot easier tonight here than I would in my bed at home, worrying whether that awful man could get in. You know what a light sleeper I am."

Rafe grinned and patted her hand affectionately. "My top dragon! I think Nialla'd feel safer with all her loyal legions on hand. Wouldn't you, dear heart?"

I felt tears threatening again, and I wondered if she'd feel the same intense loyalty if she *knew* how much truth there was to that awful threat.

"Awful man, awful man," Mrs. Garrison murmured. "I'll be right in the kitchen, Miss Nialla, if you want something else."

Rafe started to rise, and when I reached after him, patted my hand. "Mobilizing the troops to repel invaders." He dialed three numbers. "Jerry? I want the dogs out now, and if you can, I'd like you to stay on tonight. Shotgun detail. Ask Albert to bed down with the mare, right? And he's to keep his ears open for the gelding's stall. Yes, I know he won't, but I'm only asking him to keep his ears and eyes open." He listened, nodding once or twice as Jerry evidently repeated his instructions. Then he gave a snort. "No, Jerry. Not the big house. Our girth-slitting, horn-blowing, barn-burning friend is in the vicinity. Yes, I agree. Thank you!

"Now, Nialla" — and there was something daunting in his face when he joined me on the sofa again — "let's sort this out for once and for all. You heard Mrs. Garrison's reaction, and she listened to everything on the extension. I admit that you hung up before he got to specifics, but *she didn't believe him*."

"But . . . Rafe . . ."

"Shut up," he advised, not unkindly. "His threat is aimed at compromising a bride, but I already know about Marchmount. All about him. Therefore those pictures could not affect us, you and me, because I wouldn't let them."

His strong fingers forced my head up. There were angry lines at his mouth, and the frown made him look older and fierce, but his eyes were dark and, I guess, sad.

"No matter how preposterous those photos are, I've seen worse. I know the type." He gave an odd kind of a snort. "Hell, I even modeled for some at one point." He snorted again at my gasp, and looked at me with a wry grin. "I'm not a nice guy, Nialla. I told you that. That's right, shake your head, because nothing I say is going to change your opinion of me. Correct?" I nodded, and his smile curved up in a kind of smugly satisfied way. "Then, dear heart, using the same irrational logic, *nothing* can convince me you're *not* a nice girl. Fair?"

I wanted to slap his face, and I wanted to laugh because he'd talked me so neatly into that trap.

"So" — and he cradled me in his arms with the air of someone who has won a decisive victory — "we now ponder those alleged feelthy pictures from another angle. Let's assume, since that particular fateful night was mentioned, that Marchmount is the other body. Ergo, why isn't our chum peddling his wares to Marchmount? Or is that why Marchmount is not at home at the big house?"

The phone rang. I jumped as if I'd been kicked. Rafe gave me a reassuring grin as he strode to answer it.

"Good evening, Michaels. I see Cartland got my message to you. Mrs. Clery just had a threatening phone call that I tried to trace, with no cooperation from the local operator. The extortionist had some compromising photos he told Nialla he'd send me unless he got paid off. Oh, yes, he mentioned the accidents, and when she wouldn't grovel, brought up the photos. She hung up. He called back, and I answered. Told him just where he could put those faked photos. Nialla believes the blackmailer is Caps Galvano." He glanced over to me, eyebrows raised until I nodded hasty confirmation. "Yes. Yes?" There was a rather surprised look on his face. "Nialla, you're positive of your identification of Galvano?"

"If I wasn't before, I am now, and you know why," I said, speaking sharply. Fear and shame were fuel to my anger. "Why?"

"Michaels says the California police have Galvano listed as dead."

"He can't be."

"She says he can't be. When did he — ah — die, Michaels? Well, I'd find out the details. I wouldn't trust that bastard to be dead until his body started to stink. I'm not telling you your business . . . all right, I am" — and Rafe chuckled amiably — "but Nialla's positive about her identification. And there are other reasons why I'd prefer you checked more thoroughly with the California authorities on Mr. Galvano's so-convenient demise." He listened a moment. "All right, and also request the local Bell Tel to cooperate. Yes, I suppose Bob Erskine'll have to know, but I prefer my own security measures to his, Michaels, and they're in effect right now." Another pause. "Well, thanks for that, too." He said good-bye in a very cheerful voice and hung up, altogether looking pleased with the exchange.

"What was that last bit about? And how could Galvano be dead?"

"Yes, that's very interesting, isn't it?"

"What else was Michaels saying?"

"It's turned out that Pete Sankey did have an idea who started that barn fire. Mentioned it to Mac at A-Barn and Budnell on Monday, which is the last time he was seen alive."

"Then he got killed because of me. Galvano killed him. So Galvano isn't dead. Dead men can't kill. How convenient. Dead men can't be executed, because they're dead already. It's the brandy, Rafe!" He'd grabbed me and shaken me. I think I was more appalled at the imminent hysterics than at my feeling of guilt for Pete.

"Listen, Nialla, not all the keening in the world will bring Pete Sankey back, so don't carry guilt for him. After all, you didn't order him to go after the guy. And frankly, my dear, to jolt you out of that self-centered rut, Pete did it because horses were involved, not Nialla Donnelly. Pete didn't think much of the human race, but deliberate barn burning was something no horseman can tolerate."

He was right about Pete Sankey. And he was right about me, too, wallowing in self-pity and guilt.

"You've quite enough to worry about without taking on guilt for Pete Sankey's death. That's the trouble with being raised right" — and there was bitterness in Rafe's face now — "you expect everyone to operate on the same rules you were raised to respect. The 'all-men-are-brothers' routine. You're absolutely lost when something like blackmail or rape hits you, because 'people don't *do* such things.' Take a swig," he ordered me as he refilled our glasses. "Worst lesson a parent can teach a child — love one another. Now, the 'do-unto-others' bit makes slightly more sense, although I hardly want you seducing Louis Marchmount to get your own back, or blackmailing Caps Galvano. Goddamnit" — and Rafe leaned forward, elbows on his knees, glaring at the dark night beyond the windows — "why the hell is Caps bothering you? You're small fry. Even your father's insurance couldn't have been more than ten thousand dollars — twenty thousand at the most. He must have reams of stuff on Marchmount if he's taken to blackmailing. And why would he have to fake his own death? Unless . . ." He turned to me again, his eyes intense with his thoughts. "But why would a racetrack tout like Galvano need an 'out'? Unless *he* had promised to doctor a Marchmount entry! Hmm. Nialla, when Galvano came to you, he sold you some story about trying to clear your father's name? How did he know it needed clearing?"

"He said that's what they were saying around the tracks. That Russ Donnelly . . ."

"That's all he said? There wasn't anything in the papers about it?"

"Only, thank God, the usual bit about the police are following several leads. But Rafe, they *were* saying such things around the tracks. The grooms at the stable told me, and they were upset."

"Hmmm. What else did Caps ask you?"

"Ask me? About what?"

"About how you found your father, and what the police wanted to know."

"You think Caps was pumping me? You know, that's odd. He did seem more interested in what questions the police were asking me. But honestly, Rafe, I wasn't thinking straight."

"No, of course you weren't, dear heart. Tell me, though, was Galvano questioned by the police?"

"Oh, yes, he said he was, but he'd been in Tijuana at the time."

"So he says."

"What are you driving at, Rafe?"

"I'm not quite sure, Nialla." And he'd risen to pace back and forth in front of the sofa, swatting one hand into the other.

"You can't possibly imagine Caps Galvano murdered my father? Why, Dad was half a head taller and a good thirty pounds heavier. That little slimy man . . ."

"Yes, I know, Nialla." Rafe sighed, shoving his hair back impatiently. "I guess it's silly to try to relate the two things — your father's death and this spate of accidents. Blackmail *is* Galvano's line, and he found a quick buck in your situation and took it. He spotted you at Sunbury while he was trying to catch up with Louis Marchmount, and couldn't resist the chance to pick up some spare money. Not knowing, of course, that you hadn't collected your father's insurance."

"Or the money I was supposed to get from Marchmount." The brandy was reaching me, because I began to giggle. "I guess blackmailers have to eat and pay rent somewhere. Even dead men, because he certainly couldn't go make book at Belmont or Aqueduct without having his alibi exploded."

"If that goddamned operator hadn't been such a shithead, we'd've at least known the general area he was in," Rafe said, pausing to look down at me. "Drink that brandy."

"I'm getting tight, Rafe."

"I know. That's my plan." And he sat down beside me, filling the snifter. "I want you to sleep tonight, Mrs. Clery, and I won't keep barbiturates in the house, so it's drunk I'm getting you, dear heart."

"If you get me drunk, I won't know what's going on."

He gave me an odd sideways look. "Nothing's going to go on, dear heart."

I groaned, because I usually get more amorous when I drink.

"That's a girl."

In his artful way I think he coaxed half the decanter down my throat before he carried me up to bed. But by then I wasn't seeing very straight. I remember getting into bed, and I remember his chuckle in my ear. I also remember being told to stop twitching, but I was warm and comfortable, and that was all I remember.

The barking of the dogs woke me to bright daylight. Woke me and Rafe. We both listened tensely, but their calls weren't alarms; more like canine conversation, and soon stopped.

"Probably arguing over who gets which bowl." Rafe rose and stretched leisurely. "How's your head?"

"Fine! I never get hangovers."

"I'll remember that."

And our second day started much as the first. When we got down to breakfast, though, Jerry MacCrate was propping up a cabinet, a mug of coffee in one hand. He was bleary-eyed and rumpled, but when we entered, he grinned broadly at me.

"Morning! You know what that cat of yours has done, Mrs. Clery?"

"I'd never've believed it myself," Mrs. Garrison said, her

smile widening into a chuckle that set her comfortable bosom bouncing. "What do you *do* to animals, Miss Nialla?"

"What's more to the point, what has Dice done?" asked Rafe.

"Cowed those shepherds," replied Jerry, relishing the effect.

"Cowed the shepherds?" Rafe was startled.

"Yessir. I always feed 'em in the morning, you know. So I put down their food, turned around, and that damned—pardon me—cat came sauntering in as if he'd had an invitation. He walked up to Dame's pan, took his own sweet time settling himself, and ate a little while she sat on her haunches and whined."

It was so exactly the sort of trick that Dice had pulled on the Poirers' watchdog that I started laughing.

"And then," Jerry continued, waiting until I had subsided a little, "and then, he went over to Demon's pan and sampled that."

"And then"—Mrs. Garrison took up the tale—"he came here and finished off a huge dish of scraps just as if he were starving to death and hadn't been fed in a month of Sundays."

"The big bowl was too hot, and the medium bowl was too cold and . . ." Rafe began in a singsong voice, his eyes dancing.

" . . . And the enormous bowl was just right!" I capped it between spurts of laughter.

"Well, he's like no cat I ever saw, boss," Jerry said. "God, if I'd a dime for every cat those shepherds have chased off the farm, I'd retire."

"The shepherds recognize class when they see it, Jerry," I said as soberly as I could, for I could picture the actual scene clearly.

"And another thing, boss," Jerry went on, equally serious, "d'you know, he was following me during the night? Every time I made the rounds, I'd catch a glimpse of them big eyes of his in the trees, or lurking in the underbrush. Damned near scared me silly the first time, and I almost let him have a blast. Only he miaowed and came right up to me."

"He's the guy who watches the watchman," I said.

"Your loyalest legionnaire," Rafe supplied.

"It's just that I worry about him if he's got the dogs bamboozled," Jerry said, shaking his head.

"I think you'll find that the cat and the dogs have worked out some sort of an arrangement, Jerry," I told him. "He used to patrol at the Poiriers' farm in Pennsylvania. And their watchdog always let Dice sample his dish. He'd been on guard, too, after all."

"I've heard everything." Jerry did not believe everything, however. "Not that I doubt you, Mrs. Clery . . ."

"He's a special breed of cat," Rafe added. "A Maine coon cat, bred and trained to hunt raccoons."

"Well . . ." And Jerry appeared able to accept that explanation.

"He's used to hunting. He's also far more intelligent than the common shorthair cat," I went on. "But if it bothers you to have him prowling about, we can always shut him up in Orfeo's box. He's the one he's supposed to watch, not you."

"Oh, no, don't lock the beast up," Jerry told me, and I wondered from the look in his eye if he thought Dice might blame him for it. "Well, I'd better get some shut-eye."

"Nothing to report?"

Jerry shrugged. "Not even much noise up at the big house. Nothing around all night, but that cat."

Rafe nodded and thanked Jerry, who said he'd be back late this afternoon, and left.

We had a very pleasant breakfast, chatted with Mrs. Garrison. She hadn't anything to report on odd types trying to see Mr. Marchmount, but evidently Madam was some exercised over something. Mrs. Garrison's attempt at tactfulness only made her omission the more obvious. She might just as well have said that Wendy Madison was furious over Rafe's unexpected remarriage.

Well, I comforted myself, the people who apparently liked Rafe didn't seem to be upset. Bess Tomlinson had gone to considerable trouble to be a part of the ceremony, and Mrs. Garrison, who certainly cared more for Rafe than his own mother did, was already "Miss Nialla"-ing me.

We inspected the stables and the pastures more thoroughly today. Rafe preferred jumpers, and he had two old pensioners in with the mares and foals. He didn't have as many mares as he wanted, he said, but he was on the lookout for good breeding stock. We watched while Dennis Muldoon combed out Orfeo's long full tail, which hadn't been too badly thinned by the fire. Dennis also had the kind of voice, a baritone rumble, that horses prefer, and had been told to keep up a running commentary as he groomed. Orfeo stood quietly, lame hoof cocked as the boy toweled him to a high shine.

"I'll have him back to soaking again, Mrs. Clery, but I think there's an improvement already."

Rafe tipped the hoof up, and the cinder mark was definitely on the mend. When the foot was released, Orfeo put it down squarely for a few moments before easing up again. He did it absentmindedly, as if from habit and not discomfort. Rafe slapped the black rump and kept stroking forward to the withers, until his fingers reached the relaxed ears. Aware of an unfamiliar touch, Orfeo gazed around. There was a kind of wondering expression in Rafe's eyes as he returned the black's diffident stare. Then Orfeo tilted his head slightly, so that Rafe's ministering fingers caught an itchy spot at the base of one ear.

Rafe chuckled as he slapped the curving neck, and stepped back.

"He must be something over the jumps," Dennis said admiringly.

"We'll soon see." Rafe's eyes glowed.

*Would I have riz/To where I now iz/If Orfeo hadn't been mine?* I paraphrased in my mind. Then I shook my head of such thoughts and walked on to greet Phi Bete, who was whickering urgently for my offering of carrot. She chomped happily, tossing ground carrot flecks at me. Albert had already curried her, for she shone like amber, her silky forelock neatly plaited and bouncing on her forehead.

I glanced into Orfeo's stall. Dice gave a sleepy prrroww, his eyes gleaming from a dark corner for an instant before he resumed his nap.

I rode Maisie that morning, and she was a rough one. She tried every one of the same tricks on me she'd used with

Rafe the morning before, and found me quite prepared to deal with her.

"She's not very inventive, is she?" Rafe remarked as Albert led the pair away.

"No, but she's got more scope than Sadie, if she'll ever settle down."

"Yes, that was my feeling, too. Next week sometime, we'll give her a good workout on the big field," and he waved past the barns to the right.

I glanced over my shoulder at a training ring that I'd thought rather complete.

"Oh, I've got ditches, drops, water jumps, a couple of downhill approaches, stone fences, real live hedge, not that plastic garbage they use in shows. A complete setup, if I say so myself."

"A good 'chasing ground,'" I heard myself saying.

Rafe turned sharply to me, his eyes watchful, and then he gave me a small smile.

"Yes" — and that tight smile relaxed into a broad grin — "and I can't wait till you say I can try him!" That was a challenge. "Feel up to Rocking Lady?"

I was game for anything, even the workout the bay mare gave me. But my shoulders ached, and several burns smarted on my legs, irritated by perspiration. I was glad enough to hear the warning bell for lunch, though it didn't seem to me as if the morning had passed that quickly.

As we got in the front door, Mrs. Garrison met us.

"Dr. Bauman's office says they can give Miss Nialla a two-o'clock appointment, Mr. Rafe."

"Not settling with the insurance people until I'm certain you're sound of wind and limb," Rafe told me when I glared at him. "Up to the showers, m'dear," he said, pushing me toward the stairs. "Got the wolf cooked, Garry?"

"The day you catch him, I'll cook him," she replied.

By the time we got back from the doctor's office, I was beginning to be sated with the constant-companionship routine. I hadn't been alone in six days, except on the back of a horse, and that wasn't exactly alone, after all. The doctor had dressed the open burns with a few caustic remarks (didn't Rafe

know any diplomatic doctors?) about damned fools who don't
know when to take things easy. But my hemoglobin was up, and
he'd estimated that another week—without undue strain on
the burns—would see them healed. He ordered me to use A &
D ointment or I'd have scars. Rafe listened with a half-grin on
his face.

If I had "rested," I'd've gone mad. I could forget about
fires and slit girths on top of a horse—and in Rafe's arms at
night. But I felt a lot better leaving this doctor's office than I
had leaving the one in Sunbury. A few days off a solid diet of
peanut butter is to be strongly recommended.

Michaels was in the living room when we arrived. Rafe
noticed the coffee tray with slices of cake and some of Mrs.
Garrison's home-baked cookies and grinned. I doubted that
Mrs. Garrison was likely to extend hospitality to just any police
officer who identified himself. I agreed with her assessment of
him, for he was so completely different from the breed of cop
I'd contended with in San Fernando.

"Not a social call, I gather," Rafe remarked dryly.

"I didn't . . ." Michaels began, gesturing helplessly at the
tray.

"Seal of approval, Michaels, not to worry."

The man grinned then, which made him look less tired
and drawn. I wondered if he had more than one suit and if he
ever had time to get it pressed.

"Got a comprehensive on John, alias Caps, Galvano." He
handed me a sheaf of photos, typical police-type records, all the
names blocked out. "Would you please see if you can find the
man you saw at Sunbury among these?"

"Police line-up?" I asked riffling through. Caps ought to
be easy enough to spot, but my confidence was somewhat
shaken when I came across the first likely candidate. Same
weasel-type face; no, the nose was wrong. Then I got annoyed.
They didn't believe I'd seen Caps Galvano and were trying to
trick me. I took my time. And when I did come to the photo, I
was positive it was Caps; with or without the cap crammed
down over his eyes, he was unmistakable. "This is John, alias
Caps, Galvano," I said in a tone I hoped would convey my
irritation with this ploy.

Michaels gave me an apologetic nod as he took the photo.

"Now, if the gentleman will kindly remove the concealing label," Rafe said in the manner of the TV-commercial announcer, but his eyes told me he wasn't pleased either, "we will see which product this impartial witness chose."

Michaels didn't bother. "This is Galvano." He grimaced. "The California authorities aren't happy with his resurrection."

"Why?" Rafe's one word had the sharpness of a command.

Michaels sighed and leaned forward. "John, alias Caps, Galvano was presumed dead when a vehicle, registered in his name, went out of control on a hairpin turn and crashed into a canyon, where it burst into flames and exploded."

"Convenient."

"Yes. What was left to identify tallied well enough with Galvano's physical statistics. So the verdict was death by misadventure. At the time, the police had far more pressing matters than to worry about the erasure of a small-time racetrack tout."

"What pressing matters?" Rafe demanded.

"Last summer there was a massive crackdown on marijuana smuggling, and yet there was a huge supply circulating in San Fernando."

"What did you say?"

Michaels was as startled as I was by Rafe's explosive question.

"Did you say marijuana?" Rafe asked.

"Yes. You know, they've been tightening customs inspection all across the border to prevent drugs from being smuggled in. Marijuana in particular."

Rafe crowed, slapping his knees. "Particularly marijuana. And particularly at Tijuana." Rafe bounced to his feet, pointing at me. "Nialla, tell Michaels what you told me. About the hay in the station wagon?" He shook his head impatiently when I stared dumbly at him. "Nialla's father always took his own hay with him to Tijuana. He had a spotless reputation, too. No harried customs officer would have bothered the Marchmount cars or transports. Yet the day Donnelly was killed, he'd come back from Tijuana unexpectedly. Nialla said he was furious when he called her to come home. When she got to the house . . . Go on, Nialla."

I wasn't sure yet what he wanted me to say.

"Sweetheart, about the *hay*. Sorry, Nialla." And he'd whirled again to Michaels. "There was hay, *hay*, Michaels, in the station-wagon bed. And when Nialla got up to the loft . . ."

"Yes, there was hay, loose and still in blocks, spread all around. And you don't do that. You use just as many blocks in a bale as you need. I thought that was odd at the time."

"Odd? *Odd!*" Rafe was more excited than I'd ever seen him. "As odd as the hay your father accidentally separated in Tijuana. Hay is grass, Michaels!"

I understood now. "You mean, someone was smuggling marijuana into the States in my father's bales of hay?"

Rafe flopped onto the couch, smirking with satisfaction. "Exactly. And what a helluva clever way to smuggle keys of grass. God, how ingenious!" He leaned forward, striking off points on his fingers. "Donnelly'd undoubtedly bring more bales than he needed, and it would be no trouble at all for Galvano to stuff the keys in the hay blocks. Who'd suspect him? He was always around the Marchmount stables. Goddamn!"

"And you think Mr. Donnelly accidentally discovered the stash?" Michaels asked.

"What else? And came back to San Fernando to investigate. That's what infuriated your father, Nialla. He'd be livid at being used that way."

Yes, he would have, I thought. "Then who killed my father?"

"Galvano!"

"Oh, Rafe, he couldn't . . ."

"Nonsense, Nialla. Anyone can kill. There was a pitchfork handy. Makes a . . . Damnit, Nialla. I'm sorry. I'm sorry."

His arm was around me, his expression white with remorse. And all I could think of was "Do unto others." I shuddered.

"It has to be Galvano, Michaels."

"Why? It could have been the pickup man."

"True. But why else would Galvano want to play dead?"

Michaels considered that, and shrugged.

"Okay," Rafe went on grimly, "play the devil's advocate. Galvano finds out that Russ has discovered the grass. Follows him back to San Fernando. Kills him. So let's also assume that Russ has destroyed all that shipment. Galvano's in a real bind now, man. He doesn't have the grass, and he doesn't have the bread to pay for it. And he's got to answer. Sure, he'd rig an accidental death. For Christ's sake, no one has connected him with Russ Donnelly's murder yet. He even checked with Nialla to be sure she didn't see him in the loft. But if she had, she'd've told the cops, so she hadn't. My God, that little prick thought fast and smart. He even conned her into shelling out five hundred dollars."

"He extorted money from Mrs. Clery in California?"

I held my breath.

"Galvano approached Nialla with some song and dance about helping her clear her father's name."

I shot a furtive look at Michaels. Was that enough to tell him?

"Then he comes back again for more money, five thousand, wasn't it, Nialla?" I could only stare at Rafe, willing him to shut up now. "*That's* why I think things were getting so damned hot for Galvano. He had to split."

"Did you give him the five thousand dollars, Mrs. Clery?"

Numbly I shook my head.

"You realized he was extorting money from you on false pretenses?"

I could only shake my head.

"You didn't report the attempt to the authorities . . ."

"Damn it, Michaels," Rafe cut in, his voice rough with irritation, "the fuzz in San Fernando—I consider you a policeman, so you'll understand the distinction I made—gave Nialla nothing but grief. They accused her father of everything from doctoring an entry to welching on a bet. Albeit they were trying to find a motive, but they hectored Nialla so much in the process that even a lousy con artist like Caps Galvano looked good. Of course she didn't report it to the police. She left."

"Actually, Mrs. Clery ought to have informed the authorities of her leaving."

Rafe answered with a short expletive. Michaels looked at him for a long moment.

"There was no apparent motive, Mr. Clery, for Russell Donnelly's death. There were no clues. The handle of the murder weapon had been wiped clean, and all other fingerprints in the loft were accountable. When Mrs. Clery disappeared without a trace, it was logical to assume she'd been murdered too."

"Oh. That hadn't occurred to me."

Michaels smiled at me reassuringly. "If one's alive, one doesn't assume the authorities consider you the victim of foul play. But you should have told the police where you were going. They had some questions."

"Questions?"

Michaels fumbled for a flimsy sheet in his pocket, clearing his throat as he scanned it. "There were deposits of one thousand dollars made to your father's checking account on the first of September, the first of December, and . . ."

"My college money!" I stopped feeling contrite and got mad. "You mean they thought Dad was receiving payoff money."

Michaels had the grace to blush. "They didn't know what to think, Mrs. Clery. The amounts were suspicious."

"They came from the legitimate sales of stock."

"In even thousand-dollar lots?" Michaels asked.

"Yes," I replied, so sharply that Michaels blinked at me. "Mrs. du Maurier advised Dad to start a mutual fund for my education. You can sell off enough fund shares for exactly the amount you need."

Rafe nodded. "That's right."

"I just needed an answer, Mrs. Clery." And Michaels was patient with my indignation. "I have one, and you have *my* apologies. Now, would you also tell me where you were between the time you left California and arrived in Sunbury? That'll spare you another visit from me."

"I took off across country, stopped at Manhattan, Kansas, to rest me and my mare. That's where I bought the station wagon. Then I stayed with the Poiriers in West Chester until I took up circuit showing February in Florida."

"And you informed no one in California of your whereabouts?"

"There wasn't anyone left in California that I wanted informed."

"Understandably. Well, I suppose that's why Galvano didn't catch up with you until Sunbury."

"Galvano hasn't been after Nialla, Michaels," Rafe said in a quiet voice. "She's just a fringe benefit. Sorry, dear heart, but that's the way I see it. Galvano's been stalking Louis Marchmount, who was, as I told you, in Sunbury last weekend. Traveling for his health, I believe the euphemism is. And he's up at the big house right now, incommunicado."

Michaels gave a sharp nod of his head as he absorbed the impact of this information.

"Look, Michaels, take this in two segments: the murder of Russell Donnelly because he discovered the marijuana is one—right up to the point where Galvano fakes his own death, because that's the only way to get the grass ring off his neck. He's in the clear, right? Because no one has connected him with Russell Donnelly's death. But he's also without access to his usual source of income—the tracks. The moment he puts his weasel face near a betting window, he's had it. Second segment: how to make a living now. He'd already started by conning Nialla out of five hundred dollars for 'expense money.' When he realized that he'd have to split, he'd sent her to try to wheedle five thousand dollars out of Marchmount, but Marchmount doesn't give, and Nialla decamps. So I'll bet he started after Marchmount to get him a disappearing stake. And Galvano must know a bundle about Lou."

"The flaw in your argument, Mr. Clery, is that Marchmount must certainly know that Galvano died in that accident in California." Michaels consulted another set of telex sheets. "Marchmount admitted to seeing Galvano up until just after the Donnelly death. He insisted vehemently, and had the pull to make it stick, that once he discovered the man's unsavory reputation, he had had nothing more to do with him. Evidently Galvano left the Tijuana scene without paying off some bets. That's another reason why the police let his bones lie."

"Ahah, but the flaw in your flaw, Mr. Michaels, is that

blackmail is an anonymous business. Galvano doesn't have to present calling cards with what he has to peddle. Filthy pictures, protection after a score of minor accidents."

The lieutenant looked thoughtful as he rose.

"I want to get in touch with the California authorities again, Mr. Clery, on this hay-is-grass notion. I think it's a valid line of inquiry. In the meantime, I'll have copies of this mug shot of Galvano circulating in Sunbury and in this neighborhood to see if we can come up with a positive identification." He sighed.

"I'd find out whether Louis Marchmount's been paying extortion, if I were you," Rafe said, getting to his feet.

"If I were you"—and the pronouns were only slightly accented—"I'd concentrate on my home front. Not" Michaels added hastily, "that I think you have anything more to worry about from Galvano right now, Mrs. Clery."

"He sure as hell can't reach Nialla behind a Cyclone fence with K-9s patrolling," Rafe said.

The lieutenant looked about to speak and then sighed, as if he'd thought better of it.

Rafe grinned sardonically. "Galvano has a bigger fish to gaff up at the big house, Michaels."

The lieutenant ignored the jibe. "I'll keep in touch," he said, and strode out the door and down the steps to the waiting sedan.

"Oh, Rafe . . ."

His warm arms encircled me. "Dear heart, this is something we get through, and when we reach the other side, it's over and can be forgotten. I'm not letting anything . . ."

The phone rang shrilly. Rafe didn't move, holding me more firmly when I shuddered at the sound.

"You're not at home to anyone either, love."

The third ring was cut off, and we could hear Garry's voice in the kitchen. She came through the dining room, her lips firm with disapproval.

"Are you at home for Madam? She says she knows you're here."

Rafe exhaled slowly, and released me enough so we could walk to the phone. He held the receiver between us.

"Yes?"

"I *told* you to call me Wendy," she said in a sharp voice, which mellowed suddenly. "We're having an informal reception for you and" — a condescending half-laugh — "your latest bride." Again her voice altered, harder now. "I won't take a refusal from you, Ralph. *Everyone* knows about your frightfully romantic wedding, so you've forced me into a very awkward position. Just good luck I was in Sunbury with Lou this weekend. Is that chit really Russell Donnelly's daughter?"

"Yes."

"That makes some sense, then. You'll be here for cocktails at seven. And tell her to wear dark stockings. I want those horrible marks hidden. Mrs. Garrison can come up and give Mrs. Palchi a hand."

The connection was broken. The coldness in Rafe's eyes was frightening. It was worse than open hatred or anger. It was . . . I don't *know* what it was, but I had to erase it from his eyes.

"Rafe, I don't mind. Really, I don't." And I tried to laugh lightheartedly. It came out sounding like a dreadful imitation of her laughter. I put my hands to his face and forced him to look at me. "I'm really durable. After police interrogations, blackmailers, threats, arsonists, I ought to be able to survive a suburban cocktail party."

His arms almost crushed me, and his cheekbone hurt mine.

"I mind." His eyes were still on a distance invisible to me. Abruptly he refocused, but there was still that frightening reserve about him. "I know her sort of party, Nialla. And I know why she's giving it. Not for you or me, but to preserve her 'face' from the slings and arrows of outraged society. On the other hand . . ." And he began to smile. It wasn't a reassuring smile at all, and I stepped back, unsure. He looked at me again, but the empathy of a few moments ago was gone. "You'll need some rest. Garry?"

She came into the room, a tray in her hands. "Moment I heard her voice, I knew what was happening, Mr. Rafe. You'd better munch on these. Cocktails at seven? Humphf! No dinner till all hours if anyone's able to eat then. I'll just go up and give Mrs. Palchi a hand, if you don't mind. She gets so upset."

It was easy to seize on Mrs. Garrison's reaction to the call to ease through the awkwardness. We consumed most of the cheeses, all the crackers and rye bread. Rafe kept urging me to eat heartily, because Garry had the right of it; we mightn't get dinner until ten or eleven.

"Can't say who'll be there. Her crowd varies, depending on who's 'in' or who's getting divorced or dried out of one thing or another." He gave me a less acid smile. "Oh, they're not all bad, dear heart. It's just that the bitches stand out. I'll be latched to you all evening."

So I smiled at him.

"And Marchmount?"

He cocked his head at me, and there was a shade more humor in his expression now. "*If* he appears, I'll do the talking, Nialla."

He made me go up and rest, but I had too many daymares: hay blocks piling themselves over my father's prone body, while baling wire snaked around, hissing like Wendy Madison; and then, in another sequence I kept trying on dress after dress with the echo of her malicious laughter in my ears.

I had enough of that in short order and decided which of my new acquisitions I'd wear. I'd about chosen the white linen sheath and wild sandals when Rafe sauntered in, flat jeweler's box, one of the solid old-fashioned kind, in his hand.

"These suit you," he said in a very solemn voice, and flipped open the lid to display the coral necklace, earrings and bracelet. The set belonged to another, more gracious era, when young debutantes were permitted only certain adornments. Tiny seed pearls and diamonds accented the coral spikes. The earrings were for pierced ears, and Rafe was saying he'd have them altered if I didn't want my ears done.

The necklace and bracelet, however, were the perfect touch for the white linen. And damn him, he had on a deep green linen jacket and white, slightly flared pants and white boots. One of those gorgeous Italian scarves of his was carelessly knotted at the throat of his white lawn shirt. He stepped beside me so that we were both reflected in the mirror, and his grin was sheer boyish impudence. There wasn't an inch of difference in our heights.

"We look like goddamned fashion dolls. Who is it—Barbie and her friend Ken?" He gave an amused snort. "C'mon. Let's get the agony over with."

No, one didn't fool Rafe Clery at all. Except Rafe?

As we got into the car, I tried not to think of the cocktail party as an ordeal. I tried to assure myself that if Wendy Madison were so punctilious about conventions, she wouldn't be openly discourteous to me. But her dictatorial summons didn't fit in with the mutual-antagonism/hatred/contempt between her and her son.

Rafe drove right by a gate clearly heading into the big-house grounds. In fact, I had already braced myself for the car's turn, and felt a little foolish as we whizzed by.

"Gate's locked," Rafe said.

We drove a short distance to the main road and through our gate, then up the main road, to turn in at the impressive urn-topped gates, up the long white-pebbled drive to the mansion, wheeling into the parking area. Through the opening of the glassed colonnades, I could see the fountain busily spouting up, falling into the ornate marble bowl, and drooling down into the upturned stone faces of leering cherubs.

There were four expensive sports cars already parked in the wide turnaround. Rafe backed the Austin-Healey, nose out, at the far end. For a quick getaway? I asked myself.

The pebbled surface was a little hard on the sandaled feet. To my surprise, Rafe paused at the heavy wooden door with ornate knobs and nailstuds. He twisted the iron ring. A son didn't walk in? I heard the distant echo of a deep bell, but the door was opened at the same instant by a sandy-haired heavyset man in a white linen coat.

"Evening, Mr. Rafael."

"Evening, Sam. This is my wife, Nialla Donnelly Clery. Sam's an old cavalry man, Nialla. Put me on my first pony. Six days to learn equitation and sixty years at bloody well trot."

Sam's brown eyes narrowed slightly as he gave me a quick but polite stare. He bowed slightly from the hips, and though he didn't smile, I had the impression the smile was there behind the very correct alignment of his features.

"We wish you every happiness, Mrs. Clery," the man said, with the unconscious dignity of a trained servant. "They are on the terrace, Mr. Rafael, Miss Nialla."

I felt Rafe's fingers press mine as I was accorded acceptance. I wondered fleetingly what Rafe would have done if Sam had disapproved. Sam had gestured to the right, and Rafe, who surely needed no directions, led me through the Queen Anne living room, all soft purples and blues with Wedgwood lamps and elegant porcelain baskets of ceramic flowers on practically every surface. I wouldn't have thought this decor suitable to Wendy Madison's taste.

A burst of laughter came from the windows that opened onto the side terrace. Sheer glass curtains obscured the view. Rafe guided me to the left, through a smaller sitting room (morning-room variety?). French windows gave access to the terrace, which was furnished with chintz sun lounges, glass and wrought-iron tables and iron chairs, the tables shaded by enormous umbrellas in matching print. Ten elegant sun-bronzed people hovered near the portable bar set at one side of the terrace.

I was rather surprised to see that the bartender was young Dennis Muldoon, but if Wendy Madison commandeered Rafe's housekeeper and cook, it was logical for her to recruit others as well.

I caught a glimpse of Dennis, concentrating on the proportions of the drink he was mixing. His expression was neutral, unlike his friendly naturalness in the role of groom.

We had halted on the threshold while Rafe surveyed the assembled. He had just put his hand on the small of my back to escort me out, when someone caught sight of us.

"Hail to the groom! Here's Rafe!" And the curious thronged toward us.

I dislike intensely being the focus of social ogling under any circumstances, and to have all these rather tall people crowding around was bad enough. To have Louis Marchmount staring at me, desperately trying to remember my face, was more than enough. Inconceivable as it was to me, the man who had raped me did not recognize me.

Any relief was tinged with revulsion and the added shame that he had robbed me of something I'd valued and then forgot the theft and the thieved.

I found a highball glass in my hand just as Wendy Madison inserted herself between me and Rafe. She draped her arms around our shoulders, which only emphasized the difference between her height and ours.

"Don't they make a lovely couple, everyone?" my mother-in-law asked in an arch voice. (She did *not* look old enough to be a mother-in-law, but she certainly knew how to play the role with blue-ribbon insincerity.) "Let's hope it takes, this time. They have so much in common." She smiled broadly at Rafe and then accorded me the unseeing glance of the caged lioness. She hadn't accepted me as a person, much less a daughter-in-law.

They were all lifting their glasses, faces wreathed in bright, happy, winning toothpaste smiles, so I suppose I managed to smile. My face ached, as it will when I force an expression. Mercifully, the hypocritical toast was made, and people began to talk to their neighbors. To my dismay, Louis Marchmount pushed through to us.

"Thought your face was familiar t'other day," he said with false heartiness. "Friends tell me m'memory's going." His smile was suddenly uncertain with anxiety. These lapses bothered him, but I was grateful. "Meant no discourtesy, you understand."

"It worried Lou tremendously," Wendy Madison said, taking Marchmount's arm possessively. (As if I had any designs on the man!) "I won't have Lou bothered." She glared at me. "He's not been well, you know. Heart." A bright social smile returned to her face.

"Oh, that's too bad," Rafe said with a matching brittleness.

I noticed then that a heavyset, dark-complexioned man was sort of angled by Lou Marchmount. Not angled, though, as much as hovering, listening without seeming to. He saw my look, and by turning a fraction closer, became part of the group, so that Wendy Madison was aware of him.

"Mr. Stephen Urscoll; I don't believe you've had occasion to meet my son, Ralph Clery, and his . . . bride." Her introduction was grudgingly made, her manner rude. I wondered if she'd ever give me a Christian name. And I also wondered why Mr. Urscoll rated her displeasure. He was a good-looking man, well dressed, and certainly had better manners than she did. "Mr. Urscoll is . . . a friend of Lou's." The words came out in a rush, as if distasteful to her.

"My congratulations, Mr. Clery. My felicitations, *señora*," he said, with the kind of bow from the hips that was second nature to the Californian. Come to think of it, his inflection was certainly that of one whose first language had been Spanish. "I've often backed your father's yearlings to my benefit, Mrs. Clery," he added, and then suddenly stepped back, effacing himself.

"Been east long, Lou?" Rafe asked.

The question was casual enough, but the effect on Marchmount was electric. He swallowed, blinked wildly, and looked to Wendy Madison.

"Lou's been traveling, visiting friends. He had a heart attack on the Coast, and he was advised to get a change of scene. Take it easy." She patted his arm.

"Yes, yes, of course." He rallied, straightened his shoulders, and his expression looked more alert. "Been looking at likely stock in Lexington. Think I might look in at Goff's and see what's promising at Ballsbridge. Haven't been paying as much attention to my stable as I ought. Lost my trainer, you know. Best one I ever had. Was bringing along some promising colts. Damned inconvenient, losing him."

"More inconvenient for Nialla, I'd say," Rafe replied in the stunned silence.

"Lou!" Wendy Madison evinced the first honest response of my short acquaintance with her.

"Hmmm? What?" The man didn't realize what he'd said.

"Louis has not been feeling himself," Urscoll said to me, adroitly stepping into the breach. "He meant no disrespect."

"No, I'm not myself," Marchmount agreed petulantly.

"How could I be? It's too much for any man. Urscoll, I need one of my pills. I must have one. I really can't be persecuted and questioned and badgered this way. I'm not well." He put his hand to his brow, a gesture that failed to be affected, because the hand was trembling so badly.

Instantly Wendy Madison was all concern. She signed to Urscoll to take Marchmount's other arm, and with a furious glance at us for upsetting her guest, led him toward a chaise lounge on the far side of the terrace.

"Michaels might contest that statement," Rafe remarked quietly, "but I'd say Marchmount's being blackmailed."

I said nothing, watching as Mrs. Madison (I simply couldn't bring myself to call her my mother-in-law) fussed over Marchmount. He had certainly failed terribly since . . .

"Don't," Rafe said, and when I look at him questioningly, his eyes were dark. "And don't feel sorry for him, Nialla. His memory's not gone; he's high."

"He doesn't act drunk."

"Drunk? He's not drunk, Nialla. He's on drugs. Didn't you notice his eyes? The wide pupil? The vague smile and lack of association?"

"I'm for that."

"Good to see you again, Ralph," said one of those over-hearty voices that can puncture eardrums. "You always marry the prettiest girls." Before I could turn, I was whirled around and bussed with thick wet lips. "And the most kissable."

I wanted to wipe my mouth of the distasteful impression, but the man was looming over us, his presence a combination of an expensive, musky cologne, active male, and alcohol.

"I can always count on you, Paddy," Rafe said in a dry tone, gathering me back against him, away from the hearty, heavy man.

"Paddy Skerrit's the name, in case you didn't get it first time around. Wendy babbles so you can't catch names. Tied the knot Tuesday in Sunbury, I hear?"

Rafe agreed to that, making no attempt to encourage conversation.

"Going to put her to work for you, huh? I expect" — and he gave me a buffet on the shoulder which hurt — "that Russell

Donnelly's girl knows horses, eh? Never thought you'd stick the bloodstock game, Ralph, but you inherited something from Big Mike after all, I guess. Say, you didn't dump that Fairchild-Hiller stock did you? No? Good lad. Hold on to it. I *know* it's going up again. Sure can't go down further." And the man's florid face lost its bluff geniality as he introduced this sober topic.

Rafe, too, looked grave, and sipped at his drink. "I'd say it hasn't hit bottom yet." Then he launched into a discussion of debentures and coupons and percentages that was incomprehensible to me. I hadn't actually thought of Rafe as a businessman—outside of horses—but Paddy Skerrit soon stopped patronizing remarks and listened to what Rafe was saying, so I assumed he was knowledgeable indeed. Sam came by with a tray of hot hors d'oeuvres. Skerrit scooped up a fistful and began popping them into his mouth like so many peanuts.

One of those gauntly thin women who looked exceedingly elegant at twenty feet slid up to me. Very brilliant dark eyes scrutinized me from sunken sockets. The skin of her face was so tautly stretched across her face bones it looked painful. There wasn't an ash-blonde hair out of place in her teased coiffure, and not a line in her face.

"You must really mean it this time, Ralph," she said smileless, although her tone of voice indicated she was being amusing. Her eyes flicked to the coral necklace. "He never broke out the family jewels for the others, my dear," she said to me, and her hand on my arm was dry and stiff.

"You're looking well, Iona. Taken any good cures lately?" Rafe said.

She shrugged, and the neck skin wrinkled, completely destroying the illusion of youth in her face.

"I don't dare relax these days, Ralph. Too many fascinating things happening." And her eyes slid over me as she turned her head toward the tableau of Madison, Marchmount, and Urscoll. "Think she'll be next in the family, dear?" And there was malicious amusement in her slurred question.

Paddy Skerrit snorted contemptuously at the idea. "Nonsense. The man's got a bum heart."

"I think Wendy rather fancies herself in the role of the

doting, ministering angel, don't you, Ralph?" Iona's eyes glittered with a hungry expectation.

"My mother has fancied herself in many roles," Rafe replied casually.

"They say Marchmount's lost heavily since the scandal over his trainer. Ooops, sorry," she said, patting my arm with a familiarity I found very offensive. "Of course, the state of the market doesn't help much, does it? And he had all that money in railroads. I told him, and I know you did, too, Paddy, when we were at Palm Springs, that railroads are out, definitely passé. I've unloaded all I had. Transferred to airlines, though I don't like what Pan Am has been doing since they split."

"What? Eschewing foods, Iona?" Rafe asked. I couldn't believe the pun. Or that they didn't get it.

"I'm sick to death of food products," she said in a voice that was almost a snarl. She tossed off the last of her drink and called out to Sam, holding her glass up significantly.

"Now, Iona, you promised . . ." A David Niven type hurried up and took the glass from her hand. His eyes had a sort of harried, anxious look, though he smiled around pleasantly.

"What I promise, Terry, and what I decide to do are often miles apart," she said in a hard, shrewish voice.

Terry swallowed nervously, encircling her thin waist and drawing her against him placatingly.

"And this party's dead. Dead. Dead!" She went on, glaring at me, "I don't know what's happened to Wendy since she took up with Lou. She used to give good parties, with lots of fun, and people worth talking to. Now she's hiding away and being so . . . so parsimonious. I *need* a drink! Sam!" She broke away from Terry and stalked across the terrace to the bar. Terry followed.

"Gawd! She just got dried out," Paddy remarked in what he used for a stage whisper, but if Iona heard him, she was more interested in obtaining a drink.

More guests arrived at that moment, three men and a black-haired woman who kept her arm hooked through her escort's as if she would actively resist being parted from him. I was so astonished at the costume of the tallest man that I really didn't look much at the others. He was one of those long thin people who appear taller than they actually are. He affected muttonchops, long wavy hair that was clean and *probably* styled, though that style didn't suit him. He wore a white see-through lace shirt, an ornate medallion, white drill pants, and sandals that, mercifully, showed clean feet and polished nails. But he was completely out of place in this milieu.

"Ralph, darling, so you've done it again," the woman exclaimed, inclining toward me, so that I realized we were to touch cheeks. She wore an exceedingly expensive and heavy perfume. "I'm Nancy McCormack, and this is my husband, Ted." But Ted was not the man to whom she was attached. "Jeff Fermaugh"—she edged closer to him (if possible)—"and the outrageous one is Bobby Wellesley. Bobby, I told you Faith would be here. There she is at the bar."

The men had shaken my hand and said appropriate things to Rafe as she made the introductions. Abruptly Bobby Wellesley's limp hand left mine, and he lurched toward the pretty fair-haired girl talking with Dennis.

"I used to see you at Agnes du Maurier's place when you had red hair," Ted McCormack said, eyeing my cropped head.

"Nialla got singed at Sunbury," Rafe said, and I realized he liked Ted McCormack. "G-Barn finally caught fire, and Nialla went in after her gelding. Damn fool."

"You did too," I said, a little self-conscious under Ted McCormack's admiring eyes.

"Rode out of the barn on the nag's head," Rafe said, grinning.

"Horse safe?"

"Lost some hide, but so did Nialla," Rafe replied, indicating my legs. "Gelding got a cinder lodged in the off-hind, but that's healing nicely."

"Jumper?"

Rafe laughed. "You'd probably recognize him as Juggernaut, Ted."

McCormack reacted with a surprised double-take. "You don't mean this little bit of nothing rides that bastard?"

"Rides him like he was a Sunday-canter-in-the-park hack." And Rafe beamed with pride at me.

"Live up to your red hair, don't you? Sorry about your

father, Nialla. He was a damned good trainer." McCormack's eyes flicked from me to Marchmount, reclining on the glider, and his expression was perceptibly disgusted.

"Hasn't it been stifling today?" his wife said brightly, and began to steer her escort toward the bar. I gather she didn't talk horses.

But as I glanced after them, I saw another interesting situation developing at the bar. Faith, the girl Bobby Wellesley had hotfooted to see, had her back to him and was talking animatedly to Dennis Muldoon. Bobby Wellesley shifted from one foot to the other, glaring at them.

"Are they still trying to foist Bobby off on Faith?" Rafe asked Ted.

"Faith's a nice child," McCormack replied. "I'd hate to see her having to cope with Bobby's inadequacies."

"Faith's no one's fool. Good seat. Nice hands."

McCormack laughed and slapped Rafe's shoulder. "Rare praise from you, Clery. Thought for a while there you'd marry the girl and save her from her match-made destiny."

Rafe grinned as he sipped his drink, giving me a sideways look. "She didn't have enough dowry for me."

McCormack let out a bark of laughter and pounded Rafe across the back. I assumed that Faith must be wealthy.

"We'll have to come to her rescue," Rafe said, and I hastily agreed when his look required that of me.

"Shame, though. She'd be the makings of young Bobby. That boy has a good mind, Rafe, even if it is filled up with this liberal nonsense and counterculture technocracy. Oh, I suppose he has to 'find' himself," Ted McCormack went on, frowning toward the bar. "That's the current phrase, isn't it? And I suppose I'm being square when I refuse to go along with this drug phase the youth of this generation have to explore. But I haven't seen anything intelligent yet from a mind expanded by drugs. I have seen some pretty sick examples of its effects."

We all sort of turned toward Marchmount.

"You can't drop a hint to your mother, can you, Rafe?" My husband lifted his brows quizzically.

"No, I guess you can't, can you?"

"There's no calories in grass, you know," Rafe said in a low voice.

"Where's she been getting it from? I thought the FBI cracked down on the marijuana."

I felt a need to drink, and took such a hasty swallow I nearly choked.

"Gotta watch that caloric intake, Nialla," Rafe advised in a drawl as he swatted me on the shoulderblades. "Who's that Urscoll fellow? Sounds Spanish, or Mexican."

"No clue. Came with Marchmount, talks about stock sales and some of those offshore oil ventures in the West, but he doesn't quite add up." McCormack was thoughtful. "Still, I'm glad Marchmount has a traveling companion. Man's half-senile. Talks about persecution and ruin and police interrogation and all that crap."

"You don't suppose his vices have caught up with him?" Rafe asked in the most casual of voice, as if he really wasn't interested in an answer. Talk about dissembling!

"How d'you mean?" McCormack was curious.

"If he talks of persecution, ruin, and police interrogation . . ." Rafe let the question trail off diffidently.

"You mean blackmail?" Ted McCormack was both surprised and mildly contemptuous. "Bull. Everyone knows what he's like."

"Ted . . ." called his wife from the bar, making his name sound as if it had four syllables.

"Excuse me," and McCormack went off.

"I don't understand that," I said, bending toward Rafe in case anyone overheard us.

"What? Ted and Nancy? Oh, that's been going on for years. In their own way, they're devoted to each other."

"You know perfectly well what I meant, Rafe Clery." And then caught myself as he laughed. "Why would . . ."

I stopped, because Rafe's expression had turned into shocked incredulity. He was facing the French doors. I turned and beheld quite a vision—in electric-purple bell bottoms, a floral see-through shirt with flowing sleeves, ruffled at wrist and chest, accented by a white embroidered vest. The young man's face was adorned by as glorious a set of mutton chops and curling hair as any rock singer's. This paragon of East Village sartorial splendor was holding the hand of a girl with medium brown hair rippling down to her buttocks. She wore an almost indecently short purple (and the color clashed with her escort's pants) embroidered Indian shift and Indian toe sandals.

"Hellooo, there, Raffles," cried the young man, and dragged his girl over to us. In the midst of hugs and back thumpings (the boy was eight inches taller), good-natured remarks about wedding bells, I gathered that this was Rafe's youngest brother, Presby Branegg. The girl and I exchanged tolerant grins as the fraternal exuberance continued.

"My name's Sara Worrell," she said, holding out her hand rather aggressively. "I guess you're the bride, so I ought to congratulate you."

"Naw, naw," Pres said, draping one arm around Rafe, the other around Sara, "you felicitate the bride, you congratulate the groom. Now, congratulate the brother. Rafael Clery, this is Sara Worrell. We met in economics class, and I can't figure out how she could spend four years at Yale without my seeing her."

Rafe kissed the girl's lips lightly, because Pres was holding the two together. "Maybe she *studied* at Yale," he said as he broke away.

"You know, you're every bit as nice as Pres said you'd be," she said, and then blushed.

"Good things come in small packages," Rafe replied, and she blushed deeper, self-consciously trying to lessen her own inches.

" 'Bout time you found that out," his brother said crisply, "instead of going for the large economy size."

"*They* were anything but economical, brat," Rafe replied.

"Presby!" Wendy Madison's voice held a stern come-hither note, and the boy's attitude changed from good-natured chattering to anxious anticipation.

"What's her frame of mind?"

"Worried about Lou. Play it up," Rafe said, and jerked his head toward their mother, indicating the pair had better not dally.

"He's in for it," Rafe said after a moment. "God, did he have to dress like that *and* bring a girl along? Our mutual parent intensely dislikes sharing her men with any other female. And it takes more than a sweet featherweight like that to prevail against her. Poor kid."

"Doesn't the maternal edict apply to me? I'd the temerity to marry you."

Rafe regarded me in what I could only describe as an inscrutable fashion.

"Dear heart, *I* married *you*."

Before I could find an adequate comeback, a tall young man in a pale blue silk suit of impeccable cut came striding across the terrace from another side door. He was very Italianate, from his straight thick black hair, swarthy skin, and very dark eyes, to the subtle virility he exuded and the sensuality of his full, smiling lips.

"You can always count on John-boy to present the proper family image," Rafe murmured. "Nialla, my brother, John Milanesi."

Although this brother was far more sophisticated than Pres, complete with Continental bow and a kiss floating three inches above my hand, I found I preferred the mod one. The calculation in John Milanesi's eyes was almost offensive.

"I am charmed," he said, without releasing my hand, his fingers curling into my palm and caressing the skin, until I slid my hand free. "A lovely surprise . . . for me, at least." The sensuous lips curled up, as he intended me to realize that the marriage had not been well received.

"How's factory life, Giovanni?" Rafe asked with more reserve in his manner. Or maybe I was imagining it.

John shrugged, too bored to enlarge further.

"You'll lose your shirts on the midis if you insist on pushing them," Rafe said, and received his brother's full attention.

There was another diffident shrug. "It would amuse me to find the haughty fashionable deposed from their giddy heights. The maxi, at least, disguises feet of clay. And speaking of clay feet," he added, glancing toward his mother, "I see Pres made good his threat. Must you continually put that child in a position where he has to follow your example?"

Rafe frowned, glancing back from Pres's flamboyant figure to John. "He can't mean to marry that girl?"

John rolled his eyes expressively. "You'd already been divorced once by the time you were twenty-one."

"Christ! I'll have a talk with him."

"Don't bother. Wendy's ringing a peal over him right now that ought to suffice."

We couldn't hear what was being said, but there was no doubt that the conversation was unpleasant for Pres. He seemed to be contracting, and so did poor Sara. Suddenly Louis Marchmount raised a feeble hand, and Wendy turned back to him, allowing Pres and Sara to escape to the bar.

I felt John Milanesi's hand on my arm, his fingers stroking the skin.

"He hasn't accepted the AGM offer?" Rafe asked.

"Obviously not," John replied, indicating Pres's costume. "I must say, you could watch your timing, Rafael. She's not going to make life easy for anyone." His hand tightened on my arm, but I couldn't figure out any way of breaking that hold without appearing rude. "Not to offend you, my dear sister-in-law, for Rafael's no longer easily seduced; it's simply that our dear mother cannot abide marriages that aren't hers."

"D'you think she's got bells in mind for Marchmount?"

"Hardly!" John was openly contemptuous. "Although I'd've thought she'd've sent him packing long since."

"If Mrs. Madison is so possessive, why this farce of a reception?" I wanted to know, and got my arm free of John Milanesi's clutch to gesture at the terrace.

The two brothers locked glances, shrugged, and laughed.

"Our fair mother's private judgments never affect her notions of social duty," John Milanesi replied, his cynical gaze falling on his mother. I was scarcely in any position to cast stones, but his look was unhealthy. "You know, Marchmount's debility has a morbid fascination for our mother. I'd better make my duty and see what I can overhear."

"You need a fresh drink, Nialla," Rafe said, and guided me toward the bar. "I meant what I said yesterday, dear heart. The Dower House is separate from this establishment, by my choice and order."

"Then why . . ."

My rebellion waned at the warning pressure on my elbow.

"Why, because! I'm not ashamed of you as my wife, Nialla, and in the course of dealing with the woman who bore me, I've discovered that it is a far, far better thing to obey her few social demands. That's all this is—Mother's reluctant bow to convention. It's to our advantage, actually."

"Ralph dear!" The clear voice caught us just two feet from the bar. "Ralph, would you and the bride step over here a moment?"

"See?" Rafe pointed to the man following Sam onto the terrace. "The court photographer will proceed to record the event; there'll be a nice spread in the paper, describing the reception Mrs. Wendy Madison gave for her son, Rafael Clery, on the event of his marriage to Miss Nialla Donnelly, and the Goddess, Convention, will be appeased. Let's go smile for the birdie."

"So good of you to come, Mr. Arnold," Wendy Madison was saying to the photographer, who accepted her greeting with a nod and a mumble, and became very busy with his light meter.

Wendy Madison pulled John in on one side of her, glared Pres away, gestured Rafe to her other side, leaving Rafe to collect me groomily. She arranged the proper expression on her face and then smiled significantly at the photographer. He took several shots.

"I want one of the bride and groom together," he said.

This was no more to my liking than to Wendy Madison's. I turned to Rafe to protest, when I heard the click-shosh of the camera and the frame being advanced.

"How about a smile this time, Mrs. Clery? This isn't a funeral." He meant to be funny, I know.

Rafe pressed my hand encouragingly and angled me toward the camera. His mother urged me in a sharp brittle voice to smile, and I know she wished it *was* my funeral.

"Rafe," I whispered, as Wendy Madison, bubbling with social graces, bustled the photographer off for a drink, "does the photo have to go into the papers?"

"There's nothing wrong with that, dear heart. In fact, now is absolutely the best time for it to appear."

I wasn't quite sure why he should feel so, but as he signaled Sam to bring his tray of drinks over, I didn't have the chance to ask. And then Faith came up to us, obviously trying to shake Bobby Wellesley, who trailed after her. She wasn't much taller than Rafe, and kissed him with a resounding smack that made Bobby Wellesley wince.

"There!" She grinned mischievously at me. "I've been wanting an excuse to do that for years, so thanks for providing me with the opportunity. Rafe's one of my favorite people, and I really do sincerely wish you both the very best." She held out her hand to me with a forthrightness (and a firm grip) that was refreshingly candid. "Did you really tame Juggernaut? And was he the horse you rescued from the Sunbury barn fire? Is he all right?"

"That's right, Faith, show more interest in some goddamn horse than you do in a human. Talk horses with Rafe and his new wife," Bobby Wellesley said in a wild voice, pulling her roughly around to face him. "Flirt with the bar boy, do anything but talk with me. You're the only reason I came to this . . ."

"Cool it, Bob," Rafe said, and before either Faith or I could react, he had taken the agitated young man to one side of the terrace. What was said was inaudible, but there was a visible change in the boy's posture, from arrant aggression to chagrin.

"I'm sorry he's acting this way, Mrs. Clery. I like Bobby, but I don't like the company he keeps or his form of amusement," Faith said quietly. "I also don't like being forced into his company every place I go. It's . . . it's positively medieval." She glanced over her shoulder toward the Iona woman and her David-Nivenesque companion. "Mother's not a bit of help."

I was amazed. "She's your mother?"

"Remarkable, isn't it?" Faith suddenly sounded very old, very cynical, and very sad. "I'm Faith Farnham, you see."

I didn't, though.

"You mean," Faith went on, with a laugh of surprise, "you haven't grown up on Farnham's Farina, good for chick or child?"

I shook my head.

"Your poor disadvantaged darling," she said with mock concern. "You're a relief. And Rafe's such a doll. Oh, don't mistake me. I've cherished an infatuation for that man for years, but I don't fancy him as a husband. Not," she added hurriedly, "that I don't think he'd be a good one for the right sort of girl. Oh, I'm really putting my foot in it today, aren't I? Let's erase that scene. Okay? I must say, you are a relief. And Rafe's a doll . . ." Her eyes were so full of droll humor that I couldn't help but laugh with her. "He's coming down is his problem. Bobby, I mean. And I simply cannot cope with him in that condition."

"You mean, he's using drugs?"

Faith started to say something, probably caustic, from the set of her mouth, but instead she just looked at me, sort of wistfully.

"Yes, he's been using drugs . . . to expand his consciousness, because he finds himself unable to relate to present-day values and artificial standards!" She was obviously quoting something Bobby Wellesley had prated at her. "He's not the only one here, either. Look at Lou Marchmount."

"I thought Mrs. Madison said he had a bad heart."

"Yeah." And Faith's eyes were very cynical now. "From drug abuse. He's had a couple of real bummers since he's been here. I wonder how he smuggled it past his bodyguard."

"His bodyguard?"

"Steve Urscoll, of course," Faith replied, as if the man were wearing a label or something. "She must really be gone on Lou if she'd introduce a bodyguard as a house guest."

"What's this, what's this?" Rafe asked, joining us so suddenly that I almost squeaked in surprise.

"Faith says that Mr. Urscoll is a bodyguard."

"Please, Rafe, I let that slip. It can't be broadcast. Mother told me when she thought I was getting too friendly. I prefer him to Bobby. He's got his feet planted on terra firma, not some psychedelic cloud."

"Now, why would Louis Marchmount need a bodyguard, Faith?" Rafe's question was the most casual!

She gave a little laugh.

"Frankly, Rafe, I think he's just had too many bad trips and is getting flashes. Every time a phone rings, he flips his lid. But if a bodyguard makes him feel safe, why not? The man does come from a good family, after all, and I must say that I *like* a person who can take reverses like a gentleman, who faces reality."

"Bobby's really bugging you, Faith?"

She nodded rather grimly. "I'm supposed to be the making or breaking of him. And I'm sorry, Rafe, I simply don't look at the problem, or the solution, from that angle."

"Using moral blackmail on you, huh?" Rafe asked, and gave me a look that made me want to kill him—for just a split second, mind you. "You ignore that kind of shit, Faith. You're on the right track. How're your classes progressing? . . . Faith teaches equitation to handicapped children."

"I'm qualified for that," she said, still a bit grim. "What did you say to Bobby?"

"Enough. I sent him for some coffee and suggested that he was making an ass of himself. One more explosion would upset Lou."

"Oh, Rafe, how could you?"

"Why not? Wendy can put the fear of God in him when neither you nor I can! She scares him shitless."

"Who scares who?" asked John Milanesi, insinuating himself into our group. I wished he wouldn't lean over me so. "Have you seen the palatial grounds of the Herrington estate, my dear sister-in-law?"

And he took my arm and began to lead me off, nodding pleasantly to Rafe and Faith. If I had not seen my mother-in-law bearing down on us with a stormy expression on her face, I'd not have let myself be "rescued." But I did.

"You certainly are a surprise, sister dear," my new relative said, tucking my hand under his arm in a way that me wonder if I was being taken from the pan only to deal with the fire.

"In what way? You ought to have had enough practice in meeting sisters-in-law."

He laughed, and it was a sort of caressing type of laugh that disturbed me.

"You're different." He glanced down at me, his eyelids

obscuring his expression. "Nialla. That's a pretty name." He halted now that we were at the top of the sloping lawn, and gestured about, as if he were monarch of all he surveyed. "Lovely setting, isn't it?" I duly appreciated the view. "No comparable aspect from the Dower House, is there?"

Again he gave me that unsettling sideways glance.

"No, there isn't, but I prefer the Dower House. The ambience is suitable to my plebeian tastes."

"I'd've said you had . . . more ambition than that."

"I'm a horse trainer's daughter. Horses are my life, and my ambition is to deal with . . . horses . . . as much as possible. This" – I could make regal gestures, too – "is not my scene."

"My, my. Do we protest too much?"

"No, I just want to get something straight, Mr. Milanesi. When Rafe married me, I thought he was just another horse trainer."

"And here I was given to understand that this was a romance of long standing."

Rafe and his little white lies! I glared at John Milanesi now.

"What is it you want to know, Mr. Milanesi?" I asked, trying to keep my temper.

He eyed me coolly, a half-smile on his lips.

"How much you'll cost us."

"How much I'll . . . Why, you, you . . ."

"Son of a bitch?" He suggested.

I couldn't leave him fast enough, but I forced myself to walk, each step jolting through me and the pebbles of the path throwing me off balance. I told myself he was not laughing, he was not laughing, but his laughter followed me all the way back to the terrace.

Rafe was nowhere in sight. Nor, fortunately, was that bitch, his mother. John had to be acting on his mother's instructions. Or could he be so two-faced that he'd adopt one attitude in front of his half-brother and propose to buy me off when he got me alone? Either way was despicable. Despicable! Lou Marchmount was reclining in his lounge, a limp rag of a man. Paddy Skerrit was talking at a sullen Iona – who did not have a drink – and the D-N type. Pres and Sara were absent, and Bobby Wellesley, while the others were clustered about the bar.

Just then a clutch of new arrivals swirled out onto the terrace, Rafe and his mother in their midst.

One thing certain, she hadn't expected to find me back on the terrace so soon. Another thing, I wanted to go home. Now! Protocol had been satisfied, and I wanted out. If Rafe wouldn't take me, I'd walk!

Without seeming to hurry, Rafe reached me before the vanguard of the new guests. His mouth was smiling, but his eyes were blazing with anger.

"John try to buy you off?" he asked in an undertone, though the question must have been unnecessary if my face mirrored any portion of the rage inside me. "Don't blow your cool now, Nialla. I beg you!"

In the instant before we had to turn to be introduced, I got several messages. I must be, I could be, bigger than all the insults being dealt me. Rafe wanted me to be bigger. He had chosen *me*, despite two bad marital experiences. *He* was proud of me, and I could make him prouder. This whole evening, with its vicious undertones and inhospitalities, was insignificant in the fabric of our lives together. As if I were faced with a bad approach to a very difficult jump, I took a deep breath and looked up, straight ahead.

Maybe my frame of mind made the difference, plus the fact that most of the new arrivals stayed for only a drink or two, and their conversation was confined to felicitating me, congratulating Rafe, some jokes or chitchat all on a polite and jocular level. Pres's costume made a conversation piece. (I wasn't sure who looked more unhappy, Pres or Sara, but they stayed at the bar, finding sympathy in Dennis's kindred company.) Bobby Wellesley had sunk, almost out of sight, into the lounge at the edge of the terrace, and seemed almost as much of an exile as Louis Marchmount. Wendy kept everyone away from him; Lou, that is.

One older couple, the Eldicotts, were particularly outgoing. I was very sorry when they excused themselves. Of course, they were horse breeders, and I felt much happier on that subject than the ups and downs of the stock market that otherwise dominated small talk. Small talk? The figures mentioned took my breath away.

Full dark came, the terrace lights glowed before Rafe asked Sam about dinner. The party was now down to the original complement.

"A buffet is set up in the courtyard, Mr. Rafe. It's ready whenever Madam is."

"Madam is, whether she knows it or not," Rafe told him, and Sam, inclining his head with dignity, went off into the house. "Otherwise"—Rafe grinned at me—"I'll never hear the last of it from Garry."

"I'm so hungry I could even eat peanut butter."

"We can leave right after dinner, dear heart, if I can catch Urscoll by himself for a few moments."

"Urscoll?"

"Yes." And Rafe's eyes narrowed. "If he is a bodyguard, maybe he'll tell me from what is he guarding Lou Marchmount."

"He simply doesn't look or act like a bodyguard."

"You've seen too much TV, love."

"Oh, you know it all."

Rafe raised his eyebrows in polite consternation. "Hardly, but I appreciate your attitude."

Madam, my reluctant mother-in-law, was also reluctant to interrupt her drinking for dinner, but Ted McCormack greeted the announcement with such gusto that she relented, all gracious smiles, and brightly announced that everyone should follow her to the buffet.

I think, under other auspices, I'd've enjoyed that dinner. Certainly the setting was lovely, with the fountain playing under colored lights, the tables set around it; the cold soup, the delicious curry, the salads, the meringue dessert. There was champagne, too, with which our health was drunk. (I wonder she didn't choke on the bubbles, it pained her so to propose our happiness.)

We didn't get a chance to talk to Urscoll at dinner; we were seated at smaller tables, and the Madam-Marchmount-Urscoll trio did not encourage the arrival of a fourth at their table.

After dinner, however, when Madam suggested we all take coffee and liqueurs on the terrace and watch the youngsters dance, Rafe homed in on Urscoll like a magnet. Dinner had evidently revived Marchmount, because he was quite smiling and talkative.

"You and Lou are planning to make the bloodstock sales at Ballsbridge this fall?" Rafe asked as we all watched Lou and Madam trying to rock and roll.

Urscoll hesitated before answering. "That's the plan, but, ah . . . Louis isn't at all well."

"Oh, the quiet pace in Dublin might be therapeutic," Rafe said. "Give Lou a chance to really get away from it all."

Urscoll instantly tensed, then smiled. "Yes, he needs a complete change of scene."

"And not just for his health."

"What do you mean?"

We had moved somewhat into the shadows, away from the dancing area. Bobby Wellesley was dancing with Sara, while Pres partnered Faith. She knew how to dance, too.

"Would the name 'Galvano' mean anything to you?" Rafe asked casually. I thought the man would drop his glass.

"Should it?" he asked with a commendable recovery.

"Come off it, Urscoll. I'm family," Rafe replied. "Lou Marchmount has been many things, but not a paranoid. And don't give me that nonsense about a bad heart. That man is running scared. From what?"

Urscoll wet his lips, glanced at Marchmount and Wendy Madison giving a bad example of the frug, and then began to talk.

"I am not, Mr. Clery, a sportsman." And Urscoll smiled wryly. "I'm a private investigator for a West Coast firm. I was chosen because of . . . family connections and my background . . . to act as companion to Mr. Marchmount. He is being threatened by an extortionist. He has already paid substantial sums."

"Paid? Why in hell did you permit it?"

Urscoll looked unhappy too. "I realize that seems odd, Mr. Clery, but I assure you my firm has urgently recommended on several occasions that this be taken to the proper authorities. Mr. Marchmount is adamant that the police may not be involved. Frankly, Mr. Clery, he is such a sick man that anything might result in a fatal heart attack. I wish he wouldn't dance so violently, but my wishes are seldom consulted." Urscoll looked more ill at ease than ever. "My instructions are to avoid any contact with the extortionist."

"It *is* Caps Galvano, isn't it?"

Urscoll gave Rafe a long look. "I . . . think so."

"You think so?"

"When my firm checked the police records about Galvano—very discreetly—he was listed as dead. Naturally, we told Mr. Marchmount. He insisted that the man was very much alive. As Mr. Marchmount had just suffered his first heart attack, we discounted his insistence. Then Mr. Marchmount experienced a series of odd mishaps, and I was assigned to . . . to protect him from any more. On three separate occasions I have intercepted phone calls from a person whom Mr. Marchmount insists must be this Galvano. In spite of my precautions, Mr. Marchmount has paid the demands. And he absolutely refuses to let me consult with the police. I am in the difficult position of seeing—to be blunt—fear kill my client and being unable to prevent his death." Urscoll sighed. "Believe me, we usually do not operate in such a . . . an inefficient and ineffective way. But"—Urscoll gestured his hopelessness—"he is living on borrowed time right now, and if I can just keep that . . . that blackmailing Galvano away from Marchmount, I will be at least guarding the body."

"So you've been traveling?"

"Yes, by slow stages and with no advance plans and leaving no forwarding address. My suggestion. It would be harder for the extortionist to track us. Until just recently that worked. The man caught up with us two weeks ago."

"You've had another extortion demand?"

Urscoll grimaced. "For twenty thousand dollars."

"From Galvano?"

"I assume so. It was the one time I wasn't with Mr. Marchmount"—and Urscoll's regret seemed sincere—"and he took the phone call. You can see what it did to him. If it weren't for Mrs. Madison, I think the man might have died."

"Does Madam know he's being blackmailed?"

"No!" The denial was explosive, and Urscoll glanced

quickly around to see if anyone had noticed his exclamation. "She thinks he's being pestered by an ex-wife for alimony. I wanted to confide in her, in anyone, because frankly, Mr. Clery, I'm exceedingly worried about him."

"Good thing you didn't tell Mother," Rafe said. "But she seems to know that you're an employee."

"Oh, yes." And if I thought I'd suffered at Wendy Madison's hands, I ought to compare notes with Stephen Urscoll. "I realize what an imposition it is, but . . ." He shrugged. "I must protect my client."

"More from himself, I'd say, than the blackmailer."

"If he'd only let me approach the police," Urscoll said gloomily.

"Don't worry, Urscoll. The decision has been taken out of your hands."

"How so?"

Louis Marchmount's whinny of a laugh cut across the music, and we all looked over as he began the most insane contortions, totally unrelated to any dance step ever conceived.

"Lou, stop that! Remember your heart! Lou! Oh, Christ!" Wendy Madison was trying to pin his arms down, but he flailed wildly around. Urscoll ran to her aid, and just as he got to Louis, the man gave a wild scream and collapsed.

"He must have got something. He must have. My God, what did he take now?" Wendy Madison screamed. "Turn off that goddamned racket."

Someone did, as Urscoll, Rafe, and John Milanesi carried a white-faced Louis Marchmount and laid him carefully on the long couch in the living room. He was breathing stertorously, his complexion turning a green-gray.

"His heart. His heart," Wendy was moaning, clutching his hand and stroking his forehead.

"Sam's calling the doctor. Urscoll, go get a blanket." Rafe had taken command.

"That won't do any good." His mother was weeping. "He's taken something. How could he have got any drugs? I threw everything I had out. He knows it's bad for his heart. He knows . . ." Her glance fell on Bobby Wellesley, who had been,

I realized now, exhibiting the same unnatural exuberance. "What did you give him, you little turd?"

"Give him? Give him?" Bobby's voice rose to a shriek. "I didn't give him anything. He took it. He came into the bathroom and took it. I only had two tabs left. Just two, and no chance of getting more before Monday. He took it. Serves him right."

"Took what?" Rafe asked in a mild voice.

Bobby's expression turned cunning and suspicious. "No. I won't tell you. Think you can treat me like scum all evening. Turn Faith against me. Then you want *me* to help *you*. Well, man, flake off. I won't . . ."

Rafe moved toward Bobby, his hands clenched into fists.

"You little creep, you can't scare me," Bobby said, drawing himself up to his full inches. But suddenly Paddy Skerrit and Ted McCormack closed in on him from behind.

"You're all against me. Coming at me. Don't! Don't!" He had turned in a frenzied, caged-creature way that was horrifying.

"Don't, you fools!" The words were low but urgent. It was Sara who had spoken. She used the stunned silence to run closer to Bobby, her voice soothing and soft. "Bobby, Bobby, they won't crowd you any more. You need your freedom, don't you?" She cajoled him, and he watched her, almost as if she were hypnotizing him with her slow, easy advance. "You need space, don't you, man; space and air and sympathy, or everything will fall in, right?"

Rafe waved Paddy and Ted back, his eyes on Sara. She reached up and took Bobby's hand, stroking his arm, patting his face, murmuring reassurance all the time.

"If he doesn't tell us . . ." Wendy Madison began to wail.

"If you don't shut up and let Sara handle him . . ." Rafe left his threat hanging, but his harsh tone cowed his mother into silence.

"I can't think of anything meaner, Bobby, than losing your last tab like that. It's one thing to offer it to a friend, but no one should *take* it from you," she said as she pulled Bobby over to a chair and got him seated, all the time soothing his forehead and patting him. "Now, I'm right here with you, and nothing and nobody is going to bother you. You can have a safe trip. When'd you start, so I'll know when you'll be coming down? There's nothing to worry about, because I'll be right here all the time. When'd you start?"

"Just after dinner."

"Oh, then you're really just starting. Well, Sara's here, and it'll be a good trip. What're you on?"

"Berkeley Brown."

"Jesus," said Rafe in an undertone. "That's a composite. Why didn't Lou just take cyanide and forget it?"

"He took my last tab. He'd no right to do that. Not even asking, the old fart." Bobby threw off Sara's hand and staggered to his feet. Sara waved Skerrit away when he moved to cut Bobby off from the door.

"C'mon, Pres, you can help me with him. He'll trust us," she said, sweeping the room with a scathing glance. "*We* know what he's up against."

"The nerve of her!" Iona Farnham exclaimed.

"You'd better be grateful for her nerve, Mother," Faith replied in a voice of quiet condemnation. "Otherwise we'd never have found out what Bobby gave him. I'm terribly sorry for my part in this, Wendy. I knew he'd taken something, because he was more impossible than ever. But I never dreamed that Mr. Marchmount had any of it."

"I don't understand you at all, Faith," Iona said, her smooth face too composed in contrast to the outrage in her eyes, in her voice, in every line of her body. "Condoning the use of drugs."

"I don't, but is that any worse than what you're using, Mother?" Faith demanded, pointing to the brandy snifter in her mother's hand. "Liquor or drugs, they're both poison."

"What is this Berkeley Brown that Lou has taken? You know how bad his heart is!" Wendy Madison interrupted curtly. "Oh, how long does it take for Bauman to get here?"

However long it took was far too long for those of us forced to sit around. The McCormacks and the Farnham party left, with Faith repeating her anxious apology for the occurrence. She wasn't to blame, which was what Rafe told her, though Wendy's eyes followed her departure in a baleful gaze.

Maybe, I thought, Wendy Madison would now leave Faith and
Bobby Wellesley alone.

Dr. Bauman was furious when he saw Marchmount's
condition. He went livid, however, when Rafe told him what
had happened. And which drug was involved.

"A compound? Of what? Some damn fool chem major
whomping up some damn fool ingredients? How in hell can I
treat an overdose until I know what I'm counteracting?"

Rafe sent John in search of Sara and Bobby. She came
back by herself and with a kind of suppressed satisfaction (I
wouldn't have suppressed it) told the doctor what he needed to
know.

"Bobby said he took it just shortly after we finished
dinner."

"And when was that?" Bauman seemed to know the
habits of the house. "Well, then we might be able to get enough
of it out of his stomach to save his damn fool life." Bauman
glared at everyone in the room, but he patted Sara on the back.
"You know too much. Hope you don't mess with the stuff,
young lady," he added sternly.

"Anyone can mess with drugs, doctor; it's when you let
them mess you that you're in trouble."

She turned on her sandaled heel and marched out of the
living room with such dignity that I almost seconded Rafe's low
"Bravo!"

The doctor wasted no further time, but ordered an ambulance, called the hospital, and gave them swift instructions.

"Oh, no, not the hospital." Wendy Madison roused herself enough to protest.

"Yes, the hospital," the doctor snapped. "I warned you
after his last excess that his constitution could stand no further
abuses. Part of his physical condition is psychosomatic."

"But we just had a few friends in," Wendy said.

"A few friends?" Bauman rolled his eyes up in his head
and threw up his hands.

"You could hardly expect me not to give a reception for
my son's bride."

Bauman caught sight of us and merely closed his eyes.

"She ought to be resting, too. Ah, I give up on the lot of

you!" He flung out his hands impatiently and then turned back to Louis Marchmount, moving his stethoscope across the thin tanned chest. I looked away.

The ambulance arrived, siren going and lights flashing; its appearance set Wendy Madison to wailing again. I think John might have soothed her, but as luck would have it, Bobby Wellesley came roaring back through the living room, mouthing obscenities. Sara and Pres were right behind him, both showing signs of having struggled to keep him under control.

The sight of the raving young man being restrained by two husky volunteer ambulance men until Bauman could administer a sedative sent Wendy Madison into hysterics. She was also sedated and taken upstairs by Rafe and John.

Urscoll had mumbled something about staying with Louis Marchmount, so when the ambulance roared off, followed by Dr. Bauman's Lincoln (he drove more erratically than the ambulance), I was left with the notion that a barn fire was really a minor evil.

In a sort of stunned bemusement I looked around the huge empty living room, its beauty vapid and dangerous. The whole house was quiet suddenly, though I'd heard Mrs. Madison's imprecations — mainly aimed at me — clearly enough until cut off by a door.

Outside, tree frogs and night creatures chorused with the occasional muted noise of a fast car on the main road as counterpoint. I was very, very tired.

The soft thud of footsteps on the stair carpeting roused me, and glad of any company, I hurried to the hall. Rafe was swinging down the steps.

"Sorry, Nialla. Let's split this scene."

He glanced over his shoulder as if he hoped nothing would interfere with our leaving. He hauled open the heavy door, and we went out into the clean cool night.

The moment the electric eye began to open the big gate, the dogs came charging out of the underbrush. Rafe called to them, and their forbidding advance turned into a lolloping welcome. Their eyes winked red and Vaseline yellow in the headlights as we passed. When the gate had clanged shut, I saw them sniffling in the driveway, tails wagging. Then they were off again, into the shadows, at a businesslike trot.

Night lights in the stable yard illuminated a tall figure in the arch as we drove by.

"That you, boss?" I heard Jerry's voice.

"Night, Jerry."

I saw him stand there until we swung past the bushes. The porch lights and a small one in the living room showed us the path in.

"Hungry?" Rafe asked in a conversational tone.

I shook my head violently. The thought of food was nauseating.

"Nightcap?"

I just shook my head and made for the stairs.

"I'll be right up, honey," he said, and gave me a proprietary slap on the rear as he turned back to fasten the door.

I had an overwhelming urge to be alone. Completely alone. I ran up the stairs and closed the bedroom door behind me. I wanted to take a shower and get clean. I closed the bathroom door behind me, too. The room was all steam when I finally felt clean. I wrapped the thick wide bath towel around me. Abruptly the atmosphere was no longer steamy; it was suffocating. I ran out into the cool quiet dark of the bedroom.

I knew Rafe wasn't there before my eyes got used to the night, and I wavered between relief and disappointment. The ghastly evening assailed me in flashback as I lay in bed, tired and not as relaxed by the shower as I'd hoped. My blood seemed to pound through my veins, and certainly memories pounded through my brain. The only really nice people had been Faith, the Eldicotts, and Sam. Ted McCormack, possibly.

Had that sort of thing been going on in Agnes du Maurier's huge house when I was growing up, and I was just too naïve to know it? I shook my head. No. That lady had been brusque and candid, but not vicious. She'd loyally stuck by her adulterous husband (and he'd never abused an employee's daughter) until his death, and it hadn't made her like Iona Farnham or as possessive as Wendy Madison. I mopped the perspiration from my face as my body temperature gradually lowered in the cooling night air.

What made people like Louis Marchmount and Bobby Wellesley take drugs?

Where was Rafe?

I had a most persistent vision of Louis Marchmount lying on the couch, with Bobby Wellesley's twitching length superimposed on his bony chest.

Where *was* Rafe?

"I can protect you, Nialla. I want the right to protect you . . ." Rafe had told me. Was it really only four days ago?

He did well enough with police and doctors and insurance men, but in the bosom of his own family, he was a bust. (Oh, Gawd!) But the awful pun brought my humor into operation again. I needed every ounce of it I owned, with that kind of mother-in-law playing charades and sending a kid brother (not even a full brother, at that) to buy me off.

I burrowed under the sheet, for the warmth of the shower had dissipated enough to make the night air a bit chilly. I'd half-thought that Rafe might be showering, but it seemed to me he was taking a long time coming to bed. I listened until the night insects sounded louder than the distant passage of long-haul trucks on the highway half a mile beyond the farm. I could hear nothing of manmade noises. The house emanated such a deserted silence, my breathing was positively stertorous.

Where *was* he?

I slid from the bed to the window and realized that both the porch and living-room lights were off. The nearest glow welled up through the evergreens around the stable. I concentrated, discounting insect buzzes and frog chirpings, listening for any odd sound.

Where had Rafe got to? Had he learned something he didn't mention to me? Had he gone back to the big house? Perhaps that was it. Although Rafe in the role of loving son was about as ridiculous as his mother cast as Florence Nightingale — unless you made it "Martingale," and that was what she wanted to put on Louis Marchmount.

The droll notion did not restore my sense of proportion, for there was nothing really amusing about Wendy Madison. Well, at least Pres Branegg was trying to slice the silver cord, but John Milanesi's fixation was damned unhealthy.

*Where* was Rafe?

I rose again, uneasy and — yes — afraid to sleep without his protective presence. I might not be able to cope with someone like Wendy Madison in person, but once she was out of sight, I didn't have to worry about her. It was the things I couldn't see, the enemies I knew I had that really frightened me.

I paced through the upper floor of the house, peering out of each window and listening intently, trying to catch the crunch of someone on the gravel. Clever of Rafe to surround the house with gravelly paths that couldn't be jumped easily or crossed silently.

Not a noise, not a leaf stirred without the light breeze to account for its movement.

Maybe Rafe was disappointed in me?

Then . . . I heard something. The slightest bit of scraping noise. On the stairs. My throat went dry — just like they say it does — and although I couldn't seem to breathe, my pulses were pounding so hard they ought to be audible.

I could see the interruption of normal shadows on the staircase, a darker patch that advanced, not toward our bedroom but toward the back of the house, toward me, where I was standing in the west bedroom.

"Rafe!"

I raced to him, almost crying with relief and joy. I flung myself at him so hard that the breath went out of his lungs in a whoosh. Then his arms encircled, hard, comforting, and he swung me, chuckling into my ear.

"Glad to see me, huh?"

"Oh, Rafe, where have you been?"

"Sentry-go-round."

I leaned back, trying to see his face in the dark. The shadows made him seem totally different, a stern stranger, until he turned his head slightly, and I could see the gleam of his teeth and eyes.

"You were worried?"

"Not particularly," he said, which meant he had been. "Thought you'd be asleep by now."

It was the casual comment, delivered in a sort of impersonal tone, that told me how much the disastrous evening had upset Rafe. If I had dreaded the affair, he had loathed it. Yet even Rafe couldn't have foreseen the ghastly capper to the party.

Well, he'd done his filial duty, introduced his bride, and neither she not he could be compelled to make another appearance *there!*

"Asleep? You gotta be kidding, man," I said. I felt him tense slightly, saw his smile fade, and realized he misunderstood me. I tightened my arms around his neck, pressing my body against the tight muscles of his torso with what I thought was a sensuous motion. I angled my head so our noses wouldn't collide, and kissed him till our teeth grated together.

"Dear heart." He laughed as he gathered me up in his arms and made for our bedroom. "Dear heart," he repeated as he laid me very gently down on the bed. "Don't rush the fence. Sexy is soft." And his lips covered mine very lightly, his tongue caressing the edge of my mouth in a feather touch. "Very soft, until you ache for more."

And he demonstrated.

 8

I'D NO NOTION when we finally went to sleep. Who thought of wristwatches? But the morning sun slanting over the top of the windowsill through the beeches woke me. I had been so deeply asleep that for a moment I couldn't recall my whereabouts.

"Thank God tomorrow's Sunday," Rafe said close to my ear. His toes brushed mine as he arched his back in a joint-popping stretch.

"What difference does Sunday make?" I wondered. "Sun rises same as ever."

"I ignore the sun until noon on the Sabbath." Rafe threw back the covers—off me, too—and bounced to his feet. He looked down at me, a little reminiscent smile lifting the corner of his mouth. "I feel like ignoring the sun right now." He looked about to dive on top of me. I giggled. "Shameless hussy!" He didn't dive, but he had me in his arms again, his warm flesh exciting against me. But, as our chests touched, I winced. My breasts were tender. He put me from him with an oath, and there was absolutely no desire in the penitent kiss he placed on my cheek.

"Rafe?"

"We can wait. It's not going somewhere else."

With that cryptic remark he hauled me out of the bed, swatted me on the buttocks, and pushed me toward the shower.

"We gotta ride, and then I want to take you to the Locust Valley meet this afternoon at Charlie's place. That is, if you'd like to go."

"Is that where the Eldicotts are going?"

"Yes."

"I'd like to see them again especially."

"Thought you would. Old friends of my father's, and good friends of mine." Then he was off down the hall.

I showered quickly without steam effects, pleased I'd see the Eldicotts again and also watch a meet I didn't have to compete in for a change. I'd been going steady on that routine ever since Florida. But I'd plenty of points accumulated for the big trophies.

I have a tendency to forget time in a shower: I get pensive from the mesmeric beat of water on my shoulders. God knows that last few days—*few* days?—had given me a lot to think about. Incredible! I'd met Rafe only *last* Saturday, and yet, in some aspects of our days together, I felt I'd known him a great deal longer. Could I actually *have* met him when he jockeyed for Dad? And simply not singled him out of the gaggle of short men who drifted in and out of the Du Maurier paddocks? I shivered with erotic memories of last night. Unlikely that I'd have met Rafe and not remembered. No, now, Nialla, you'd've been twelve? Thirteen? You weren't noticing boys in *that* way . . . only horses.

I was also a little nonplussed that Rafe hadn't taken me again this morning. He certainly looked like he wanted to. I wouldn't have minded the hurting: it was perversely stimulating, I'd discovered. But if Rafe was considerate of me, he hadn't married me just for *that*. (I couldn't any longer use the contemptuous vulgar words with which I was used to referring

to the sex act—not after being pleasured by Rafael Clery.
"Pleasured"—that was exactly the right word, too.)

I ruthlessly turned on the cold tap. The sharp needles of
water stung my breasts, and I turned my back on *that*. Neither
Maisie nor Sadie was I. Speaking of whom . . .

I was losing time ruminating again, and just as I stepped
from the stall shower, there was a discreet tapping on the door.
He was leaning against the jamb, a wistful expression on his face.

"I'm so sorry, Rafe. I get started thinking under a shower
and lose all track of time."

"So long as you think of me," he said, pushing himself
erect and speaking with an exaggeration that put me instantly
in mind of a Rudolph Valentino movie.

"Of you, my lord, of you and no other," I replied with
matching extravagance, and flourishing my hand to my brow,
pretended to swoon.

"I have you in my power, my proud beauty! Must I be
valet as well as lover?" quoth he, bending me back until my
head nearly touched the floor. "But I won't have much power
if I don't get my Cheerios!" he added petulantly, pulling me up
and letting me go so suddenly I nearly fell. He steadied me, his
eyes merry with our fooling.

We were both laughing as we went downstairs. I thought
of last night's harrowing scenes and decided to forget them
completely.

But there were too many reminders. Jerry, sleepy and
disgusted, sipping coffee in the kitchen, waiting to report that
not a damned thing had happened last night. It was his opinion
the blackmailer was just talking. Rafe reminded him that a slit
girth, a blaring horn, and a barn fire couldn't be classed as
"talk," and perhaps the absence of activity was designed to
relax our vigilance.

"Ask Dennis to take over if these late hours are getting
you down," Rafe suggested half-jokingly.

"His Sue Jan's baby-sitting this week for the Perdues,"
Mrs. Garrison said, turning from the pancakes she was watching.

Jerry grumbled something about a boy taking a man's job
and said he'd sleep on it. I tried not to giggle, and heard Rafe

clearing his throat, but Jerry wandered off, yawning, oblivious to the play on words.

After Rafe finished nine pancakes—and Mrs. Garrison's were not the chintzy restaurant size—I slyly suggested Cheerios and meekly endured her lecture on empty calorie foods and starving on a full stomach of such blown-up garbage. Rafe had to assure her I was teasing, and we both insisted that she sit down for coffee.

"Well, I could just tell *something* was going to happen last night, Mr. Rafe," she said, "and I was that scared it might be trouble for you and Miss Nialla."

Inadvertently my eyes met Rafe's.

"I don't mean to sound unfeeling about Mr. Marchmount—who's holding his own, I heard—but I guess it could have been worse. It's *her's* not well today."

Rafe's eyebrows rose in polite inquiry.

"Yes. Mamzelle said she was in a fine state of hysterics, carrying on about being disgraced and ruined all because Dr. Bauman insisted on taking Mr. Marchmount to Nassau County Hospital and making that Wellesley child go, too, and what would the Wellesleys think of her when they heard he'd been taken ill in her house. Taken ill!" Mrs. Garrison snorted contemptuously at the euphemism. "As if his people wouldn't know what that young feller's been doing, the way he dresses and all. As if they didn't know what she does now and again. My lands, how can people fool themselves . . . That photographer had left by then, hadn't he?"

We nodded.

"That's a mercy. And young Dennis had gone, too. I'm just as glad of that."

"And you think Dennis doesn't know about grass?" I asked before I stopped to think.

Mrs. Garrison looked at me, her lips firm with disapproval. "I expect he does, Miss Nialla, but he's got more sense than to use it. Grass is for horses to eat, not people to smoke."

I wondered if she had failed to catch an essential difference, but I wasn't the one and this wasn't the time to explain.

"I expect," Rafe said, grinning at me, "Dennis agrees with you, Garry."

"I should hope so. He's a nice boy. I know he was kept up pretty late bartending, but he was here right on time this morning. Oh, and Mr. Rafe, about those race types, Mrs. Palchi said there haven't been any at the house."

"Phone calls?"

"I told you about that, Mr. Rafe. Sam's to say Mr. Marchmount's not there, same as before."

"To work, to work," Rafe said, clapping his hand together. "We'll put the string through a quick workout and then run over to Locust Valley. Garry, can you put lunch forward to about one, one-thirty?"

"Of course, Mr. Rafe. It's going to be a scorcher, according to the weatherman"—and she wasn't too certain about his ability—"so I'd planned something cool and light, Miss Nialla. Doesn't pay to eat too heavy in hot weather."

"That sounds fine," I murmured, and Rafe and I left.

"While you were lost in that shower," Rafe said as we walked briskly through the still-cool morning air, "I called the hospital. Spoke to Urscoll and told him about your extortion call. His bosses can't fault him if Marchmount's involved, sidereally, as it were, and Marchmount, if he lives through this relapse, can't say they abrogated his confidence. But I'm not having my wife threatened, even as a fringe benefit for some ex-racetrack-tout. Meanwhile, back at the ranch"—and his arm tightened around my waist—"let's you and me concentrate on some steeds."

"Going to be a scorcher," Dennis said in greeting. He'd just finished grooming Orfeo in the passageway. Dice was watching, yawning sleepily. "He had a hard night, that one."

Rafe loosened the halter rope and led the gelding out into the sun, his hide gleaming with dark rosettes.

"He's stepping out well," Rafe remarked. "Dennis, move him about."

We stood and watched as Dennis ran with the gelding, but he was still, just a little, favoring the off-hind. Rafe took the lead from Dennis and gestured for me to look at the hoof. It was almost healed, the char all but gone from the sole and barely noticeable where the cinder had burned into the frog a little.

"He'll be as good as new in a few days," I allowed.

Rafe was communing with Orfeo; he didn't even seem aware I'd spoken. There was excitement in Rafe's eyes, and the hands that caressed my black gelding were as possessive and gentle as his hands on me. I felt a surge of conflicting emotions: jealousy, regret (Orfeo was *my* accomplishment), envy, irritation, impatience, unworthy feelings; I suppressed them. Orfeo was no less mine if Rafe rode and won on him, and I damned well couldn't chase him.

"Rafe, would you ride Phi Bete this morning for me? She needs some exercise, and I'd like you to try her," I heard myself saying.

Orfeo tossed his head, and I didn't see Rafe's expression.

"Well, since you ask me so nicely, I don't mind if I do," was what he said, and there was an odd ripple in his voice. And a kind of pleased smile on his face when Orfeo moved back.

Rocking Lady worked better for me this morning, though she seemed very spooky. Maybe it was me, for I was constantly craning my neck to see if Phi Bete was performing properly. (I mean, you can get awful silly about a horse you've trained, who's had only you on her back, to the point where it's absurd.)

"You ride that damned bay," Rafe muttered under his breath as we were walking the jumper after a steady round, "and let me ride your precious darling." The deep smile on his face belied the words. He reached over impulsively and kissed me on the lips, right in front of the delighted Dennis. He patted Phi Bete's curved neck, too. "She's as beautifully trained a jumper as I've ever sat, Nialla. You can be proud of her. And stop worrying. I need you to take the rough edges off that bay bitch."

"You're sure . . . "

"Stop frowning. I goddamn well don't put the Clery seal of approval on any spavined ring-boned blown hack simply because I married her owner." What he didn't say — "It's Orfeo I want your permission to ride" — hung as clearly to me in the silence as if he had spoken the words. And, for the life of me, I couldn't see why I had any hesitation in offering.

We worked the grays next, until all four of us were

sweating heavily. The weatherman had been right, and by eleven the sun scorched hot through the heavy humid air.

"Let's call it a day, Nialla. I feel stewed in my own juices. And the jumping will be hot at Locust Valley. We ought to go watch awhile. You may be riding against some of the winners later on."

Dennis appeared to take the sweating horses from us, listening carefully to Rafe's instructions about cooling them.

I seemed to have spent a good portion of the last week in a shower—far better than a pail in the ladies'—but this time I made a conscious effort to stick to cleaning and rinsing, without deviation.

I'd have to improve if I wanted to beat Rafe, for he was tapping at the bathroom door, black hair still wet but sleekly combed. He also looked disgustingly cool in a tissue-thin blue jersey pullover and elegant walk shorts, twirling ebony-framed sunglasses in one hand. He presented me with a matching pair.

"Reduce the glare. Charlie's place usually has a nice breeze, but there's not much air stirring on the island today."

Charlie's place happened to be one of those huge estates that still boast ten-foot, glass-topped concrete walls. Only a discreet sign in gay-nineties printing, "Horse Show," gave any hint of the doings those walls hid.

We turned obliquely left, before the drive that led to a gorgeous Georgian brick mansion, past an elaborate swimming pool glimpsed through screening rose arbors, around the estate's stable complex, before we came to the open fields, with the usual appointments of horse trailers, cars, people, horses, temporary rings, children, and even a mobile sandwich truck.

Some events were already in progress as Rafe stopped at the improvised box office of card table and elderly gatekeeper. The loudspeaker was urging Numbers 18, 23, 36, and 72 to come to Ring Number Four, if you please!

"Nice to see you holding up after last winter, Willie," Rafe said, handing over money and accepting two programs.

"Hot weather's good for me, Mr. Clery. It's the cold bothers my chest."

"Ought to be hot enough today."

"Just right. Just right," the old man agreed, mopping his brow.

As the Austin-Healey made its low, slow way over the rough ground, I suddenly wished I were on horseback among all these strangers. Rafe's chuckle, pure devilment, distracted me.

"This'll be good. George's here."

"George?"

"Uh-huh. One of the top jump trainers in the world. Look at him! Flaunting enough ribbons to set up a shop!"

I followed his gesture to the big blue horse van whose side doors had been rigged with a line on which hung an impressive array of reds, blues, and damned few lesser shades. Two youngsters were sitting in the camp chairs, bootless legs stretched out, fanning themselves. Four pink hunting jackets and several plain linen ones hung on a bar across the back of the van.

"George runs one of the best jump clinics on the East Coast. He's got young hopefuls from all over, saying yessir and nosir, ready to swallow their pride and their fathers' almighty dollars to qualify for Madison Square or Chagrin Valley. God, there are some people who'll make a racket out of anything."

"George?"

"No!" Rafe seemed almost annoyed, not realizing that his aspersion was ambiguous. "The prestige-seekers, the status-claimers. 'My kid won a blue jumping at Broken Tooth.' Takes all the joy out of it."

The one clump of shade by the larger of the two iron-picketed rings had been preempted by the show officials. They had even moved the equipment from the loudspeaker truck, which would have been a glass-walled steambath.

Four separate rings were in operation, I realized, looking over my program as Rafe parked the car on the far side of the ring and began to study his. There was a small ring beyond the main field for the pony classes, a huge meadow with five substantial hunt-class jumps, and the one permanent ring, set under some magnificent oaks, where flat riding was being judged. One could see the dust clouds, at any rate, and the spectators were standing well back from the railing. I wondered that the judges could see a thing in such smog.

"Ray just informed me," the announcer informed the county, "that unless 18, 36, and 72 are at Ring Number One gate in one minute, Class 23 will be closed. What's that? Oh, well, we'll give her one more minute to change tack." Then, sort of off-mike, "We're not giving them enough time between classes, Ray."

Just as Rafe suggested that we drift around, someone hailed him. I was delighted to see the Eldicotts coming over. They were such a handsome couple, bearing gracefully the years which Iona Farnham and Wendy Madison tried to deny.

"Anne, you sneaked away far too soon last night," Rafe said, kissing her hand and then shaking Steve Eldicott's.

"Just as well, I gather," Steve replied in a dry voice.

"Oh?"

Anne Eldicott smiled reassuringly and patted Rafe's hand, for he hadn't released hers. "The show is a gossip kettle, Rafe. They'd make soup from a stone. They'd have it that the Herrington estate was raided by narcotics agents last night, and half a dozen people were rushed to the hospital. That's the worst you'll hear. Ran into Ted McCormack, and he told us that Lou had a mild seizure."

Rafe gave her a long look. "Lou's heart is bad, and he did have a seizure last night, and Bauman rushed him to Nassau County. He's holding his own."

"Bob Wellesley has heart trouble, too?" Steve asked, his expression very bland.

Rafe began to chuckle. "Bob, you might say, has heart trouble, too. Faith."

"Hope and Charity," mocked Steve.

"We really were sorry we couldn't stay longer last night," Anne told me, without seeming to change the subject. "Rafe's one of our favorite people, so very much like his father."

"And all the time I thought it was my winning personality."

"Ha!" said Steve with a disparaging snort, then addressed me. "Pure self-interest on Anne's part. She's an inveterate gambler, and used to treble her betting fund every time Rafe rode."

Rafe cast a despairing look at Anne. "It wasn't my big blue eyes?"

"Sorry, chum," Anne said with an unpenitent grin. "Have you noticed that Korlin is *still* trying."

Rafe looked around, spotted a tall, graying man warming up a chestnut. "He'll never make it that way. I keep telling him bargains in horseflesh aren't bargains if you're after jump trophies."

We walked along the rail, seeking a spot that gave us the best view of the set jumps. The entries were by now all assembled, and the first contestant did her round. The Eldicotts knew most of the entrants. There was a preponderance of younger riders in this open class, all hoping to win enough points to qualify for the events in the bigger regional horse shows, and finally Madison Square, come November. Some of the kids were good; certainly all were well-mounted.

"One of George's," Rafe said to me as a girl trotted by on a well-bred dark dappled gray with an uncommonly white mane and tail.

"How can you tell?"

"Look at George." He pointed across the ring, where a man stood, arms on the top metal strap, intently taking the jumps with the contestant. When the girl made a flawless round, the man relaxed but did not smile.

Although Rafe and the Eldicotts chatted about mutual acquaintances and training troubles, I never felt left out, though I had few comments to offer. We were all interested in the class's progress. The judge's indecision between the two first-place contenders was exactly mine. He asked them to switch mounts. The gray moved out as well for the boy as for the girl. She had to keep the boy's mount well in hand, for the chestnut showed in inclination to refuse, which she thwarted with nice leg work. She took the blue. George's face seemed to indicate that there'd been no question at all in his mind. And then I saw the second-placer joining George's small knot of adherents. His rather flat voice carried across the ring as he discussed the class, gesturing from one rider to another as he remarked on the aggregate performance.

The announcer was calling another class, juniors sixteen or under, limit only. It was a large class, half the kids nervous and communicating it to their mounts. The raw-boned bay was almost on me before I recognized the colored Tomlinson headstall and saw Bess Tomlinson's daughter go by.

"I thought I'd find the bride and groom here," called a cheery voice. I whirled to see Bess herself bearing down on us. As usual she had one freckled arm loaded with bangles. They cut into my back as she embraced me warmly. She really did seem pleased, too, her grin threatening to split the biggest freckles on her cheeks. "By God, you look a thousand percent better already. If Rafe hadn't been taking care of you . . . " Her threat trailed off. "Anne, you look disgustingly young; how's Jeffrey?"

Mention of this person seemed to dampen everyone's spirits.

"Jeff's just fine," Steve replied, but Anne's gentle smile and Steve's stock reply told me that "just fine" wasn't all that good. "Your girl up on old Majority?"

"Yes. I try to keep her out of the game, but she's determined to compete with her old mother."

There was a kind of taut determination in the lumpy girl's straightly held shoulders.

"I used to think excitement followed Rafe," Bess was saying to me, "but you manage to gather a fair amount of it yourself. Recovered from the fire? How's that leaping fool of a Juggernaut?"

"Juggernaut? Thought he went to glue years ago," Steve said.

"No, as a matter of fact," Rafe said in the manner of someone who's held on to a surprise, "he's up at my place. Nialla is actually a white witch and worked a spell on him. On me, too. But she jumped him to a blue at Sunbury . . . ."

"*You* were in that fire?" Anne exclaimed with concern. "Oh, your legs and arms." She could now admit she'd noticed them.

"The girl's a real heroine," Bess went on proudly, and launched into a reasonably accurate account of the fire and my part in it. All the time she had one eye on her daughter.

"Actually, if Rafe hadn't come to my aid, I'd never have got Orfeo out," I said, obliged to tone down her exaggerations.

"Rode the damned horse's head to keep the blanket on," Rafe added.

"Did you lose any stock?"

"No horses."

"But a lot of peanut butter," Rafe put in with a straight face. "And all her clothes and tack. I got me a bride with only tatters to cover her . . ."

"I'd've thought you'd remedy *that*," Bess said outrageously. I didn't dare look around. "However, Rafe Clery, you did get Juggernaut and that sweet-moving sorrel mare. Say, they haven't discovered who killed old Pete, have they? And what's all this about Louis Marchmount taking an overdose of drugs? I saw him with Wendy in charge at the Marshalls'." Bess grimaced. "She was put out . . . " Bess broke off, her eyes flicking to mine, and she flushed. "Oh, good girl!"

We all concentrated very intently on the jumping.

"She is still letting him crowd his fences," Bess said with a dismal groan. "And she wobbled all over the saddle on the hurdle jump. If she'd lose ten pounds, she'd be able to get her thighs into the saddle properly. But that doesn't get you off the hook, Clery," she continued, jabbing Rafe in the shoulder with a bony forefinger. "Girth cut, horn blaring, barn burning . . . not to mention old Pete with his head broken. I don't believe that hogwash about spontaneous combustion, either."

"Bess, you're a love, and I promise not to compete against your string all summer, but I can't give you answers I don't have," Rafe said, his expression grim.

Bess looked at his arm around my waist and raised her sun-bleached eyebrows.

"Well, I see you're intent on guarding your own interests and counsel. Just remember, *I* stood up for this girl, and I dislike having *my* arrangements broken."

"Mrs. — Bess" — I corrected myself as she glared at me — "was my matron of honor," I told the Eldicotts, who were politely hoping for an explanation of something. "D'you know, she brought me her veil and flowers?"

"D'you blame me for rushing Nialla off her feet?" Rafe said, giving me a rather shameless leer.

"If she's got that black jumper, no. You always swore you

only needed a chance at him to get him working properly,"
Steve said. "I admit I thought Brader would take your offer. Six
thousand was a damned good price for that beast, considering
his manners."

Six thousand? I'd paid forty dollars for Orfeo because
that's all I had on me that day. And I expect that the farm who'd
been holding Orfeo for the knackers considered that a bargain
for taking a near corpse off his hands.

"Steve!" His wife regarded him with mock horror, then
smiled at me. Had my face revealed something? "You'll make
Nialla think Rafe's mercenary."

"As far as horseflesh is concerned, he is," Steve said in a
succinct fashion, softening by the smile he gave me. "However,
I think he's met his match on all points in Russ Donnelly's
daughter." Steve frowned then, his eyes going from my face to
Rafe's, but whatever he thought, he said nothing, although
from time to time he watched me intently.

I'd been genuinely glad to see Bess Tomlinson, but her
questions, however well intentioned, only brought back the
shadows which the show had briefly banished.

"Gawd, it's boiling here. C'mon, Nialla. Spot you to a
Coke," Rafe said when the judges had announced their
decisions.

Bess's girl had a fifth-place ribbon and looked rather put
out. She'd had stiffer competition here, though, since it was a
class in equitation rather than the horse's performance.

"That'll knock Madam's yarn," Rafe chuckled as we got
out of earshot of the Eldicotts and Bess. "Though why she
wanted to be at the wedding is beyond me."

"She didn't go to the others?" The words were out of my
mouth before I could stop them. Rafe looked perversely
pleased.

"No indeed. But then," he told me in a bland voice, "I've
never been to any of hers." His arm linked though mine, and
he matched my stride. "Bess is worried about you, dear heart.
People do, you know, besides me. And the Eldicotts really like
you, or they'd have stayed away from us today. They tend to
keep to themselves."

"Why? Because of this Jeff?"

Rafe's glance was warmly approving. "Jeff's their only child. We used to go to the same school till I got 'asked to leave.' He's a paraplegic from Korea. I drop in now and again."

And that was all he wanted to say on that subject.

He stepped up to the counter of the mobile snack truck, greeting the older of the men working there, chatting as he waited for the Cokes to be found in the cooler. Rafe couldn't be as unconcerned over the rampant gossip about us as he appeared. I mean, it might not matter to the Eldicotts, who had problems of their own, or Bess Tomlinson that his wife was obviously connected to some fatal incidents. But this business-as-usual might be misconstrued as indifference. And last night's episode, while scarcely any fault of mine, made me feel a real Jonah.

"There's a time, Nialla, when you don't look for more problems," Rafe said, handing me the Coke with a flourish at variance with his serious advice. He tipped his bottle back for a long swallow. "Boy, that hits the spot. Hotter'n the hinges of hell here." We moved to the shadow cast by a big horse van. It wasn't any cooler, but the sun didn't bite my shoulders and arms.

"I should have known Bess would be here, and her usual games-mistress self. But nothing will affect her opinion of you." He chuckled, because he knew he'd read my mind a-right. "Dear heart, I *know* you, inside-outside-hindside-near-side. And *that's* why we're at a show today. It's the only thing will take your mind off what's bothering us both. Also" — and he glanced around us — "we're in a big, safe crowd. And if you think I'm going to leave your side for a moment, you're wrong."

I wasn't just imagining it; there was affection in the depths of those disconcertingly blue eyes. Damn the six thousand dollars. It wasn't because of Orfeo.

"So let's divert ourselves for another half-hour and then go home and eat. Unless you'd rather pick up a hot dog here. Garry won't mind."

I looked at the snack truck and then at the people milling around. Somehow this place seemed safer than the quiet Dower House for all the gates and the guard dogs.

"Of course, it's damned hot, and the house is air-conditioned. We can leave here anytime. You want to go swimming or something? Come to think of it" — and there was astonishingly enough a shade of apology in Rafe's rueful admission — "I don't remember asking what *you'd* like to do."

"You don't have to — mind-reader."

He gave me a quick kiss on the cheek, and evidently the matter was settled, for he suggested that we see what the Hunter Class was doing, all gussied up in pink coats (they must be boiling), breeks, hunting boots, whip, gloves, hat, saddle accessories. They were waiting in the ruthless sun for the judges to check the appointments.

We managed to get some shade from the high hedges in the corner of the hunting meadow, Ring 4. And, watching the contestants stretching their horses over the ground between hurdles, I did manage to forget the omnipresent shadow of fear. I didn't connect the slowly approaching police car with my involvement, even when it pulled up near us.

"Clery! Hey, Clery."

I didn't react to the name the first time, because I wasn't used to thinking of myself as a Clery.

"Well, if it isn't Bob Erskine," Rafe said, nodding pleasantly to the heavyset police officer who heaved himself out of the back of the sedan. His badge said "Sheriff," and that's how he was introduced to me.

"Sorry to trouble you, Mrs. Clery" — he must take lessons from my mother-in-law — "but I've a few questions to ask you."

"Thanks all the same, Bob. You don't need to assign a man to protect Nialla."

"Protect . . ." Erskine floundered momentarily. "I'm talking to your wife, Mr. Clery. Are you Irene Nialla Donnelly, otherwise known as Nialla Dunn, and did you reside in San Fernando Valley at Merrymount Estate? . . . "

The noon-high sun could not thaw the chill that sprang from the pit of my stomach and spread rapidly to my hands and feet.

"I'm not sure I like your tone of voice, Erskine," Rafe said in a dangerously soft one.

I caught Rafe's hand, his fingers contracting around mine, instead of into a fist. I wouldn't let his hand go.

"I *was* Irene Nialla Donnelly, and I have used the name Nialla Dunn in the show ring," I said quickly. The cold receded rapidly before the anger I felt toward this paunchy bully, sweating in the hot sun. "I did reside in San Fernando. Why?" I felt Rafe relax at the crispness of my counterquestion.

"Seems like you left without notifying the authorities in charge of investigating a murder."

"I did leave California after my father's murder, that's true. But I also had been thoroughly interrogated by the police and left a signed statement with them. No one told me I couldn't leave the state, and so I'd no idea I was committing any kind of crime or misdemeanor."

"I didn't say you was—"

"You didn't *say* it," I replied, grabbing Rafe's hand again, and staring back at Erskine without wavering. "But your 'questions' imply it. I know that Detective Lieutenant Michaels has been in touch with you, so you must be aware of the facts."

"Now, there's no reason to get—"

"Isn't there?" I demanded, imbued with unexpected confidence and cool. This man was not one whit different from the disagreeable bullies who had harassed me in California. Only I wasn't a fool any longer. "When you accost me here, at a sports event? If you knew I was Mrs. Clery, then you knew the rest, Sheriff Erskine. Believe me, I am quite willing to cooperate with the authorities. Ask Detective Lieutenant Michaels. But I really do not think that this is the time or the place."

"Doesn't that about cover it, Erskine?" Rafe asked, using that soft dangerous tone. "Or should I ask Korlin to step over here a moment? He's right over there." And Rafe jerked his head back toward Ring 1, where the next class was lined up to enter. "You have more official questions? My wife will answer them, but since she has not broken any law by being the victim of planned accidents and an extortion attempt, the time will be convenient to her and her attorney. Now, good afternoon."

Rafe swung me back toward the ringside and began to comment on the form of the rider then approaching the stone fence in the far corner. I could feel fury in the shadow the Sheriff cast over us. It seemed an age before we heard the car

door slam and the squawking of power steering as the auto
backed around and bounced away over the rough ground.

"Rafe . . ."

"Nialla"—and for the first time he sounded impatient
with me—"Bob Erskine is an officious oaf, hanging on to his
office by the tips of his hairy fingers. Half his precinct is
drug-ridden, from the college kids experimenting with electric
punch to the upper-income brackets tripping on esoteric com-
pounds. He can't touch the one because the campus goes up
like a rocket. He can't touch the others because they consis-
tently buy either him or the judge off. All the fervent puritans
in the township and the narks in Mineola are breathing down
his neck. But he can't pull that kind of a law-and-order arrogance with me—or you." Then he smiled at me. "You
couldn't have answered him better."

"Those answers I have."

I'd felt unusually secure (for me) while I was actually
confronting the Sheriff, but now, in reaction to the tension, I
needed to find a ladies' room fast.

"The house isn't open," Rafe told me when I asked, "but
I know there's a john in the stable. I'll show you."

We were halfway there when Rafe was hailed by the
McCormacks. He urged me to go along to the stable—it was
only a couple of hundred yards farther up the track.

I found a gay-nineties-style sign of a hand, the index
finger pointed toward an open door at the back of the stable.
The whimsy amused me. I entered a wide, cobbled passageway
with six loose boxes along the right. On the left a double-barn
door was barred from the inside, but at the end of the corridor
was a second hand-sign pointing to the L of the stable. Two
horses stuck their heads out of the stalls to investigate me: a
rangy bay and a timorous gray. I made my duties to them, and
they whiffled in response.

The john itself was a long narrow room, undoubtedly
constructed for another use entirely but now serving as
lavatory, kitchenette, and animal dispensary. The toilet was an
original, same vintage as the hand signs, complete with upper
water tank, pull chain, and golden oak trimmings. I had, as a
matter of habit, thrown the bolt on the door, so when the

handle rattled, I called out that I'd be only a minute. There was no reply, and I guiltily remembered monopolizing the one good toilet at Sunbury. I completed my use of the facilities and opened the door. To my chagrin, there was no one waiting in the passageway. It might have been a child with a far more urgent need . . .

Hands grabbed me from behind, fingers pressing into my windpipe with brutal strength, shaking me off my feet so that I fell to my knees, too startled to cry out with what breath remained, too terrified to do more than claw at the hands that were choking me.

"High and mighty, are you?" The words were no more than an anonymous hiss on a garlicky repellent breath. "Think you're safe with high gates and dogs? Too big, are you? Unless you pay up, you'll never be safe!"

I heard another voice, someone calling — calling me? — just as I passed out.

When I came to, I was propped in Bess Tomlinson's lap, her bracelets jangling in my face. Rafe was bending over me; he looked white and strained. My throat felt as if it was torn out, and hurt enough to make me wish it were. I couldn't swallow, and even air hurt in my throat, and I wanted to cry, and the air was stifling.

"Easy, darling." Rafe's fingers curled around my wrist, firm and gentle. "You'll be all right. Don't try to talk."

Which was fine by me. Bess Tomlinson's hand kept smoothing my hair back from my forehead, her charms jingling in an oddly comforting fashion. Her hand was very soft and cool. She used Ma Griffe perfume, and that reminded me of the sour-hay smell, the acrid odor of wool and sweat I'd smelled as my assailant was strangling me.

Someone came along the passageway at a run, followed by others moving with equal haste.

"The guy got away, Rafe," a man said, gasping for breath.

"Get a good look at him?"

"At his back, yes, but nothing I could swear to."

"Was he wearing a cap?"

"Huh?"

"Think, man! Was he wearing a cap or a hat?"

"Hell, I didn't *see*. I was *running*!"

"Here, move away now. You, too, Rafe!"

I stared up at Dr. Bauman's worried face. He was sweating under a patina of tanning oil. His hands were considerably more gentle with me than they'd been with Lou Marchmount or Bob Wellesley.

"I've been summoned in many ways, but not by a Paul Revere before," he said wryly as he turned my head very carefully from side to side, running fingertips lightly along my neck. "It'll hurt, but can you swallow, Mrs. Clery?"

I could, but the effort brought tears to my eyes. He patted my shoulder.

"No obvious damage to the thorax that I can tell, Rafe, but she's going to have a sore, bruised throat for a few days. Let's get her out of here." He rose, and his shirttails extended down thin hairy legs. As he gestured people out of the way, I realized that he did have on a bathing suit, but the total effect gave me the urge to laugh, which hurt, and the tears just flowed down my cheeks. "Here," the doctor said, "you two muscle boys, give us a hand."

I grabbed for Rafe's hand, and he had me up in his arms before the doctor could finish organizing assistance.

"Here, now, just a moment. What's going on here?" the rasping voice of Sheriff Erskine demanded.

"Someone just tried to strangle Nialla Clery," Bess Tomlinson replied in a disgusted tone. She stepped forward, an arm outstretched to make room for Rafe and me, but the Sheriff blocked the way.

"Now, just a moment. Where are you taking her?"

"Home, you damned fool," Bess answered.

"Not before I hear what happened," Erskine said, taking a stance.

"Out of the way, Bob," Rafe said in that very quiet voice that made Erskine shift his feet.

"Oh, for Christ's sake, Bob," Dr. Bauman exclaimed with exasperation. "Look at her throat! She's been strangled half to death. She damned well can't talk. Bess probably saw more than Mrs. Clery did, anyhow. Fellow grabbed her from behind . . ."

"Grabbed Mrs. Tomlinson?" the Sheriff asked.

"No, you idiot, Mrs. Clery! She's the one got strangled."

I clung to Rafe, burying my face in his neck.

"I had to use the loo," Bess said in a rapid voice, but she was furious with Erskine. "When I got inside, I heard odd scuffling, and someone choking, so I called out. Some of the kids eat too much junk from that snack truck. I thought someone was sick. Then I heard someone slamming through the other door, and by then I'd seen Nialla."

"And yelled bloody blue murder," a young man spoke up. "I was coming up the road, so I took off after him. Only I thought it was just a purse-snatcher or something. I'd've run faster if I'd known, but God, in this heat . . . "

"I'm taking Nialla home," Rafe said, and angling my feet past the Sheriff, carried me out of the stable, through the small crowd that had gathered.

"My car's here, Rafe," Bauman said.

"Fine by me," Rafe answered in a grim tone. "Keep your head down, Nialla," he added as he bent to slide into the front seat. It was a big car, so there wasn't much bending necessary.

It was also air-conditioned, for which I was intensely grateful. The cooled air was easier to breathe. I clutched Rafe, knowing a desperation I hadn't felt since the day after Dad had been killed and the police had ruthlessly questioned me, trying to find a motive and suggesting reasons, each more infamous than the last.

Would I ever live normally again? Could I ever be alone without being terrified—even in such a simple act as going to a john?

I felt Rafe's lips on my cheek; then he raised my hand to his mouth, the arm around my shoulders tightening reassuringly. What had he got himself in for when he married me? A lifetime job as a bodyguard?

The way the trees and telephone lines flashed by, the doctor must drive like an acid-head, but there was very little motion to be felt inside the big Lincoln, and the air-conditioning muffled exterior noise.

We were facing the gate in next to no time. The doctor cursed modern technology, and a blast of hot air hit me before the gate was swung open and the doctor had driven us inside. Safe! "Safe behind high gates and dogs?"

The sneering whisper made me squirm in Rafe's arms. He tightened his grip, and I relaxed. I *was* safe behind high gates and dogs. I was!

There was a minimum of protest from Garry after her initial outburst, but her face was very angry as she and Rafe bundled me into bed. Then the doctor was swabbing my arm, and I tried to protest. Because suddenly I didn't want to be asleep, unconscious, absolutely vulnerable behind high gates and with dogs!

"I'm not leaving this room," Rafe said, holding my free hand.

I started to shake my head, but it hurt. I tried releasing his grip. He mustn't feel he was tied to me. I *was* safe. I'd make myself believe I was safe, but whatever existed between us would sour if Rafe felt tied to me.

More coherent thought, not that I was thinking straight then, was impossible, for whatever the doctor had pumped into my arm worked with speed.

I woke, my throat parched, my tongue swollen, my neck a band of sore fire. There was a weight across my chest, and another at my feet. I cried out, or rather, a strangled sound left me. There was a grunt in my ear and a prrroww at my feet.

"What's wrong, Nialla?"

The weight across my chest moved, and Rafe propped himself up on his elbow, smoothing hair from my face.

"Thirsty." How he could understand that croak, I don't know. Perhaps it was only logical I'd be thirsty. At any rate, a sliver of ice was popped into my mouth.

"It'll hurt to swallow, love; let the ice melt in your mouth and trickle down your throat." He gently adjusted the pillow under my head so I was higher.

The lump across my feet stirred, and Dice's eyes glowed as he queried me again.

"Damned cat sat and pounded on the living-room window—with his nose, no less—until Garry heard and let him in. How in hell did he know?" Rafe's low voice was rippling with laughter. Another ice sliver was poked through my lips. The first had gone too fast to do any good, but the cold and the wet of the second began to relieve the awful desert of my mouth. Then a cold moist cloth was laid gently on my neck. I exclaimed at the contact, but held it there when Rafe tried to remove it. It felt good after the initial shock.

My eyes were used to the dark now, and I could see Rafe shaking his head, his lips in a grim line.

"Don't try to talk, Nialla. See, Dice? She's all right," he told the cat, who walked up to check anyhow, his cold nose touching my ear. He sniffed at my eyebrow (I never have figured out why my brows fascinate Dice), gave it a lick with his rough tongue, and sat down at my shoulder, purring like some mad motor. I tickled him under the chin, and the purr went up three decibels.

"You approve, sir?" Rafe asked, and snorted when Dice miaowed, a raucous noise in the quiet of the room. "Damned cat all but speaks English."

I opened my mouth, but Rafe popped more ice in before I could get throat to work on making a sound.

"I told you, no talking, Nialla, that's an order." He gave the tip of my nose an admonitory push. "However, I can appreciate your thirst for information. No, we have not caught the assailant. Yes, you'll be all right in a day or two. Nothing in your throat broken, though I don't imagine you believe me." Then he chuckled, only it wasn't his usual amused chuckle; it was a nasty one. "You'll be interested to hear that Bob Erskine is furious that you could be attacked while he was still on the premises, so to speak. He had half a dozen men there in record time, searching the woods for the intruder. They didn't find anyone, of course." Rafe's voice conveyed contempt and anger. "Goddamnit." And he gave the mattress a closed-fist pound. "*I'm* right there, and you nearly get killed."

I shook him by the shoulder, and when he turned to me, pulled his head so I could whisper in his ear.

"Blackmailer. Wanted to scare me. Wants to be paid! I'm safe here, behind the fence, with the dogs."

I had to repeat some of it twice, but when Rafe did understand, he was madder than ever.

"Pay? *He'll* pay! He'll pay for every moment he's made

you miserable. Just wait till I get my hands on him! We'll see who pays! It was Caps Galvano, wasn't it?"

"Who else could it be?" I whispered. "His breath was horrible!"

I wanted to laugh at Rafe's rejoinder, but I couldn't. Dice was rubbing his head into my cheek sympathetically, and then, prrrowwing earnestly, jumped down and made his way to the door, where he stopped and prrrowwed more quizzically.

"And you expect me to get up and let you out?" Rafe asked. "You've got one helluva lot of gall, cat."

Dice agreed affably, making an umbrella hook of his tail as he waited for action. His prrroww turned more acid, and his tail switched impatiently when Rafe refused to move.

"He wants to get back to Orfeo," I whispered, pushing at Rafe.

"I am *not* a cat butler," Rafe cried, even as his feet hit the floor. Dice bounced away, ahead of him, down the stairs. I heard the door slam as Rafe emphasized his disgruntlement with the exercise. His heels pounded on the bare floor as he stalked back to bed. But he was chuckling as he resettled himself beside me.

"Wish that damned cat did speak English. His conversation is more to the point than most people's. More ice, Nialla?"

I shook my head, and then he pulled me into the curve of his shoulder.

"Get some more sleep, dear heart; it's only two." A huge yawn interrupted him. "God, you're getting old, Clery," he told himself.

I tapped his chest to indicate disagreement, and felt the chuckle deep in his chest as he turned to look at me.

"I'm not getting old?" He kissed my fingers. "Not with you in my bed, at any rate." He shifted his body slightly and closed his eyes.

It wasn't very long, it seemed to me, before he was asleep, for the arm around me got heavy as the muscles relaxed completely, and his breathing was slow and shallow.

## 9

I WAS MANAGING to swallow soft scrambled egg at brunch (we got up at a scandalous ten o'clock) when Dennis phoned on the intercom to say that a Mr. Michaels was at the gate, and could he come in?

Jim Michaels did have another suit — or rather a second pair of pants and a seersucker jacket. He got far enough inside the house to feel the air conditioning, and sighed with relief. Then he exhibited real dismay at interrupting our meal.

"It *is* Sunday," Rafe said, ushering him to a chair and urging him to try the cornbread with his coffee.

He accepted with a grin, which faded when he saw my throat.

"I'm a walking fingerprint gallery," I said in the un-projected tone that put no strain on my throat.

He nodded, but his expression was a little fierce.

"Can you identify the assailant?"

"It has to be Caps Galvano."

His eyelids dropped briefly, and he sighed again. "Which means, Mrs. Clery, that you didn't see his face?"

"Who else could it be?" Rafe asked caustically.

Michaels shrugged. "A would-be rapist, a purse-snatcher, take your choice."

"It *was* him," I said. "He said if I thought I was safe behind a high fence with dogs, I was wrong. He said I'd never be safe unless I paid him. His breath was concentrated garlic."

"It was Galvano, Michaels, because Galvano is the only one who knows what the blackmailer told Nialla." Rafe was becoming impatient with the detective's caution. "For Christ's sake, Michaels, does she have to be murdered before the cops take action?"

Michaels looked uncomfortable and smoothed back his already well-groomed hair.

"You ought to know the handicaps under which police operate these days, Mr. Clery. However, Galvano has been positively identified by half a dozen people. He was definitely at the Sunbury fairgrounds. He also forgot to wipe all his fingerprints off the station wagon when he tried to frighten Mrs. Clery's gelding. It's a blurred print, but it's his."

"Then you believe me."

"I always have believed you, Mrs. Clery," Michaels replied in a rather grim voice, "but belief is not admissible evidence. And it doesn't help me find the guy. He's at an advantage there. You're stationary, he's not. We've got to catch him, and we've either got to have proof positive — like fingerprints on the blunt instrument used on Pete Sankey — or Galvano's confession."

"Speaking of being stationary, Lieutenant, Louis Marchmount has been on the run, with a bodyguard. A Stephen Urscoll admitted to us that Louis Marchmount has been paying extortion. To Caps Galvano."

Michaels nodded. "Some eighty thousand dollars, to be precise. I keep busy."

Rafe whistled in surprise at the sum involved, and then almost pounced. "Then why in hell is Galvano threatening Nialla? With eighty thousand dollars, he ought to have skipped to one of the Latin-American countries by now! Particularly when he has very carefully arranged his own death to get the grass ring off his back."

"I admit that baffles us, too, Mr. Clery. Eighty thou for a man like Galvano is good bread. Enough to buy a fake passport for a dead man. He certainly can't afford to spend freely, because that would attract notice. And he can't afford to do that."

"He does attract attention," I whispered. "He stinks as if he hadn't changed clothes in weeks, and his breath is vile."

"That's not a criminal offense, Mrs. Clery," Michaels said with a glint in his eyes. "Were you aware, Mrs. Clery, that Mr. Marchmount was visiting near Sunbury?"

I shook my head too hard; it hurt my neck.

"We saw him first Monday night, at a distance, in the Charcoal Grill at Sunbury," Rafe said, "but that was the first we knew he was there."

"So it is conceivable that Galvano had been tracking

Marchmount and then saw Mrs. Clery . . ." Michaels paused, rubbing his lower lip thoughtfully. "However, this is where motive falters. Mrs. Clery was not Mrs. Clery then, I understand, and candidly in no position to pay any extortion . . ."

"If he'd take peanut butter," Rafe said with such a bland face I wanted to smack him.

Michaels gave a fleeting grin. "I suppose we have to assume that Galvano indulged in malicious mischief while waiting to nail Marchmount, then."

"Whatever the reason, Michaels" — and all humor vanished from Rafe's face — "we've had enough of this kind of trick or treat. Marchmount has, too. Will you kindly arrest that bastard before there's a third death? Marchmount's or . . . Galvano's."

"There is a third death, Mr. Clery. Whoever was in that car in California. But as I said, we have to find him first, Mr. Clery," Michaels said wearily. "If he hadn't broken with all previous associations, that wouldn't be so difficult."

"Apply to the nearest racetrack and ask?"

"Quite. But unless we can force him into the open . . ." Michaels raised his hands, palms up, expressively.

"He'll have to, to collect," Rafe said. "He's got two possible sources of income — Louis Marchmount and Nialla. True, we've told him to shove it, and so, in effect, has Louis Marchmount. But Lou collapsed last night" — Michaels nodded, as if this were not new to him — "You know? Good. So that rules him out as a source of revenue for the greedy Galvano. And leaves us — Nialla."

"As you said, Rafe, I've had about enough of trick or treat." My voice came out in squeaks, and my incautious vocalizing hurt. I put my hands to my throat, a little scared and more than a little angry at the trend of their talk.

"Understandably, Mrs. Clery, but this time we can control the action."

"Nialla, honey, he may come near you, but he won't ever touch you again!"

I looked from one man to the other, not knowing which I despised more, and in that silence we all heard a car braking to a tire-stripping halt. A shrill voice was raised in vituperation, and then two people came clattering up the stairs. The door was flung open, and there stood Wendy Madison, her eyes round with anger, her face suffused with blood, and every inch of her thin body involved with her fury. Dennis, his face white and scared, stood behind her.

"Tell this . . . this . . . effing bastard that he's fired," she demanded. "Tell him right now, Ralph Clery!" She whirled and slapped Dennis across the mouth. It wasn't the first time: I now saw other marks on the boy's face. "There, you effing bastard. You'll never disobey an order from me again."

"That's enough, Madam, and Dennis is not fired. He was acting under my orders. No one was to pass that gate without checking here."

Wendy Madison stalked into the room, trembling with fury, straight up to Rafe, as if she meant to slap his face, too. Then she saw me, and before I knew what she meant, she'd swooped down, waving something wildly above her head, and slapped me with stunning force across my face.

"You bitch, you little gutter whore! I'll have you—Oww!"

Her hand was sweeping back to strike me again when Rafe caught it and twisted it behind her back so swiftly that she let go what she was clutching, and glossy photographs rained on the floor.

"Madam, I'll break your arm, mother or not, if you don't control yourself." He had her pinned in a chair. She writhed and tried to hit at him, until he gave her arm another little wrench. With a cry she bit her lip and sat, her back arching to ease the strain on her arm. "No one speaks to my wife that way. No one. Especially you."

"Just wait, Ralph Clery. Just wait until you've seen those photos. Then we'll see how we speak to your *wife*."

Rafe didn't ease his hold on her an inch, but he craned his neck to look at the photo nearest him. I knew what they must be! I think I knew the moment I saw her waving them as she entered. I wanted to die!

"Oh, for Christ's sake," Rafe said with utter disgust and annoyance, letting his mother go. "And you fell for them?"

Wendy Madison's jaw dropped. His reaction took away all her impetus.

"Fell for them?" A glance at me stoked her anger again. "I'm supposed to pay twenty thousand dollars to keep them from being circulated. *I'm* supposed to pay because you . . . you horny dwarf . . . married some cheap . . ."

Rafe's hand curled on her shoulder so fiercely that she cried out and shot him a glance full of fear and surprise.

"Madam, if you ever even *think* of my wife in those terms . . ."

"Ralph, you're hurting me." And tears began to fall from her brimming eyes. She was very sincere. Then her attitude changed to misunderstood and abused innocence. "You're brutal and unfeeling. *I'm* being blackmailed! Forced to protect the family name, all on account of your . . . latest wife." She didn't need to use foul language when she could inject such venom into a simple noun.

Out of the corner of my eye I saw Michaels shift, and Rafe gestured him curtly to be quiet.

"Exactly what happened?" Rafe demanded in a cold, hard voice.

"These . . ." She gestured to the strewn photos. I couldn't even look to see how many had fallen face up. ". . . came special delivery . . . through the mails" — and that obviously doubled the outrage — "with a note. If I didn't wish to have them circulated, I must be prepared to pay twenty thousand dollars."

"Where's the note?"

Wendy Madison's eyes flashed. "That won't tell you anything. Block printing on cheap pad paper." Then her face crumbled again. "Ralph, I can't have my name linked with your . . . wife's . . . in this sordid manner. I'd be ruined socially. Give me the twenty thousand dollars" — her eyes blazed as anger overcame fear of disgrace — "because I most certainly am not going . . ."

"Madam . . ."

She winced as his fingers dug into her shoulder again.

"Really, Ralph" — and I winced to hear the whine in her cultivated voice — "she's your wife. You married her. I didn't. I didn't even know about it, and then, when I try to put a good face on it, give a reception for her, introduce her to my closest friends . . ." She dabbed at her eyes again, emulating distressed virtue.

"If you really need a scapegoat, Madam," Rafe said, and scooping up the photos, shoved them under her nose again, "look at the man involved. Because I can assure you, Nialla is blameless."

I wanted to die. We should have paid the man yesterday. How could Rafe do this to me?

But when I heard Wendy Madison's gasp of stunned and incredulous horror, heard her moan and knew that there was nothing feigned in that piteous cry, I was almost glad.

"Oh, no," she cried, half-doubled in anguish. "Oh, no, it couldn't be. It just couldn't be. Oh, no, Lou wouldn't." Suddenly she straightened, her face wiped clear of expression. She pulled her shoulders back and lifted her chin. "They're fakes," she said with the absolute certainty and fantastic dignity of one who has perceived a truth. "Obviously retouched fakes." She rose, in regal dismissal. "Burn them."

"Hold it," Rafe said, standing in her way. "You're not going anywhere yet. First you will make Nialla profound apology for your insults."

I couldn't see her face, but even the muscles in her slender legs tensed. Rafe just kept looking at her. If he ever looked at me that way . . . She turned slowly, like an automaton not wound tightly enough, and her face was a strained caricature of the courtesy she was forced to perform. "I apologize for my hasty words."

I nodded my head once, twice, my slapped cheek stinging as if her reluctant words physically impacted on me.

She turned again, desperate to leave, but now Rafe took her by the arm and escorted her, willy-nilly, back to the chair.

"Now, Lieutenant Michaels, here's your opportunity to catch a murdering blackmailer."

"Lieutenant Michaels?" Her voice was no more than a whisper, as pained a whisper as I'd been forced to use. This second shock sent color flaming to the roots of her blonde hair. One hand on her throat, the other clutching the chair arm, she slowly turned her head toward Jim Michaels.

"Your precipitate arrival, Madam, prevented me from

making an introduction. May I now present Lieutenant Detective James Michaels of the Sunbury Police."

"Police. Oh, my God, Ralph, the police mustn't know."

Michaels inclined his head in silent apology for the fact that he already did know.

"Extortion threats are best handled with police assistance, ma'am," he said in a quiet voice. The woman looked absolutely shattered.

"The police! Oh, my God."

Rafe strode to the bar cabinet and poured a stiff drink, which he gave her. She knocked it back in a dazed fashion and then seemed to get a second grip on herself.

"Mrs. Madison, if you will cooperate with us, we will see that . . ."

"But he's threatened to send the negatives to the newspapers and *Vogue* and *Harper's Bazaar* . . ." And she began to rock back and forth in the chair.

"Mrs. Madison," James Michaels went on, still in that quiet calm voice, "those negatives would never be printed even if they did reach a publisher's office. The newspapers and magazines are very cooperative in these instances, believe me. What is more important is to apprehend this man before he victimizes anyone else. Before he does more harm." Michaels gestured toward me, and for the first time, I think, Wendy Madison saw the marks on my throat, and her eyes widened.

"He attacked her?"

"Yes, Madam. He tried to kill Nialla at Charlie's place yesterday."

Her hands went out to Rafe appealingly. "I need protection," she said in a breathless whimper. "Ralph. I'm totally unprotected up there. There's only John and Pres. You've got to let me stay here. You've got the fence, the dogs."

Rafe took her hands down. His face . . . his face showed the most awful lack of expression. "You'll have ample police protection." He moved back, away from her outstretched hand.

Michaels quickly started to assure her that she would be guarded night and day, but she didn't seem to hear him, still begging Rafe silently for sanctuary in this house.

"I'm afraid you'll have to stay in your own home, Mrs.

Madison," Michaels told her. He could afford to be kinder. He wasn't related to her. "The extortionist will be calling you now that his little . . . bombshell has been delivered. You'll have to stay home. We'll arrange for a wire tap to trace the call, have men guarding you night and day . . ." He noticed the rise of her eyebrow as his words and meaning penetrated her fear. " . . . and a policewoman in your room. There won't be any chance of your being—ah-hem—having any personal dealings with him."

"A burglar-alarm system was installed in the house some time ago, Lieutenant," Rafe said, disregarding any attempt of his mother to get his attention. "There's also a trained private investigator."

"This Urscoll fellow?"

"Ralph, how could you?" Her protest was a shocked wail.

"You can dispense with the pose of outrage, Madam. Two . . . three . . . men have already been murdered, my wife has been physically attacked, and Lou Marchmount driven to the edge of insanity. If . . ."

"Lou? You mean, that man has already approached Lou?"

Rafe stared at her with incredulity. "Why did you think Marchmount hired Urscoll?"

"Why, to keep his second wife—that awful Lorette person—from besieging him with her hypochrondriacal demands."

"And you believed him?"

"Of course, I'd believe Louis Marchmount. Why should I ever doubt his word?"

"You were quick enough to doubt my wife's honor," Rafe replied harshly. For the first time fury broke through the icy coldness with which he had been treating her. "And quick enough to call those pictures 'fakes' when you thought Lou was involved. For God's sake, Madam, don't be so naïve. You know Marchmount's reputation . . ."

"You mean, those pictures were real?"

"No, ma'am, they're not," Michaels said rather forceful-ly. "Good fakes, yes, but fakes they are. Our lab can blow them up and show where the heads were stripped in. Clever, but the joins are there."

"As I said earlier, Wendy" — and Rafe made her name into a cold, hard epithet — "Nialla is not to blame for the insidious position in which you now find yourself."

"Then all his talk about ruin and persecution wasn't . . ." Wendy Madison shut her mouth with sudden discretion. She rose again. "I want to get out of this ridiculous position. How do I cooperate with you, Lieutenant? Ralph, you will have the courtesy to call your brother Michael instantly and tell him to come at once. Lieutenant, I want these photos destroyed. I don't want everyone gawking . . ."

"I can't destroy evidence, Mrs. Madison, but I assure you that all discretion will be used to protect Mrs. Clery,"

"Mrs. Clery?" She was stunned, and looked around at me as if I'd no right to be discussed at all.

"And Mr. Marchmount," the lieutenant added diplomatically. But as he escorted her to the door, his attitude toward her had changed. Rafe was gathering up the photos quickly.

Dennis, I realized, had disappeared some time ago. I wondered in a sick fashion if he'd had a good look at those poses when she'd been brandishing them about. But Michaels had said they were obvious fakes. How had he known? How obvious? Had he just said that? I wished — no, I didn't wish. No! I didn't ever want to see them.

"Nialla," Rafe's voice recalled me from the grotesque push-pull. "I won't be long."

I numbly gestured acceptance, but the moment he was out the door, I wanted to cry out to him to come back. He was leaving me alone.

"Get a grip on yourself, Nialla," I whispered out loud. Garry's in the house. I could hear her quick steps, and then she started down the stairs, moving more slowly then, as heavy people do. When I saw her face, her brows puckered in an angry frown, I realized that she'd heard everything, and I looked away, anywhere but at her.

"I can't pretend I'm deaf and didn't hear a thing, Miss Nialla." Her voice reached me because I couldn't unhear.

"Madam's gone too far this time. Storming in here like it was all your fault and speaking to you in such a way. It was all I could do to keep quiet. Anyone'd think you'd arranged the whole thing to put shame on her. Now, you just sit quiet till Mr. Rafe gets back. Imagine, someone with spit enough to try blackmailing the Madam. No wonder that poor Mr. Marchmount took to drugs with that hanging over his head. Well, Madam won't see his heels fast enough, I reckon. Good thing, too. I only hope Dennis didn't stay?" I shook my head. "There, there, you poor child. Why, you look dreadful. You're as white as a sheet. A cup of tea? No, maybe you need some of that brandy!"

I shook my head, pointing to my neck.

"Yes, of course. I was forgetting. I'll just make you something nice and cool. That'll make you feel better, and you can forget this whole terrible thing." With that she marched out of the room.

Just as if a drink or a cup of tea would, could, put everything to rights. I leaned my head back against the couch, feeling drawn and quartered and strengthless. Would to God Mrs. Garrison had some magical potion. I wished I'd been consumed in that barn fire. I wished I had been strangled the day before. I wished I'd never let Rafe talk me into going to dinner that first night. But I'd been so tired of peanut butter . . . If only I'd refused—even that second time—and just packed up and left the grounds, prize money forfeited and everything. Pete Sankey wouldn't be dead . . .

"If you're feeling sorry for yourself . . ."

I gave a convulsive leap, crying out in surprise before I realized it was Rafe. One look at the awful expression on his face, and self-pity was the furthest thing from my mind. He looked a hundred and two, every line in his well-used face graven deeply. His eyes lacked even a touch of blue.

"Anyone'd think you'd arranged the whole thing to put shame on her." Mrs. Garrison had pointed to the wrong woman.

"Actually, I was thinking that a peanut-butter-and-jelly sandwich would taste damned good about now," I said, taking a deep breath. "And trying to figure out how Lieutenant Michaels could sound so sure that those pictures were fakes."

Rafe blinked suddenly, a slight frown creasing his brows still more, but the color came back into his eyes and his jaw relaxed. I'd managed to surprise him, too.

"For one thing," he said, coming across the room, "the girl so lewdly portrayed was very gaudy. Not at all neat." There was even the faintest suspicion of a smile at his mouth. "Which the lieutenant wouldn't necessarily guess. But you are five-foot-four, my dear heart, and that girl was an Amazon."

I was suddenly consumed with fury. "Then how could anyone . . ."

Rafe roared with laughter at my reaction. "Shock value. If Wendy Madison had thought twice, she'd have realized it, too. All she saw were the faces and the postures." He turned serious again and gathered me into his arms, his eyes blue and oddly sad. "You've been at the more serious disadvantage, my dear, because you knew Lou Marchmount had raped you and there was just the possibility that there had been a photograph taken."

"Oh, Rafe, if I should ever have to testify . . ."

He pulled my cheek against his and held me tightly, reassuringly.

"*If* that should ever happen, you simply do not tell the whole truth. Lou Marchmount is in no condition to contradict you. And I sure as hell will gladly perjure myself on the score of your virtue."

He held me away, framing my face with his hands, looking deep into my eyes.

"Because, dear heart, you are." He gave me another long searching look and then lightly kissed my cheek — the one his mother had struck.

I wanted to say something, I knew I was supposed to say something, and it wasn't connected with his mother, but I didn't know what it was he expected of me. Then all of a sudden Mrs. Garrison came bustling in from the kitchen, and the moment was shattered.

"Don't you ever ask for peanut butter and jelly here,

Nialla, or we'll lose the best cook in Nassau County," Rafe said in a hurried undertone.

Mrs. Garrison's notion of therapeutic food turned out to be raspberry sherbet, which went down easily, coolingly, and I could actually taste it.

Rafe filled a mug of coffee for himself and settled down to the Sunday papers with an air that clearly said, "At last!"

There appeared to be two copies of *The New York Times*, one each of lesser Sunday editions. For kicks I turned to the society pages. And there we were. Only it was just Rafe and me. I appeared to be hanging on his arm, the very model of the blushing bride, while Rafe was beaming directly into the camera with fatuous pride. He *hadn't* been, but that's the way the shot came out. There was only a caption with our names, listing Rafael Clery as noted sportsman and horse breeder. We weren't the only bridal couple who'd been feted, I noticed, glancing at the long columns headed by studio portraits of faces fresh or stern under misty veils. The datelines were all the "right" ones from East Hampton, south to Roanoke, north to Boston, with a few San Franciscos, Washingtons, and New Yorks to leaven the rise.

The group picture appeared in several of the Long Island papers: somehow the counterfeit grins looked genuine, and the general impression was of society enjoying its "in" tribal customs and rites, graciously consenting to make their festivities known to the lesser breeds.

The Long Island papers ran some background material on Rafe. (They bloody well had nothing to say about me, except to mention that my father was the late Russell Donnelly, noted trainer. Bess Tomlinson [Mrs. Augustus] was given as matron of honor, also the fact that I had used her family veil. A Gerald MacCrate, sportsman, had been the groom's best man. The ceremony had been private.) Rafe graduated from the University of Virginia? With honors, no less. And he'd been a *captain* in Korea? I hadn't known that either. Nor that he'd earned a DSC with a cluster.

Rafe evidently believed in reading every word of the news fit to print. He made a lot of noise, too, turning pages, but whenever I glanced around mine, it was an absentminded, not attention-getting-irritated rustling. At one point he got up, took some black bound books from the breakfront desk, and busied himself making notations.

This placid sabbatical scene was interrupted by the phone. I'd been so absorbed in an article on the emergence of pop art and its primary perpetrators that the sound lifted me up out of the sofa like an elevator.

"Hey, your nerves are shot," he said solicitously as he rose to answer it. "Sure, Dennis. You can let Michaels in anytime."

The detective refused coffee, even iced, when he arrived, but a few minutes in the air-conditioned house seemed to revive him. I was glad I didn't have to go outside today.

"I've got surveillance for your mother, Mr. Clery, and the phone tap is set up, so you don't have to worry about her."

"Thanks." Michaels grinned slightly at Rafe's caustic comment.

"I checked in at Nassau County Hospital, but Louis Marchmount is in no condition to be questioned. I've also arranged for a relief man for that private investigator, because" — and here Michaels exhaled deeply — "I'm not the only person who'd like to speak to Marchmount. Someone tried to get in to see him on Saturday morning. In fact, he was so adamant that the hospital guard had to assist him off the premises." Michaels grinned at me. "Both the guard and the nurses' aide at the desk remembered that he had a very bad case of halitosis."

"There!"

"More important. They identified the mug shot of Galvano."

"Saturday morning?" Rafe asked.

"Yes" — and Michaels was grim again — "with plenty of time for him to get to the show and attack Mrs. Clery. How he knew where to find you is not clear."

"The Austin-Healey is distinctive," Rafe remarked. "There're plenty of places on the main road for him to watch for it if that was his game."

"I had a talk with Urscoll."

"And?" Rafe urged politely, because something was troubling Michaels.

"Well, he confirmed what you told me. Said it's only a matter of time before Marchmount is carried off by a heart attack. The excitement of apprehending the extortionist might be the fatal stroke, which is the only reason why Urscoll's company went along with Marchmount's demand. Urscoll said he was awfully worried, because the man's memory is failing. He said he did all he could to prevent Marchmount from becoming excited and getting hold of any drugs. But . . ." Michaels shrugged.

"What I don't understand," Rafe said, "is how, if Urscoll was so eager to guard Marchmount, Galvano could have picked him for eighty thousand dollars?"

"One man can't guard another every minute of the day," Michael said, rising. "I've got to get back."

"Don't envy you the trip in this heat."

"Oh, it's not so bad." Michaels grinned smugly. "I borrowed one of the traffic helicopters. That's why I have to get back before the millions swarm back into the city."

"So, how do things stand?"

"We . . . you . . . wait, I'm afraid."

"With Erskine handling the local protection?"

Michaels nodded, an odd gleam in his eyes. "He seems very keen on helping."

"Yes, the good, jovial, up-for-reelection Sheriff Erskine would."

"I really have to work through the local authorities at this juncture, Mr. Clery."

Rafe gestured, absolving Michaels. "Standing guard is one thing Erskine's men ought to do well. They even went to college on it."

Michaels stared at Rafe a moment and then guffawed heartily.

"We've only to wait until the blackmailer gets in touch with Mrs. Madison now. And if he's as desperate as he acts, that oughtn't to be too long," he said as he reached the door.

I wished I could feel as confident as Michaels sounded. But I did trust him.

The hot air was like a furnace blast as the door closed. Helicopter or not, I didn't envy the weary detective his trip.

Rafe snatched up his paper and settled in the couch, beside me, our thighs touching lightly, our shoulders brushing now and then as Rafe turned the pages of his newspaper. The light contact had the effect of . . . of what? Not possession, really. More. "I'm here because I want to be."

I sneaked a sideways glance at my husband's profile. He was too absorbed in his article to be aware of my scrutiny. I hadn't had too much opportunity to really look at him, what with his habit of being attached to me all the time. He wasn't handsome, certainly; he didn't have to be, with those compelling blue eyes. There was character in the straight sweep of his jaw, the firm chin, the well-shaped wide lips, the aquiline nose, the slight bulge of the brow; he'd be even handsomer in a few years. I was close enough to notice the fine lines under and at the corner of his eye, the few bristles his razor had missed that morning, and the fact that his sideburns needed trimming. Would he let me do it?

This Sunday's quiet, read-the-paper routine was so "married" to me — something I remembered from childhood as part of a Sunday's inevitable order. Mother reading the papers beside Dad on the sofa, with the Sunday symphony rolling through an otherwise silent scene.

Suddenly Rafe swore under his breath and reached for the account books he'd abandoned when Michaels came in. He did some rough figuring on the margin of the newspaper, and swore again. The numerals, written in a bold hand, were plain to read: $7,578.98. He swore again and closed the open book with a slap, tossing it negligently to the footstool.

Fragments of conversations on loss and margin, shares depreciating, came back to me, coordinated with Rafe's continuous interest in news items and stock-market pages. And I correlated a few other facts — like this comfortable house, Mrs. Garrison, three men in the stables, new horse trailers, and such. $7,578.98 was a lot of money.

"Did you lose that much on stocks in this recession?"

Rafe regarded me with mild surprise.

"Oh, the seven thousand? That's that electronic company Paddy Skerrit's touting. There's a piece here about a copyright-infringement action they've launched against a rival company that got the government contract they were hoping for. The stock's down now, and it may drop further."

"Can you afford to lose that much money?"

"Dear heart, I haven't 'lost' it yet. The company's sound. I've generally had good luck in the electronics field. Bought into Xerox when it first went public"—and there was twinkle in his eyes—"despite what I was told. Why?" He looked at me squarely, a sort of waiting look.

"Well, it's just that . . . well, there's that insurance money, and the rest of the funds, if you were at all worried . . ."

"God bless you, Nialla darling," and he gathered me into his arms, pressing his face into my hair, even then remembering to be careful of my neck.

I've heard of "heart swelling," and mine certainly did then.

"Dear heart, you simply haven't got a clue, have you?" Something amused him; laughter rippled in his voice as he rocked me back and forth in his arms.

"A clue about what?" I didn't want him laughing right then. I wanted him as serious as I felt.

He held me a little from him so he could look down into my eyes. His were dancing with devilment.

"Maybe it's just as well you don't know."

"Know what? I guess ten thousand dollars doesn't seem like a lot to you . . ."

He realized what he'd done and hugged me tightly again. "It is a lot of money, Nialla, but I really don't need it. That's a paper loss and doesn't particularly affect my income."

"Income?"

"God love us, it is an innocent." He sighed and explained succinctly that, due to the perspicacity and ruthlessness of several ancestors, he had a large private income which, due to some equally perspicacious investing of his own, he had increased. "Money tends to beget money, Nialla, and I'm in the bracket where an occasional loss saves me taxes." He looked deep into my eyes again, the slight upturning smile of his lips engagingly boyish. "I do really appreciate your offer, dear heart, but I'd rather *you*" — and he kissed me lightly — "had money of your own."

"You're rich, then, aren't you?" (Gawd, that sounded like an accusation, didn't it?) "In spite of what you said about the acres being mortgaged?"

He frowned in surprise. "When did I say that?"

"Wednesday. Or did you mean" — I broke off and then realized I'd better continue — "a moral mortgage?"

"A moral mortgage?" He seemed startled. "Because Wendy Madison lives in the house next door? Yes." And a shadow of the awful expression I so hated crossed his face. "She has the right to live in that place until her death, but the property is mine. Grandfather Herrington stipulated it was to go to the first male issue of his three daughters." He looked beyond me to that desperate distance in his life which had been so bleak and miserable, and brutally lonely. "I wasn't exactly what Grandfather or Mother had in mind as Lord of the Mansion, so she's welcome to it."

"It isn't a mortgage she holds over you, Rafe, it's blackmail. Did you ever think of it in those terms?"

He looked at me suddenly, his hands sliding around me.

"Not until this morning, dear heart. I guess that's what albatrosses are — blackmail by conscience."

Then he began kissing me, starting out with a sort of an apologetic pressure of lips on mine. But the gentleness quickly gave way to a mutual inflammation.

"Nialla?" His soft query was right in my ear as his hands began to caress my body urgently. I'd got mine under his shirt, caressing the warm smooth hide of him. He felt so good. But when I tried to disentangle us so we could go upstairs, he held me tightly. "We can't be seen. The couch is high-backed." He chuckled as he unbuttoned my shirt and released my breasts from the bra.

"Mrs. Garrison?"

"Gone! I wanted you to myself for the rest of the day. Got any more objections?" He said it half-teasing, half-irritated. Was I being coy?

I pulled him to me, slipping my hands inside his pants, inside the cotton briefs, all the time straining my breast against the exciting rough texture of his shirt. He turned rough suddenly, rousing me so deftly that my need of him was not a whit less than his. Rafe was unbuckling his belt when the sound of banging on the front door penetrated our absorption.

The language Rafe used as he hastily buckled his belt and yanked his shirt down appalled me, but I felt exactly the same way.

"I'll get rid of whoever it is," Rafe vowed as he pounded across the floor. Had he kept his shoes on all that time on the couch?

I made an effort to cover myself, just in case. And I glanced at the back of the couch to be sure I wasn't visible, but I couldn't even see the front door, so I relaxed, praying that the caller could be summarily dismissed and we could take up where we'd been so rudely interrupted.

"Dennis, if . . ."

"Mr. Clery, the west meadow's on fire!"

"Christ!" Rafe's single explosive curse was followed by an incoherent stream of invective.

"Jerry's called the fire department and gone on ahead with Albert."

"Where in hell were the dogs?" Rafe demanded, as he seemed to be wrecking a piece of furniture.

"They were loose, Mr. Clery, but in this heat, it could be spontaneous."

"Spontaneous, my . . ." I heard the unmistakable sound of a revolver chamber turning fast. "Okay, okay. Jerry bring shovels?"

"And brooms and wet blankets."

"Good. Nialla, just in case, don't you dare leave this house. I don't know how he could have got in, but don't you leave this house. Check all the doors and the windows. I'll throw the night latch on this. You go up to our room, stay by the phone. No one can get up those stairs without them creaking. First creak that doesn't call you in my voice, you pick up that phone and dial 999."

He was out of the house and then shaking the door handle. It was well and truly locked.

I was trembling, but not from lust anymore. I got my

clothing reassembled, suddenly cold in the air-conditioned atmosphere. I checked the front door myself, and every window on the first floor, the back and side doors, and shoved chairs under the handles as an added precaution. I'd heard that worked.

Then I went upstairs and did those windows, peering out and not seeing much because of the trees that surrounded the house. There were black clouds far off to the west. It could rain.

By the time I got back to our room, I was exceedingly unhappy about this new development. I wished I'd gone with Rafe. Anything was preferable to sitting here, waiting, like a tied kid. The west meadow afire? The grass was dry and sere. But . . .

I touched my bruised throat. Galvano was not supposed to be after me now. He was supposed to be phoning Wendy Madison and extorting from her for a change. And all the guards were up at the big house, protecting her.

I dialed 999 and asked for the police station.

"This is Mrs. Rafael Clery." (Gawd, I sounded like the cat's pajamas with that erratic break in my voice.) "Our west meadow is on fire." (That sounded even worse.)

"Then call the fire department, lady."

"I did, but the fire could have been deliberately set, and I'm alone in the house. You see, I was assaulted yesterday at . . . at . . ." (I couldn't very well say Charlie's place, could I?)

"Who is this?"

"This is Mrs. Rafael Clery, Nialla."

"Good God, lady, why didn't you say so in the first place?"

The connection went dead. I *had* told him who I was.

"Mrs. Clery . . ." Sheriff Erskine's unmistakable baritone leaped out of the earpiece and forced me to hold the phone a few inches from my deadened ear. "What's this about a fire at *your* place?"

"The west meadow's on fire. My husband and the men are there. But I thought you should know . . . ."

"But . . . but we've got the Herrington place staked out." He sounded aggrieved.

"I realize that, Sheriff, but, well, is it possible for you to investigate here?"

"Are you alone in the house?" He was furious now.

"Yes, but the place is tightly locked up. I checked all the doors and windows myself."

"Then you stay there. Forest, I want . . ." And the connection was broken.

Your kindly police force is mobilizing. Relax. Help is on the way!

Relax?

I sighed and thrust the ends of my shirt into my shorts. Damn it!

"This is Mrs. Rafael Clery."

That had a very satisfactory sound to it.

It wasn't a creaking I heard; it was a tapping. I froze so solid I could hear the pulse of the air conditioner turning on in the basement. Did this house have a basement door? One I hadn't locked?

I crept to the staircase. Nothing! I went down a few steps, still hearing that tap-tapping, rhythmic, insistent, demanding. I got down far enough to see the front door and the porch. There wasn't anyone there. I went to the kitchen, but halfway across it I couldn't hear the tapping.

It was louder in the hallway, and louder still as I crept back up the stairs, over the creak.

As I came level with the second story, I saw Dice at the dormer window of our room, tapping the pane with his nose.

I rushed to throw open the sash. "Dice, you scared me to death!" One overhanging beech limb swayed up and down. He'd taken the upper route. He wouldn't come in. He weaved in and out, more garrulous that I'd ever heard him. I peered as far as I could over the roof, but the ground below was invisible. The air was suffocatingly sultry. "Rafe send you to keep watch? Come on in, boy. Come in."

He ran a few steps down the roof, prrrowwing agitatedly. He must have smelled the meadow fire. I glanced up now, but this room faced east, and the meadow fire was to the west . . . Then why was I seeing a thin plume of smoke! A thin plume? From a meadow fire?

I wondered later that I hadn't tripped over Dice as we took those stairs in a mad plunge down. Dice's excited prancing didn't help as I fumbled with the double latch, double-hatched, double-damned door. The phone began to ring. I got the upper half open. To hell with the bottom, although I scratched my thigh on the brass weatherstripping as I vaulted over.

The pebbles of the drive made me excruciatingly aware that I had no shoes on, but I merely took to the grass, following Dice. He didn't need paths, and led me through the beeches and underplantings to the back of the stable.

I could hear sirens on the highway. I could hear, more acutely, the kicking and whinnying of fire-scared horses. And the dominant piercing note of Orfeo's bugling.

I remember grabbing a sheet from the drying rack, and I guess I grabbed the pitchfork as I raced past the manure pile. And stopped. Because the fire was not *in* the stable. It was outside. Someone had heaped hay and straw in the fifty-gallon oil can used as a water barrel for the roof drains. More smoke than fire. Not that it mattered to Orfeo, because the smoke, blowing in his window, was sufficient to start him going. The fire had been deliberately set to lure *me* here.

The meadow blaze had been started to draw the men from the house and the stable. How had Galvano got past the gate? The dogs? Where was he now?

Dice leaped to the small barred window at the back of Orfeo's box, wriggling to get his hips through the bars. The frantic gelding was plunging and kicking, shrieking with fear. The whole stable was in an uproar.

I shoveled manure into the barrel. The stench was incredible, but the sheer sopping wet mass would put out the fire.

I hefted the pitchfork, ready to commit a little mayhem myself with it when I found Galvano. I tried not to think of Orfeo's terror. He was in no present danger, whatever he thought.

Galvano'd got rid of the men, probably watched them leave so he could be sure I was alone in the house. Had he tried to enter and found it locked? Probably. But if he'd seen the windows locked and closed, how had he planned to lure me out with smoke? The phone! It'd been ringing as I climbed over the door hatch. He could've called from the stable phone in the tack room. The intercom dialing system was printed beside the receiver.

I picked my way back to the front of the stable, wishing I'd had wit enough to put sandals on. And there was no way for me to peek into the tack room from the outside of the stable rectangle. The windows were small and high and impossible to reach because of the dense foundation plantings. I started for the main archway and halted. That would be the route Galvano expected me to take.

I raced around the stable again, wincing as I passed Orfeo's stall. From the sound of it, he'd angled his kicks at the stall door now. It wouldn't last long. The upper hatch was open, and the bottom was nowhere near as substantial as the doors in G-Barn.

I pressed myself against the wall of the pasture gate, easing my way carefully forward until I could see the tack-room door. He had to be in there. That was where the phone was. And he must be expecting me through the main arch. Or had he gone up to the house to check?

I had to catch him now. A sudden ripping of wood close by told me that very shortly the yard would be full of frightened horses! Horses. I glanced quickly at the tack-room door and darted around the corner, keeping low. I peeked at the first box. Bay heels lashed at the door. Which one was Sadie? I flipped the hatch lock free and ran on. Loose horses would bring Galvano out and the men back! Gray hooves battered the next door. Praying that this wasn't Maisie, I waited for the next kick and then slipped in as fast as I could move. The gray had her head down for another go when I grabbed the loose halter rope and jerked her head up. Flipping the end over her neck, I managed to jam it through the nose-band ring on the other side. This must be Sadie. She was calming with a human near her.

Wood was splintering all over the yard now. I turned the mare, vaulted to her back, nearly spiking her with the pitchfork, and then kicked her out of the stall, just as the bay in the first box erupted into the yard, with Maisie on my right charging to freedom a second later.

I had headed the excited Sadie toward the tack room when hell really broke loose. Orfeo splintered the last crosspiece of the hatch, banged hysterically about in the box a moment more, and tore into the yard just as the skinny figure of Caps Galvano emerged from the empty stall on the other side of him. He collided against the flank of the fire-crazed horse. Behind the gelding streaked the mighty Eurydice, his tail enormous, every hair of his spine as erect as a porcupine's fighting crest. I couldn't imagine what Dice thought he'd accomplish by chasing after Orfeo. But then, I wasn't all too sure what I was trying to do, having the devil's own time keeping my seat on Sadie's smooth bare back (how in hell had knights managed lances?) without skewering myself or the mare. The sweat pouring down my face half-blinded me as well.

As it was, the dogs made the "capture." Orfeo, witless as all horses are when fire-scared, came thundering back to his own stall in time to knock Galvano down again. Rafe and Dennis, legs pumping, arms flailing, narrowly missed the bay's stampeding exit as they came through the arch. Maisie had found her way out the pasture door, and Orfeo, Dice gamely a jump behind, crashed after her. I remember thinking that there was nothing impeding his use of that off-hind now.

Rafe and Dennis got to Galvano before the dogs were thoroughly roused by the blood pouring from his nose and mouth. Sadie kept rearing, and I got a round-about glimpse of Jerry's arrival, but Rafe bellowed at him to investigate the fire. Dennis appeared to be trying to protect Galvano from Rafe's flying fists when a bullhorn blasted the confusion. The staunch defenders of law and order had arrived, stopped by the electronically sealed gate.

Albert was now clinging to Sadie's bridle, yelling to me something about the pitchfork. I nearly skewered him, but he wrenched it from my hand. Then Dennis was shouting at me to get off so he could let the cops in.

And really, the whole scene was unbelievable. And got more so. There was Albert, like some diabolic gnome, holding a pitchfork inches from Galvano's chest as the man lay groaning in the dust; Dennis riding like a centaur out of the yard; and

Jerry coping with the unwieldy bulk of a foam extinguisher, demanding to know where the goddamned fire was.

Rafe caught hold of my wrist, jerking me half off my feet and into Orfeo's stall. He flipped me over his knee and proceeded to pound my bottom with a hard and merciless hand until I begged him to stop.

"I told you to stay in the house, goddamnit, Nialla."

"You love me. You love me. You love me," I screamed at him from the straw, weeping with joy and pain.

He grabbed me up and began shaking me, his face a blur of soot-streaked white, his blazing eyes my point of focus.

"You ever, *ever* disobey me like that again, Nialla Clery, and I will wear the hide off your ass with a crop."

"You love me. Say it. You love me!"

He stopped shaking me, glaring ferociously.

"Of course I love you!" He roared it louder than the bullhorn. "Why in hell did you think I married you, you witless woman?"

He was dragging me out of the stall just as Sheriff Erskine heaved himself out of the first squad car.

"Mrs. Clery wasn't harmed, was she?"

"Harmed?" Rafe snapped the word out so violently Erskine backed up hastily. "No, she's not *harmed*!" Then Rafe took a deep breath and a tighter hold on my wrist, pulling me past Erskine to where two troopers were hauling the dazed and bleeding Galvano to his feet.

Before anyone could interfere, Rafe had grabbed Galvano by the jacket front.

"What in hell were you trying to do to my wife . . . you . . ."

Galvano started screaming for help, the cops tried to peel Rafe's hand loose, stepping on my bare feet because Rafe had *not* let go of my wrist, and there were all these heavy bodies crushing me.

I'm not sure how everyone got untangled, but then Galvano was sobbing out that he hadn't been doing anything wrong. Rafe yelled louder that he was a murderer, a pyro. Only the troopers got Galvano into the police car and jack rabbited off.

"Now, just a goddamned minute there, Clery," Erskine

started bellowing, because Rafe transferred his fury to Erskine, but Dennis and Jerry intervened. "You cool off or you'll get served with assaulting an officer."

"Berserk" was the only word for the expression on Rafe's face. I was sick with fear. And staggering, started to fall. Fainting!

I didn't, but it had the desired effect. Rafe even caught me before I hit the ground.

"Nialla! Nialla! Now look what you've done, you god-damned fuzz head. Jerry. Get Bauman here!"

Rafe practically raced to the house with me, all the time Erskine bellowing his ineffectual, "Now, just a minute there, Clery," in our wake.

It seemed advisable to come to my senses the moment Rafe laid me on the couch so he'd think of something else besides his quarrel with the sheriff. I groaned and waggled my head, but I couldn't look Rafe in the eye after pulling such a stunt. I caught glimpses of Erskine's pale face, though. Was he scared of swooning women, or had he just realized what a beating I'd saved him?

At any rate, by the time Bauman arrived, everyone had calmed down, and sane conversation was possible.

I was one mass of bruises and lacerations. I wasn't very comfortable lying down either, but I could hardly explain *that* to the doctor. However, he did bandage the worst cuts on my feet and put something aromatic on my incipient bruises, all the time scolding me for being such a goddamned fool. I couldn't defend myself at all because the screaming excitement earlier had rendered me mute. So I lay wan, tired, and disgustingly smug while the others hashed over the events.

Michaels was contacted and had advised us he was returning immediately. Suddenly a stickler for the forms of law, Erskine said he could charge Galvano only with trespass, arson, and assault and battery. I had perjured myself with a nod to the fact that I recognized him as my attacker in the stable.

How he got on the property was a trifle embarrassing for Rafe, because in an effort to get Wendy Madison back in her own house quickly, Rafe had unlocked the side gate, leaving it unlocked while he and Michaels drove her home. Galvano had evidently been hiding on the grounds, seen his opportunity, and taken it. He'd made it to the west meadow and set the dry grass afire. When Rafe and the others arrived, with the dogs, he'd hightailed it up to the house. Only it was locked. So he'd set the barrel fire and phoned me to be sure I knew the peril in which my horse was. What he intended to do when he'd captured me, we never knew. I don't like to speculate.

Michaels landed in the charred west meadow, and his arrival cleared everyone out of the house. The thunder I could hear outside was nothing to the storm in my husband's face. My fanny began to smart, and I slipped my hands over it protectingly, trying to make myself very small in the couch as he loomed, Big Chief Lightning Eyes, over me.

"All right, Nialla Donnelly, you've been getting away with murder, but the crisis is now over, and you, young lady, are going to behave yourself. If you *ever* disobey a direct and reasonable order from me again, and if you ever pull another stunt like that stagy faint . . ." Then his grim expression softened, and he was sitting on the couch and pulling me into his arms, his hands roughly tender. "Of course I love you, Nialla Clery."

"But you never said it."

"Did I have to?" he demanded fiercely, looking deeply into my eyes. "It's so easy to say." His lips twisted bitterly.

I thought of two discarded wives, Amazons who'd been anything but economical. I thought of his mother, and I wanted to kill her and them. Instead I held his soot-smeared face in my hands and tried to iron out the bitter lines with my fingertips.

"No, it's not easy to say, Rafe Clery. If you mean it and it's all you have to offer."

"All you have . . ." The twist in his smile straightened out. "If you do mean it, Nialla, say it?"

In his eyes was that unexpected vulnerability and wariness that I'd glimpsed before, and an intense yearning that had nothing whatever to do with physical lust. In the second I had this clear view to the core of a complex personality, I experienced an elation, a humility, and a womanly wisdom that made me simultaneously maternal, wanton, and sad.

"I love you, Rafe Clery. I love you very much in many

ways I didn't know a woman could love a man. I fell in love with you when you walked into the stall beside Orfeo. I hated every woman who had ever ridden in that car and worn your scarves. I nearly cried when you walked out of the stable after dinner like an operatic Prussian. And after we rode together that morning—as if we'd done it all our lives—I hated myself because I was so damned inadequate for you. No, you shut up and listen. It was absolutely indecent of you to appear in that excuse of a bathing suit you wear. It was a dirty, dirty trick, Rafael Clery, and I only just realized that you knew exactly what you were doing to me, even then . . ."

The smile in his eyes, on his lips, was real, and his hands seemed to move with joy on my body as he swung me around, cradling my head on his chest in the crook of his arm. My voice was coming back, but still breaking now and then, and he cuddled me, with this idiotic smile on his face.

"I damn near flipped," he said, low-voiced, "when I realized you'd been raped. I thought I'd do something wrong and spoil any chance of waking you up again."

I laughed, suddenly very sure of myself with this man for the first time.

"Then you didn't realize I gave up the moment you sat down on that lounge like some damp eunuch?"

He threw his head back, laughing. "Damp eunuch? I'll eunuch you," he said with a growl, but I held him off.

"You will have the courtesy to hear my declaration of love and affection all the way through."

His eyes remained brilliant with laughter and love, but his face was a mixture of astonished delight.

"Then you waltzed up to me with that girth, and that clinched it! Ooops, I'm doing it now!"

"I love you, I love, love you, Nialla," he crowed. "I was so afraid that it was only gratitude you felt . . ."

"Gratitude?" I sat up so fast I almost clobbered him under the chin. "For the misery you've put me through the last few days, wondering if you married me only because you felt some responsibility for Russ Donnelly's orphaned kid, or because you wanted to own Orfeo."

His face was abruptly grave. "When I saw you from the

stands in Sunbury, Nialla, on that sorrel, I was positive I knew you. And I couldn't imagine who I knew who rode like that or who owned that gorgeous sorrel mare. That's why I came to G-Barn. I had to find out who you were." His smile was ineffably tender as he stroked my cheek. "I didn't know it, but I was hoping to find a gawky redheaded tomboy I'd seen on an old show horse in Agnes du Maurier's pasture. She told me to keep my cottonpickin' hands off her trainer's daughter for at least ten years. I was pretty bitter right then—I'd just paid through the nose to get rid of Amazon Number Two. You know how Agnes talked, blunt and to the point. She'd a few choice remarks to make about my life and habits, and wound up giving me some stringent advice. I've never been sorry I took it. Her final words went something like this: 'And the next time you pick a wife, pick one who rides, one you can mount without a ladder. Don't pick a shower, pick a winner. Like that nice kid down there.' And she pointed toward you."

"You mean, you didn't make that up . . . about waiting for me to grow up?"

He shook his head slowly. "I don't bother with social lies."

"You mean, you knew who I was all along?"

He shook his head again, ruffling my hair. "No, I was looking for red hair, remember? But after we rode that morning, I had my suspicions. Your father taught you a lot of his distinctive style, Nialla. I almost asked you flat out, the morning after the fire, only . . ." He hugged me very hard, his lips moving softly against my cheek. "God, Nialla, I can't believe my luck."

It was so very magical to be held close, knowing I was really safe, with his arms locked around me, our tired bodies comfortable, our minds attuned. I've no idea how long we might have stayed that way if Jerry hadn't come running up the front stairs, knocked urgently on the front door.

"Jesus, can't I ever have you to myself?" Rafe released me reluctantly.

"Boss, we've caught all the loose stock but . . . Orfeo. And, boss, he's in such a state I can't get near him. You know damned well Albert won't help, and Dennis . . . well . . ."

"Have you located him?" I asked, amazed at how revived I was when I got to my feet.

"In the jump pasture, ma'am, and we can't get near him."

"He hasn't hurt himself?"

"Gawd, no." Jerry sounded disgusted.

"And the cat?" Rafe asked.

Jerry swore under his breath. "He's sitting on the stone fence laughing. Honest, boss, he's sitting there laughing!"

He probably was, if I knew Dice. But that meant that Orfeo was really okay.

"Rafe, we really ought to get him in."

"I brought the hackamore and a rope," Jerry said, holding them out helpfully. "There's one helluva storm ready to break, too."

"Get your shoes on this time, Nialla."

One was under the couch, and I finally located the other under the end cushion.

By the time we started for the jump pasture, the sky was completely black with thunderheads, roiling and growing if you glanced up at them. Orfeo wasn't usually bothered by thunderstorms, but . . .

"We can put him in the orchard pasture shed overnight, Nialla," Rafe said as we half-trotted, half-walked along. "Jerry says the smoke smell in his stall is very noticeable. The rain may wash it away, but a night in the orchard shed won't hurt him. A night in a smoke-filled stall might."

Lightning crackled open the sky above us; thunder rolled a peal a few heartbeats later. But we were at the jump pasture, and the flare outlined Orfeo midfield. When the thunder died away, I called him and saw the magnificent head turn. A cat's complaint wafted across the storm-silenced field. I called again, and almost cried out with relief as the horse began to move toward us.

"Now, if that thunder'll shut up . . ." Rafe said as we ducked under the fence slats.

I kept calling encouragingly to Orfeo, walking slowly to meet him, Rafe at my side. Thunder rumbled much too near, and the black gelding tossed his head, whinnying sharply. He began to trot, Dice veering to run beside him, and Orfeo bent his head briefly to check on the cat. Fifty feet from us another clap of thunder sent him shying away, galloping off at a tangent.

I waited until the thunder died and called him again. Almost as if he recognized that I was the only safety in this darkening, terrible-noised world, Orfeo wheeled back, racing to me, showering my legs with cut turf as he slid to a halt.

For a horrible instant I thought Rafe might move too swiftly to secure the gelding. I ought to have known better. Rafe still considered Orfeo my horse, and only I had the right to manage him.

I got the hackamore over the gelding's nose, up over his ears, talking to him quietly. Orfeo snorted restlessly, the prestorm tension swirling around us.

"You'd best ride him back, Nialla," Rafe said, and laced his fingers to give me a leg up.

On sudden impulse I shoved the bunched reins at Rafe.

"I can't *sit*. On him or anything, you damned sadistic wife-beater. You ride him."

Rafe gave me such a look I shall never forget, and then, as if he was afraid I'd change my mind or something, vaulted to the gelding's back like a circus rider. Instantly he was stroking the startled gelding's neck, crooning to him, letting him accept the weight of an unfamiliar rider. Cautiously he took the reins, making contact with Orfeo.

Thunder boomed, lightning crashed, illuminating Rafe's exultant face. Orfeo pivoted, not from the unaccustomed rider, but away from the sound. Rain pelted down, huge, heavy gobbets of water.

I stepped back. "Go on, Rafe. I'll follow." Dice brushed against my legs, miaowing with distaste for the rain, and then plunged in mad leaps across the pasture to the fence.

"The gate's over to the right, Nialla. About ten feet."

"Gate?" I demanded, laughing. " 'Fraid of a little bitty fence, steeplechaser?"

"I love you, Nialla," Rafe shouted above the thunder.

I saw him lean forward, watched Orfeo move out, lift into a canter in a few strides.

There was more than one fence in the path Rafe took to the perimeter of that pasture. And lightning obliged as they took the double hurdle. They were dark shapes across the storm-black field at the broad water jump. I could feel the beat of speeding hooves through the soles of my sandals as Rafe headed Orfeo toward the pasture fence. Orfeo squealed as he tucked his hooves under him and soared over. It was an expression of surprise, not fear or fright, as if he approved of the fearlessness of his rider as much as I did.

I trotted after them, lifting my face to the sky to be washed in the torrents that fell, warm and soft.

Dice reached the shed before me and was already ensconced on the rafter above the two straight stalls. He was licking himself furiously, growling displeasure at the soaking.

Rafe was wiping Orfeo down with clean straw as the gelding lipped hay from the manger as placidly as if he hadn't been hysterically insane with fear a scant hour before. I arrived in the shed's open end just as lightning flashed and thunder cracked.

"Easy, lad," Rafe soothed Orfeo's restless dancing. "My God, look what swam in!" And he went right on tending the gelding.

Well, I couldn't fight that. Didn't want to. I got into the shed and began to wipe rain from my arms and legs, wringing out my shirttails before I sagged wearily into the bedding of the other stall. And rose up with a pain-filled gasp. I really couldn't sit on anything, especially straw.

"What's the matter?" Rafe asked.

"You wife-beater. You miserable sadistic brute."

A bunched horse sheet was launched at me, accompanied by his pleased (damn him) chuckle. "Try this!"

I spread the sheet, doubled it after a moment's close thought, and then carefully settled down again.

"Did you see how he took that pasture fence, Nialla?" Rafe asked, his voice excited, as he couldn't restrain his enthusiasm any longer. "He's fantastic. He's incredible. And you're right about the speed in him. Good thing I know every inch of this farm, or we'd've come a cropper. And responsive? No wonder you can ride him with a hackamore. He's like a goddamn cutting horse. And I *knew* it! Ask Ted or Steve. I kept telling them all this horse needed was the right handling. You are a white witch, my dearest. A proper white witch."

A gust of wind whipped rain on my legs, so I scooted back into the stall. Lightning outlined Rafe coming toward me.

"Where are you?" His hand connected with my ankle, and then he flopped over on his back beside me, tiredly, reaching for my hand. "That's some storm. Well" — and he exhaled deeply — "no possibility of that meadow fire smoldering with that drenching. Probably clear the stench from the stable, too. Couldn't you have found anything better than manure to douse that fire with, Nialla?"

"No." I couldn't have cared less. I was tired, my feet stung, my butt smarted, my throat throbbed, but Rafe was lying beside me, and all I could *feel* was his hand on mine.

"Did I really hurt you?" Rafe asked suddenly in a penitent voice.

"Yes. No."

He propped himself up on his elbow, grinning down at me in the gloom, and lifted my hand to his lips.

"Yes *and* no?"

"Yes, because it did hurt. No, because the hurt didn't matter because I knew you wouldn't have whaled me so if you didn't love me."

His eyes glittered as his hand dropped to my breast, slid inside the wet blouse and bra, gently exciting me.

"A good thing I admitted my fatal passion for you before I rode Orfeo, huh?"

"Mmmm." I turned toward him eagerly.

He made an abrupt movement upward. "Let's get back to . . . No!" And he was back beside me again. "No one can interrupt us here, by God, and I've been aching for you all day." His hands were busy with my shirt, but no busier than mine. The wet shorts tore, and I giggled, struggling with his. But our wet skins were touching at last, and I could rub my palms up and down the smooth hard muscles of his back, down to his waist and around. Suddenly his fingers dug into my buttocks. I gasped, and he gave me several sharp little slaps. Incredibly aroused by that, I seemed to go mad, desperate for him, infuriated by his delighted chuckle for my wanton response. He was slapping me again, but now he was within, his lips fastened on one breast as I arched my back, straining to him.

Thunder and lightning were all around us, and in us. Fire and noise were part of the storm that seized us both and drowned individuality into one single, fused entity.

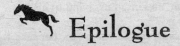 Epilogue

WE WERE SITTING down to a perfectly normal, every-Monday-morning-type breakfast when James Michaels knocked on the door.

"Well, the honeymoon is over," Rafe remarked, shoving back his chair, but the grin in his eyes was positively lecherous as he rose to greet the detective. "My God, man, you look ghastly. Get him some coffee, Mrs. Garrison. Better still, get him a steak."

One look at the man's face, and I shooed Mrs. Garrison to the stove for the steak and poured the coffee myself.

"I've been up all night."

"We wouldn't have guessed," Rafe said, but our eyes caught over his head, and I could feel myself blushing. We hadn't got back to the house ourselves until nearly five. Our occupation had at least been . . . well . . .

"What happened? Besides Galvano denying everything?" Rafe asked.

Michaels grimaced, sipping eagerly at the coffee. "I expected that. But what I didn't expect was that he was telling the truth part of the time."

"Ah, come on, Michaels."

"This turned out to be a bit more complicated than any of us could have foreseen, Mr. Clery."

"Explain."

"Please," I added, and Michaels gave me a very weary smile.

"John, alias Caps, Galvano, did murder your father, Mrs. Clery. And he confessed to it this morning, but only because we threatened to charge him with the murder of an unidentified man in a car registered in his name."

Rafe whistled tonelessly through his teeth.

"And it was as you suggested, Mr. Clery. Galvano found out that Russell Donnelly had discovered the hidden kilos of grass in the unused bales of hay. Galvano said he didn't mean to kill your father . . ."

"Kind of him!"

Michaels flushed at Rafe's sarcasm. "I'm not defending him, Mr. Clery, but it is one thing to kill in a cold, premeditated way, another to . . . Well, all Galvano wanted was to recover the grass. Your father rushed at him, and he grabbed up the pitchfork and . . ." Michaels' eyes asked me to accept the confession.

I nodded. Michaels didn't need any lumps for telling me.

"Galvano got back to Mexico without anyone being aware he'd left, because he'd paid a cousin to circulate the track wearing his clothes. And no, he did *not* bump off the cousin to keep him from talking," Michaels said, holding up a hand to forestall Rafe's protest. "You'd better let me tell it my way, Mr. Clery. It's rather complicated, you see." Rafe settled back, resigned to listening. "Galvano, having established an alibi, was still not certain whether you'd seen him, Mrs. Clery. And he also had to produce either the money or the marijuana. When he was questioned by the police, along with anyone else connected with the Marchmount stables and your father, Galvano realized that you hadn't seen him leaving the loft. But he was still in grave trouble with the grass ring.

"I gathered" — and Michaels grinned sardonically — "that Marchmount had more or less dispensed with Galvano's auxiliary services over the few months preceding your father's death. In fact, that was what drove Galvano to venture into drug-running. Now, he had some time before the drug contact would want payment, but he had to find money. Bizarre as it seems, Mrs. Clery, it was Marchmount himself who gave Galvano the idea of extorting money from you. He contacted Galvano and paid him one thousand dollars — in expense money — to do some quiet investigating for the purpose of clearing the good name of Marchmount; not, I'm afraid, Russell Donnelly."

Rafe swore under his breath and stroked my arm soothingly. I nodded in a sort of numbed way, remembering now how startled and furious Marchmount had been when I stammered out the reason for my need of money.

"So Galvano approached you, Mrs. Clery. He knew your father wasn't poor, but he didn't count on the probate delay. You gave him five hundred dollars the first time, I understand."

Michaels' eyes met mine squarely. I nodded.

"And I presume that Marchmount refused to give you anything because he realized the source of the suggestion?"

Rafe squeezed my hand imperceptibly.

"I didn't get any money from Marchmount, Mr. Michaels."

"And you left the state that night?" There was no shadow of blame or cynicism in Michaels' tired eyes, merely the expectation of an answer to a calm question.

"There seemed nothing left for me to do under the circumstances," I replied as calmly.

Michaels sat back a little. "Galvano underestimated both you and Marchmount, Mrs. Clery. But he was essentially a stupid man, scared enough to try anything to get the grass ring off his neck."

"Including faking his own death?" asked Rafe.

Michaels shook his head, taking another swallow of coffee. He kept the cup cradled in one hand, as if the warmth of the coffee helped.

"He didn't. The grass ring" — Michaels grimaced —

"obliged. Or so Galvano assumes. Which I'll buy. The man killed was the same cousin who stood in for him at Mexico. Who felt he could borrow Galvano's Pontiac without permission. Only someone had thoughtfully drained the brake fluid. Galvano was so furious remembering the loss of the car he'd planned to use to leave the state, that I believe he's telling the truth. Of course, draining brake fluid suggests premeditation in homicide, which was why he was quite willing to confess to the second-degree-murder charge."

"Hey, just a minute," Rafe demanded, half-rising from his chair. "What do you mean, second-degree murder? And what about Pete Sankey, too? And . . ."

"Galvano did not kill Pete Sankey," Michaels said so firmly that Rafe was momentarily silenced. "I hope you don't think me callous, Mrs. Clery, but we had to force the truth from Galvano. He will have to stand trial for your father's murder."

I put my hand on Michaels', understanding what he was unable to come out and say. I no longer wanted a death for a death, even if Rafe was still out for vengeance for my sake. I wanted only that the trial cleared my father's name. And I did not want the trial to ruin mine. Therefore I had to practice compassion or expect none myself.

"Rafe, that's what I want. That's all I want."

The anger faded from my husband's face, and he nodded slowly.

"All right, how come Galvano didn't kill Pete Sankey?"

"In a moment. He did admit that he slit the girth and tried to spook the black, Mrs. Clery. He was motivated by sheer malice. He recognized the sorrel mare, found out you owned the gelding, and decided he owed you a thing or two because your father had ruined him. But he was rather . . . incensed . . . to be charged with barn-burning."

"What? Who else could it have been? And why?"

"Someone else who knew a great deal about Nialla and Russ Donnelly, Caps Galvano, and Marchmount was in Sunbury that weekend."

"You must mean Marchmount?"

"No, I don't." And the faintest suspicion of satisfaction in stumping Rafe crossed the lieutenant's face. "Remember that Galvano had to go into hiding after his 'death,' and all he had was the thousand dollars from Marchmount and the five hundred from Mrs. Clery. That wasn't enough to get him out of the country, although he was now beyond the grass ring. He had plenty on Marchmount and had those photos faked. He had Nialla's face stripped in because he felt he could use that as a further lever against Marchmount. And then, as he tells it, he got to wondering why Marchmount was so eager to clear his own name. He knew all Marchmount's haunts, and with a little discreet phoning, found out that Marchmount had been in San Fernando at the time of Russell Donnelly's murder, and *not* at the hotel in Tijuana as he claimed. So Galvano pretended to be his cousin, the one so conveniently murdered in his place, who had come across some photos in Galvano's effects which would give a very good motive for Russell Donnelly's death. He asked for five thousand dollars and got it so fast, he realized he could have got much more. Marchmount was scared to death. He waited a week and called again, but that was when Marchmount had the first heart attack. So Galvano was forced to wait until Marchmount was out of the hospital. By then, Marchmount had applied to the Secrest Agency, a very reputable firm, by the way."

"Urscoll!" Rafe pounded the table so hard, everything jumped but the coffee cup Michaels was holding.

"Right!"

Rafe's face went through a variety of changes, from surprise, awe, disappointment, to tight-lipped fury.

"Why, that bastard!"

"Yes, he had found a unique situation and was exploiting it all he could."

Rafe angrily waved his hand. "Pete Sankey was worth four of Marchmount. And burning a barn around horses! Bastard!"

Michaels nodded sadly. "Urscoll spotted Galvano at the fairgrounds when he was leaving the station wagon. He'd been well briefed, of course, on the case, and had seen the mug shots I showed you, Mrs. Clery. He also knew exactly how Galvano was blackmailing Marchmount, and applied his knowledge. However, if he were going to cover his tracks, there was his chance. By getting Galvano to bear all the suspicion, he'd be blameless. So he burned the barn, an act aimed completely at you, Nialla Donnelly Clery, because it didn't take long for Urscoll to figure out why there'd been two attempts on your life. He also knew that Marchmount wouldn't last much longer. Then, when Mrs. Madison drove Marchmount down here, he followed in Marchmount's car . . . and gave a certain hitchhiker a ride all the way from Sunbury to Locust Valley, even pointed out the various estates to his passenger."

"How do you know this?"

Michaels looked at Rafe a long moment after the quiet, deadly question.

"Urscoll told us. We caught him." Michaels gave a sigh of justifiable satisfaction. "At the airport, during a routine preflight inspection. He had a thirty-eight on him, for which he produced his license, but he also had fifty thousand dollars in cash he couldn't explain so easily."

"But the phone call . . . and . . . those awful photos . . ." My hand went to my throat.

"Oh, that was Galvano. He couldn't reach Marchmount in a terminal coma—he died this morning—and he was desperate. You'd married money, he had incriminating photos. Twenty thousand dollars would set him up nicely in Canada."

"And he never knew that Urscoll had raked in all that money?"

"How would he? Urscoll had cleverly been keeping Marchmount on the move. Galvano was following, yes, because he could guess where Marchmount might go, but he didn't really catch up until Sunbury."

"God, the colossal nerve of the man!"

"Except for the airlines' nervousness, he'd have got away."

"He didn't seem that kind of a man," I said, rather horrified. Who could you trust? "I mean, he seemed honestly worried about Mr. Marchmount."

"He was," Rafe replied sardonically. "He had a bankroll at stake."

"How can people be that way?"

Rafe cocked an eyebrow at me, a cynical expression in his eyes.

"So," he asked Michaels, "what happens now?"

"Galvano stands trial in California, and Urscoll in New York State."

"And Nialla will have to appear in both?"

Michaels nodded unhappily. "But the cases are both open-and-shut, with signed confessions. Nothing to worry about." And he meant that.

Mrs. Garrison set down a sizzling steak platter in front of the startled man.

"My God, I thought you were joking," he said.

"Rafe rarely jokes about steaks," I told him, receiving my steak with a great deal of anticipation.

Michaels did look better when we'd finished breakfast, and he said he had to get back to Sunbury.

"Will you have a chance to rest now?" I asked, rather worried about him.

"With a little luck," he said, shaking the hand I offered him.

"You deserve a great deal."

He ducked his head with embarrassment and walked quickly toward the door, but Rafe got to it first and held it shut.

"Jim . . ." Rafe's hand went out, and he was displaying one of those fantastically winning smiles of his " . . . I have never bribed a policeman" — and the emphasis was complimentary — "before, but if a quiet cabin on a secluded lake in the Adirondacks would ensure a couple of weeks of rest and relaxation, there could be a first time."

There was the barest hesitation before Michaels shook his head.

"However," Rafe continued, as if Michaels had made no response at all, "since I never have bribed a policeman, I won't start now. But a close personal friend, Jim Michaels, is under no such restraint."

"Mis . . ."

"How's that again, Jim?"

Oh, Rafe can be . . . be . . . unswervable.

"You arrange some vacation time with the captain, Jim. Nialla and I won't take no for your answer."

"We'll see," Jim Michaels replied with a faint grin.

"Indeed we will." And Rafe accepted the challenge.

The storm the night before had cleared the air of humidity and noxious odors. Michaels kind of shook himself as he walked across the porch and down the stairs to the car. We stood, arms about each other, until he was out of sight.

"Okay, Mrs. Clery. Shall we go school some horses now?"

I answered the smile and the cocky gleam in those brilliant eyes the only way possible.

"Sure, Mr. Clery."

# THE
# MARK OF
# MERLIN

# ❦ 1

I WAS AWARE that I should be more grateful. The train was after all headed in the right direction. Track was laid from Boston to the end of Cape Cod and eventually this train, too, would arrive at its destination. Maybe not on the day of embarkation, March 18, 1945, but sometime. Such vague reassurance didn't make the journey from Boston to East Orleans in a frigid baggage car any less cold and dreary.

Not that this was the first trip I had made in a baggage car. Merlin and I had traveled that way all over the United States, including the territory of Alaska. But this time the ignominy of forcing a gentleman like Merlin among common crates, bales, and boxes, and having to have him muzzled and chained, was one more insult to the injuries of spirit I had already sustained. My rebellion was complete. The only living thing it did not touch was Merlin. He was, all totaled, the one being who cared for me, Carlysle Murdock. I should say, James Carlysle Murdock, driving that particular thorn deeper into my side.

Merlin sensed my rising inner turmoil and whined sympathetically, his tongue cramped up against the confines of that indecent muzzle. At Merlin's remark, the imbecilic baggageman cast a nervous look in our direction. I ignored him. As I had ignored his attempt to bully me into confining Merlin in a cage.

I knew how useless it was to explain that Merlin had had the benefit of schooling under the leading canine trainers in the world. That he had far better manners than three-fourths the travelers today, including service personnel. Merlin's size and his breed predisposed people immediately against him. It is difficult, I agree, to reassure the timid that one hundred and

255

twenty pounds of silver-black German shepherd was in actual
fact a driveling coward. I could show his K-9 papers discharging
him on the ground of "insufficiently aggressive behavior" and
I would find people ready to discredit the word of the under-
secretary of war.

Oh, I could have caged him and sat forward in comfort
and warmth with the human passengers but some perverse
streak in me reveled in the martyrdom of this segregation. I
knew I was acting childishly, that I was not adhering to the strict
"chin-up" code in which I had been raised, but that was another
facet of this whole humiliating, terrible journey.

Tears, never far from my eyes these days, dribbled down
my cheeks. Rather than let the baggageman misconstrue my
weakness, I buried my head in Merlin's ruff, choking back the
lump in my throat. Merlin's soft whine was more understanding
than all the sympathy of the dean and the hospital staff at
college, or the commiseration of my boardinghouse colleagues.
None of these people had ever met my father so how did they
know how much I was going to miss him? How could they
understand this crushing loneliness that overwhelmed me?

Here I was, sick with grief and not yet recovered from the
strep throat infection that had stricken me at midterms, advised by the dean to take the rest of the spring term off "to get
my bearings," on my way to meet a guardian whom I earnestly
wished to hell.

And *he* had perpetrated the final indignity. He had not
even had the grace to come get me, though he had certainly
known from the dean's letter how sick I had been. I refused to
allow him the one benefit of doubt to which I knew, in my heart,
he was entitled. He did, after all, believe me to be a boy. Who
wouldn't? With a name like James Carlysle Murdock? Was he
in for a surprise! And, damn my dear father anyway, not only
for inflicting such a name on me in the first place, but for not
explaining to the friend he had happily conned into "guardian-
ing" me that his beloved Carlysle—Dad had never called me
"Carla" as my friends did—was actually a girl and not a boy.
Major Regan Laird was in for a mighty big surprise at the
station at Orleans. That is, if he condescended to come meet
me there!

Remember, my better half reminded me, he's just been invalided home himself. He might not be able to drive, assuming first, he has a car and second, he is able to wheedle gas out of the local ration board.

I was not to be mollified so easily. I was bound and determined to be as miserable, disagreeable, and awful as I could. That would repay the much decorated Major Regan Laird for his ridiculous letters, urging me to join the service and finish my college later.

"Apply for O.C.S. and be a credit to you father!" Indeed. What did the service ever do for Dad but kill him?

"Enlistees have tangible advantages over draftees." Sure, Major, but I'd love to see your face signing a WAC application form as my guardian. I smiled to myself, smugly sure of startling the hell out of the patronizing, insufferable, egocentric major-my-guardian.

What had my father been thinking of? Couldn't he have appointed someone I knew? Captain Erskine, for instance: He was in Fort Jay. For a year I could even put up with simpering Alice Erskine. But this unknown major? That rankled!

Now, said myself to me, your father had been mentioning this Major Laird ever since he wangled Laird's transfer to his own regiment. Laird had been praised, appreciated, blessed by Dad for two years. Two soulmates, that's what my father and the major had been. Two minds but with a single preoccupation — infantry: the proper disposition and use thereof in battle.

If it did nothing else for me, this line of thought kept me so agitated I did not feel that damp, raw sea-cold that seeped through the ill-closed baggage door as the train bucked and squealed slowly over the icy tracks. I heard the conductor calling "Yannis" at the next station. Not bad. A mere three hours late to Hyannis. Chatham would be next and finally, at long overdue last, Orleans. This endless journey to the long-delayed meeting with my unknown guardian was drawing to its conclusion.

I leaned into Merlin's warm body as the baggagemaster swung open the door to the icy March evening. No appreciable effort had been made here to clear the depot or the street visible just beyond. Drifts were piled high around the baggage entrance; a narrow aisle, shovel-width, led to the passenger side of the station. Two Railway Express trucks were backed into four-foot drifts and a green mail truck was revving its motor noisily, gusts of its exhaust odors mingling with the smell of overheated oily steam drifting back from the hardworking engine. My stomach churned spasmodically.

Immersed in this slough of self-pity, I envisioned myself trudging drearily, freezing cold, down the deserted snow-heaped streets of Orleans, trying to find my way to Major Laird's house, Merlin, his silvery coat white with snow, pacing wolflike behind me.

"Gawd, what is it? A wolf?" a masculine voice demanded in a broad down-east twang as the door creaked wide.

"Nar, the gul's dawg," the baggageman said, giving me a dirtier look than usual. He had been questioned at every stop and was as irritated by now as I.

"Should be caged. Reg'lations."

Before the baggageman could open his mouth with another of his simpleton remarks, I answered.

"They don't build cages that big."

"Bulieve it. Better keep that'un chained down heyah, miss. Someone's shoot'm fer a wuff. Would indeed."

"He never leaves my side," I replied coldly, looping one arm loyally around Merlin's neck. He had watched the exchange, cocking his head right and left, ears pricking forward. He looked soulfully up at me and tried to lick his lips through the muzzle. Frustrated, he stretched his front paws out and eased his huge barrel down, resting his insultingly packaged head on his front legs.

There was the usual endless routine of waybills and did Mrs. Parson's package make this train and when did they expect the shipment of Brown's and so on and on. I supposed acidly to myself that without the summer visitors to gossip about they had to make do with such banal topics. But it was driving me nuts. I didn't want to get to Orleans and yet I couldn't wait to confound Major Laird. I was supremely tired of train riding. I was thoroughly bored with baggage cars and I was exhausted, very cold and very hungry. Since we'd left South Station in Boston at eleven this morning I had had one single cup of lousy coffee and nothing else. The moron of a bag- gageman wouldn't let me leave Merlin long enough to get so much as a sandwich.

The raw sea-cold chilled me despite ski pants, boots, and heavy mackinaw. I felt deprived of muscle and bone; I was a frozen amalgam of tissue, supported upright by solid ice par- ticles within. I had to admit that the college doctor and the dean were correct in their insistence on a term-long convales- cence. I had driven myself too hard at my studies, using them to dull my senses to the fact of my father's death and my awareness of the loss of all familial relationship. I would rest now, hole up in the major's lair, and come back for the summer term. It would be asinine to suffer the defeat of poor grades when I had made dean's list every term so far.

I forced myself to ignore the exchange of platitudes between railroad officials until the baggage car was finally closed and I heard the conductor's muffled "Ar board . . . ."

Surprisingly, the train picked up speed between Hyannis and Chatham. And *mirabile dictu* there were only two crates to be unloaded at that small town. Either the threat of Nazi submarines had scared fishers inland to war plants or everyone was too poor to buy a thing. I didn't really pursue the blessing.

"Ohleens, next," the conductor intoned and I could see relief parade across the baggageman's face. He even went so far as to assemble my battered bags at the rattling door to make it easier to speed his departing guest.

"That's very kind of you," I said so sweetly he didn't get the sarcasm and mumbled a "You're welcome."

Merlin sensed the end of the journey and rose, stretching with majestic indolence. The baggageman made a strategic withdrawal to the far side of the car.

The train jolted to a stop, braked wheels spinning on the icy track. As the baggageman threw open the door, I slipped off the hateful muzzle and hand-signaled Merlin out of the car. The look of pure terror on the man's face as Merlin, free, darted out, made up for some of the indignities we had endured according to the gospel of regulations. Merlin plunged around in the snow, tail lashing with pleasure at liberty. I jumped down from the lip of the baggage car, disdaining the help of the stationkeeper. I pushed him aside discourteously, lifting my bags down and staggering with them to the corner of the station which seemed somewhat protected from the winds. It was snowing heavily again and the wind gusted it like sand, hard and cold, into my face. I signaled Merlin to stay by the bags. I didn't want him disappearing in a strange town on a stormy night no matter how much he needed some exercise.

The stationman and the baggageman were already deep in their endless trivia. The wind blew to fragments most of their sentences about soggy mailbags and frozen parcel posts. I peered up and down the platform, straining to see through the blown snow. In spite of my inner conversations, I knew I had counted heavily on the major meeting us. But there was no one in sight. As the wind tore at my legs, I felt the additional chill of disappointment.

A heavy woman, muffled in a Hudson Bay blanket coat of ancient vintage, struggled down the high steps of the single passenger car and trudged through the snow to the street. She ducked awkwardly under the roadguard and disappeared into the wind-driven snow and darkness.

Lights shone from a taxi office, a restaurant, and a stationery store lining the far side of the snowy street. Behind the station on my side of the road I could discern the cheerful snowclad rectangles and crosses of the town's old cemetery. A lone truck stood outside the store but, as far as I could see in the darkness beyond, the street was empty of vehicles and pedestrians.

I swallowed against the pressure of more ridiculous tears. It would spoil my confrontation with the major completely if he were to find me weeping childishly. The sense of desolation and frightful loneliness was intense.

Merlin whined and rocked back and forth, yearning to break position. My gratitude for his company, much less his empathy, routed the tears. Merlin didn't need explanations. Merlin was never away when I needed him. Yet had he been as wise as his namesake, he was still not a human and his wordless sympathy was not quite enough. Although God knows, I had no other.

So complete was the sense of abandonment that self-pity deserted me. I tried desperately to find excuses for the major's absence. I had written him a week ago to confirm my coming. This morning I had wired him from South Station to expect me. I had to admit the train was a trifling matter of three hours and twenty-five minutes late but the weather was atrocious enough to account for a far longer delay. He would surely have had sense enough to call the station and check the e.t.a.

Well, I argued, he might not have a phone. He might have waited for hours and then gone home. It was past seven. No, he had gone home to eat and would be back. Home! How could I conceivably call the major's house "home"? I was an army brat. Home was where my hat was, nowhere else. No, home was where Merlin was, I amended.

Perhaps the major didn't have a car. I swung around toward the taxi stand. It was empty. Perhaps it had gone for him now the train was finally in. And if the major did have a car, it was possible, entirely probable, that he might have had engine trouble in this weather. Or got stuck in a drift on his way here. There were umpteen dozen reasons why the major was not here. None of them made much difference to the sick, cold, frightened lump in the pit of my empty, cold, churning stomach.

The train started up and pulled out of the station with metallic complaints about the effort required to pull its half-frozen cars along the icy rails. The roadguard went up. I peered into the gloom on the other side of the track and saw only the dark hulks of cars parked in the station lot. Just then I heard the station door open and shut with a bang. A figure came charging up to the stationmaster who was wrestling with the frozen mail sacks.

"Any passengers get off, Mr. Barnstable?" a muffled voice asked.

"Jist Miz Brewster, and a gal and a big dawg from the baggage car." The stationman brushed by the figure with an apology, hurrying to get himself and his unwieldy sacks into the warmth.

The other man was the major. His stance was unmistakably military despite his bulky clothing. The relief I felt at knowing he had met the train was mingled unpleasantly with the distressing fact that he was not looking for a girl, or a girl with a dawg, and he was not happy.

"Damn young squirt's missed the train after all." His voice drifted towards me. He caught sight of me and hesitated, undecided by the sexless figure bundled in pants and mackinaw. Merlin whined and the major stamped back around the corner of the station. Just as he passed from my view, the flood of light from the window caught his face briefly. I was glad, then, that I was a distance from him, that the gusty wind covered my gasp of shock at the sight of his ruined face. Shrapnel, more than likely, had gouged through cheek and jaw. Raw heavy scar tissue drew the right eye down at the corner and twisted the mouth into a permanent half smile. No wonder he had never mentioned the nature of his wounds. No wonder he had not wanted to come to Cambridge to meet me. All plans for petty vengeance disappeared from my mind.

"Major Laird," I cried, hurrying across the intervening space.

He stopped and turned, his hand already on the doorknob. This time I saw the other half of his face and experienced a second shock. It was obvious that the major had been a handsome man. Plastic surgery would repair most of the cruel scar on the right but that anyone, man or woman, should have to endure, however briefly, such disfigurement was the other side of enough.

He said nothing but waited till I reached him. Nor did he make any move to obscure the damaged profile as he faced me.

"Major Laird," I began and impulsively thrust out my hand, "I'm Carla Murdock."

His eyes narrowed angrily and he frowned; at least, one side of his face frowned.

"Is this some kind of a joke?" he snapped.

"No, no joke," I hurried to say. "At least, not on you. If there is a joke, it's on father for having a girl and giving her the name he planned for his firstborn son, James Carlysle Murdock."

I resisted the impulse, prompted by the disbelief on his face, to reach into my shoulder bag and drag out the dog-eared birth certificate, the baptismal papers, and the sworn statement of the commandant of Fort Bragg, addressed to all draft boards, that I was legally James Carlysle Murdock and unequivocally female.

He stared intensely at me as I was sure he had stared at incompetent junior officers and privates. Only I had seen my father use this unnerving technique too often to dissolve into the nervous stammer of self-defense it usually provoked.

"You had your fun, didn't you?" he said finally in a cold scornful voice. I knew he meant the letters he had written to an unknown boy. It would have been far more polite of me to have disabused him of his error immediately.

"And why this lie about going to Harvard?"

"I *do* go to Harvard. Radcliffe College is a college of Harvard University," I retorted, stung out of remorse by his unfair accusations.

"Your mailing address . . . ."

"I can't live on campus . . . with him." I pointed at Merlin. He interpreted the gesture as a release and came over.

"That doesn't excuse you from deliberately misleading me."

"You misled yourself," I snapped, trying to keep my teeth from chattering. "My father may have called me Carlysle but I'll bet at some time or other he had to use the female pronoun. You just didn't hear. You just didn't think, mister. Most of all, you wouldn't want to be a guardian to a girl! Sweet suffering Pete," I cried, "do you think I haven't *wanted* to be a boy, if only for Dad's sake?" He blinked as I unconsciously used a pet expression of my father's.

I stood glaring at him and, despite the firmest clamp on my jaws, my teeth began to chatter. Merlin whined questioningly, licking his chops, shifting his paws restlessly on the snowy platform. Almost absentmindedly, the major held out a gloved hand for Merlin to sniff and as offhandedly patted Merlin's head.

"We can't stand here all night. You'll have to come with me now," the major said. "I'll decide what to do later."

He pulled me around, a rough hand under my elbow, and pointed towards the blurred but unmistakable outline of a jeep in the parking lot.

"The jeep's mine," he said, bending to pick up my suitcases. I tried to take one from him but he glared at me fiercely. "I'm not crippled," he said with a definite accent on the final word.

Rebuffed and feeling that perhaps frozen solitude was preferable to his present company, I trudged behind him to the jeep. He tossed the bags easily into the back before sliding into the driver's seat. With cold fingers, I fumbled endlessly at the stiff handle on my side. With an exclamation of exasperation he reached over and opened the door. Merlin, without order, leaped into the backseat, sitting straight up, his tongue out, watching first me, then the major. It infuriated me that Merlin appeared to have accepted the major at first sniff.

Expertly the major backed the jeep in the treacherously drifted snow. He bisected old frozen ruts and crossed the railroad track as the jeep's four-wheel drive found what traction there existed on the bad surface of the unplowed road. He waited patiently for the traffic light to change although there wasn't anything moving anywhere on the abandoned road.

The jeep must have been standing forever in the parking lot for inside the car it was colder than outside. The isinglass curtains were none too tight and gusts of frigid air lashed in particles of snow. I sat huddled with my arms hugging my sides, trying to make myself believe I was warm. I shivered spasmodically. Whatever reception I had anticipated, I had got more than I'd planned. Actually I never had gone beyond the first moment when the major discovered my sex. That's the problem with daydreams. They are not the least bit practical.

In all honesty I had to admit that the major had more justice on his side. I had had fun deliberately encouraging his misconception. Based on his information, he had given good advice in suggesting that his ward join the army. Faced with an inevitable draft, it would be smart for a young man to volunteer. The Allies had broken out of the Belgian Bulge and were racing across Germany to meet up with the Russian forces. Undoubtedly the war in Europe would end by spring. Then the entire concentration of Allied military strength would sweep over the Japanese positions and end the Pacific campaign. A man joining the service right now would get through basic and probably have a short tour on occupation forces. Then he'd have the G.I. Bill to see him through college.

I now realized that the major had very carefully thought out that first letter of condolence to a boy suddenly orphaned. It had been a kind letter, if devoid of emotion. He had, bluntly it is true, described the fatal injury my father had received on a routine trip at night between his command post and a bivouac he wanted to inspect. The major had gone into detail about the brief ceremony in the little Lutheran cemetery at Siersdorf where my father had been buried. Every man in the regiment who was not on duty had crowded in. The description might have read like the orders of the day but the picture evoked had been equally clear. The major had gone on to ask me what my immediate expenses were and how much I would need to finish the term. I was not to worry about staying in college, if that was what I wanted. He hadn't seen my father's will yet, but there would be enough in the National Service Insurance to see to my education. If I had damned the major for insensitivity to my grieving I had done him an injustice, for he had done the courtesy of assuming the boy was a man. I knew, now I had seen the major, that he would have written an entirely different letter had he known I was a girl.

However, neither of us had entertained the possibility that he too might be wounded or that I would work myself into ill health. Dad had been killed November 18, 1944. The major was critically wounded on December 7 in the Sportplatz near Jülich. I hadn't known of that until mid-January when he wrote me from an English convalescent camp. Neither of us had thought of meeting before the summer when he expected to have enough points to get home. Now here we were, thrust together in late March under the worst of conditions.

I like to think that had he not been wounded, had I not gotten ill, I would have soon told him the truth. It was spiteful of me not to have told him. Whatever excuse I might hide behind, the fact remained I had put myself in a very bad light. My egotism had inflicted hurt on someone already badly injured. I was deeply ashamed of myself and I could think of no immediate way of convincing the major of that.

How he found his way I do not know for the full dark of deep winter was further complicated by the wind-driven snow, lowering visibility to a point just a few inches beyond the slitted headlights. The jeep growled in low gear as he inched it along. We had the road to ourselves. There weren't so much as tire marks from previous travelers to guide us for the wind swept continually over the road.

Major Laird didn't swear to himself as Dad would have, driving under such conditions. Against the isinglass window his profile was silhouetted boldly, the disfigurement hidden in the gloom. It was a strong face, dominated by an aquiline nose and a sweeping jawline, the sternness alleviated by a sensitive mouth and a full, sensuous lower lip. He was a lot more man than what drifted around campus at Harvard.

I cast about in my mind, trying to think of something to say, some way to apologize, but I was sensible enough to realize his mood was unreceptive and the conditions of the night made silence valuable. I noticed he kept glancing down at the dashboard.

"I've either overshot the turn in this foul weather or it's just ahead. You'll have to walk point till we find that blank crossroad. It's an oblique right."

You don't argue with orders given in that tone of voice. Not if you're army raised. It doesn't matter that you're cold already. He knows that, because he is, too. It doesn't matter you're not quite over a bad illness and this could make you sicker. He's taken that into consideration. I just got out and, with one hand on the right headlight, walked along the side of the road, peering through the sudden flurries, making out the black looming boxes of houses, the half-covered telephone poles, match-slim, until, fortunately not too far ahead of us, I found the turn. The brief walk had been stimulating. My toes burned and my fingers tingled. When I got back into the car, Merlin nuzzled my ear, crooning softly, deep in his throat.

The jeep proceeded a little faster until we reached another point predetermined by the odometer. Laird stopped the car and turned his head expectantly towards me. I got out, not even irritated with him when he held Merlin back from joining me. At the next crossroads we bore right again.

This road, even in the obscuring snow, had a different character: no houses, no trees, but, despite gusty winds, visibility improved. I could sense openness, could occasionally trace the horizon by the difference of the gray-white of land, the gray-black of wintry sky. Far on the left I caught a vagrant gleam of light quickly extinguished, for all Cape Cod observed strict blackout precautions. Once on the downslope to the right, I made out the tossing field of sea as it sent tentative fingers up coves on the forearm of Cape Cod. The road dipped here and there and we had to gun the car through drifts at the bottom. Sometimes the top of the road was swept clear, down to the macadam. Bay bushes thrust stark branches out to reflect the yellow slits of headlight. I don't know how far we went along this road. It must have been some distance for the warmth exercise had generated in my hands and feet had dissipated. The snow, constantly thrown against the windshield, had a mesmeric quality to it. The crow-flight distance from Orleans to Pull-in Point was approximately eight miles, and only ten by road under normal conditions. No self-respecting crow was a-wing and these were not normal conditions. I only know that it had been about seven when the train pulled into the station. When we finally entered the kitchen, the clock said eight thirty-five.

I had one more short march as point for the final left-hand turn to Pull-in Point Road above Nauset Beach. The Laird house, which in fair weather had a full view of the sea over the tops of Nauset's then substantial dunes, was partially protected by the lay of the land from the full brunt of the blizzard. Now its slanting saltbox roof was heavily laden with the accumulation of several snowstorms. It loomed blackly to our left, a solid bulk against the surrounding grayness.

"Find the driveway. There's a post on the right-hand edge to guide you."

I had trouble unbending my cramped knees. I got out very slowly, very stiffly. I came close to falling onto the post. Merlin bolted out the door as if he understood we had reached our destination. He promptly left a message at the beachplum bushes that formed the front hedge. As he barked ecstatically, snapping at the falling snow and rolling in it puppyishly, Major Laird revved the jeep for the dash up the rise to the garage I now distinguished in the gloom.

The major succeeded the second time. He gunned the motor peremptorily, recalling me to my senses, gesturing at the garage door. I slipped several times in the drifts, spitting out snow and cursing it as it leaked into my gloves and up my sleeves. I got a grip on the door handle and yanked. The top-hinged door stayed stubbornly shut. I made several more futile attempts and finally turned to the major, stretching my hands out in a show of helplessness. I heard him cursing with disgust as he crawled down from the jeep. There was some consolation in the fact that it took both of us, kicking and tugging, to loosen the frozen door.

He gave me a push towards the door in the rear of the garage. Unquestioningly I stumbled towards it as he drove the car in. My wet gloves slipped on the doorknob but I got it open the second time, gasping as warmth and light hit my face.

I lurched stiffly in, my entry hampered by Merlin who had had enough of playing around in the cold and barged past me. We entered a small back hall filled with fishing gear, hunting paraphernalia, oars, a well-greased motor, an imposing pile of cordwood, heavy-weather boots, and a filled meat safe high on the wall.

"Go on in," the major ordered impatiently as I blocked his way to warmth.

I hastily opened the door and entered a welcoming kitchen. I hurried over to the huge black wood stove, drawn like a needle by the magnet of its heat-radiating bulk. A Dutch oven squatted at the back of the range and from it came the odor of rich meat stew. Turning to present the rear of me to the stove, I saw the major clump into a corridor. I found later that it ran along the back of the house, separating the kitchen, bathroom, and a small study from the living room, dining room, and front hall. From where I stood by the hot stove I could see only doors and an area for coats and boots.

The major beckoned to me. "Hang your wet things out here," he said, less a suggestion than an order.

Mechanically I obeyed, fumbling with the ski-boot fastenings. My other shoes were in the suitcases which he placed just inside the dining room. I decided it was too much effort to rummage through the luggage for mere shoes. I got my boots off. My socks were either very wet or very cold; my toes were too numb to know the difference. I hung up my heavy mackinaw and scarf and walked like an automaton back to the kitchen. I sat stiffly down at the old honey-colored table in the chair nearest the stove.

The major had filled two plates with stew and two mugs with coffee from a pot that had also been kept warm at the back of the stove. He served me and himself, then ladled out another bowl, splashing it with water to cool it quickly. He put this down by the hall door and whistled.

Merlin had gone on his own private reconnaissance through the house and, although he had never been whistled at in that particular arpeggio, he knew he was being paged. I heard his claws clicking against bare floors. He came into the kitchen, head high, eyes curious, darting, taking in everything in a sweeping gaze. He looked up at the major, at me, and then went to the bowl of food. He sniffed at it and sat down, tongue hanging out.

"Eat, Merlin," I said and he rose and approached the food in earnest.

I had made it a point that Merlin should never accept food without my permission. I had trained him this way after two of his litter brothers were poisoned "by person or persons unknown." Ha! I'd known. The disadvantage to this discipline was that I could not leave Merlin for more than forty-eight hours. He simply would not eat. When the strep throat had been at its worst and I was delirious, Merlin had stubbornly fasted for four days. Then one of my friends had brought him to the window outside the infirmary. Receiving my permission, though how he recognized me by the croak my voice had become I don't know, the poor dog had wolfed down three pounds of horsemeat.

Right now he acted equally starved and I realized how hungry I was. Part of my depression must be due as much to hunger as cold. The stew had simmered into a semisolid mass, tasty, hot, restoring. The coffee, like any respectable army brew, was strong enough to have floated the stove. I cleaned my plate twice and felt infinitely more like facing the problem of the major.

In my concentration on the meal I had said nothing to him and had managed to forget his existence beyond the click of silverware against china. My attention was drawn back to him when a pack of cigarettes was thrust under my nose.

"Smoke?"

"I don't."

He lit one, the smoke he exhaled shadowing briefly the injured cheek. His look, without the disfiguration, would have been somber enough. I noticed that his hand bore scars, too, and I later learned that he had taken mine fragments all through the right arm and chest. He had, it turned out, been trying to drag the man in front of him out of the minefield.

"The situation is this, Miss Murdock," he said bluntly, leaning forward slightly. "It was perfectly all right for me to extend hospitality to my male ward of twenty. Quite another thing when that ward is female. There is no one in the house but me. And while this may be wartime, there are still proprieties to be observed."

"But . . . we barely made it here," I exclaimed, gesturing out at the whirling night.

He shook his head impatiently. "Not tonight, of course, you idiot. I'll find a place in the village tomorrow."

"I'm sorry I was so silly not to tell you," I babbled, unable to meet his eyes. "And I'll be twenty-one in less than a year so you won't be bothered with me long. Oh, the whole thing is ridiculous," I cried, jumping up, annoyed because I couldn't even make a decent apology to him.

He looked up at me with less rancor. He reached out one hand and reseated me.

"It's not that I am bothered with you, my dear ward. To be truthful, I couldn't do enough to repay the debt I owe Jim — your father. It's just that it would be so much easier if you were a boy."

"That's what father always said," I muttered sullenly.

"You make a much prettier girl . . . or would if you had

some flesh on you. That dean didn't exaggerate when she said you were run down."

"Her!" I grated out between my teeth. I'd had my run-ins with crab-eyes. Some of my resentment must have been reflected in my expression for he suddenly smiled at me.

"From the tone of her letter, I gather she considered me her contemporary," he remarked dryly.

"Fatherly and white-haired, suitable guardian to a well brought-up army brat," I replied in a simpering voice, up to the last two words which I spat out.

"Brat is right," he agreed firmly. "And as your guardian and by the few gray hairs I possess as of this moment, you get to bed."

"It isn't even ten yet," I complained, glancing at the clock.

"The time is immaterial, the way you look. I'll show you your room."

"The way I look indeed," I murmured to myself but I followed him.

"Which bag do you need tonight?" he asked and I pointed.

He led the way through the corridor into the dining room, to the front hall beyond. As I entered the foyer, I saw on my left the most unusually lovely stairway I have ever seen. A short flight of steps, parallel to the front door, ended on a low landing where the stairs continued, again parallel to the front door, to an intermediate landing, then switched on a short leg of a Z to the upper level. The balustrade over the stairwell was slightly bowed out, the spindles gracefully and unusually turned. It was a clever variation which fitted into a smaller space than conventional flights.

Major Laird noticed my surprise and pointed out the chandelier hanging over the stairwell.

"I mean to get the house electrified one day but not that. With candles in it, it is lovely to behold. Electricity would spoil it. This house is fairly old, added onto during the course of the eighteen hundreds. The oldest part is between the kitchen and the garage. I'll show you tomorrow."

We climbed the stairs and I stopped at each level, turning to see the effect.

The major shoved open an H-hinged door into a room at the front of the house, to the right of the stairs. Merlin padded in ahead and circled the room. The major ducked mechanically where the roof sloped down in front of the house. He lit the kerosene light on a massive old cherry bureau and laid my case at the foot of the four-poster spool bed with its quilted coverlet.

"It's a lovely room," I murmured, glancing around at the sparse but good furnishings, noticing the handmade braided rugs on the wide planked floors.

"My mother enjoyed this sort of stuff," he commented, implying that he did not.

"Bathroom's down the hall, second door on the right. Colder'n Croesus, I warn you. No way to heat it." He turned to the fireplace in this room, its coals glowing warmly. He threw on more wood and the fire flared up obediently.

"More blankets in here if you're cold," he told me, tapping the blanket chest at the foot of the bed.

I sat down wearily on the high bed. Merlin jumped up and I was about to order him down, looking up at the major apprehensively. Even if he didn't approve of the antiques, he might not want a dog on his mother's patchwork quilt.

"I wish I had him to keep me warm tonight," he said, grinning ruefully as he closed the door behind him. He stuck his head back in. "We're on total blackout here, so keep your curtains drawn."

"In a blizzard?"

"In a blizzard!"

I waited until I heard his footsteps on the stairs. Fatigue seeped through me. I pulled myself up by a bedpost and struggled to open the suitcase. I found slippers and a flannel nightgown. I shed my clothes and kicked them out of my way under the bed and the hellwiththem tonight.

I shuddered as the cold sheets chilled me even through the heavy flannel. Merlin did his usual act of stretching out beside me. He was longer than I. His warmth spread soothingly through the heavy blankets and he squirmed on his back to get comfortable against me. His warm moist nose prodded my ear in a canine kiss. Fine life when only your dog wishes you goodnight, I thought as I closed my eyes.

# 🐌 2

It was a combination of the cold and the wind that roused me. And once half conscious, I felt a vague nausea develop rapidly from chronic to acute. I staggered from the bed, barely aware of my surroundings. Merlin was instantly alert, whining a concerned question. I fumbled for the door latch, managed to open the door, and ran down the hallway. The upper hall was narrow and I barely avoided tumbling down the stairs, dizzy with nausea as well as sleep.

"Second door, second door," I heard myself mumbling and swallowed against the rising substance in my gorge. I slammed open the door and saw the gleam of the toilet bowl. I just made it.

Merlin thrust an inquisitive nose at my arm and I pushed him away impatiently. He was no use to me. I heard his nails scrabbling against the bare floor. I kept on being ill. I kept on being ill and then I started to shiver, because the bathroom was colder'n Croesus. I started to shiver and I couldn't stop and it was a toss-up between shivering and dry-retching. I didn't have the strength to crawl back to bed. I huddled weakly against the toilet seat.

My eyes had just become accustomed to the dark when I caught a glimpse of light over my shoulder. I groaned at the humiliation of having the major find me in such a condition. I groaned and my teeth chattered and I retched futilely.

"God, what next?" I heard him say as he paused on the threshold. I felt his warm hand on my forehead, the skin rough with the uneven scar tissue.

"You're freezing."

I chattered back at him.

"Through being ill?"

I nodded, swallowing against the reflexive spasm that seized my diaphragm. He took my hand in his and drew me to my feet. His wool bathrobe was warm under my hands. He slipped an arm under my knees and picked me up. He also cracked my head against the door frame as he maneuvered me out.

"For the love of webfooted friends in the forest," I complained. His hands tightened spasmodically on my knees and shoulder. It was another of my father's favorites.

Laird was more careful angling me into my room, but he stopped half-way in. I was shivering uncontrollably now, grabbing tightly at his neck and arm to still the shakes.

"Colder'n hell in here," he muttered and backed out.

Downstairs, through the dining room, out into the corridor he carried me, kicking open a door into what had been the original house. The room was about twenty feet square, narrow windows high in the walls just under the ceiling. A huge fireplace, its coals banked for the night, radiated tremendous warmth. As the major lowered me to the studio couch, I had a revolving impression of the doors and bookshelves and Merlin sniffing around the room.

The major covered me tightly with the blankets, holding them down against my shaking body.

"Chilled riding that goddamfool baggage car with your overgrown wolf. Made a pig of yourself with stew so what else can you expect from a half-well organism like your body," he muttered.

I tried to will myself to relax to the warmth that surrounded me. He pressed the covers more tightly to me. Then, with the queer whistle he could make without compressing his lips, he ordered Merlin up beside me. In the variable light from the dying fire his face assumed satanic qualities, the flames alternately flaring to illumine the scarred surface, then dying to cast it completely in shadow.

With a snort of impatience he turned to the fireplace. He came back with a shot glass full of liquor.

"If you haven't started drinking, you're about to learn at the insistence of your guardian." He held the glass against my lower lip and tilted it deftly, so that despite my chattering the fluid got into my mouth. I gulped it down, grateful for the burning stuff although I'm not fond of Scotch. It always tastes to me the way ants smell . . . formic acidy.

"It's a dog's dose," he remarked, "but I've got to warm you up. You're so thin you'll break bones shaking like that."

He poured another stiff drink, and disregarding my weak protest, propped my head in the crook of his arm and kept forcing the Scotch down my throat.

By the third shot I couldn't focus and I didn't bother to resist. But the shivering had stopped and I felt exceedingly warm and cozy. I was also sure that there was, somehow or other, a coating of ice, smooth and unbreakable, over my entire body. I told him so. I suggested that he stand me upright in the fireplace. If I put my head in the chimney I'd fit and then the ice would melt before I could get burned.

I remember he had a very pleasant laugh which was the first pleasant thing I had noticed about him. I told him so and was rewarded by another laugh. Something caught me by the back of the neck in one convulsing jerk and I remember that he held me against him and patted my head gently. He talked about a girl who had a curl in the middle of her forehead. I felt insulted enough to point out that I had too damned many curls all over my head and he was welcome to all he wanted to help hide his scar. I remember his hand over my mouth and that I was very very warm and very very sleepy.

Something heavy lay across my chest and my right arm was asleep. I woke up. I must not have been completely sober at that point because I looked down, quite calmly, at the major's arm across my breasts. It didn't seem at all improper that I was in the same bed with him because I was warm. This had been terribly important some long past time ago.

A kerosene lamp, flickering as the wick used up the last of the fuel in the well, gave a feeble light from the shelf over our heads. The major's pajama sleeve had slid up and I could see the terrible gashes, rawly red, where shrapnel had sliced through the fleshy part of the arm. Yet his hand was long-fingered, well shaped, and strong, the nails flat, deep, and well kept. My father had always watched a man's hands as he saluted or shook, not the face. Dad always maintained he could separate men into categories by the shape and care they took of their hands.

Regan Laird would surely have passed that test with honors. So his face didn't matter and the surgeons would work their minor miracles and put him back together again. In repose his right profile lost some of the distortion it had in waking. The eye did not seem so drawn nor the grin such a travesty. He had lost half his right eyebrow, which gave him a curiously bald look. The scar tissue extended up into the hair-line but his thick black hair had been carefully cut to hide most of it. The worst furrows of keloidal tissue stretched across the cheekbone down to the jawline. I remember my father men-tioning how Regan took care of the petticoat problems in the regiment. An ambiguous statement. Now I had seen the major's good side, I imagined all manner of interpretations.

Scarred or not, Regan Laird was *muy hombre* as old Turtle Bailey would have said in that gravel-pit voice of his. So different, I sighed to myself, from what infested the campus. Irresistibly tempted, I carefully twitched a long piece of hair away before it ticked his nose and roused him. His hair was unexpectedly fine and silky under my fingers and, feeling foolish, I stroked his hair back over the scar. He moved and, startled, I withdrew my hand. But I didn't remove the arm he had thrown across me. Big warm heavy Merlin was firmly planted along my left side so I was wedged between two male bodies. Would Merlin constitute a chaperon in Mrs. Grundy's eyes, I wondered?

The kerosene lamp flickered and went out. The quiet hiss of the fire lulled me. Warm and feeling safe for the first time since Dad had shipped out three years before, I slept.

A loud crack-pop woke me. A log had split on the fire. I looked around, startled to find neither the major nor Merlin in the room. The kerosene lamp, filled and trimmed, burned brightly on the shelf. Gray light filtered in from the high win-dows, the gray light of a stormy day, not early morning.

I was warm but the memory of last night's chill had not receded far enough for me to want to rise from the comfort of the bed. I heard Merlin's nails clicking. I heard a door open to the accompaniment of Merlin's glad barking. I pictured him outside, trying to bite snowflakes, leaping and twisting his big frame in an awkward return to puppyhood. I imagined him sniffcasing the yard, leaving "sign" on every likely bush and stone.

The door to the back hall opened, letting in a billow of frigid air. The major entered, his hands occupied with a tray, adroitly kicking the door closed with a deft foot.

"Is there anything that dog doesn't know about you?"

"Hmmm?"

"He's been sitting in front of the door for the last hour," the major explained as I struggled to a sitting position so he could put the tray on my lap.

"Tea?" I cried in horror.

"Better for your stomach after last night. Yes, Merlin told me in plain language you were awake. He considered he could be relieved of sentry duty and he wanted out."

I grinned at the major.

"Dad always said Merlin had more sense than most sergeants even if he didn't take to K-9 training."

The major raised his left eyebrow questioningly. The right one did not move. His face, plainly visible in the daylight, did not seem so grotesque. I suppose you can get used to anything to the point where you don't even see it.

"Yes," I went on, stirring plenty of sugar in the tea to take the curse off it, "Merlin chickened out of K-9 training. He wouldn't attack."

"'Damn all sugar in our tea?'" the major asked, pointedly watching the teaspoonfuls I ladled into the cup. "So they discharged him, huh?"

"Yes, insufficiently aggressive for active duty was the euphemism. Dad said the dog had too much sense to attack a stuffed dummy that hadn't done anything. Merlin is fast enough if a live'un raises a gun, though."

Major Laird snorted sympathy for the fine distinction.

"I might not believe you if I hadn't seen his performance this morning. But I do. I'm sure I'll agree more as our acquaintance deepens. But the dog must have complicated your life no end. No, eat all of it!"

"I don't like eggs in the morning," I said enunciating clearly. "Particularly soft-boiled eggs."

"I don't care what you don't like. This diet is designed to reintroduce your stomach to solids. I've a suspicion you've ignored all basic convalescent rules or you wouldn't have got so ill last night."

"Your cooking!"

"My cooking my . . . sainted aunt," he replied, frowning as I laughed over his hurried substitution of a politer phrase. But his face told me he would shove the eggs down my throat if I demurred so I gagged the mixture down, hoping it would regurgitate and annoyed because it tasted surprisingly good.

"I had quite a row with the college about Merlin," I remarked, picking up the original subject. "That's why I ended up at a boardinghouse instead of a dorm. And I had a helluva time finding—"

"You don't need to swear."

"If I feel like it, I will—a house that would accept him." I chuckled smugly. "When I was sick, Mrs. Everett was very glad he was in her house. Someone tried to burgle it twice. Merlin nearly broke the window in my room when the thief tried to get in from the roof."

The major looked at me sharply, frowning, "Into *your* room?"

"Eyah. My room gives onto the back porch roof."

The Major's frown deepened, on the left side, that is. "I gather Merlin dissuaded him thoroughly?"

I grimaced. "No. He got away. Now if Mrs. Everett had had the sense God gave little apples, she'd have let Merlin loose and told him to go get the man. But," and I shrugged philosophically, "she didn't and he escaped."

The major was thoughtful as he refilled my cup.

"I don't want any more."

"Immaterial. You need fluids. You're dehydrated. Stir hard. I don't mind the noise and you've two months' rations on the bottom of the cup."

"I am not dehydrated."

"Want a mirror?"

I closed my mouth with a snap and sullenly spooned more sugar in the cup, stirring with as much noise as I could make.

"Bathroom's down the corridor," the major said, throwing a heavy wool bathrobe on the bed. "You'd better stay here today. I can keep it warmer."

"But . . . I thought . . ."

"Blizzard!" and he took the tray back to the kitchen.

Snowbound with the major. How romantic! I thought acidly.

By the time I finished the second mug of oversweet tea, common sense had asserted itself. I knew that I had been outflanked and outranked and it didn't happen often enough to sit well. But I would snitch some coffee. Him and his tea! No one as thoroughly indoctrinated in army ways as I was could consider starting a day without coffee. I slid down under the covers again, gathering warmth for what was surely going to be a cold dash for a freezing bathroom.

The corridor was really frigid but not the bathroom. It backed against the kitchen and a vent from the stove kept the room, probably converted from an old shed, luxuriously warm. A huge raised tub, pull-chain toilet, and ornate lavatory indicated that someone in the Victorian era had preferred not to brave the rigors of Cape Cod winters for trips to the outhouse. I was deeply grateful. And *mirabile dictu!* hot water steamed out of the spigot. I jerked my hand back in time to avoid being scalded. I'd have preferred a bath but, in view of my weakened condition and the chilly corridor back to the warm study, decided against it. It was morally comforting to know the facilities existed.

A mirror, badly in need of resilvering, told me I was no Cinderella. As a matter of fact, I wouldn't have made it as Apple Witch. My eyes were dark holes in my face, my cheeks drawn and gaunt. Perhaps it was the effect of the shot-silver. I'd never looked that desiccated before!

Men's toiletries took up the small shelf above the sink. I made bold to pull the major's comb through the tangle of my hair. Great wads pulled loose as they had ever since my fever. I'd be bald, I was sure, despite the doctor's reassurance that there would be new growth coming in. All fringe benefits of the high fever. Maybe my hair would grow back in straight, I mused hopefully, and pulled at a curl experimentally. It flopped back into place with disgusting resilience. I made a face at my reflection which was almost an improvement. Why did my lipstick have to be up under my bed? I needed all the color I could get.

When I opened the bathroom door, a smell of coffee wafted up the corridor. I could go back to the study by way of the kitchen. I had been a good girl and I had kept my eggs down. Maybe I could have coffee as a reward.

A muted thudding caught my attention and I ducked back to the window, parting the blind. The major, bundled up in a bright hunting coat, was right outside splitting kindling. He threw a piece out towards the scrub bushes for Merlin to retrieve. The major's good profile was towards me and I could see his grin, the flash of his even teeth as he watched my idiot dog romping. Given half a chance by people who are not cowed by his size and apparent ferocity, Merlin was as agreeable a companion as you'd want. The major was not the least intimidated and Merlin was taking full advantage of the relaxed atmosphere.

I thought of Mrs. Everett who never quite trusted him in the same room with her. Merlin was always the gentleman in her house, instinctively aware of her anxiety. On campus he knew which of my classes he could sneak into, lying quietly under my chair. He also knew which lecture halls to avoid completely, returning after the hour was up to escort me home or to the next class. He had become, very shortly, as much a campus feature as the two legitimate seeing-eye dogs. He ignored them studiously. They were working.

Of course, Mrs. Everett's attitude had changed after Merlin had routed the prowler. She had even unbent enough to pat his head tentatively as she accompanied me to the taxi the day before. Day before! It seemed like years ago. Time had been suspended during that incredible train ride and that ageless drive in the jeep.

"You will be coming back, won't you, dearie?" Mrs. Everett had asked anxiously through the taxi window.

I had roomed with her for two years, summer and winter. She had been kind and comforting when she discovered my lack of family. I would always remember the terrible stricken look on her face when she brought me the telegram informing me of

Dad's death. She had known instinctively what news that telegram contained. She'd had one herself for her navy son. She and Mr. Everett had done more than true relatives would have for their "poor orphaned lamb." Kay Alexander who roomed down the hall told me that's what the Everetts called me.

I was not above milking such reactions. To tell the truth, kindly boardinghouse ladies had been mother surrogates since my own had died when I was five. What none of them would admit was that I was perfectly capable of taking care of myself. Dad had seen to that. However, when I occasionally needed a female ally against some of Dad's purely masculine directives, I was bald-faced enough to use any nearby sympathetic soul to achieve the ends in mind: dating, long dresses, less childish clothes, more spending money, dancing lessons, and the rest of these absolutely essential items an army colonel could not have imagined. Consequently I had a handpicked string of courtesy aunts and uncles all over the country. There were few cities near large army installations in the United States and its territories where I could not find a roof to shelter me off base. And Dad had to name Laird my guardian!

But those people had only been buffers against Dad's idiosyncracies. He had always been there, somewhere, on maneuvers, on duty, but there. Alive. Now I was really on my own, despite the legal farce of Major Regan Laird.

I wondered how old the major was. The war had graven such terrible marks on him it was impossible to guess accurately. Late thirties? Perhaps. Old!

I heard him pounding snow off his boots on the back porch and I cleaned my hair from his comb, putting it back precisely in the military brush from which I had filched it.

I scampered down the hall, to the kitchen, hoping to snag some coffee before he reentered. He had come straight to the stove with his armload of kindling.

"Close the damn hall door, girl," he ordered as I stood there, thwarted. I slammed the door and stayed firm. He might leave.

He dumped his burden into the woodbox and poked several sticks into the stove. He glanced up and caught me staring at the coffeepot. He grinned.

"Stomach feel normal?"

I nodded.

"All right then. Fix me a cup, too. It's . . . hmmmm . . . it's cold out there and snowing again."

"Sorry to cramp your style," I remarked sweetly as I found cups in the cabinet beside the kitchen sink. I couldn't quite reach the shelf so I hoisted myself onto the counter. The major's long arm intercepted my grasp and I glared around at him.

"You are a little bit of a thing," he said, handing me the cups.

He looked at me as though seeing me clearly for the first time. He would pick right now when I looked ghastly. I tugged for him to release the cups to me. He held onto them, regarding me steadily. It was difficult for me, in returning his gaze, to resist the compulsion to drop my glance slightly to the furrows of his wounded cheek. He smiled, the smile echoing in his gray eyes.

"A little bit of a cocky thing," he repeated. He meant it, as Turtle Bailey, Dad's sergeant, always did, as a compliment.

He let go of the cups and, picking me up at the elbows, lifted me off the counter. "Next time, use the step stool by the door," he commented, nodding in its direction. "Like mine black and sweet."

"And we are grad-u-ally, fading away," I warbled as I poured the coffee.

Merlin, who had crawled under the table, flipped onto his side with a great groan, as if deploring my singing. He let out a huge sigh and fell asleep.

"Are we really snowbound?" I asked mischievously.

"Yes, indeed. We were damned lucky not to go off that road last night. Coast Guard had plowed, fortunately, right up to the final turnoff or I'd never have made it out. Damn train being late nearly sewed us up in town. There's only the one inn in Orleans." He reflected a moment. "Probably been better if we had stayed there though it's no Waldorf."

"You're a good guardian, protecting my virtue," I taunted him.

"Don't kid yourself about *that*," he snapped, annoyed by my flippancy.

"I can take care of myself," I lashed back. "I'm a colonel's daughter and the day I can't handle a mere major . . ."

He saw the humor in the situation quicker than I did and threw back his head to laugh. He sobered as quickly.

"All kidding aside, Carlysle . . ."

"Carla," I corrected him automatically.

"I'm too used to thinking of you as 'Carlysle' and male to change both at once . . . All kidding aside, it'd be better for you not to stay on here any longer than the storm."

I got the feeling then that it was not the proprieties that worried him. I couldn't imagine what did. Then he confirmed a nagging doubt I'd had.

"You said there were two attempts to enter your rooming house? Was it the first or second time that Merlin interfered?"

"The second. Why do you ask?"

"Oh, nothing."

"That's the kind of nothing that's something," I replied with exasperation.

He raised an eyebrow but made no explanation.

"Did you bring everything you own with you?" he asked, nodding towards the corridor where my other suitcases still lay. "Or did you leave things with Mrs. Everett?"

"I left all my college books." I grimaced sullenly. "And my summer clothes are stored in a trunk in her cellar."

"You'll be back in the summer and you'll make up this term. For Christ's sake, the dean was justified," he exploded as I turned obdurately sulky over that hotly contested decision. "You're nothing but skin and bones. Worn out. Mentally, too, I'll wager. Book fatigue, nothing more. Tired minds make mistakes and risk lives."

"I'm not in a position to risk lives," I replied angrily.

"No, you're risking more. Your education and your future."

"You know so much about it?"

He glared back at me, refusing to budge an inch. "In that letter, your dean—"

"Oh? Really, and you never tumbled from her letterhead that I was at Radcliffe, not Harvard . . . ." I sneered.

"I thought it was a wartime exigency. So many professors drafted, the Radcliffe faculty pitching in to fill the gaps . . . ."

"A likely tale. You didn't want me to be female any more than my father did."

"Damn well told," he shouted, his carefully contained temper erupting, "and it'd be a piece of infantile foolishness for you to jeopardize a dean's list record with your bullheadedness."

The fact that he was absolutely right and rational only infuriated me more. The decision had been forced on me and I resented coercion bitterly.

"You'll obey me in this, young lady. Legally I'm your guardian, and I'll decide what's right for you when you're too stubborn blind stupid to see the forest for the trees. You'll take this term off if I have to lock you up."

"I'm not in the goddamned army," I yelled, jumping to my feet.

"Too damned bad you're not. You'd've learned to obey if you were!"

There we were, both on our feet, glaring at each other, our faces inches apart. The tension reached Merlin's sleeping senses and he barked sharply twice. That brought us to our senses. I blinked at the major's angry face, the cords of his neck taut and the ridges of the keloidal tissue red and angry-looking.

I was instantly heartily ashamed at my outburst. He was assuming a disagreeable responsibility and I was being a silly little fool not to make things as easy as possible for him. I sat down abruptly, stirring my coffee vigorously.

"I'm sorry," I said, sincerely contrite. "I am behaving childishly. I'm being unfair to you. You're right. I am worn out. I'll behave."

He remained standing for a moment so I couldn't see his face. He sat down slowly. His unscarred left hand covered mine with a brief reassuring squeeze.

"I'll make an arrangement for you in town and then you'd better go back to the Everetts after I leave."

I looked at him stupidly. "After you leave?"

"I'm to report to Walter Reed in a few weeks," he said tonelessly. In spite of myself my eyes went to his scarred face. He returned my startled look expressionlessly.

"But I could stay here then."

He shook his head violently, frowning savagely.

"You can't stay here alone."

"Why not?" I insisted. "Merlin won't let anyone he doesn't know . . . ."

Major Laird closed his mouth with a snap.

"You said . . ." and he leaned forward to me, angry again, "you said you'd behave. Just leave it that I have good and sufficient reason for wanting you . . . in . . . town." He hesitated just enough to clue me he was evading. He knew I caught it but refused to give me the satisfaction of a direct answer or an explanation. I was forced to bide by my agreement to behave.

I swallowed my hasty words. I wanted to say that I was well able to take care of myself. He'd've tossed them back to me.

"How long will you be gone?" I asked instead.

He shook his head, a curt negative. I couldn't see why he wouldn't welcome the plastic surgery which surely must be the reason for his hospitalization. He couldn't like looking this way. Why else had he come to such a remote place as this? He had been a very handsome man before his injury. Vanity, self-respect alone — unless his personality had unexpectedly warped — would demand that he take advantage of a facial restoration. It was incomprehensible why he was reluctant to go to Walter Reed. I wondered if he just didn't want to leave Pull-in Point.

"When the snow stops," he said heavily, "I'll make arrangements for you in town. Or maybe over in Chatham." He gave a short mirthless laugh. "They have a movie house. Runs a show every weekend."

"And church bingo on Thursdays. Big deal!"

We finished our coffee in strained silence. The cold of the house was suddenly more preferable. I jumped to my feet, trying to act normal, and walked with unnaturally stiff legs to rinse my cup in the sink.

"I'll get dressed and wash these up," I said in a falsely bright voice as I added the mug to the stacks on the drainboard.

"I'd appreciate it," and his voice had a rueful sound. "It's rather . . . ahem . . . beneath the dignity of a major," he mocked his rank in an effort to lighten the atmosphere of the room, "to do KP."

I gave him a grin that was not too off-center normal and plunged out into the cold hall.

# 🍎 3

THE MAJOR had stoked up the fire in my bedroom so it was warm enough to dress. I dug out army issue longjohns and officer pinks I had had tailored for me when Dad got new uniforms just before going overseas. I forced myself not to dwell on that inadvertent association. I pulled on a green long-sleeved sweater and then a gray sweatshirt. It was too cold to be feminine. I dug out heavy socks and the mukluks Dad sent from his Alaskan inspection trip. I even had a fur parka from that jaunt, exceedingly practical for crossing frigid Cambridge common.

I set up the pictures of Dad and Mother and a couple of little mementos I always carry with me to make hotel and boarding rooms *mine* no matter how short a time I inhabited them. Dad, in an expansive mood, used to call me "Pussy" because I was able to make myself at home the minute I entered a new place. Turtle had taught me that flexibility and I was overwhelmed with a desire to see that old reprobate. Because he was part and parcel of my life with Dad, I crowded down that longing. Turtle was overseas anyway. I wouldn't see him till after the war. If he survived this one.

Such gloomy thoughts were disastrous and I hastily scrambled under the bed for the clothes I had thrown there last night. I made the bed and, slamming the cover down on my suitcase, felt free to leave.

I decided to do a reconnaissance of the upper floor as an antidote to my nostalgia. The first door on the right opened into another period-perfect room, dominated by a spindle four-poster bed complete with muslin canopy. I'd've moved my things right in if my relations with the major had been better. I'd wanted a four-poster canopy bed since I was a little girl.

There'd been one in a boardinghouse near Benning. I'd thought the canopy was to keep dreams in and obviously the bed was fit for a princess. For months afterwards I'd plagued Dad to get me a "princess bed." Mother'd squashed that notion the first and every time I brought it up. She hated living on post and avoided it by not having any furnishings at all. We'd always lived in boardinghouses off base. There were advantages. Army wives used to say they never made a move without losing the one valuable piece they owned or having their best china pulverized. Misdirected personal belongings were standard operating procedure so you were better off carrying what you owned with you, whenever possible.

Mother invariably managed to find temporary quarters which included my care. As a small child, I'd adored my mother — but always at a distance that wouldn't muss her dress or smudge her makeup. Now I see her as a frivolous woman, unsuited for motherhood, and selfish. I never let my father know I had overheard the gossip that mother had been killed on her way to meet another man. It had made me love my father more, excuse him his tempers and his eccentricities. Perhaps if he had loved the army less, he would have kept his wife. There I was again, reminiscing.

I closed that door and went on, looking in briefly at the bathroom. It was larger than a conventional one, so I assumed it had been added much later in the house's life. It might have originally been a nursery or a sewing room but it made a most luxurious bathroom.

The first room in the rear of the house was a catchall; cedar chests and a wardrobe I didn't investigate. I was turning to go when I saw the army footlockers. There were three, one on top of the other. The camouflaged paint pattern on one of them was strangely familiar. I walked over. The middle one. The old stenciling had been masked out with a smear of army green and the new legend gave Major Regan Laird's name, serial number, and this address. The other two were newer and obviously his but I could have sworn the middle one was my father's.

Only one small box, tucked right now in the outside pocket of my bomber bag downstairs, had come back to me, containing his most personal effects. I had assumed Turtle disposed of the uniforms and clothing. I certainly didn't want to see them again. I'd better ask the major though. There were some things of Dad's, his stamps, for instance, that had not come back yet. I'd been too ill when the first package came to pursue the matter. The major would know. I'd ask him.

There were two other bedrooms on the floor, frigid but furnished, dusty with long disuse. In the front bedroom I paused to look out the window, over the frozen drifts to the gun-green sea tossing whitecaps beyond the protecting dunes of Nauset strand. The poles of a small wharf stuck up through the snow across the way so there must be a navigable cove for the neighbors further down the Point.

A movement, barely discernible through the veil of falling snow, caught my eye. I peered out but the angle was wrong and I couldn't see far enough on the road to distinguish man, beast, or car. Just then Merlin barked.

I raced around the hall and thundered down the stairs, skidding on the bare treads in the slick-soled mukluks. Between my noise and Merlin's, the major came whipping out of the study. Merlin, tail a-wag, came bounding in from the kitchen and propped his front feet on the windowsill, craning his head, barking furiously.

"Whoever it is, Merlin knows him," I said in surprise, pointing to Merlin's lashing tail.

The major, his face anxious, leaned around Merlin's head to squint through the shifting snow.

"Whoever it is is coming here," I exclaimed.

"You must be mistaken," he said, half in anger.

"I'm not mistaken and furthermore, it's an infantryman. You can't mistake that gait," I asserted, peering through the window beside him.

The figure swung clumsy arms up and down to warm himself as he trudged head down against the swirling snow. Suddenly the angle of the head, the attitude of the whole figure were incredibly familiar. Merlin barked twice, his voice carrying through the walls into the air outside. The man stopped, looked up at the house.

I dashed for the front door, flinging it open, heedless of the snow blown in on the freezing wind.

"Turtle! In here! On the double!" I shrieked.

"Gawd, that can't be Little Bit!" Waving an arm in violent greeting, Turtle lumbered forward, floundering in the drifts, half staggering, half slipping up the incline. I would have leaped out to help him but the major grabbed my arm. Merlin leaped into the snow, raucously welcoming Sergeant Edward Turtle Bailey. I wrenched myself free of the major's grip as Turtle waddled up to the door. Flinging myself at him, I was suddenly choking on tears of relief and nostalgia. The old familiar Turtle Bailey, so constantly my father's companion, brought home at last the fact that Dad would not return from this tour of duty.

Instead of me ushering Turtle in, it was Turtle and the major carrying a hysterical me back to the fire.

"He's gone, Turtle! He's gone! He said he'd always come back and he won't! He's not going to come back this time," I wailed.

"Yessir, Bit, I know," Turtle's gravelly voice muttered, roughened by the tears that coursed down his own stubbly cheeks. He looked gray and stricken and every year of his age. The major must have taken off his overcoat because the fruit salad on Turtle's chest scratched my face as I abandoned myself to grief.

"He's not coming back! He bought it! He bought it," I cried.

"Honest, sir, this isn't like her. She was always the soldier, a regular little bit of a soldier. Even when her mother died."

Turtle's huge hands held me with great tenderness. He dabbed at my streaming cheeks with a khaki handkerchief, then blotted his own brimming eyes.

"She's been rather sick," the major murmured understandingly.

That made me blubber worse. It was all too true. Maybe that's why I broke up so completely, seeing Turtle. Dad had been out on summer war games in the wilds of southern Jersey when mother had been killed in a car accident. We'd been based at Dix. Turtle had been in the O.D.'s office on some errand from the games when the local police had called in to report the accident. It had been Turtle who had called me from a sand fight, I remember that very well, to tell me about my mother. At five, I hadn't fully understood what he had tried to explain. So naturally I hadn't cried. Now I did. Perhaps I cried for my mother, too.

"C'mon now, Bit. This ain't like you," Turtle growled. "Sick er not."

"Give her this," I heard the major say.

"Knock it back the way I taughtcha," Turtle ordered, handing me the shot glass.

Still boohooing, I looked first at the resolute major and then at an equally determined Turtle. The Scotch did the trick because I had to stop sobbing or choke. Once I could stop crying, I was thoroughly ashamed of myself. But, honestly, it was Turtle who touched it off. Certainly I'd prefer not to blubber in front of the major, my guardian, Regan Laird.

"Oh, Turtle! I'm so liquid. Major, give him a shot, too. He must be frozen. Don't tell me you slogged it all the way from the station?" I demanded, fussing in my turn over the sergeant. I pushed him into the leather chair by the fire, handed him the drink the major poured, and then started to strip off his combat boots, soaking despite their waterproofing.

"Major don't have no phone. Only a couple of miles. No great thing," Turtle grated out in that marvelous-to-hear, indescribable broken voice of his.

A flood of memories, held back because up to now I had carefully avoided associations that would remind me of those times, came charging back. But this time I controlled myself.

"Hey, Bit, y'ain't waiting on me!" Turtle bellowed, batting halfheartedly at my hands as I unlaced his boots. I knew, despite his show of embarrassment, he was pleased. I'd done it before.

"And why not? Your fingers are too cold to do it and if you don't get these wet things off, you'll get pee-new-monia."

"*Me!*" roared Turtle, indignant at the mere suggestion of such frailty. "Not on your _____ life."

"Sergeant!" The major's voice crackled.

"Leave him be." I grinned up at Turtle. "The sergeant's not himself without four-letter words. However, to ease your guardian conscience, the one and only time I mimicked him, he soaped my mouth out with army issue." I shuddered at the memory of that taste.

"That's right, Major, begging your pardon," Turtle put in, mindful that the major's one word had been tantamount to a direct order.

"At ease," the major said, mollified.

I bridled at such offhanded assumption of complete authority over *my* Turtle Bailey. United States Army notwithstanding, my claim on Turtle predated the major's. Turtle grinned at my bristling defense and laid a soothing hand on my shoulder. Another thought struck me and I stared at Turtle, torn between surprise and irritation.

"Turtle, why in God's green world didn't you tell Major Laird that James Carlysle Murdock is a girl?"

"Huh?" Turtle was so astonished I knew he couldn't be acting. I'd seen him pull incredible performances on visiting generals and colonel's wives. But he was not shamming now. "Didn't he know?"

I rocked back on my heels as the second boot suddenly released its watery grip on Turtle's foot.

"No, he didn't," I said with a sideways glance at the major as I propped up the soaking footgear by the fireplace.

"Bailey didn't know your father had appointed me your guardian either," Laird put in, absolving Turtle of all guilt. It also left me unable to pass the buck. "I was wounded not long after your father . . . died, you know. Between his death and the push towards Jülich, there wasn't much time for talk."

It was then I noticed the purple heart bar among the stuff on Turtle's barrel chest. I stared, grabbing the sergeant's arm, and pointed to it.

"Turtle, where?" I gasped.

"Huh? Aw, knock it off, Bit," Turtle growled. "I only took it fer points. I wanted out."

I shook his arm because I didn't believe for a moment that was the reason. It was then I began to wonder. What on earth was Turtle doing looking up a major on a stormy day at the elbow of Cape Cod? Furthermore they were both looking awfully ill at ease. Which had nothing to do with a silly girl's tears. They were hiding something from me. In that moment I began to feel the first tendrils of an honest fear. Merlin picked up my embryonic apprehension and growled softly in his throat. He's uncanny in his ability to sense mood shifts and not just in me. His soft growl intensified my uneasiness. The dog and I exchanged glances just as the major and Turtle did.

"I didn't know you'd copped it," Laird remarked. He proffered cigarettes but Turtle shook his head, reaching into his breast pocket for the ghastly Fatimas he preferred. His battered face broke into a grin as he pointed to his ear. I saw then that the tip of his ear was missing as well as the first joint of his index finger on the left hand, the stump barely healed.

"Goddamnedest fool _____ piece of luck. We mopped up at Jülich after you got hit, Major. Then hooked up with the Hundred and Sixteenth because the krauts had shot the hell out of the unit in those _____ _____ _____ beetfields. You know some rear echelon fart named Warren a light colonel after you got clobbered?"

The major nodded solemnly, his jaw muscles working.

"Jeeze, Bit, I thought the general had that _____ pegged for what he was," Turtle hissed at me through his teeth. " _____ rear echelon—"

"Knock it off!" the major ordered curtly, his eyes flashing.

Turtle was not going to be intimidated by any rank lower than four stars and he was only polite then.

"Wal," he continued blandly, "we were knocking the _____ out of a block in Jülich. Snipers on the roof, in the cellar, you know the drill. I was waving the squad up," he demonstrated, "when some _____ sniper winged me. Got the BAR man behind me though, right through the eye."

"You mean, you . . ." I gasped, utterly unable to believe the indestructible Bailey pulled a blighty for an earlobe and a finger joint.

" _____ no!" Turtle exploded indignantly. "I didn't even report it till I got the major's letter. Then I hunted up the medic and took my points."

"What letter?" I asked suspiciously.

"The letter that the major was invalided stateside." Turtle was evading now and he knew I knew it even if the major didn't.

Obviously I wouldn't get Turtle to come clean with the major hanging on every word. Whatever was going on between those two did concern me. Of that much I was sure. How, why, I hadn't an inkling but I wasn't going to leave this house until I found out. I had the feeling it also concerned Dad. But, if Dad were involved and he had never been anything but a *good* soldier, why wouldn't Turtle level with me? Unless, of course, the major had antiquated ideas about helpless females or me blabbing about company business.

"Well," I said rising abruptly, "with *two* guardians, one of them totally above reproach, I can stay on here."

"*No!*" they chorused explosively.

"Now you two knock it off. I don't know what gives between you but I want you to know, you're not fooling me for one split second."

"This isn't a woman's concern," Laird answered hotly, the ridges of his scars reddening.

"Women. Ha! Have you men done so well with the world?" I asked with fine scorn. I turned on Turtle who had the grace to look abashed. "I'll bet *you* never even stopped to eat in town," I accused him. Turtle shook his head in quick affirmation.

"Well, I'll fix you something to eat," I offered grudgingly. "Get some clean socks from the major. You both appear to wear the same size shoe when your feet aren't in your mouths." I flounced out of the room, slamming the door with a satisfactorily resounding crash.

I'd get it out of Turtle in my own way and the hell with the major. I poked unnecessary wood in the range, burning my finger on the hot plate-iron top. With more caution, I pulled the coffeepot onto a front ring and hunted in the icebox for the Dutch kettle. I knew we hadn't consumed all the stew last night. Turtle was very partial to stew. The idea of Turtle trying to put one over on me, I muttered to myself.

The stew was not, absolutely not, in the refrigerator. Congealed messes, improperly covered, and some partially molded over, two bunches of good carrots and four limp stalks of celery, a half-gallon metal can of milk almost full, a huge wheel of butter, a bowl of eggs, a slab of bacon, and an indecent quantity of beer completed the inventory of the box, but no stew.

"If I were stew, where would I go?" I asked myself à la Stanislavsky.

Merlin whined at the back porch door. I guessed that the men had let him out the study door. Exasperated, I let him in.

Now I can't say he overheard me muttering, but as I opened the door I caught sight of the iron kettle perched on the shelving on the back porch. I peered inside and the contents were frozen solid. Naturally, important things like beer should be kept at a proper degree of refrigeration, I muttered to myself, whereas relatively unimportant items like a meat stew, not to mention the chickens I had also observed in cold storage and the hunk of meat, would be left to their own devices against the weather. First things first.

By the time I had washed up the backlog of dishes, the stew had thawed and was simmering. There was more than enough for all three of us to eat our fill. The major's culinary skill seemed limited to making up quantities of one thing that would last for days. That might be all right for him, himself alone, but not this li'l chile.

I gave a chow yell and heard Turtle hop to with a "Yo." He padded down the corridor in, I hoped, fresh-stockinged feet. I heard his oath as the steaming hot water in the bathroom sink caught him by surprise.

When he and the major entered the kitchen, they both had that look about them which meant they'd confirmed their idiotic boy scout pact. They made a determined effort to fore-stall any reopening of the subject while I was equally deter-mined to ignore the whole ploy.

I served Turtle first, grinning at the gusto with which he attacked the meal.

"Major," he said around a generous mouthful of meat and potato, "you make the best goddam stew this side of the Divide. That includes . . . hmmmmah . . . all Europe." He pointed his fork at me, waving the potato speared on it like a baton. "Bit, you shoulda tasted the rabbit stew the major scrounged up near Montcornet." (He mutilated the French pronunciation.) "Jeezuz but that tasted good." He smacked his lips retrospectively. "Marty got the rabbit. Big bastards over there, they are."

"Was it Landrel or the Bum who liberated the vegetables?" the major asked, grinning.

"The Bum," and the curt way Turtle answered indicated both men were now dead.

"That one could scrounge from St. Peter," was the major's admiring accolade. Turtle nodded his head, his mouth too full to speak.

"Bosworth swapped K rations for some vin ordinaire as I recall," and there was nothing wrong with the major's accent. Regan Laird took up the tale, "and M. LeMaitre loaned us a pot . . . against his wife's better judgement."

Gravy spilled out of the corners of Turtle's mouth as he grinned at the memory. He caught the gravy deftly with a hunk of bread, then popped bread and all in his mouth, licking his fingers.

"And then," Turtle shook with malicious mirth, "the mutts in the village cornered Warren and he never did get anything to eat. Then he tried to get the colonel to give us hell because we weren't supposed to be bivouacking *in* the village, annoying," Turtle snorted with contempt, "annoying the inhabitants. Annoying? Hell, they adopted us!"

Mention of Warren was sobering. It improved my opinion of the major that he shared our dislike of Major . . . no, damn it, Colonel Donald Warren.

I had always hated Warren myself. No one ever succeeded in convincing me that he hadn't poisoned Merlin's litter brothers. He was irrationally frightened of dogs, any dog, down to and including a Chihuahua. And I knew for certain he had been instrumental in putting away Morgan le Fay, Merlin's dam. Warren could swear and allege all he wanted to but I'd never believed Morgan had bitten him. She had more sense. *She'd've* got blood poisoning. Dad had been off post at the time and, because Marian Warren was toadying up to the C.O.'s wife, neither Turtle, I, nor the Downingtons, who owned Morgan, could change the edict.

It infuriated me that Warren had assumed Dad's command, however briefly, after Major Laird had been wounded. It was intolerably bitter to me that Donald Warren still walked the earth and my father was under it. War is not only hell, it is too damned indiscriminate in its victims.

"I always wanted to know, Bailey," the major was saying, his eyes twinkling, "if you and Casey had anything to do with the bedroll problem?"

"Bedroll . . . ." Turtle was seized with a violent paroxysm of choking, complicated by a fit of laughter that brought tears to his eyes.

"Bedroll?" I asked suspiciously.

Regan Laird's grin threatened to break open scar tissue. Chuckling, he managed to explain.

"Ah, Major Warren seemed to have trouble keeping his bedroll free of . . . ah . . . ."

"Messages?" I cried, delighted.

"Messages," Laird agreed. That set Turtle off again so I had to pound his shoulder blades before he choked to an untimely end. Laird managed to straighten his face before he continued. "DeLord was of the opinion the dogs homed in on him. That right, Bailey?"

Turtle choked again, turning bright red, and this time Major Laird swatted him smartly on the back. Turtle finally got his breath back, downing a full can of beer to set things right.

"That . . . DeLord," he gasped finally, belching noisily. "'Scuse it. That DeLord! I can't figure him."

"Why not? Damn good officer. Thought on his feet."

"Yeah. Well, guess who got mighty thick with Warren after you got clobbered?"

"Not DeLord?" The major frowned in surprise.

"Yeah, DeLord," Turtle confirmed sourly. "I never figgered he'd suck up to Warren after the colonel was . . . buried."

Turtle looked stricken. He swallowed furiously, glancing nervously at the major. The major stared back at him angrily, his eyes snapping, and awkward silence settled on the room. I still wasn't up to discussing Dad's death, particularly with Turtle. And obviously the subject was as painful to the sergeant as it was to me.

"Is that . . . Dad's footlocker upstairs?" I asked.

Both men turned sharply around to glare at me. The major recovered first.

"Yes it is, Carlysle," he said quietly. "I spotted it at Division HQ and had it sent on with mine. Some idiot painted my name over it. The key should have been sent back with the other personal effects."

"Yes. I have it with me," I admitted before I realized this was exactly the information he wanted.

"You'll want to go through it, to make sure everything's accounted for."

"Yes, I will. When it warms up upstairs."

"Sure," the major agreed easily. I didn't miss the looks they exchanged as I rose to clear the dishes.

"I need some sacktime, Major," Turtle announced, kicking back his chair. He caught it with an experienced hand before it clattered to the floor.

"Colder'n a . . . cold upstairs," the major corrected himself.

"Oh, Turtle can use my room for a while," I suggested. "It's warm in there and this kitchen is a positive disgrace . . . even for a KP-less major."

"Good," exclaimed the major, rising purposefully. "I'll build a fire now in the back bedroom. Take the chill off."

They stomped away, glad to be out of my company. Merlin trotted off with them, infected by my irritation with the male sex. He gave me a backward look, chastened and reproachful. I didn't call him back but I wasn't angry with *him*.

# 🍃 4

MY SCOTCH FORBEARS would have regarded my day's work with as much satisfaction as I did. I literally peeled accumulated scum off cabinets, walls, floors, pots, pans, cans, bottles, glasses. I cursed unknown predecessors for slovenly habits even as I ignored the plain fact that probably the house had been untenanted for several years. I knew that Regan Laird had not been back from Europe for very long but even he must have been aware the kitchen was incredibly dirty.

Mother Bailey, Turtle's mother, had always scrubbed, caroling a lusty revival hymn in time with her strokes. It had been part of her philosophy that singing hymns was prayerful and being prayerful made work go faster, combining two virtues at one and the same time, rewarding doubly. I had spent two years with her in West Roxbury just after Mother's death, until I was school age. I know those few years were my happiest although I missed Dad sorely. However, I had uncles and aunts and cousins and grandparents galore. Ma Bailey's favorite for floor scrubbing was "Rock of Ages" which could set the crockery rattling as her volume increased in direct proportion to the amount of mud and dirt on the floor. She had a fine resonant contralto and her one criticism of her religion was that the Catholics had few decent "tunes" for scrubbing. As a matter of fact, she confided in me shortly after I came to her that she had felt it on her conscience to be singing Protestant hymns and had taken the matter up with her parish priest. Looking back, I can see the humor of the situation and wonder how the priest had managed to control his mirth at such a question. Ma Bailey did receive the dispensation although she was scrupulous about choosing "nondenominational" anthems and avoiding any which mentioned the Trinity or the Virgin Mary. I might have turned Catholic in that household had I not heard how Turtle got his voice. Or rather, got the one he now used.

Despite all latrine gossip to the contrary, Master Sergeant Edward Bailey's voice was not the product of years of parade ground drilling nor was his undamnable flow of blasphemy the result of frustration with "stupid squads." Born in Boston just before the turn of the century, of poor but honest folk, young Edward Bailey had been a handsome lad, a devout Catholic and, as soon as he was old enough, an altar boy. The parish priest had noticed the lovely quality of young Ed's voice in the repetition of the responses. It became apparent by the time he was ten that he was possessed of a naturally sweet, true soprano. He was quickly exploited and became known throughout the Boston metropolitan area, singing at high masses, weddings, funerals, association meetings, and such, billed as Boston's McCormack, a true Irishman. A brilliant career was projected for him, including entrance to a fine Catholic high school and college.

One evening, on his way home from a music lesson, a bunch of roughs, out on the prowl for any Irishman they could "put in his place" (for those were the days of the terrible Irish pogroms in Boston) attacked him, beating him so severely about the face and throat that his voice box was smashed and his face so brutally mutilated he bore no resemblance to the old tintype his mother cherished of her Eddie.

For months after the incident he could barely talk. But his early vocal training gave him one advantage, he could force air from his diaphragm for a semblance of speech. Gradually he was able to use his vocal cords again but the glorious voice was gone. The Church, without noticeable regret, canceled the scholarships. At sixteen, a battered-faced, embittered boy had lied about his age and enlisted in time to fight in the first World War. He had wanted to die but fate had assigned him to my father's first command. A comradeship was established at that Plattsburg training camp which had lasted my father's lifetime and seemed to spill over to include me.

Child though I was when I heard that story, I knew who had hurt my Turtle Bailey the most and the Catholics lost me. Turtle was even then my special haven. As a matter of fact, I was responsible for the nickname. Somewhere, somewhen, a biblical phrase had been repeated in my hearing, the one about "and lo, the voice of the turtle was heard in the land." I'm told that I asked Sergeant Bailey if *he* had a turtle's voice and once the notion stuck in my mind, I never got rid of it.

Ma Bailey always claimed that one of the fringe benefits of floor scrubbing was solving problems. It only solved one of mine today, cleaning the floor. But I did cast the problems up and down, around and sideways, which could be considered the first step towards solving them. If you happened to be of an optimistic nature.

My first problem was staying on in this house. Then finding out what was going on between the major and the sergeant. Did it have to do with my father? And why? Did it have something to with the burglar? The footlocker?

The floor was drying. The walls and cabinets were sparklingly clean and everything within them. The rest of the house was too cold to assault with mop and pail except for the bathroom. So I launched a major offensive against it, whipping it into a sanitary state in next to no time. I came back to the nice clean kitchen and slumped down in a chair, to revive myself with coffee and mull over dinner. In Ma Bailey's lexicon, cleanliness was next to godliness but food was what a man wanted next to him. At least, that was the version I learned at six.

I brought the chickens in from the back porch, the poor things. I must tell the major, war or not, he was not to patronize again whoever sold him those birds. They'd obviously been running around since the last war. The only decent thing to be done with them was stew. As I recalled it, Turtle was partial to my dumplings. At the moment I had no desire to satisfy my guardian's preferences. Then, too, there was nothing like a full stomach to tempt a man to lose his discretion.

My years of boardinghouse living had had several hazards. One was that if the proprietress was widowed or single, she made a play for my father. This usually began with intense concern for the well-being of his daughter, with much discussion about my lack of feminine skills such as housekeeping, cooking, and sewing. I don't know whether I learned to cook in my self-defense or Father's but I also don't remember not knowing how to cook. Once each new aspirant discovered me versed in fundamentals, she would undertake to instruct me in fine points so I had acquired culinary arts above the ordinary. In fact, I earned all my spending money now cooking, with two regular dinner jobs a week and two lunchtime positions.

Even my skill was challenged by these fowl. Fortunately the larder was not bare of herbs, in fact, the inventory was extraordinary. The inequalities included five half-used boxes of paprika, nine thyme, three rosemary, but no marjoram. Lots of oregano, but no basil. Still I had enough of the right things. It looked to me as if the summer renters had always brought their own spices and then left them behind in the hectic windup of seasonal withdrawal.

I made a cake, reveling in the unusual amount of honest-to-gosh butter. As I slid the cake pans into the oven, I realized there was no heat gauge. The oversupply of wood I had petulantly rammed in had burned off and the oven innards did not seem overhot on my skin. If Grandma could do it, I could!

The cake rose and rose, unevenly to be sure, but it was a home-baked product and they could like it or lump it. I heard stamping on the back porch and when I peered out of the crystal-clear window, the major glanced at me questioningly. When I smiled, he pointed to the woodbox. I shook my head. He loaded up and I heard him crashing back in again, slamming the door to his study. Then the kitchen door opened.

"Have you . . . hey, what happened to the kitchen?" he asked, coming all the way in and looking around with a pleased smile.

"Where's your white glove?"

His grin broadened. "No need. I appreciate this, I really do. I've been trying to get a woman out here but no luck." He opened a cabinet and peered in. He whistled, his fingers absently stroking the now greaseless wood.

I held the coffeepot aloft suggestively. Just then he spotted the cake cooling on the table. There was a curious look on his face as he reached mechanically for a cup.

"Maybe I'm glad you're not James Carlysle," he said, looking down at me as I poured his coffee. A shadow of an odd expression flitted across his face.

"Oh, I've been promoted to human status?" I asked.

He lifted his mug in a toast. The lid of the Dutch kettle rattled, drawing his eyes from mine to the stove. He took a deep sniff.

"That mouth-watering aroma cannot possibly come from those desiccated carcasses in the hall?" he inquired.

I shrugged nonchalantly. "Naturally. Even retreads from the last war cannot daunt Chef Murdock."

He winced. "I know what you mean. And, at that, the farmer assured me it was a favor from one vet to another."

"Favors like that you don't need! Particularly in wartime."

He tilted the lid, breathing deeply.

"Ambrosial! You put my efforts to shame."

"You've merely lacked the touch of a woman about the house."

He straightened quickly, his face cold.

"I wouldn't be too sure of that," he said in a flat voice and turning on his heel went directly back to his study.

I stared after him, curiously sensitive to his rebuff. He hadn't mentioned a wife and he wore no ring. If he were married, it wouldn't have bothered him that I was unchaperoned. Surely he'd want his wife with him right now .. or maybe he wouldn't with his face like that. No, I couldn't buy that theory. You don't marry a guy just for his good looks. Can that, too, Carla. You know damned well some girls have married guys for the set of their shoulders in a military tunic.

I iced the cake unenthusiastically, the edge of my pleasure blunted by the incident. I regarded the respectable product of my labors with a jaundiced eye and put it on the sideboard. I tasted the stew and salted it again. After I had peeled carrots and potatoes and added them, I set the table for dinner.

The kitchen clock said six although it felt earlier. Because, I supposed, the day had begun late. I peeked out into the hall and noticed my other bag. The side pocket of the B-29 canvas bag bulged with the box of Dad's personal effects. That reminded me that the key to the footlocker was at hand and the footlocker above my head in the back room.

Well, I might as well clean up that detail. If the inventory of my father's effects was going to reduce me to tears, at least there were sympathetic shoulders at hand. And I might just find out what it was the major thought I'd find in that locker.

By the time I had wrestled the bomber bag up the stairs, the chill of the house had taken away the heat of my desire to circumvent the major. I really didn't want to look through that locker. For that matter, I hadn't even looked very carefully past the first layer of the box. The sight of Dad's West Point ring, tied to the end of the liberty scarf he'd bought me in England, had been too much for me. I had shoved the V-mail letters and the photo case that formed the first layer over the scarf and closed the box. I hadn't been able to open it up again.

Irresolute, I stared at the door to the back room. The stamp albums must be in the footlocker; the box was too small for them. And the stamps were valuable. I wasn't the philatelist my father had been but I'd learned enough about stamps so that I wouldn't be cheated much if I were forced to sell the collection. Stamps didn't depreciate and if diamonds were a girl's best friends, stamps were a man's . . . or a refugee's. He'd mentioned picking up some surcharged Polish stamps and three French Colonial oddities in Paris the one time he'd had leave there. I'd better ask the major if the stamps oughtn't to be evaluated. Wartime or not, there were certain formalities for a hero's heir.

Come to think of it, Dad had mentioned that this DeLord had been with him on that Parisian foray. Dad's opinion of DeLord had been favorable and Dad was an infallible judge of men. Why were the major and Turtle contemptuous of the lieutenant? Of course, if the man were so ill-advised as to consort with Warren, I could understand their dislike. But, if Dad had liked DeLord, why was DeLord cozying up to Warren? Oh, it made no sense. Irritated by my indecision, I kicked the bomber bag against the wall. It could stay there. It was too cold to go through Dad's things. Even basically impersonal things such as stamps. I turned on my heel and went to my own room.

I knocked. I banged. I pounded. Well, Turtle always could sleep up a storm when he put his mind to it. I opened the door, closing it quickly because the room was warmer by noticeable degrees than the hall.

Turtle was snortingly asleep, a quilt half covering his husky frame. He was lying on his back, his head to one side, one hand across his chest, the other tucked under the pillow. Never a lovely sight, with his broken thick nose, the heavy, undershot jaw, the pitted scarred face with its shadow of new beard growth, he made Lon Chaney look like Robert Taylor by comparison. With the familiarity of our friendship, I marched up to the bed and shook him by the shoulder. The next thing I knew, a Luger was pressed to my temple and a beefy hand was tight on my throat.

"For Pete's sweet suffering sake," I managed to say in a normal voice although I was never more startled in my life. Had I struggled or screamed, I think I might have been killed.

"Chrissake, Carla," Turtle exploded in an angry roar of

relief, "never do that to a combat fighter. I'd've blown your brains out. Chrisssst!" and he snapped the safety on and flopped back onto the bed, as shaken as I by the incident.

I sat down limply on the foot of the bed, rubbing my throat.

"I knocked," I explained plaintively. "Then I banged and I pounded, Turtle."

He nodded understandingly. "I'm too used to sleeping through barrages, Bit." He rubbed the back of his neck and jerked his head around sharply so that something cracked hollowly. This made him feel better but it made me nervous. "Best thing to do is call me by name."

"Sergeant? Or," and I grinned maliciously, "Turtle?"

His glower dissolved into an affectionate grin.

"Sarge," he suggested with a gravelly growl. He raised himself up, deftly knocking a single cigarette from the pack to his lips. "Jeez but it's good to see you, Little Bit. You're as thin as a stick but you look great to this old horse."

"It's wonderful to see you, too," I agreed, "but I don't exack-a-tally like you hobnobbing with the brass before coming to see *me*."

Turtle scowled, his glance sliding from mine before he looked back. "I did. I called your boardinghouse and you'd gone out somewhere."

"When?" I exclaimed, annoyed I hadn't been told of his call and sick I hadn't seen him earlier.

"Day before yesterday. I'd just got in."

"Day before . . . Oh, yes. Mrs. Everett did say I'd had a couple of phone calls. I was at the dean's," and I grimaced at the memory of that "take-it-easy-now" interview. "You called twice."

"Naw," he contradicted, surprised. "Just once. Like I said. The lady didn't know when you'd be back. And I got . . . involved."

I grinned at him and he waved off the suggestion in my smile that he'd gone off on a bat.

"When I called yesterday morning, you'd just left for the major's. So I came on down. Lined up my targets."

"Why did you have to see the major?" I asked as casually as I could.

Turtle looked at me squarely in the face, his jaw set, his eyes bleak.

"Comp'ny business," he growled in a flat no-nonsense voice.

"One of my father's companies?" I asked.

Turtle didn't so much as blink.

"I've known you since you were an hour old, James Carlysle Murdock. This is company business and that's all you'll get from me. Flat out!"

There is nothing stubborner than a Boston Irishman when he gets set. I'd seen Turtle like this a couple of times before. Once with an inspecting general and it wasn't Turtle who gave in. I acknowledged his obstinacy by standing up abruptly.

"Made you chicken 'n' dumplings. And the sun's over the yardarm."

Turtle's face broke into a slow, grateful smile. He cuffed me affectionately on the shoulder. "Good girl."

He rose and said, through a massive yawn, "Sprung a bottle loose from my sister's bastard of a bartending husband. God, what a stingy _____ he is."

"She must like him. She married him."

"Ha! Don't remember René very well do you? She had to!" Turtle's mirthless laugh was accompanied by the multiple crackling of his knuckles.

"Oh, you know I hate that sound, Turtle. Speaking of marriage, is the major?"

Turtle looked at me sharply.

"Or is that company business too?" I added sweetly.

Turtle shook his head. "He *was* married." The sergeant paused thoughtfully. "But it broke up sometime before Pearl. He's been in a while but he's no Pointer."

His bachelor status was more of a relief to me than it should have been, considering our brief association. His not being an Academy man was a surprise. I could usually spot the ninety-day wonders. The way Turtle looked at me then decided me against further pumping. It was natural for me to want to know the scuttlebutt about my guardian but if Turtle was reticent about the major, there was no surer indication of the old sergeant's respect for him.

"Major well liked?"

Turtle nodded solemnly and I left it at that. As Turtle rummaged in his bag for the bottle, I closed the door quietly. I got the locker key from my B-29 and turned resolutely to the back room. If they won't tell me, I'll find out myself.

An old chest of drawers had been pushed next to the three footlockers. So, with some pushing and shoving, I got the top locker onto the chest. The major was probably in his study so he wouldn't hear me rumbling things.

The key fit into the lock all right enough but it took me a little time to get the key to turn the tumblers. Salt air probably, plus the freezing temperatures of the room.

Gritting my teeth, I threw the lid up, exposing the compartmented tray on top. I sighed deeply; there certainly wasn't much to cry about in this assortment of badly mimeographed orders of the day, manuals, language dictionaries, torn map fragments, handkerchiefs and unmatched socks, thready shoulder patches. I could even regard Dad's Sam Browne belt sanguinely. I poked around unenthusiastically until I realized I was evading the issue.

I lifted the tray out and below it were things that had meaning for me. Stolidly I lifted out the top stamp album. It was, naturally, the very one I'd given him for Christmas three years ago. I found myself stroking the red leather, tracing the gold tooling with an idiot finger as my throat began to tighten. I shook my head, resolved not to cry again, and leafed carefully through the pages. These were his commemoratives and consequently incomplete. I put it carefully aside, my fingers trembling as I reached for the two blue albums, recalling how often they had appeared on the evenings which Dad and I had spent companionably together. He'd spread them out on a table or the bed, losing himself in his hobby for hours of patient study and arrangement, cursing because he missed the one vital stamp that would double the worth of the unit. Beneath the two blue books was the shabby brown one which had been his first. I lifted it a few inches and then dropped it hurriedly. For it covered the triangular shape of a folded flag and that was too much.

Hastily I put the other three album backs in place and started to unpack the other end of the locker. A canvas-wrapped rectangle disclosed a handsome, blue leather, gold-tooled volume bearing the inscription "Briefmarken." This must have been the German album he had picked up in Paris which had excited him so much. I opened it and two pieces of foolscap fell out. In Dad's handwriting at the top of the first sheet was the initial "D." D for Dad? Dog Company?

Below was a list headed "French China," broken into several categories. The first was headed "handstamped," carmine and purple, 1903, 1900, 1902–4. The second included stamps from 1 centime to 75, with the 75 underscored heavily to Tchongking, Mong-tseu, Yunnan Sen (Yunnanfu) also Packhoi.

I dredged up what I could remember of half-heard philately lectures from Dad. The 75-centimes was something special but I couldn't remember what. I did remember that before the Boxer Rebellion in 1900 many of the foreign countries involved in that blatant exploitation had maintained their own postal offices, quite rightly distrusting the vagaries of the Chinese system. Had Dad actually run across a complete series? Oh, that would be a find. I leafed through the album carefully. There were even some of the 75-centimes stamps from each of the various French-China offices, a rather odd combination of deep violet and orange.

I looked back at the list. Just before the carmine and purple handstamp on the 1900 category and the 75-centimes in all the French-China divisions was a tiny check mark. I glanced again into the album but the ones checked were there. Well, I'd have to dig out the Scott Stamp Catalogue and see what exactly he meant. Perhaps these were more valuable. Although even as it stood these particular stamps were valuable by themselves if I remembered correctly.

Beneath the Briefmarken volume were two more rectangular shapes, carefully wrapped in heavy paper, neatly tied with thin cord. I felt the edges, assuming these were more albums; evidently the covers were made of wood. Or these might be the little surprise Dad had bought and never had time to mail to

me. Well, I couldn't look at them right now. I pushed them to
one side and there, half hidden by underwear and socks, were
several boxes of forty-five shells and Dad's service revolver,
holster and all. Turtle was slipping up badly, sending live ammunition and a gun. I'd roast him for it.

I grabbed up the gun, replaced the albums and the tray,
and closed and locked the trunk. I eased the top locker back
into place, more because I was used to putting everything back
the way I'd found it than because I wished to hide the fact I'd
been inspecting it.

I was halfway across the dining room when I heard Turtle
roaring in a voice that could have penetrated armor plate.
"Proof? Christ, what d'ya need proof for? Who else could have
done it?"

"Proof to stand up in a court-martial, damn it, Bailey," I
heard the major's equally incensed voice reply. Outside the
house, Merlin barked, a sharp punctuation to their dispute.

"You can't be judge, jury, and executioner, Bailey," the
major continued urgently. "And don't try it again."

Merlin barked again and I heard someone let him in.
Then he scratched at the corridor door in front of me, sensing
my presence even if the men did not.

"Major, if you think I'm going to let that murdering . . ."

"Can it, Bailey," Regan Laird warned curtly. Before I
could move, he had jerked the door open. Merlin, delighted,
wove around me, crooning, nosing my dangling hands. Regan
Laird, his face stern, his eyes narrowing slightly, looked down
at me accusingly. Wordlessly, he pushed the door wide for me
to enter.

His face flushed with anger, Turtle was standing stolidly
in the center of the room. Merlin circled me nervously, whining
a demand for reassurance in the midst of the taut silence.

"Who's a murdering so-and-so, Turtle? What kind of
proof do you need? For whose court-martial?"

Turtle's face closed down implacably.

"Where did you get that?" the major snapped, snagging
the holstered revolver out of my hand. The cryptic conversation
I'd overheard had put it out of my mind.

"From Dad's footlocker."

Turtle looked as if something had caught him a solid blow in the solar plexus. As the major drew the gun from its holster, Turtle poised as if he wanted to grab it out of the major's hands. Laird broke open the gun. The cylinder was empty. He flipped the gun to the ceiling, squinting up the barrel. He and Turtle looked at each other over the weapon. They were both angry and disturbed.

"That's not my father's gun," I exclaimed, puzzled.

"No?" The major looked sharply at Turtle for confirmation. Reluctantly Turtle took the Colt, turning it in his hand to expose the handle.

"That isn't Dad's," I repeated, firmly. I knew the gun well, I'd cleaned it often enough, and the major's dubiety was irritating. "The right side of the handle was cracked. Here." I pointed out where the flaw should have been.

"She's right, all right, Major," Turtle stared at the gun as if it were evil. He dumped it back into the major's waiting hand as if he couldn't get rid of it soon enough. "Besides, I turned the colonel's Colt in to Ordnance before the corporal picked up his locker to take it back to Division." He stopped, his eyes widened, then he snapped his mouth shut.

Very slowly the major reholstered the gun as if he, too, found contact with it distasteful.

"If it isn't my father's gun, whose is it and why do you both act as if it were . . . poison or something?"

I glared at Turtle but he returned my stare, his eyes stubborn, his lips set in a thin line. I grabbed Laird's arm as he made to turn away.

"You've got to answer me. I demand to know!" I cried.

Laird looked down at me, the left side of his face towards me, his expression both pitying and angry.

"The gun is poison . . . if it's the one that killed your father."

# 🍒 5

"CHRIST, MAJOR," Turtle groaned in a hoarse voice, his face drained of all color, "she didn't have to know."

"I don't know what you mean," I said, dazed. I felt unreal. The words he had just said were not making any sense. *My* fathered murdered? He'd been killed. Killed! Not murdered!

The major put the gun on the mantelpiece before he looked at me again. When he did, his face hadn't changed. He had meant what he just said.

"No, Bailey, she should know because she'd find out anyhow." He sighed heavily. "Your father was killed by a forty-five slug."

"A forty-five slug?"

He nodded. I glanced, bewildered, at Turtle. Gray-faced, the sergeant confirmed it.

"No. No! *No!*" I cried, turning from both of them, hugging my arms to my sides. Merlin whined urgently and I thrust him away, whirling back to the men. "I just won't believe it. It doesn't make sense. I could see someone shooting Warren. God knows he was hated but not my father. Not Dad. The men loved him. He ran a good regiment. No one ever complained about Dad, did they, Turtle?"

Turtle nodded slowly.

"Maybe it was a sniper . . . got hold of a forty-five?" I suggested frantically. "It *was* a mistake? It wasn't murder!"

The major took me by the shoulders and gave me a hard shake; his eyes were compassionate but I hated him.

"No, Carlysle, it was no sniper. It *could* have been a mistake," he admitted slowly, heavily, as if he wished wholeheartedly he could accept that. "DeLord was driving your father to Warren. It was late. God knows . . . but Bailey and I now have reason to think it was murder."

"I don't understand," I cried, trying to twist away from the major, wanting to go to Turtle who stood so immovable, so silent, his stricken eyes dominating his white face. "I just don't understand."

My eyes lighted on the gun.

"Why did you say *that* gun killed my father?"

"I didn't. I said it might have. Now listen to me. Your father was still alive when DeLord brought him in. We got the medic but there wasn't anything he could do. But a Colt, particularly at short range, makes a recognizable . . " he broke off, struggling to make this horrible recitation easier on my feelings. "It was a forty-five, not a rifle, not a German handgun. After your father died . . . the slug proved it."

"Turtle, you *know* who killed Dad. Who was it?" I shrieked, struggling to break the major's grip.

"You're as trigger-happy as he is," the major bellowed, his eyes blazing, his hands like bruising iron grapples I couldn't shake. "Now you listen to me, Carlysle. I'm just as anxious as you two to get your father's killer but I'm not so much the fool as to take matters into my own hands. With a little patience, I can get the law to do it. That Colt may be all we need to do it legally, properly. War *doesn't* give license to settle private quarrels." He glared significantly at Turtle.

"Why not?" I cried, one part of me white-hot for vengeance, the other shocked at such hysteria. "Why didn't you settle things then and there, the night Dad was killed? Why wait four months? Why let the murderer get scot-free?"

Laird gave me another bone-jolting shake.

"We had a war on!"

The cliché brought me up short. I hated it for one thing: It had been used as the excuse for so much inefficiency and stupidity. Right now it was so revoltingly trite it made me nauseous. Yet I knew what he actually meant by the phrase and I was too army to ignore the significance. Sensing the change in me, Laird let me go.

"Now, sit down. You, too, Bailey, and we'll attempt to talk about this sensibly. There've been quite enough half-ass actions and assumptions." The major pinned Bailey with a withering stare. He looked back at me and saw my rebellion getting a second wind and pointed peremptorily at the couch. "Sit!"

I did, holding myself stiffly erect, disdaining the cushions inches behind me. Merlin, deciding the crisis was over, curled around by my feet and lay down. The major waited pointedly until Turtle seated himself on the other end of the couch.

"Now, Carlysle—"

"Would you have told me straight out if I had been a boy?" I interrupted him bitterly.

"Yes," the major agreed. "That would have been necessary."

"But not necessary for a girl, huh?" I retorted sarcastically.

"Bit . . . ," Turtle pleaded, speaking for the first time.

I cut him off impatiently. "A girl may not avenge her father's murder—"

"There will be no *avenging*," the major snapped violently.

"It's an archaic distinction. He was my father, boy or girl. I'm not delicate, not sheltered, not stupid."

The major cocked an eyebrow at me. "Then shut up and listen," he suggested in a dangerously soft voice.

I shut my mouth and folded my arms across my chest, glaring at him.

"The night your father died, we were bivouacked just north of Siersdorf. Your father had set up his command post in a shack near a coal mine we'd cleaned out two days before. The regiment was spread out all over the area. I'd been sent up with some units to help the One Hundred and Sixteenth at Setterich. Now, Bailey says DeLord was with your father for about an hour. Then a call came in from Division for your father. DeLord was sent to get Warren—"

"What was the call about?" I demanded.

The major took a deep breath. "I don't know. Right now I want you to understand the events as we have pieced them together. DeLord was sent to get Warren. But your father changed his mind and had DeLord drive him."

I glanced at Turtle who usually knew all my father's business whether Dad intended him to or not. Turtle gave a negative shake of his head.

"The sergeant was called to check on the ammo and rations that had just come up. When he got back to the post, how long, Bailey?"

"Half hour maybe."

"When Bailey got back, your father was gone and so was his jeep and his usual driver was fast asleep."

The major paused. "I was on my way to report myself back from Setterich when DeLord came in with your father."

I tried to force the picture out of my mind, of Dad unconscious and dying.

"At first we assumed it was a sniper," the major was saying in a dull voice. "We'd had a helluva time cleaning out some kraut positions, north of the mine. Two men in a jeep, late at night on a forest road."

My imagination drew another horrible picture . . . the jeep bucketing along the dark, shaded road, the sudden crack of a . . . . I closed my eyes and leaned wearily into the pillows behind me.

"As I said, the medic noticed the kind of wound and . . . removed the slug. Turtle and I made him keep quiet. We checked every single side arm in the area within the next couple of hours. None had been fired that recently and none were missing."

"But that one," I began, pointing to the fireplace, "where did it come from?"

Laird shook his head, sighing.

"Someone stashed it away," Turtle growled. He emphasized "someone" just enough to make me certain he knew who "someone" was.

"Knock it off, Bailey,"

"Stashed it away," Turtle continued stubbornly, "so we wouldn't find it that night and then slipped it into the colonel's footlocker. Safest place in the world, you think about it."

"Ballistics can easily prove if that Colt killed your father," the major went on, ignoring Turtle's bitter aside. "The serial number will tell us who it was issued to. We go on from there."

Turtle snorted.

"Yeah, and suppose the Colt turns out to belong to some poor slob got killed back on the Cotentin," he sneered. "Where's your theory then? I tell you—"

"Bailey!" There was something about Regan Laird that daunted even Turtle. "That gun is important—"

"Fingerprints!" I cried out. "You smeared all the fingerprints just now."

The major dismissed that with an impatient wave of his hand.

"I am more interested in the two attempts made to break into your boardinghouse, Carlysle."

I stared at him blankly.

"Tell me, how long after your father's things arrived was the first attempt?"

"Just a day or two," I said, startled. "But I just had the box. And I only found the gun in the locker, today."

"Eyah," agreed the major pointedly, "but the thief didn't know the locker was delivered here."

"Chrissake!" Turtle exclaimed, scowling. "Colonel died in November. This is March. Took long enough."

"Oh, that's ridiculous. Why would the burglar—"

"If that gun does identify the murderer . . . If he did put it among your father's things as the safest place to hide it . . ."

"Look, Major, I packed the colonel's things myself . . . ."

"It's there now and as I remember it, we had to leave the locker open until Division had gone through it."

"Then someone in Division could have put it in and it needn't be connected with my father at all," I remarked sourly.

"Then why the two attempts to break into your room? What else were they after?"

I shrugged, having no answer at all. I still didn't feel the incidents could be related. There wasn't anything else of value in the locker or in the box. It would be a sophisticated burglar who wanted my father's stamp collection and he'd've had to know the stamps were in my possession.

"That doesn't answer why my father was murdered," I said finally into the silence of the room.

"No, it doesn't, and that is what has bothered me ever since it happened," the major said, in a defeated voice. "It makes no sense. He was a damned good officer. Hell, he was wounded—"

"Wounded?" The word came out of me like a shriek. "Wounded?" I stared in horror at Turtle who flushed violently red. "Wounded! When?"

The major sat-down, running his hand back through his hair. Elbows on his knees, he leaned forward to me.

"He'd got winged two days before, bullet grazed him in the ribs. He made the medic patch him and then pulled rank so it wouldn't be reported."

It was so like my father.

"Goddamned fool'd be alive today if he'd listened to reason," Turtle suddenly exploded, unleashing his accumulated tensions. "Chrissake, Gerhardt *knew*! Warren'd never got the regiment. Why'n hell did the colonel have to stay on the line?"

Turtle hurled himself away towards the fireplace, futilely pounding at the heavy mantel. The gun bounced.

"Warren got the regiment? What d'you mean?"

The major shook his head from side to side, sighing again. "It's hard to piece this all together for someone who wasn't there. So much was happening so fast. That's why we made out it had been a sniper's bullet. The morale of the regiment was shot to hell after the beetfield massacre . . . ."

"Beetfields?"

"Look, let me explain and don't interrupt," and the major held up a cautionary hand. I nodded agreement.

"Our objective at the time was to join other elements of the Division for a major assault at Setterich. But we had to clear Siersdorf out beetfield by beetfield. We hadn't been warned there would be so much opposition. Company B and C were to advance. They hadn't got more than two hundred yards before the crossfire was murderous. Emsh . . . you remember Emsh?"

"Sure, who else ran Warren's company while Warren was sucking up to the C.O. of whatever post we were on?" I asked.

"Shut up. Emsh wanted to pull out and called back to the command post. Jim had gone up to see what was holding up the advance so Warren got on the walkie-talkie and started in on Emsh. Whatever was said, Emsh moved Charlie Company out again. They got pinned down in the rows of the beetfield. The krauts were taking a bead on the bulge of the combat packs. DeLord ordered his company to shed theirs but he had to pull Baker back and Charlie was pinned flat. Your father got there and was grazed by a ricochet. By the time we mopped up the two German emplacements, there were only twenty men left of Charlie Company. Emsh was not one of them."

Turtle started swearing, softly, bitterly, accentuating each expletive with a dull thudding blow of his fist against the mantel until I was sure he'd bring his hand away bloody. He and Emsh had been boozing buddies; rivals in everything else. He would feel Emsh's loss as perhaps no one else ever could.

"Goddamned Warren killed him, that's what," Turtle said savagely.

"We had to wait for tank support to pulverize the krauts' positions before we could move up in that sector." The major winced, his face dark with suppressed anger. "That was another reason why Jim stayed on the line," he said.

"Gerhardt had rocks in his head. If only he'd known . . ." Turtle began.

"If he'd known, yes, but he didn't."

"Known what?" I demanded of the major.

"Known your father was wounded. Instead he reamed him."

"Who? General Gerhardt? Reamed Dad? What for?"

"Failing to push on towards Setterich. Jim was told to quit fooling around, stop arguing about things . . . like beet-fields . . . to quit stalling, pull up our socks, and get with it."

I stared at the major, incredulous at the general's reprimand. For one thing, my father was a helluva good line officer. The regiment had many citations. Surely the general must have known that my father's judgment was to be trusted.

"What the general didn't know was that not only was the colonel wounded, not that that mattered in the advance, but we hadn't enough officers. Captain Hainey was killed, Major Dunbar was badly wounded, and that left only Colonel Gregory, Major Sorowitz, me and —"

"Warren!" I inserted, beginning to understand. "So Father plays the hero because he won't let Warren get command of the regiment."

"Battalion," the major corrected me. "I was Exec."

"Why didn't Dad just transfer Warren back to Division HQ?"

The major shook his head impatiently.

"We didn't know, Carlysle. God knows, I suggested it, hinted at it, and when we moved into action at Baesweiler, I came right out with it. I told the colonel if he wanted the regiment to move out with any confidence, he'd better transfer Warren."

"And?"

The major grinned ruefully. Turtle looked disgusted.

"We got our heads handed to us," Turtle finally said.

"In no uncertain terms," the major said humorlessly, "we were told that Colonel Murdock still commanded the regiment. And until his command was challenged by the commanding general, he felt no need to explain decisions."

I blinked, visualizing the scene, picturing Dad's lean face, expressionless as he always was when agitated.

"His wound?" I asked tentatively, wishing to excuse my father's unusual autocracy.

Both the major and Turtle shook their heads slowly.

"Something *was* worrying him, Major," Turtle said slowly, frowning in concentration. "And I didn't have no clue. Not a one." Turtle's face reflected the hurt of this unusual reticence.

"He wouldn't have worried about turning the regiment over to you, Major," I remarked, "even with only a few officers."

"I think," the major began slowly, "it was more than relinquishing command just then . . . although the morale was pretty bad after the beetfield incident. Near as I can remember, the colonel started getting edgy around October."

"DeLord joined us in October," Turtle suggested.

The major shook his head violently. "DeLord's all right. I'd bet my bottom dollar on that."

"Dad liked him a lot."

"He sucked up to Warren when your dad was dead!" Turtle growled.

"C'mon Bailey, you must know what the colonel and DeLord were cooking up? They had too damned many quiet conferences."

Turtle glowered unhappily. "All I know's something about looting."

"If DeLord was the looter," I jumped on the idea, "and

Dad was trying to make him make good, maybe DeLord killed him to keep HQ from finding out."

Both the major and Turtle dismissed that notion instantly.

"DeLord preferred a thirty-eight," Turtle said.

"And . . . he was . . . crying when he brought your father in," the major added softly.

The silence that followed those words was punctuated by the wind outside, by the spatter of snow driven against the windowpanes. It made no sense, Dad's murder. Maybe it had been a mistake.

If Dad, after Donald Warren had goaded Emsh into disregarding his judgment about sending Charlie Company into the beetfield, had finally decided the man was too much of a menace in the regiment, had gone to order Warren back to the rear, why would Warren kill him? That was too straightforward an act for Donald Warren. His *modus operandi* would have been to slyly report my father's wounded condition to Division HQ and have Gerhardt order Dad relieved of duty. But Regan Laird would have assumed command, unless Warren tried to kill him, too, which made even less sense. For Warren, though he had never made any bones that he considered himself a superlative officer and a clever tactician, was not fond of the hazards of actual line duty. He didn't want to get killed. No, Warren would not have killed Dad to prevent his transfer.

Now possibly someone else, hearing Dad send DeLord for Warren, might have decided that the dark road was a good place to remove Warren permanently.

"How many were around when Dad sent DeLord for Warren?"

Turtle swiveled around, startled, his jaw dropping, his eyes blinking nervously.

"Huh? Half of headquarters company, but we all left to check the ammo and rations."

"Supposing," I suggested, hunching forward, "someone decided it was time to transfer Warren permanently?"

The major sighed. "I'd considered that as the strongest possibility until . . . Turtle found out about the looting."

"Looting?"

"Looting on an extensive scale."

"Yeah, Bit. The regiment was sometimes first into an area. Like the Cotentin lorry." He nodded to Major Laird who acknowledged the example. "A whole kraut truck trailer crowded with 'liberated' things. The CAO sent out directives every third day about what to look for in the kraut transports, stuff they'd made off with, what monuments not to bomb, that kind of crap. Kind of stuff your father detailed over to Warren to keep him out of the line. Only some of the stuff wasn't turning up at Division HQ."

"What does that have to do with Dad's . . . death?"

Turtle screwed his face up in thought. "I think the colonel got worried that someone in the regiment was holding back. One time I caught him planting some things on a bombed-out kraut truck near Baesweiler. Told me to forget what I saw and shut up." Turtle shrugged expressively.

I knew what he meant. Dad could be mighty short when he was worried and not even as long-standing an associate as Ed Bailey dared him in that mood.

"An officer?" I suggested, thinking of DeLord.

"Could have been anyone," Turtle replied. "Hell, all the guys swarmed over the stuff. We all lifted things here and there." He saw the major's glare and rose to the accusation blandly. "Sure, me too." Then his face hardened. "Until that _____ Warren started searching combat packs. Lousy _____!"

"Warren?" I asked, sitting up, my mind flipping through the possibilities. I might not feature Warren as a murderer but a thief? It was Regan Laird who pricked this theory.

"No, I saw the quantities of things the searches turned up. You could hide a piece here and there but not that much. Some of those wagon trailers had big canvases, heavy carved chests, old books," he explained. "Not stuff you could hide in a money belt or your shirt."

"Warren had a footlocker, didn't he?" I pursued.

Laird shook his head firmly. "Yes, but they don't hold much. And he'd have no way of getting loot back from the line. Does you no good to steal something you can't hide and can't send on. Beside, how would someone like Warren know what would be valuable?"

I gave a harsh laugh. "Same way the krauts would. And I suppose, if the krauts felt it worthwhile lifting from the French, it would be worth Warren's while, too."

"A point," Laird allowed but he was not convinced. He leaned forward, then, tapping me lightly on the shoulder. "Just remember, Carlysle, all this is only supposition. If it had been normal times, or even in an assembly area, we would have reported it to the MPs or the CID. But we couldn't." He glanced over my head to Turtle. "I know Bailey has it in for Warren but I'm afraid he's allowed other elements to cloud his judgment. Oh . . ." and he raised a hand to quell Turtle's resenting guttural, "that's one reason Turtle came down here, to enlist me in going after Warren and forcing a confession from him."

"But there's the gun now," I reminded him.

"Yes, there's the gun and there've been two attempts to burglarize your room. I'm asking why and although I can't figure out yet why someone would murder Jim Murdock, I can no longer believe it was a sniper. If there was widescale looting traced to our regiment, if Colonel Murdock knew about it and wanted to find the looter, that would account for him not wanting to leave the line for any reason. He had laid a trap . . ."

"Yeah, and he sent DeLord for Warren," Turtle reminded him.

". . . which would be an ample reason for Warren shooting father . . . ."

"But," the major interrupted us, "your father never got to Warren that night. He was killed on his way there."

"Then, if Warren isn't the looter, though I like that theory very much," I grinned wickedly, having many private reasons for hating Donald Warren, "whoever put that gun in my dad's locker knows it will connect him — Warren — with the murder."

"Exactly. But who's back?" the major asked sardonically.

"I am. Turtle is . . ."

"DeLord's back and so is Warren," Turtle remarked in a very quiet voice.

"Warren?" I exclaimed.

"Yeah," and I have never seen such a horrible expression on Turtle's battered face. Involuntarily I drew back. "Yeah,

Warren's back. He got wounded, you know, Bit," and the sergeant grinned knowingly at the major.

"Bailey?"

Turtle's eyes rounded with innocence. "He got hit at Aachen when we was clearing out each house in a block."

"Badly, I hope," I said vengefully.

"Smashed his shoulder real bad," Turtle replied, shaking his head ruefully.

"Not low enough, huh?"

"Carlysle!" Laird bellowed.

I grinned at him. "I have absolutely no use for Donald Warren."

"Neither do I but your indiscretion is inappropriate for a young girl—"

"But not a young boy?" I asked sweetly.

The major's eyes were snapping with anger and he was barely containing his own temper.

"All right, Bailey. I'm here, you're here, Warren's back, and so is DeLord. What we have to do is get that revolver out to Edwards and run a ballistics check—"

"When the storm settles down," Turtle interrupted.

The wind had indeed risen in volume and ferocity, as if stirred by the tenor of our arguments. Snow lashed at the windows, some particles sifting in around the old casements. Regan Laird turned towards the windows, listening to the storm's violence. His mouth curled in a faint smile as he realized the elements had abetted the sergeant's moratorium.

"That's a real cold sound, Major," Turtle said blandly.

I wondered if the major knew Ed Bailey as well as I did, because I knew that nothing was going to stop Turtle from killing Donald Warren. And I had no intention of apprising the major of that knowledge.

Regan Laird looked speculatively at me. Abruptly I got to my feet, to break his train of thought lest I inadvertently betray myself.

"Good God, dinner!" I exclaimed with real feeling and dashed to the kitchen.

# 6

"SIR, shall we break out the bottle?" I heard Turtle suggest as I left.

"Indeed!"

They followed me into the kitchen.

"Oh, man oh man, that smells like prime eating," Turtle ground out in a full bellow, rubbing his hands together in anticipation.

"Neat, water, or soda?" asked the major, getting out ice and glasses as I mixed dumplings.

"Neat . . . oh, that's when, sir. I want to *taste* that chicken."

"Soda for me," I put in.

The major hesitated briefly, the bottle poised over the glass. I saw Turtle's hamlike hand tilt the bottle generously into the glass. He gave it a courtesy dash of soda and some ice and handed it to me. Then his heels came together, his shoulders snapped back as he came to rigid attention, glass raised.

"The colonel . . . God bless him!" His voice made it more of a supplication than an invocation. I blinked the sudden tears from my eyes, raised the glass to touch theirs, and swallowed a stiff jolt.

"Did you hear what Timmerman said when he was told to cross that railway bridge at Remagen?" Turtle growled with suppressed amusement. He twisted a chair, its back towards the table, and seated himself, propping his heavy arms on the curved back of the chair.

The major, a smile twitching at the good side of his mouth, moved a chair catercorner from the table, stretching his long legs out just where I'd have to walk over them to get to the sink and back to the stove.

"Tell me," he urged.

I'm not sure it was Turtle's voice that made the story or Turtle's unusual vocabulary. Probably both plus the added fillip that both men knew the personalities involved and could enjoy an "inside" that I didn't have.

This Lieutenant Timmerman had discovered that although the railroad bridge at Remagen had been a target of the Allied air forces and had suffered some damage, it was back in commission. The Germans were flowing in retreat over it. When the enemy with their own curious logic decided the Americans would strike somewhere else, they withdrew the considerable strength at the Remagen bridgehead. Timmerman consequently found the bridge intact. Later that day the units supporting him controlled enough of the town to turn their attention to the bridge. The Germans were frantically preparing to blow it up. Timmerman was ordered to get across it before the Germans could succeed.

"And Major, get this. The lieutenant says to the general, 'What if the bridge blows up in my face?' Get it, blows up in my face? A lieutenant says *that* to a general! That's your _____ new army for you," Turtle remarked with trenchant disapproval.

"Did it blow up?" I asked. After Dad's death I hadn't paid much attention to the First Army's advance.

"Naw, not then, It got shook up some, that's all. We crossed it. But I knew it wasn't the same army or the same war and I got out as soon as I could. Charlie Company was five men by the time we got to Coblenz. I'd had it."

I didn't for a minute doubt that once Turtle made up his mind to it, he could get sent home. He was such an old hand at red-tape cutting, I'm sure it was ostensibly legitimate. It just didn't sound like the Ed Bailey I knew.

I served their dinner and there was no more talk of war or any talk at all. Turtle paid me the compliment of eating with great concentration and gusto, passing his plate back three times. I had to whip up a second batch of dumplings as the major, though a more elegant trencherman, was equally hungry. Turtle's capacity had been a private joke for years but after three helpings of chicken 'n' dumplings, I hardly expected him to find room for three pieces of cake, too.

Merlin, who had napped on the far side of the stove while we were eating, woke. He stretched, walked majestically first to thrust his nose under Turtle's hand, then the major's, and then sat down expectantly by the kitchen door.

"Say, didn't he get volunteered for the K-9 Corps?" Turtle inquired, indicating Merlin with a cake-filled fork.

"He didn't make it," I grimaced, filling Merlin's bowl with what was left of the noontime stew.

"Naw!" Turtle's eyes went round with amazement. He hitched his chair around to get a full view of the shepherd. "You don't mean it. Him? I'd've though he'd be a good kraut killer."

"I did pull rank on them," I explained, "and made them give him an *honorable* discharge. But the fact remains he was considered of 'an insufficiently aggressive personality' for the Corps."

Turtle made a rude gesture. I giggled because the major glared so fiercely.

"If you were regular army," I told Laird, "you would know that army brats like me can't be shocked by mere sergeants."

"I don't get it," and Turtle shook his head sorrowfully, "he had half the rookies and two thirds of officers' row at Riley scared puking."

"Particularly Warren," I chortled nastily. "I swear, Turtle, he poisoned those other pups when he found out base families were going to take them. You know as well as I do that he made the Downingtons put Morgan away. She never bit him. She had more sense."

"Didn't I go to the C.O. myself?" demanded Turtle, his eyes wide at the implication he hadn't helped.

"That you did. Honest to God though, why couldn't it have been Warren who got killed?" I cried angrily. Turtle looked away.

"Any coffee?" the major asked, breaking the uncomfortable silence.

I slammed across the room for cups and back to the stove for the pot. The major's raised eyebrows cautioned me to get a hold of myself. I poured carefully.

"Warren's back, too, you said?"

"As a matter of fact," drawled Turtle, stirring spoonful after spoonful of sugar into his cup, "he came back on the same

ship I did." He put his spoon very carefully down, right next to
the knife he had not used. He straightened both so they were
precisely aligned and then looked the major in the eye.

The major sipped his hot coffee, his eyes never leaving
the sergeant's. His left eyebrow arched slightly.

"He joined his missus in Boston day before yesterday. I
believe he planned to pay a courtesy call on Miss James Carlysle Murdock."

"Of all the insufferable, patronizing, condescending,
ridiculous, hypocritical, vicious, egregious, inconsiderate, vile,
contemptible, despicable . . . ." I sputtered, rigid with indignation, unable to categorize what I felt from my guts about
Lieutenant Colonel Donald Warren.

"I think that's very interesting," the major remarked
when I momentarily ran out of appropriate adjectives. He
didn't, however, mean my descriptive venom. He meant that
Warren was in Boston and proposing to call on me. "I'd very
much like to know *why* he felt constrained to call on you."

That drew me up short for I had been about to launch
into another tirade, having recovered my eloquence. I glanced
at Turtle and then did a double take on him. The look on his
face was a killing one, a hating one, far more expressive of what
I felt for Warren than any word fashioned by man to express
inner violences.

"You do think Warren killed my father, don't you Ed
Bailey?"

Turtle's head turned sharply around to me and I saw the
deadly hatred in his eyes, and something else, unfathomable
and unfamiliar.

"He only *thinks* so," Major Laird interposed in a steely
voice. "But I want to know *why* first. There is more to this whole
goddamned mess than a fine man's death. I want to know what.
Is that clear, Bailey?" The major spaced those last words out
very carefully, as if cutting the orders of the day ineradicably on
Turtle's consciousness.

Turtle swung his head slowly back to face the major.

"Yes sir," he grated out softly. "Very clear, sir."

Merlin, sensing the aura permeating the room, looked up
from his dinner and growled deep in his throat.

# ❦ 7

THE DETAILS of living got us through the rest of the evening. I washed the dishes while the two men chopped wood and replenished the fireplaces and wood buckets throughout the house. Thanks to a fall survey course in English literature I cleverly thought of heating bricks to warm the beds.

The wind had risen higher with nightfall and the snow was swirling and howling around the Point where occasionally whitecapped waves lunged to the top of the protective dunes. Within the house, despite its chilling discussions, there was warmth and companionship.

By the time the chores had been done and Merlin let out for a brief run, we were all ready to turn in for the night. Perhaps as much to be alone with our various thoughts as to sleep. Maybe the others felt, as I did, that all should sleep on what had been said and suspected.

My room was warm and the wrapped hot brick did take the clammy chill off the sheets. With Merlin stretched comfortingly beside me, I should have slept. I think I did but it was a restless slumber and shallow, for any crackling of the fire or sudden whine of the wind at the shutters roused me.

I was awake when I heard the minute clink of the latch moving on its tracks. Merlin raised his head briefly but his body did not tense. He didn't even mutter a growl. He put his head back down, sighed, and slept. I could feel the cold from the hallway and, through slitted eyes, I saw a figure cross the room. The dying fire lit the gargoyle side of the major's face as he softly stepped across the floor. He bent over the fire and quietly added more logs. He turned back, I closed my eyes tightly, then remembered to relax the muscles of my face. I could feel a difference in air pressure as he stood right by my bed. I could feel Merlin turn his head and I felt motion through Merlin's body against mine as the major scratched the shepherd's muzzle. Then lightly, so gently I couldn't be sure whether it was his fingers or just the air current preceding the withdrawal of his hand, I felt him touch my hair, much as I had his the previous night.

When he had left, I wondered if he were mocking me. Had he seen my eyes a trifle open? Had he been awake last night when I had caressed him in similar fashion? Caress, I suddenly admitted to myself, was the proper word. Because caress implies tenderness, affection, desire. I could chide myself all the way from Orleans to Boston on any cold, uncomfortable baggage car, yet not escape the fact that the major was more man than I had been next to in a long time and I was—to be blunt—man-hungry. These years when I should have been dating, dancing, having fun with boys were empty. The boys were embattled in far places. I remained in chaste loneliness. By virtue of a life as an army child, I understood the world of men better than most girls, but I understood it as a child and not as a woman. The major, wounded and embittered, was a magnificently romantic figure. This whole crazy situation of his being my guardian was *romantic* in the Gothic tradition. Ridiculous when my father must have known exactly . . .

My train of thought stopped with an icy jerk. The realization that my father *had* known exactly what he was doing in assigning me to Laird's guardianship dawned on me. He'd've known that the major's type was attractive to me. He'd had plenty of opportunity to judge what kind of man I liked, or what kind of man he'd prefer me to like. I had, after all, dated regularly on most of our posts after I was fourteen. Well, Dad had provided me with his choice and thrown us together by the simple expedient of making the Chosen my guardian, in case he shouldn't be around to introduce us. Of course, Dad was a fatalist so he would have done just as he had to make sure Regan Laird and I met. Had he anticipated the fact that I would divine his complicity? Probably. Dad never underestimated my intelligence, which is why I worked so bloody hard at getting good marks. He'd insisted on a proper good education even to the point of putting me in day schools when the post facilities were inadequate. And he'd insisted I try for Radcliffe. Always aim high, he'd said.

I gave Dad full marks for a mighty shrewd campaign. I wondered if the major had tumbled to Dad's strategy. Probably not. Dad kept his cards hidden. He'd always made money playing poker even against Turtle. But now I understood why the major had been deluded about my sex. Dad had intended to imply that I was a boy so the major would be easily gulled into the guardian routine.

Wait a moment. Did Dad have a precognition of his death? No, I dismissed that notion as foreign to his character. A cautious soldier always leaves a bolt-hole.

Silly tears came to my eyes, tears of longing and gratitude for this silly, magnificent gesture. I turned my head into my pillow and sobbed bitterly for his loss, for the utter wastefulness of his manner of dying. Merlin shifted his body, nuzzling me with ready sympathy. I buried my head in his silky ruff and he endured my rough embrace and sobs with devoted patience. I finally cried myself into an exhausted sleep.

I drifted back to consciousness in a curious state of mind. I had evidently argued with myself while sleeping and I had the silliest impression I was picking up the argument at a point where I had dropped off to sleep. I was saying to myself, as consciousness increased, that if Dad had never underestimated my intelligence, he had overestimated my physical charms. What guarantee had I that I had any appeal for the major? Now there, I found myself commenting, was the crux of the matter. It was all very well for Dad to slap the white man's burden on Major Regan Laird but did he intend to leave the seducing to me? And did my father feel I was up to such carrying-on?

For one thing, I was twenty and the major must be fifteen or so years my senior. If not more. He was a damned good-looking man, or would be again, when the surgeons at Walter Reed had a go at him. The good Major Laird might have certain plans in mind that did not include the five feet two inches, one hundred and a half pounds of curly-haired imp. Imp was what I had self-styled myself from the day I had regretfully decided at sixteen that I was stuck down at five feet two inches. The major was a well-built six foot one. The angle of elevation made his height deceptive. It was a pet peeve of mine to see tall men guiding around little girls. It seemed a waste, particularly when I considered some of my lengthy friends forced to wear flats so as not to tower above their dates.

Of course, once this fool war got finished up, taller men might reappear on the scene. In the meantime, it was close to indecent for five foot two to run around under the waistband of six foot one. That was approximately eleven inches going to waste, right there and, as we are forever being told, don't waste manpower. This put me in mind of a very obscene joke I'd overheard. Which put me in a very good frame of mind. Which reminded me of how I had fallen asleep.

My grief over my father had taken a curious shift somewhere during the subconscious moments of the night. Perhaps I had admitted that Dad had forever passed beyond recall. Perhaps I had let go the trappings of grief to take up the banner of just retribution and vengeance. Of perhaps time, in its inevitable way, had moved me past the initial plateau of sorrow. Turtle Bailey's appearance had completed my acceptance, allowing me the vital catharsis of tears coupled with pleasanter reminders.

My remorse over things omitted and committed in relation to Dad had been painfully keen. The letters I had not found time to write that would have reached him in a moment of desolation. The meals I had elected not to spend in his company. All the petty things that rise to plague the mourner were now done with.

It would be ridiculous to chalk up my new spirit to one isolated incident. It seemed plain silly to waste time analyzing the whys and wherefores. Just accept the blessing graciously and get yourself out of bed, I told myself.

I looked at my watch.

"Ten o'clock!" I exclaimed, sitting up. With some astonishment I realized Merlin had left. My exploring hand told me it must have been some time ago for the impression his body had made was cold.

A shutter, its fastening broken or loosened by the continual pounding of the storm winds, swung leisurely ajar. The day was fair with curious brilliance of reflected snow. Someone had mended the fire again for new logs burned warmly on the grate.

I dragged clean clothes out of my suitcase, loath to leave the warmth of bed. I managed to dress under the bedclothes, no mean feat. I rued the fact that slacks and pullovers are not exactly siren togs but I could not fancy any man enjoying the embrace of an ice maiden, however chic in her dress. Presuming, of course, I could entice the major within my skinny arms in the first place.

I stared at my image in the mirror over the dresser. There had been no overnight physical metamorphosis. I sighed. The color in my cheeks was only the product of the nippy air and the freckles stood out like beauty marks. The dark circles under my green eyes had receded by perhaps a quarter of an inch. I brushed my black hair vigorously, hoping it might condescend to fluff out. Instead, the friction in the cold air only made it lie flatter to my skull. I looked more like Joan of Arc than Helen of Troy. I gave up and decided to put my trust in good cooking, hoping that the major was so suitably indoctrinated into infantryitis as to remember that every army moves on its stomach.

"Forward, Joan," I urged and opened my door with a dramatic flourish.

The major, about to knock, teetered precariously in an effort not to knock on my forehead and to recapture his balance in order not to spill the coffee in his hand.

"And what does Joan have to do with the morning?" he asked, a droll expression in his eyes.

"I have absolutely no idea," I lied. "How sweet of you!" I took the coffee from him gratefully.

He was dressed in an assortment of heavy clothing, wide-wale corduroy trousers tucked into infantry boots, a well-worn red blanket-coat, sweater cuffs showing at the wrists which indicated he wore several layers under the jacket, a muffler, and a hunting hat with earflaps turned down. Heavy gloves were stuffed in one pocket.

"Don't tell me mine is the only fire in the house?" I asked, indicating his outdoor costume. He reached over my shoulder, reminding me again of the difference in our heights, and closed the door to my bedroom.

"No. There are several islands against the sub-zero weather," he assured me. "But we won't keep them long if Bailey and I don't bring home some more wood. I neglected to plan on so many houseguests, to say nothing of that storm when I last chopped up a woodpile."

"One of these years we must put in central heating," I said and suppressed the astonishment I felt at hearing myself so possessively impudent.

He hesitated a brief instant, giving me a measuring look before he smiled politely. "Yes, we must." There was the briefest lingering on the pronoun.

With what poise I could muster after that gaffe, I glided to the stairs and hurried to the kitchen, hoping the devil was not at my heels.

Merlin was having words with Turtle when I entered from the hall. Merlin was extremely pleased with himself, his tail pumping violently while he barked fit to clear the chimneys of soot. Turtle, too, was dressed for heavy weather work. He needed the padding to roughhouse with Merlin. The kitchen chairs had been knocked askew and the heavy wood bucket had been pushed back under the kitchen sink.

"Good for you, Turtle," I cheered as Merlin made a lunge which Turtle dodged expertly. "He had to give up that sort of play with me when he was eight months old or there would have been crushed Carlysle to spoon up from the floor. And he loves to fight."

"This dog has 'an insufficiently aggressive temperament'?" asked Regan Laird dryly, hands on his hips, watching the dog's snarling face.

Turtle looked up just long enough to be distracted. Merlin took advantage and sank his teeth into the sergeant's forearm.

"You overgrown son of a bitch," Turtle roared. "Leggo." Merlin promptly obliged.

The sergeant rubbed his forearm thoughtfully, frowning at the dog with new respect. He had felt that bite even through the layers of clothing.

I was laughing too hard to be sympathetic although I did hand signal Merlin to sit. He didn't want to but he did. Glancing at the major, I caught my breath, my laughter trailing off. He had turned up his jacket collar, preparatory to braving the cold outside, and only his good profile showed. I abruptly gave up all hope that I could ever interest him in little old Little Bit.

"Ready, Major?" Turtle picked up an ax from the kitchen table, the edge gleaming with newly sharpened steel. "Keep the coffee hot, Bit," he enjoined me and the two started out.

Merlin whined expectantly, rocking back and forth as he reluctantly maintained the sit. I waved him out.

"Wait a minute. I want him here with you," the major objected, extending his leg across Merlin's path. The shepherd stopped, whining plaintively.

"Oh, for Pete's sweet suffering sake," I exclaimed in exasperation. "And what panzer division are you expecting today?" I waved out the window at the snow-fast land.

The major deliberated, shrugged, and slapped the side of his leg to encourage Merlin. The three stamped out through the back. As they lurched up the slippery slope behind the house into the scrubby beach pines, I saw a sled trailing behind the major. High slatted sides had been fastened on to make it an excellent wood carrier on either snow or sand. Once it must have been young Regan's and I wondered what kind of a boy he'd been.

"Maxim two," I muttered to myself, "the infantry moves on its belly and they will be mighty hungry 'footsojers' when they get back . . . probably on their bellies."

I brought meat in from the freezing porch and eyed it. I might as well pop it into the oven now. Eventually it would have to thaw. I found a pan and, a little dismayed at the size and solidity of the meat, put it in the oven, closed the door, and crossed my fingers.

I remembered seeing some dried apples so I put them to soak and got out piecrust makings. Oh, but it was nice to have butter to cook with again.

When I put the pie in, there was the barest hint of tan on the meat. Fork testing proved that approximately one thirty-second of an inch had thawed. This was a hopeful sign. I fed the stove a few sticks of wood and did dishes. It then occurred to me that men were men in blizzard and in war. I went to find what I could do with the state of the major's socks, et cetera.

This little job was taken care of and distributed neatly,

festooning the bathroom, after a solid hour of scrubbing and rinsing in the tub. The pie had cooked perhaps a trifle too crisply brown but it smelled heavenly. The meat was doing far better than I expected so I fed the stove again and went to straighten up the study.

One of the nicer things about a good fire is that it burns. It burns dust, cigarette butts, and dirt. By the time I had finished, the major's room actually looked respectable. I had also changed the sheets after an intensive recon for a linen closet. I was coming down the stairs with fresh towels when I saw what must have been a snow mirage. I covered my eyes with my hand for a moment and looked out again.

The figure plodding down the road was no mirage. It also walked like an infantryman. I caught the glint of metal at the shoulder, but the face was hunched in the protection of the collar, chin tucked down so that I couldn't distinguish any features.

The more I looked the more apprehensive I became. It was ridiculous to assume the man was looking for any other house but this. All the others were boarded up so tightly and no one would survive in this weather without a fire. Our chimneys were all blooming with smoke.

The stranger was no one I knew. Not even Warren. Not that you'd have caught Warren walking very far. Certainly not in weather like this. Warren loudly bemoaned the fact officers no longer rode thoroughbred steeds into battle, spurring valiantly into the fray, saber held high. He was a frustrated Jeb Stuart-ite. However, he had accepted the jeep as an endurable alternative to walking.

No, this wasn't Warren but it was somebody looking for the major. I deeply regretted my generosity with Merlin. I'd have faced my mythical panzer unit with no qualms with that shepherd at my side.

The man had come abreast of the house now. He looked towards it, examining the sloping approach. He made a decision and started up, removing his hands from his pockets as the tricky footing required additional balance. He slipped and went down on one knee. As he got to his feet I saw his face for the first time. He was no one I knew but his face, not handsome like the major's, was attractive and there was an openness in the exasperated determination on his face that I liked.

I threw back the bolts on the front door and pulled it open.

"May I help you?" I asked, conscious of the triteness of that remark.

He looked up, startled, grinned broadly as he brushed snow off his legs.

"You sure can, Mrs. Laird," he agreed warmly with a trace of a southern accent in his tone. "You are Mrs. Laird, aren't you?" he asked with concern when he saw the startled expression on my face.

"No!" I said flatly, wondering if I looked that old in the light.

"I beg your pardon, ma'am, but this is Major Regan Laird's house. Or did I take the wrong turn?" and he looked over his shoulder at the road in dismay.

"No, this is the right house."

He was almost to the front door now, and the ground under the drifts was even. He got up to the windswept front stoop and stamped the snow off his boots and trousers.

"Actually, while I do want to see the major, I was told that his ward, James Murdock, would be here."

"That's right."

"I served with the lad's father in France," he said quietly, "and I wanted to see him."

"That does you credit," I said, gesturing at the drifts and trying not to sound sarcastic.

He regarded me with a disconcerting directness in his clear light-green eyes.

"May I come in? I'd hate to cool the house off," and, at my invitation, he pushed the door wider and stepped in.

"There's not an appreciable difference in this part of the house," I explained, suddenly aware of the load of towels in my arms. "Follow me, Lieutenant . . . ?"

"DeLord, Robert DeLord, ma'am."

The towels fell in a mosaic on the floor as I turned to stare at him, the temperature within me matching that of this part of the house.

# 🍂 8

"I'M SORRY. Did I do that?" he apologized, bending quickly to pick up the towels before the snow from his boots could melt into them. I held out my arm stupidly while he piled them up.

"The kitchen is warm," I managed to say and, in a daze, led the way.

"Apple pie," he exclaimed, sniffing deeply as he entered. "That smells good and proper."

"Been back long?" I asked inanely, putting the towels down on the cabinet and getting a mug down for him. My inner thoughts were too chaotic to sort out. I had the feeling of being on a treadmill. I had to keep moving faster or I'd fall off altogether. Like Alice, running as fast as she could to stay in the same place. Only, as of right now, I wasn't even in the same place.

"Got in a week ago," he replied genially.

"Take your things off."

He divested himself, grinning apologetically as he kept peeling off layers. When he had got down to uniform tunic, he turned to take the coffee I poured him.

"Just black, thank you, ma'am," he smiled and edged close to the stove. "That was one mighty cold walk," he continued sociably, his glance dropping to the pie and away. "I got a lift from the railroad station to the first crossroads. The Coast Guard. Oh, near forgot, the stationmaster gave me some mail for the major and young Murdock," he said, and having found the letters in his pocket, handed them over to me. "Special Delivery." His grin was frank and broad.

"You weren't kidding." A stupid remark, for one of them, addressed to me, was liberally covered with special delivery stamps. It was from Mrs. Everett and thick. She had probably forwarded me some letters, I thought. It was sweet of her to go to so much trouble. I put the letters down on the sideboard.

"No, ma'am," he said, turning this way and that to warm all angles of him at the stove.

He had crisp blond hair cut close to his scalp, and I could see the line of a bullet crease along the top of his head. He was stockily built and shorter than the major but still six or seven inches the better of me. He seemed to be waiting expectantly and I realized he wondered why I didn't call "the Murdock lad" or the major.

"The men are out after wood," I explained hastily and gestured him to the chair nearest the stove. He thanked me again and sat down, hands curled around the hot mug.

"You sure would need it, day like today."

"Day like the last several."

"Ah," he began self-consciously, clearing his throat, "how's the kid taking his father's . . . death?"

"I think I'd better set you straight, Lieutenant DeLord," I said deliberately. He looked apprehensive. I held up my hand. "Now this may come as a surprise to you but—I'm James Carlysle Murdock."

"Well, I'm pleased to . . ." and he did a perfect double take. "Did I hear you right, ma'am? You're James Carlysle Murdock?"

"Oh, yes, if you knew my father for very long, lieutenant, or very well, you probably discovered he had an odd sense of humor."

The light green eyes regarded me seriously.

"He was also somewhat stubborn. He had chosen an appropriate name for his firstborn, so it didn't occur to him to change the name simply because he was disappointed in the sex of the child. I have been James Carlysle Murdock all my life and there have been times, especially since Pearl Harbor, when it has been a liability, believe me."

The green eyes began to twinkle although the face had not changed expression. The twinkle turned to laughter and then the mouth turned up at the corners as Lieutenant DeLord started to laugh. He continued to laugh until the infectious quality of his mirth caught me up, too, dispersing entirely my apprehension about him.

"James Carlysle Murdock, well, that's one on me," he said.

"No," I contradicted him, grinning, "that's one on me."

This set him off again and I joined in so wholeheartedly

that neither of us heard the men approaching until the back door burst open and Merlin came charging into the room.

The moment the shepherd saw the newcomer he changed from a happy dog in from a mad morning of fun into a guard animal, alert, intent, moving slowly, purposefully, towards the stranger.

I'll say this for DeLord, he didn't move a muscle. It took a strong will not to retreat from the sight he was facing.

"At ease, Merlin!" I said sharply.

The hackles on Merlin's back dropped, his muscles relaxed and he came forward at a normal pace, to sniff the hand DeLord slowly extended.

"Friend," I added, having just decided that. Merlin was already making a new acquaintance.

This had all happened very quickly so that both Turtle and the major had just reached the doorway when Merlin touched DeLord's hand with an inquisitive nose. DeLord got to his feet.

"The lieutenant, by God," Turtle ground out.

"Major," the lieutenant acknowledged gravely. "Bailey. Didn't realize you were back, sergeant."

"No, sir, just got back. Excuse me, Major," and Turtle pushed in with the load of logs he was lugging.

Regan Laird, also laden, came in too, hooking the door shut with his foot. There was a clatter as Turtle dropped his burden into the wood basket.

"What brings you to this neck of the woods?" the major asked, stalking—yes, that was the term—stalking across to dump his own load.

"Young James Carlysle Murdock," drawled the lieutenant, moving to one side to let the men warm themselves at the stove. He leaned back, against the inner wall, one hand holding the coffee mug, the other thrust into his pocket. He seemed far more at ease than either the major or Turtle.

At the mention of my full name, the major frowned, first at me and then at the lieutenant.

"He thought I was Mrs. Laird," I giggled nervously.

"Issat apple pie?" Turtle cried, pointing to it.

"No," I told him, making a face, "it's monkey meat."

Turtle grinned, turning to Laird with a satisfied smile.

"I tol'ya we'd eat good when we got back."

I pushed them both out of the way to check on the roast. The fork went in smoothly, two full inches.

"I'd have given odds this meat wouldn't thaw before late tomorrow," I commented, closing the door slowly on the delicious aroma. I was very conscious of the major's alertness, DeLord's almost insolent ease, and the fact that Turtle wanted to improve the situation.

"Yorkshire pudding?" Turtle asked hopefully.

"If this ever cooks," I promised, poking the meat again. "It'll probably be red-raw in the middle."

"Only way to eat it," Turtle replied, rubbing his hands together and licking his lips. "Right, Major?"

"Yes," the major agreed absently. "Could we have some coffee, Carlysle?"

"Yes, yes." I went to the cupboard, planting my hands on the counter to lever myself up.

"The stool, Carlysle. Use the stool," the major said in a grating voice that sounded more like Turtle's.

"Allow me," said the lieutenant smoothly and handed me down two mugs. I thanked him sweetly, carefully avoiding Regan Laird's eyes. The air fairly crackled with his annoyance.

"The lieutenant hitched a ride in with the Coast Guard," I said conversationally as I filled the mugs. "He brought us some mail, too. Special delivery." I glanced over at DeLord with a special grin for our inside joke.

Picking up the packet of letters, I rifled through them. Two for Regan Laird were in the brown manila envelopes, franked for official business, U.S. Army. There were two V-mail envelopes for me plus Mrs. Everett's letter and one with a local postmark.

"If you'll excuse me a minute, I'll see what my nice landlady has to say," I said, drawing up a chair to the far end of the table, "since she was 'specialing' it to me."

One envelope, addressed in an unfamiliar handwriting, fell out of the pages and pages of lined tablet paper that had been folded over it.

"Jesus," I exclaimed angrily, "what does that bastard want with me?"

"Bit, can it," Turtle growled at me.

I pursed my lips. "Warren!" I flung the envelope distastefully to the table, "Guardian, *you* read it."

I picked up Mrs. Everett's bulky pages; her platitudes and homey admonitions ought to calm me down. I had got the first four phrases deciphered when I realized what she was babbling about.

"Good heavens," I cried out, staring at the men. "Someone did get in the house. Mrs. Everett says my room was torn apart. Damn," I added because she went on to say that all my college notes had been thrown around the room.

All your books [I read on] were scattered and it was the most awful mess. Really, Carla, I was terribly upset. Naturally Father insisted on calling the police and they came and questioned every one of us. I felt simply awful. I don't know what the neighbors will think, much less your dean. They are so particular at the college where the girls stay. And it *was* only *your* room that was searched. That's what the police say. That your room was *searched*. I know you'll be hearing from them because they *have* to know what might be missing. I *explained* to the detective that you were convalescing on Cape Cod with your guardian. I *told* him that you had left *only* your books because you were *not* to study, but *rest*. But I didn't want you to think that we aren't careful of your things. You know how I always lock the doors, particularly since we had that scare before. You know, dear Carla, I find I miss that dog when things like this can happen. He may have upset me a little when you first came here, but I can *see* now why he's been such a comfort to you.

Upset was a euphemism for scared sick. Her fear of the dog had warred with her desire to mother the war orphan. I had sensed this and had waved the flag violently. Considering how most army personnel were treated before the war, I had no compunctions about exploiting the new status.

Mrs. Everett did not believe in paragraphs nor in much

punctuation. Her style, while very like her, lacked the additional flavor of her broad Dorchester accent, but I had a vivid
picture of her standing indignantly before me as I read the
letter. Embarrassed over the notoriety, concerned over the
possible repercussions on her carefully maintained reputation.

So don't be alarmed, Carla, when the police call to ask
you about your things. Kay Alexander was so sweet and came
and helped me pick things up and put the room back together
again. You'll be glad to know that nothing was really damaged
[I interpreted this to mean the furnishings and linens escaped
harm] and everything is back in place just as you like it.

Now, I know Mrs. Laird will cook good nourishing meals
for you. I always said you never ate enough to keep a bird alive,
and you so [she had crossed out a word with many lines] slim
anyway.

I looked up from my letter, having deleted the last paragraph from my running commentary of her remarks. The major
was scowling, Turtle growled deep in his throat, sounding like
Merlin, and the lieutenant was watching. Just watching, but I
was certain no detail on anyone's reaction missed his scrutiny.

"Was there anything you wouldn't like to find missing?"
asked Regan Laird slowly.

"I told you," I began, "I brought everything down here
but books, as ordered," and I glared at him, "and you have
the . . . ." The look on the major's face stopped me. "That's the
trouble with majors," I complained to the lieutenant, trying to
make this sudden switch appear spontaneous. If the major was
worried about DeLord's possible complicity with Warren, I had
already said too much. But the expression on DeLord's face
was one of polite interest, nothing more. "The trouble with
majors," I repeated, giving Laird a dirty look, "is that they don't
have enough responsibility to make them humble and too
much authority to make them human."

DeLord burst out laughing. This certainly wouldn't improve his relations with Laird but when Turtle joined in, the
major had to grin at my deprecating description.

"You have to get up early to put one over on Little Bit," Turtle announced proudly. "But I don't like this burglary."

I shrugged. "There wasn't anything for him to take but, if my Government 18 notes are all fouled up, I'll . . . ." I trailed off as I saw the major opening Warren's letter.

He read it quickly, the muscles around his mouth tightening with distaste. He tossed it over to me.

"Innocuous enough," he said in a flat voice.

I thought I caught a gleam of interest in DeLord's eyes but he maintained his incurious pose.

I didn't pick the letter up. For one thing it had floated to my side of the table, right side up, so I wasn't forced to touch it to read it.

I made an impolite sound in my throat as I read the opening paragraph:

> Dear Carla,
>
> Marian and I wish to express again our deeply sympathy for your orphaned state. I admired your father . . .

"You hated his guts!"

> . . . and respected his ability to command . . .

"Which is why you often ignored his orders and snafued everything with your own."

> I was deeply shocked and grieved at his death.

"You probably got roaring drunk with delight."

> You may not have heard that I sustained a wound in Aachen.

"And hoped you were! With no pain-killers."

> *. . . and have been relieved, temporarily*
> *you may be sure, of my command.*

"Permanently unless Bradley wants the V Corps to go mass AWOL."

> *Marian and I happen to be coming to Bos-*
> *ton on the 28th . . .*

"I wonder which general's wife she's sucking up to now."
"Carlysle!" The major snapped.

> *. . . and would very much like to see you*
> *for old time's sake. I will call when we ar-*
> *rive and arrange a date.*

> *Affectionately yours,*
> LT. COL. DONALD H. WARREN

"Affectionately? He debased the word."

DeLord's green eyes were sparking and the hint of a grin twitched at his lips.

"Well," I said with great satisfaction, "isn't it a pity I missed them? My timing is superb." I flicked a finger at the letter and it drifted across the table to Turtle. "Burn it, Bailey."

Turtle was about to comply when the major retrieved it. He replaced it in the envelope.

"You know Colonel Warren?" DeLord asked me with the most innocent expression I have ever seen on a lieutenant's face. Even Turtle blinked respectfully.

"Carlysle," the major cautioned me, his eyes angry.

"I'm all too well acquainted with Lieutenant Colonel Warren," I replied, stressing the rank with acid scorn, ignoring my guardian deliberately. "The very idea that he was given my father's command—even for a day—turns my stomach."

"Carlysle!" the major said more forcefully.

DeLord's expectant look was an added goad to my defiance.

"I was ignored by him until I reached adolescence and

learned, like every other young girl on the post, to keep something solid between me and him. I've been condescendingly chaperoned and mothered," I shuddered violently, "by his dear Marian who'd sell herself to a corporal if it would look good on her Donnie's 201 file."

This time the major grabbed me by the arm and shook me. I swung around long enough to wrench my arm free.

"I'm not army anymore and I can say what I want to now about Lieutenant Colonel Donald Warren. And I can say it to whomever I please!"

Merlin began to growl in his throat.

"You see, the dog agrees. He'd love to sink his teeth into Warren and I wouldn't call him off. Warren's had it coming a long, long time."

"That is quite enough from you, young lady," the major said in a steely voice. He meant it and for one fleeting second I was positive he'd slap me across the mouth if I said one more word.

Considering he had a very poor opinion of Warren, I couldn't see why he objected until I recalled that he, or Turtle, had mentioned that DeLord had been thick with Warren after Dad's death. Well, green-eyed DeLord would bloody well know where I stood as far as Warren was concerned. Discretion be damned.

Turtle had kept his mouth shut during my tirade. DeLord had ducked his head as if that would help him avoid participating in the tense scene. I saw DeLord tenderly finger the bullet score on his head as if it suddenly bothered him.

"Well," I said, turning my attack to him, "now how do you think James Carlysle Murdock is adjusting to her father's death?"

The lieutenant shot me a penetrating look, compounded of surprise and shock. I saw him dart a glance at Laird and then at Turtle. He pulled himself back into the pose he adopted—I was sure now it was a pose—and laughed nervously.

"No comment."

"Chicken!"

He threw up both hands in a mock defense. "I'll take

krauts any day against a colonel's daughter." For the first time I noticed the West Point ring on his finger.

"A typical career man's remark!" I scoffed. "It just volunteered you for KP. Turtle, we need wood everywhere."

"Sounds like the colonel, too," DeLord muttered goodnaturedly to Turtle. "Yes, sir, ma'am, sir," he said, saluting me repeatedly.

"I'll unload the sled," the major offered before I could pointedly ignore him in my summary disposition of duties.

"Dinner in an hour, *with* Yorkshire pudding," and I cocked a finger at Turtle.

One of the basic facts I had learned from the years with my father was that occasionally men enjoy being ordered around by a woman. Just occasionally. Whether it's a voluntary return to the status of small, naughty boys or whether it's just a relief not to have to make decisions, I don't know. But I often found it worked with my father. However, he was quick enough to tell me when I was out of line, if I did not sense it first.

I seized upon this ploy because I wanted some time to think. I wanted the air to clear between Major Laird and myself, now that the unexpected arrival of DeLord had erased the nice sense of companionship between Turtle, Laird, and me.

Whatever those two said, I could not place Robert De-Lord in Warren's camp. He was a very cool man and his green eyes missed nothing. I was certain he was sensitive to a lot of what was not being discussed.

The major did not seem to trust him nor want him to know that we suspected Dad had been murdered—there, I could actually think it without wincing—and that all my father's effects were under this roof. It was compatible with the respect in which my father's men had held him that they would make the duty call, however painful, on his daughter were they able to. That sufficiently explained DeLord's reason for seeking me out. I had myself, at Dad's instigation, made several calls on Boston families of combat fatalities. I had been rather surprised to learn that Mrs. Colonel Warren had also paid such visits. She didn't live in Boston. I wondered what had got into her. Bucking for Warren's chicken wings, probably.

In the meantime, I set the lieutenant to peeling potatoes.

"I didn't really intend to impose on your hospitality, Miss Carlysle."

"Carla," I corrected automatically. I couldn't get that message through to the major but the lieutenant was going to start out right.

"Carla."

"And don't give me any nonsense about imposing. If a man has the decency to hunt up his colonel's daughter, he is entitled to one good meal. Especially when he braves blizzards to pay his respects."

"Yes, ma'am," was all he said to that but his eyes sparkled.

I didn't want him to get the idea that I was too stupid to realize he had some double purpose.

"How long is your leave?" I went on, not letting him reform his thoughts.

"Oh, I'm entitled to quite a bit," he temporized.

"You're peeling them too thick. Didn't you learn anything at the Point?"

His grin widened. He concentrated on his peeling.

"I certainly look forward to a piece of your apple pie." He reverted to his original trend of thought.

"Yes, I'd noticed."

He stopped peeling a moment, looking at the middle distance as he reflected.

"It's funny ma'am, apple pie was one of the things you're supposed to miss."

I snorted.

"Actually, what I craved most was an Idaho baked potato!"

"Not hominy grits?"

He gave me a rueful grin. "I keep trying to live down my rebel origins. No, a baked potato, hot and fluffy inside, with buckets of butter!"

"The major must have an 'in' with the local cow," I commented, showing him the wheel of butter.

His eyes widened with delight at such a supply.

"In Europe," he continued, peeling carefully, "the potatoes are small and yellow. When you can get 'em at all. Oh, all right in stews and such but they don't bake." He turned the potato over in his hand. The russet was not exactly in prime condition nor very large, but the flesh was white. "Your father was a good rough cook. Did you know?"

I snorted. "And who do you think taught him?"

"I got a few days off in October and made for Paree." I expected him to respond to his reminiscences in some typically military fashion, a smirk, a smile, or a grimace. But he went on, "And, of all people, guess who I met?" He slapped his thigh for emphasis, a gesture entirely out of character. "Who did I run into but Colonel Murdock? Never guessed then he'd be my C.O. in a few weeks' time. And guess where?"

"You tell me."

He looked at me squarely for a moment, wonderingly.

"Buying stamps!"

He paused and deliberately finished peeling the potato. I said nothing.

"Yes, ma'am. We were fellow philatelists." He glanced up at me. "He was lucky that day. He picked up some departing German officer's abandoned collection. Has it been returned to you?"

He was regarding me squarely, his eyes on mine, his face grave.

"Yes, Lieutenant, it has." I failed to add that the two onionskin lists were in my pocket, one with his name in pencil at the top.

He heaved a counterfeit sigh of relief. It irritated me beyond measure that he continued his playacting. He must be aware I was not fooled by it.

"I'm very glad, Miss Carla, because I know some of those stamps were valuable. Your father was very pleased to get the French-Chinese 1900 issues."

That gave me pause for those were some of the items Dad had listed and checked off.

"I was afraid," the lieutenant continued, concentrating on his potato for a moment, "that it might have gone astray in the shuffle at Division HQ. Or that someone might have offered you a good price for it?" He gave me a quick look.

"The peels are getting thick again." I remarked caustically.

He paid attention to his peeling.

"Or maybe," he suggested softly, "you know enough about stamps to realize the collection is valuable?"

"Yes, I do know Dad's stamps are valuable."

"The ones he got in France?" and DeLord scanned my face.

"I haven't gone through them closely but I thank you for the warning. No one will get them without paying a lot for them."

We were looking directly in each other's eyes now. I couldn't tell what he was thinking or what reaction he had been trying to get from me. He was forewarned, at any rate, if his part in all this was devious.

I had a sudden urge to level with Robert DeLord completely. I disliked underhanded dealings and hidden meanings. I liked things open and understood. I preferred to know where I stood with people and I wanted them to know where they were with me. My instinct was to trust DeLord. Dad had. He might even have trusted DeLord with information he didn't pass on to Turtle or the major for some peculiar reason. He might even have charged DeLord with keeping an eye on Warren—which would account for DeLord's interest in that man. If Dad had been conscious as DeLord had been bringing him back in the jeep, he might have told DeLord something, even who murdered him. And if DeLord had buddy-buddied Warren . . . maybe there was a damned good reason. It would certainly explain DeLord's line of questioning as well as his efforts to reach me. And the major? Oh, no. No!

"Good," DeLord was saying, accepting my implied warning.

"By any chance," I replied, twisting my dig a little, "would you be interested in buying them?"

"Me? No, ma'am," he answered with honest surprise. "Not on a lieutenant's pay."

Turtle came in. He looked sardonically at the lieutenant's labor but said nothing, passing through to the back porch. I heard him rumbling on to the major. The conversation with

DeLord had been punctuated with the cracks of an ax against wood and the thud as logs were piled against the side of the back porch. As I heard the clumping of several pairs of feet approaching, I switched to more general conversation. I could see that it rubbed my guardian exactly the wrong way to find me and Robert DeLord in congenial good spirits. I paid Major Regan Laird no attention whatsoever as he stood peeling off layers of clothing.

"Sun's over the yardarm, Turtle," I announced when the sergeant came in.

I ignored Turtle's startled look at the use of his nickname. He shot a menacing glance at the lieutenant who did not so much as flutter a muscle. The sobriquet might never be used by anyone but me but I'll bet anything the whole regiment knew it.

"Gotta wash," the sergeant mumbled. He and the major disappeared.

I listened for the major's explosion when he entered the bathroom. His profanity, muffled but unmistakable, startled the lieutenant. I gave him no explanation and continued blithely to set the table as I pumped him.

"You never saw Camp . . . Fort Dix . . . I'll never get that straight," I groaned, "before its new exalted position, did you?"

"No, Miss Carla."

"Just Holabird and Benning?"

"That's right."

"But Holabird was provost marshall school, wasn't it?"

"Oh, I reckon so, but they took in other units just before Pearl, about the time I got there."

"I see." And I was beginning to. And I wondered if I liked that conclusion. If Major Laird and Turtle had their doubts about DeLord, maybe they had a good reason, apart from the one they gave, for distrusting him. But Dad hadn't and, as regimental C.O., he would have known that DeLord was provost marshal. But why should a secret P.M. be attached to the regiment? Warren had pulled an awfully costly blunder at Bois de Collette in the Cotentin Peninsula that had decimated two companies, but to warrant a P.M.? No. There had been *some* extenuating circumstances. If Dad had *only* got rid of Warren . . . the man had been an albatross forever. He had a way of giving orders that positively antagonized officer and enlisted man alike. He was the greatest refugee from the Civil War since Custer and he never had been able to understand the necessity for changing tactics that had been successful in Napoleon's day. For instance, the need for tank support of infantry (Warren, Dad had told me, considered tanks a Buck Roger's lunacy) and the necessity of sustaining an artillery barrage until visible casualties among your own men—these new tricks of warfare Warren simply could not accept. But Dad had gone to the Point with Warren and Dad had his own Scotch ideas of loyalty. Well, they had cost him his life. Did DeLord suspect that? That would have brought down a provost marshal. But DeLord had been with the regiment long before that. Why?

Nor could I see any connection between provost marshal and a perfectly respectable stamp hobby. Not unless Dad had taken blocks of stamps from the French postal service and they were raising a Gallic fuss. But Dad was discriminating and large blocks didn't interest him. And, anyway, Dad had been in Paris before DeLord joined the outfit, not after. So it wasn't stamps . . . exactly . . . .

I heard the major's heavy step in the corridor. There was no mistaking the suppressed anger in that determined thump. I wondered if he wanted to rake me over the coals for doing the laundry, or for festooning it in the bathroom. At any rate, he was livid, or the scar was a very reliable pressure gauge. And I just didn't care.

It did seem a little ungrateful of him when you considered the efforts I had saved his majorial dignity. I couldn't picture *him* bending over a steamy washboard. And there is nothing like combat boots to foul up socks for fair. But oh, he was mad.

Fortunately, DeLord's presence was inhibiting and, though the major's eyes blazed with fury, he said nothing. He stalked over to the cabinet and got out three glasses. I was about to remind him there were four of us when he swung his body around, shot a frown at DeLord, and took down one more.

"Soda?" he barked at the lieutenant.

"Neat!"

This, too, annoyed the major. He put the glasses on the table with a thud which roused Merlin. He had been snoozing under the table but sat upright with a throaty growl, aware of the undercurrent in the room.

Major Laird, until that moment unaware of Merlin's presence, sprang backwards, hunching, his hand automatically seeking a nonexistent gunbutt at his hip, all his combat reflexes alerted by the unexpected noise. For one split second I wondered if he would be foolhardy enough to lash out at Merlin. Even as that outrageous thought cross my mind, I realized how unworthy it was. Mad at me the major might be, but he was not the sort of person who slapped down the next guy in line for someone else's fault.

"Easy, fella," he said although the admonition went to the wrong person. Merlin sneezed and lay back down.

I wondered if the major realized he looked a trifle foolish, at least to me he did, overreacting to a dog's growl. I glanced at the lieutenant out of the corner of my eye. I amended my thought and decided I was foolish. The lieutenant approved the major's quickness. It was analogous to Turtle's reflex attack on me yesterday. I was the one at fault, I chided myself, being very childish, selfish and thoughtless. These men had been in combat. Their nerves were still wire-tight and battle-honed. I had no right to play on their emotions and set up situations that increased their tensions.

"Oh," I exclaimed, as if suddenly remembering, "I'm sorry about the bathroom, Major. I left stuff all over. I hope you didn't mind my taking over like that. Force of habit. I always did it for Dad."

"Thank you," the major said stiffly, his head barely inclining in my direction. "It was kindly meant, I'm sure, but unnecessary."

"Dry yet?"

He shook his head and continued fixing the drinks. Turtle barged into the kitchen.

"Freezing upstairs," he croaked, warming his hands over the stove.

The major handed drinks around. The lieutenant hopped

up nimbly for a man who affected a languorous attitude most of the time.

"The colonel, God bless him," grated out Turtle, raising his glass. It still had the quality of a prayer, not a toast. Was Turtle getting religion?

My inner question helped me over the moment. No tears and only a slight constriction in my throat, so it surprised me to see a grimness in the lieutenant's mouth. It passed so quickly I may have been reading more than was there.

Turtle reversed a chair as he usually did, and, seeing Merlin sprawled under the table, arranged his feet carefully.

"Wore him out, we did," the sergeant laughed, taking a long swig. "Good stuff. By God, good stuff."

"I didn't realize that shepherds had retriever instincts," was the major's comment, relaxing for the first time since the lieutenant's arrival.

"Oh, Merlin is full of surprises. Did you think to make a sled dog out of him on the way back? He's strong enough to pull quite a heavy load."

Turtle cleared his throat, grinning wickedly at the major.

"We *tried*," the sergeant admitted.

The major grinned, glancing under the table.

"He didn't seem to think too much of the idea."

"He's been cooped up so much lately, he may just have needed the run," I decided.

"Swim," the major corrected me. "He didn't stay in long, though."

I laughed heartily. "He's a frustrated lifeguard. I remember one time Dad and I went over to Wildwood Beach . . . that's Jersey coast. Merlin wouldn't let me in the water. The sea wasn't rough or anything and Merlin'd been in. We couldn't understand it. Then Dad tried and he wouldn't let Dad in. Dad was furious. A boy, about four or five, started to wade in and Merlin ran around him until the child was so terrified he went screaming back to his parents. I want to tell you we had quite a time. The lifeguards called the police and wouldn't listen when Dad and I kept trying to explain that Merlin was not rabid, had had all his shots, was a trustworthy animal and . . . you know." I nodded significantly at Turtle who nodded back sagely. "They were all set to take Merlin by force when someone started screaming out in the ocean. Come to find out, Merlin wasn't so stupid. There were swarms of jellyfish and men-of-war coming in with the tide." I shuddered at the thought of those slimy, stinging tentacles. "How Merlin knew they constituted a danger, I don't know. But he wasn't going to let me or Dad or that child in the water. The others, already swimming, I guess he figured he couldn't help."

"Dog's near human," the lieutenant commented appreciatively.

Merlin, who knew we were talking about him, laughed happily up at us, his tongue dangling sideways out of his mouth.

The eggy aroma of Yorkshire pudding now overlaid the combined smells of meat and woodsmoke. I hastily checked my dinner.

"Sure do admire pioneer women, coping with these things," I groaned, trying to avoid the blast of hot air from the oven. "We got to eat right now."

"No complaints here," Turtle assured me.

# ❦ 9

MERLIN WOKE ME. The very manner in which he woke me, his cold nose butting into my eyes, told me he was on the alert. He kept butting me in the neck when he saw my eyes open. Assured I was awake, he carefully got down from the bed, turned back, and imperiously nudged my shoulder. Shivering, I dragged my dressing robe around my shoulders and slid into it. Merlin went to the door. No sound, not so much as the click of a toenail on the bare floor.

I opened the door cautiously, grimacing at the effort of keeping the metal latch silent. He slipped out as soon as there was enough space for his body. He went towards the back of the house. I grabbed his neckchain as we passed Turtle's door. I hesitated briefly. Merlin's manner told me someone unannounced was either in the house or trying to get in. He had not barked but had awakened me for further orders. I couldn't imagine who was trying to get in the house, snowbound and isolated as it was.

Even if Lieutenant DeLord, presumably fast asleep in the kitchen as the other two bedrooms had no fireplaces, were prowling about, Merlin was not likely to have been alarmed. He trusted DeLord and had been given no orders restricting the lieutenant to the kitchen.

I'm sure if the major had known I could specify DeLord was to be kept kitchenbound by Merlin, he would have suggested it. But we had had a very convivial evening after all. I don't know when the men got to bed, because I left early. They were well into the bottle when I went up. Perhaps, in their cups, Major Laird might have reconciled his differences with Robert DeLord.

Also, if Lieutenant DeLord was so fascinated by my father's stamps, there were easier ways for him to get a look at them than crawling around a frigid house in the dark. The albums could be anywhere.

So here I was, prowling the freezing hall myself. I paused by Turtle's door and listened, ear against the cold wood. I was rewarded with the sound of fantastic snores, each bigger or more intricately breathed than the last. I was not going to wake him if the only way I could do was to yell "Sarge" or risk my brains blown out.

I passed the room by. Merlin stopped at the bathroom. I could see his eyes gleam as he turned his head back to me expectantly. I tried to remember if the roof of the kitchen extended below the bathroom. Someone could climb it to the second story. If someone had scouted the first floor, he would have seen the lieutenant asleep in the kitchen and decided against that. The back door wasn't locked though the front was, an unnecessary precaution in this weather and on the Cape. No, the back room, where the footlockers were, gave onto the kitchen roof, not this bathroom.

I snapped my finger softly at Merlin and started towards the back room, certain now that would be the point of entry. The next thing I knew someone's hand was over my mouth and I was being yanked back into the bathroom.

I struggled, wondering with amazement why Merlin

wasn't ferociously attacking my assailant. I tried to bite the
hand over my mouth just as I heard him snap "Quiet!" in a
tonelessness that was too low on the audible threshold to be
called a whisper. It was the major. He was fully dressed except
for boots and wore his heavy outer coat. He had a gun in his
hand, a little Luger from the size of it. His lips were at my ear
and he released my mouth.

"What's wrong?" he asked in a below-sound word that
was really enunciated air.

"Merlin's on the alert," I said, trying to duplicate his
near-silent communication. "Why are you here?" I demanded.

"Not now." And, steely fingers around my arm, he
propelled me to the back room, Merlin padding soundlessly
beside us.

The door creaked as the cold hinges complained in the
wood. Then Merlin erupted into the room, launching himself,
a silvery projectile, against the back window. There was no
doubting the presence of the intruder. His body was silhouetted in the window against the snow on the slope behind
the house. Merlin had leaped in silence but the moment he
connected with the barrier of glass he burst into enraged snarls.
The figure hesitated only briefly and then turned, slipping
down the incline of the roof and dropping off into the drifted
snow below. Merlin clawed frantically at the window, snarling,
bilked of an immediate capture. He had more wit than we did,
for he did an end-for-end switch to get out of the room and
down the stairs.

But the room was small and crowded, with one hundred
twenty pounds of shepherd, me in a full-skirted robe, and the
major. The door got closed. The major and I in a comedy of
errors both tried to find the latch and let the frantic dog out.
When we did, Merlin tore around the hallway, no attempt at
quiet progress now. He didn't stop at the front door and even
as the major, a few steps ahead of me all the time, followed him,
we heard Merlin crashing against the kitchen door, barking
urgently.

Just as the major reached the kitchen door it opened,
revealing the lieutenant, hair tousled, down to his heavy underwear, obviously not the one who had tried to enter the back

room. He stepped aside for Merlin and the major. Merlin, his feet scrabbling an impatient tattoo, danced at the back door. The major, his arm fully extended, flipped up the latch and followed the dog's mad flight to the final door out. Merlin took off across the snow with my voice roaring a command after him.

"Hold him, Merlin, hold him and guard!"

As the major started after the dog, I screamed at him, "Your boots. Get your boots. Merlin'll hold whoever it is."

The major caught at the door frame to stop his forward momentum as he, too, realized he was no good in that deep snow in stocking feet. Before he could, I had rushed into the study and retrieved his boots by the fireplace. He dropped to the floor, jamming his feet in, lacing them part way.

The lieutenant was no laggard. He had thrown on pants, shirt, boots, and jacket. He was out after the major before Turtle, roused by the barking and clatter, entered the kitchen, also dressing as he ran. He was somewhat hampered by the service revolver in one hand.

The three men, almost evenly spaced in their order of pursuit, staggered and plunged through the drifts, guided by Merlin's clear cry.

Shivering as much from cold as excitement, I stood in the doorway, straining to follow the chase. But the night was moonless and the snow cast up deceiving images. I waited, frustrated, angry, hopeful.

I heard Merlin's now distant bark change to an attacking snarl. Despite the confusion in the room and all the doors, he had made up the burglar's head start.

A shot rang out in the still night. I gasped, leaned against the door for support. I heard another shot. Then two more in quick succession, I heard a motor revving and the squeal of protesting metal. Another shot and then a pained yip.

I sank, stricken, to the cold planking of the porch, grabbing the doorframe until I felt my fingernails bend at the quick from the pressure. Merlin! Not Merlin, too! Oh, please God, let me hear him bark, or snarl, or even yip again.

More shots broke the night stillness. I closed my eyes, limp with despair.

"Kill him, kill him," I heard myself shriek. "If he's hurt Merlin, kill him. *Kill him!*"

And then I curled in on myself, sobbing. I couldn't have sat there very long but I might have. The convulsions of wild crying gave way to the violent shaking of shivers. The tears were runnels of ice down my face. I got myself to my feet and forced myself to stop crying. I closed the porch door. I went back to the door of the major's room and closed it. I marched woodenly into the kitchen, closed the door behind me. I leaned against it for a moment, shaking with cold. Then I closed the hall door Turtle had left open. I drew the curtains. I went over to the table and lit the kerosene light, its bright glow a false note in the room. I threw wood on the fire. I couldn't stop shivering so I took the whiskey bottle and poured myself a stiff shot. I stood there, trying to swallow the first mouthful, dreading what the men would tell me when they returned.

Over and over in my brain spun prayer words for Merlin. It wasn't fair, it just wasn't fair, for Merlin to be taken from me, too. Memories of him as a long-eared awkward pup crowded into mind. The foolishness, the folly, the fun of the insolent intelligent beastie. The trials I had undergone to keep him by me from crowded baggage cars to the sometimes third-rate boardinghouses that would accept pets. The times when Dad's allotment check didn't reach me and we had little to eat, too proud to approach acquaintances. All the many, many facets of a relationship that was blessed with an uncanny rapport, transcending his lack of speech. I could not be deprived of that by so mean an instrument as a petty burglar.

I heard motion outside the kitchen. Disregarding the blackout, I spread myself flat against the window, straining to see but the light within the room made the outside indistinct. All I saw were two figures carrying something. I whirled to snatch the porch door open.

"He's hurt but not badly," the major said swiftly, as he and DeLord edged sideways to bring the limp dog-body in.

I swept the lamp from the table, holding it high so they could put Merlin down. I clamped my teeth on my lips, covered my mouth to dampen the sound of the sobs rising in my throat. I widened my eyes to keep them clear of tears.

"Hold the light over here, Miss Carla," the lieutenant ordered, pointing to Merlin's head. He was bending over the dog, shedding his gloves and jacket so he could work better. "He got creased in the scalp. Like me," and he threw me a hasty reassuring grin, "and, I think, in the shoulder. Major, got a first-aid kit?"

"Coming."

The lieutenant's hands were quick but gentle as he felt the unconscious dog's shoulder.

"Yeah, here. Oohoo, that's quite a furrow. Hold the light a little higher."

The major returned, another lamp in one hand, first-aid kit in the other. In the augmented light, the gash was visible, and more.

"He's got a slug in him," the lieutenant said, his fingers locating the lump. "Not deep, though," he reassured me.

When the major put an arm around me, I realized I was swaying. I caught myself upright.

"You'll have to get it out, won't you?" I said in a tight voice.

"No sweat. We've all done field surgery. Even on colonels. Right, Major?"

"Right," the major's deeper voice assured me. His hand pressed comfortingly against my waist. "Merlin had him by the arm, too, but the man in the car shot him. Shot him twice," and the major's voice turned hard and cold. "To make sure."

The lieutenant muttered under his breath. He sighed and straightened up, looking at the major.

"I'll need a good sharp knife, sterilized. Is that a field kit, Laird?"

"Yes, it's got a probe."

"Good. Hope he stays out. His teeth are sharp as I'm sure our catman found out," and the lieutenant bared his own teeth in a malicious grin. He washed his hands very carefully.

"Merlin won't bite you," I declared.

"All in a good cause," the lieutenant said lightly, using a sink brush vigorously on his nails. "Many men have survived my tender ministrations, Miss Carla, and walked away to fight again. We got him in out of the cold which could be bad for open wounds."

He dried his hands and looked critically at Merlin.

"It'll be easier on all of us if he sleeps on."

"He wouldn't bite you even if he did wake," I reasserted loyally.

"Of course not. The dog's got more sense than most humans. Here's Turtle now."

Turtle stamped in, breathing stertorously. His language, even for him, was incredible, his expressiveness therapeutic. He came right up to Merlin, glancing anxiously at the two officers. When he saw their confident expressions, he straightened up.

"Snow slowed me. They got clean away, the _____ ," he said curtly.

"Now, Miss Carla, you hold both lights, like so." The lieutenant positioned my hands. "I want you two to be ready to hold him. Put your full weight on him if necessary. Bailey, you lean across his shoulders, to keep his head down. Major, take his hips. His frame is strong. The important thing will be to keep him from moving while I'm probing. Ready?"

"Wouldn't more light be better?" I asked fearfully.

"This is more than we usually have," Turtle grunted.

The major held up an ampoule of morphine from the field kit.

"This might help," he suggested.

"Dose isn't calibrated for a dog, damnitall." The lieutenant rejected the idea with the first swear words I'd heard him use. He picked up the knife, a wicked-looking gleam running its sharp length in the lamplight. He took a deep preliminary breath and, with sensitive fingers, felt around the slug where it bulged slightly in the fleshy part of the shoulder.

Soon my arms, numbed by being held so high so long, began to tremble. The major took the lamps from me, leaving me standing stupidly useless.

The bullet had creased Merlin's head between his ears. A little lower and it would have entered the brain. For a wild shot on a dark night it had been all too close! I turned quickly to the counter and fumbled along it for the half-filled glass of whiskey. I took a deep swallow.

"There," said the lieutenant's voice, full of relief for the task accomplished. "That'll fix him. I wonder, do dogs get headaches? By rights, he'll have a beauty."

"Thanks," I said in so low a voice I wondered if anyone could hear me. "Thanks," I croaked again only this time my voice sounded too loud and very unsteady.

Two hands closed firmly around my shoulders. I thought for one moment it was the lieutenant but, as I leaned back grateful for the sympathy conveyed by the gesture, I realized it was Major Laird.

"Take another jolt, Carlysle," he murmured softly, giving me a little squeeze. I felt his hand brush my hair, half caress, half reassurance.

I obeyed and then turned around. Over Merlin's still form, the lieutenant caught my eyes. He draped a blanket loosely over the dog, his gestures quick and sure despite the strain he'd been under.

"Protecting him from shock will be the important thing. He didn't lose much blood and we got him out of the cold quickly."

DeLord skirted the table and began to wash his hands. The major and Turtle were conferring. Then Turtle left the kitchen as the major experimentally sloshed the coffeepot.

"You're very knowledgeable about animals," I said inanely to DeLord, trying to get out a phrase that might possibly express a gratitude too deeply felt to voice. I put my hand impulsively on his damp forearm, instinctively trying to communicate my sincerity by touch alone.

"Raised on a farm, Miss Carla. Bound to learn how to take care of sick and injured critters." He patted my hand understandingly.

"I can't ever thank you enough."

He shrugged. "I'd feel better if we could have a professional check that over," he sighed, glancing over at Merlin. "Sutures could be tighter."

"He hasn't come to," I said, biting my lip anxiously.

"That was a clout, bullet notwithstanding," the major

remarked, putting a coffee cup in my hand. "Irish coffee," he added when he saw me looking around for my whiskey. "You got creased, DeLord. Tell Carlysle how long you were out."

Grinning with boyish ruefulness, the lieutenant's hand had flown to his head, gingerly touching the scar.

"Several hours, they do say," he replied. "Now, don't you worry," he admonished me kindly.

Turtle clumped back in with a bundle of quilts.

"Over here by the stove, sergeant," the major ordered and I watched, vestiges of outraged housewifely conscience rising to protest as valuable handpieced quilts were laid down as a sickbed for my dog. Even if Mrs. Laird's ghost was turning in its grave, my estimation of the major rose.

"We don't want him falling off the table," DeLord said.

With great care the three men settled my Merlin on the quilts, covering him meticulously as if he had been a valued human buddy.

I was about to sit down beside him, preparing to be by his side the rest of the night, when the major took a firm hold on my arm, propelling me towards the study.

"Oh no you don't."

"But he'll need me," I protested, trying to escape.

"Old Doc DeLord's volunteered for this detail," the lieutenant put in, dodging around the table to take my other arm.

I couldn't fight both of them, not that I had the strength to.

"You've been through quite enough tonight," Regan Laird continued inexorably. He seated me on his bed, throwing a spare blanket around me. "Now you'll finish your coffee and then go to bed. Sergeant, did you get the license on the truck?"

"Naw, sir. Either they covered it up or it was plain too dark. Night like tonight, I couldn't tell what color the car was but it was a Chevvie body. I'd say about 1938. I lost them by the time they reached the second turn onto the good road. Geez, I coulda sworn I'd punctured the gas tank."

The major turned expectantly to DeLord.

"Your eyesight's failing, Bailey. The truck was light gray. The burglar was about five nine, slight build, too muffled in clothing to tell much more. But he sure could move in the snow," DeLord remarked. "I think I winged the driver. I'm not sure but he gave up shooting and started cussing."

The major nodded, digesting the information.

"Driver was just a dark blob," he added and then exploded unexpectedly. "Goddamit, DeLord, where do you fit in all this?"

I was feeling all relaxed suddenly and the fact that the major hadn't guessed was extraordinarily funny.

"He's provost marshal, guardian dear. Maybe even CID."

All three men turned to me with various expressions of astonishment on their faces. I found it difficult to focus my eyes and blinked to clear my vision.

"Provost marshal?" Turtle bellowed, half rising from his chair, disbelief and desperation on his face. "CID?"

The lieutenant ducked his head, his fingers smoothing down the crease scar.

"She's right, I'm afraid."

"Course I'm ri . . . right . . . ." I was having the hardest time enunciating. "Summuns wron wi' me," and I felt myself falling sideways into darkness. The last thing I saw was the major's satisfied grin and I knew that there was more in that coffee than whiskey.

# ❧ 10

WHEN I WOKE, the room was brilliant with sunlight reflecting off snow. I hadn't realized my windows faced due east. I lay there for a moment, logy in brain and body. I yawned fit to pop my jaw, covering my mouth belatedly. My watch registered ten and, positive it had stopped the previous night, I wound it. Then I realized Merlin was absent.

I was out of the bed in a single motion, grabbing my robe on the way to the door. The floor was icy under my bare feet as I flew down the stairs and burst into the kitchen, ignoring the three men, eyes only for Merlin in the corner.

He raised his head weakly, whining a greeting. I could see him gathering his body to rise. The pain of his wounds forced a yip out of him. I signaled him to stay, hurt to the quick that my entrance caused him the least unnecessary pain.

I fell on my knees beside him, crooning softly, stroking his muzzle and ears, kissing him, talking to him, in an excessive display of relieved affection. He licked my face, something he rarely did, and lay back with a sigh, letting me fuss over him, answering me with his own version of a croon, deep in his throat.

"He's all right," I told the world, dashing tears from my cheeks, only that moment aware I was crying with relief. "He's all right?" I questioned, turning to DeLord for confirmation.

"Fine. Drank a half gallon of water," DeLord nodded. "Very good patient. I know plenty could take lessons from this dog."

"You bet," Turtle rumbled.

"You!" I began, pointing to the major at the far end of the table. I got to my feet and marched myself over to him, for once at an advantage because he was seated. "You drugged that coffee."

"Damn well told," the major agreed. "You were out on your feet and too damned stubborn a little fool to know it." Having delivered this considered opinion, he calmly continued to eat his breakfast.

"Flapjacks, Little Bit?" asked Turtle, rising and going to the stove.

I glared at him, indecisively. The major wasn't going to let me pick a quarrel with him and neither was Turtle.

"Okay, okay," I said, not the least bit gracious, flopping into a chair. "Pull your diversionary tactics. I'll wait."

The lieutenant, with what I now realized was a habitual gesture on his part, ducked his head and smoothed the scar crease. I sighed with exasperation.

"You are all alike, all of you, and that includes my fine four-footed friend." Merlin answered with a placating whine, raising his head from his quilt a few inches before he sighed plaintively and laid down again. I jerked my finger over my shoulder at him, tapping my foot. "Can't say anything around here."

"Sleep well?" asked the major politely, but even his mouth twitched in an effort not to laugh at my frustration.

"No fault of yours." I glared.

"Drink this and shut up," Turtle ordered, putting coffee in front of me.

"Is it safe?" I asked sarcastically.

Turtle snorted and turned to tend his flapjacks. I sipped rebelliously because I was not going to get anywhere. They had been perfectly justified and I had better adjust to it. As if he sensed my softening, the major leaned forward, touching my arm lightly, so I'd look at him.

"Do you remember identifying DeLord last night?"

I glanced, startled, at the lieutenant and then remembered. That did much to restore my battered self-esteem.

"Yes, and I was right, wasn't I?"

The lieutenant nodded.

"Well," Major Laird continued, scratching the back of his neck with his forefinger, "he told us why he was masquerading. And it is serious."

"Dad?" I cried out so sharply Merlin whined. I absently signaled him to stay down.

"No, no, your father knew about it," DeLord hastened to say. "Although to be quite candid, I had to suspect him, too."

"The stamps?" I queried, adding facts up.

The major held up his hand for me to slow down with wild guessing. The lieutenant grinned.

"She's quick."

"Let us explain the whole thing, will you, Carlysle," the major suggested patiently.

"Then Dad *was* murdered!"

"Car-*lysle!*" the major snapped in an authoritative tone.

DeLord's hand went up to interrupt the major's reprimand.

"Yes, only I didn't know that until last night. It puts another complexion on the whole situation." His fingers lightly pressed my hand. "Believe me, had we any idea that would happen, we would have acted with more dispatch. But we had only circumstantial evidence that points to the One Hundred and Fifteenth Regiment. As far as my superiors were concerned, it was serious but not an acute situation. Naturally, I could take only the colonel into my confidence when I was assigned to the case. Matter of fact," and he grinned ruefully, "the major was one of my prime suspects."

Incredulous, I stared at my guardian.

"You see, Miss Carla, it had to be someone with enough sophistication to know *what* to loot."

"Loot? It was looting?" I glanced at Turtle.

"Yes, looting. Not just trinkets or ghoul jobs on corpses. But items of intrinsic or tangible value. Jewels, stamps as you suggested, even some rare letters and a rare and immeasurably valuable Book of the Hours. Very old, more than priceless to its custodian. These are things an educated man would know to steal."

"But why was my father murdered?"

"Your father had identified the thief . . . to his satisfaction. He was obviously murdered to keep from disclosing what he knew."

"For a mess of jewelry and stamps?" I cried, appalled at the horrible, horrible wastefulness.

The lieutenant shook his head slowly from side to side.

"I'm afraid it was more than a mess of jewelry and stamps. The estimated value of the losses is close to several hundred thousand dollars."

I stared in silence at the lieutenant.

"It took us some time to narrow down our search when the initial reports came in after the Falaise-Argentan pocket was wiped out. There were items stolen by the German Seventh Army that should have been recovered in their baggage vans and weren't. I was detached from CAO to the MF Double A S . . ."

"The what?" I asked.

"The Monuments, Fine Arts and Archives Section. So the French wouldn't find their art treasures on a quick trip overseas to America. All soldiers are light-fingered. Then we found ourselves with too many potential masterminds." The lieutenant stroked his head but he didn't smile. "When your father and I crossed paths in Paris that time, I eliminated him completely. I asked him to request a replacement and I'd make sure it was me. Then I could work directly in the regiment without being suspected. We checked everyone. Including you, Major."

The major was frowning in concentration and suddenly his face cleared. He pointed directly at the lieutenant, snapping his fingers as his thoughts crystallized.

"That lecture on autographs! Bonaparte, Louis, ye gods. I thought you'd gone into battle shock. We were at the assembly area at Montcarnet, right?"

The lieutenant nodded. Regan Laird's face clouded again, the muscles tightened along his jaw, and his eyes turned bleak.

"That leaves us with . . ."

"That's right, Laird."

"Warren!" I exploded out of my chair. "Warren killed my father."

"We believe so," DeLord said quietly.

"Believe so?" I echoed, aggravated at his calmness.

He sighed. "Believe me, I sympathize, Miss Carla. Unfortunately, although my earnest private desire is to arrest Warren immediately—"

"But weren't you and Dad on the way to arrest Warren the night he murdered Dad?"

DeLord shook his head. "Your father had laid a trap for the looter with several valuable stamps and some jeweled crosses. We had to find them in the thief's possession, you know, to press charges. Frankly, I hadn't suspected Warren. I had my eye on one of the Third Battalion smart operators. I thought at the time your father was going to order Warren back to HQ. He should've after that stunt with the beetfields!" The lieutenant's face was grim. "Now I know why, against all logic, your father had to keep Warren on the line."

"Fer Chrissake!" Turtle growled softly.

"So after your father . . . died, I had to go on alone, set up another trap which also meant the necessity of—"

"Sucking up to Warren?" Turtle interrupted again, his eyes narrowing.

DeLord nodded. "The bait was taken and then I couldn't find it!" He grimaced with distaste and dismay. "And that was the hardest blow. It has to be Warren because he was the last person to handle the items. But he didn't have them and I searched, believe me, I searched. I even drugged his coffee one night to search him personally. And I had to find out how he disposed of the loot. There were some mighty valuable pieces involved by then and they've got to be recovered."

"And my father's murder is less important than—"

"No, no," DeLord hastily interrupted, his eyes shocked at that suggestion. "But *I* didn't know that until last night. Now the serial number has been filed off that Colt but I think we can get enough to reconstruct it and trace the issue. Unfortunately, Miss Carla, we have to have proof to bring an officer to court-martial. Proof of murder and proof of grand larceny."

"But I'm no longer army," I said through my gritted teeth, "and I don't need any further proof. Warren's waiting for me in Boston."

I swung my chair around, grabbing for the pile of letters on the sideboard. The major caught my arm as I passed him and jerked me sharply to my feet. I tried to twist free but he was on his feet, hands on my shoulders, shaking me hard.

"But I'm not having my ward up for murder. Now you stop this ranting around . . . right now . . . ." He gave me a neck-snapping shake, bruising my shoulders with his powerful hands. "You're army as long as I'm your guardian. Just remember that, Carlysle. And *I* give the orders. *I* expect them to be obeyed."

He forced my chin up, his eyes glinting angrily down at me.

"You don't go off half-cocked into a battle if you want to win it." Again he shook me but not so hard, because I knew he was right and he sensed it. "You want Warren? Not half as bad as DeLord, Bailey, I and the U.S. Army want him. And you're going to help get him because, my dear ward, you're the new bait. Someone tried to burgle this house last night. Two attempts . . . no three, were made in Cambridge. Now sit down and listen."

He gave me a little push and I stumbled back into my chair, rubbing my shoulders absently.

"We think he's after the gun. DeLord thinks he might be after more than that . . . ."

Merlin interrupted with a bark. His head was turned towards the front of the house and his manner, despite his weakened condition, was alert. He barked again with more strength and struggled to rise.

Turtle was halfway through the corridor before I could force Merlin down. The open door gave a clear view of the front windows and the police car that slid sideways on the snow to a stop in front of the house.

"The shots last night?" DeLord asked.

"The burglary at Mrs. Everett's," I countered flatly.

Merlin growled, an angry frustrated snarl of a growl. His head slewed around to the rear of the house. I grabbed at the major's arm, pointing.

"We're surrounded," I cried out, for a navy patrol, led by two Dobermans straining on their leashes, came tramping out of the scrub at the rear of the house.

"Those shots!" the major said conclusively.

"Christ! Shore Patrol!" Turtle grated out. Two blue jeeps had drawn up beside the police car and armed men were piling out of all three cars.

The policeman gesticulating at the house was cut off bluntly by a gesture from the SP officer. Just then Turtle yanked open the door.

"Whaddya want?"

And the second patrol banged on the back door.

I fell on Merlin to keep him down. DeLord came to my assistance as the major, his face set, went to deal with the rear assault group.

"Let's see your papers, Major," a stern voice ordered Laird through Merlin's snarls.

The Dobermans, aware of another dog's presence, set up a deafening hullabaloo. I heard a noisy scrambling over the incensed barking and the back door was slammed, cutting the canine chorus down appreciably.

"This is all snafu." DeLord grinned at me over Merlin's writhing body.

"Goddamitall, Merlin, *at ease!*" I ordered, slapping his

muzzle in my desperation to keep him from opening his wounds. He whined piteously at the unexpectedly severe reprimand. With an aggressive expression in his eyes, he had to content himself with growling at the Dobermans who were still roaring outside.

"Come in, Ensign," Laird was saying. "May I inquire why my house has been surrounded?"

"Your papers, Major!" the shore patrolman repeated flintily. The man had entered the back hall far enough to see the lieutenant and me sprawled over Merlin's body. He stared at us, turning slightly to expose the drawn thirty-eight in his hand.

"Shut your dogs up, Ensign," I cried. "Mine's been wounded and I've got to keep him quiet." With those Dobermans sounding off, Merlin would not relax.

"Ensign, I'm Lieutenant Robert DeLord, Provost Marshall, on special assignment with Major Laird and Sergeant Bailey." The authority in his voice was incongruous with his semirecumbent position.

The coastguardsman had to crouch to see the lieutenant.

"If you'll muzzle your dogs, I can get up and show you my identification."

"Belay those dogs, mister!" the ensign bellowed, his volume equal to Turtle's parade voice. The Dobermans were silenced.

At this point, Turtle stomped back into the kitchen, his face black with indignant anger. A police officer and another shore patrol j.g. followed him. I could see two men taking positions at the front door. One carried a tommy gun at the ready.

"You get up, Merlin, and I'll whip you. Whip you. Hear?" I muttered savagely before I scrambled to my feet. Cold air swirled around my bare toes.

"Close that door!" I cried.

"Chrissake, Lieutenant, they think we're Nazis, landed by sub last night!" announced Turtle at the top of his lungs, his Dorchester accent unmistakable. No Nazi was that good an imitator.

Laird was now showing the ensign his orders. The sandpeep's manners thawed considerably.

"Thank you, sir. Lieutenant?" and the ensign took the major's papers over to his j.g.

The kitchen, large enough for many, seemed awfully crowded with armed and angry men.

"These *look* all right," the j.g. remarked dubiously, passing them on to the policeman who waved them aside. He had been staring in an unpleasant way at the major.

"Eyah. I know Laird."

At the curiously antagonistic comment, Regan Laird turned his face slightly to the left so that his good profile was in full view of the policeman. The man nodded coldly.

"Eyah, that's Regan Laird."

"Beatty," the major said by way of greeting.

"Who are these others, then?" demanded the j.g.

The policeman lifted heavy shoulders in a shrug.

"I'll vouch for them," the major said quickly. "Both the sergeant and the lieutenant served with me in the Fifth Corps."

"The lieutenant says he's provost marshal," the ensign tacked on.

DeLord bore the keen scrutiny with poise.

"Know about the shooting last night?" the shore patrolman asked.

"Yes." DeLord's flat answer was intended to discourage further questions.

"I have to ask for an explanation, lieutenant," the j.g. insisted, shifting his weight.

"Will you tell them to shut that front door?" I hissed, seizing my opportunity.

"Who are you?" the policeman asked.

"I'm James Carlysle Murdock," I said, with a grimace, steeling myself for the inevitable reaction.

"My ward," the major inserted. "The daughter of my commanding officer who was killed in Europe."

Questions were effectively silenced and the intruders shuffled nervously. I saw the j.g. give a signal and I heard the door close.

The policeman was looking at me speculatively now.

"I want to know about those shots, too," he asserted, looking from me to the major. Laird gestured to DeLord.

I made a quick bet with myself, and won. DeLord ducked his head and fingered his scar.

"We had an unexpected visitor last night," the lieutenant said, having gathered his thoughts together. "Naturally we took off after him. So did the dog and when the burglar's accomplice took a shot at Merlin, well, naturally we took defensive action."

"Did it occur to you that you would alarm the coast with such unauthorized gunfire?" the j.g. snapped in an acid voice. "Don't you guys know there's a . . . ." He stopped. He had the decency to look abashed as his eyes darted to the major's ruined face. His own countenance turned bright red with embarrassment. Turtle's surly growl indicated his opinion of the navy.

"No, I'm afraid it didn't," DeLord replied with more humility than I'd have used under the circumstances. "For one thing," and I couldn't see why he felt he had to justify our actions, "Miss Murdock's dog was seriously wounded. For another, we have no way of communicating with the authorities."

"Well," the j.g. grumbled, "this isn't our jurisdiction at all then." He saluted the major, jerked his head significantly at the ensign in lieu of an order. The front-door party of patrolmen withdrew with what I considered rather bad grace since we were not at fault.

"A moment, Ensign," DeLord said after Turtle closed the hall door on the first group. "Any of your men trained in veterinary skills? I'd appreciate someone looking at the shepherd."

"Sure, Lieutenant, just a minute." The ensign was not at all disgruntled.

"That can wait," said the policeman officiously. "I've a few questions."

"They've waited this long, they can wait a little longer," I retorted, glaring at him.

He turned his head in my direction slowly and gave me a long look, compounded of annoyance that I had spoken in the first place, then insolence as he realized I was older than I looked.

"It won't take a moment," the lieutenant assured Beatty diplomatically.

I began not to like this young man suddenly.

Beatty ignored the lieutenant, pulling a slip of paper out of his pocket. He consulted it for a moment.

"I've been asked by the Cambridge police to question a James Carlysle Murdock concerning a burglary in her boarding-ghouse room . . . Burglary! And you had one last night, too? Whatinhell's going on here?" and he glared around menacingly.

The ensign returned with a sailor who pushed past the major with a polite excuse and suppressed curiosity.

"Evans has had some training, miss," the ensign said and we all stepped aside for the sailor to look at Merlin.

"Merlin! Friend," I told the dog as Evans, his face lighting with admiration for the shepherd, bent slowly, his hand extended.

Merlin whined, licked his lips, but let the sailor examine his head.

"That's a bad crease, miss, but it's clean."

"We dug a bullet out of his shoulder," the lieutenant said.

Evans turned back the quilt and whistled. I heard him pull in his breath sharply as he saw the wound. He put the quilt back and stood up.

"That's beyond me, sir. And he's too good a dog not to have the best."

Evans turned to me, his face eager. "Ever thought of donating him to the K-9 Corps?"

Turtle snorted. I held up a warning hand.

"He's been in, sailor," I said gravely.

I know it was outrageous to imply that Merlin had seen service and been retired honorably but I didn't want him belittled any further with explanations after his heroism of the night before.

Evan's eyes widened and he saluted.

"There's a good vet in Hyannis, miss. With the ensign's permission, I'll give him a call. He'll come out if I say so."

"We'd appreciate it, sailor," the major said smoothly,

moving to my side, his manner, for some reason, protective. I glanced up at him inquiringly and caught, out of the side of my vision, the smirk on Beatty's face. I didn't like it.

"Thank you, Evans," I said, not to let the major do the honors for me exclusively.

The Coast Guard contingent left with expressions of apology and good will. Merlin growled low in his throat as the Dobermans' baying announced withdrawal.

"All right, now," Beatty said. He pulled a chair from the table and sat himself down, opening his heavy coat, taking out report forms, and a pen, his long, lantern-jawed, mulish face disagreeable.

"I want a few things cleared up *on the civilian level*," he said nastily.

I saw the lieutenant ease himself out to the study.

"There's been some hanky-panky heyah that I don't miss even if you pulled rank and all on them sandpeeps."

"I'm sorry, officer," the lieutenant said smoothly. He held out to the policeman a small leather case and a folded sheet of army issue paper. "This matter is now classified."

"Whatinhell you say?" He reluctantly took the papers from DeLord. His eyes widened with outraged surprise. "I don't believe it. Burglaries? Classified?"

"I'm working out of Fort Edwards at the moment. Call CID for verification. This is my code number."

I began to like the lieutenant again.

"I don't like it," Beatty said flatly. He thrust the chair back angrily as he rose. "I don't like it one bit." He waved a finger under DeLord's nose, his anger growing with each shake. "And don't think for one moment, Lieutenant, that I'm not going to call Edwards. There's something godalmighty fishy about this. Burglaries! Shooting!" He turned to include me in his catalog. "Wards! Hell. I know you too well, Regan Laird."

"Now, wait a minute," Turtle growled, placing himself belligerently in Beatty's path. "You don't —"

"You look familiar, Sergeant," Beatty interrupted him pugnaciously, his lantern jaw jutting out. "You at Edwards?"

"Bailey's just back from Germany," Laird intervened. At

his stern look, Turtle stood aside as Beatty, casting one more meaningful sneer over his shoulder, stalked out the door. Merlin's soft snarl summed up my feelings exactly.

"I don't think we've seen the last of him," the lieutenant remarked ruefully, his hand reaching for his head.

"Leave that damn thing alone," I snapped with irritation, pulling a chair near the stove and curling my cold feet under me.

"Edwards does know?" the major asked hopefully.

"Oh, indeed, they do," DeLord replied. "You know this Beatty fellow?"

The major sat down heavily, lighting a cigarette and inhaling deeply before he answered. "Beatty and I have had a few run-ins before."

"Speeding?" I taunted flippantly.

The major shook his head. "Long before I started driving, Carlysle, and long before he got on the force. I came here for summers as a child, you know."

"No, I didn't know," I said caustically.

He ignored me. "If my memory serves me correctly, the initial engagement was fought over some crabs."

"Crabs?" Turtle exploded. Merlin barked.

"Crabs," the major reaffirmed, amusement lighting his face. The lieutenant began to chuckle. "I believe we were about ten at the time. I lost all the crabs I'd caught—a whole morning's work—and came home without the net and with a black eye."

"And Beatty?" I prompted hopefully.

"Oh, he was crabless, too, and minus a front tooth."

"And you're still fighting over that?"

"No," Laird allowed, setting his jaw against what he had no intention of discussing. "There were a few other . . . minor . . . disagreements."

Turtle chuckled understandingly and had that special look which I had learned meant members of my sex were involved.

"However," and the major's attitude changed abruptly as he turned to me, "it only points up my reasons for wanting you out of here."

"That?" I exclaimed, gesturing at the door where Beatty had exited.

"That!" Laird repeated emphatically. "I don't trust Beatty's discretion any further than I can throw him. And I would if it'd serve any purpose. It's going to be all over Orleans that I have a good-looking adolescent ward—"

"I am not adolescent," I objected strenuously. I did not fail to catch the other adjective and treasured it.

"Shut up. And that's going to ruin your reputation."

"But Turtle and the lieutenant are here . . ."

"Turtle possibly constitutes a chaperon but the lieutenant? Sorry, Mrs. Grundy says no."

"A backhanded compliment if ever I had one." DeLord chuckled and then hastened, spurred by Major Laird's angry look, to add his weight to the argument. "But the major's right, Miss Carla. Beatty is no gentleman."

"Now, wait a minute," I suggested, my dander rising on several fronts, "there's one helluva lot more at stake than my reputation. About which I'm *not* worried." I glared at all of them impartially. "Have you so easily forgotten my father's murder? You started to outline what we were going to do next to trap Warren. And I warn you, all of you, I'm not giving up that little item. I want Warren up for court-martial, you, the major, the shore patrol, Beatty, and the entire town of Orleans notwithstanding." I looked at each man belligerently, knowing I had a very strong case.

"Furthermore, Merlin can't be moved. And if I'm not here, he plain won't eat. You're not going to sacrifice him to convention, are you? Because I won't."

"That C.G. rating said he'd call the vet," the major said evasively. "Maybe he can be moved."

"Over snowy roads, in a jeep?" I asked sarcastically. "Ever done it, wounded?" and bit my lip because the look on Turtle's face, not to mention the major's, gave me a definitive answer to that. I swallowed and changed my tactics. "That burglar last night wasn't Warren because Donald Warren would have frozen solid with fright if Merlin were anywhere near him. But I'll bet Warren hired him."

"How would Warren know where you were?" the major countered.

"Ahh," I cried in exasperation. "He wrote me at the Cambridge address, didn't he? He was to be in Boston the twenty-eighth, he and his precious Marian. One quick phone call to Mrs. Everett to arrange a state visit from Lieutenant Colonel and Mrs. Donald Warren, sweetly simpering, sympathetic, solicitous . . . sickening!" I waved my hands, erasing the scene. "And Mrs. Everett who is a sweet lady is not very bright. 'Oh, I'm so sorry. But she's staying with her guardian on Cape Cod,'" and I mimicked the Dorchester accent. "Sure they know where I am. And you may be damned sure they didn't tell their second-story man my dog was here, particularly if it's the same thug who tried to burgle Mrs. Everett's."

"Which brings up another point," the lieutenant interrupted. "I'd like your permission to go through your father's footlocker, Miss Carla."

"Of course. We've been theorizing entirely too much."

"Get dressed first, Carlysle," the major ordered as I led the way upstairs.

I got as far as the door to the little back room before Regan Laird caught up with me. He picked me up bodily and turned me around. He marched me back to my bedroom and thrust me inside. The room was frigid as I'd left the door open.

"It's freezing in here," I complained as he shut me in.

"Too bad. Teach you to shut doors in the future. But you don't leave that room until you're warmly dressed."

"I want to be there when—"

"We won't touch your father's things till you're present," he snapped. "Now dress. On the double."

# ❦ 11

With fingers which fumbled from cold and frustration, I threw on clothes, stamped into boots, and threw open the door. The major was leaning against the jamb, a pleased expression on his face. I could have slapped him.

"Better put a few logs on the fire while you're at it. Warm the room up for later."

I glared at him, tapped my foot and, seeing my irritation only amused him further, I whirled and slammed some logs on the grate. Of course, then I had to sweep up the scattered coals and clinkers.

"Haste makes waste," he chanted from the door.

I raised the fire tongs menacingly and gasped as he instinctively crouched. He strode across the room, his eyes flashing, and jerked the tongs out of my hand.

"That's just enough of that, young lady." He gripped me at the elbows and gave me a hard shake. "I've put up with your bad temper, your moodiness, your insolence because I've been sorry for you. Honestly sorry. But enough is enough. You keep that temper under control or I'll turn you over my knee. Do I make myself clear?"

I was scared of him. And ashamed of myself. I lowered my eyes and swallowed hard.

"I'm truly sorry, Major. I've behaved abominably and I do apologize."

He gave me another little shake, accepting my penitence.

"All right then. Your father saw fit, God knows why, to make me your guardian. As you say, you're nearly twenty-one so our association will be brief. I'd rather it was as pleasant as possible because it is my intention to discharge my duties to the best of my ability. In spite of you."

I still couldn't look at him. He was absolutely right. I had been a self-centered, childish, irresponsible brat. He drew in a deep breath and let it out in a rush, holding out his right hand.

"Now, let's call a truce."

I put my hand gratefully in his and he covered it with his left, pressing it in a friendly way. Then he tipped my face up so I had to look him in the eye. He regarded me seriously for a moment and then smiled slowly.

"You've got pretty eyes, brat," as if he had just noticed I had eyes at all.

He put one arm around my shoulders companionably and led me downstairs.

Turtle and DeLord had cleared the kitchen table and placed the army locker on it. We went through the footlocker, and the lieutenant and I checked through the three albums carefully.

"There's nothing in here. I don't see stamps that are particularly valuable," I said.

The major who had watched for a while decided to make coffee. As he opened the canister he started to swear.

"That tears it. No coffee. Okay, ration stamps everybody."

Turtle flushed. "Left mine with my sister-in-law, Major. Didn't expect to be here so long."

"I've some," the lieutenant said.

"Mine are upstairs but you don't need stamps for coffee," I exclaimed, turning back at the door.

"I need them for meat and sugar, Carlysle. And I'm not making a trip into Orleans for just coffee. I didn't plan on so many guests." His grin belied any inhospitality.

I dashed upstairs for my ration cards, throwing aside last night's disordered clothing as I rummaged through my suitcase for the folder. My hand crumpled some paper. I remembered the two sheets in the German album. I retrieved the lists, jubilant. They must mean something and possibly DeLord would know. I did remember to snatch up the ration books and came triumphantly back downstairs.

"I've got something," I babbled, pressing the ration books in the major's hand for he was all dressed to leave. I waved the sheets in DeLord's face, crowing in triumph.

"At ease, at ease," laughed the lieutenant, unable to see why I was excited.

"If I don't get started now, I'll never go," the major said. "Explain it to me later."

"Go, go, go," I crowed as the lieutenant took the sheets from me, frowning at first and then beginning to smile.

"This is it. These are the lists of the first trap your father set. The reason I was in Paris and doing the rounds of the stamp merchants was to see if some valuable stamps and old books known to have been appropriated by four high-ranking German officers had turned up yet," DeLord said. "I ran into your father in a little store near the Plaza Athénée. You can imagine my surprise at seeing someone from the suspected regiment in a stamp shop." DeLord rolled his eyes expressively. "It didn't take me very long to realize your father was not the looter."

"I should hope so."

"Well, remember, he had both the knowledge and the opportunity. Now, these particular stamps and the rare illuminated books should have been 'liberated' when we erased the Falaise-Argentan retreat alley the Germans managed to keep open so long. A lot of kraut baggage transports were captured and the stuff should have turned up. And the unit which came on the transports first was the One Hundred and Fifteenth."

"Yeah," and Turtle looked off into the middle distance, remembering. "Yeah. That figgers. I remember."

"It does figger, doesn't it?" DeLord agreed gravely, "and the Third Battalion overtook that train, too."

Turtle continued to nod as though more pieces of the puzzle were fitting together.

"Yeah, I'm remembering a lot now," and his face twisted into an ugly expression of distaste. "Yeah. And Major Warren was so _____ set on inspections to keep looting down to a minimum in *his* regiment. He even snafued me with a . . . ." He stopped as he caught the lieutenant's glance. "Christ, Lieutenant, spoils of war! But, when I think of the angle that lousy _____ bastard worked, so high and _____ righteous . . . ." He pulled his head between his shoulders belligerently and cracked his knuckles sharply as if he wished they were Warren's neckbones. "Yeah, he knew _____ well we wouldn't question him! And _____ part of it is, we didn't. We thought that _____ bastard turned everything over to regimental when they came around on pickup." Turtle's laugh was ugly. "Christ, but I'm glad I . . . ." and he broke off, blinking, and looked around at me with a basilisk stare.

I don't know what he intended to say but I know he felt he had said too much already. The lieutenant had not been paying attention for he had been deep in his own ruminations. He slapped the sheet he held.

"Help me with this list, Miss Carla. Those stamps must be somewhere in this locker. Bailey, remember when you caught the colonel coming in from a recon near Baesweiler?"

Turtle nodded.

"Well, we'd just planted the stamps on an abandoned baggage lorry which Recon had spotted on an aerial sweep. The colonel planned to do a thorough search of anyone who got near it. I thought the trap had failed because I remember Warren pulled a search before we could. And he made such an issue of sending the stuff back to HQ. The call that Colonel Murdock got just as he ordered me to go get Warren was to tell him that the planted bait had *not* reappeared at HQ. He called me back and we both went to get Warren. Only, at the time, I thought the colonel had finally made up his mind to transfer Warren out of the line. And, of course, we never got to Warren."

Turtle cursed under his breath.

I bent hastily over the German album, straightening a stamp in its treads. This particular album was made with strips to retain the stamps in place without gummed tabs. As I fooled needlessly to cover my inner pain, I pushed it to one side and . . . disclosed the stamp carefully inserted behind it. The second stamp was not a duplicate. Furthermore it was one of the violet-orange 75-centimes French-Chinese stamps and as valuable as it could be! *The 75-centimes was inverted!* Information was triggered in my mind and I didn't need any Scott to remind me this little piece of pretty paper was worth several thousand dollars. In fact, the French at that time seemed to have a problem with the 75-centimes stamps all along the line and the inversions were as valuable as they were rare.

"Look!" I gabbled excitely. "Here's our proof. Here's one of them. See, the seventy-five centimes is inverted. They're priceless. All by themselves." I had difficulty keeping my fingers careful as I discovered more of the rare inversions. And, sure enough, amid some perfectly unexceptional French Egyptian stamps were some of the valuable carmine and purple handstamped Tchongking of 1900.

"Gawd," I exclaimed, spreading the finds out delicately on the table for them all to see, "Dad must've just died to find these. Oh!" I closed my eyes against the pain of that imbecilic idiom.

"What are these paper-wrapped packages?" DeLord asked evenly.

I forced myself to see what he held. "I haven't looked yet."

The lieutenant undid the string. Pushing back the paper, he whistled in amazement. I glanced up and my eyes widened with surprise. That was no album.

"Whatinhell's that?" Turtle growled.

Reverently, the lieutenant opened the heavy tooled cover, exposing the first illuminated sheet with its elaborate and beautiful titles, red, black, and gold. Even the borders were in gold. There were about eighteen or so lines, arranged in one column on the back, framed by those magnificently intricate, monk-conceived borders.

"Confessio Santa Fulgentii . . ." the lieutenant read hesitantly as he deciphered the ancient script. He whistled again, carefully turning the next page of heavy but brittle-looking vellum. Some of the gold in the border on this page had faded and the green background showed through.

"That's one of those Books of Hours or something," I said in an awed voice.

"No wonder the MFAAC had me assigned to find out what was happening." The lieutenant's eyes were wide. "This thing is priceless."

"Can't even read it," Turtle remarked dourly.

There were two other wrapped packages which we lifted out with great reverence. One was quite small but rather thick for the leaves were heavy vellum. The illumination was even more elaborate than the "Confesssio," purple bands, gold lettering, the most intricate initials and borders. Pictures in many colors with silvery borders. Just beautiful and so old, so lovingly, meticulously crafted. The lieutenant and I decided it must be the Gospels, although between the unfamiliar calligraphy and our rusty Latin it was difficult to tell.

The third was unquestionably a Bible, two columns of the black Latin script on each page. The capitals were gold and red, the titles daintier in design than the others. Lots of vines in the borders and much gold with more varied colors than the other two had boasted so the effect was more brilliant.

When I learned later what they actually were, I felt I had blasphemed even to gaze at them. The last one was an eighth- or ninth-century book of Gospels, stolen from the Bibliothèque de Tours. It had been used when the monarchs of France took their oaths as honorary canons of St. Martins. The smallest one was also dated in the ninth century and also Gospels, but a bedside copy.

The "Confessio" was, again, ninth century, done at St. Germain des Prés. I guess it was the brilliant golds and colors that attracted Warren and made him think they were valuable. They were but he could never have sold them. The Germans, of course, hadn't worried about selling them. They just wanted to have them.

"Those things look like money," Turtle remarked after we had carefully rewrapped the old books and put them back on the footlocker. "But these things?" and he picked up one of the "trap" stamps, a 75-centimes inverted.

"They're a fine investment," DeLord assured him, collecting the squares carefully. As he reached for a transparent envelope his leg brushed against one of the cartridge boxes we had put to one side. It fell and the sound it made striking the floor drew our attention.

Fascinated I stared down. One of the shells had lost its lead tip and two gemstones winked up at me.

"Chrissake!" Turtle gasped.

We grabbed up the shells and when we had finished opening them, a glittering assortment of jewels lay before us. The second box, apparently not even sealed, contained heavy gold and gem-encrusted crosses of ancient design.

"Willya look at that!" Turtle said as we lined up the impressive array of wealth.

The lieutenant was shaking his head slowly from side to side.

"The man was clever. I'll give him that. We've been looking for these since the Cotentin. They're why PM assigned me to the case. Tell me, Miss Carla, let's suppose Warren did call on you. Did bring up the subject of the footlocker. I suppose he could have inquired whether you got your father's things back safely. He might even have inquired what was returned. Would you have been likely to turn over to him the gun and the cartridge boxes?"

"Well," I said with a heavy sigh, "probably yes. You're not supposed to keep a service Colt and he'd know I know it. Yes, I probably would have handed him over a fortune in gems and the gun that killed my own father."

Pure hatred flooded me.

"But those books? How would he have got *them* back?"

DeLord grinned at me. "I only just found that out myself. Let me backtrack a bit to where we left off before the navy landed. What had puzzled us was how the missing valuables were getting out of Europe. Even when I knew that Warren was the only possible suspect, and I didn't know that until I'd planted my own trap, I still didn't know how. I felt I was close to the solution when the colonel got wounded at Aachen."

Turtle's laugh was very unpleasant.

"I told my superiors my suspicions and a very close check was kept on Warren's movements, contacts, and mail, while he was recuperating in the hospital. We arranged to have him transferred stateside, knowing he would have to lead us to the loot eventually if he was to realize any profit. By then, one or two items had turned up in pawnshops and in respectable antique shops. When Warren inquired when the next shipment of casualties' effects was being made, we had our first real break. He tried to arrange his passage on the same ship but we switched him to another at the last moment." DeLord's eyes danced maliciously.

"But, wait a minute, Dad's footlocker came in four weeks ago and Warren wrote me only on the twenty-sixth."

"Ah," the lieutenant said, "but when was your first burglary?"

"Oh," and there my theory blew up in my face. "About two days after it arrived. But I was in the hospital. What if I had gone through it . . . ."

"Did you?" asked the lieutenant quietly.

"I couldn't bear to."

"Exactly. And I'm sure Warren counted on this. Shock alone would keep you from examining it very closely."

"Wait a minute, you mean you knew something must be among my father's things?"

DeLord shook his head. "Not exactly, but your father's footlocker, being a colonel's and being his, would not be inspected closely, if at all. Remember, even the gun was at the bottom. The albums, the legitimate ones, were carefully on top of the illegal bibles. It wasn't until I realized that Warren, in addition 'to keeping the looting down,' also handled the effects of the fatalities that I knew how he was getting things out. Then I had to find out how he recovered them."

"Chrissake, and the colonel put him into Headquarters Company to keep him out of trouble."

"Hmmm," and DeLord hurried on. "After Jülich I realized he added things to packs. This meant someone had to intercept on this side."

"Marian Warren," I exclaimed. "You know, I thought it was awful strange that she'd bother to call on those families in the Boston area. Do you mean she was picking up loot? How would she know? How did she do it?"

"Well, we started intercepting letters from him to his wife or anyone else he wrote."

"You mean he told that harpy right out . . . ."

"Oh, no, he was discreet enough. Just suggested she go visit so-and-so's family. He had a code worked out, too, because we noticed he'd use several phrases over and over. 'He was a fine soldier,' 'he died bravely,' and 'I shall miss his leadership qualities.' When the provost marshall over here got with it and did some checking, they tracked down quite a pack smuggled through. The really valuable items, a few fine rings, a silver communion chalice dating from the fifteenth century, some very rare stamps, all came in officers' packs. They also connected several burglaries with the arrival of footlockers. Nothing had been disturbed in the house, nothing apparently was missing. But there had been burglaries just after shipments."

"'Miss his leadership' ..." I gasped in outrage. "But ... he said in his letter to me something about Dad's ability to command. Ye gods."

"Repeats himself, doesn't he." DeLord chuckled. "At any rate, we have it pretty well lined out now; opportunity, motive, *modus operandi*, but we haven't caught him with the goods and we have to or our case won't stand up."

"And why not?" I demanded indignantly. "He murdered to protect his racket."

DeLord shook his head patiently. "Circumstantial although we know now he had a motive for killing your father but, Miss Carla, until last night I didn't know your father had been murdered." He shot a significant look at Turtle.

Turtle's face drained of blood and he spun away to the stove to pour himself a cup of coffee.

"All I was out to catch was a thief who was causing some bad feelings with our allies." DeLord's voice dropped to a quiet sad tone.

I sighed deeply, shook off my apathy.

"All right, why don't you take the jeep when the major gets back and get that gun traced?"

DeLord nodded. "I've the slug that murdered your father, too," and he touched his breast pocket briefly. "I'll run a ballistics check on it as well. We'll maybe have conclusive proof."

"You mean I can't help trap Warren?" I felt cheated.

Merlin growled at that point and we turned to look at him. He continued growling, his head cocked towards the front of the house.

"Now what?" Turtle demanded wearily. "The Marines?"

"No," I cried, jumping up with relief. "The vet the gob promised."

I raced to the front door, vowing to think more kindly of the Coast Guard from now on. I pulled the door open and stopped. Two cars had pulled up. One of them was an army jeep, an officer and two burly MPs filing out. The other car was Beatty's and there was a self-satisfied expression on his face as he plowed back up the swath he had cut through the snow that morning.

"What's on your mind?" I snapped.

"You'll find out soon enough, Miss Murdock," and he made the formal title an insult. His voice, brash and loud, reached Turtle's ears.

Before I realized what it was all about, Beatty had pushed me roughly back and waved in the two MPs who entered, revolvers drawn.

"There's your man!" and he pointed straight at Turtle.

Turtle went into an instinctive crouch. I think he would have tried to make it out through the kitchen but, unwittingly, the lieutenant stepped into the doorway, blocking his retreat. Turtle straightened. The MP lieutenant came up to him.

"Name, rank, and serial number," he asked formally.

Turtle rattled them off, defeat written in his posture.

"You're to accompany me to Camp Edwards, Sergeant."

"For the attempted murder of Lt. Col. Donald Warren," sneered Beatty.

Someone screamed and it must have been me as I ducked around Beatty and flew to Turtle, my arms around him in a futile effort to protect him.

"You can't, you can't. He served my father for twenty-eight years!"

"Sorry, miss."

"Here's the AWOL list," Beatty offered too helpfully. "Resisted arrest at Aachen and disappeared. Only they thought he was still in Europe. I never forget a face."

"May I see it?" DeLord's voice, steely and authoritative, cut across Beatty's abusive triumph.

"You can't arrest him. You can't. You've got to prove it," I screamed.

"Bit, knock it off," said Turtle, disengaging my arms from his neck.

I looked at him. I read the truth which I had before only happily suspected. He had shot Warren. But Warren had deserved to die. Warren had killed my father. It was too damned bad Turtle had missed.

"Thank you," DeLord said, his face grim as he returned

the incriminating sheet to the smug policeman. "If you've no objection," and DeLord flashed his own identification, "I'd like to accompany Sergeant Bailey. I have evidence to present." His hand brushed his breast pocket.

"As you wish, DeLord," the MP said. "Get your things, Sergeant."

I had to watch as they stood over my Turtle Edward Bailey while he shrugged into his outer clothes. I had to witness the gloating expression on Beatty's face. Why did he have to show up at all, with his petty informer's nature and goddamned good memory? I had no conscience about the moralities involved in Turtle playing executioner. I was only sorry Turtle had failed. My horror was that Turtle might have to pay too dearly for that rough disposition of justice.

It was intolerable to watch Beatty delighting in the scene. I stalked over to him stiffly.

"You get out of here, you hear me."

He glanced down at me, as if surprised I dared approach him at all.

"I'm talking to you, Beatty. You have no warrant to enter this house and no business in it. Now get yourself out of here or I'll call my dog on you for trespassing."

"Your dog's too sick to move," he sneered, slowly, insultingly.

"I'm not," DeLord said, moving me gently to one side, facing Beatty. His body was poised lightly on his toes and in his hands he held the holstered forty-five Colt. Beatty would have no way of knowing it was unloaded but he would appreciate that DeLord was in a fighting mood. "Miss Carla asked you to leave and if you do not leave . . . ." He did not complete the threat.

Beatty shot a hurried glance behind Robert DeLord. What he evidently saw in the faces of the MPs was enough to know that they would not support him. They had come for their prisoner on his information but they didn't think very much of Police Officer Beatty.

Beatty backed out of the house, his angry eyes and set lantern jaw boding no good for me. I didn't care.

Turtle was ready and he was marched out of the house, eyes front. Beatty stood to one side of the stoop to watch Turtle positioned between the two MPs in the back of the jeep. DeLord gripped my arm, gave me a reassuring squeeze.

"I'll be back as soon as I can. I've got some talking to do to Colonel Calderone. Tell Laird I'll see about the gun's issue, too." The lieutenant squinted down the road anxiously. "He ought to be back soon. Don't worry, honey."

I stood helplessly as he, too, climbed into the jeep. I watched as the wheels spun in the snow, as it turned and slid up the road. Then I realized Beatty's car was still there and he was standing near me.

"I said get out."

"All your protectors are gone now, girlie," he laughed nastily, striding back up the stoop.

A vicious snarl at my side caught him midstep and he backed hastily, his eyes wide. Merlin stood there, spread-legged, snarling, no question of his intention. I don't know if Beatty would have drawn the gun he started for. I think he would have and Merlin might have died in the attempt but Regan Laird, his jeep skidding to a snow-splaying stop, changed the odds in our favor.

"I'll be back, girlie," Beatty warned me again and walked quickly to his car while Laird watched from his jeep. Once certain Beatty was on his way out of Pull-in Point, the major jockeyed the jeep into the garage. He slammed out of the car and to me on the double.

Despite his ferocious attitude, Merlin was barely able to stand, his side bleeding from exertion. I supported him as best I could until Regan Laird reached us and tenderly lifted the dog up.

"Whatinhell happened, Carlysle? Why were DeLord and Bailey in an MP jeep?" he asked as he gently pressed new gauze pads on Merlin's bleeding side.

I explained as lucidly as I could, trying to control both temper and tears although I was so stunned by the rapid succession of events I didn't think I was making much sense.

"They arrested Turtle and DeLord went with him to see what he could do. Said he had something to explain to the C.O."

"Beatty's favorite reading always was government mail

posters. I guess he's added AWOL notices as his part of the war effort."

I stared stupidly at the major. "But they arrested Turtle for attempted homicide . . . ."

"Whose?"

"Warren's."

He didn't seemed surprised at the victim.

"That explains the AWOL then. I thought Master Sergeant Edward Bailey had changed character. The regiment always meant as much to him as it did to your father." Accidentally he pressed too hard against Merlin's side and the dog let out a cry, turning his head to lick the major's hand as if he realized the hurt was unintentional. Laird stroked the dog's ears apologetically. "I wish that vet would come. He's torn open the sutures DeLord made."

I knelt beside Merlin, stroking the muzzle he immediately buried into my lap.

"But what I don't understand, Major, is how they could *know* Turtle shot Warren?"

The major rocked back on his heels, looking me squarely, in the eyes.

"Warren could have seen Bailey take aim at him. To be honest, Carlysle, I knocked Bailey's gun up once when he'd a bead on Warren."

"Oh, no."

"It was just after your father's death when we had moved up on Setterich. Bailey and I were the only ones that knew your father had been killed by a forty-five slug. Bailey had been bitter enough at Warren when Emsh got killed and he took the colonel's death very hard. I thought he'd go out of his mind when DeLord came in with your dad. Christ, the heart went out of all the men. Bailey acted as if Warren were the Jonah for everything, from the losses of the Third Battalion at Bois de Collette to the beetfields right up to and including your father's death. But I checked Warren's side arm myself and it wasn't even clean, much less fired recently."

The major's eyes turned cold and bleak.

"I myself find it very hard to forgive Warren a few things. D'you know, he actually tried to assume command the next morning after we got back from the cemetery? Oldest in grade, logical choice. Ha! I got through to Division and Gerhardt and scotched that."

I don't think I heard all he had been saying. I was so torn by the despair that had driven Turtle, in loyalty to his colonel, to desertion and attempted homicide. And his capture.

"How could Turtle get back here . . . to the States? He had no travel orders or . . . ."

Laird gave a mirthless chuckle. "After twenty-eight years in the army do you think a little thing like proper travel orders would stop Bailey? He probably forged them. And did a good job, too, I'll bet."

"It's awful, it's just awful," I muttered hopelessly. I felt limp, bereft, numbed, not even angry anymore.

He took me by the shoulders, only this time he held me gently and bent over to look in my face.

"I think I'd rather have you ranting and raving than woebegone like this, Carlysle," he said quietly. He tipped my head back, his eyes searching my face. "Damn it, girl, I can't keep on buoying you up with booze and knocking you out with seconal." He shook his head slowly from side to side. "But you've been clobbered good and often. As a guardian I'm doing one helluva poor job of it. Whereas you, short of mucking about with my socks," his voice quickened, "and, young lady, don't ever let me catch you doing that again; a laundress I don't need." He sounded forceful. "Is that straight?" and he gave my chin a punch. I jerked my head away.

"Yeah." His manner demanded an answer.

"As I said, you've been doing a pretty good job of taking care of me. Now, I brought in supplies and I think the best thing that could happen to what's left of this squad is to feed it. Right? I did go after coffee and food before this latest skirmish."

He paused at the door.

"C'mon, Carlysle. Lend a hand."

He said it in a way that precluded disobedience. My legs moved of their own volition and I followed him out to the jeep.

# 🐚 12

REGAN LAIRD WAS RIGHT to get me busy with the mechanics
of daily routine. We fetched in the groceries and put them
away. I noticed numbly that he had found Idaho baking
potatoes, and this put me in mind of Robert DeLord and his
mission. I put that out of my mind and washed and put the
potatoes in to bake. I made a hearty meat loaf, vaguely wondering at all the stamps such a generous amount had taken. The
major had brought in fresh cod and flounder but I was tired of
fish. There were some fresh vegetables and oranges. I didn't
examine the canned goods closely, except the dogfood.

   "I didn't have much choice for Merlin," the major said
apologetically.

   "I know."

   We were both marking time until DeLord got back. I
wondered idly, anything to think about but DeLord and . . . I
wondered why Evans had been so certain a vet would come to
this point off the coast of nowhere for any dog, much less a
civilian's. The major busied himself by bringing in more and
more wood and spending lots of time policing the fireplaces. I
made beds and straightened rooms, pretending that Turtle's
belonged to someone else. Then, as darkness was falling on the
snow-bright world, there was no more busy work to be done. I
sat down at the kitchen table near my dog and folded my hands
in my lap.

   The major came in with one more, unnecessary load of
wood and shed his outer clothes.

   "Say," he began as pulled up a chair to the table, "what
did you find in the locker? Anything valuable?"

   I looked at him blankly and then twisted around, wondering where the locker was.

   "That's funny. It was here in the room."

   "Yes, but did you find anything in it?"

   "You just bet we did. Ancient bibles, hundreds of years

old, some absolutely unique French Colonial stamps, and guess what was in those cartridge boxes?"

"What?"

"Jewels stuck in dud shells and a boxful of gold and jeweled crosses."

The major whistled expressively. I got up, peered out into the corridor, rummaged in the back porch, ducked my head into the study.

"I don't understand it."

"Think back, Carlysle. You say you went to the door? Had you finished with the footlocker?"

"Almost. Most of the stuff was back in for lack of a better place to put it."

"Bailey and DeLord stayed in the kitchen when you went to the door, then? Long enough to clear the rest?"

"I think so. But where could they have put it then?"

"Did the MPs come into the kitchen at all?"

I closed my eyes to concentrate. "I saw Turtle come to the door of the dining room, stand, crouch, turn, to be blocked by the lieutenant. Then the MPs came up, DeLord stayed in the doorway until Turtle went to get his coat from the back hall. One of the MPs must have gone with him but that's when Beatty got so nasty. Then . . . ."

"Beatty got nasty? How?" demanded the major and I realized I'd rehearsed that scene out loud.

"Just nasty," I said, waving aside his interruption. "Then Turtle went with them. No, I'd gone to Turtle but I didn't think to look in the kitchen. Yes, and the lieutenant showed them his papers and asked to come along. They agreed he could so he went to get his things. He took the Colt along, too."

"When I drove up," the major said thoughtfully, looking at me out of the one corner of his eye, "you were at the door, Merlin was snarling, and Beatty was on the front stoop."

"I'm only sorry Merlin was so weak," I said with regret.

"So what happened to the locker?"

"There was no one else in the house. No one came in the back because Merlin would have warned me."

"Well, somehow, between the time you went to the door and the time the MPs got in here, the locker got stashed away."

Merlin growled, his head up, ears alert. I let out a disgusted breath.

"Oh, now what?"

The major turned quickly to me, a half smile on his face.

"That sounds more like my ward."

We both went to check, of one mind on the advisability of screening visitors to this house. Merlin's growl rumbled after us and cut off with a yip.

"Down Merlin. Stay!" I ordered. He whined a protest but stayed.

A wood-paneled station wagon cautiously slowed to a halt on the snowy road. It appeared distorted, top-heavy. The slit lights went off and we saw the over-tall door open. No one emerged. The door hung ajar. Then a figure got out and seemed to keep on standing up like a cartoon drawing unexpectedly elongating. The door was closed and as the shadow of the tall figure separated from the shadow of the top-heavy car, we could see a familiar medical case swinging from the end of one long, long arm.

"The vet did come," and I think I was as surprised as the major sounded.

He hastily opened the front door and, for all his own six-foot odd height, he had to look up at the tall, tall man who entered.

"Major Laird?" an unexpectedly tenor voice asked.

"Dr. Karsh."

"Have we met?" and the voice was unusually musical with no trace of a down-east accent.

"No, but I've heard of you."

"Hmmm. Wouldn't doubt it for a minute."

Merlin barked.

"My patient is in good voice."

Merlin yipped because he had disobeyed me.

"Spoke too soon."

The veterinarian ducked under the archway separating hall and dining room. I backed up instinctively so as not to have to crook my neck to see his face.

"My ward, Carlysle Murdock. Merlin is hers."

"Quite a beast, I'm told. Twice told, young lady. Once

by an excited coastguardsman of my acquaintance and once by a lieutenant, a calmer man but equally insistent that I should come."

He swooshed his bag at me to indicate I should lead him to his patient. I scurried ahead into the kitchen.

Merlin got to his feet and stood there, swaying slightly, the major's bandage bloody.

"Merlin, if you weren't so sick, I'd beat you. You were told to stay."

Ashamed, Merlin dropped his head, peering up at me with a woeful expression in his eyes. Then he jerked his head up, his jaw dropping as his dog face registered surprise.

"Ooooh," and the doctor's voice was a croon of delighted interest. "Now you are a magnificent fellow. You are indeed."

The doctor's voice was a marvelous singsong. He ignored us completely, heaving his bag to set it with a very soft plump on the kitchen table, although it must have been very heavy. Then he dropped to his knees by Merlin in a fluid movement. He didn't attempt to touch the shepherd but he bent this way and that so he could see Merlin's points in the undiffused kerosene light.

"What a dog! What a superb dog! Have you any idea, Merlin, what a sight you are to these tired eyes?"

Merlin was watching him, absolutely mesmerized.

"He's hypnotized Merlin," the major whispered, bending his head to my ear.

"I've never seen Merlin behave like this with anyone," I murmured back, not wishing to interrupt this significant meeting.

Dr. Karsh placed his long-fingered hand under Merlin's chin, his over-length thumb stroking the soft fur of the muzzle. Merlin's eyes drooped sleepily, his head leaning into the supporting hand much as a tired child will cradle himself against his mother. With his free hand, the doctor explored Merlin's body, the deep chest, the long back, the well-placed hips.

"Will you clear the table?" the doctor crooned, not changing his voice one decibel from the tone he was using to soothe Merlin. It took me a moment to realize he was talking to the humans in the room. The major and I jumped to his bidding.

With a deftness and speed that was an astonishing blend of individual motions, Dr. Karsh had lifted Merlin and placed him on his good side.

"The lights, so and so," the doctor directed, waving fingers at two distinct levels. We complied.

"Now, young fellow me lad, let's get a look at this outrage on one of nature's grandest. As the lieutenant said, his was rough field surgery but I think he did extremely well. It's only that you do not obey your mistress' order to stay."

The major and I found we had to pay close attention to this dialogue, delivered in a rippling Irish tenor-like *tessitura*, for sometimes he was talking only to Merlin and sometimes to us. The doctor had by now washed his hands thoroughly and donned rubber gloves.

"Now this will not be pleasant, my sagacious friend Merlin—a marvelous name for a magnificent specimen of *Canis familiaris*. I congratulate you, young Miss Carla," and he paused briefly to prepared his curved needle with black gut, "on your perspicacity in seeing in a bumbling puppy the dignity of the adult dog to come. Or perhaps you created a personality for him to grow up to . . . . Steady, this will hurt but not for long. There! Merlin is a sensible creature and knows that my hurt will cure . . . . By eschewing the Rover-Chief-Rin-tin-tin mania, you gave him a goal of wisdom to acquire. For Merlin was a great magician and there is magic in the heart of a dog when he will defend his against the mechanical madnesses of men. Oh, one more and the worst of my ministrations are over. You can do yourself no more damage, my silver shepherd. This wound will heal, given God's good time and what appears to be a superb constitution. There. Good boy! Not a word out of you. Brave lad."

Dr. Karsh straightened, having bent double to work, interminably it seemed to me, on his patient. The shadows of the kerosene lamps jumped around as his upward ascent caused a draft. The doctor took two long strides to the sink and stripped off the gloves. He had to stand sideways as he did not fit under the canopy across the sink. As I hurriedly got him a towel, still speechless, I realized I came only to his belt. I hastily backed away. Way up, he smiled down at me as he handed back the towel. Then he turned and scooped Merlin up again, depositing him on his quilts, giving the dog a stern signal to stay. Merlin licked his chops, whined very softly, rolled to his good side, sighed, and fell asleep.

Dr. Karsh stood staring down at his patient and, pivoting in place, favored us with his full attention.

"Evans was right to say I should see Merlin myself. I do not mean to imply," he hastily assured me in his mellifluous way, "that the dog is in any danger . . . no, no . . . not to deprive you of his company, but as fit mate for a lovely young thing of my own. I had despaired of ever matching her size and color, not to mention her temperament for she is, above all, amiable and affectionate. Evans knew at a glance that Merlin was *the* dog to husband her. I am grateful to him."

"I'd be willing, very willing, Dr. Karsh," I answered breathlessly. My voice, which I had always considered rather light and childish in tone, sounded unexpectedly harsh in contrast to his. "I'd be delighted. I never thought you'd actually come so far on such a miserable day."

"My dear, I serve the animal needs of this community and my patients rarely can come to me. They are not your pampered bench pets in shows. They are working beasts and when they are ill, they need me," he said simply. He started to leave. "My word, I am so forgetful. The lieutenant who called to add an unnecessary but concerned plea that I attend brave Merlin asked me to tell you he will be back tomorrow. He said to say that something unusual has developed that he must check out. I trust his cryptic message reassures you. His tone was confident. I know I remembered his phrasing right, once I remembered I was to tell you something."

"Yes, yes, thank you," I assured him, bemused.

He started to bend out of the room.

"Keep him as quiet as you can. And major, for his *comfort*, carry him outside soon. By morning, he'll be no worse for wear."

And he was leaving. The major and I started after him but, with his long strides, he was out the front door before we could cross the dining room. "He'll know when he's well enough to be active. Feed him what he wants. I'll look in later this week, never fear, to feast my eyes again on a fine, fine dog."

He said these last words as he telescoped back into his car. Both the major and I stood, half dazed on the front step, oblivious to the cold, as he drove off slowly, in second gear, up the snowy road.

"He's unbelievable," I muttered. It was the sight of my breath in the cold that broke the spell. I moved out of the doorway and the major closed it, hurrying me by the arm back into the kitchen.

"I'd heard about him but I didn't believe it until now," the major said, slowly shaking his head.

"Merlin just *let* him sew him up," I exclaimed.

"I think I would, too," the major admitted with a bemused chuckle.

"I can't get over Merlin just *letting* him. The man's a genius," I said dazedly, and went to check the dinner in the oven. "Did you notice his car?"

"What about it?"

"It was top-heavy."

"It'd have to be for that beanpole."

"How can you say that?"

"Don't get your back up. Stands to reason he wouldn't fit in a regular car."

"He doesn't fit, period. He's unique. You said you'd heard about him?"

The major had poured himself a drink, offering me one which I declined. He settled himself at the table while I set our places.

"He's one of the local legends."

"He hasn't got a local accent."

"Educated. I don't have one either and I've lived around here all my life."

I said nothing but the major obviously hadn't *heard* himself speak. Still he didn't have much of an accent.

"In Orleans?" I asked hastily.

"Summers. Winters in Waltham."

"And you'd never seen Dr. Karsh?"

"At a distance. Never been introduced."

"Are there other vets around?"

"No, just never had any reason to call one."

I stared at him. "Didn't you have a dog as a boy?"

He grinned at me and the expression, distorted by the scar, reminded me I had all but forgotten his wound. He sensed the distraction and his smile faded. He leaned back, his bad side hidden in the shadows.

"No," and his voice was flat with a return of the cold cautious neutrality that had marked his manner towards me until just recently. I felt ill that I had been so gauche.

"Maybe . . . one of Merlin's pups?" I tendered in a small voice.

He looked at me, quick to sense this obtuse apology for my unintentional offense. He thawed.

"I'm sorry, Carlysle. You didn't deserve that of me. I've come to understand, in a way I never would have before, why Karsh prefers the quiet life here where people are so used to him they no longer notice his extreme height. He's accepted in a community that would defend him to a man against outsiders' curiosity. And he is a downright genius with animals. I knew that long before I heard a mutter about his size." He took a long pull at his drink. "It was all so easy when I thought you were a boy. It wouldn't be wrong to bury you down here along with me for a few months. But it won't work out now!" He drank again, his mood bitter.

I sank into the chair by him, just listening because I couldn't think of a thing to say although there was much I'd've liked to say.

"I'll have to reopen the house in Waltham and get a housekeeper." A return to Waltham appeared to be exceedingly distasteful to him.

"But you've lived a long time there? Surely they know you," I suggested, implying that his friends and acquaintances certainly wouldn't avoid him because of his scars.

His lips compressed into a thin line and I knew I was wrong. He drained the glass.

"Oh! How could they!" I cried angrily.

His glass came down to the surface of the table with a

loud crack. He splashed in more whiskey, moodily swirling it around the ice cubes.

"I never considered I was particularly vain before this," and for the first time in our acquaintance, he fingered the scarred side of his face. "But then, war changes a lot of values."

"You're going to Walter Reed soon and they'll be . . . ."

He glared at me, opened his mouth to snap something out, and stopped.

"They might even improve on the original," I suggested ruthlessly, suddenly conscious that sympathy was the worst comfort I could offer him. "Your nose is a bit too aquiline. While they're about it, can't they reduce that hook?" I reached over and tapped his very aristocratic nose disparagingly. "I think you might possibly be able to achieve a Robert Taylor, smooth, suave look of distinction. Or perhaps the rough-hewed Gary Cooper type. You haven't got the basic structure for Cary Grant, of course. And next time, do get a proper haircut. The length is disgraceful," and I flipped up the long hair that covered the baldness of the scar tissue.

His fingers caught my wrist in such a vise I thought he'd break bones. The anger in him was white hot and I glared right back at him, daring him, knowing the anger he would vent on me was anger suppressed from whatever hurt he had suffered elsewhere.

The fury drained out of him. He closed his eyes and shook his head, breathing deeply to disperse the inner tension. His fingers loosened but he didn't release my wrist. When he opened his eyes again, his face had cleared of both bitterness and anger.

"I'd forgotten an incident I should always remember," he said in a low normal voice. "When I was in the hospital out in the Newtons, a woman came into the ward. We were facial injuries, all of us. I was not the worst one by a long shot. There was a fighter pilot who'd had—" he broke off. "She was a good-looking woman and obviously had plenty of money. I remember she swept in with furs, smelling of fine perfume, every hair on her head in place. She was everything none of us wanted any part of. Not the way we looked. Well, she introduced herself and then proceeded to take off her hair, take out her teeth, and pass around photos of herself before and after her accident, before and after surgery."

He swallowed, his face still. Then he looked at me. "There wasn't a man in that ward, with the exception of that pilot, who wasn't better off than she had been. God, her face had been sliced and mashed cruelly. And there she was, looking like a goddamned junior league virgin. She spent the whole afternoon with us, talking. She made us feel her face where the grafts had healed, showed us the tiny scars in her hairline. She told us this could be done to us, too. And she said go ahead and make any improvements we wanted, just for laughs. When that lady left, every one of us stood up and saluted her. She didn't have to come, she didn't have to do what she did but she came often. There's all kinds of courage in the world."

He picked up my wrist in both hands and gently stroked the angry marks his fingers had made.

"Thanks, Carlysle, for reminding me of her."

"Any time," I said lightly, because I was embarrassed and flustered by his confidence. I felt I had learned more about Major Regan Laird in the past few moments than I'd discovered in the last few days.

Merlin stirred in his sleep, his feet twitching in the urgency of some dream sequence.

"God, I'd better get him outside," the major said, rising. "When that's taken care of, dinner will be ready."

# ❦ 13

WHEN MAJOR LAIRD came back in, Merlin was walking stiffly beside him. Regan Laird's face was suffused with mirth.

"The poor damn dog," he chuckled as I looked at him questioningly. "That poor dog." The major sat down, trying to stop laughing.

Merlin moved to his bed with what might be considered injured dignity. He paid no attention to us, curled himself around and lay down again, a deep sigh forced from his lungs as he settled. He lay with his head towards us, blinked his eyes once, and then closed them.

"That poor damn dog," the major repeated for the third time.

"Enough's enough," I exclaimed for Merlin's sake.

"Dinner smells good," Laird said, controlling his amusement with effort.

"Learned this recipe from a gentle lady of good background but impoverished circumstances near Bragg," I explained, passing him the meatloaf. "Oh, and the lieutenant had missed baked potatoes so much."

The major covered my hand with his, giving a little squeeze.

"I'm just as worried as you, Carlysle, in spite of the doctor's message. But I can't change it by worrying about it so I don't. Takes practice but it saves a lot of wasted time and effort."

He cut a massive slice of meat loaf for himself. I was appalled at such liberality, being used to meatlessness.

"Eat, drink, and be merry, for tomorrow who knows?" I asked.

He nodded agreement so I helped myself to an equally huge portion, and we dug in with good appetites.

The events of the past few days had blunted quite a few sharp edges and sent several shoulder-carried chips flying. Tonight for the first time I felt at ease alone with Regan Laird and he was at ease with me. It was a nice harmonious feeling. I hoped it wouldn't be fragile, that possibly it could last a while.

I was surprised to learn that he had a B.S. degree from Boston University in civil engineering. He had joined the army in 1939 when he couldn't get a job.

"With typical army efficiency, they put me in infantry O.C.S." He grinned.

He had an older sister, married and living in Texas, but she was now his only relative, their parents having died several years ago. He had been married but he'd sued for divorce in 1941. I never learned more than that.

He had joined up with the First Army in the fall of 1941. He had met Dad and liked him but it wasn't until September of

'43 that Dad had wangled Regan Laird's transfer into the regiment.

"Are you going to stay in?"

"I could. Retire at forty-one with full pension? Not bad. They'll have occupying forces for years when this is settled. Here and in the Orient."

"That's what Dad wrote," I put in eagerly. "I'm majoring in government. Dad is . . . Dad was sure he could wangle me a job as a civilian employee in the occupation force. My German's good and my French is fair."

"I got your midterm marks. You're a better student than I was," he remarked, proud, if vicariously, of my scholarship.

"Don't sound so patronizing," I suggested because I'd just figured out he was only twenty-nine, not in his mid-thirties as I'd assumed.

"The prerogative of my experience and position!"

"You're only twenty-nine."

"Thirty in June!"

"You make yourself sound ancient." I laughed at him. "Of course, you are," I added, "compared to the male population I'm used to."

"Really?"

"There's this math genius on the campus," I said with some feeling, "who's not more than fourteen. So help me! *He* tells the math instructors where *their* errors are."

"That must endear him no end to the faculty."

"And he loves nothing better than to matchmake at dances."

"For you?"

I glared at my guardian. "He's exactly my height. And his best friend, for whom he tries to make a match — is a seventeen-year-old, pimple-faced Latin scholar."

The major's eyes twinkled. "I think I had better get a chaperon. To protect me, from you."

"Go mend a fire!"

He left chuckling. I looked at the closed door, not the least bit annoyed. Rather I was extremely pleased. I felt alive again, and good, and somehow tomorrow *would* take care of itself. Even the terrible reality of Turtle's arrest and the grim delight of indicting Warren. The depressions that had plagued me, the indecisions that had worried could no longer overwhelm me.

I suppose I had been so badly put down by circumstance, there was no place to go but up. I couldn't attribute it all to having cleared the air and achieved a nice relationship with the major. But that helped. So did the curious magic of Dr. Karsh. The aura of his incredible personality seemed to linger although I couldn't have described his face, what color his coat had been, or even whether he had been dressed in business clothes or a garage overall. The impression he gave of immeasurable depths of kindness and understanding, for humans as well as animals, was more palpable than such details as color or texture.

I fixed some of the meat loaf for Merlin, justifying this extravagance as both reward for his heroism and a necessity for his convalescence. The smell of food under his nose roused him. As he ate, I stroked him lovingly, telling him how wonderful he was. He ate all I gave him but didn't look greedily for more. He laid his head on my shoulder briefly and then sighed very deeply, rolling his eyes to gaze at me wistfully.

"Okay, go back to sleep."

He curled around and settled back again. I busied myself cleaning up the stove. I sloshed the coffeepot to measure its contents. The sound was suggestive and the idea of more coffee was appealing.

I glanced over my shoulder at the step stool on the far side of the porch door, remembering the major's injunction. I wrinkled my nose disrespectfully.

I was levering myself up onto the counter when Regan Laird returned. He grabbed up the stool and marched over to me. He set the stool on the floor under my dangling feet. Spanning my waist with his two hands, he picked me up and set me joltingly on the top step. His eyes blazed a few inches from mine.

"If I've told you once, I've told you a dozen times to use that stool. I don't want you breaking your fool neck."

"Stop sounding like a father," I snapped irritably, our previous rapport shattered.

"My feelings towards you at the moment are scarcely paternal," he retorted heatedly, his jaws clenched.

When he had encircled my waist, my hands had automatically gone to his shoulders for balance. Furious at his proprietary manner, I dug my nails into his shoulders.

"Why you little . . ." and before I knew it, he had hooked an arm around my waist, roughly jerking me against him. He wound the fingers of the other hand in my tangled hair and pulled my head towards his.

His mouth fastened angrily on mine. He must have intended that kiss as a disciplinary affront. But the moment our lips met, the moment I responded, his intentions changed. I could feel it in the tenderness of his mouth on mine, in the longing strength of his arms as they tightened about me. I had never been kissed like this before, not even by the acknowledged lady-killer of Riley. And Regan was no less hungry for such caresses than I.

I found my hands were kneading the muscles along his shoulders and back, gripping his strong arms in an instinctive desire to be as close to him as possible. My whole being was concentrated on the warm, hard pressure of his mouth covering mine, his hand burning at my waist, his fingers in my hair. Time was a curious new dimension of contact points that thrilled and ached as we clung to each other. Beneath my urgent hands I felt his body begin to tremble. Deep within him I heard a soft groan begin. Very gently, most reluctantly, he loosened the tight embrace. His face, a blur above me, became separate features, his eyes achingly tender and gentle as he searched my face.

My feet were back on the stool and he framed my face with his hands, one thumb stroking my temple where a frantic pulse beat. A very, very gentle smile touched his lips.

"Talk about surprises," he murmured in a husky voice.

He leaned forward again slowly, giving me time to evade him if I wished. He bent his head to kiss the base of my neck. I felt the rough scar tissue against the skin of my throat and quickly pressed his head against me, my lips on the wound by his forehead. I felt him stiffen slightly and then relax as his lips continued to move along my throat. He suddenly stopped, raised his head, and looked at me with a peculiar expression.

"I can't go on like this. I'm supposed to be your guardian, not your seducer."

I looked at him with what I hoped was a solemn expression but exultation surged within me.

"There is a way in which you may be both legally," I said and held my breath at the conflicting emotions that crossed his face. He started to draw back but I tightened my hands around his neck.

"Unless, of course, you've been trifling with my affections . . . ."

He gathered me tightly to him again, his lips against my hair, my head pressed against his good cheek.

"No, by God, I'm not trifling with you, Carla. But I'm a one-time loser already. I'm not a good husband candidate."

"If it makes any difference, my father didn't think so."

Startled, Regan tilted me in his arms so that he could see my face.

"How in hell do you figure that?"

"Why in hell do you think my father went to such asinine lengths to throw us together? I don't need a guardian."

Amazement flooded his face.

"Why the old—of all the crazy . . . . Oh, Carla, I'm in love with you all right enough. I know it's rushing things but watching you cook, flounce around my kitchen . . . even your funny moods . . . . I was so mad when you washed my socks . . . I . . . I . . . ." and his lips covered mine which was what I wanted very, very much.

He kissed all kinds of ways that gave me intense delight. My pulses raced so violently I couldn't breathe. Then he set me very carefully on the counter and backed up to the table. He sank to the surface, rubbing his hands along his thighs, regarding me.

"That's enough of that for tonight," he said decisively. And, I thought, considering the sweetness of the moment, a little grimly. I knew what he meant for I was aroused and he surely must be.

"No nonsense now, Carla. You'll *have* to go somewhere else until we can be married. For a little bit of a thing you're much woman."

I beamed at him. "Only three days for blood test and license. I've got my guardian's consent."

"Three days! Wait a minute," Regan said, holding up a restraining hand. "I'm due down at Walter Reed."

I jumped down from the counter and, before he guessed my intention. I put my hands on his head and kissed his scarred cheek.

"I don't want anyone to say I married you for your good looks," I said softly, earnest despite the light tone. He remained so still I dropped my hands uncertainly. His eyes were closed and he held his head back stiffly. I could see the pulse in his neck beating strongly. Then his head came forward slowly as he expelled a deep breath.

Frightened, I wondered if I had offended him with my impulsiveness; if I had gone on one of my headlong plunges unaccompanied. Just when I was afraid he would never break the silence, he held his hand out to me.

"You unman me," he murmured and I shall treasure forever the look he gave me.

Hastily I placed my hand in his and we stood that way, just looking at each other. Slowly, after a very long moment, he drew me gently to him and kissed my forehead.

"If you don't leave me ... now ... Carla ...."

I was half tempted to stay, fully aware of the consequences, when the rational part of me insisted this would be unfair to Regan's New England conscience. I was at the door when I remembered another obligation.

"Merlin!"

I saw Regan grip the table edge with both hands.

"Get out of here, Carla. I swear I'll take *him* to bed with me. I'll order him to guard me. But, Carla darling, don't let me hear your voice again until morning." The room echoed with the intense emotion in his order.

I really didn't want to leave but I did, closing the kitchen door softly behind me, the blood still hammering in my veins. When Regan did claim me, I wanted him to have no reservations, no dying qualms of guardianly conscience; a curious switch of conventional positions!

# ❦ 14

I WOKE the next morning, alert as I had not been in a long time, alert and eager for the day to begin. It was early in the morning for the sun was just up over the edge of the dunes sheltering the Point from Nauset Beach. My watch said quarter of eight.

The fire was almost out and I rose hastily in the cold to build it up. I smiled to myself as I realized Regan had not mended it as he had done every night since I arrived. His abstention endeared him further to me. Despite the chill in the room, I stretched fully and luxuriously, curling my cold toes up, away from the frigid floor.

I rummaged through my suitcase to see what I had to wear that was more appropriate to my improved status than pants and layers of concealing sweaters.

I had lost enough weight during the bout with strep throat to make both my wool dresses hang badly. Really, my wardrobe was sadly lacking in anything suitable. I had either skirts and sweaters for classes, cocktail and dancing length dresses, or pants. I had to settle on a kilt, Dress Mary plaid in red and green. At least the full pleats gave me some semblance of curved femininity. I had matching pullover and cardigan to wear with it. Quite British, but the garnet red of the sweaters lent a warm color to my face. As a concession to the unheated house, I tugged on knee-length socks and loafers.

I almost skipped down the stairs but restrained myself into befitting dignity. I'd be very quiet and sedate and have breakfast ready for Regan when he woke. But when I went to feed the stove, I found fresh wood just catching fire from the banked coals. Merlin was barking outside. Then the sound of water rushing in the bathroom warned me that Regan was already up.

Well, I could still get breakfast so I started fresh coffee. I sorted thriftily through the stale bread to make French toast. I had the table set when I heard Regan's steps in the hall. I felt myself blushing and I certainly experienced what was once termed "palpitations of the heart."

He was coming down the hall, he was at the door, his hand was turning the knob. I couldn't bear to stand there, barefaced, waiting so I whirled to the stove, pretending much industry over the spider. The door opened and he must have stopped at the threshold. Did I make the proper picture, I wondered?

"Morning," I said cheerfully without looking round.

The door closed.

"Breakfast is nearly ready," I added, making great work of turning the crisping bread.

He advanced towards me and then I could feel him so close that if I leaned a fraction backwards, I would have rested against him. Above the rich smell of French toast, I caught the odor of piney soap and shaving cream, clean linen and after-shave lotion, a combination excessively masculine and very stimulating.

Then his hands cupped my shoulders, his fingers tightening one by one. He bent and kissed the right side of my neck where the sweater ended.

"Now," he said softly, his voice rich with laughter and love, "let's see what my Little Bit looks like dressed as a girl?"

His hands turned me and so help me, I was suddenly too shy to look up at him. With one hand he pushed the frying spider off the burner. Inadvertently following the motion of his hand, I looked at him.

He laughed, deep in his throat. His eyes, more blue than gray this morning, were gleaming with good humor and affection. Still laughing, he spanned my waist with his hands and lifted me high. I gasped, grabbing his hands for balance before he set me down with my feet on the stool, his face level with mine.

"Now, try to avoid the issue," he dared and, turning his head slightly to one side, drew me into his kiss.

The kiss was no less thrilling than the anticipation of it. I wished I could just melt into him. I certainly tried to. This morning he was master of the situation whereas last night's encounter had been spontaneous. His attack on my senses was as deliberate as it was skillful. By the time he released me, I was the one trembling.

The expression in his eyes told me this was exactly what he intended and I quickly searched for some diversion to give myself a breather. My glance fell to his chin where he had cut himself shaving below the unshavable scar. As he saw my eyes drop, I felt his arms stiffen. The muscles of his mouth tightened into the thin line of withdrawal.

I wasn't going to put up with this. If I wanted to look at Regan Laird I was not going to have to put on blinkers until he'd had plastic surgery.

I put a finger on his chin and gave a little push.

> Something I owe to the soil that grew
> More to the life that fed.
> But most to Allah who gave me two
> Separate sides to my head.

Kipling was furthest from his mind at such a moment. He gave a shout of laughter, hugging me exuberantly to him, swinging me around and depositing me on the floor again.

"Message received, over and out. I'm hungry," and he gave me an affectionate shove towards the stove before he sat down.

Merlin barked at the back door and I let him in. He nosed his face into my hand in greeting. If his walk was stiff and slow, he was again operating under his own power. He went up to Regan, laid his head on Regan's knee to have his ears scratched. That attended to, he went back to his quilts and sank down with an enormous canine sigh.

"I took a look at the sutures this morning before I let him out," Regan remarked. "Doing fine."

"Anything else would be a surprise to me," I said with complete confidence in the skill of Dr. Karsh.

We had taken our time over breakfast, the problems to be met today remote from our talk. Regan was dressing to go for more wood when Merlin came alert, a bark in his throat. Regan glanced at me inquiringly.

"Friend, whoever it is," I said. "DeLord!" We both moved swiftly to the front of the house. A Navy jeep was idling in the driveway, but there was no sign of its driver. Just then there was a knock on the back door and someone hallooed.

Merlin barked twice. Evans, the good Samaritan, stood in the kitchen doorway, grinning down at Merlin who had walked stiffly over to greet him.

"Gee, miss, he looks so much better. Dr. Karsh get here?"

"He certainly did, Evans," Regan replied as he shook the young coastguardsman's hand gratefully.

"I'll have to revise my conditioned opinion of the Coast Guard," I remarked. "Particularly since you sent us that incredible man."

Evans' eyes shone. "Aint he something magic? Say, did he like Merlin?"

"Love at first sight. Do you know he stitched Merlin's side and that dog didn't so much as flinch?"

"Believe it. I believe it," Evans assured us fervently. "Oh, Major. A call came in to the station for you. You don't have a phone, I know. I left the jeep running and we can make it back to the station in no time."

"DeLord, I imagine. I'll be right with you, Evans."

As the sandpeep hesitated, Regan ushered him to the door, closing it firmly behind him.

"Why'd you do that?" I asked, surprised at his behavior. It bordered rudeness.

"Because, my dear ward, I do not wish to complicate your position on the Cape any further by having the Coast Guard witness our passionate farewell," he said as he folded me into his arms. He lifted me clear of the floor, grinning broadly at the disparity in our heights.

"You'll have to wear those clog-heels like Carmen Miranda," he teased as he bent his head.

And a passionate farewell it was for we had not kissed often enough to be the least bit casual about it. We both intended to be brief but Evans revved the motor loudly and I was set on my feet so quickly I had to clutch the edge of the table to keep my balance.

"I'll need that cold ride," Regan muttered as he strode out the door.

By the time I had the table cleared and was starting the dishes, I had recovered my wits enough to start worrying. Regan had jumped to the conclusion that it was DeLord who had called. Well, if he had good news, why wouldn't he just come back here? I chided myself for being pessimistic. Maybe DeLord needed Regan's supportive evidence. No, Regan had been wounded before Aachen. Oh, I'd find out soon enough. No use borrowing more trouble until I knew there was some. Besides, it was difficult to stray long from the engrossing subject of Regan and me.

How incredibly delightful to contemplate the prospects. Oh, the dean was going to be livid. She hated married students. They were always giving birth in the middle of exams. We could live at the Waltham house and I'd take the summer session to finish my junior year. I assumed Regan would want me to get my degree. That was but one of the hundreds of things we would have to discuss. It was good I did have the rest of the term off at that. A nuisance to worry about a wedding and studies at the same time the way one of the girls had had to. Boy, was she a nervous wreck.

I was so wound up with projections that Merlin had growled twice before it registered as a warning.

"Easy, boy," I said for Merlin had risen. "Down! I'll go see who it is."

I carefully closed the kitchen door to keep him in and preserve the warmth. I was still so bemused I didn't so much as glance out the dining room window. I even opened the front door wide. When I realized who my visitors were, it was too late to slam it. Beatty's foot was across the sill. Just behind him stood Marian and Donald Warren.

"Alone, Miss Murdock?" Beatty smirked.

I knew then that he knew I was. Fleetingly I wondered about the phone call Regan had gone to answer at the station. Merlin started to bark furiously. I heard his claws scrabbling on the kitchen door.

"Constable Beatty was kind enough to drive us out here,"

Lieutenant Colonel Donald Warren announced in that patronizing nasal voice I remembered all too well.

"You look so wan, dear Carlysle," Marian Warren said, insipidly correct.

Beatty firmly pushed the door wider and stood aside for Marian to enter. The three of them stood indecisively in the hallway. I said nothing.

"My, it's cold here," Marian Warren said pointedly.

Merlin barked continuously.

"Oh, I was hoping you didn't have that beast here with you," she said, shuddering delicately. "I hope you have him chained up. Donnie always swore he was vicious. He certainly sounds like it."

I glanced at Warren whose face had taken on that look of intense strain which proximity to Merlin always produced. In spite of that, Lieutenant Colonel Warren looked revoltingly fit, his wounded arm carried conspicuously in a black silk sling.

Warren was not an ill-favored man. His face was full, his features even, and he carried himself well. He looked the proper officer image and if you didn't know what an indecisive person he was, what little insight he had into anything beyond the end of his rather Roman nose or the pages of the Manual of Arms, you'd have been reassured about the quality of officers running the war. As a matter of fact, he looked more the model of the proper officer than my father had. The natural gauntness of Dad's rough face always seemed forbidding. Dad, although the same height and general build as Warren, appeared too thin, his tunic dropping from bony shoulders to a hipless torso. The comparison was even more distasteful to me now.

"Isn't there any *warm* room in this house?" Marian Warren demanded petulantly, drawing her thick Persian lamb coat tighter to her.

She hadn't changed. She still looked skillfully plucked and painted. I'd bet anything she was wearing a crepe dress, floral pattern, under that coat. Naturally she wore silk stockings and had high heels on under the rubbers she wore as a concession to the unplowed countryside.

Merlin gave voice to unrestrained displeasure at the sound of her voice.

"Don't worry, Mrs. Warren," Beatty said, his hooded eyes glinting smugly. "That dog's too hurt to stand on his feet."

I didn't bother to contradict him because I felt I could handle Beatty without Merlin's help today. He wouldn't dare anything in front of the Warrens.

Another fact registered with me. Donald Warren was aware that Merlin was seriously injured. It was probably the only reason he had come under the same roof. He not only hated Merlin; he was terrified of him.

"Shut him up, Carlysle," Warren ordered through set lips, "no one can hear a word with that racket going on."

I allowed sufficient time to pass for Warren to realize I issued the command on my own, not because he ordered me to.

"I'm so cold, Carlysle," Marian Warren complained again.

"I'll light a fire in the living room," I said with no graciousness and continued with a bald lie. "The only other room we keep warm is the kitchen. And Merlin's in there."

Beatty opened the living room door, displaying a familiarity with the house that I didn't like. He strode over to the fireplace and knelt to light the fire.

"If Beatty would be so kind to light the fire for us," I suggested sarcastically.

The room was more than chilly; it was frigid. The clammy damp cold seeped through my double sweaters. I refused to budge from this room and ignored the desire to shiver.

"There. This fireplace draws well. Take the chill off the room in a sec," Beatty said genially.

"Unless your presence is official . . . ." I said acidly to Beatty.

"It is," Warren replied with unctuous mien. He planted his square body directly in front of the fireplace, hugging any warmth.

Beatty looked at me, a smirk on his mule's face. His eyes took in the fact that I was dressed in a skirt and sweaters. I inwardly cursed the fact that I had no protection from such insolence.

"I fear I am forced to exercise a most unpleasant duty," Warren continued. Beatty's smutty look was driven from my mind. "I must recover some stolen property from you."

"Stolen property? What stolen property?" I demanded.

"Oh, come now, Carlysle. You received your father's footlocker and his personal effects. You don't imagine those parchment books and those valuable stamps are legitimate spoils of war? I know he thought to make restitution —"

"What are you talking about?"

"I told Division that I would handle the matter as tactfully as possible," His face lengthened with simulated regret. "There will be no publicity and, in view of your father's otherwise satisfactory record as an officer, this will be forgotten. But only if restitution can be made to the French authorities."

"What are you saying?" I demanded, the chill forgotten as anger rose in me — hot white anger at the snide implication in Warren's words. "How the hell can you imply anything so ridiculous?"

"Come off it, girlie," Beatty put in jeeringly. "You hand the stuff over and we'll leave. Otherwise I have a search warrant right here. You defy it and I'll have you in jail."

"Go ahead. Search. You won't find anything stolen here."

If Regan and I hadn't been able to find that locker, they couldn't.

"Come now, Carlysle," Warren snapped, his pose abandoned, "don't be tedious. We know you have all your things here."

"Because your second-story man couldn't find them at Mrs. Everett's?" I taunted.

"I told you she'd be difficult," Marian said.

"You're damned right I'll be difficult. The very idea of you two ghouls coming here, slandering my father when all the time . . . ."

My voice had risen in outrage and roused Merlin who began barking frantically, banging his body against the door.

"Shut that goddamned dog up," Warren bellowed, his face white, his eyes darkening with apprehension.

"Only because he's wounded and don't think I don't know who caused that," I cried. "Merlin, shut up!"

Merlin whined in protest, but he stopped barking and battering the door.

"Search the house, Constable," Warren directed Beatty

in the offhand manner he used with anyone below his own rank. His manner did not set well with Beatty whose good opinion of himself did not include subservience to anyone. I did not miss that quick flare of irritation as Beatty trudged down the back hall. As he passed the kitchen door, Merlin growled. Beatty cursed him but continued.

"Really, Carlysle, you're making a difficult duty very unpleasant for Donnie. Only the fact that your father served so many years with him persuaded Donnie he must intervene, for the reputation of the regiment. Why your father—"

"Spare me your interpretation of duty," I snapped. I never could stand the sound of that woman's voice; there was a whiny edge that grated on my nerves.

Marian Warren blinked at the outright animosity and looked appealingly at Warren.

"I'm distressed you're taking this stand, Carlysle," Warren said, switching to the father-confessor pose. "Marian and I wanted to spare you."

He appeared to deliberate, turning to his wife, shaking his head regretfully, shrugging his uninjured shoulder to show he had been forced into a difficult position.

"I have to tell her, Marian. Maybe then she will cooperate. After all, her father was only trying to shield the insubordinate sergeant of his—"

"What has Ed Bailey got to do with this?"

Marian Warren gasped, her mascaraed eyes wide. "She doesn't know?"

Warren's hand had gone significantly to his wounded shoulder. He wore a pained expression.

"We were called down from Boston yesterday to Camp Edwards to identify Bailey. I'm afraid, my dear," his reluctance was pure crap, "that not only did Bailey loot thousands of dollars of valuable stamps and irreplaceable manuscripts from German baggage trains, but he tried to kill me when I accused him."

"Stamps? Manuscripts? Bailey?" I repeated inanely, dimly realizing that Warren was harping on minor items.

"Your father must have realized it first, of course."

"Go ahead, Donnie," Marian spat out viciously, her cold eyes fastened on my face. "Tell her! It'll serve her right, the way she's acted towards us. Just as if her father were chief of staff . . ."

"My dear," and he had the nerve to come over and put an arm around my shoulders. I stepped aside, showing my revulsion openly. He stiffened, his eyes narrowing. "All right," he snapped, his voice taking on the same edge as Marian's. "Your father was murdered."

He paused to see what effect his words had on me. I stared back my hatred. He evidently mistook this for shock because he continued. "By none other than your precious Sergeant Bailey. And I have proof."

I couldn't help it. I laughed in his face. I laughed at the outrageous invention of it, leaning weakly against the fireplace.

"Don't you dare laugh at my husband," Marian Warren screeched, her sharp thin fingers digging through my sweaters as she jerked me around to face her.

"She's hysterical, Marian."

"She is not, the little bitch. She's laughing at you, you fool," and Marian Warren slapped me across the face.

It stopped my laughter but the look on my face dissuaded her against slapping me again. She lowered her hand just as Beatty came back into the room.

"There's a much warmer room just off the dining room," he said, his eyes sliding up and down my body.

"Did you find anything?" Warren snapped, without taking his eyes from me.

"No."

"Search upstairs."

His peremptory tone caused Beatty to hesitate.

"You deal with her, Donald, I'm going to get warm," Marian announced loftily. "The sooner we find what we came after, Officer, the sooner we can all leave this icebox of a house," and she smiled conciliatorily at Beatty. "This is all very upsetting for the colonel. I just know his shoulder is bothering him. Do hurry and search the second floor."

Those two left. I heard Beatty clumping upstairs as Marian's heels clattered on the hall floor. Merlin crashed against the kitchen door as she hurried past.

"You can't think me stupid enough to swallow that accusation, Donald Warren," I said, surprised at the dead calm I felt.

He began to smile unpleasantly.

"And if you think Division will believe such a tale about my father, from *you*, you don't know your reputation in the Fifth Corps."

His smile broadened. "On the contrary. There is incontrovertible evidence. The obliging lieutenant brought along the slug that the medic dug out of your father's body. It matches the one that wounded me. Both were fired from Bailey's service revolver which was taken from him when he was arrested in Aachen, and tallies with the number issued to him."

He spoke with such conviction that a cold uncertainty paralyzed me. It must have shown in my face for he smiled his toothy smile, showing teeth badly discolored.

He must be wrong, I told myself. Whose was the forty-five we found in Dad's locker? Turtle Bailey could not have murdered my father. That was impossible!

Besides, it was Warren who had done the looting. Turtle hadn't. DeLord had proved that. He was completely satisfied it was Warren. And Dad had known it, too. That's why Warren had shot him.

"Bailey escaped in Aachen. If he'd been innocent, why would he run?" Warren's voice hammered at me and then he shook my arm roughly. "Now stop protecting that murderer and tell me where those things are or I'll see your father's name smeared. He was shielding a looter. He knew, too, how much money was involved. He was obstructing justice. I'll see his name—"

"You try it, Warren, you just try it," I shouted, losing all control, "and I'll give that court-martial proof of the many times my father shielded your reputation, covered up your mistakes. I'll tell them what happened at Bois de Collette when you lost ninety-five men because you couldn't give a decent order to save your own neck. I'll tell . . . ."

His eyes widened as the impact of my words reached him. He raised his hand, palm flat, to clout me when Merlin's body lunged past me, knocking him to the floor. He screamed, a curiously high-pitched, womanish scream, terror-ridden.

"Hold, Merlin! Guard!" I ordered, grimly satisfied by the look of abject terror on Warren's wide-eyed white face.

Merlin crouched, one paw lightly resting on Warren's throat. He snarled, his fangs a scant inch from the man's chin. Warren moved once and Merlin's jaws snapped without meeting flesh. Warren lay still, his staring eyes never leaving the dog's menacing face.

"Hold, Merlin. Just hold!"

I heard the back door crash open and Regan was shouting for me. I ran for the safety and sanity of Regan's arms, slamming the living room door behind me, knowing that Merlin would keep Warren there until I heard from Regan's lips how absurd that man's charge was.

"Carla, Carla, thank God," Regan cried, embracing me roughly with relief. "The phone call was a fraud. To get me out of the house. Bailey hasn't shown up, has he?"

Marian Warren came stalking out of the study into the back porch.

"Major Laird," she began imperiously and was effectively silenced by his look.

"Regan, they're saying awful things about Turtle," I cried, "and that Beatty man is searching the house."

Regan's face was grim, his eyes terrible.

"What's the matter?" I wailed. "Where is Turtle?"

"He escaped. When I realized the phone call was a fraud, and you were here alone, I got suspicious. I called DeLord at Edwards. He was just leaving to warn us."

"Warn us?"

"Sweetheart, listen. Turtle is armed and he's . . . desperate. He's sick. He knocked the guard out when they brought his breakfast, stole a jeep, and is on his way here. He's after Warren."

"Donnie? Bailey's after my husband?" Marian Warren cried shrilly.

She barged past Regan on her way to the living room but he grabbed her and propelled her back into the study.

"You stay in there, lock the doors, and don't come out unless you're aching for a stray bullet."

As if to give added urgency to his warning, we heard

distant gunfire. Evans, who'd been standing in the door, withdrew hastily. I saw his patrol spreading out, crouching low behind the slope of the land, seeking cover.

Marian Warren shrieked again and slammed the study door. I heard the lock click and her frightened squeals as she raced to bar the study's front door.

"Regan, *please* tell me what's happened?" I begged, pulling at his arm because he had turned to join Evans. "Warren was saying Turtle killed my father! That the bullets match?" I yearned for denial.

Regan gently disengaged my hands.

"According to DeLord, Warren is right. I hate to think so, Carla—"

"It isn't so. It can't be so," I screamed.

Regan jerked his head around at the sound of another volley and indistinguishable shouts. He dashed out the door. Beatty came striding into the kitchen.

"Now whatinhell's going on here?" he demanded.

I stepped aside, gestured him out the door, too shaken to speak. As soon as he had barged past me, I grabbed up an old coat from the door and followed him out. There were more shots, from just down the road.

I could see distant figures spreading out, advancing purposefully, black against the scintillating snow. I could see the white smoke-blossoms before I heard the crack of rifle fire. Then I caught a glimpse of the running man, crouched low but all too familiar. Sergeant Edward Bailey!

The coastguardsmen opened up from their positions at the edge of the scrub bushes surrounding the house. Horrified I saw the sergeant's body jerk and spin, lurch with a second jolt, and then sink slowly to the snowy ground.

The rough shakes were icy beneath my hands as I backed against the house for support. I stared at the distant dark form in the snow until tears dimmed the sight.

Numbed and blinded, I closed my eyes. When I opened them again, I saw men converge on the sergeant's body. Saw them take it away in a jeep. Another car picked up the remaining men and started towards the house. Then Beatty came around the corner. I instinctively drew back but he saw me and halted.

"Well, your murdering sergeant got his. Now let's—"

"One more word, Beatty . . ." and Regan left the threat hanging as he thumbed back the safety on the thirty-eight he carried.

Beatty paused only a moment before he backed slowly away from me, standing at a distance. Regan, his hands gentle, led me back into the house and sat me at the kitchen table.

"DeLord's coming," he said, his voice heavy and flat.

A jeep motor whined up the snowy slope to the garage. I wasn't sobbing anymore but my eyes were full of tears that wouldn't go away so that I couldn't see, but my other senses became excessively acute. Heavy boots banged against a metal running board. Men were tramping with grating sounds across the garage cement. The door handle rattled and the hinges squeaked as the door was opened. Cold air beat on my shoulders. There was a heavy smell of cordite from recently fired guns, wet wool, and sour sweat. There was the distinct feel of many people pressing in around the room and the air was close.

"I see Beatty got here. I gather he brought the Warrens," Robert DeLord said as he slid sideways into the chair beside me. "I missed them by a hair at Edwards and then had to help trace Bailey." He, too, smelled of cordite and cold air and snow. His cold fingers touched my arm lightly and, obediently, I looked up at him. His face was very tired and his green eyes sad. There was no trace of any boyishness right now.

"Bailey's dead, Miss Carla," he said gently.

I managed to nod that I understood him.

"He told me he had fired the shot that killed your father."

"No." I contradicted him flatly.

DeLord's hand tightened. "Yes, Miss Carla. But he *thought* he was shooting Warren. You see, he heard your father ask me to go get Warren just as he was called to check out the ammo and rations. He didn't hear your father call me back. Instead, Bailey found a good place for an ambush and when your father and I came along the road, he assumed I was driving Warren back, not your father *to* Warren.

"You see, Colonel Murdock had just had a call from HQ. I found out later it was to tell him that the bait, those stamps and one of the Gospels, had not turned up at Division HQ with the other liberated valuables. So your father had proof it was Warren. If only the colonel'd told me then . . . that it was Warren he suspected . . . but I do understand why he felt he couldn't confide in me until he had definite proof. And he was mighty upset when he called me back and said he'd go with me."

DeLord leaned forward towards me, his face anxious, his eyes begging me to understand. "Bailey was only trying to protect your dad. He felt that if he killed Warren, your father'd report himself to the base hospital and recover from the wound. But he knew your father would never leave the regiment if Warren were here, the way the men felt about Warren just then. But Bailey's been faking eyesight tests for years. Your father was the same height and general build as Warren and in the dark . . ."

"Bailey wouldn't have killed my dad," I repeated stupidly, unable to accept the truth.

Regan's arm came around my shoulders and I realized he had been sitting quietly on the other side of me.

"No, Carla, he wouldn't have. He was out to kill Warren. By mistake, he killed . . . someone else . . . someone he worshipped. It isn't far off the truth to say Bailey went into battle shock. He talked himself into believing Warren had actually fired the shot and he nearly talked me into it except I couldn't see Warren killing like that. But, in a way, Warren really was guilty of your father's death. If he hadn't caused so much trouble, Bailey wouldn't have been driven to killing him."

Emotionally I could accept that interpretation. Maybe later . . . when it didn't twist and hurt so much . . . .

"Turtle did shoot Warren?" I asked finally.

"Yes," DeLord confirmed. "And the attempt at Aachen was not the first one, either, was it, Laird?"

"No," Regan admitted. "I knocked his hand up once near Jülich, and the lieutenant who replaced Garcia in Able Company told me he caught Bailey taking aim on Warren. Told me later he was sorry he'd deflected the sergeant's arm. We all knew Bailey hated Warren. I felt I knew why but I was only half right."

"Is it safe to come out now?" a muffled voice quavered into the dead silence that followed.

"God, I forgot her," Regan muttered, rising. "Yes, come out, Mrs. Warren."

We heard her slide back the bolt and then she peered cautiously out. When she saw who was grouped in the kitchen, she pulled the door wide and pranced out, her face suddenly as livid with anger as it had been white with fear.

"Well, who are you?" she demanded.

"Robert DeLord, ma'am," and the lieutenant had risen, the polite Southerner no matter what. "This is Regan Laird."

"Well?" she demanded her voice harsh. "Have you captured that maniac? Where's Constable Beatty? Has he found that locker yet? Where's Donnie?"

"Yes, where is Colonel Warren?" asked DeLord, exchanging a look over my head with Regan.

"In the living room," I gasped. "He's in the living room. He tried to slap me. Merlin's holding him."

"That monster? Ah!" screeched Marian Warren, her eyes bulging with terror as she ran, ungainly in the high-heeled galoshes. Regan and DeLord followed, breaking into a run at her hysterical shriek. There was a ring of horror, so unlike Marian's usual pitch, it snapped me out of the paralysis that held me. I ran to the living room.

"Merlin, heel!" I heard Regan order and then, more softly, "Colonel? Colonel Warren? Answer me, man!"

Marian kept on shrieking.

"What's happened?" I demanded, pushing past the lieutenant who had halted mid-room. "Merlin hasn't . . ."

Merlin hadn't done anything. That was it, I guess. But Warren's abject fear of dogs had. The colonel was in a fixed-eye state of shock, his face gray, spittle dripping down the side of his slack mouth as he lay on the floor. Merlin had scared him out of his wits.

As the two men got the colonel, unresisting, to his feet and sat him on a chair, Marian, still shrieking, ran out. She came back in, dancing in a frenzied rage, towing Beatty behind her.

"Shoot him! Shoot that mad dog. He'll kill us all. Look what he's done to my husband. Shoot him! Shoot him!"

Beatty did go for his gun. I threw myself on Merlin, keeping my body between the officer and the dog.

"That'll be enough, Beatty," Regan snapped.

"Shoot him! Shoot him!" Marian Warren kept screaming.

DeLord strode over to her and, muttering an apology, slapped her quickly and smartly on both cheeks. It effectively calmed her.

"If you have a radio in that police car of yours, Beatty, call an ambulance. The colonel's had a shock. And keep that gun holstered in my house!"

There was an authoritative knock on the front door.

"Come in," Regan shouted, without taking his eyes from Beatty's face.

"Colonel Calderone," DeLord said, waving in a wiry, Italianate man.

"Thank God you came, Colonel," Marian Warren babbled. "Everyone here's mad. That dog is, too. They've been mistreating me and just look at Donnie." Then she stopped, her hand going to her mouth as she absorbed the look of cold contempt on Colonel Calderone's face.

"You were right about the truck, DeLord," he said turning his back deliberately on the woman. "There were three slugs in the gas tank. We've picked up the men." He turned back to Marian Warren. "There are a few questions I would like to put to you and Colonel Warren." He looked at the passive figure in the chair. "Colonel?" he said, his face puzzled by the lack of response.

"Warren has gone into shock, Colonel," Regan said. "No doubt," and he swung towards Beatty, "due to the untenable position in which he finds himself."

Beatty was the first to drop his eyes. When he did, as if sensing she no longer had a single champion, Marian Warren began to cry softly. Beatty glanced contemptuously at her.

"I came here to recover stolen goods," he said stubbornly.

"Yes, where is that footlocker?" Regan asked, looking at DeLord questioningly.

A shadow of a smile touched the lieutenant's mouth.

"Under the woodpile, of course!"

# 🍎 15

"SHE SAID NOTHING to me about any jewels," was Beatty's angry comment later when Colonel Calderone took official charge of the illegal shipment.

"Of course she didn't," DeLord answered. "They could righteously turn all this over to the authorities," and he waved at the array of treasures on the kitchen table. "I imagine Warren would have innocently suggested he take charge of the service Colt and the ammo and return them to Edwards. And neatly retrieve what he was really after."

Beatty snorted, shuffling his feet. Neither he nor Regan looked near each other and he avoided my glances studiously.

"What'll happen to that colonel?" he asked.

"If he recovers," Colonel Calderone answered him, "he'll stand a court-martial."

"And her?"

"She's been an accomplice in armed robbery. The civil courts will handle her. *After,*" and the colonel grinned mirthlessly, "we find out how much more of this sort of stuff is still unrecovered from grieving relatives." He held up one of the ruby-jeweled crosses, the stones catching fire from the sunlight. "I heard a part of the list one burglar was giving the sheriff. Quite a racket they had. Well, I'll take this, Miss Murdock, and be on my way. Coming, DeLord?"

The lieutenant glanced expectantly towards Regan who nodded.

"I'll be along later, Colonel, if you've no objections."

"Colonel," I blurted out. "About Turtle?"

"Yes, Miss Murdock?"

"He . . . had such a fine record. He didn't mean to kill my father. They had been together since 1917. I even lived with his family after my mother died. Does . . . do you . . ." I couldn't continue. I whirled appealingly to Regan, towards Robert DeLord.

Regan came around the table and held me tightly, looking towards the colonel. The man sighed, shaking his head slowly.

"The family will be told he died in line of duty. In a way, I guess that's the truth after what you all have told me. And considering what Warren and his wife were doing I expect I don't begrudge the sergeant that potshot at Aachen." He gave me a one-sided grin of reassurance. "Look, I'll do what I can."

"He was a murderer," Beatty growled, his eyes darting around the room suspiciously.

"I'd watch that talk, Beatty, if I were you," Calderone said in a quick, harsh voice. The man was not tall but there was a confidence and subtle strength about him that was more impressive than mere size. "Your nose isn't too clean in this affair. An officer of the law involved in receiving stolen property?"

"Receiving?" Beatty gagged.

"That would be my testimony if one word of the circumstances around Bailey's death ever gets mentioned in this county!" Calderone's words had the crispness of deadly earnest. "Good afternoon, Constable Beatty!" And Beatty left.

Calderone turned to me, his face reflecting sympathy.

"That'll settle his hash. Now, Miss Murdock, if Warren recovers there will have to be an investigation but courts-martial, thank God, are not public. That's all I can do for you and Bailey."

"Thank you, Colonel."

He raised his hand to his cap in an informal salute, gathered up the treasure, and left.

I leaned weakly against Regan, so terribly grateful there was someone to lean on. I didn't have to be the brave little soldier anymore. I could be a grieving, tired, weeping girl. But, oddly enough, though the double tragedy of Turtle and my father was leaden in my heart, I was dry-eyed.

"It seems like such a terrible, terrible error," I said slowly. "It has to be corrected. It has to come out fair."

"Here, honey, drink this," DeLord suggested.

I looked at the cup of coffee he was offering me.

"So help me," he vowed, "there's nothing but bourbon in it."

Regan gently seated me. I had felt him go tense at

DeLord's endearment and it penetrated my numb mind that he was jealous.

"Yes, it was a terrible, tragic set of errors," Regan said quietly, thanking DeLord for the coffee the lieutenant handed him. "Doubly terrible for you, Carla. Now take a good drink. It's cool enough to swallow. You look transparent." His brisk command was leavened by a tone rough with suppressed feeling. "If your father hadn't been such an honorable fool, trying to protect a worthless brother officer simply because they were classmates, maybe this whole fiasco wouldn't have happened. The colonel would sure as hell have transferred any other incompetent replacement so fast the man wouldn't have known his sergeant's name. But that goddamned Pointer tradition, honor and duty . . . ."

I stared at Regan, astonished and dismayed at the scornful vehemence in his voice.

"What's the matter with honor and tradition and duty?" I demanded, stung and hurt.

"There," and Regan smiled broadly at me, "that's better. I can't stand you looking like a woebegone elf." He encircled my shoulders and drew me as close to him as our chairs would allow. "Your father's dead, Carlysle, and don't ever for moment think I haven't mourned him and missed him. He was a great man, a real soldier and a patriot. There are very few of his mold in any century. Bailey's dead, too, but he courted death. Killing Warren was one way to achieve it and revenge his error about your dad."

"What bothered Bailey most," the lieutenant put in quietly, "was what you would think when you found out what had actually happened. He was a broken man . . . tired and old and bitter."

"He didn't really kill my father. Warren did," I said, when I could get words over the lumps in my throat. The tears just fell down my cheeks into my hand.

"Oh, Carla darling," Regan whispered, kissing my cheek. "We're both pretty battered around right now but, in time, the worst hurt heals."

"Ohho," DeLord drawled in an altered voice. "Have I been outmaneuvered?"

Whether he meant it or not, the absurdity penetrated my grief.

"Rank has a few privileges," Regan retorted quickly.

"Well," DeLord chuckled, looking at our faces, "that would have pleased the Old Man no end." He laughed again at our expressions. "I know. In Paris he was bending my ear either about Miss Carla—he always called you Carlysle—or you, Laird. I didn't get the significance until I met you, Miss Carla," and grinning mischievously, DeLord inclined his head graciously at me.

"Then, Bob, would you give me away, kind of *in loco parentis*?"

For a brief second DeLord looked startled. Then he smiled broadly.

"Miss Carla, it would be my honor. But unless you two plan on an early wedding. I might not be able to oblige. I don't know how long I can string out the wrap-up of this assignment."

"It only takes three days . . . ." I pleaded with Regan.

"Shotgun wedding, by God!" he complained dramatically.

"Wouldn't be the first time for you, I imagine," I teased coolly back, rewarded by the look of shocked dismay on the major's face.

"Why, you impudent little bit of a thing. It was no such . . . ." Then Regan caught himself as he realized he'd fallen for the bait.

The noise had roused Merlin who barked joyously, wagging his tail and cavorting stiff-leggedly around.

"Ah," Bob DeLord put in tentatively, "would you mind, Miss Carla, if I fixed myself a little something to eat? I left Edwards in rather a hurry this morning and—"

"Holy Moses, it's nearly lunchtime," I cried. "You both must be ravenous. There's some canned soup. Will that take the edge off your appetite while I fix something more substantial?"

I flung open a cupboard door, standing on tiptoe to read the labels.

"That sounds just fine, Miss Carla."

I had both hands on the countertop to give myself a boost upward when Regan roared at me.

"James Carlysle Murdock, if I've told you once I've—"

"— told you a thousand times to use the stool," I finished for him, ducking guiltily and turning to grimace at my love.

As he swung me up to the top of the stool to kiss me, I had one brief glimpse of Bob DeLord, ducking his head to soothe the bullet crease with careful fingers.

# THE
# KILTERNAN
# LEGACY

# 1

AUNT IRENE TEASEY, great aunt Teasey, solved my problem: She died. She died in Ireland, and left all that she died possessed of to me.

"Good heavens," my mother said when I phoned her to see if there was anything to be possessed, "I don't know. Your father used to say that Irene was the only smart female the Teaseys ever produced. Although why she'd leave you everything when she'd all those relatives . . . hmmm. Maybe that's why."

"Why what?" I asked—patiently, because Mother's thought processes had driven Father to an early grave, although he had once admitted to me in utter confusion that he found my mother's conclusions fascinatingly accurate.

"Why she did. I named you after her because your father liked her so much, and I *had* run out of interesting girl names [I've four sisters] and the one time I met Irene, I quite liked the old girl. Very independent sort, you know. Never married."

I wasn't certain from Mother's tone whether it was because of her independence that Irene had not married, or whether she'd developed the habit because she'd remained single.

"Well, is she likely to have left anything?"

"Quite possible. Doesn't the lawyer man give you any inkling?"

"No precise figures. I must establish my identity as Miss Teasey's great-niece first, and I'm executrix of the will, and there're death duties to pay, and—"

"You'd better go there, then. Always does to be on the spot, especially with lawyers—no, barristers—no, *they* plead

431

cases before the bar, don't they? Solicitors is what you'd have to deal with. But she does solve your problem, Rene."

"By having to go to Ireland to consort with bewigged men?"

"*Men*, dear, is the relevant word."

"Oh, Mother!"

"Oh, Daughter! You were complaining only the other day that you didn't know who stood where in relation to you or Teddie-boy since the divorce. Why bother to find out? The ones who'll stay by you are too dull, or married and don't have the contacts you need, and the ones who side with Teddie you don't want to know."

She was, of course, massively correct.

"Besides, I read somewhere recently that a removal from the marital area is often a very constructive step. If taken in the proper direction."

I could tell that Mother now considered Ireland, of all places, to be the proper direction.

"There're men there," she said, again darkly suggestive.

"There're men everywhere, Mother."

"Not what *I'd* call men."

"Mother!"

"Nonsense, dear. Besides, think how broadening it would be for the twins!"

I gulped. "The twins are quite broadened enough."

"I don't mean precocious, love. I mean, broad in outlook and culture."

"You ought to know Teddie's opinion of Ireland by now."

"And I thank God that the jet set hasn't discovered Ireland yet. They do have good schools, and no drug problem."

"True, but they do have a minor religious war."

"Darling, it *isn't* religious. It's socioeconomic, hidden under clerical skirts, I read somewhere . . . And besides, you'd be in the south."

"Mother, I'm not certain that I want to go anywhere right now."

"What? Another six months in your lair licking your wounds, dear?" Mother can be disconcertingly acute at times. "Consult the twins."

I did. I'll never figure out how she got to them before I did. After all, they were in school in Westfield, and she was in New York City. Their reaction was so affirmative that Simon was booking flights while Snow listed the clothes I had to bring. As she was constantly garbed in sweaters, shirts, and pants, her packing posed no mental exertions.

"But, children, you don't want to leave all your friends . . ."

"Why not?" asked Snow, her gorgeous, big, light-green eyes very adult in expression. "Everyone will be away for vacations in a week. It'd be great. You'll have to get some dresses, Mother. These are just too much!"

Snow was conventionally christened Sara Virginia, after Mother and my mother-in-law. At the party after the baptismal double-header, one of her uncles had observed the sleeping child, all lacy in the family christening gown, her wealth of curly black hair escaping the cap, and renamed her Snow White. She was only a half-hour younger than her brother, but the difference might have been two separate pregnancies. Simon was dark too, but not as dramatically so. His skin was ruddy, not white, and his eyes more gray than green. Curiously enough, their personalities belied their looks, for Simon tended to be the dreamer, and Snow had a fine sense of everyday expediencies. Teddie had complained that she was revoltingly precocious. She was. He had made her so by showing off his "fairy-tale princess" to bored sophisticates.

It was when Teddie began to . . . well, never mind. That sort of consideration was behind me now. And, fortunately, behind Snow. Yes, going to Ireland would solve many of my problems, all right. And pose others.

One of them was Teddie's reaction to having his children removed from his sphere of influence. Neither he nor that expensive and indolent lawyer of his had put any clause in the divorce papers restricting me to be domiciled exclusively in Westfield, New Jersey, or the continental U.S.A. I could not put the children in a boarding school, but that was the only restriction.

"What about my visitation rights?" Teddie had shouted.

"You haven't exercised those rights in three weeks!"

"Now see here, Irene, you can't just snatch my kids from under my nose without my permission—"

"I don't need your permission, and I'm courteously informing you of my summer plans. I'm going to Ireland for a month at the longest, and the children are going with me. I'm just telling you, and that's that."

Then, before I could become embroiled in one of those impossible arguments in which I always end up being wrong, ineffective, stupid or ludicrous, I hung up on him. It had taken me six months of divorced bliss to achieve such decisiveness. I'd always had the feeling that if only Teddie would really listen to my side of an argument, we might be able to patch up our faltering marriage. Only, my rebuttals had lacked the ingenuity of his ad-agency-trained responses, and I always lost.

Fortunately his lawyer had not discarded an iota of his laziness, and Simon and Snow overrode my hesitation, so we were on the plane to Ireland in ten days' time, the passport photos barely dry under the stamps. My lawyer had walked them through Immigration. I suppose Hank had had a notion of what Teddie might do if he were really as annoyed as he said he was about my taking *his* children from him. An injunction restraining me from removing Simon Richard and Sara Virginia Stanford from the continental U.S.A. was issued the day after we left. Had I known of it beforehand, I couldn't even have applied for passports for Snow and Simon. Later I wondered whether the children's efficiency had been prompted by a "get Mother moving" campaign or an inside knowledge of their father's reactions.

We were in Dublin at 11, and in a taxi to the hotel by 11:30. We'd been booked into the Hotel Montrose, typical Americana, but comfortable. I phoned the solicitor, Mr. Noonan, and was informed that he was in court.

"I thought he was a solicitor."

"He is indeed, but he's attending a client in court."

That didn't make much sense to me, but I was in no shape to pursue the subject. "Please tell him that Irene Teasey is at the Hotel Montrose, and I'd like to see him as soon as possible."

"Mrs. Teasey?" There was a startled squeak in the girl's soft voice.

"The American one. The great-niece." Silence. "I'm to see him about inheriting my great-aunt's property at Kilternan." Silence. "This is Noonan, Turner, and Pearsall's office, isn't it?"

"Oh, yes, it certainly is."

"Then please give Mr. Noonan my message and say that I'm anxious to see him as soon as possible." Again the rather stunned silence. "Is anything wrong?"

"No, no. Of course not, ma'am."

Well, I was too tired to chew that over.

So the twins thought, too, because Snow took the phone out of my hand, replaced it, and pushed me back onto the bed, and Simon shook a coverlet over me.

"You rest."

"But I can't leave you two alone in—"

"Why not? The natives sound friendly."

"And I'm hungry," added Snow.

"There's a grill downstairs, and a bank."

I'd given them each some money, American and Irish.

"You sleep!" said Simon in a stern, masculine voice.

I didn't really expect to, and was therefore more than a little annoyed to be roused from a very deep slumber by the insistent burring of a phone by my ear. Sleepily I grabbed at it to shut it up.

"Would I be speaking to Irene Teasey?"

"Yes!" I wasn't too sure myself, but the tone of the male voice implied that I'd better be Irene Teasey.

"I understand that Hillside Lodge is for sale," the man said.

"Hillside Lodge?" Where was that? Where was I? "Who is this speaking?"

"I'm Brian Kelley, of T K & B, and I've a client who's making a firm offer of—"

"Now, wait just a minute. I just got to Dublin this morning, and I haven't seen the place."

"Well, Miss Teasey, then I can be of service to you in several ways—by helping you wind up your business quickly, selling at a profit, and you'll have plenty of time to enjoy some sightseeing before you go back." The man had spoken with a wheedling pseudo-charm which I knew all too well.

"Mr. Kelley, you are rushing things."

"Why now, and I thought you Americans liked a direct approach."

Not when I'm half asleep I don't. "I have just had a tiring journey from the States, and I'm in no mood to discuss business at this moment. I suggest—"

"It's just evening now," he said with a conciliatory smoothness, and I glanced hurriedly at my watch, which read 3:30. "Let me welcome you to Ireland with a few jars. Say around nine? It would be worth your while, I assure you. Shall I ring your room?"

I stammered out an affirmative and then, when I realized that I had been guided into agreeing, I tried to retract and found the phone had gone dead.

Good Lord! I'd hardly expected such a problem, and I did wish that the solicitor had been in. I didn't have a clue as to whether I should even listen to offers. Grab the first sucker, or hang out for top development prices? Did they develop in Ireland? Ah, yes, I did recall rows of identical semidetached houses on the way from the airport.

Three-thirty is evening in Ireland? I rose, washed my face, put on eyebrows and lips, and decided that if this was evening in Ireland, there might be tea—preferably coffee— served somewhere. And where were my children?

That proved easiest to establish. They had gone out, the sweet-voiced receptionist told me, and gave me the impression that Snow and Simon had been laying on the charm right, left, and center. Good. There had to be some fringe benefits of life with Teddie . . . like public-relations-minded children. *"Preserve the Image!"*

Yes, I could have tea or coffee served in the lounge bar. So I had coffee and thin sandwiches while browsing through the Irish *Times*. A large section of the paper was devoted to real estate. The intelligence slowly penetrated my brain that "auctioneers" were also agents for selling and renting houses. T K & B translated into Thomas, Keogh, and Brennan, evidently a large and active firm, so friend Brian Kelley was a sharp operator, moving in quickly on a prime prospect. But wasn't it a shade too quickly? There seemed to be no dearth of houses in Dublin, or south Dublin. I did some hasty pounds-into-dollars conversions and found that many of the houses advertised were about $25,000. Not that that helped me, because, obviously, location had something to do with price, as did the age of the house. The range was all the way from £3,000 to £12,000.

And how had Brian Kelley known that Irene Teasey was in Dublin? And here only for the purpose of selling? Something Irene Teasey hadn't even decided.

After all, the only person who'd known I was here was . . . ah, was that why the girl in the solicitor's office had been so silent? Had she been tipped to report my arrival to "interested parties"? Surely Hillside Lodge couldn't be so valuable as to require such cloak-and-dagger tactics!

Mother never had been explicit on that score, but she'd been very disquieting about lots of relations who'd be unhappy about my inheriting. I'd tried several times to nail her down to specifics, without luck. Not even I can understand Mother's crypticisms. She'd interspersed her rambles with odd remarks and advice such as: "Her sisters were the worst—they'd greedy little clutching paws, and petty minds. Dublin's no more than a small town. Everyone knows everyone else, and all their business. You'll find that out. Never tell 'em anything. That's probably why your grandfather got out of Ireland. There was one other brother but he died. Your father often mentioned his uncle Beebee. His name was really Richard. At any rate, don't sell a thing, a stick, until you've had sound legal counsel. I expect the lawyer's good. Irene Teasey was no fool. Probably why she never married an Irishman. Or maybe *because* she never married an Irishman." This distinction puzzled Mother, and interrupted that particular discourse.

"This is, however, exactly what you need, Rene. A complete change, a new challenge. You're only thirty-six, the one advantage in marrying young."

I might be only thirty-six, but I felt a hundred even after two cups of strong coffee. As for the challenge of coming to Ireland, did I really need it? I sort of sank into my chair, feeling small.

Fortunately for my trend of thought, Snow and Simon came through the entrance, with Snow pointing at me dramatically in her "See? She's all right" gesture. Simon shrugged and then brandished something which turned out to be two maps, one of Dublin and one of Ireland.

"This is Dublin proper but Kilternan doesn't appear on it, much less Swann's Lane," Simon said, spreading out the map across the small lounge tables. "See, it's down in here," and he illustrated. "Nice country, I'm told."

"Who told you?" I asked, curious.

"We did a little adroit questioning," Snow said.

"Where?"

"Oh, up the road a piece is a largish shopping center," and Simon jerked his thumb over his shoulder rightishly.

"Not bad specialty shops, either," added Snow.

"How'd you get there?"

"Walked up, bused back." Simon flourished a bus schedule. "They're all double-deckers!" He beamed. "Thirsty work."

I got the hint and signaled the waiter. Snow did some flirt-practicing, and the man responded visibly until I gave her an adroit kick. She might be only fourteen but she looked much, much older. So did Simon, I realized, seeing him against an unfamiliar background. He'd shot up to a respectable five foot ten in the last six months, and recently complained that he had to shave. I suggested a beard, and he haughtily replied that everyone was bearded. Ergo, *he* couldn't be.

"And there's a rental-car place." Simon handed over another folder. "These are the rates."

"I should hire you as leg man," I said, but Simon knew I was grateful.

"They want your arm for new cars here," Simon said, shaking his head. I knew he'd had delusions about our driving a Mercedes or a Jaguar while we were here. "All those small foreign cars cost a fortune."

"All those small foreign cars are native, Simple Simon," his twin said with a remonstrating snort.

"Now, wait a minute, children, I'm not buying a car."

"Who suggested?" Simon was honestly surprised. "Just

compared prices, that's all, but you will want something to get around in. This," and he tapped the bus schedule, "is supposedly an old Irish legend."

"What do you mean?"

Simon snorted, and Snow giggled. "You should have heard them at the bus stop! 'Sure now, an' I've been waiting the half-hour or more!' [Snow has an ear for dialect] I mean, Mom, and there's no route that takes us to our part of Kilternan."

"How do you know?" I waved at the Kilternanless map.

"Big area map in the Hertz place. Swann's Lane is" — and Simon walked his fingers down a road marked TO CABIN-TEELY — "approximately here," and his fingers hovered over a large rose in the carpet, five inches from the map edge.

"Hmmm."

"So, we'd need a car," Simon said.

"And you know the one I should have?"

"Well, you always liked Gammy's little Renault. They have the same model . . . Of course, it's right-hand drive, but you'd cope, Mother."

Simon has a most satisfactory way of assuming all kinds of abilities that I'm not so sure I possess until he indicates that I do, and then I do.

"And they've a Renault all ready and waiting for me tomorrow?"

Simon grinned. "Well, I didn't see any harm in asking. And they do."

"Garnet red," said Snow approvingly.

"Well, that's one thing settled. However . . ." and I told them about Mr. Kelley's call.

"I wouldn't see the man," said Snow autocratically.

"That's a bit quick, isn't it, Mother? Sounds fishy." Simon was giving me that too-intent look, which meant that he and Snow had been conspiring.

"Okay, what's with you two?"

"Well, we've all summer to do nothing in, why not do it in Ireland?" she asked guilelessly. "If that cottage is habitable at all, it'll do as a base for any touring we want to do."

"You don't like the Westfield routine any more anyhow, Mom," Simon said. "Swimming club and that nonsense."

He didn't add "and running into your ex-husband and his new wife."

"You haven't been in Ireland more than . . ." I glanced at my watch, but Simon covered it, his expression very earnest.

"It's the feeling about it," Snow said, raising her hands in an unconscious effort to enfold the new experience, "and the people have time to talk to you, and answer questions, and *listen*."

"And give advice." Simon's grin was suddenly a faint echo of Teddie's I've-got-this-account-sewed-up smile. "I mean, they're *nice*, Mom."

"They know we're tourists," I said, to cushion their eventual disillusionment.

"Even if that's the case, it's a very welcome change!" Snow's eyes flashed, and her lips compressed against the increasingly frequent and distressing incidents that her young beauty provoked. If she felt less threatened in Ireland . . .

"Look, let's not go leaping without looking."

"Aw, Mom, Ireland's nice," Simon said, as if that were the definitive reason.

"I'm not saying no, I'm just—"

"Temporizing as usual," Snow finished for me.

"Really, Sara!"

She subsided, making a face, because usually she is not pert with me.

"Getting back to Mr. Kelley," Simon said adroitly, "you're not going to talk with him?"

"How can I avoid it? He was very insistent."

"Nine o'clock, you said? Well, you can be a number of places at nine. I think his insistence is a bit suspicious."

"So do I, but it doesn't hurt to listen."

The twins were dubious; they know how soft I am.

"Got an idea," said Snow. "You said he'd ring your room? Okay, nineishly, Sim sits in the lobby where he can hear. You sit in here, where you can see. Kelley announces himself at the desk, asks for you. Simon opens the map . . . wide. You see if you like Kelley's looks, and if you don't, when you get paged you don't answer. The girl at the desk can't find you if you're not here."

"That is rude. I mean, what if he is nice, and on the level..."

"So call him at T K & B and apologize. You were out for dinner and it took longer than you expected. Basic!" said the practical Snow.

I really wasn't up to meeting Mr. Kelley and being pressured, and the children knew it, so in the end I agreed that the plan was sensible.

Then we pored over the map to get some bearings. Dublin wasn't very big compared to New York (or, for that matter, Westfield, New Jersey), but the streets were irregular, and I could see that finding places might be a problem. And that led to looking at the full-scale map, and by the time we'd finished dinner the twins had plotted quite a tour of Ireland. Really, I could see their point. If we had a base, we could take short forays to historical sites, and it wouldn't be all that expensive — certainly no more than living in Westfield and shelling out five dollars a day at the pool — and more for air conditioning — or for trips to cousins. Well, I made no promises, but the twins knew me well enough to realize that they'd half persuaded me to stay.

"That is, if all goes well," I said, trying to be firm.

There were variables. For instance, how much cash would be left over after death duties and stuff from Aunt Irene's estate? I am *not* mercenary, but the trip over had taken most of my sinking fund. Of course, the support money from Teddie would be in on the first of July, and that would probably go further in Ireland than in New Jersey.

I suppose it was because everything was grown in a different soil, or maybe not to such homogeneous standards, but the peas at dinner were heavenly, the steak tender and delicious, and even the french fries ["Chips, Mom, chips," Simon corrected me] which I don't usually like, tasted superb!

"Maybe I was just hungry," I said, finishing the coffee with a sigh of repletion, and then saw my watch. "Oh, dear."

"Stations, everyone. Snow, you stay with Mother."

Simon put the maps under his arm and strode masterfully

into the lobby and ensconced himself on the small sofa facing the entrance.

There weren't many people in the lounge yet as Snow solicitously ushered me in. We had a choice of seats, so I took one where, by leaning slightly forward, I could see anyone at the desk but I couldn't be seen from the desk. I was nervous, for I don't like deceptions of this sort.

"You wouldn't have Canadian Club whiskey, would you?" I heard Snow asking, and turned around in shocked surprise. "Oh, for you, Mom. Relax. Dutch courage."

"With ice?" asked the waiter.

"If you have it," replied Snow, at her most regal. Then she grinned impishly at the waiter, who winked back conspiratorially.

"Would you be wanting something, miss?"

"A Coke, please."

"How you can consume all that Coke and not blow up into a balloon, Snow, is beyond me." I remembered myself at her age, rather dumpy, and terrified of eating *anything*, for everything I ate seemed to go to my hips. If a mother is fortunate enough to have daughters (and that's what my mother *always* said, with the five girls and one boy), she is doubly blessed to have beautiful, slim, elegant ones. Eventually, I too made the grade.

"Oh, Mother," my darling daughter said airily, "I burn it off. That's what you always say."

"Snow!"

She grinned, and then I knew her impertinence had been to distract me. Just as well: Sim's map was flapping as if it would take off. Snow craned her neck beyond me to see the importunate Mr. Kelley.

His broad back was to us.

"Wouldn't you just know!" said Snow irascibly.

I put my glasses on, and the man was well-enough dressed from this distance: dark-haired, a mackintosh thrown over one arm. He turned his head slightly, and I could see long sideburns, slightly darker than his head hair; and the plane of his left cheek. Suddenly I was aware that Simon was shaking his head violently behind the map.

The barman came with our drinks, an ill-timed interruption. I couldn't seem to find the proper change, and finally Snow grabbed a pound note. By the time I could devote any attention to Mr. Kelley, he had turned his back fully toward us. And Simon kept shaking his head.

"Oh, dear." I mean, Simon is only fourteen, and, having lost that wonderful intuitive sense of judgment that small children have, he hadn't yet developed mature criteria.

Suddenly I was being paged, and I shriveled up against the overpadded seat. The waiter came back with the change.

"Aren't you being paged, Mrs. Teasey?"

"Yes, but we don't want to be bothered by that man," Snow said in a stern voice. "Do we, Mommy?"

"Well, that is, no. I'd rather not." I was horribly embarrassed.

"Well now. Not to worry," the waiter said, very understanding, and he walked quickly to the bar. To my continuing mortification, the waiter and the barman had a conversation, the barman picked up the phone, and in a few seconds Mr. Kelley had been given the word. I watched his reaction, and he seemed to be giving the nice receptionist a very hard time. Relenting, I was about to get to my feet when he suddenly turned, and I was very glad I'd refused to see him. He was an angry man with a sort of piggy face on which sideburns only increased the porcine resemblance. Yes, he was furious at this check in his sale. By the way he strode out of the hotel, fists clenched, mouth pursed, I'd the feeling that he'd be awfully persistent.

"You just leave it to us, missus. If anyone comes bothering you that you don't want to see, you just tell us," said the waiter, back again in front of the table.

"It's just that I'm so tired after the plane trip." I felt obliged to give some explanation — he'd been so cooperative — but I trailed off as he nodded understandingly.

"You look awfully tired, Mom," Snow said. "And we've such a lot to do tomorrow. You just finish that drink and off to bed with you."

"Really, Snow . . ."

But the waiter seemed to approve. Basically, so did I. Then Simon joined us, maps folded neatly under his arm.

"Hands," he said in cryptic disapproval.

"Really?" asked Snow. "He looked the type."

"Simon, *how* can you judge a person just by his hands?" I asked.

"Never wrong." Simon looked at me with mild rebuke. "Besides, you should've heard the time he gave the receptionist. He wanted seeing you bad!"

"Simon, please speak English."

"Why? You speak Amurrican."

"What's with you two tonight?" I was suddenly very tired, and the whole improbable trip became impossible.

"With us is you, Mom," replied Simon, knowing perfectly well what I meant. "C'mon, Sis, we better behave. She's plum tuckered out. Sorry, Mother." He slipped the map into his jacket pocket and stood up. "Let's get this wreck of the Hesperus to bed. We can watch the telly in the lounge."

With my children on either side of me, tugs for the wreck that I honestly felt myself to be, I left the lounge.

"Oh, here's Mrs. Teasey now," the receptionist was saying.

I groaned in horror and sagged against the children. Mr. Kelley *was* persistent. How had he known that I—

"It's a girl, Mother," Snow said.

If I hadn't wanted to meet Mr. Kelley, this young girl certainly didn't want to meet me. She looked scared stiff.

"Here, Miss Teasey. The keys to Hillside Lodge." She held out at arm's length a ring of keys, some old, some shiny-new, attached by a thick string to a tag. "Mr. Noonan won't be free until half two tomorrow. He suggests that you might like to look at the property. Oh, the map." She fumbled in her pocket, an operation hampered by the fact that she had to juggle a motorcycle helmet and heavy gloves. I took the keys.

"Yes, I'd be relieved to see him. At two thirty?"

She nodded, still scared, got the map free of her pocket, and stepped up close. As she shoved the paper into my hand, she blurted out, "If Brian Kelley calls you, don't promise anything. Please! Not until you've spoken to Mr. Noonan. Oh dear!" With that she turned and ran from the lobby. In a matter of seconds we heard the explosive roar of a heavy motorcycle gunning, then varooming out of the parking lot.

"Get that!" Simon's eyes were wide with amazement.

"That was odd," Snow said. "What an elegant key!" She took the set from my limp hand, holding up an old key, long and wrought iron, with a curlicue in the handle and huge teeth in the business end: a real honest-to-God lock-the-door-against-invaders key. "What's the map say?" And she opened it, Simon craning his neck to look too. The mileage was clearly marked between checkpoints, and landmarks were indicated.

There was also a second small map, marked *OFFICE*, showing me how to get to Noonan's, just off the Grand Canal on Baggot Street.

"I didn't know Dublin had a canal," I remarked.

Snow shook her head dolefully. "The essential mother hath not changed. Let's put her to bed and hope for an improvement overnight."

They did. And oh, how quickly I was asleep, not troubling my conscience over the fact that I was leaving two fourteen-year-olds on their own in a hotel in a strange city.

 2

SIMON IS a born organizer. The Renault was ready at the Hertz place at 9 in the morning. All I had to do was sign. I did try to explain how nervous I was about driving on the wrong side of the road, and that I'd be very careful, but Snow and Simon interrupted me. (Preserve the Image.)

So, planting Simon as map reader and conscience in the front seat, and sternly abjuring him to watch my left-hand side and keep me on and in the right, I drove off. And tried to shift with my right hand.

"Here, Mother, here," Simon said, grabbing my left hand and placing it on the gear shift.

By the time we were on a dual highway, I had the hang of shifting left-handedly and some notion of judging distance on the left side of the car. Just as well, because we turned off the wide road where minor errors were easily correctable onto a very narrow one with walls and high earthen banks, and winds and turns and cars coming down at me on the wrong side.

"There it is!" Simon cried, his arm across me indicating frantically to make a right turn.

"Where is what?" I cried, jamming on the brakes in reflex action. There was a screech behind me, and I shuddered, expecting the angry blast of a horn. When nothing happened, I bravely used the right-turn indicator and hastily did what I said I was going to do.

Swann's Lane was narrower and dirt.

"Are you positive it's Swann's Lane?" I had a glimpse of incomprehensible syllables on a green-and-white sign imbedded in the low stone wall.

"Yeah, the first line's in Irish, Mother."

"This is nice!" Snow said.

I had the impression that it was, but I was watching the road to avoid the rocks and ruts.

"Look at the old horse! He's sweet!"

I got a glimpse of brown rump and tail, and then saw the cottages nestled into the cut of the hillside. And another one on the right side of the lane.

"Is that where we're going?" Snow was dismayed.

"Naw," Simon replied with contempt, "that one's where we're going," and he pointed to my left where a sandy-colored house loomed beyond some thick hedges and small trees, quite separate from the nest of cottages. As we drove up, a small sign at the corner of the wall confirmed that this was indeed Hillside Lodge.

The house had a forlorn look, unfinished sort of, despite the fact that (as I later learned) it was two hundred years old and a good example of farmhouse Georgian; I suppose I had envisioned a thatched cottage, charmingly rose-covered. There were gardens front and rear, and a lawn in front which had obviously been seeded when the house was built, because it had that velvet integrity so much prized. But the house wasn't at all what I had expected. Then I chided myself: Who was I to look gift houses in the face?

The front door was reached through a small glassed porch which was shelved with plants, all carefully potted and recently moistened. Someone was tending the place. There was a huge modern padlock on the front door and the older large keyhole. The door paint wasn't new, but it had been washed scrupulously clean.

Inside smelled musty. Well, Aunt Irene had been dead nearly two months. In front of us was a small hall with stairs, and doors on either side. To the right was a long sitting room, with fireplace, lace curtains, and the incredible combination of wall papers that I learned was an Irish failing. There wasn't much furniture: a Victorian two-seater, a modern fireside chair and hassock, a good mahogany table, a small desk, several lamps, an electric heater, and a few worn pieces of carpeting. Everything was immaculate, discounting the fine layer of dust.

"It's a pretty room," said Snow in a dubious tone.

"It could be."

To the left of the front door was a dining room with a nice old round table in its center, the buffet to one side, and a second fireplace with an enclosed stove. We could see beyond to the kitchen; the sink facing the front of the house was at a backbreaking height. Good God, how could any decent cook function? I groaned.

"Hey!" Snow stopped at the kitchen door in surprise.

I hurriedly joined her, and beheld a wonder. The sink might not have been altered, but beyond it were beautifully constructed cabinets, Formica-topped, a modern countertop fridge, a lovely gas range, and wall cabinets the length of the kitchen to the back door.

"Mom? More rooms back here," called Simon, and Snow and I, still flabbergasted by the splendid kitchen, turned back toward Simon's beckoning arm.

One of the two rooms was an office, with an old desk, an ancient file cabinet, several shelves of books (the dull-looking type), and some ledgers.

A snitch of carpet, well swept but its original motif dimmed by usage, led down the small hall to the solidly barred back door. Hooks and a boot rack held worn raiment of a durable farm type.

The second room was full of old trunks and boxes, a few discarded bits of harness, and a well-patched saddle and bridle.

"Maybe the old horse was hers?" asked Snow, her eyes brightening. I knew what she was thinking. She'd always wanted to ride.

High windows looked out on a back yard, the barn and stable, and the garage, in which the blue trunk of an old car was visible.

"Let's go upstairs," said Snow excitedly. I couldn't see why she was so eager, but I caught some of her contagion.

Except for the kitchen, there were evidences of what I'd call pride-poverty, and it distressed me to think that my great-aunt might have been in want during her last years. But that kitchen . . .

There were three bedrooms above.

"Three's all we need," cried Snow, bouncing up and down on the left-hand-room bed. "Wow! It's hard!" She was up and peeking into the little bathroom which fitted in the space over the front hall. "Well, everything we need." The bathroom's fittings were old, except for the john. She flushed it experimentally, and a rush of water answered the summons.

"And indoors," I said. I'd half expected a privy out back.

The bedroom over the kitchen-dining room had obviously been my aunt's: the double bed was old cherry wood, with a beautifully crocheted spread, and the Victorian dresser and chair, the marble-topped, very shallow chests, and a huge ornate wardrobe were *good* pieces. The wide-planked floor was almost hidden by the one fine rug in the whole house: an Axminster with warm blues and reds. A good-sized electric heater stood against one wall, and Snow saw the electric-blanket attachment and whooped.

"How incongruous!"

"How practical!" I said, feeling relieved about Aunt Irene's last days.

The third bedroom was long and narrow, with a sloping ceiling. A recently built wardrobe stretched across one wall, but apart from that, only a narrow cot, a very small chest, and a chair occupied the room.

"I'd like this room," said Sim thoughtfully, his eyes

roving about. He had to bend to see through the small rear window into the yard. "Say, there's a vegetable garden behind the stable. We eat!"

"I don't know if we can stay here yet, children."

"Why not?" asked Snow.

"There are such things as death duties, and I may be wise to take the first buyer that comes along with ready money in his hand."

"That girl didn't want you to talk to Kelley," Snow said.

"Mom has a point, Sis. We'll find out this afternoon from the lawyer. But I do like this room!"

"I'll switch beds with you," Snow said to her brother. "You like yours rock-hard."

"You sprawl." Simon pointed to the narrow cot. "You'd be on the floor half the time."

"Better than feeling like a corpse . . . whoops! Sorry, Mom."

For I'd given a shudder, not so much for her untimely simile as for my growing sense of trespass, unwelcome, and trouble. My right hand itched intolerably. I mastered the desire to scratch, because Sim and Snow would know I had one of my itches again.

A loud clanging, rattling, rumbling distracted us, and, curious, we all made for the front of the house. A huge construction bulldozer was churning up the lane, figuratively and literally, because you could see the tread marks on the unpaved road. I groaned. The springs on the Renault were not good enough to take that mess. Suddenly the bulldozer stopped. Or, I should say, was stopped. Craning my neck, I could see a stocky figure standing resolutely in its path.

Simon inched the window open. It was very tight, judging by his grunts and groans.

"This is a private road," Stalwart Defender was saying, "owned by Miss Teasey and not to be used by commercial vehicles."

"I was told to take Swann's Lane," said the driver, angrily gunning his engine for emphasis.

"By whom?"

"By Kerrigan. He owns the field there," and the man

pointed up the lane. I couldn't see what lay at the end. But I'd all too often seen what havoc bulldozers made in fields before they got strewn with ticky-tacky boxes. Suddenly I very much did *not* want a development around this lovely pastoral setting.

"That wall also belongs to Miss Teasey."

"She's dead. Who're you?"

"I own that cottage. I also own a right of way on this lane. Kerrigan does not."

"I can't give a damn who owns what. I got orders to use this lane to get into that field!"

"Get out!" said Stalwart Defender. "Miss Teasey wouldn't give Kerrigan the right to spit on her land, much less use this lane. So get out!"

"You and who else'll make me?" and the driver began to fiddle ominously with his gears, activating the plow end.

"Hey, he'll run the guy down with that thing!" said Simon.

I started to reassure him, and then wasn't so certain myself. There was an obstinate just to the driver's jaw, and he was beet-red with frustration.

"I'll make you, young man," I shouted from the window. "You just stay where you are!"

As I turned from the window, I heard a startled "Jasus, preserve me" from Stalwart Defender.

The three of us rattled down the steps. "Did either of you see a phone in the house?"

"There!" Simon pointed to a hand set on the small hall table. "And here!" He detached a shotgun from the wall above it.

I took the gun and started out the door, armed to defend my property, though I'd never held a weapon before in my life. I suppose the Irish air imbued me with this sort of courage and rebellion; certainly I'd never experienced it before.

"I'm Irene Teasey," I said, foursquare on the steps. Over the wall I could see the man on the seat of the bulldozer, but not Stalwart Defender. The driver looked startled at the sight of the gun in my hands, and my loyal cohorts. "That thing of yours is making a mess of my lane. You will kindly back down this instant or I'll have the police here immediately."

He was still goggling when I fumbled my way through the gate — rusty from long disuse — and onto the (*my*) lane. Maybe that's what added to my sense of power: owning the way into my own demesne.

"Now clear out! That thing's a mortal nuisance!"

He opened his mouth to protest.

"Simon, haven't you reached the police yet?"

That settled the driver, for he couldn't tell at this distance that Simon was only fourteen. A gun and two men to contend with, plus police interference, were more than he liked as odds. The bulldozer churned more mud as it rumblingly clanged its destructive way back down my lane.

"Your timing is fantastic, Mrs. Teasey," said the baritone voice of Stalwart Defender.

"Yes, thanks, even if I don't know the rest of the script," I replied, turning to get an eyeful of beard and body. Stalwart Defender was not much taller than I, and mostly shaggy beard and hair the last foot of that, but he looked big. He wore what I soon came to recognize as uniform for a lot of Irishmen: cord britches, heavy sweater, and a knit cap. He had very bright, light-green eyes, like Snow's, and well-shaped lips hidden in the face-fur. He also had hands!

"You spoke your lines with true conviction and have thus foiled the enemy!" I was accorded a slight bow and a wide grin.

"I'm the heir — heiress, I guess."

There was a startled blink of the green eyes.

"I really am Irene Teasey, you know."

"There's no doubt of it. I'm Kieron Thornton," only it sounded like "T'ornton." My hand was engulfed in one large, strong, scaly paw while the other neatly twitched the shotgun away from me. "Kerrigan may call the Garda. Swear on a stack of bibles that I had the shotgun. You've no permit."

"Huh?"

Snow and Simon now arrived to be presented.

"Say, how come we can stop that thing?" Snow asked, beaming at Stalwart Thornton, who politely ignored her and turned to me.

"You own the lane and you've the right to stop Kerrigan. I don't."

"Who's Kerrigan?" I asked.

Thronton hesitated. "You've not seen the solicitor?" He considered his next words. "He owns the fields beyond that wall," and Kieron pointed up the lane to its abrupt end. "He bought the property last fall, and was on to Irene to sell him the right of way through this lane. He's got prime development property there, and the owner of the only other way in, from the Glenamuck Road, is asking five thousand pounds for a right of way."

Simon whistled, and Thornton grinned at him.

"Yes, that's a lot of money. Irene suggested that if he paid *her* the five thousand pounds he'd save on the paving costs of a much shorter road."

"But you said my great-aunt wouldn't sell to him." I was rather confused.

Kieron Thornton grinned. "So I did. And so she wouldn't."

"Oh," I said, not much wiser.

"Then you don't intend to sell?"

"Sell what? The right of way?"

"No, the queendom?"

"The queendom?"

Kieron Thornton frowned, as one will at an idiot child. "This" — his gesture included the lane, the house, the cottages, and the fields beyond — "is what your Great-aunt Irene called her queendom."

"I didn't know that." Then I caught his look of exasperated disapproval — so much like that mood of Teddie's that I quaked and hastily began to explain. "Please, I only arrived yesterday. We've only just now looked through the house. I haven't a clue . . . And then there's this man bothering me with an offer."

Simon and Snow stepped closer to me, their protectiveness registering with Thornton, who made a slight bow of acknowledgment.

"I'm not talking out of turn by saying that this property is worth a great deal, Mrs. Teasey, to the wrong people. A great deal more, not necessarily in terms of money, to the right ones. I was very fond of your great-aunt. She asked me to protect her

queendom"—and he smiled gently as he used the odd word—
"until you got here. Then she asked me—" He stopped, changing his mind with a rueful smile.

"You were about to say, Mr. Thornton?"

"She asked me to help you, if I could and you would."

"My great-aunt and I never met. That's why I can't understand any of this."

"No more can others I could name."

"The relatives?" I asked, feeling sick with apprehension.

He nodded. "I won't say more on this subject, Mrs.
Teasey. My judgments are colored by my partiality for your
aunt. You may have an entirely different view."

"Wait . . ." I put my hand on his arm, for he'd given me a
little bow and taken a step away. "At least show me what I've
inherited, for good or bad. You'd know and, apart from the
house, and this lane, I don't."

"Your solicitor can tell you."

"And undoubtedly will, but in an office with a surveyor's
map or some such two-dimensionality. That doesn't tell me
*what*," and I held up my hands to express a need for tactile
assimilation.

He gave me a long look, then shrugged and turned
toward the house. "As you will."

He led us back into the house long enough to replace the
shotgun, warning the twins to stick to the story that he had held
the weapon. I was to apply instantly at the local Garda station—by the traffic lights in Cabinteely—for a permit.

"If it was Aunt Irene's gun, how can you use it?"

"I've a permit. More than one person can have a permit
on the same gun, you see, but everyone who uses the gun must
have a permit for that gun. Complicated. And if the troubles up
north get worse, you may be asked to surrender it to the
Garda."

That made Simon bristle. "Surrender my gun to the
police?"

Very politely, Kieron Thornton asked Simon how old he
was, and then said that the age for gun permits was eighteen.

Simon muttered under his breath. He had been mad
crazy to own a gun ever since that weekend in Pennsylvania

with some of Teddie's friends who'd had a skeet shoot. Simon had shown a tremendous aptitude for marksmanship, outclassing his father, which hadn't set too well (Preserve the Image!). I'd managed to point out to Simon that he couldn't very well have a skeet shoot in suburban Westfield, but I'd been backed into promising that if he ever lived in the country, he could have a rifle. Well, we wouldn't be staying in Ireland that long.

Kieron Thornton knew the house and property well. He spared us the worst of the muddy parts and a very close look at the four cottages nestled in the hillside. These were rented, and he said that I'd have a chance to see the tenants later on. He owned the cottage he lived in and the land within its fences, having purchased the place from my great-aunt three years ago.

Now he led us past the house and the barn, which was well stocked with hay and straw, to the flourishing vegetable garden.

"I planted that for Irene. She wasn't well enough, and the lack worried her." His unspoken comment was that he'd known that my great-aunt wouldn't survive to enjoy the produce, but he'd humored her in the planting.

"Yummy. Fresh vegetables," said Snow. She was devastatingly pert all through the tour, ignoring my disapproving looks and Simon's disgusted snorts. However, she failed to attract Kieron Thornton's amused interest, and I was beginning to think that Ireland might be very beneficial for my precocious daughter if the males over twenty-one kept reminding Snow that she was still a child.

"Now," Kieron said, "the land extends another three acres beyond this," and he laid his hand on the earth-and-stone fence, "to the west, and down to the road, from there to the field across the lane. There're natural springs, plus the stream."

"Whose is the horse?" asked Snow, less affectedly.

"Your mother's . . . now. Horseface."

"Horseface?" Both Snow and Simon whooped with laughter.

Kieron laughed too, a nice rich real laugh. "I believe he has another name in the registry, but that's what he answers to."

"My aunt rode him?" He looked very big.

"Yes indeed, right up to her first stroke, and gently when

she'd recovered completely from it. He's about twenty now, I'd say. In their prime, Irene hunted him." Kieron turned to me. "Call him. He answers to his name."

"Me?" But I raised my voice. To my utter surprise, the beast raised his head instantly, looked unerringly in my direction, and whinnied.

"You see, he does know his name," Thornton said as the horse trotted eagerly to the pasture fence.

"Hey, Horseface," called Snow, and she and Simon went off to meet him, gathering fresh handfuls of grass to feed him.

I caught a suspicious gleam in Thornton's eyes, which I couldn't account for. I was about to question him when we were startled by the angry blasting of a car horn.

"Hmmm. I was expecting that," said Thornton, taking me by the arm and guiding me back to the house. "The visitor is impatient," he added as the horn continued to break the pleasant soft noises of the countryside.

"Who is it?"

"Can't you guess?"

I stopped short. "Mr. Kerrigan?" Kelley and now Kerrigan? And with no real idea of what to do! "Mr. Thornton, couldn't you . . ."

"Mrs. Teasey," and he gave me a stern, reproving look, "you own this property. Admittedly, I have caused you an embarrassment by more or less forcing you to stop that bulldozer. But I knew that was what your aunt would have done. I did not know you were in the house. You may, after an appraisal of the situation, want to let Kerrigan have that right of way. I only ask that you wait until you've had time to arrive at a fair decision. Or maybe you Yanks like acres of houses all around you." He had managed to hurry me through the yard, and now he gave me a push toward the kitchen door.

"Oh, don't leave me!"

He gave me an amused look, disengaging my hands from his arm. "Believe me, you don't need *my* help." And he was away.

The car horn was still blaring, in a fashion guaranteed to irritate, and I was already annoyed at Kieron Thornton for landing me in such a compromising situation with an unknown and infuriated man. I raced around the side of the house to the front. A man was standing on the driver's side of a blue Jag, bent slightly so that he could lean on the horn. The car, the arrogance of the action, plus memories of other helpless moments like this, combined to give me unusual courage.

"Stop that infernal racket," I shouted, and it was cut off instantly.

The man who stared at me across the blue Jag top was as handsome as sin. Sandy-haired with a well-trimmed, slightly darker moustache and very black eyebrows, my importunate caller was elegantly dressed in a blazer and slim trousers, a trendy patterned shirt, and a solid-color cravat.

"You're not Irene Teasey," he said in a flat, surprised voice.

"I most certainly am."

Suddenly his angry expression turned into a smile. "Oh, but of course. You're the niece. The American."

"Yes, I'm the American *great*-niece."

"Well," and he walked toward me, all smiles, hand extended. "Welcome to Ireland — *cead mille failte*. That means a hundred thousand welcomes, Miss Teasey."

"Was that why you were blasting the horn? A royal salute?"

"I'm Shamus Kerrigan. I'm afraid there's been a bit of a misunderstanding."

"Was that your frightful bulldozer thing that tore up my lane?" I asked, trying hard to be severe, for Kerrigan had the sort of charm that is very difficult to resist.

He turned to survey the damage as if he hadn't just had to tool the Jaguar very carefully over the ruts.

"I do apologize. But it would only be the one transit. Once the dozer is in the field, it wouldn't have to come out."

"Oh?" I looked pointedly at the stout stone wall. "How had you planned to get across that?"

"Well, rather, through it," he admitted, smiling ingenuously. "Of course, we'd build the wall back up again behind it."

"What comes in must go out, Mr. Kerrigan."

"Oh, I expect to get permission to use the other road."

"All the way from Glenamuck?" I asked, delighting in the surprise in his face at my knowledge, however spotty it was. "Surely you know that this is a private lane, Mr. Kerrigan, and that even one transit—much less knocking down my wall—constitutes trespass?"

He nodded and then smiled reassuringly. "Actually, I did have permission."

"From whom?" I was suddenly suspicious of Kieron Thornton. I'd only his word that my great-aunt hadn't wanted Kerrigan to have the right of way. Maybe the solicitor . . .

"From a relative. You see after Miss Teasey died . . ." and he looked appropriately regretful.

"No false condolences, please. I'd never met my great-aunt."

"I had, Mrs. Teasey," and there was suddenly nothing of the suppliant in Mr. Kerrigan's manner. "She was a most admirable woman."

Because she'd refused him? I wondered privately.

"I tried to find out who had inherited the property so I could have my solicitor make the proper application. I've got a lot of money tied up in that land."

There was now a flash of impatience in his voice, which he covered instantly with his facile charm.

"Yes, that would be a consideration," I said agreeably.

"So," and his smile was hearty again, "when I learned that it was yourself, and you in America and no one knew where, I tried to find someone in the family who could give me permission to use the lane."

"If *I* had inherited the property, Mr. Kerrigan, none of the relations here had any authority to give you permission for anything." I wasn't certain of that, but, by the expression in his eyes, I was within my rights.

"That's why I apologize," and he bowed with contrition. "Because the relative assured me that he had the right to grant me the one use of the lane."

"Who was the so obliging relative?"

He smiled again. "I don't think that would be fair, do you, until this has all been sorted out?"

"Fair to whom, Mr. Kerrigan?"

He smiled more broadly. "You wouldn't consider my using the lane today, since I've the equipment laid on and all?"

I shook my head, smiling back. "I'm so sorry."

"Oh, you're a wise one, you are," he said finally, the grin still firmly in place. "But I feel we could sort the problems out," and he nodded at the battered road and the stone fence, "and very soon. Say, this evening? At half seven? Over dinner?"

"A very good suggestion." I emphasized the last word slightly, and saw that he took my meaning. "I'm at the Montrose." By the expression in his eyes, I guessed that he knew that.

"You're certain about the dozer?" he asked, with winning wistfulness.

"Positive. You're taking an unfair advantage of me, Mr. Kerrigan, for all your thousand welcomes."

"You Yanks!" I wasn't certain if that was a compliment or not. Nonetheless, he left, bumping the Jag carefully over the ruts.

Snow and Simon erupted out of the hedge where they'd been hiding.

"Who he?"

"Didn't you hear all?"

"Arrived late."

"And why didn't you come out?"

Simon shrugged. "You were handling him just great."

"Hmmmm."

"So we all get a free dinner tonight, huh?" asked Snow, her eyes wide.

"Yes indeedy. This pore li'l ol' Amurrican needs chaperones from that big Irish woof!"

Snow giggled.

"Sure has a beautiful Jag," and Simon whistled softly. "Say, Mom, that car in Aunt Irene's garage is a Mercedes! It's in beautiful condition inside. It's up on blocks and all, and the tires are there too."

"Really?"

"Horseface is just darling, Mom. Can I learn how to ride him? I mean, is twenty years too old for a horse to be ridden?"

3

I SUPPOSE our fate had already been decided that morning but I don't see such events with an awareness of their immediate and future significance. Teddie always did, and my obtuseness irritated him. Just as well he was safely three thousand miles from me — and someone else's problem now.

We went through the house again, peering into cupboards this time. And bare they were. I kept telling myself that it was because no one had been tenanting the place that there was only a dusting of sugar in the bowl, a half cup of flour in the canister, a small tin of curried beans, an inch of ketchup, a fingernail of salt and the same of pepper. The fridge had been cleared and unplugged. Snow turned it on with a dramatically uttered "There! We can shop later. That'll be fun."

"Expensive, too," I said, knowing my daughter's proclivity for impulse buying. However, we did have to eat.

Snow was rattling on enthusiastically about redecorating, which would mean more outlay of cash. I *could* see the merit of her suggestions (take a positive attitude, Rene). A touch here, some paint there, new curtains at those windows, some judiciously placed new carpet, and new vinyl and paint in the kitchen would give the house a much more cheerful atmosphere. Simon volunteered to paint the outside trim, Snow to weed the neat garden, and both were so generally enthusiastic that by lunchtime I could relax and appreciate the potential charm of the house.

I locked up and we piled into the car. As we bumped down the lane, Simon cursed the bulldozer and I wondered which of my relatives had had the audacity to give Shamus Kerrigan permission.

On the off chance that Brian Kelley would be haunting the hotel, we ate in town, at a charming restaurant just off St. Stephen's Green. Then we did some gawking down Grafton Street. People hurried, as on other streets, but as many more sort of lounged down the sidewalks, utterly unconcerned about reaching their ultimate destinations. Double-decker buses roared down the narrow street, occasionally puffing hot exhaust around our legs, but not with the horrid urgency of the New York counterpart. Altogether, Dublin was exercising much charm to soothe this savage colonial breast.

We arrived on the solicitor's street, and I suddenly felt very Georgette Heyer, looking at the beautiful Georgian fronts with the lovely fanlights above the doors. Finding the right number was not hard, but finding a spot to park the Renault did take time.

Michael Noonan looked more like a jet-set playboy than a solicitor, but, fortunately for my peace of mind, his manner and cogent explanations (as far as he went) dispelled any further comparison. He wore his dark hair short on top and close cut but long in the back, with well-trimmed sideburns, which added to his rakish appearance. His eyes behind the heavy black-framed glasses missed nothing of my appearance or my children's as he welcomed us each with a firm handshake. Despite myself, I looked down at his hands, as the children did, and knew their opinion before I saw it in their eyes. He had hands.

He also had brains.

Ceremoniously I tendered him my identification and my grandfather's naturalization papers, which clearly established Granda as the late Irene Teasey's brother Michael Maurice Teasey.

He handed me a parcel of long, folded documents. "Your copy of the will, which makes you principal heir and co-executrix with this office, myself in particular, the authenticated list of the belongings in the house and on the property, and their estimated value for death duties."

I dutifully opened the uppermost document, and flinched at the whereases and second parts and all that overwhelmingly confusing legalese.

"There were other bequests?"

"Some minor ones in the will, and I've a letter here for you which your great-aunt directed me to hand you personally," and I received a square envelope of heavy paper. "And here" — he was passing me another long, legal-feeling document — "is the trust-fund report."

"Trust fund?"

"Yes, and it ought to more than settle the death duties. We were exceedingly lucky with the appraisals, despite the fact that your great-aunt's property had appreciated a good deal over the past few years. The duties could have been atrocious, so I'm very relieved that the fund should prove ample." He saw my amazement and grinned. "I'm sure it's a common enough practice in the States too, Mrs. Teasey. Provided the trust is set up, as this one was, five years prior to decease, the money is tax-free."

"Excuse me, you mean I've been the heir that long?"

Mr. Noonan smiled very kindly. "Yes, Mrs. Teasey, you have. Certainly ever since I took over your great-aunt's affairs, seven years ago."

"Well!" The twins breathed out "Wows!"

"Mrs. Teasey? Don't ever feel that you have usurped anyone else's claims."

"Well, it was a great surprise to me. I never knew my great-aunt at all. I mean . . ."

"She knew about you. And she had good reasons for leaving her" — he smiled again, with mischief in his eyes — "her queendom to you. Now, we haven't received the exact figure for the death duties yet. They must be paid within this year, but not to worry. You've the trust."

"Then it's unlikely that I'd have to sell the property to satisfy the duties?" And why were there no supplies in the house?

He looked startled. "Good Lord, no. That was the whole purpose of the trust fund."

"Is the property intrinsically valuable, Mr. Noonan?"

"Yes, quite." He riffled some papers.

"I don't need the exact figure. I was just asking because Mr. Kelley — "

"Brian Kelley?" There was surprise as well as steel in Mr. Noonan's query.

"Yes. He was most insistent about seeing me."

"Did you?" Mr. Noonan's hands were suspended in his paper search.

"No. I decided against it. I didn't like his looks. Nor his insistence."

Relief smoothed the crows'-feet from the corners of Mr. Noonan's eyes. "How the devil did he know you were in town? You only arrived yesterday morning."

"I wouldn't know," I said, although all three of us had a fair idea from the pleading look in the receptionist's eyes. She had been the motorcyclist with the keys to my . . . queendom.

"If it had been at all possible, Mrs. Teasey, I would have met you at the airport. But you gave me no warning of your arrival." Mr. Noonan rattled the papers before him in a testy fashion.

"The children had finished school, there were seats on a flight, and so . . . we just came."

"As well you did. All things being equal, you'd best take possession of the house instantly. I mean by that, physical possession. There is a variety of conflicting interests."

"One of them named Kerrigan?" I asked.

He dropped the papers and slapped both palms against the desk, staring at me with amazement.

"Kelley *and* Kerrigan?"

"Hmmm. I assume that they're both prime contenders?"

He cleared his throat and said, with a slight, unhappy smile, "Essentially but not actually. To be blunt, Mrs. Teasey, almost every one of your great-aunt's adult relatives, and she had innumerable, believes that he or she should have been left the estate rather than yourself."

"Me too."

"Your great-aunt knew what she was doing, and, believe me, no matter what you might hear to the contrary, had every right to dispose of her property and possessions as she wished."

He was so emphatic that I was instantly more apprehensive. Teddie always said that I have no powers of dissembling, which he thought remarkable, since I had acted. He never could understand that I was playing a particular part then, whereas I was just me off the stage. My thoughts were, as usual, painfully obvious.

Mr. Noonan leaned toward me. "Now, not to worry, Mrs. Teasey. Your position is secure."

"It isn't her position that worries Mother," said Snow in her most protective manner. "We've just got her through a very messy divorce scene, and she doesn't need the greedy-relatives bit."

Mr. Noonan eyed my outspoken daughter with, I thought, more approval than prejudice.

"I think you've no cause for worry."

I heard, as clear as his spoken words, the tag "not yet."

He cleared his throat. "Now, how did you encounter Shay Kerrigan?"

"Trying to get a bulldozer up the lane."

"Oh. He did try."

"You knew he would?"

"Might. He was rather anxious to get in touch with the heir. My letter to you about his offer must have crossed your coming. I had arranged with one of the residents on the lane —"

"Mr. Thornton?"

"Naturally, you've had the chance to meet him, too."

"Oh yes, he actually stopped the bulldozer this morning. I just seconded it."

"And you landed here yesterday at noontime? Well!"

"I don't usually operate at such a high level, Mr. Noonan," I felt obliged to say, and then saw that he was more amused than critical.

"Mr. T'ornton showed us around the estate," Snow said, mimicking the accent. She went on, in one of her maliciously guileless moods, "He had a shotgun." I stared appreciatively at my daughter, and so did her brother. (Create the Image?) "But it was Mother who made the guy take that thing back down. You should've seen what it did to the lane."

"I'm sorry to hear that Shay Kerrigan would try that." Mr. Noonan was annoyed. He had the intense look of a man swearing silently.

"He came later . . . in person," Snow said brightly. "To apologize."

"Be quiet, dear," I said to her, and meant it. "I did have

the right to refuse him the use, didn't I? He gave me some nonsense about having applied to a relative for permission."

"What?" Mr. Noonan was now furious. "Who?"

"He wouldn't say. But maybe I can find out at dinner tonight. He's taking" — I paused and then indicated the twins — "us."

Noonan was sharp, and his laughing eyes applauded my stratagem.

"If you can find out which relative it was, it might be helpful later."

"You mean, there may be litigation about this?"

"That's possible, Mrs. Teasey. As I said, your great-aunt's little queendom is now quite valuable. Where pounds and pence are concerned, blood has a tendency to curdle."

I groaned. I wasn't certain that I was up to more nasty court proceedings and complaints and countercharges. Not twice in one year!

"You can, of course, sell out as soon as the will is probated."

His expression plainly told me that he'd be disappointed if I chose that course.

"Your great-aunt rather hoped that you'd like to take your time about selling — if that was your final decision."

The letter from Great-aunt Irene burned in my hand. I was both reluctant and eager to open it.

"Mr. Noonan? About my great-aunt . . . Did she . . . I mean . . . she didn't linger or go without anything?"

He shook his head. "No. The final stroke was quick. She'd had one last December. Thornton found her and rushed her to hospital. Saved her life. She'd pretty well recovered by March, and was getting around much as usual when she'd the second stroke. That disabled her completely, and a week later the third one took her life. She was a delightful person," and Mr. Noonan's smile was that of regret.

"You liked her," said Snow.

"Yes, Miss Stanford, I liked her very much. She was a most unusual woman."

Then he turned his keen eyes on me. "I know substantially what's in that letter, Mrs. Teasey. I hope that you'll find it agreeable to you, and possible, but I am required to advise you that you are in no way legally constrained to follow those instructions. As soon as the will is probated, you can sell the estate to whomever you choose."

"And I do have the right to refuse Mr. Kerrigan the use of the lane?"

"Yes, indeed. That's private property. Yours . . . or yours legally . . . when the will has been probated."

"Until then?"

"The use of the lane was denied Kerrigan by Miss Teasey, and her order stands until yours rescinds or reinforces it. But you can't do anything until the will is probated."

"Mr. Noonan, in simple language, how much is the property worth?"

"It's still not simple, Mrs. Teasey. You could probably sell the house and its immediate gardens, the stableyard, and the back field for, roughly, say twenty-five thousand pounds." Snow whistled, and I shushed her. "Mr. Thornton owns his cottage and the two roods of land on which it stands. There are four other cottages, now renting from one to seven pounds a month. I do know that Mrs. Teasey was offered three thousand pounds for one of them recently, but with sitting tenants in all four the value is considerably reduced."

I thought dazedly of the sturdy cottages and then of the modern semidetached places selling for twice that and wondered.

Snow frowned. "A pound a month is less than three bucks!" She was round-eyed with indignant surprise.

I gathered from Mr. Noonan's expression that the rent *was* ridiculously low.

"I believe Miss Teasey mentions that offer in her letter to you. Now, the acreage on the roadside would bring in about three thousand pounds an acre."

"Three thousand pounds?" I was stunned at the difference in three dollars a month rent for a cottage already built that might *sell* for three thousand pounds, and then the same sum for just the land!

"That's sixty-five hundred dollars an acre, Mom," Snow

said helpfully. "And you could charge Mr. Kerrigan a bundle for a right of way if he's getting that kind of money for houses."

"Hush, Snow, you're distracting me."

"Mother isn't interested in the *money*," Simon said, entering the discussion.

"I'll bet all the relatives are, not to mention Kelley and Kerrigan," continued my irrepressible daughter. "Those Jags cost money."

Mr. Noonan chuckled again. "Your daughter has the way of it, Mrs. Teasey. Of course, nothing can be done until the will has been probated."

"You keep saying that, Mr. Noonan. Is there another problem?"

"Technically, no." He leaned forward, his eyes intent on my face, an exercise I found rather disconcerting. "Read your great-aunt's letter, Mrs. Teasey, before you make any further assumptions or decisions. Think carefully about what she asks of you. Miss Teasey was a wonderful person. She was ahead of her times in some ways, but she had certain . . . shall we say, peeves, with which you may not be in sympathy. You are, you say, seeing Shamus Kerrigan this evening. Undoubtedly Mr. Kelley will be on to you again with his proposition. I don't know whom he represents in this matter, but there's no harm in listening to both of them. And you can do nothing until probate is filed." He smiled reassuringly.

"Which is my defense and alibi?"

"If you choose."

"How do I get a permit for the shotgun?"

He looked startled.

"I come from pioneer stock. There may be Injuns," I said in a deadpan voice. "No, actually, Mr. Thornton said that I shouldn't wave the gun about until I have a permit."

"I don't believe you'll need a gun against Shay Kerrigan, Mrs. Teasey," and his eyes were dancing with suppressed amusement. "However, speak to the sergeant at the Cabinteely Garda station. You're over twenty-one, and you have a place to shoot. There'll be no problem. Miss Teasey felt obliged to . . . discourage . . . . ah . . ."

"Invaders?" asked Snow. "Invaders of our queendom, threatening to lay siege?"

"With only a shotgun?" asked Simon. "Nuts!"

Michael Noonan chuckled as he rose, and extended his hand to me. "After you've read the letter and the will, please don't hesitate to phone me if you've any questions."

"That's kind of you, Mr. Noonan, because I've a feeling that I've inherited a lot of problems and will need many answers."

His smile corroborated my assumption and did my morale no good. Then he courteously ushered us out.

"You know, Mom," said Snow as we got into the Renault, "we don't know that much more than we did when we got here."

"He does," said Simon with a laugh. "Maybe the letter tells it all."

"Hmmmm. I'm not, I repeat, *not* opening that letter till we get back to the hotel."

"And close to some Dutch courage," said Snow, as I gave first Simon and then her a forbidding look.

When we got back to the hotel, there were five messages from Brian Kelley asking me to phone him as soon as possible. The last was timed three minutes before our return.

"Read the letter first, Mom," said Snow, frowning at the message slips.

I turned to the girl at the desk. "If Mr. Kelley calls before I get a chance to catch my breath . . . please, I'm still not in?"

"Ah, not to worry, Mrs. Teasey." Obviously she did not much care for Mr. Kelley.

The twins ensconced themselves on either side of me on the lounge settee so that we all read the letter together.

The letter, dated March 3, was penned in such a beautiful copperplate handwriting that I admired the look of it before I got down to the reading.

My dear Namesake,

I had so hoped to be able to meet you, for
it was my intention to invite you and your
children to visit me this summer. But dear Mr.
Fleetwood is so cheerful, and careful to say
nothing to the point, that I realize I will not
have another reprieve.

Now I must let dry pen and ink speak lines
I had so often rehearsed. We have much more
in common, my dear Irene, than our names.
Originally I willed you my little property for the
sake of our mutual name. You were the only
child in three generations and five lots named
for me. I confess I was inordinately pleased that
you resumed your maiden name after your
divorce. Thank goodness such relief was permitted *you*.

"What does she mean by that?" asked Snow, who was
reading faster than Simon and I.
"Hush and read!" said her brother.
"Hush, the pair of you!"

I am now more sure than ever of the fitness
of making you heir to my queendom. I shall try
to set as much in order as I can in the time left
to me, but you are American and I am confident that your upbringing will help you solve
what problems remain with good Yankee common sense.

You could do worse, dear Irene, than to
make this queendom your home and to remain

here in Ireland. You will not need to depend on any man. Carefully managed, this realm can give you independence wherever you wish to live, if not in Ireland.

If you are not of a mind to stay, however, do me three favours: do not sell my faithful horse to the knackers but have him put down and buried in the back pasture. Ann Purdee will know how to go about that. Unlike the horse, you cannot shoot my Mercedes, which is a valuable old car. But do sell it to someone who cares for the car herself, not merely her monetary value. Gerry Hegarty, for instance.

My third request may seem to you to be spiteful. I am not at liberty to divulge the reasons behind this, since they affect someone else's reputation, but do not give access up the lane to Shamus Kerrigan.

"Wow!" said Snow. "That's laying it on the line."
"Yeah, but not why," said Simon.
What Aunt Irene hadn't said, but what I felt, was a curious anger in her wording.

If you decide to stay and circumstances permit, please continue the present tenants of Swallow and Lark cottages for as long as need be. You will understand very quickly and, if you are the girl I take you to be, agree. George Boardman, however, is quite willing, and able, to give £3,000 for Finch or Thrush cottages, whichever comes vacant first. Michael Noonan can help you secure them, but I have had to let the proceedings drop to keep death duties down.

I know that you will meet discord among the relatives—yours too, though mercifully removed by distance and marriage—for few will be pleased with the disposition of my property. There were several of the youngest generation who deserve something of me for their kindness and friendship, but for me to single them out would be unkind. When the swearing ceases and they have turned to other trivia, you may care to ease circumstances. By that time, you'll know who I mean.

You are, my dear Irene, the only logical successor to my queendom. God bless and keep you.

Your affectionate aunt,
Irene.

"Long live Queen Irene the Second," said Snow, but her tone was by no means facetious.

"She didn't want that bulldozer up the lane."

"Yeah, but I wonder why," said Snow darkly. "As if we'd put down that lovely Horseface! I couldn't!" She glared dramatically at me.

"I like her," said Simon, having deliberated on the matter. "I mean, a woman who can recognize that a car has a personality, isn't just a mechanical object. I don't like this bit about the relatives, though. Five lots? That sounds like too many, and we've got a horde as it is."

"Cheer up, Simon, maybe they'll stay away in their droves and dozenses. And besides, we're not staying long."

"Ah, Mom, you promised." They both rounded me.

"*I* did no such thing." Before I knew it, I was embroiled

in a series of entreaties and promises and evasions (on my part) that lasted through checking out of the hotel and driving back to Hillside Lodge. But I held up the stream of argument long enough to tell the nice desk clerk to inform Mr. Kelley that I had checked out and would phone him tomorrow.

"He may want to know where he can reach you," she said with diplomatic subtlety.

"Then tell him I'm staying at the home of a relative."

I was halfway to Hillside Lodge before I realized that I'd told Shamus Kerrigan to meet me at the Montrose. Snow said that was no big problem—we'd get settled in and go back and meet Mr. Kerrigan in the lobby.

We found a small general store and picked up milk in plastic bottles (you had to give glass ones to get glass ones), eggs, butter, bread (a crescent loaf that smelled delectable and some good Irish brown bread), bacon, Coke, and instant coffee. We'd do a major shopping the next morning.

And so, bag and baggage, we took possession of a queendom.

Fortunately, the lights worked, and so did the telephone. (I found out much later that I owed those services to the motorcycle girl—penance?) We all made beds together from lavender-scented linens found in the closet with the hot-water tank. It was stone cold, and I couldn't figure out where it got heated.

"Simon," I said in despair, for I longed for a hot bath before braving Kerrigan, "go ask Mr. Thornton how to get hot water. He's likely to know."

"May I help you, Mrs. Teasey?" asked a soft voice from the back door.

In America one hears that the typical Irish colleen is a reasonably buxom, apple-cheeked miss, constantly smiling, so this slim, tiny, solemn girl with the delicate features and coloring of an equally typical Dresden shepherdess was a surprise. In fact, nothing about Ann Purdee was ever what it seemed.

"If you know how to get the water hot, yes," I told her.

She smiled in a brief, polite way and stepped quickly past us into the dining room, where she knelt by the fireplace.

"This stove will heat the boiler," she said, lighting a match from the package on the top of the enclosed fireplace and deftly inserting it. Flames licked around white cubes. "If you open the door in a few moments, so, once the firelighters have taken, the draft will start a nice blaze. You'll have hot water in an hour. If you aren't going to use too much, you must bank the fire with slack." She saw the uncomprehending look on our faces. "To the left of the kitchen door is the coal bunker. The small pebbly stuff is slack, and you use it for slowing a fire down." She plunged the shovel into the coal bucket and showed us the fine stuff. "Would you be wanting the beds made and all?" she asked, wiping her hands carefully on her apron.

I expect the twins had checked those hands first off, but I was appalled at how bone-thin they were, red and cracked from hard work and cold water. A thin gold band on the third finger rolled loosely up and down between the knuckles.

"That much we figured out," Snow said with a little giggle, and there was an answering gleam in Ann Purdee's lovely blue eyes.

"We've old-fashioned ways of doing things here, don't you know? No bother once you've the way of it, but strangelike at first. Kieron T'ornton said you'd been by this morning."

What she was hoping to hear was as plain as day to me.

"We'll be staying on a while, Mrs. Purdee," and I was surprised when she flushed. "I want to take my time before I decide what to do."

"I want to learn how to ride Horseface," said Snow, bubbling into the sudden, rather awkward silence. "He isn't too old, is he?"

Some of the stiff stillness went out of Mrs. Purdee's body and she looked at Snow. "I can teach you for sure, he's not that old. I used to exercise Horseface," she told me, "when Miss Teasey couldn't. I've been taking care of him till you came. Not that there's much taking care like, with him on grass now. He's a grand old lad, you know."

Abruptly she reached into the pocket of her housecoat. "I have the rent for you, Mrs. Teasey. I was going to send it on to Mr. Noonan again, but as *you're* here . . ." and she put a pound note and a column of coins on the dining-room table.

"Oh, thank you." I was somehow embarrassed, never

having been a landlady before. "Do you need a receipt or anything?"

Ann Purdee was watching me with a very disconcerting keenness. She swallowed now before she answered.

"No." She gulped. "There's no lease, you see."

"Is one needed? I mean, if my great-aunt rented to you . . . and I don't know anything about horse keeping, and . . ." The relief in her eyes was so intense that I became almost as upset as she'd been. "Besides, Aunt Irene specifically said that you should stay on."

"That's what worries me, Mrs. Teasey. You shouldn't feel yourself bound by what herself said."

"And why not? My aunt seems to have had good reasons for most of the things she did. I don't know the setup here, and I'm not about to make arbitrary changes."

From Ann Purdee's expression, I gathered that reassurance didn't reassure.

"I can't stop long now, for the bahbee's waking any time now. May I come back tomorrow? For there're some things I'm to tell yourself alone. But sure, you've only to step down to the cottage if you need to know anything like, where things are and all."

When she'd slipped out, I looked down at the money. Two pounds was roughly five dollars, and that didn't seem like a lot of money for a cottage that'd sell for three thousand pounds cash, but I knew that two pounds was a great deal of money to Ann Purdee.

I didn't have time to think about that now. It was almost seven o'clock. I sent the children scurrying to change into something elegant, and I slipped into what Snow considered the most acceptable of my new clothes. "You gotta be a Merry Widow, Ma!" (Construct the Image?)

We arrived at the Montrose at 7:20, parking the Renault. The receptionist told me that Mr. Kelley had indeed phoned back, and had been rather upset about my sudden departure. He'd wanted to know which relative had picked us up and what she had looked like.

"Ahha," said Snow with a chortle, "a 'she' he suspects."

She made another of those incredible noises acquired from watching too many late horror shows.

The receptionist tried not to giggle.

"I'm sorry if he was unpleasant," I told the girl.

She shrugged. "Not to worry, Mrs. Teasey. I'm used to his sort."

Simon saw the blue Jag before I did, and dug me in the ribs warningly.

"Honey, you'll break my ribs doing that one day," I told him, rather more irritably than the situation warranted. "You're so strong . . ." I was scared stiff about meeting Shamus-Shay Kerrigan. Unless I have the lines, I can't act the part. And I'm never at ease with ruthless men. When I realized that Kerrigan must have a lot of money tied up in acres that he couldn't reach, I could see myself being ruthlessed. Probably not in front of my children . . . I was very glad to have their supporting presence.

Kerrigan was not. In fact, he was dumfounded, a condition he undoubtedly seldom found himself in. He covered quickly, I'll give him credit, and professed to be delighted, saying all kinds of flattering things about my youth with two such adult children, and yes of course, he realized that I couldn't very well leave them alone on their second night in Ireland, but if he'd known he'd've brought his young nephew as company. So I was doubly glad that I hadn't told him.

He seated Snow in the Jag with the same courtesy he accorded me—a ploy which went down well with her—and chatted amiably with Simon about the performance level of the Jaguar as opposed to a Mercedes 220, which my son had previously considered his favorite foreign car.

"We're dining at the Lamb Doyle's," Shamus Kerrigan said as we wound past slower traffic. "Superb view of Dublin in the evening. You haven't been in Ireland before, have you, Mrs. Teasey?"

I told him no, and then we bandied the usual "Good flight? No customs problems?" et cetera back and forth until we turned on to a less settled road and began to climb up the hill, which he identified as Ticknock, the site of a mysterious murder in the twenties. Then we were at the restaurant, which did have a commanding view of the city. And of all the developments sprouting up in the near valley: row after row after appalling row with postage-stamp sized space between them.

I began to see why someone would offer £3,000 for one of my aunt's—no, my—cottages. Shamus Kerrigan's bulldozer simply wasn't going to rape the land around me if I could stop it.

Lamb Doyle's was not, thank goodness, modern Americana. We went upstairs to the cocktail bar and settled down to admire the panorama and have a pre-dinner drink. The handsome headwaiter came around with leatherbound menus, and Snow assumed her blasé act. I could see that Simon wanted to kick her too, but I managed to catch her eye before her brother's critical expression irritated her. She got my message loud and clear, and subsided.

All the while Mr. Kerrigan set out to charm us. And he did. I noticed that Simon was watching the man's hands, and realized that this criterion was evidently not giving the expected result. Well, there's always an exception.

"Have you any vacation plans in mind, Mrs. Teasey?" Shay Kerrigan asked me when he'd given our orders.

"Oh, we let our fingers do some walking—on the maps— last night," I told him.

"I hope you'll do more than that," he said eagerly, leaning toward me across the table. In his enthusiasm, his deep blue eyes sparkled, crinkling at their corners when he smiled and widening for emphasis as he talked. He was a great one for the wide hand gesture. (*Must* Snow stare at his hands so?) "We're a poor country, industrially speaking, Mrs. Teasey, and way behind the rest of the world, but we've got some of the most beautiful scenery. If you go nowhere else, you ought to go down to Dingle, do the Ring of Kerry, particularly this time of year, though it's beautiful year long. Then turn north toward Galway—don't let the song turn you off, because it's all true. Sunset in Galway Bay has to be seen. Oh, grand"—he broke off to return a greeting—"how's yourself?" When the man smiled pleasantly at us and moved on, Shamus Kerrigan remarked that he owned the restaurant. "I used to race motorbikes with Reg, before he gave it up."

If Simon wanted anything in the world more than a gun, it was a motorbike.

"*You* ride motorcycles?" Simon shot me a glance that said, "You see, good guys ride bikes too."

Kerrigan grinned at Simon's reaction. "Got a Bultaco 250 cc right now."

"A trial bike?" Simon was ecstatic.

"Spot on."

"Would there be any scrambles or trials going on here soon?"

Kerrigan was grinning more broadly now, with sideways glances at my reaction. "Every Saturday and Sunday, somewhere in Ireland, there's something going on. In fact, there's a trial on at the Curragh this Saturday. If you'd really like to go . . ."

Simon turned pleading eyes to me, his face screwing up the way he had had as a small boy desperately wanting what seemed unreachable. I groaned inwardly, wondering what expression on my face was being read by the others. Conflicting emotions, I hoped. Certainly Simon must realize the awkwardness in my being beholden to this man. And it would be—for Simon—a slap at his father, for Teddie had been almost apoplectic that *his* son could be interested in anything so plebeian and disreputable as motorbikes. Evidently bike racing was in better odor in Ireland than in the States.

"I've promised to take my nephew, Mrs. Teasey," Kerrigan was saying, his expression bland and innocent. Then he winked at Snow. "He's fifteen. If you'd like to come too, Snow?"

She played it cool. "Thank you very much, Mr. Kerrigan, but if Simon cares to go, I think I ought to keep Mother company."

"If we could persuade your mother to join us, would you come then?" That dratted man was clever enough not to condescend to my daughter but to approach her on a conspiratorial level that suggested I'd be missing a treat by refusing.

Snow rolled me a look of "What can we lose, Mom?"

"The Curragh is really worth the trip, Mrs. Teasey. I'd be obliged if you came. Think of me outnumbered by *three* teen-agers!"

He was a guileful soul, was Shamus Kerrigan. I'd half a mind to say no thank you, but both children were so intense suddenly that I stammered out an acceptance. No sooner had I done so than I saw the gleam of what could only be triumph in his eyes, and regretted my capitulation. I might have stymied him from talking business at dinner tonight, but he'd neatly manuevered me into a more vulnerable position.

Then he and Simon got into a discussion about motor-bikes until the headwaiter announced that our table was ready.

"Are your children too young for bike races?" I asked him after we were settled.

Kerrigan gave me a stunned look before he smiled. "I'm not married yet, Mrs. Teasey." His smile became self-mocking. "You'll find that Irishmen tend to marry fairly late, sometimes not till they're forty, forty-five."

"They should be old enough to know better, then," said Simon with unexpected bitterness. He'd started making such remarks even before I'd given the twins any idea that I was thinking of divorce. They'd always seemed fond of their father, which was one reason I'd hesitated long after I knew our marriage had turned into a sham. But suddenly their affections for Teddie had suffered quite a change. Ever since the night of the Harrisons' party . . .

"I shan't marry until I'm at least thirty," said Snow loftily. "And only if I've known the man a long, long time and can assess his weaknesses."

Simon snorted, but Shay Kerrigan, to my surprise, took Snow's comment seriously and agreed that it was very wise to look for weaknesses. If you loved someone in spite of such flaws, the affection must be secure.

"Of course, you have to be able to *admit* you can make mistakes, which is a mature attitude," she went on, while Simon rolled his eyes in exasperation at her present role. "Oh, cut it out," she said to him irritably.

My feelings were rather mixed. I wished she hadn't come out with such statements in front of a complete stranger; she was using phrases with which I had explained my divorce plans to my children, and Shamus Kerrigan was regarding her with a good deal of interest.

"They don't have divorce here in Ireland, do they?" she went on to Kerrigan. "Say, Mother, is your divorce legal in Ireland?"

"Shut up, Snow," said Simon. "Mother?" He appealed to me to assert maternal authority.

"I could ask, if you'd like," Shamus said, studiously avoiding my eyes.

"If she isn't, then if Daddy came to Ireland with that gushy woman he married, he'd be a bigamist and could be arrested, couldn't he?" And she gave a funny little laugh, not at all the sound of a fourteen-year-old girl. I got the feeling that Snow would very much like to see her father in jail!

"Here's the food," said Simon. "Stop jabbering and eat. This is too good to waste."

As though to prevent any more shock waves in the social situation, Shamus Kerrigan initiated other conversational gambits. He was good at it without being heavy-handed in directing the talk. If only I hadn't been bothered by the fact that he was doing the pretty only to get me to give him access up the lane, I'd've thoroughly enjoyed myself. To give him his due, not once did a hint of the matter arise during dinner. Nor on the drive home. I mean, to the hotel.

The twins and I were properly appreciative of the evening, and he confirmed the Saturday date. Then, as he tooled the big Jag slowly out of the parking lot, we swept into the hotel just as if we ought to. When I figured he must be clear of the intersection, we ducked back out and into the parking lot for the Renault.

 4

I DON'T SLEEP WELL in strange houses on unfamiliar beds. At least, that's what I told myself when I was still wide awake at three. I was damned well lying to myself. I disliked taking the sleeping pills which my doctor had sympathetically given me after I'd innocently complained about insomnia. I'd been rather aghast when he'd obliquely advised me to "get around more," meet new people, form new attachments, "however brief." Mother'd suggested that she was very broad-minded and this was a permissive society. I'd not been nearly as horrified at her tacit advice to take a lover as I had been at Dr. Grimeson's. After that, however, I couldn't chalk up my sleeplessness to nerves or not enough exercise: I had to admit it was the lack of sex.

Sex, or lack of it, had never been a problem while I was married to Teddie. He liked to exercise his rights and occasionally was rather brutal about exercising them, even after I tumbled to the fact that he was having affairs and in no pain. I'm not a prude — well, not for *other* people — but I wasn't going to play the suburban game, particularly after I'd decided to divorce him. I certainly wouldn't give him a chance to get custody of the twins because of any indiscretion he could lay on me. So I sweated it out. Then — and now.

I'd about dulled my sex drive before coming to Ireland, so it was heartily discouraging to find a resurgence after just a few hours in the company of an attractive man. It just wasn't fair.

While I was prowling about the first floor of the house, trying to wear out my restlessness, I noticed two other patches of light in the darkness: one at Thornton's cottage and the other at Ann Purdee's. I also heard the thin wail of a sick child. That brought back other memories: of me desperately trying to cope with two screaming, teething infants while Teddie snored on in oblivion and then berated me the next day for looking haggard.

I forced myself away from such reminiscences. "Remember the good times," I'd been advised by another divorced friend. "Hating him, or the if-I-had-he-might-not-have routine, is a waste of think-energy," Betty had told me. "You loved him enough once to marry him, so you must have seen something good in the man — remember that! And let the trivia decay. Otherwise, you end up with a fine case of soul-pollution. Which, honey, is a good way to scare off *any* decent chance at remarriage."

"I don't want to get married again, Betty," I'd told her vehemently.

She'd given me a sideways glance and ostentatiously fingered her new wedding band. "Oh yeah? Convince me!"

Betty'd had a singularly dirty divorce (and given me tips on how *not* to have one), picked herself up, joined a singles club in Westfield, and married a widower with five children. She had four of her own, and they bought a huge house and all got on extremely well.

"Oh, you're at the I-hate-all-men stage right now," she'd said. "Can't blame you. But it passes, lassie, it passes. And then everything and anything in pants stimulates the old sex appeal." She caught my astonished look and laughed. She was tall and rather gangly, inclined to wear old tweed skirts or blue jeans. "Even this old mare! At least you're not one of those I-can't-cope-alone wailers! Soon enough you'll begin to wish you did have a male around. It's awfully nice to have a shoulder to cry on when you damned well know you've been stupid."

"Teddie was never cried on."

"I don't doubt it," and she rolled her eyes, for she'd known Teddie rather well. "Which is to your advantage right now. You've been used to coping."

"That doesn't mean I make the right decisions," I said, thinking glumly of the horror of an apartment I'd taken. The walls were paper-thin. The next-door neighbors had whining kids and played their stereo so loud that we didn't need to turn ours on except when their choice of music left a lot to be desired. The apartment had been the best of a bad selection, but I'd been so obsessed with the desire to leave the "matrimonial home" and all its associations that I'd taken the first available accommodation. The twins had been very tolerant, and we'd moved as soon as possible into an old, thick-walled house, newly converted into apartments.

"That doesn't mean a man will decide right the first time either," Betty had said in her droll way. "Say, why don't you join a singles club?"

"Betty!" and I gave her a warning look.

"Honey, you don't have to *marry* the first man. You'd be a fool if you did. That's how mistakes get compounded. No, you need to get back into circulation, and by that I mean just seeing a lot of different people, women and men." Then she regarded me thoughtfully. "Your big problem, Rene, will be pleasing yourself for a change."

"I don't understand."

"I mean, don't try to be what you *think* the guy wants in a woman. Just be yourself."

"I still don't understand you."

She gave me another long, searching look. "What-your-best-friend-had-better-tell-you department," she said with a sigh. "Now, look, I'm not the only one who thought you were getting the bad end of the stick from Teddie-boy. I *don't* mean the fact that he was sleeping around. I wanted to bash him in the teeth for the way he'd speak to you. My God, who did he think he was? The Pasha of Persia? And you were too well-mannered to retaliate." Betty's breath started to get rough with suppressed anger. "And I *am* taking you to the next meeting at the singles club!"

Betty would have—if it'd meant dragging me all the way—but news of the legacy arrived, and she was jubilant for my sake—and aligned herself with my kids to see that I didn't back out at the last moment.

"Irishmen are gorgeous," she told me enthusiastically. "Just what you need to get back into practice."

In the dead of night, I wondered if she had foreseen someone like Shay Kerrigan. I'd have to write her. She'd be highly entertained. And at this distance she couldn't match-make very actively. But such thoughts were not soothing me to sleep.

I went back to the kitchen and started the kettle. A hot toddy might help. Damn! No whiskey. Well, hot milk would be okay.

The pots fell out of the cupboard with a clatter. I nearly joined them when I heard a tap at the back door.

"Whoooo . . . who is it?"

"Kieron T'ornton, Mrs. Teasey."

"Oh, good grief! Come in."

As he entered, he looked down at the door latch. "You'd best be locking that door at night, Mrs. Teasey. We've a lot of tinkers on the long acre, and you could lose the best things in the house for sleeping."

I stood there, pot in hand, staring at him because he'd a

brown bottle, unmistakably the kind which held spirits, in his hand. He noticed my gaze and grinned.

"The bahbee's teething, and a little of this helps."

"I'm not teething, but if you could spare a thimbleful . . ."

He strode into the room, looking blockier and shaggier than ever in the small space.

"If you'll permit me to drink with you? A pretty woman shouldn't ever have to drink alone." Then he chuckled. "That's what I'd tell your aunt."

"My aunt drank?"

He threw back his head to roar with laughter, but I made hushing noises and pointed up to indicate he shouldn't wake my kids. He covered his mouth until the laughter subsided. "Sure and she did!"

"Hmm. I didn't mean to imply that she was prudish . . . but somehow one doesn't think of old-lady aunts as drinkers."

"Don't think of your great-aunt Irene as an old-lady aunt," and there was strong feeling in the grin on his face. "She was a grand gal. Had she been younger or I older . . ." He gave me a mischievous wink and, with accustomed ease, slipped into a chair at the small table.

Strangely enough, I didn't feel the least bit embarrassed by Kieron Thornton's presence in my kitchen. What harm could I come to with a man who succored teething babies and distraught mothers at all hours?

"Is it Ann Purdee's baby?" I asked.

He hesitated before he said, "Poor little tike."

Then I nearly let the milk boil over, because it suddenly struck me as odd that Kieron Thornton was at Ann Purdee's. Had she no husband?

"She's no man in the house, you know," he said in a slow drawl, and I wondered if I'd been thinking aloud again. "Which is as well," he added slowly, his eyes on mine. "One more such beating and there'd've been bloody little left of her, there being not much of her except willpower anyway."

"She dropped in on us this afternoon," I said, matching his casualness. "To pay the rent."

He caught and held my eyes. "*You've* no objection to her staying on then?" There was something he didn't add.

I shook my head, and he smiled with relief and approval. "There's a story about Ann Purdee?"

"I'm not wide in the mouth, Mrs. Teasey, not about other people's affairs, Irene, your aunt, was satisfied, let's say, and helped out a bit now and again. No more than was neighborlylike."

I caught the hint and nodded. Ann Purdee had already struck me as a proud person whom well-meant but ill-timed generosities could wound deeply.

"I'm pleased you thought to move in right away," he said, taking a judicious sip of the hot milk and whiskey. "Hmmm. Very tasty." I'd doctored it with a bit of nutmeg and sugar. "Possession is nine points of the law in any country."

"And there'll be trouble?"

"Have you spoken with Mihall Noonan?"

"Yes, for all the good it did. I'm just as confused. And then, my aunt left a letter of instruction."

He was nodding, so I gathered he'd known about it. After all, Mr. Noonan had said he'd saved her life.

"Do you think," I asked him urgently, "that there'll be trouble with the relatives?"

"Not to worry, Mrs. Teasey. You were always to inherit, or so she told us time and again. God rest Queen Irene! God save Queen Irene!" And he raised the mug in a toast. "Not to worry, I said. You've loyal subjects here." He inclined the upper part of his body in a bow. "Given half the chance, we'll defend you to the death."

"Good God, it won't come to that?" I was half teasing, and yet I could hear the warning, the resolution to defend, in his tone.

"Finish your drink, pet. Get the good of it," he said in a sort of paternal tone, and lifted my hand off the table. "It's chilly, and you should be abed."

I could feel the cold even with the warm, laced milk in my tummy. And I could see the lightening of the sky through the kitchen window. "Good Lord, what time is it?"

"Half three. We've short nights in the summers here." He downed his drink and rose, pocketing the bottle of liquor. "Sleep sound, and God bless!"

He was out the door, softly humming a tune that was vaguely familiar.

I did sleep soundly. Very soundly. Until the thudding on the front door penetrated my sleep, and I felt Simon shaking my shoulder urgently.

"Mom, it's that Kelley guy."

The presumptuous manner of knocking added to my fury at his unheralded arrival. Perhaps it was close to ten in the morning, but I don't fancy being awakened by people I'm avoiding. I tried to open the window, but it was too tight.

"I'll tell him to go away," Simon said, starting down the stairs.

"No, I'll handle him!" I grabbed up my coat, more concealing than my flimsy dressing gown, and nearly tripped down the steep, short stairs. "What do you mean by pounding on my door in that fashion?" I demanded as I threw it open.

Brian Kelley, hand poised for another whack on the panels, stared at me, popeyed, his face gone white. Only for a moment, though, for he rapidly recovered his poise, his ruddy complexion, and his accumulated frustration.

"Are *you* Irene Teasey?"

"And whom else were you expecting in this house? And why have you been pursuing me? I left specific instructions that *I* would contact *you*." Then I belatedly realized that I shouldn't know what Brian Kelley looked like. "I assume, that is, that you *are* the persistent Brian Kelley."

"I am." He made a movement as if to enter the house, and I closed the door just slightly to emphasize unwelcome. Simon and Snow had ranged themselves on the stairs, and I was glad of their moral support.

"Well?" I said, tapping my foot.

"I have been trying to get in touch with you, Miss Teasey, to present a very fair offer."

"For what?"

"Why, for this," and he spread his chunky-fingered hand to indicate the house and grounds. "A very good offer, considering there are sitting tenants, and your circumstances."

"Which circumstances?"

"Why, that you have to sell."

"Who told you that I have to sell?"

"Well, you've the death duties to be paid. I happen to know that they'll be pretty stiff on a property like this."

"Will they?"

He wasn't liking my attitude at all. "I've a firm offer of twenty-five thousand pounds. That would be sixty-five thousand dollars!" He seemed impressed, and I refused to be. "You'd still get home with money in your pocket."

"Mr. Kelley, you seem to know a lot more about my affairs and my plans than I do. Among other points, you've neglected to take into consideration that my great-aunt's will has not yet been probated. Until it is, nothing can be done about buying or selling."

"If you accept this offer, Miss Teasey, you might find that probate is only a question of time." He was unctuously implying aid.

"I'm given to understand that it's only a question of time anyhow."

"You're in Ireland now, Miss Teasey." The threat was stated now.

"So I am, come to take up my inheritance, and comply with the terms of my great aunt's will . . ." The piggy eyes informed me that Mr. Kelley knew the terms of that will. "... And her letter of specific instruction, which I intend to follow to the spirit and law." Well, he didn't know about any letter, that was certain. "Now, if you do not leave my premises I shall be forced to get the shotgun for which I obtained a license from the Cabinteely Gardai yesterday." That really shook him, and he backed out of the doorway and the small porch.

"You'll be sorry you turned that offer down, miss."

I slammed the door behind him, and while Simon was shaking the clasped hands of victory above his head, we heard the choleric Mr. Kelley stalling his car.

"Mom, you were great!" Snow said, chortling with pleasure.

"Who does he think he is, threatening you? Could he really hold up probate, Mom?" Simon wasn't the least bit upset about that prospect.

"Don't know and I don't care, but I'll ask Mr. Noonan," I said, inordinately pleased that I had actually outfaced a man.

"Among other things, you'd better get that license today," Snow said, then sighed. "If only you'd stood up to Dad like that once in a while . . ."

"It would only have delayed matters," Simon said, glaring angrily at his sister. "Besides, Dad would have made Mother sell Kelley this place for sixty-five thousand bucks!"

"Oh no!" Snow didn't fancy that alternative.

My sudden triumph turned to doubt. "Do *you* think I did the right thing?"

"About Kelley?" Simon's outraged response answered the wrong question. "Oh . . ." and then he realized what I had meant and put both arms awkwardly but sweetly about me. My, he was getting tall. I had to look up at him. "Mother, you did exactly the right thing. With Kelley and with Dad. Sara and I have no regrets. None!" His serious face was suddenly split by an inimitably Simonesque grin. "Hell, Dad had no real use for us except to show off 'his twins' or prove his authority by snapping his fingers and having us, and you, waiting on him hand and foot. And I will *never* forgive him for that night in December—"

"Simon!" Snow's voice was sharp and scared.

I'd known that something had happened to the children the night they'd gone with their father to the Harrisons' party, but they'd never talked about it. I'd been flat on my back with one of those sudden, terribly debilitating stomach viruses. Teddie'd been furious with me because he'd wanted to go to the Harrisons' "do"; they always "did" so extravagantly. I knew he hated going to parties alone, as he was at his best scoring off a foil—like me. In desperation, and because the Harrisons had a daughter the twins' age, I suggested that he take the children. They'd come home about midnight: I'd been listening for their return, but they'd whispered in the hall outside my room without coming in. Which was unusual in itself, but I'd chalked it up that night to their concern about my health. I didn't know until much later that Teddie hadn't brought them home. Indeed, I didn't learn until after I'd initiated divorce proceedings that Teddie'd been put to bed at the Harrisons' stoned out of his mind, and was never invited there again. Something devastating had indeed happened, which the children were determined to keep from me.

Now Simon's face softened, and he patted me on the shoulder.

"No, Mother dearest of them all, you did the right thing. *We're* not sorry. You're a real tough mother!" And he kissed me.

"And I'm starved!" Snow said, as if Simon's overt show of affection irritated her. She was the less-demonstrative child. Now she marched toward the kitchen.

"Say, who does that Kelley character think he is," asked Snow into a pause at the breakfast table. "This place is worth a lot more than any old twenty-five thousand pounds."

"Did Kelley mean just the house, Mom? Because it would be a pretty good price that way."

"No, Simon, he meant the whole property."

Simon considered that momentarily. "Then he's a crook. Particularly threatening you with no probate unless you played his game."

"You don't suppose he's acting for Shay Kerrigan, do you?" asked Snow. "No," she answered herself, even as Simon exploded with a negative.

"Shamus Kerrigan's not that sort of guy. He wouldn't sneak about—"

"Well, he tried to sneak a bulldozer up our lane."

"Children, children!" I called them to order, but I had to admit that Snow's suggestion of Shay Kerrigan as Kelley's client had also occurred to me—and been discarded. "I agree with Simon, as far as Mr. Kerrigan's concerned, Snow. But that Mr. Kelley knew too much . . ."

"He didn't know about the trust fund, did he?" said Simon. "And that Mom wouldn't *have* to sell to pay the death duties!"

"Come to think of it, I don't know what's in the will."

"You said you did."

"I said I'd comply with it . . . Where *did* I put it down?"

Snow swished from the kitchen and flounced back again in very short order with the document and Aunt Irene's letter. The will was considerably less dramatic, and fairly straightforward, once you discounted all those whereases and thingies. I was named co-executrix with a representative of the solicitors. We were to pay all her just debts and death duties. I was to administer the Brandel trust as long as necessary. Otherwise, everything, lock, stock, and barrel, was left to me, Irene Teasey Stanford.

As I could plainly see, the will had been signed ten years ago. That had been rather a hellish year for me. If I'd known of Aunt Irene's bequest, I'd've endured it with a stouter heart. That was the year I'd been sure I couldn't stick marriage with Teddie, when he'd flaunted that Joan creature all over town. However, you can put up with rather more than you think you can.

"What's the Brandel trust? Mr. Noonan said nothing about that yesterday," said Snow.

"That's another thing I'll have to ask him."

"If this Kelley character can hold up probate, do we get to stay on in Ireland?" asked Simon, eyes wide with hopefulness.

"*If* he can hold it up, we'll have to see how long . . . but however long, you two have to be back in school come September ninth, and don't forget it."

That unholy pair exchanged glances, and I had the suspicion that I'd already acceded too much.

"I don't know why you're so keen to stay here when obviously there's a lot of trouble brewing," I said, feeling a bit put out with their connivery.

"Aw, Mom, it's a lot better here than Westfield."

"Right *now*." I hinted at their well-known boredom.

"Ha!" Simon was contemptuous of my skepticism. "With trials and scrambles on every weekend?"

"And a horse for me to ride?" piped up Snow.

"We'll see, we'll see! Now let's get organized."

We'd tidied up and dressed and were going out the front door when I heard the phone ringing.

"Damn!"

"Mom!" Snow's tone was exasperated. "It's probably that Kelley character."

It was nearly noon, and though I honestly doubted that Kelley would be presumptuous enough to beard me again, I didn't want to put it to the test. So I left the phone ringing.

We found the nearest supermarket, which was more a discount house than a grocery. You could buy everything, including a TV. We had two huge shopping carts full, and I forked over £32 and odd pence, which didn't seem like much to me until Snow did a rapid calculation and said we'd spent over $75. I was flabbergasted, but, as Snow pointed out, it was cheaper than eating out.

I must say, it was fun putting things away in our new kitchen, making discoveries in the dining room like the beautiful Staffordshire dinner set and the delicate Beleek tea service. We kept some of the table linens for our use and carried the rest upstairs to store. The closets were already fairly full of my great-aunt's clothing. She couldn't have been a very large person, and certainly hadn't been given to frivolous clothes: Everything had a hard, durable look, though nothing appeared worn. Snow went into hysterics over the long-john winter drawers and knitted vests, but I advised her not to laugh.

"I wonder how much it would cost to put in central heating," said Snow when I explained about Irish winters.

"A bundle probably, and don't start planning a winter here, too, my girl. School beckons in September."

Snow gave me one of her wide-eyed innocent looks.

"Surely they have schools in Ireland, Mother."

"We all need some lunch," I said firmly, and went downstairs.

We grilled chops, made french fries out of the best frying potatoes I'd ever tasted, had marvelous frozen but fresh-tasting peas and a smallish green melon that was very sweet. We were all in such good moods that the meal became an event; even the washing up afterward went painlessly. Had I known how much the Staffordshire was worth, I don't think I'd've let Simon do the washing. But no harm was done.

I did call Michael Noonan, but he was engaged at court. The children wanted to do some sightseeing in Dublin, but I wanted to write Mother to inform her of our address and all the news, so I sent the twins out exploring until I could finish. I made a bet with myself as I heard them clattering out the back door. By the time I got upstairs and could peek out Simon's window, I'd won. He was in the garage examining the Mercedes, and Snow was halfway down the track to Horseface's pasture, the plastic bag of sugar lumps swinging from one hand.

 5

WHEN WE GOT BACK from our tour at eight o'clock, there was a card pushed through the mail slot.

"'Called to see you. Will call again.' signed 'Imelda.'" I turned to the children. "Have you met an Imelda you haven't told me about?"

Snow took the card from my hand, turned it over, and pointed to the printed name.

"Mrs. Robert Maginnis. Who she?"

"I haven't a clue."

"Maybe Kieron has," Simon said, and we took ourselves down to Kieron's cottage.

I don't know what I expected, but when he insisted that we come in and sit down awhile, I was stunned, and not a little embarrassed, by the unexpected charm of the room. The walls were finished off in a creamy paint, the beams darkened for contrast. There was an old-fashioned settee, and a beautiful small teak chest whose design was echoed by the bookcase and side tables. There was, of all things, a rocking chair, from which Kieron Thornton must have just risen, for it rocked to and fro on the braided rug. Pewter, copper, and brass ornaments gleamed on the mantel and table tops. It was a very finished room for a bachelor. He must have seen that opinion in my reaction, but he was gracious.

"This is embarrassing," I said, getting down to the reason for our visit. "We don't know who this is, and ought we to?"

He glanced at the message and the name, and snorted.

"One of your great-aunts, Irene's older sister." He handed back the card, and I could tell that while he was amused, he was also annoyed. At Mrs. Maginnis, not us.

"You seem surprised."

"I am. That's the first time she's called at that house in twenty years."

"Twenty years? Her own sister? Why?" I might wish that at least one of my sisters would make herself that scarce.

Kieron's eyes twinkled as he replied. "Originally I believe it was because Irene was stupid enough to buy property so far from the city."

"Originally?" I asked, hoping he'd go on. "Oh, please, you do know? And I'm dumped here in a real bag of weasels and Aunt Irene said that you'd help me. In her letter."

That obliged him to answer, although he was reluctant. "Irene's sisters didn't like the company she kept, nor her tenants."

I thought of Ann Purdee's delicate features, her work-roughened hands, and the two pounds, which was a lot of money to her.

"My aunt's letter expressly instructed me to keep on the present tenants in Swallow and Lark cottages." He was nodding, so that wasn't news to him. "Unless I find very good reasons for disobeying those instructions, I intend to honor them."

Something close to relief passed quickly across his face.

"Do you mean to tell us," began Snow indignantly, "that her sisters didn't come here when she was sick last winter?"

Kieron's expression was not friendly. "I believe they did visit her in hospital."

"Probably to see if she was dying and if they could get her money and property," Snow went on, disgusted. Her surmise was accurate, judging by the slight narrowing of Kieron's eyes. "It was *you* who saved her life. Mr. Noonan told us."

"Irene Teasey . . ." and he stopped, grinning at me, the second Irene Teasey.

"Wouldn't it be easier if you called me Rene?"

He nodded, smiling warmly, and began again. "Irene Teasey was a remarkable woman for her own age, and even this one. She had tremendous vitality and compassion—not the treacly sort, but down-to-earth, practical compassion—" He broke off, hesitating as he tried to explain. "Ireland's a good fifty years behind the rest of the world, you know."

"Part of its charm," I murmured as he paused again.

"Not necessarily, Rene," and he was critical.

"Are you trying to tell us that Irene wasn't conventional?" I asked.

"And that she liked her own sort of people on her queendom instead of the stuffy petty ones like her sisters?" piped up Snow.

Kieron nodded vigorously.

"Well!" said my daughter, as if that settled her preference. "And I'll just bet it made them stinking mad to think her place was worth more than theirs."

"Yes, but it wasn't until Shay Kerrigan paid an atrocious price for the Donnigan land . . ."

"Why wouldn't my aunt give Mr. Kerrigan access to the lane?" I asked, and he gave me such an intense, alert look that I added, "She specifically instructed me, in that letter, not to, even if it seemed spiteful."

"Just that?"

I wondered what else she could have said, but then he asked if we'd driven around the county very much, if we'd seen the housing schemes.

"Oh no, not ticky-tacky boxes," groaned Snow.

Kieron was nodding, but, to be honest, I wouldn't've thought squashed-up building developments were Shamus Kerrigan's thing. He was very elegant himself. I *could* see Brian Kelley's type throwing up ticky-tacky.

"Is that why Brian Kelley's so mad-keen to buy this place?" I asked.

"Kelley?" Kieron was irritated. "How'd he know about you?"

"What do you mean?"

"Irene chased him away no end of times. And I threw him out of the house last February."

"He offered Mom a lousy twenty-five thousand pounds," said Snow scornfully. "The place's worth much more than *that*!"

"Sure and it is." Then he laughed. "And when you know that Irene paid five hundred pounds for the thirty acres in 1945 . . ."

"Wow!" Snow was impressed, and Simon whistled.

"No wonder her relatives were annoyed," I said. "But, if

they also didn't like her tenants, you weren't one then, were you?"

"My mother was." And there was a shadow of old anger and sadness in his eyes, and hurt.

"What is it that the relatives don't like about Ann Purdee?" asked Snow belligerently.

"You're in Ireland now, young lady, and people have different ways of looking at things."

Snow made a grimace.

"What matters is that the relatives, for reasons best known to . . . and appreciated by . . . themselves, did not approve of my great-aunt's way of life," I said, and Kieron nodded. "It also didn't sit well with them that she was the smarter businesswoman." Kieron nodded again. "Well, I could see being annoyed, but not cutting off the association . . . even if it is Ireland and they do things differently . . ." Ah, yes, there was more that Kieron Thornton wasn't telling me. "So I suppose," and I brandished the calling card, "they're going to see if I'm more amenable." Kieron nodded; he was beginning to look like one of those stupid drinking birds. "So if you'd be so kind as to tell me who my relatives are, then I can separate them from the real-estate people who want to con my land out of me."

"Irene kept the family bible up to date, but let's see. Irene had two sisters, Imelda Maginnis and Alice Hegarty, and two brothers, your own grandfather, Michael, and Richard. He's dead now but his widow's alive, Winnie. Each of them had about six kids apiece . . ."

"So did Great-granddad's," said Snow with a long-suffering groan. "And none of 'em are Catholics."

"None of them here are either," said Kieron. "You could take tea with a different set of cousins for a month or two."

Snow rolled her eyes. "Who'd want to?"

"Sara! Really, Kieron, I'd no idea we had so much family left in Ireland."

"I thought you Yanks prided yourselves on your Irish ancestry."

"Not all of us can claim a Timahogue or two," I said, a bit annoyed. "In America, it's more what you can do — "

"Or who you know," chimed in Snow.

"—than where you came from and who's your family."

"It's who you know here too," Kieron said, grinning at Snow for her impudent observation. "Imelda and Alice are the ones to be right careful with. Winnie's a good sort; she means well."

"Are the sisters in bad circumstances? Financially?" I asked, still feeling guilty over inheriting from someone I'd never met.

"Jasus, no. Even Winnie's well-off. She watches the family fish business like a gull. None of 'em's pinched. They're just greedy. They can't take it in that Irene could possibly leave her property to a rich Yank simply because the gel was named after her."

"To begin with, I'm not rich."

"You are now," Kieron said.

"Not until probate. Which reminds me—Brian Kelley hinted I'd get probate a lot faster if I accepted his offer."

"Could he really do something nasty and obstructive?" asked Snow. We didn't need a verbal answer with the look on Kieron's face.

"I'd speak to Mihall Noonan on that point, as soon as possible. I don't know who Brian Kelley knows. But Alice's daughter's husband works for the same firm. *It's* reputable enough, but Kelley . . ."

"Is not," Snow said, making grubbing gestures with her fingers. "Sausage fingers and sweating palms and a piggy face to go with it."

"Would you fancy a cup of coffee and some biscuits?" asked Kieron, rising and politely changing the conversation.

I started to refuse, but Snow informed Kieron that I took coffee any time, anywhere, but I was choosy about my company, and while I was getting my breath back she boldly asked if she could peek through the rest of his beautiful home. She'd never been in a real Irish cottage before.

Any thought of resemblance between his home and a "real Irish cottage" was corrected. I wondered how Kieron Thornton supported himself, but by the time we got to his kitchen, through the beautifully appointed dining room, I did know that he'd made the cabinets in Aunt Irene's house and all the furnishings in this one. He said flatly that he worked only when and on what he wished to, and for whom he chose. I began to understand how charges of unconventionality could be leveled at this one of Aunt Irene's friends.

"You're too neat," said Snow approvingly as we continued upstairs and into Kieron's room.

"Why can't men be neat?" asked Simon, bristling.

"No reason for them not to, they're just too used to having a woman do it all for them," she said condescendingly.

"I was in the army," said Kieron, to interrupt the skirmishing. "And I happen to like things in order."

"So there," said Simon.

"He'll make some woman a good husband, then," his sister went on, determined to have the last word.

"The kettle's boiled." Our host hurried down the stairs, urging us to join him.

"Sara, you are impossible sometimes," I said, giving her arm a painful pinch. Ouching, she went down the stairs, well in front of both of us.

"What's that for?" she asked, pointing to a large copper cylinder and an electrical motor in the pantry.

"Heating water and pumping it out of the well. Irene had well water piped into all the cottages."

"Doesn't everybody?"

"Not in Ireland."

"Good grief!" Snow was amazed, but then, so was I.

Then Simon spotted the motorcycle in the lean-to. "Hey, what is it?"

"Honda 250. You like bikes?"

"Do I like bikes?"

"Simon is mad-crazy for bikes," Snow said rapidly, because both of us could sense that Simon was about to mention Saturday's outing, and in the present company, with the most recent disclosures, that seemed a sort of treachery. I'd have to figure out how to withdraw courteously from that invitation.

"Know how to ride?"

"No," Simon replied glumly.

"If your mother is willing, I'll teach you."

"But he can't drive it. He's only fourteen."

"You'd never know it to look at him. And in his own lane it doesn't matter." Kieron warmed to the idea. "Look, Rene, I'll give him a few lessons, he can't hurt himself. And he is on holiday."

With Simon looking so pleadingly wistful and Kieron's half smile egging him on, I was weakening.

As Kieron Thornton brewed the coffee in a filter pot, Simon was restlessly poking around the living room.

"Hey, this one isn't finished," he said, picking up an eight-inch carved figure à la chinoise from a group with several others which were completed and stained.

"Why, they're chess pieces," said Snow, jumping up to examine them. "*You're* doing 'em!" she said, pointing an accusing finger at Kieron.

They were lovely indeed: a queen and two bishops, and Simon had picked up the embryo knight. I stared at Kieron with awed respect.

"Good things to have on hand when you can't sleep," he said, without so much as a glance in my direction.

"Well, get her!" said Snow, affecting a haughty face like the queen's and then dissolving into giggles as she handed the piece to me. It was a delightful face, giving the queen a definite personality.

"Do you play chess, too?" asked Simon because his sister was getting on his nerves.

Kieron did, and Simon forthwith challenged him to a game, but they didn't start until we had spent a good bit of time admiring the individual figures.

"Are these ancient Celts?" I asked, trying to identify the costumes.

Kieron grinned approvingly at me and stroked his beard. "You got Brian Boru, and Conchobuir's there."

"Which one's Cuchulain?"

"So you know your Irish legends?"

"Some of them. Is the Red Queen Deirdre of the Sorrows?"

"Indeed and she is, and the white one's Maeve."

As I passed them from the box to the board, glancing at

each pawn and major piece, I realized that they had quite distinct faces and expressions. Maeve, of course, was positively malevolent, and looked about to weep. Cuchulain was a knight with a sort of Steve McQueenish visage; I wondered if Cuchulain would have ridden a motorbike instead of a chariot. His opposite red number bore a marked resemblance to John Wayne.

"Cuchulain *could* have looked like Steve McQueen," began Snow thoughtfully.

"You mean the other way round, don't you? Cuchulain came first," said Simon, "by a couple of thousand years."

"Who knows?" said Kieron. "There're only so many basic facial types, and, certain temperaments are attracted to certain occupations. And then, temperament stamps a face with distinctive lines: the blandness of the politician, the alertness of the competitive businessman, the stance of the professional athlete, the jowls of a singer, the—"

"The long hair of the singer, you mean." Simon grinned.

"Not pop, *trained* singer."

"You mean, you don't *like* rock and roll?" Snow began to bristle.

"I said 'trained singer,' and that's what I meant, so don't be bold, pet. Most rock and roll singers, until they get very good, don't bother to protect their biggest asset. By the time half of them are thirty, they won't be able to sing a note because they've misused their voices."

"You aren't a trained singer yourself, are you?" I asked.

Kieron turned to me, his eyes laughing, his lips twitching the corner of his beard. "No, but your aunt was."

"Aunt Irene? Sang?" Was that part of the unconventionality that had annoyed her relatives?

"You didn't know?" Kieron frowned.

"No. I told you that I didn't know anything about her. Look, my mother met Aunt Irene once, when she was abroad before the war. She liked her. I've four older sisters, and a brother, all married now, with bundles of kids. Mother came from a large family, and so did my father, and I can't keep *them* straight. So when I came along, Mother'd run out of interesting names and thought it fun to name me after my great-aunt Irene." I flushed, because my initials had made me an IT girl, a plaguey nuisance in high school. "That's why I was so dumbfounded when she left everything to me." I stood up. "Oh, I'll just turn it over to—"

There were shocked cries of "Mother!" "You couldn't!" and Kieron Thornton leaned forward to grab my hand, and pulled me, rather hard, back into the chair.

"That's enough foolishness. Irene had very sound reasons for doing as she did. I've no right to fault you for not knowing about her, and I don't. But I was surprised that you didn't know of her career. That's how she was able to buy this land and keep it."

"What did she sing? Opera?" asked Snow.

Kieron's eyes twinkled. "Guess again." He looked at me.

Then suddenly, I remembered what Mother had said.

"Good Lord, she sang Gilbert and Sullivan. At Covent Garden!"

"Bang on!" And Kieron laughed at the shock on the twins' faces.

"She didn't?"

"She did," Kieron and I said together.

Snow and Simon both turned to stare at me, mouths slightly agape.

"Mother sang G and S, too, before we arrived."

"I know," said Kieron blithely. "Check," he added, having caught Simon's king in a well-laid trap.

"Hey!"

"I'll give you the chance to beat me again," Kieron said, standing up. "I'd like to make it now, but I've an engagement at half nine."

We hastily thanked him for the hospitality, the gossip, and the game, and walked back up the slight rise to the Lodge. I was even beginning to think of it as home.

"Nine thirty and the sun's still up," Simon said. "Crazy country! Crazy country!"

6

WE WERE ENJOYING a nice leisurely breakfast when there was a knock at the back door, which Simon answered.

"Come on in, Mrs. Purdee."

She gave him a very solemn greeting and then came straight to me, holding out a small cardboard box and a key.

"You were out yesterday when I came by, Mrs. Teasey. And I know the tax appraisers have been here, so it's safe to give you these now. This," and she put the box on the table, "is the missing carburetor"—she pronounced it with a different accent, so that at first I didn't know what she meant—"for the Mercedes," and she nodded toward the garage. "And this is the key to the boot. We put the silver tea service and flatware there."

"Why?"

Mrs. Purdee eyed me very solemnly, as one does an idiot. "Sure, the silver's worth a small fortune, Mrs. Teasey, which your great-auntie didn't want to give the government. And Kieron told 'em the car wouldn't go for want of a carburetor and that part not available, but perhaps the new owner could sell it for parts."

Simon began to whoop and clap, appreciating the subterfuge, but I (they say I am occasionally square) was aghast.

"Your auntie wanted us to do it—*before* they came to lock up the house. And before the *others* got here."

Tax officials came off with a slightly better odor than my relatives if I correctly interpreted her pronouns; she plainly had little use for either.

"Will that Mercedes run if the carburetor's put back?" Simon asked.

"Oh, it will so." Her slight smile was tinged with a bit of malice. "There were only about three hundred made of that particular model, you see, and your auntie kept it in super condition. Kieron'll fix it for you if you want him to. You're to say that you ordered the part from the States." Then she started toward the door.

"Is your baby better?"

"My baby?" She whirled, startled.

"Yes, Kieron said it was teething the other night. I'd heard a child crying, you see."

"Oh, yes, well, you know how it is and all. She's easy now."

She couldn't get out of the house fast enough, and Simon and Snow both noticed it. I hadn't told them what Kieron had said about Ann being beaten by her husband, so I distracted their questions by suggesting we all go find our treasure.

And treasure it was! A superb tea service, complete with an immense tray, and an enormous box of tableware: place settings for twelve, and the most confusing array of forks, spoons, knives that I've ever seen.

The intelligence that the Mercedes was operable was very good news, and before we unloaded the silver from the boot, we took a closer look at the car.

It was curiously modern for a car built in 1956, and, to again rearrange my mental picture of Great-aunt Irene, it was a sports coupe, undoubtedly very dashing when it first came out. There wasn't a blemish on the leather upholstery—under the dust—and only signs of key-scratch on the dashboard. There seemed to be more dial faces than were familiar, but Simon told me—nonchalantly preserving his own image—that there were tachometers and things that measure motor revolutions per minute for rally driving and . . .

"If it runs, that's the only important thing," I told him, and banged at the neatly stored tires.

We were wondering where to store all the silver when Simon discovered that the center portion of the buffet obviously accommodated the silver chest. So in it went. The silver tea service could repose importantly on the buffet top, and suddenly the rather drab room took on elegance.

"Now, Mother," said Snow in her let's-get-down-to-brass-tacks voice, "if this room were, say, a soft Wedgwood green . . ."

"Yes, yes, you're right," I agreed, with unsimulated enthusiasm, and ran an experimental hand along the wallpaper. It was old and brittle. A good steaming ought to lift it.

An odd rasping sound penetrated my concentration.

Snow looked up from her arrangement of the tea and coffee pots . . . they must be Georgian . . . and then her face cleared. "It's the doorbell, Mother!"

"Kelley?" I groaned.

"Simon, we need you," said Snow. "Who else would be calling at eleven thirty?"

As I marched to the door I took a deep breath to support my anger, and exhaled it hastily in the face of a shortish woman wearing one of those matronly knit combinations in a deadly blue, which did not compliment her frizzy blondish hair and florid complexion. Her eyes, a faded green, missed nothing, giving my tunic-slack outfit a quick and disapproving once-over. She arranged her mouth in a smile, which her eyes didn't echo.

"I'd know you anywhere. You're so obviously Michael's child."

"Michael's grandchild," I replied, correcting her because she was the sort of person you have to correct, want to correct. "And you are . . . ?"

"My dear, I'm your . . . ah . . . Auntie Imelda," and she shifted her feet for a forward movement.

"Oh, you left your card yesterday."

"Indeed and I did, because I'd only just learned that my dear dead sister's namesake was actually here in Ireland." She looked reproachfully at me. I found her sorrowful "dear dead sister" routine to be overdone.

"I'm pleased to meet you, but I'm afraid we're in such a mess inside . . . unpacking, you know . . ."

"Not to worry in the least, my dear Irene," and with that she brushed by me into the small hall.

It wasn't entirely the surprise of encountering the twins which halted her forward motion. I *knew* that she'd never been in this house before. Score #1. The coup obscurely pleased me.

"Your children, my dear?" She was clearly astounded at the size and beauty of my offspring. Score #2.

"This way to the living room, Mrs. Maginnis," I said, smoothly leading the way. Simon followed her, and Snow caught my nod and closed the half-open dining-room door, then brought up the rear of the procession.

"This is my son, Simon Stanford, and my daughter, Sara."

Mrs. Imelda Maginnis was far more interested in her surroundings than in my introduction. She acknowledged them with a cursory bob of her head. She managed to look down a very short nose as if it were a Medici hook. I could see her mentally inventorying the value of the furnishings. When I urged her to take the small settee, she settled herself tentatively on the edge with an almost audible sniff, as if she expected dust to billow out. Then she asked Snow how old she was, in a condescending tone that made me want to spit.

I could see Simon closing his eyes and cringing as we both wondered how Snow was going to respond. She behaved herself, undoubtedly for some malicious purpose.

"My," said Mrs. Maginnis in that arch tone, "you're well grown for fourteen. And how old are you, Simon?"

"Fourteen."

Mrs. Maginnis pursed her lips, uncertain whether she was being mocked.

"They're twins, Mrs. Maginnis. Don't let their looks or size fool you."

"How very intr'usting!"

Good heavens, I wondered, didn't "nice" people in Ireland have twins?

"Well, now, you've cousins the same age as yourselves who would be so glad to take you about while you're in Dublin," said their great-great-aunt, again insufferably patronizing. It was obvious that she felt we wouldn't, or shouldn't, be staying here very long.

I caught Snow's eye warningly.

"Sure and we'd like that so very much," said my dutiful daughter with an alarmingly Irish brogue. "We hope to do such a lot of sightseeing . . . while we're here."

"In fact, my dear," and Mrs. Maginnis turned to me, shifting her buttocks on the slippery sofa upholstery, "my sisters and I would like to give you a little welcome party. At *my* house."

So, her house was the best of the lot? I mumbled something appropriate and wondered how I could graciously decline. Then I realized that I was overreacting. They *were* my relations; Mrs. Maginnis was obviously trying to be hospitable, however much against her better judgment. And Aunt Irene had said that I should "do" something for the younger ones who'd been kind to her.

"It's not proper, of course, to do much entertaining, like. With Irene gone so soon." She sniffed pathetically as she eyed the carpet. Her nose wiggled to acquaint us with her low opinion of the thing. "Would Sunday suit? For tea?"

I was forced to say how kind she was, how thoughtful.

"We must do what we can to make you welcome while you're in Ireland, even in such sad circumstances. And then too, my dear, you'll need help settling and selling up the estate, won't you?"

"Actually, Mrs. Maginnis—"

"Please, Irene—Auntie Imelda."

I choked out the syllables as directed. "... I can't do anything about selling until the will has been probated, you know."

Clearly she didn't, and her eyes went very round and dissatisfied.

"Oh, but of course," she recovered quickly, with a nervous giggle. "Well, you'll be able to rely on us, you know, because you'll want to clear all the cottages of those tenants." She managed a ladylike shudder of revulsion. "And there're more deserving—"

"My great-aunt specifically requested me to keep on most of the present tenants."

"She what?" Great-aunt Imelda was not pleased to learn of instructions beyond the grave. "My dear sister had suffered several strokes, you know," and then she tapped her forehead, nodding her head significantly.

"This letter predates her illness," I replied mendaciously.

"Well, this isn't the time to discuss such delicate matters. And the men are not here to give you the benefit of their good advice. You'll need it, my dear Irene. Ireland's a man's country!" She rose; I wasn't quite sure if it was in deference to Ireland's being a man's country. There was, at any rate, a disagreeable hint of smugness in her expression as she glanced around her again, as if she were obliquely pleased by the spartan furnishings. "I can't imagine why you're not stopping at the Montrose. Such a nice hotel. So American."

"That's why we're staying here," Snow said.

As Mrs. Maginnis stomped to the door, her expression said plainly, "And that won't be for long."

Somehow Snow got between her great-great-aunt and the dining-room door. The woman undoubtedly had every intention of looking in. Foiled, she smiled sourly at me, and glanced up the stairs, which told her nothing.

"Until Sunday, then?"

"What time is Irish tea on Sunday?" asked Snow in her little-girl voice.

"Why, half four, of course."

"Oh?" In that one surprised, haughty syllable, Snow managed to convey how unaccustomed she was to taking tea at such an unfashionable hour. Nor was the implication lost on our relative.

"You mustn't go to too much trouble for our sake," I felt obliged to say, but I would not be hypocritical and reprimand Snow. It had been too delicious of her.

"My husband will collect you, for sure you'd never find your way." And Mrs. Robert Maginnis stalked down the lane.

"Well, ain't she somethin'?" Snow said, glaring at the portly retreating figure. "She was dying of curiosity about the house. I wonder who she thinks ought to inherit?"

"One of the 'more deserving'?" asked Simon. He altered his voice to a falsetto imitation of his great-great-aunt: "'And there're cousins the same ages as yourselves' . . . Yeah." He went bass again. "I can just imagine. Do we *have* to, Mother?"

"Well, yes we do. We accepted, for one thing. For another, *we* might find out more than they want to." I shook a warning finger at my daughter. "And you'd better watch your manners, missy. I gather that children are seen and not heard here."

"I'll behave . . . if I can."

"You know, she's the second person who's suggested that we'd be selling . . . I must get hold of Michael Noonan." But he was out.

"You know something," Snow said musingly as she sat on the steps and peered at me through the rail, "she didn't take her gloves off, but I'll just bet anything she's got grabby little fat-fingered paws."

"Oh, let's not start *that* one again," I begged, which reminded me that Shay Kerrigan's long-fingered, well-shaped hands did *not* obey the twins' much-vaunted criterion.

"Say, Mom, didn't Kieron mention something about Aunt Irene keeping tabs on our kith and kin in the family bible?"

"Yes, he did, Sim."

"We might as well have the sheet to keep score on."

We found the family bible readily enough in the little desk in the living room, complete with family-tree chart, branches, twigs, and leaves all neatly name-tagged. I could only hope that we weren't going to meet *all* the relatives listed. Objectively, I could appreciate why Imelda Maginnis might be miffed with the property going out of the immediate family . . . the immediate Irish family.

"How was it Great-great Irene put it?" asked Snow. "'Out of three generations and five lots'? Well, there sure isn't another Irene. And look, she knew about cousin Linda's baby! Who could've told her?"

I followed Snow's pointing finger. Aunt Irene had been up-to-date, all right. I knew Mother had too much else to do to correspond with anyone regularly. Then Simon thought of looking for any mail in the back-room office desk.

We didn't find any correspondence, but there were receipted bills from previous years, all neatly bound, as well as old ledgers—but none for the previous and current years.

"Probably the tax people took them away. Or Mr. Noonan," Snow said. Which seemed logical. Then she found the worn leather address book and the problem was solved. My eldest sister, Jenny, was listed with all her changes of address.

"That figures," said Snow. "No, it doesn't. Why would Aunt Jen be so big with letters?"

"I dunno. Except she's the clubwoman type. Organized," said her twin.

Simon was still pondering the family tree. "Grandpa wasn't the only wild goose to leave the family nest. There's a slew of others, if this 'E' means emigrated. It's after a lot of names."

"Unless it means 'E' for egress and they'd died."

"Naw! Boy, look at how Imelda produced. Six!"

"Alice and Winnie were as good. Now where would you put six kids in a house this size?" Snow wanted to know.

"I wonder what did happen to her letters," I said, noticing a good supply of nice notepaper. It probably *was* Mr. Noonan. I tried reaching him again, but this time he was engaged with a client, so I didn't think it would do any harm to ask his secretary what had happened to my aunt's private papers.

"Anything to do with the estate, or income taxes, is here, Mrs. Teasey, and will be returned to you. I believe that one of the tenants burned all Miss Teasey's private correspondence, at her request. Shall I have Mr. Noonan return your call when he's free?"

I said yes, because I wanted to find out about this probate business and Kelley's threat. Just as I hung up, a leatherbound scrapbook was thrust at me. I held it off far enough to distinguish a headline and realized that this contained my aunt's professional clippings.

"Wow!"

Irene Teasey in a hundred photographs . . . costumed and made up for her stage performances as one of the leading lyric sopranos of the Covent Garden D'Oyly Carte Operetta Company.

"Gee, she was pretty!" said Snow.

"And small. Look at her. Who was she here, Mom?"

"Probably Mabel in *Pirates*," I said, considering the parasol and the pantalettes.

Some rather lovely—and painful—memories surged up out of storage. I had a vivid recollection of Mother's expression when she saw me costumed as Mabel for my first performance in *Pirates*.

"I suppose it just skipped generations, dear, but you manage to sound exactly like your aunt Irene Teasey. She was *good!*" Until now, sitting in Great-aunt Irene's living room, I really hadn't thought past the approving note in Mother's voice (for Mother has very high standards in theater). "Odd that that break in both your speaking voices never occurs when you sing. You did very well, my dear. Very well."

That was the trouble. I did do very well. The Jan Hus production of *Pirates of Penzance* was extremely well received by the off-Broadway critics. There was talk of the group turning into a professional repertory company and doing tours of G & S. Teddie was just starting with the agency, and he was torn between wondering if my career was good for his, and pride that he could show off a wife of star caliber. I certainly wasn't making any money at it. And I wasn't really any good at anything else musical. I had the perfect G & S ingenue voice, I looked Victorian, especially my figure, and, I was often told, I had the natural style of G & S. When the craze in musical tent circuses for summer circuit was going strong, I had one very exhausting, nerve-wracking, divine summer before I happily discovered I was pregnant. In spite of the fact that Simon was his spittin' image, Teddie had had a drunken habit of casting doubt on the paternity of the twins, acidly remarking that bitches could get pups from a number of dogs and I'd had plenty of opportunities to be unfaithful to him with my stage cronies. I don't know where he thought I'd've got the energy, with the schedule we had: rehearsals during the day and just enough time to bathe, eat dinner, and get made up for the evening's show, after which we were too tired to do much more than eat a hurried supper and fall into bed—alone. Of course, I had much the same routine once the twins were born—only, no applause. And the cruel criticism of a frustrated husband.

"You don't suppose she made any recordings, do you?" asked Snow, hauling me back to the present.

"She didn't sing in the Dark Ages, love, and there *are* recordings of Caruso, you know."

My great-aunt had done all the lead roles from Angela to Yum-Yum. There were press clippings, including those of a tour, until a final notice, a few sentences really, dated March 1944, which told me why my aunt's career had been ended. She'd been injured in a buzz-bomb blast.

"How?" asked Snow.

"It doesn't say."

"Must have been bad," suggested Simon. "Remember, Kieron said she bought the queendom in 1945."

"Her face?" asked Snow, flipping through the final

pages. "No. Here she is, standing in front of the house. We could ask Ann Purdee."

"We could, but should we?"

"Why not? It's not your fault that we don't *know* very much about Aunt Irene. I think we *should* be curious now. It's only grateful."

"Aw, c'mon, stop the yammering," said Simon, and shooed us out of the house before him.

Then we all stopped, our progress impeded by ignorance.

"Which is Swallow cottage?" asked Snow.

"She comes to the back door," Simon said, and pointed to the path and the small pasture gate. "That way, George!"

It seemed logical, and it was. When we had gone through the little gate and started down the steep path to the row of cottages, I had sudden second thoughts about the venture.

Three cottages were in a line, terrace cottages, they call them, the fourth (which I sincerely hoped was Ann Purdee's) at right angles to the others. Each cottage had a fenced-off rear yard, but only one looked cared for at all. The other two were junk heaps, with all sorts of rusting, molding, decaying garbage. The right-angled cottage was completely different: The palings had been secured, and there was a flourishing garden. Neat lines held a variety of children's garments flapping in the breeze. We had to go all the way around the house to get to the first of the two doors.

In the kitchen, Ann Purdee was up to her elbows in flour. Two very small and beautiful children were sitting on a braided rug, playing with cooking utensils and a cocoa can. A carry-cot on a small chest wobbled from its occupant's motion. Kieron Thornton's handiwork was obvious in the cupboards, the table and banquette benches, the shelving by the cooking range.

Ann Purdee and I stared at each other, and I was somehow embarrassed. She seemed surprised and apprehensive.

"I'm so sorry to bother you," I said, and tried to back us out.

"Don't *go*!" She hurriedly dusted her hands. Then Snow saw the children and started to squeal with compliments, demanding of Ann if the children minded strangers, could she play with them, weren't they gorgeous, and what a lovely kitchen, was it bread she was baking? Real Irish brown bread?

Snow's exuberance is infectious, and Ann Purdee's initial shock dissolved.

"We have come at a bad time, Snow . . ."

"To be sure, you're always welcome here, Mrs. Teasey." The emphasis was unmistakable.

I couldn't help wondering who *wasn't* welcome. However, it wasn't something I could ask Ann Purdee . . . yet.

"Please don't stop what you're doing," I said, for she'd been about to wash her hands, and that bread still required kneading. "We only dropped in because . . . I mean . . ."

"What Mother's stumbling over is that we want to gossip a bit with you. No one tells us anything!" Snow rolled her eyes in exaggeration and then beamed at the small child she'd placed in her lap. "What's her name?"

"Fiona."

"Such magnificent eyes! See, Mom?"

Simon and I had taken places at the table. I nodded vigorous approval.

"What was it you wanted to know?" Ann asked me, pounding the dough expertly.

"For starters," Snow began, seeing me floundering again, "the accident Aunt Irene had, the one that ended her career — why did it make her give up singing?"

Of all the questions in the world that we could have asked, that was evidently the one Ann least expected, for her hands poised a long moment above the dough. She also looked relieved.

"It was a terrible thing that, and would have been no bother to anyone but your auntie. She was hit by splinters of glass from a shattering window."

"But there's no mark on her face."

"She protected her face like, and her eyes with her arms. They were scarred, but the splinters pierced her throat."

"Her vocal cords!" I cried, and my hand went to my throat protectingly. I had that awful stomach-sinking of utter regret. "How awful for her!"

Ann shrugged. "She *said* it was as well. She'd had the best of the cream, and had no fancy to do character roles."

"Did she ever make recordings?" asked Snow.

"I believe so, but she'd none in the house, nor player."

"By preference?" I could see that it would be easier to give up music altogether.

"I 'spect so. She never did mention the matter."

"Did any of her relatives visit her often?"

Ann's expression became angry. "Neither of her sisters bothered their barneys about her until the solicitor phoned to say she was in hospital. Then they flocked up the lane like . . ."

"Vultures?" Snow suggested helpfully when Ann faltered.

"Yes. And when . . . she died . . . why, they'd've stripped the house and turned—" She stopped, snapping her teeth closed over what she'd been about to say. But I heard it. "' . . . turned us out.'" Why on earth would Ann Purdee be considered an undesirable tenant?

"But you and Kieron had hidden the silver by then, hadn't you?" Snow was asking.

There were defiant tears in Ann's eyes, which she blinked away furiously. "She'd told us over and over that we were to hide it all from the tax people. Just as well. Had *they* ever seen it . . ."

"None of her relatives were ever in the house to see the silver?" I asked that so very innocently that Simon gave me an odd look.

"No, I couldn't say that. There were several came around often . . ."

"Which ones?"

Ann Purdee looked at me sternly. "I'm in no state to cast stones." She sighed, and gave the bread a punch.

"Well, then," said Snow, her resigned voice at variance with the grin she was giving the child she held, "we have to enter the Maginnis den without knowing friend from foe."

"Maginnis?" Ann was startled enough so that all the color left her face. "Mrs. Robert Maginnis?"

"None other, in her best bib and knit suit," said Snow. "Commanding us to tea on Sunday at *her* house."

"She was here?" Ann could not absorb the information.

"And has gone," Simon put in, "with a grinding of gears."

"Oh!" All the life had drained out of her.

I went on briskly. "Mrs. Maginnis—I cannot for the life of me bring myself to call her Auntie Imelda—"

At my exasperated tone, Ann seemed to pull herself together.

"Whoever named *her*?" Snow wanted to know.

"She can't drive worth a dime," Simon added, sensing what we were trying to do.

"At any rate, she seems to think that I'll oust my perfectly good tenants on her say-so because I'm in Ireland now and the men in the family will tell me how to go on."

Snow hooted with derision, and then Simon leaped to his feet and advanced ominously toward Ann. "So, my gel, behave with me!" He twirled an imaginary moustache and leered down at her, until she had to smile. "I'm the *man* in *this* family, you know."

"You are not to worry over what Mrs. Maginnis may say, Ann Purdee."

"'My, you're well grown for fourteen,'" said my irrepressible daughter in Mrs. Maginnis's bright accent, "'Twins? How intrusting!'" She went on, although she accidentally slipped into the role of Lady Bracknell discussing handbags and railway stations, but she had Ann Purdee actually laughing, getting her face all floury when she raised her hand to cover her mouth.

I decided we had said enough on that subject and rose. "The other thing was, did someone dispose of my aunt's old letters and correspondence?"

"She told me to burn all her letters. She made me promise I would . . ."

"Oh, please don't misunderstand me, Mrs. Purdee. We just noticed the absence of letters in the desk. We were looking for the family bible." I didn't want her to think we were pawing through my aunt's things.

"She'd burned a great lot herself when she recovered from the first stroke, you see. Said she didn't want anyone laughing at her mementoes."

"I'll bet Great-great's mail would have made fab reading," said Snow.

I reprimanded her, but Ann Purdee smiled and went on

shaping the loaves, slapping them negligently on the baking tray before she deftly sliced the tops with a heavy knife.

"I'll be bold American — may I buy a loaf from you when they're done?"

"Sure, and I'm baking one with your name on for welcome!"

"Wow!" came from Snow and Simon.

"C'mon, kids," and I signaled them. "We've got a lot to do, and so does Mrs. Purdee."

Ann didn't try to stop us, so I knew my guess was accurate. Snow pleaded to stay with the babies and keep them out of Ann's way, but I insisted on her coming with me. Ann Purdee was a well-organized body, and I'd bet her children kept out of her way, young as they were, until she had time for them. Just as we were about to leave, I heard the sleepy cry of a young child upstairs, so I hurried my twins out the door. When Ann Purdee realized that we were going to walk down the front of the cottage row, she — almost frantically — suggested that it was shorter the way we had come.

"I thought I'd see if I could meet the other tenants," I explained. "Which one is Lark?"

"Ah, oh, the end one, but Mary'd be at work. And no one else is at home either."

I wondered why she was apprehensive, but the child cried again and Ann just closed the kitchen door.

"Great-great only said Swallow and Lark cottages should stay, and I can see why the others could go," Snow said, pointing to the litter in front of the one immediately to the right of Ann's.

The back seats of two cars, stuffing coming out through the rents in the upholstery fabric, were propped up against the wall, under the two dirty windows. Muddy bottles crowded the windowsills; cracked pots held dead branches and assortments of rusty tools and shredded paintbrushes. Propping up one end of a wooden bench were several rusty, corroded gallon paint buckets. The only door was bare of paint in places. I wasn't very happy with the appearance, and wondered how Aunt Irene had let the tenant get away with such slovenliness. Although I knocked on the door, I hoped that no one was in.

"Hey, Mom, we gotta do something about this," Simon said, and I agreed. "Maybe this is who Auntie Imelda meant as 'those' tenants . . ."

"Nonsense, I distinctly remember she said *all* the cottages," said Snow.

"Well, their days here are numbered," I said, glaring at the disreputable place.

The next cottage was not as bad, although the tenant was still no great shakes as a householder. I knocked on the door and was surprised to hear a querulous voice telling me to go away.

"It's Irene Teasey, your landlady. I'd like to speak to you."

"Who?" The voice was terror-stricken. "Who? Go away! For the love of God, go away!" And I caught fragments of a feverish recited prayer litany. "Go away!"

"Well!"

"No sale there, Mom. I'd better try next time," said Simon. "They may think you're Aunt Irene back to haunt them!"

"If I were, I would."

The last cottage was more in the style of Ann Purdee's, with two doors, but there was sufficient evidence of order to reassure me that Lark cottage would suffer no change of occupant. No one was at home.

"So much for making like a landlady," said Snow. "C'mon, I'm hungry."

"You just had breakfast."

"If breakfast is over, can lunch be far away? I can't wait to taste Mrs. Purdee's bread!"

When we got into the house, Simon elected to see if Irish chopped meat (minced steak?) made suitable American burgers. Snow volunteered to do the french fries, and I could just see myself getting hog-fat and wondered if I cared.

Suddenly there was an unmerciful pounding at the front door, and a loud and abusive shouting for me to open the door.

"Now just a living minute!" Simon roared back. He pushed me out of the way and jerked open the front door. "Who the hell do you think you are using such language?"

Simon doesn't look fourteen, and Teddie's training had given him a good deal of self-assurance beyond that chronological age. He's also a responsible young man, and considers himself the man of our house. He has never used vulgar language in my presence, though I've heard him curse in Teddie's best manner when Sim thought I wasn't within hearing distance.

"And who the hell might you be?" asked the big, flame-faced man belligerently poised on my threshold, sizing up my son.

"I'm Simon Stanford. What's your business here?"

"I want to know who's been frightening the hell out of my old mother. What kind of people are you to frighten an old woman with ghosts? What business have you here in the first place? Where's the bitch who's playing that fucking trick on my poor mammy?"

"No trick was played on your mother," I said, coming to the door.

The man's eyes bugged out at the sound of my voice, and he turned very pale. "Who are you?" he demanded in a hoarse whisper.

"I'm Irene Teasey."

"You're not!" He said it emphatically, denying my existence with a wild wave of his arms. He took two steps backward, stumbling against the potted plants as I stepped beside Simon.

"I most certainly am Irene Teasey. My great-aunt willed me this property, and I only called at your cottage to introduce myself. I'm not a ghost, and I don't go about frightening people. Besides, Mrs. Purdee—"

"Her!" and the color flooded back into his now contemptuous face. "We've no dealings with the likes of them two." He stepped forward now, leaning toward me with a confidential air. He reeked of beer and cigarette smoke. "You wouldn't, a'course, know about *them* yet. But you'd do well to turf her out of that cottage and put in decent folk. I was on to your great-auntie about it many's the time. I don't want me old mammy having to—"

"My great-aunt specifically requested me to keep the tenant of Swallow cottage," I said, and had the satisfaction of knowing that he caught my emphasis.

He gave me a slit-eyed look. He had a mean mouth, I thought and tried not to glance at his hands. What I saw of his stained jacket, dirty sweater, and oily tie were sufficient character references.

"Truth be known, missus, your auntie wasn't all that right in the head after her first attack. Aye, that's the truth of the matter." He jerked his chin to his chest two or three times to give weight to his statement. "I can see you're a respectable lady and all, and you shouldn't associate with that lot."

"Mr. . . . ?"

"Slaney's the name, missus. Tom Slaney."

"Will you please explain to your mother, Mr. Slaney, how sorry I am that I caused her a moment's alarm? I only wanted to get to know her."

His eyes, which had been wandering over me, came back to my face, and his whole body was still a moment. Then he relaxed and began to smirk.

"Sure now, and you won't be staying on any longer an' you sell the place? With all them wanting it so?"

"Mr. Slaney, I've made no plans at all. Now, if you'll excuse me, my lunch is ready."

He touched his forehead. "Sure'n I'm only home meself fer me dinner."

There was more he wanted to add, but I closed the door firmly.

"He's something, isn't he, Mom? Did you hear his language?"

"All too clearly." I gave my son a big hug, very grateful for his presence and his size. If I'd been there on my own, I doubt that I'd have had an easy time with Mr. Tom Slaney.

After lunch, we were poring over the map to see where we would wander that afternoon when the phone rang. It was Mr. Noonan.

"It's kind of you to ring, and I'm glad you did, because something else has come up," I said. After he'd confirmed having all the business correspondence and records, I went on. "That Brian Kelley character was back again, offering twenty-five thousand pounds for the entire place. He intimated that if I didn't accept his offer . . ."

"You did mention that the will had not yet been probated and you couldn't sell?"

"Yes, and he intimated that probate wouldn't occur unless I did accept the offer."

"Oh, did he so?"

"He did! Can he?"

"Ah, it is possible to delay probate," he finally said, slowly. "But two can play at that game, Mrs. Teasey. Not to worry."

"With someone like Mr. Kelley, I do."

He chuckled, but the sound wasn't as reassuring as I'd have liked. Still, I did trust Michael Noonan.

"I'd also like to know who my tenants are, besides Ann Purdee. And she's paid me the rent direct. What about the others?"

"Ah yes, Mrs. Teasey."

"Oh dear." His tone clearly said "problem."

"Not to worry. Something can be done about them, you know."

"I hope so. Two of the cottages look as if pigs live there."

"Slaneys and Faheys."

"I don't know about Faheys, but I've met Tom Slaney." I gave the solicitor the details.

"Good Lord!" And then Mr. Noonan began to laugh. He'd a very nice one, rich and deep. "To be truthful, Mrs. Teasey, you do sound extraordinarily like your great-aunt. You startled my receptionist out of her wits, so it's easy to see the effect you'd have, knocking up Mrs. Slaney. The poor ol' thing's half-witted as it is."

"You mean, my aunt tolerated *him* for her sake?"

"He made himself bloody scarce while your aunt was alive."

"Well, can you contrive to make him bloody scarce again? What are the Faheys like?" I'd better get all the bad news at once.

"The trouble with them is more absence than presence. Your aunt had initiated proceedings to have the cottage returned to her, but she died and the matter was not pursued. You've met Ann Purdee?"

"Yes. Now, she's charming. And she gave us the silver and the carburetor."

"Silver? Silver? I don't know anything about any silver,

Mrs. Teasey." That's what he said, but the laugh in his voice indicated that that was only his official position.

"Slaney's not very complimentary about 'the likes of her.'"

"Slaney wouldn't be," and Noonan's voice turned hard. "Also, his mother is five months in arrears on the rent."

"He looks the type to drink up every cent in the house."

"You can do something about him. But I think we'd better arrange a meeting so that you understand the entire position."

"Oh dear, problems!"

"Not really, Mrs. Teasey. And the tenants of Lark are absolutely reliable. The Cuniffs, a mother and daughter. No worry there."

"Two out of four isn't a good batting average."

"I beg your pardon?"

"An Americanism, I'm sorry."

"Would tomorrow, Friday, at half twelve be convenient?"

"I've nothing planned. Yes."

"Fair enough. See you then."

 7

SINCE I'D BE SEEING Noonan tomorrow, we decided to leave Trinity College viewing until the next day and fare south by road now.

We were just piling into the Renault when a squat and stolid black Morris Minor pulled past the gate. So we piled out and intercepted a dumpy, short woman whose faded features nevertheless bore a familial resemblance to Imelda Maginnis. For the life of me, I couldn't remember this one's name.

"She's the Alice, I'll bet," Snow told me sotto voce, and then assumed her little-girl-innocent pose.

Just as the aunt saw us, another woman came through the gate, turning around and craning her neck in such a way as to suggest that this was her first visit here, and something more.

"May I help you?" I inquired.

Both women stopped, mouths dropping open, and stared

at me. I sighed. This was getting to be the stock reaction to me, or at least to the sound of my voice.

"You're Michael's child."

"Grandchild. And you'd be my Aunt Alice."

Thanks to Snow's memory, the identification was accurate. Ignorance would have been tantamount to insult to one of Alice's nature.

"Of course I am." She didn't introduce the other woman, who seemed accustomed to such treatment — or should I know who she was? Aunt Alice also didn't offer to shake hands, or, fortunately, to kiss me. She stood on the pathway, we on the grass — a demilitarized zone, as Simon later styled it.

"We were just about to leave . . ."

"Dublin?" Hope livened Great-aunt Alice's faded features.

"No," said Snow, all surprise. "Sightseeing."

Aunt Alice's lips pursed. "We *had* expected that you would get in touch with us."

"Oh?"

"We didn't know your address, and there are so many Hegartys in the phone book," said my clever daughter.

That was not quite enough justification to suit Aunt Alice's sense of self-consequence. That anyone should fail to know the address of chief relatives was unthinkable.

"*We* [there was never a more regal pronoun] have arranged a family gathering on Sunday, at teatime, so that you can meet with your cousins and get proper advice."

I couldn't resist the temptation. "Proper advice on what?"

"Why, the arrangements that must be made for this!" She gestured with contempt at the house and land. "It wouldn't do to leave the house unoccupied while probate is pending. Tinkers! I think it's possible that Jimmy and Maeve here might move in. They need a large house." So that was the unidentified quality to Mouse-face's look: seeing if she liked the house her mother had promised her.

Snow was having some sort of spasm beside me. I think Simon had kicked her.

"And once those . . . those . . . persons are turfed out of the cottages, I don't doubt but what you'd get a decent return from the properties instead of the pittance that satisfied Irene. Certainly you could realize enough to pay the rates until you can sell up."

"Sell up?"

"Well, you'll have to sell up to pay the death duties." Then my dear great-aunt stopped and stared hard at me. "I suppose that *you* could pay that out-of-pocket and never miss it."

"No, I couldn't pay those death duties out-of-pocket and not miss it. I don't know why you should think all Americans have gold mines."

"Michael did very well in America. Everyone knows that."

"My grandfather's business is none of mine."

She sniffed and crossed her hands — oh dear, they were paws — at her waist, as if girding her loins for another attack.

"You'd be well advised to listen to what the men have to say to you on Sunday. Property values being what they are, you'd do well to take the first decent offer you get."

"I have to wait until probate . . ."

"So you do, but if, for instance, Jimmy made you an offer on the place, it being in the family and all, the details could be worked out to everyone's satisfaction."

The last person I'd sell my house to was vacant-eyed mousy Maeve.

"So far, my solicitor has been quite capable of advising me, though you're very kind."

"That young man is too bold by half," said my great-aunt, so firmly that I suspected she'd run up against Michael Noonan's unrufflable intelligence already. "These are *your* children?" she continued.

"No one else's."

She snorted at my flippancy as I performed the introductions. She gave another snort but made no attempt to introduce Maeve properly.

"And you'll need someone very keen to break that ridiculous Brandel trust! Well, you're to be collected Sunday afternoon. Be sure you're ready at half four sharp."

She wheeled, made a peremptory gesture to the shadow Maeve, and was gone before I could get breath enough to say that I found I had other arrangements for Sunday. And what was the Brandel trust anyway, that I should break it? I'd forgotten to ask Michael. Oh, well, I was seeing that bold young man tomorrow.

"Wow!" was Simon's heartfelt response. "With relatives like that, who needs enemies?"

"That poor Maeve," said Snow.

"Poor Maeve nothing!" replied Simon. "She's panting to get into our house."

"Well, she won't!" I said definitively.

The time we got as far as the turn into the . . . my lane. And the car was an Austin, which was hurriedly braked, as much to avoid ramming us as because the driver was in a flap to stop us.

"Oh, wait, please wait!" the woman cried, and raced around her car to me. "Please, I know my sister-in-law was just here. I saw her car in the lane and pulled out of sight till she'd gone. I'm Winnie Teasey, your uncle Richard's widow. And please, please, do say you'll come Sunday? I'd be glad to collect you. No, Bob is to do that. I've wanted so to meet you. You *are* Irene Stanford, aren't you?" And suddenly the flustered woman was blushing with additional confusion. There was something very appealing and sweet about her disorganization. One had the urge to reassure her at all costs.

"Yes, I'm Irene, and I'm very pleased to meet you."

"Oh, Alice has been *that* way." Her face contorted with distress. "I knew it. You see, she'd been certain that it would all come to her, being the oldest surviving sister like, and she'd already decided that Maeve and Jimmy must have the Lodge, and Tom and Michael would have the row cottages, and Betty the big end one. Oh dear, I probably shouldn't have said that, but you'd find out soon enough *any*how. But I mean, Alice has very *good* qualities . . . she's a pillar of the church, it's just that *tact* was never her long suit, and she gives such a different impression than she should." She paused long enough to take a breath, and seemed to notice Snow beside me for the first time. Then Simon.

"Are you Sara? And that must be Simon. How clever of you to have twins. And how charming you are! And only fourteen? My, whatever do you feed your children to make them so big? Now please don't let Alice put you off coming this Sunday. There are so many of us who *want* to make your acquaintance that you can simply ignore her and talk to us. And Tom — that's Alice's husband — doesn't let her run on so when he's about. But we all want to meet Michael's children. Not that I knew Michael, you understand . . ."

In a way, Winnie was as overwhelming as her sister-in-law.

"Michael'd left before Beebee — that's what Richard was called — married me."

"I'll be truthful, Aunt Winnie, I never heard anything about my Irish relatives, except that I had some, until Aunt Irene left me her queendom."

Winnie's still pretty face illuminated in a rather astonishing way, showing us that she must have been a lovely young woman.

"Irene's queendom!" Tears filled her eyes. "She was such a good person. So understanding of people's problems. And I *told* them that Irene was quite right in the head when she made you her heiress, for I can just *imagine* what would have happened had she chosen any one of us. I mean to say, it would have been just desperate. If only Beebee had been alive!" She sighed. "Oh dear, there I go on, but I did *try* to get out early before Alice was likely to come."

"Auntie Imelda beat Auntie Alice," said Snow in a sweet voice that dripped acid.

Winnie's mouth opened in an "oh" of surprise. "Imelda's been here?"

"Between you and me, Aunt Winnie," my daughter went on before I could answer, "there's not much to choose between 'em."

"Oh, there is, there is!" Winnie was plainly upset that both sisters-in-law had had the jump on her. "Oh dear, oh dear, and really they're not *like* that."

"Money's involved," remarked Snow in a knowing tone.

"Oh, and you couldn't be more right. How clever you are. Oh, but please do come. I've a granddaughter, just your age, not nearly as pretty, and a grandson, *my* Betty's oldest, who's Simon's age. I suppose you're wild about motorbikes too?"

She couldn't have uttered wiser words to change Simon's mind about going to the tea.

"And don't ever tell Alice's Betty, but her second boy has a motorbike. He hides it in a friend's shed." Aunt Winnie said this as if she were certain Alice's ears were still tuned to the happenings on Swann's Lane. "So please *do* come."

"We'll come, Aunt Winnie. I promise."

Her relief was so intense that tears started in her eyes again. "Oh, you are good. Just like dear Irene. I miss her so much. Now I must run. I've these things to give Ann for the children. Such darlings!"

She dragged clothing out of the back of the Austin, and, with her arms full, she paused once more by the window. "Ann's related, too, you know."

Before I could ask how, why, when, where, because I was quite delighted to claim a relationship with Ann Purdee, Winnie was off down the lane at a shamble-run.

"Well, will surprises never cease!" said Snow, grinning with delight.

"Mom, get the hell outa here before someone else descends on us," said Simon in a long-suffering tone of voice.

We did.

8

"YOUR POSITION is somewhat difficult in this, Mrs. Teasey," Michael Noonan said as he began riffling through a bulky file of papers. "In September of last year, the elder Mr. Fahey informed your aunt that he was relinquishing the cottage, but he did not hand over the key. Your aunt telephoned him at his new address, and he said he'd mail it to her, only he never did so. By then George Boardman had offered her three thousand pounds.

"After your aunt suffered the first stroke, she asked me to press Fahey for the key. He again refused, saying . . ." Mr. Noonan cleared his throat and gave us an expurgated edition of the saying. ". . . He'd changed his mind and would keep the cottage as a summer residence. Legally he is not entitled to do so, since he is a veteran, living now in veterans' housing, and he can't hold two properties at once."

"Can't you evict people here in Ireland for non-payment of rent?" asked Snow.

"But of course you can. However, Fahey has paid the rent on the cottage until September. The amount is twelve pounds per annum."

"Twelve pounds? And Great-great was offered three thousand?" Snow's practical mind rebelled.

"In addition, he is claiming the amount that he had paid out for a new roof."

"To be blunt about it, is he by any chance blackmailing us for a lump sum, after which he'd quit?" I asked.

"That's about the size of it."

"Don't let him get away with it, Mom. The way they've left the place, they ought to pay *us* to get out of the lease."

"Slaney's is worse," said Snow.

"But Slaney is not the leaseholder," Michael Noonan explained. "His mother is. And the rent has been overdue since Tom Slaney returned."

"Since he returned?"

"He's a thoroughly bad lot, drinks heavily, is out of work more often than he's in, but his mother was Miss Teasey's cook until she became too feeble. Then she stayed on in the cottage."

"Aunt Irene said nothing about keeping on the tenant in that cottage," I said.

"Not surprising. Old Mrs. Slaney was very ill last winter, and not expected to last. Of course, you can do as you wish. Actually, it might be a blessing to put the old lady in an old-people's home, out of the reach of her son."

"I'd have to think about that," I said, feeling Ugly American.

"The Cuniffs in Lark are no problem. The rent is paid monthly by banker's order into your aunt's account, and there's never been a lapse."

"How much do they pay?" asked Snow.

"Seven pounds a month."

"That's still not much against a purchase price of three

thousand pounds. You'd get more interest with your money in a savings account. Or would you?"

"Good heavens, Snow. What will Mr. Noonan think?"

"That Americans raise their children to be practical, Mrs. Teasey," he replied, with a twinkle in his eyes. "She's right, you know. The rents are absurd, due partly to the Rent Control Act and partly to your aunt, who had her own reasons."

"Which she didn't vouchsafe to us, and no one else will tell us."

"As soon as the will has been probated, you can sell any of those cottages and let the new owner worry about eviction. And as for Brian Kelley, that may be all wind and stuff. He even badgered your great-aunt when she was in hospital—until T'ornton"—he dropped h's too—"turfed him out."

"Mr. Noonan, in my situation, about which none of the relatives are happy, could probate be contested? Aside from Brian Kelley's threats, I mean."

Reluctantly he conceded that it could.

"Because I've been getting clues."

"We've been inundated by elderly disapproving auntie relatives," explained Snow, with complete disgust.

Michael Noonan's expressive lips twitched, suggesting that he knew exactly whom she meant.

"We've been commanded to a family tea on Sunday, at half past four," my daughter continued. "It seems we've cousins our ages." She sounded so thoroughly bored that Michael Noonan did chuckle.

"Well, Mr. Noonan? I've already had broad hints that, when I go back to the States, Jimmy and Maeve might be willing to caretake the house for me, or buy it, and that once 'those' tenants have been chucked out of the cottages, decent rents might be earned. And they know tenants who are desirable, respectable, and solvent."

"We do things a little differently in Ireland, Mrs. Teasey."

"I've been apprised of that fact too."

"Please. I can appreciate how uncomfortable it could be for you but, as my client, you should be aware that there is a very good chance that one or another of your great-aunt's relatives may decide to contest the will formally—unless you'd be willing to *seem* to give them what they want until probate has been secured."

"I gather they think I have to sell it to pay the death duties, so they're counting on my accepting a very low offer."

Michael Noonan chuckled again as he leaned forward across his desk in a decisive manner. "Fair enough. Give them no indication to the contrary. The trust fund is *not* public information. And if they become too insistent, refer them to me."

I sighed. Snow, however, gave one of her giggles, and then composed her face into a mask oddly resembling her Great-great-auntie Alice.

" 'That young man is too bold by half!' " she said, in such an excellent imitation that Mr. Noonan roared with laughter. "You've met her!"

"I'm just no good at dissembling, Mr. Noonan," I said, worried.

"Ah, Mom, it'll be fun stringing them along. You let me and Simon handle it."

Our solicitor cleared his throat.

"Yeah, yeah, I know," Snow went on, "children are seen and not heard in Ireland, but *that's* an advantage."

"*Mom*?" said Simon in that "she's off again" tone.

"Oh, Sim, we'll *help* Mother. I mean, you don't want Auntie Alice's Maeve in our house, do you?"

"Actually, Mrs. Teasey, simply say that you can do nothing until the will is probated."

However, I saw Michael Noonan and my conniving daughter exchange understanding glances.

"Naw, Mom, just slide away from the question," said Simon, making the proper gesture with his hand. "You do *that* very well."

I knew what he meant, and I *could* evade very well. Teddie had taught me how, but I didn't want to discuss that any more.

"Mr. Noonan, there was mention in the will of the Brandel trust."

"That's the one Great-great-auntie Alice wants you to break," said Snow to me.

"She couldn't an' she wanted to, Miss Stanford," said Michael Noonan, the sharpness in his tone directed against Aunt

Alice. "The Ladies Brandel are sisters, very old friends of your great-aunt's," and it was patent that he thought them charming. "They're well into their nineties, and as spry as sparrows. Both have their eyesight and hearing, and although they walk slowly, they still get about under their own steam."

"They're not relatives?" asked Snow, hopefully but suspiciously.

"Not at all!" He rocked back and forth in his chair. "No, they're devotees of Gilbert and Sullivan. I believe that they encouraged your aunt when she was first considering a stage career. I know that she always sent them tickets to the Rath-mines-Rathgar G-and-S shows, said they'd been going since Gilbert first met Sullivan. For them *not* to see their annual operettas would mean that the end of the world had at last come. Irene Teasey inaugurated the trust under my father. I believe she discovered that they were existing on the produce of their garden patch and tinned cat food."

"But—but—" Snow was sputtering with indignation. "What about welfare?"

"The Brandel Ladies dispensed charity, Miss Stanford, they didn't receive it." You could see that he was repeating someone else's gently intoned dictum.

"But old-age assistance isn't charity."

"In their book, the same thing." He gave a very gentle shudder at such a degrading notion. Mr. Noonan was unfolding as a very interesting personality. "Such Old World principles are very much alive in Ireland, Miss Stanford. There's never a winter goes by but some elderly person is discovered dead of starvation, too proud to appeal to the agencies set up to help."

"And my aunt helped?" I asked.

"Subtly. She unearthed a distant cousin. That was necessary, because there's nothing stupid about the Ladies Maud and Mary Brandel."

"It would be Maud and Mary," said Snow, with an appreciative giggle. "And are they really 'ladies'?"

"Oh, indeed they are. They consulted the family bible," Mr. Noonan continued, "to see if there was indeed a Robert Esquith Brandel. Of course, there was, because Irene had done her research first. He had just died. Without a will, too. So Irene Teasey and my father connived to set up a fund, allegedly the estate of this deceased cousin. The monies came from several sources, actually, all masterminded by Miss Teasey: benefit performances, their legal old-age pension, which my father applied for without their knowledge, and some"—he gave that sly grin again—"windfalls which Miss Teasey contributed."

"And they've never caught on?" asked Snow. "I like that. I think I'd've loved my Great-great-aunt Irene, Mother."

"Me too."

"It is a grave shame you never met," said Mr. Noonan, and then rattled his papers as if he'd said too much.

"Can we meet the Brandels?" I asked, as much to rescue him as to divert my returned sense of guilt.

"I do wish you would. In fact, you should, as you now administer the trust. However, you must never reveal that."

"Will Aunt Alice spill the beans?" asked Snow, horrified.

"I'm inclined to doubt that she is received by the Ladies Brandel," said Mr. Noonan blandly. "Miss Teasey, of course, had the excuse of long acquaintanceship and a mutual interest in G and S."

"Mother sang G and S in the States," said Snow with the air of one springing a tremendous surprise.

"Yes, I know."

"You do?" Snow was utterly downed.

"Miss Teasey told me. And, as her heiress and also some-one keen on G and S, it would be quite normal for you to pay them a call. Incidentally, the G and S Society here is very good. They give a season every year in December."

"Mom, think of the effect if Irene Teasey appeared again." Snow's eyes went round in anticipation of the reaction.

"For mercy's sake, Snow, we won't *be* here in December. But, Mr. Noonan, suppose they do contest the will . . ."

"Let's worry about that if they do, Mrs. Teasey." Just then his phone rang. "Yes, please, tell them I'll be with them short-ly." He turned back to me. "They might try to contest the will, but succeeding is another matter entirely."

"How long would probate take?"

"A month or two more, with luck."

"Good heavens. That long?"

"In Ireland, the only thing that moves quickly is the weather." He shook my hand, very warmly, and Snow's, with a grin, and Simon's, man-to-man. "Don't hesitate to ring me if you've anything else that puzzles you about the way we do things in Ireland."

"Where do the Ladies Brandel live?" asked Simon.

Mr. Noonan grinned. "In Stepaside, in a cottage called Innisfree. It's rose-covered, with a blue gate set in a yew hedge." There followed a rather complicated set of directions, ending with the usual "You can't miss it."

I could and did. As Simon pointed out the third time we retraced the route, if we'd been walking we'd've seen the neat little gate, but in a car, zip, turn your head, and you're past.

One of the Ladies was in the garden, weeding the roses, and the other quickly appeared from the house. They were undeniably twins: Lady Maud the elder, we were soon apprised. They were tiny, coming no higher than Snow's shoulder, with bright faces, smooth-skinned despite their advanced years, and sparkling eyes that twinkled young. Their welcome, when they discovered our identity (indeed, once the twins appeared, they seemed to assume who we must be), was ecstatic.

"But, my dear, I nearly fainted when I heard your voice . . . that dear familiar tone . . ." I think it was Lady Maud—yes, Lady Maud had been weeding . . .

"So like dear Irene's. How extraordinary!" Lady Mary chimed in, her voice slightly deeper than her sister's. "That's why I *rushed* to the door. Because, although we *know* dear Irene has passed on," and there was a delicate dab at her eyes, "you sounded so like her . . . The heart does hope . . ."

"We do miss her visits so much . . ."

Nothing would do but that we come in and take a cup of tea.

"One only needs the excuse, my dears, and I've done my chore for the day," said Lady Maud, briskly stripping off her gardening gloves and placing them neatly in the wicker basket with her tools. "If you'd just drop these in the potting shed, dear," and she handed the basket to Simon, who trotted off. "On the bench, dear boy," she called after him, then beamed at me. "Such a nice child. So kind, so handsome."

I caught Snow's eyes as we entered, for I had a feeling of Brobdingnagian trespass into another era, a wonderland. Everything in the room was scaled to the size of its residents, from the diminutive Victorian sofa and chairs to the slightly lower tables with their exquisite pieces of Dresden china and silver ornaments. Even the fireplace was miniature.

As one, Snow and I moved to the sofa, which looked sturdier than the delicate chairs. A miniature Empire clock daintily chimed the half-hour. Before I could summon up a reason not to partake of their hospitality, Lady Mary and Lady Maud had each brought out a small tray, one with tea accouterments, the other with plates of bread and butter (sliced by the millimeter), fruitcake, and tiny iced lady cakes.

Simon loomed massively in the doorway and instinctively seemed to fold up his large and manly frame. I didn't know how to warn him tactfully from the delicate furniture but then Lady Maud was having him clear one small table for the tea and place another on her right for the goodies.

Lady Maud smiled her thanks. "Such a nicely mannered young man, you must be very proud of him, Mrs. Teasey — or do we still address you as 'Mrs. Stanford'?"

"Don't you remember, Maud dear? Young Irene *resumed* her maiden name," said Lady Mary, her smile approving. "Remember how *thrilled* Irene was. *Such* a compliment, my dear, you've no *idea* how *gratified* Irene was that you wanted to be Irene *Teasey* again." Lady Mary spoke with a lilting quality.

"It's almost as if — if you'll pardon me, dear Mrs. Teasey — Queen Irene is dead! Long live Queen Irene!" Lady Maud's tiny hand was raised in a regal gesture.

"Long live the queen on her queendom!" cried Simon and Snow with outrageous spontaneity, and the Sisters Brandel applauded, their small hands pattering.

"Irene was overjoyed, my dear," said Lady Maud, her lovely eyes swimming with unshed tears, "to think that you too would occupy her queendom."

"I'm actually very humble and embarrassed, Lady

Maud," I said, because I'd become increasingly uncomfortable in the midst of this gentle jubilation. "I mean, I'd never even met my great-aunt. And for her to leave me everything . . ."

"To whom else would she leave her queendom?" they demanded in indignant duet.

"To those grasping sisters?" asked Lady Maud.

"Or *their* namby-pamby daughters?" Lady Mary was appalled.

"Now, Mary, there's that quite charming child . . ."

"*She's* a granddaughter."

"Of course, how could I forget . . ."

"When you've seen as many generations as you must have," said Snow, "it must be awfully difficult to keep them straight."

The two ladies beamed at my daughter; then Lady Mary leaned over and patted one of the long black curls.

"Snow White — how very, very like the illustrations in our nursery books, so many years ago."

Snow was startled. "How did you know my nickname?"

"Oh, my dear child, we *know* so *much* about you." Lady Mary's twinkle now included Simon. "So to speak, we are *very* close despite only *meeting* today. Twins are *that* way, you *must* know."

Then all four of them began one of those disjointed dialogues in what I had long ago termed "twin short-speech." For a bit I was totally ignored, and pleased to be.

"My dear, if you had to be burdened with children," said Lady Maud, "at least you managed the felicity of twins. In our day it was a shocking breech of etiquette for any well-born lady to produce twins."

"*Nanny* was mortified," said Lady Mary.

"Not half as much as Papa," added Lady Maud, and there was a dry, almost harsh quality to her voice. She turned to me. "You must never reproach yourself, my dear, over the terms of Irene's will. Ah, I see it has worried you."

"I had no idea of her intentions."

"*She* didn't intend that *you* should, my dear Irene . . . if I may . . ." Lady Mary picked up the conversation, laying a gentle hand on mine for permission to address me familiarly. "She wanted it to be such a *surprise*. A *welcome* surprise. Your being *another* Irene Teasey, your children, not to *mention* the fact that you *too* had sung Gilbert and Sullivan operettas, *all* and *every single* one of these considerations served to reinforce her sense of the fitness of her bequest."

"She'd never the least intention of any other course," said Lady Maud, "once you were named for her."

"That far back?" I was astounded. "But the will—"

"Pshaw!" said Lady Maud. "More tea, dear?" she asked Simon, who held out his cup.

"Irene *gave* them *all* a chance," said Lady Mary, uncharacteristically stern. "*Such* a *commotion* when *she* went on the *stage*!"

"More of a commotion when she refused to live with any of them after the accident . . ."

"With *each* of the sisters *certain* that *all* Irene *could* do was mind *their* children . . ."

"She accepted our hospitality," said Lady Maud, "when she first returned from England." An expression of intense sorrow robbed her face of all youthfulness and joy. "Her voice"—a hand gestured with ineffable, graceful regret—"was gone."

"Yet we *never* heard a single *word* of complaint for what she had so *tragically, needlessly* lost. That's *why* it was such a *reviving* thought to her that *you* also *sang* Gilbert and Sullivan."

"It was as if," Lady Maud said, pausing dramatically, "her voice had not been lost, merely passed on."

"But you see, Lady Maud, I didn't even know she was a singer."

"It was in your blood, my dear Irene. You couldn't deny the promptings of your inheritance any more than you should now deny the rightfulness of inheriting."

"I see you've a phonograph, Lady Maud," said Simon quickly.

I hadn't noticed one, and followed his glance to the shadow on the far wall: a horned, crank-type gramophone.

Lady Mary bounced to her feet. "*Indeed* we do. And *we've all* Irene's records! She was *so* generous to us in that *respect*."

"Could we hear one? Please?" begged Snow.

"Certainly," said Lady Maud, airily gesturing her permission. "It's so nice to have someone who can wind it, for, truth to tell, the spring is much too tight for either of us any more."

Simon was on his feet, carefully picking his way past the small-scale furniture, like a giant in a doll's house.

"What is your favorite?" Lady Maud asked me courteously.

"My favorite of Mother's is 'Poor Wandr'ing One,'" said Snow, and when I hastily agreed, Lady Mary told Simon where to find that album. (Afterward Simon told me that the Ladies Brandel's 78 albums would make a collector flip his wig. "Mom, they had Caruso imprints worth a fortune!")

He found the right side of the heavy old record, which he handled with awed care, where Frederick is entreating "one whose homely face and bad complection/have caused all hope to disappear/of ever winning man's affection."

"Not one!"

"Not one?" pleads Frederick.

"Yes, one," and I gasped with shock at the voice. What one hears of one's own voice differs from what others hear out in front. I'd thought I was accustomed enough to hearing my recorded voice. And there was "I" singing as I had always wanted to. For, to be utterly candid, I simply hadn't the training or the great natural voice that my great-aunt had had. I could hear the difference.

I recovered enough from the shock to smile reassuringly at the delighted ladies.

"I *knew* you'd be *amazed* that you *sound* so *much* alike!" said Lady Mary in a hoarse whisper.

"Do listen, Mary dear," said Lady Maud with gentle reproach.

Talk about infatuation with the sound of one's own voice! I only wished it *were* my voice.

They insisted that we hear the rest of the first act. And there was more tea in our cups, and more bread and butter, until I worried that we might be eating the dear ladies out of house and home. I hadn't a clue how fat the trust fund was, but at one point Snow leaped to answer the kettle's summons, and on her return caught my anxious eye and reassured me. I made a mental note to find out the exact details from Mr. Noonan.

These ladies must be preserved as long as possible, although they seemed to be doing a good job by themselves.

With considerable reluctance, we made our adieus at six o'clock.

 9

I FELT RELIEVED about the circumstances of my inheritance. The good Ladies had reasserted Kieron's valid reasons for Aunt Irene's decision, eccentric as they seemed to me and unfair in the eyes of her disappointed relatives.

Irene Teasey had dared to be what she wanted—a singer when such a profession was not *quite* respectable—she'd made money doing so (which was construed in some oblique way to be wrong in the eyes of her conventional family), and she had managed—despite her femininity—to have invested it so wisely that she was now condemned for the success of that perspicacity. That figured, as Simon would say.

To add insult to injury, she had left her so much despised and unexpectedly valuable property outside the immediate family. The gesture was not so much of spite as a wish to continue the tradition of her independent spirit with the only one of her relatives (me?) whom she felt qualified to ascend. Well, she had earned the right to dispose of her possessions any way she chose. And she had chosen me.

I would go on Sunday to the relative tea and observe. I would nod, smile, and ooze (as Snow said) from any commitments. I'd see if I could spot those of the younger generation whom Irene had wanted to assist. I was beginning to comprehend why she hadn't named them . . . with specimens like Imelda and Alice looming large and rapacious on the horizon.

Yes, we'd do the pretty on Sunday and then forget about the whole kit and caboodle. We'd tour until the probate was accomplished, and get home in time for the twins' school opening. We'd've had a relatively inexpensive holiday. I'd half decided not to sell the queendom—at least not this year. I could rent the main house and have Ann and Kieron keep their eyes open—even make Ann my agent, with a small stipend to ease her situation. Such fun I'd have in Westfield, talking about my Irish holdings. And Teddie would be livid at my luck. (Preserve the Image!) I did want to evict the Faheys, and I would see if I liked George Boardman and could make a deal with him. I wanted to meet the Cuniffs, and I'd better brief Simon and Snow and have *them* speak with old Mrs. Slaney.

Really, the similarity between our singing voices was uncanny, I'd *have* to try to find copies of those recordings. Of course, I wouldn't actually say they were of *my* voice . . . and while I thought that, I could feel the temptation to perform welling up. Ah, well! If only I *could* sing like that . . . And, at thirty-six, I was far too old to be a G and S ingenue.

"Hey, Mom! Mom!"

Simon's voice jerked me out of my reverie.

"Telephone. For you."

"Who?"

"It's safe. It's Shamus Kerrigan."

I had been bombarded with so many new impressions that day that I had to stop a moment and think who might Shamus Kerrigan be. Then I hurriedly took the phone.

He was a smoothie! My half-formed notion to evade his invitation was neatly spiked. He said that if I were still game enough to be seen in his company, he'd collect us at half ten, and that we should bring raincoats just in case the weather blessed us.

"Which in Ireland is a certainty," he added with a laugh, and then rang off before I could demur.

"You were going to cancel," said Simon in a very stern mood.

I gulped. "Well, yes. Because he's just one more complication on top of the relatives."

"Ah, Mom, cool it! He won't bother you about the lane. I'm sure of it."

I knew that he had no way of substantiating that opinion except that he would will Shay Kerrigan not to.

"Well, even if he does, it won't get him anywhere until after probate."

"Then why are you looking under the K's in the phone book?"

"Well, that won't do me any good anyhow, there are too many S. Kerrigans," I said, closing the book with a *sssshlap*. "I yearn to see a Schwartz or Chang in the phone book."

"Too many damned Irishmen, huh?" said Simon, grinning, and he put his arms around me. "Now don't you worry, Mother."

"You're so good to me, Simon!"

He gave a self-deprecating snort and a quick, awkward kiss.

"I'm hungry. Bread and butter is *not* enough."

"You know, so am I."

"Maybe that's what's wrong with you. I'll peel the spuds."

I was fixing cabbage with caraway seeds when I heard Snow babbling away in her luring tone of voice. "Good Lord, who's she found?" I asked Simon.

He looked up from peeling his spuds and shrugged his shoulders. Then Snow appeared in the back door.

"Mother," she called in the "highbred" tone she can affect, "you'll never guess who's surfaced."

"Really, I am intruding," said a very male, deliciously baritone voice, and then my darling daughter was hauling a complete stranger into the room.

I've always been fascinated by prematurely silver hair, which is apparently a Celtic trait. Snow's victim had a head of wavy, shiningly silver hair, set off by very black eyebrows and a gorgeously trimmed black-and-silver handlebar moustache. He was laughing as she dragged him into the kitchen, reluctant to intrude.

"Oh no, you're not. We've been wanting to meet you. Mother, this is the man who wants to buy the cottage."

"Oh, good Lord, Sara . . ."

"I told you, young lady, that I didn't think this was the time to intrude, and I still think so. If you'll excuse me, Mrs. Teasey . . ."

"No, please, Mr. Boardman . . ."

"No, please, Mrs. Teasey," and his eyes were bright with

amusement. "I've the habit of looking in on Horseface of a Friday evening, and your charming daughter apprehended me."

"He's *hunted* Horseface." There was no quelling Snow. "*And* he sings Gilbert and Sullivan!"

The upshot of that was that George Boardman, who was as nice as his looks, joined us for supper. He reassured Snow that twenty was far from being decrepit in a horse and that he had indeed hunted the beast last year, albeit a fairly quiet hunt, but that Horseface had a good few years in him, in which Snow could learn how to ride. He'd become acquainted with my great-aunt when she'd still been active in the Rathmines & Rathgar Gilbert & Sullivan Society. He was forced by Snow to admit that he'd sung with them—still sang with them, for that matter. I wasn't surprised—his speaking voice hinted at musicality.

"She coached me," he said, warmly reminiscent, "in Covent Garden's best fashion, and she was superb! How she could imitate a baritone!" He laughed at some outrageous memory. "It's such a shame that you never met."

"Now, Mother," said Simon, patting my hand. "Cut it out. Mother feels guilty."

"She oughtn't," replied George Boardman flatly. "Irene was pleased as punch to have a relative who sang G and S. Those sisters of hers never saw her on stage, and they'd the gall to criticize her for it. No, don't you worry your head over inheriting. Just follow in Irene's footsteps. Her loss is sorely felt."

I thought he was hinting at something, but Snow interrupted the flow of the feeling.

"You want to buy one of the cottages, don't you?" She said it more than asked.

George Boardman glanced quickly from her to me.

"Aunt Irene said you did," Snow went on. "Well, don't you? Mother wants to get the Slaneys and the Faheys out."

"You're a bold miss for sure," he said, not altogether approvingly.

"Snow has a good practical head on her shoulders, if little tact," I said, seeing my daughter's flush. "She's not jumping the gun, because I have already asked Mr. Noonan to find out if you still want to buy. Aunt Irene left me a letter, and I should like to comply with her instructions."

Ah, that was it. He knew about the letter.

"Of course," I went on, "there's all this business about probate, but Mr. Noonan said that possibly you'd buy now and pay later on a caretaker basis."

"I'd like to buy on any terms you think best."

"Even with the place as big a mess as it looks?" asked Snow.

He gave her another long look, and she flushed again, subsiding into the chair. I saw Simon give George Boardman a look of intense respect. Simon, poor dear, often felt at a loss as to how to handle two women at once.

"The place has tremendous potential, Mrs. Teasey."

"Rene, please."

He smiled wryly. "It seems odd to hear such a request in that voice. You do realize that you and your great-aunt sound fantastically alike."

"Yes. I seem to have scared poor old Mrs. Slaney into thinking I was the ghost of Irene Teasey."

He sat up, startled. "Yes, you would. The poor old thing. Have you reassured her?"

"More or less," said Simon. "Her son—"

"Tom Slaney's about?" For some reason this irritated George. "I'll look in on her myself. Poor old wight."

"Wouldn't she be better off in an old-people's home?" I asked hopefully. I'd already had doubts about putting out any tenant Aunt Irene had favored.

"She'd certainly be safer, and her bit of money wouldn't be spent on drink..." but I could tell George Boardman didn't really think I should evict the poor old lady.

There followed one of those awkward pauses, which Simon broke by remarking that we'd heard the Ladies Brandel's recordings of Irene.

"Aren't they pets?" George said, his face lighting up with a smile of extraordinary delight. "I was going to suggest that you visit them. Which album did you hear?"

"*Pirates.*"

"I say, did you ever sing Mabel?"

"Yes."

"'I am a pirate king . . .'" he sang, and he had a very good rich baritone. With his looks, he'd've made a fine Pirate King.

We got a trifle off the subject of his buying the cottage with a discussion of which roles he and I had sung. We ended up singing snitches and snatches of arias and choruses. I hadn't sung in so long that my voice tightened up quickly, but if he noticed, he gave no sign. Then too, Simon and Snow know as much G & S as I, and so we were all singing away, fairly shouting out the Policeman's Chorus.

"You've got to audition this fall for the Society," he said. "I'd give anything to see their faces when Irene Teasey appears on stage!"

"Oh, but we're only here to settle the estate," I said.

"Oh, I hadn't realized. Then you'll be selling up?"

"Oh, no. Just the cottage to you. I'll probably get a good tenant for the house here."

"You're not selling anything else?" He was very intent.

"Oh, no."

"I think Mother's getting used to the notion of a queendom of her own," said Simon teasingly.

"Mother's stubborn too," said Snow, unaffectedly this time. "Too many people want her to sell."

"Oh?" And George Boardman very much wanted to know who.

"You wouldn't happen to know of a Brian Kelley?" I asked.

"Indeed I do. Kieron usually bounces him off the place as soon as he shows up."

"Kieron can't play my watchdog all the time," I said, a little glumly, because I didn't want to run into Tom Slaney again.

"Not to worry. Slaney comes floating in about the first of the month, gets fluttered, and ends up in the nick."

"Make an edict, Queen Irene," said Snow with a giggle. "No Slaneys, Kelleys, and bulldozers welcome here!"

"Bulldozers?"

"Yes," said Simon before I could, "we warned off a bulldozer our first day here. Do you know a guy named Shamus Kerrigan?"

George was very serious as he looked toward me. "I know Shay Kerrigan very well. So did your great-aunt. In fact, he bought that property because she'd give him access up this lane."

"What?" we all said in chorus.

"But—but—in her letter to Mother she said *not* to give Shamus Kerrigan access to the lane."

"*Was* he going to put ticky-tacky boxes on that land?" asked Snow, rather more aggressively than need be.

"No, he most certainly was not, because I'm his architect and I won't design that sort of house." George Boardman was equally adamant.

"That's a relief!" said Snow, heaving an appropriate sigh.

"Your great-aunt knew of our intention," George said to me. "That's why her sudden reversal was such a surprise. I tried to speak about it, and she wouldn't even hear Shay's name. Then she had those strokes, and neither of us cared to pursue the matter. Shay's about shelved the whole project." George looked at me thoughtfully. "I suppose that's why it's such a relief to know she'd still let me have the cottage. Frankly, I was beginning to think we were both in her black book, and neither of us could figure out why." He rose. "I really must be going now. I've an engagement."

While it was a relief to me to have him go after that unfortunate turn of conversation, we all tried to make him feel that his return would be very welcome. He assured me that we'd see a lot of him, one way or another.

 10

THE CURRAGH was a topologically astonishing area, and the "soft" air (that means very fine misty drizzle) lent it an additional mystery. We had come down an ordinary road which wound through typical small Irish towns, and were thrust onto a smooth, rolling plain, a vast prospect, at first seeming to flow limitlessly into the mist-obscured distance.

The "softness" of the day was lifting, giving deceptive prominence to sheep grazing at the top of the next rise, so that they stood in bold relief against the brightening sky, looking much larger than they actually were. To our right was the distant raceground of the Curragh, also limned bigger than actual size.

"This is where the high kings of Ireland used to hold chariot races," said Jimmy Kerrigan, Shay's engagingly personable nephew. "You get out here early enough and you can see them training the race horses."

Shay Kerrigan had arrived on our lane only fifteen minutes late, charming and rather overpoweringly attractive in an Arran sweater, matching cap, old corduroys, and heavy boots. His slightly built nephew, a dark curly-haired lad with traces of his uncle's charm in his smile, was also regulation-Arran-sweatered, wearing bell bottom pants of which Snow and Simon instantly approved. Jimmy's fascination with Snow was patent, but his readiness to align himself with Simon against her became apparent in the first exchanges. Jimmy had been as apprehensive about meeting Snow and Simon as they had been about him, but all shyness dissolved with an adroit comment or two by Shay. The three hadn't stopped talking since we'd left Dublin proper and headed southwest toward Naas and Kildare.

I had entertained the hope that Kieron Thornton and Ann Purdee might not be abroad when Shay Kerrigan picked us up. I did not want to disrupt the fragile friendships developing by appearing to associate with a man who'd been in my aunt's black book. George Boardman had indicated that Shay had once enjoyed her favor, and I was consumed with curiosity to discover why he had fallen from grace.

However, Rene's Law came crashingly into operation: In short, anything that could go wrong did. No sooner was Shay Kerrigan's Jag driving up the lane than Kieron Thornton emerged from his cottage.

To confound me further, Kieron waved cheerfully at Shay, who hollered a greeting back. Both were smiling in the friendliest fashion. I had no chance to comment, what with the bustle of introductions and settling us in the Jag. Shay was deftly turning the Jag when Ann Purdee, astride her bicycle, came whizzing down from the cottages. I had a glimpse of her startled, even fearful expression, and then we were away. The fat, fer sure, was in the fire.

Fortunately, the children were babbling away at such a rate that my silence wasn't—I hoped—noticeable. I managed to smile amiably and made any responses in monosyllables. Kerrigan must have seen Ann Purdee—he'd swerved to give her clearance, but his expression had been "driver concentration" rather than concern. Oh well, I'd have to explain later. Right now I was determined to enjoy the day. The twins were in such good spirits. And as a passenger I'd get to see some sights, instead of just road signs.

Shay Kerrigan was a considerate driver. To my relief, he was not the sort of driver who keeps up a running commentary on, or swears under his breath at, the erratic movements of other drivers. He just drove, handling the big Jag easily. He did, it's true, jam down the gas pedal on the big double highway beyond Clondalkin, but that was a road engineered for speed, and it was fun to sail along. I could relax with such driving.

The twins had embarked on one of their duet stories, and Jimmy was utterly entranced, looking from one to the other (he sat between them on the bump) as the twins switched the story-ball. Before Simon's voice changed, you couldn't tell which one was speaking, a circumstance which had disconcerted their father to the point of fury. But then, Teddie hated anyone interrupting him and, I supposed, thought everyone had the same dislike. I don't think the twins even noticed who said what in their favorite stories.

"Do you two always carry on like this?" asked Jimmy when he'd stopped laughing over the punch line.

"Like what?" asked Simon, all innocence.

"Like that. One saying half a sentence and the other the other."

The two shrugged together. "We're twins, you know."

"Yes, but that's not going on forever, is it?" said Jimmy.

"Look at Lady Maud and Lady Mary," said Shay, glancing in the rear-view mirror at his passengers.

"Do you know *them*?" asked the twins in concert.

"Of course," replied Jimmy with a "doesn't everyone?" look. "Uncle Shay's their chauffeur for all state occasions."

I don't know which of us three was the most startled.

"Have *you* met them?" asked Jimmy.

"Yes," said Simon with, I thought, admirable sang-froid. "Took tea with them yesterday."

"They're a gas, aren't they? Do you know *why* they live in a teeny cottage like that? They used to live in a castle."

"No, why?" Snow was dying to find out.

"Well, Lady Maud got betrothed"—Jimmy stumbled a bit on the archaic term—"to a chap she didn't like. Her father did it. Fathers could when *they* were young . . ." Jimmy made the good Ladies centuries old. "And she refused to marry away from her sister. So he disowned her. And Lady Mary walked out too. They bought that little cottage, and they've lived there ever since. They used to have more money, and a huge old touring car, and a gardener and a maid, but Mum says that was before the war. And they used to be invited to all the big balls and official functions, because they were related to Queen Victoria somehow or other. That was before the war too." Then Jimmy stopped, as if he'd been about to say something he wasn't certain he could discuss.

"The Brandel trust stops only with their deaths, Jimmy. I told you that," said Shay Kerrigan. "Apart from that, Jimmy-lad, I believe that this Irene Teasey isn't the sort of person who would disobey her great-aunt's last wishes." He took his eyes from the road long enough to give me a very cryptic look. "Would you?"

"No one can revoke it. It continues."

"You just bet it does," Simon said emphatically.

"If *we* had to eat cat food, they'd eat meat," finished Snow. "Aren't they terrific? I mean, fairy godmothers should look like them, so dainty and so valiant. They're unique."

We were entering the Curragh now, and fell silent with wonder. Sheep grazed by the unfenced road, nibbling so disastrously close to the flow of traffic that I gasped a couple of times. Jimmy regaled us with the near misses they'd had. True, Shay slowed the car and wore a very alert expression. Then he turned off the road and we went beyond the rolling ground into very rough country. We came around a bend, and there were twenty or thirty cars, some with trailer frames, pulled up in a rough line.

"Here we are," Shay said, and a heavy motorbike varoomed an echo.

I was glad of my heavy sweater and slacks as Shay and I followed the young people toward the spot where the riders were readying their bikes. There was a chilliness in the air that seemed to ignore clothing: It felt more like autumn than nearly summer. When I recalled the stifling heat we'd had in New Jersey in early June, I resolved to enjoy all this coolth. Suddenly the sun broke through the clouds. Faces turned toward the brightness, and Shamus muttered something about it's not lasting. Which it didn't. I had no desire to complain, since we'd had good weather all week, when I'd been told to expect nothing but rain in Ireland.

I wouldn't have thought that my darling daughter knew anything about motorbikes, but she was chattering with her brother and Jimmy as if she'd osmosed pertinent knowledge from her twin's brain.

"That pair of yours is incredible, Mrs. Teasey."

"Would you make it Rene, please?"

"Rene?" Shay Kerrigan stopped being distant for a moment and actually saw me.

"Yes, that's what my family calls me. Irenes are supposed to be tall and stately."

"They are?" and the twinkle in his eyes reminded me that my Aunt Irene had not been tall.

"Well, in the States they are."

"Rene, then. Jimmy's rather odd man out in his family. Hates sports, loves to read, and he doesn't usually talk much."

We grinned at each other at the way he'd babbled on the trip.

"Simon's more introverted than Snow, but when they're both on the same wave length . . ." I raised my hands in surrender, and Shay Kerrigan chuckled.

He put a hand under my elbow to steer me across some stony footing, and I was suddenly struck by a curious observation: His gesture was protective, helpful without any of the "you're too stupid or clumsy to do it properly on your own" attitude that had marked such gestures of Teddie's.

"I brought along a picnic basket, because there's no place about that serves a quick meal. Oh, the Jockey, if you'd want several hours to enjoy the food, but the Red House doesn't do lunches any more. I hope you don't mind."

Of course I didn't, but again Shay Kerrigan's attitude was the reverse of what I'd expected; if I protested, I was sure, he would take me along to the Jockey for my lunch — no, the Irish eat dinner midday.

The picnic, as far as I was concerned, was a real feast: cold chicken and ham and sliced roast beef, three types of cake, Cokes for the kids, hot coffee from a huge thermos flask for us.

By then a huge number of spectators, mainly males of assorted ages, had gathered and a few more bikes had arrived to be tuned up. Jimmy and Shay explained the course to me, and it looked frightening. I mean, straight up rocky slopes and down steep, curving tracks that goats would have had trouble with.

And "scramble" was the operative word. My goodness, how those riders stayed aboard their bikes, I don't know. Glue, I privately suspected, but where? because half of them rode in a standing position. Maybe they had suction cups on their knees, but I'll bet they had blisters and bruises, particularly when they bounced and banged up slopes. The going down was obviously easier, and unnervingly faster. I had to close my eyes several times.

Simon and Snow cheered and scrambled from one vantage point to another. I think the spectators were more active than the riders. I noticed one group which had walkie-talkie units, with members at strategic points so that what one person missed seeing he at least heard about.

I gave up counting to see if all the contestants made each checkpoint, but, all in all, it was a stimulating way to spend an afternoon. I certainly ended the experience with a great deal more respect for motorbike riders than I'd've thought possible. Hell's Angels these people were not.

While the scramble had been going on we'd had to move about a good deal, but once the events were over I began to feel the chill.

"I say, that won't do," Shay said with real solicitude, and he immediately rounded up the young people, ignoring their pleas to speak to this racer or find out if that bike had been badly damaged.

The heater in the Jag was very effective, and I was beginning to thaw out and enjoy the countryside when we pulled into a pub parking lot.

The place was called The Hideaway, in the town of Kilcullen. The pride of the establishment was someone's desiccated, mummified arm. The man had been a renowned boxer with an extraordinary reach. (I'd rather been told than shown, but Simon and Snow were not so squeamish.) We had a few drinks and then supper, and didn't get back to our house until the sun was out of the sky—which was, I discovered to my amazement, half past ten.

"I didn't mean to impose on you for the whole day," I told Shay, rather appalled.

He had my hand in his, and his very strong fingers managed to caress as well as hold.

"Impose? Sure and you didn't," he said, sounding excessively Irish for a moment instead of well-bred English. "For all of that, it's a pleasure to see young Jim getting on so well. You'll probably have him round in the morning again. He doesn't live that far away."

"Jimmy's welcome any time," I assured his uncle. "And the morning's fine, but we've got to go to tea with those relatives."

"What?" Shay's expression was amusement and concern. "The haughty sisters?"

"They all came to invite me the other morning."

"Came here?" He was surprised.

"Yes, and I gather that was a first."

"Not for Winnie. She was here now and then."

"You know them all?"

He nodded.

"You're not distantly related to me too, are you?"

Shay threw back his head with laughter and stroked my hand reassuringly. "God love you, no."

"Then how do you know so much about them? And how come Aunt Irene wouldn't give you right of way up the lane?" I just blurted it out.

The amusement drained out of his face. "I don't know, Rene. We were good friends until just before her stroke. I don't know what happened to turn her so against me. At first I thought it was the aftereffects of the stroke. Jasus, I bought the land up there only because I thought we could work out a deal about the access. And then . . ." He made a disappearing gesture with his fingers.

"So what are you going to do now?"

"That's for me to know and you to guess, pet." He raised my hand to his lips, and the salute was rather disconcerting. "Come along, James. I'll be on to you again during the week, Rene."

My children ranged beside me to say their farewells and give their thanks. We truly had had a marvelous day.

 11

SUNDAY STARTED OUT so peacefully that perhaps I hadn't caught up with myself by the time we got to the tea. Which was just as well, I suppose.

I awoke around eleven to hear voices below and outside: Snow's excited soprano rang clear above the others—children's voices and something male. *That* had better be Kieron Thornton. Whose children? Ann Purdee's surely weren't old enough.

"Hey, Mom, did you sleep well?" asked Simon as I appeared in the kitchen door. Jimmy Kerrigan shot to his feet.

"I hope you don't mind, Mrs. Teasey, my coming back so soon . . ."

"Good heavens, no!"

Simon was plugging in the electric kettle, and it must have been warm, because I had a steaming cup of coffee in front of me in moments.

"What is Snow up to?"

The boys grinned. "Her first riding lesson," said Simon, and I heard that he had something else, momentous, that he wasn't saying.

"Well?"

He gave Jimmy a jab in the ribs. "What did I tell you? Mom hears what I don't say." He grinned bigger. "It'll be more fun if you find out yourself."

"Simon Stanford, Sunday morning is no time for unexpected surprises. We've had quite enough for one week."

"Oh, Snow'll tell all. Soon as she claps eyes on you. First have some coffee."

Except for the Slaneys and Faheys, the resident population of my queendom was assembled at the small pasture gate. I already knew Kieron Thornton and Ann Purdee. There were two other women, one holding a small baby, the other with her hands on the shoulders of a girl about eight or nine. Snow was astride Horseface, who was bridled but not saddled, and she had one child in front, clinging to the mane, and another behind her with a death grip on Snow's already tight jeans. The old horse was walking most sedately around the pasture, his neck gracefully bowed and his tail switching in a manner that I thought indicated satisfaction. His lovely small ears were twitching back and forth to the sound of the laughing children. But he was taking his task seriously. I had the additional impression that he was placing his feet very precisely so as not to dislodge his giggling riders.

Kieron saw me first, touched Ann Purdee on the arm, and pointed in my direction. The movement caught the attention of the other two women. One smiled welcomingly; the other tried to.

Ann Purdee, as one determined to face an unpleasant task squarely, took the darker woman's arm, and they both advanced on me. Kieron angled himself as their rear guard. Or that's the impression I received.

"Oh dear, you look so solemn, Mrs. Purdee. Whatever is

the matter?" And I instantly remembered her seeing Shay Kerrigan.

"I told you," said Kieron, encouragingly cryptic.

"Mrs. Teasey, may I introduce my housemate, Sally Hanahoe."

"I'm very pleased to meet you, Mrs. Hanahoe," I said, holding out my hand.

The young woman blushed all shades, looked about to die, and then jerked her chin up bravely. "I'm not a 'Mrs.'"

I stared at her a moment, mystified, and then several matters became clear. "Those" tenants, "that lot," Aunt Irene setting up the tenants of *her* queendom as she chose, with very low rents. The baby Sally held was the little one in the carry cot, who'd been teething. I had been unconsciously wondering how Ann Purdee could have three so-young children, even in a Catholic country. And it also struck me that an unmarried girl with a baby in holy Ireland might have a very rough time of it. That accounted for Sally's defensiveness.

"Well! Well, I think you're a very brave girl to keep your baby. You must love her very much. And I think it's marvelous of you, Mrs. Purdee, to help her. Or are you related?"

"Only by trouble," said Ann in a rather grim voice. "Then you don't object?"

"To what? Why should I? Aunt Irene knew?"

"Irene knew," said Kieron, stepping forward. "She knew whom she wanted in her queendom."

"That's more or less why Molly and I are here, too," said the other woman, coming forward with her hand outstretched. She had a mature, serene face, but the lines at her mouth and her eyes spoke of deep sorrows past. "I'm Mary Cuniff and this is my daughter, Molly. I was a little luckier than Sally. I do have marriage lines, for all the good they do me." She gave Sally a cryptic smile.

"Well, I appreciate your telling me, but I can't see that it matters much—at least to me."

"What worries Ann at the moment is that you're taking tea with the relatives," Kieron said, and nodded toward Snow as his source of information.

"And? Winnie Teasey brought you clothes," I said to

Ann, "and seems to know you—" I started to ask what degree of kinship we enjoyed but Ann interrupted.

"Winnie Teasey is a good woman with a guilty conscience." Then she caught herself. "Oh, that sounds nasty, but she knows I need the clothes and all, and it makes her feel better to give them to me than to the tinkers."

I cast about for something to say to ease the dreadful bitterness in Ann Purdee's voice.

"We're well met, then, Ann, Sally, Mary. I'm scarcely in a position to cast a stone. After all, I got rid of my husband only because I'm lucky enough to live in a country where separation and divorce are possible. And where a woman can bring up a child without too much censure. Furthermore, I'm not about to undo what my Aunt Irene did without very good reason. More than just those greedy relations' opinions of you." Kieron was giving Sally a reassuring hug. "And how did you get in, Kieron? Or were you a deserted husband?" I asked, trying for a lighthearted note.

"Oh, I suspect I'm useful as a gatekeeper, chucker-out, and odd-jobs body."

"Don't believe him," said Ann sharply. "He came back to take care of his mother when his sisters turfed her out as useless. You've a collection of outcasts in your cottages, Mrs. Teasey: unwed mothers, deserted wives, and"—she flashed another look at Kieron—"layabouts. And Tom Slaney's been back again. You're not even doing that job right."

"No, I threw him out on the roadway yesterday evening. Drink-taken."

"He's only dared to be back here because he knew Irene was dead. She'd have the Gardai on him!" Ann said.

"You know, I think my great-aunt was women's lib!" I said.

Mary Cuniff laughed, a very warm contralto sound. Sally Hanahoe was first startled and then giggled, but Ann Purdee looked upset.

"No," she said slowly, thoughtfully. "She didn't like them all that much. She believed that when you had made a decision you had to stick by it. You had to accept all the responsibility for your actions and never blame anyone else. Like your mother spoiled you, or your father didn't understand, or this or that. She felt that a lot of the women's-lib movement was trying to evade responsibility by saying men put them down."

"Ann, you're simplifying it again," said Mary gently. "You know what a desperate situation we [and she meant women] have in Ireland. You know what I'm paid and what that lout Feeney gets, and I do most of his work."

"There, that's just what Irene meant."

"Girls, girls!" said Kieron. "Sure and 'tis the Sabbath! And that's not what Irene meant."

"A squeaky wheel gets oiled," said Mary, and from the look on Ann's face I thought the next argument would be launched immediately.

"Hey, Mom, look at me! I'm riding a horse!" cried my daughter as the circle Horseface had been following brought her around to where she saw me.

Dutifully, and thankfully, we all went to the fence to make appropriate comments. Ann didn't seem at all nervous that her children were in the keeping of an absolute novice.

"Don't bang so with your heels, Snow. And sit very straight. That's better. Shorten your reins. You need more contact." Ann slipped in under the rail and shortened the reins to suit herself.

Kieron stepped closer to me and said in a quiet voice, as if commenting on the lesson, "You won't be taken in by the relatives and their notions of how you should dispose of your property, now, would you?"

"You own your house, so why should you care?"

"Those girls've all had desperate hard times. They don't complain, but it would be cruel to see what they've built so carefully together destroyed by that group of biddies." He put his hand under my arm and led me away. I wondered what he'd look like without all the face fur. He had such nice eyes. He was guiding me toward the garden patch, as if we were discussing that. "You see, Ann can't work away from home. There's no one to leave the children with, and she'd lose her Deserted Wives' Allowance. Not that it's much. Sally works in the supermarket. She pays board to Ann for herself and the bahbee. Ann minds Molly for Mary, who's a cashier at the Montrose. They all look after Mrs. Slaney, who's a desperate poor creature, can barely see or walk . . ."

"Would Mrs. Slaney be better off in a home?"

"No. She knows us and all. Leave her be the while." He glanced over toward Faheys'. "But them . . ."

"Mr. Noonan's getting them out. And how does George Boardman get into this queendom?"

Kieron laughed. "Sure an' haven't you guessed yet?" His twinkling eyes enjoyed my puzzlement. "Irene was immensely practical too. Go on, give a guess."

"I can't."

"I'm the tenor . . ." And when he saw my amazement: "Ann's the soprano, Mary the alto . . ."

"And George is the baritone? But Irene's dead, why have a quartet?"

"Why not? Long winter evenings, you know. Good crack. No, now, I'm teasin'. Irene liked George, and Fahey'd turned so sour in his old age he was no more use to her at all. It's only to be nasty he's kept on there." Kieron waved at the messy garden. "So when George offered her three thousand for the place, she told Mihall to get Fahey out. I'm not here as often as Ann makes out, and there should be someone about the place. You see," and Kieron turned dead serious again, "there could be desperate trouble for Ann, and maybe Mary. We know Ann's husband's been looking for her when his ship's in. He's a right bastard, and he'd move in on her just so's she'd lose her allowance, which she would do, even if he spent only one night. And he'd beat her again."

Not if Kieron saw him first, I heard plain as day.

"Is he in Ireland?"

"No, he took the boat."

"Took the boat?"

"That's an Irish divorce," Kieron said with a bitter snort. "Fella takes the boat from Ireland to England and he can't be forced to pay support for a wife in Ireland."

"Good Lord." I wondered for a frantic moment if Teddie-boy might get some ideas. But Hank wouldn't let that happen. "They can get away with that?"

"Oh, indeed they can. The last time was two years ago,

when she was pregnant with Michael. Winnie brought her here. The big cottage had just gone vacant." He gave a wicked grin. "Never have figured out if Irene approved or disapproved of her girl graduates. But it saved Ann's life, no question."

"You're on her side?"

"Don't sound so surprised. Fair's fair. Add to that, I owe the girls a trick or two." A muscle began to jump in his cheek. "They cared for my mother until I got home."

I started to inquire about his sisters, pure curiosity on my part while Kieron was in this expansive mood, but a wild shriek interrupted me. It was only Snow, sliding off the shoulder of the horse. She wasn't hurt; in fact, she was howling with laughter as we dusted her off and hoisted her onto Horseface again. The horse dipped his soft muzzle into my hand, sort of inquiringly, and made the most endearing whicker. I patted his smooth nose encouragingly and said something affectionate. He snorted with more force.

"He likes you," said Snow, almost resentfully.

"He thinks he recognizes my voice, that's all. But I don't seem to smell right."

"You do sound much like Irene," said Ann. Then, as if she'd said too much, she turned briskly to my daughter.

The littler ones had gone off to play with Molly Cuniff. Mary wasn't anywhere in sight, but just then Kieron saw the two boys peering around the Mercedes and excused himself. That was just as well. I had quite enough to digest right now.

If Aunt Irene had wanted to protect her subjects, it was logical to choose as successor someone whose ways were not as inflexible as the relatives'. But how could she be sure I'd not be as hard-nosed? On the basis of our names? Or an interest in G & S? Good heavens! Simply because one sang G & S didn't necessarily mean one went along with their sniping at Victorian mores.

I had just turned two eggs into the plate for my belated breakfast when Snow came bouncing in, declaring that she was about to expire from starvation. She was also full of incidental information.

"Great-great didn't like men—"

"With Kieron on the property?"

" — in general," and her expression chided me for interrupting. "Particularly Irishmen. Can't be trusted. Always believe the worst of a man and you won't be disappointed." She tried to snag a piece of eggy toast from my plate until I signaled her to make her own.

"Was she crossed in love?"

Snow shrugged. "Probably, but Ann said that she'd heard that Great-great always had a lot of beaux, and turned 'em all away. Ann said it was because they were after her money, and she always said *her* money wasn't for any man to drink up. Sally's not married, didja know?" I nodded. "Mary's been here since before Molly was born. *Her* husband was a bigamist, only he wasn't because the Church annulled his first marriage. Mary knew about that, but what she didn't know was that the State didn't recognize the annulment, so now she's married only as far as the Church is concerned, not the State."

"Why doesn't she get an annulment from him because he married her under false pretenses?"

"I dunno. I suspect it costs money, and he went through most of hers and then started going with someone else and she found them in bed together — "

"Sara Virginia! They haven't been talking — "

"Heavens no, Mother. They're too square, but I can hear just as well as you what people don't say. Anyway, Mary up and left him when she was seven months gone with Molly. I mean, gee, that takes real guts. Do you know what divorce Irish-style is, Mom?" asked my all-too-precocious daughter. "Taking the boat!"

"Oh, you mean skipping to England, where the man doesn't have to pay support?"

"Oh!" That deflated Snow. "You were smart to be an American, Mom. Daddy can't do that." Her eyes widened. "Can he?"

"I don't think he could slip anything past Hank van Vliet." It was easier to reassure Snow than it was to quell that niggle of fearful worry in my own breast.

"Mommy, aren't there any nice Irishmen?"

"Heavens, yes. Look at Kieron and George and Shay and Mr. Noonan."

"Yeah! But there's something that Ann doesn't like about Shay Kerrigan."

"Ohhhh?"

"She sorta tried to find out if he'd be coming around much. I told her you weren't giving him any right of way, because you didn't want a lot of traffic and ticky-tacky boxes lousing up the queendom, and that *seemed* to be what she wanted to hear. Then Sally appeared and Ann clammed up. Did you know Ann knits Arrans like zappo, it's finished? Only the Deserted Wives people can't find out, or they'd reduce what they give her. She does get medical free, but with the price of things going up so . . . Sally's got a friend who's a fisherman, and he always brings up a sack full of fresh-caught stuff Saturdays, and Sally brings in bruised vegs and stuff from the supermarket, but, honest, Mom . . .

"So then when Ann heard we were all going to this relative tea this afternoon, she flipped. *They* had big notions of a clean sweep in this quarter before Great-great was even in the ground. And the relative who was supposed to get Ann's cottage would only sell it anyway, because she's already got a luxury-type bungalow in Cabinteely. And Ann didn't say it, but she's still scared you'll change your mind, or you'll be coerced by the death duties to sell hunks of the queendom."

Snow's vivacity suddenly drained from her face, and she looked woebegone.

"Sara Virginia, you know perfectly well I won't. Certainly not to that crowd. But we do have to put in an appearance today. Besides, there're the young people that Aunt Irene wanted to help. How're we going to know who they are if we don't go where they are?"

"I hope they're there. Unrelieved Great-aunts Alice and Imelda are indigestion-making. Ugh!" She gave an expressive shudder, but her spirits did not revive.

Nothing will make me rise to battle stations faster than the need to cheer up Snow. I hurriedly distracted her by asking how we should redecorate the kitchen. This worked like a charm, although I wasn't certain that Aunt Irene would have liked purple trim.

"Fer Pete's sake, Mother, are we always going to be

dominated by what Great-great would have wanted, done, said?"

"Well, no, of course not. I was just making—"

"Definitely." She ignored me and pivoted slowly about the room. "Purple in the kitchen, and we'll find a purple design—they *must* have contact paper in Ireland."

Simon strolled in, saying that he was hungry and were we going out to dinner or did we have to wait to stock up at the tea.

"What color do you want in your room?" Snow asked.

By the time we'd figuratively redecorated the entire house it was almost four o'clock, and we scattered to get suitably attired for the relative tea.

Robert Maginnis drove a sober black Ford Zodiac. "Not that he drove it well," Simon said later. For my own peace of mind, Robert Maginnis was a most pleasant-spoken, amiable man, with a ruddy complexion, a shock of rumpled white hair, and a very sweet manner.

"By golly," he said, "you do sound like Irene." He placed a hand under my elbow to guide me to the car. "You put quite a fright up Melly, I can tell you." I had to quell the twins with a stern eye, because his accent, not to mention his calling Imelda "Melly," made the phrases rhyme. "Hope we won't be too much for you all at one blow, like. We're a long-tailed family, we are."

Uncle Bob, as he asked to be called by the time we were halfway up the Kilternan Road, was a beef merchant, buying from farmers, fattening steers, and selling to local independent butchers. He had a chain of meat shops, but said he preferred the buying end.

"Gets me up early, like, to attend the auctions. Keeps me feeling young, y'know."

He was so affable, so jolly, so completely different from what I'd expected Aunt Imelda's husband to be that I was glad he was so talkative. I was too surprised to do more than make the proper responses.

I couldn't have found my way to the Maginnis house, and whether I'd want to find my way back there again would remain a moot point. The house was distinctive, set in its own grounds, surrounded by fields and a high stone wall. We drove into the stableyard, past nearly empty hay barns and cattle sheds, onto a flagged drive that led to the two-storied house of such varied design that I guessed amateur architects had enlarged it to suit their particular tastes.

We entered through the kitchen, which had been extended to incorporate a back room; the separating beams were a constant danger to six-footers, of whom there soon appeared to be many. There were seven people seated at the round table chatting with Aunt Imelda, who rose to greet us most effusively. Just as she was introducing me and explaining the degree of cousinship to the people at the table, Alice came barging in, two steps ahead of an anxious-faced Winnie. Winnie hovered for a moment, seemed to be reassured, and made off with the twins, whom she wanted to introduce to the younger set in the parlor. Uncle Bob was asking me what I'd like to drink. I thought tea or coffee, and there was a large guffaw from one of the men. I was then apprised that tea in Ireland does not necessarily mean the beverage tea; it can very easily—as this evening proved—be an excuse to have a party.

One of the men at the table had risen when Alice and Winnie arrived—I couldn't remember his name just then—and he took me by the shoulders and guided me to the seat next to him, rather beyond Alice's conversational arc.

"I'm your second cousin at a couple of removes, Gerry Hegarty, and you stay by me and I'll protect you," he said, with an engaging grin and the most incredible blue eyes.

"Watch out now for Gerry," said the black-moustachioed man across from me, offering me a cigarette. "I'll protect you from him."

"And who's to protect her from you?" asked Gerry as he lit my cigarette, waving aside the other man's lighter.

"My wife!"

"I'll see that my dad doesn't slip you any poteen," said Gerry with mischievous solemnity.

"What's poteen?"

"What's that she says?" Gerry repeated as if amazed. "Sure and you don't know what poteen is?"

"Mountain dew!" said the other man, rolling his eyes wildly to indicate potency.

Well, I knew what that was, so I eyed the drink set before me with suspicion. Gerry sniffed it and handed it back to me with a reassuring shake of his head.

"Safe! Weak Irish!"

Encouraged, I took a sip. "Safe?" I cried when I could speak again, wondering what form of distilled lightning I'd got.

"Stir it" was Gerry's suggestion.

I did, and took a very cautious sip. Evidently no one had stirred the mixer properly: I'd got a mouthful of pure Irish.

"You'll not be telling me this is the first drink you've had in Ireland?" Gerry asked, having watched my performance with intent curiosity.

I was framing a reply when I heard the black-moustachioed man speaking to Aunt Alice, who was leaning toward him with all the attitude of a private conversation.

"Sure and I'll have a chat with her soon's Gerry gives me the chance. Isn't that Maureen coming now?" And he pointed out the window.

With that, Aunt Alice muttered something under her breath and then flounced off — if a woman of that build and age could be said to flounce.

"What're you and Mammy cooking up there?" Gerry asked the man.

"Aunt Alice is your mother?" I was astounded, dismayed, and mortally glad I'd not had the chance to put my foot in my mouth.

"I'm her bahbee," he said draping his hands across his chest and giving me the eye, for all the world like a bashful three-year-old.

"I'm Jim Kenny," said black-moustaches beside me, "for I'm sure you'd not manage to remember all the names flung at you before. And I want to make one thing very plain to you." He glanced over his shoulder to see where Aunt Alice was. "Nothing would get me to move out of my modern, unpaid-for, centrally heated, four-bedroom house in Blackrock to a cold hillside far from the delights of town." As I stared at him, shock vying with relief, he went on. "I'm Maeve's husband, and while she's a darling girl an' all, she will get caught up in those rainbow schemes of her mother's."

"What we're trying to say," put in Gerry on my other side, "is that we know what *she's* about," and he nodded his head toward his mother, busy talking (and nodding in my direction) to two new arrivals. "And you're not to worry. Never a soft word for Irene in her life, plenty of tears at the wake, oh my yes, and a different sort of noise altogether when the will was read."

The letter! "Oh, you're the Gerry who's to have the Mercedes," I said, suddenly recalling Aunt Irene's instructions.

"Oh, no way. You're the Irene that still has the Mercedes."

"No, I'm Rene."

"Praise be! It's got so the very word 'Irene' puts any decent one of us running in the opposite direction. Seriously now, Rene, that car is a gem. Kieron did give back the carburetor, did he not?"

"Aunt Irene specifically said . . ." I can stick to the point too.

He shook his head firmly. "This is not a day, either, for repeating what Irene said . . . though God bless the woman . . ." and he tilted his glass in a quick toast, as did Jim Kenny. Were these the "young" people she'd wanted to help? "We've all been Irened to the death of us. *This* is the day to meet your cousins over the waters, chat 'em all up, and get stocious. Now, tell me how you like Ireland. How long do you plan to stay, and are those large young people really *your* children?"

I jumped at the opportunity to answer innocuous questions. (Hide *behind* the Image!) On top of my relief at discovering that these male cousins of mine were singularly unconcerned about the eccentric will of our mutual relation, I found that they were delightful company. Shortly, however (and I'd noticed the pair keeping a surreptitious eye on Aunt Alice), they maneuvered me out of the kitchen, away from her notice, and into the living room.

When I didn't see my twins among the assorted younger people — there was an incredible number of children of all sizes and descriptions — I got apprehensive, until one of the women said the twins had gone to inspect young Tom's new motorbike and wasn't the racket frightful?

It was all very pleasant but I seemed to be getting too

many refills on that drink, so I was very glad when someone asked me if I wanted a bite to eat. Gerry guided me to the dining room, where there was a turkey and a ham, sandwiches, and bread and cake and cookies. A platoon of teacups stood ready on the sideboard. I was very much in need of something to sop up all that liquor.

Snow and Simon descended on the buffet with six young people, chattering a hundred to the dozen. Snow heaped an indecent amount of food on her plate, but others had collected as much if not more. My conception of ladylike teas went through another upheaval.

Snow sidled up to me in her best conspiratorial fashion. "Boy, have I got a lot of gossip for you, Mom." Then she got snatched away by a grinning black-haired boy before she could elaborate.

No sooner had the multitude been fed and tea-ed than the table was removed and chairs pushed back. A red-haired man started to fiddle a come-all-ye, and another man hauled out an accordion.

Gerry was all for seizing me for a wild reel, but I firmly held him off and asked where the ladies room was.

"I'll take you, Mrs. Teasey," said a soft voice beside me. It was the motorcycling receptionist. She'd been waiting for a chance to get me aside, I suspected.

"I hope you don't mind, Mrs. Teasey," she said as she threw the bolt in the bathroom door behind her, "but I've been trying all the evening to get to talk to you. I wanted to explain and to thank you."

"There's nothing to explain, really," I told her, wanting very very much to use the toilet.

She turned to the mirror and began to fiddle with her hair, giving me a chance.

"You see, my grandmother . . ."

"Oh Lord, *which* one is *your* grandmother? I'm hopelessly lost with all these relations."

"My grandmother's Alice Hegarty. I'm Maureen, Tom's daughter. Brian Kelley's my father's boss. I had orders to let him know when you got here. I had to do that, you see. I didn't want to, but my dad said I had to, and there'd be no harm done.

You do understand?" She was so pathetically conscience-stricken. "And you should've heard *them* when she died! Parceling out *her* things, her money—*if there was any.*" Her tone mimicked the original speaker. "And they were so positively *glad* to turf Ann and Mary out, you wouldn't believe!" Her eyes were sparkling with remembered outrage. She gave a sharply expelled breath, her expression both sad and cynical. "I know how people can behave, because I've been in a solicitor's office long enough, but when they're your own kin, and it was Auntie Irene . . ." Tears sparkled in her eyes, but she controlled them. "You'd better go out first, Mrs. Teasey."

"Oh, for Pete's sake, Maureen, we *are* related, please call me Rene?"

She gave me a soggy smile and nodded.

"And come see us soon at the queendom. Please? I need your help, for Aunt Irene's sake."

She agreed and I left the bathroom, much relieved on several counts. Such a sweet child. She must have been one of those my aunt had wanted to help and didn't dare: The vultures would have descended instantly.

Gerry was leaning against the hall arch, a drink in each hand. Beyond there was singing; the tune was familiar, but the words escaped me.

"C'mon, you've to do your party piece," he said, taking me by the arm and wheeling me toward the dining room. Protests availed me nothing.

My Uncle Bob was in the middle of the floor, vigorously directing the singing, his face flushed and sweaty with effort. His tenor was strong, if not precisely true; he sang with enough vivacity and enthusiasm to overcome any faults. He beckoned Gerry to lead me forth. The last thing I wanted to do was sing in front of this audience.

"No, no, I couldn't sing," I said urgently to Gerry, and held my glass up. "I'm too tight."

"Sure and what are the rest of us? What'll you sing? My dad can play anything on that squeezebox of his."

Uncle Bob seconded Gerry's insistence, and the man with the accordion obligingly came over, said he was my Uncle

Tom, and told me to sing anything I wanted in any key and he'd do his best.

Snow came running up to me. "Oh, do sing, Mommie," she said sweetly (the traitor), but the message in her eyes amounted to a royal command.

I don't like to sing cold, without a chance to warm the voice up properly. And I hadn't done any real singing, except the other night with George Boardman, in such a long time that I knew I'd sound stiff. Then I saw the faces of Imelda and Alice, politely composed to endure listening to the visiting Yankee relative whom they cordially wished to the devil. Well, I'd show them.

"Would you object to a Yank singing an Irish song?" I asked.

"Not at all," the men assured me, and the accordionist ran a few encouraging chords as a guarantee.

I told him the key, and when he looked slightly blank, I asked for a chord in B-flat, which he understood. And began to sing "Kathleen Mavourneen," which, believe me, was the only Irish song I could think of at that particular moment.

The babble courteously died. Then, as the quality of my voice became audible, I had an accurate count of which relatives had heard my aunt sing. A small gust of gasps occurred behind me, and, turning, I saw Gerry staring at me as if I'd erupted from the grave. His father gave a startled squeeze on his instrument. Uncle Bob's jaw dropped a foot. Neither sister turned a hair, their faces still polite, exhibiting merely surprise that I could sing creditably, but Winnie Teasey began to cry.

"By golly," said Uncle Bob, his eyes moist, as he pumped my hand during the applause, "you sounded exactly like Irene."

Then everyone was clamoring for more, for me to sing this song or that ballad. I had—to myself—sung well, but I wouldn't be able to sing long before lack of practice showed up in faulty breathing and projection. But I wasn't allowed to leave the floor until they had coaxed, then threatened, half a dozen songs from me. Then I got away because I simply walked out of the dining room and out of the house.

Gerry followed me. "Do you know how much you sound like Auntie Irene?"

"Did you hear her, or just the recordings?"

"Once as a small lad I heard her sing. But it's incredible. Did she know?"

"She knew I'd sung in G and S."

He gave a funny laugh. "Well, it's no wonder — the name, the voice, and all."

"Oh God, not the will again."

"Now, not to worry, Rene," and I didn't hear hypocrisy. "They've precious little to do except gossip. I told them they hadn't a chance in hell of inheriting."

"You knew . . . about me?"

"Sure, most of Irene's friends did." Gerry had a rich laugh. Then he solemnly took my hand in his. "And look you, you don't know our ways here in Ireland, so ignore the half of what you hear and discount the other fifty percent."

"What on earth do you mean?"

He jerked his head back at the house. "That lot has come up with some pretty silly notions, and they've hatched another tonight." He stroked my hand and grinned down at me. "They've decided to try to marry you into the family."

"What?"

"Not to worry, not to worry."

"Who?" I was appalled, furious, and somehow it was all hilariously funny.

"Me," he said in a squeaky voice.

"That's right, you're the widower."

All humor left his face. "Irishmen make devilish bad husbands, Rene. Never marry an Irishman. We're spoiled rotten, self-centered, and hard on a woman. Sell up, rent out, do what you like with the queendom, but don't marry here."

I felt awful suddenly, and awkward, too full of drink to cope with any more shocks, surprises, or contretemps.

"Oh, Gerry . . ."

"I'm warning you so's you'll know not to worry. I like being single again!" And he grinned in the most engaging fashion.

All I could think of was my mother sending me off to Ireland because men were men here. They certainly were, and

I began to wish that I could go off quietly somewhere and sleep, not have to be diplomatic with these incredible relatives.

"Come, pet, I'll drive you home. Can you come back in, just the minute, so's my mother won't take offense at the guest of honor's leaving so?"

"Oh, my children! I've got a pair about here somewhere..." The fresh air was not helping my wits at all, an effect which became even more noticeable when I got back into the close, hot atmosphere of the kitchen. Gerry's masterful manner—or maybe the fact that the relatives were only too happy to have him escorting me someplace—got me through the leave-taking formalities. Surprisingly, considering their dread at coming to the tea, the twins begged to stay on a bit. I was informed that someone would see them home, and then everyone was kissing me, especially the men, only it wasn't offensive, and I was saying over and over that I'd had a lovely time, and then Gerry had me out in the fresh air again and in a car and I suddenly realized that I *had* had a lovely time.

 12

THE NEXT MORNING was not a lovely time. I felt slightly ill, my mouth tasted like last winter's unaired snowboots, my feet felt bloated and too heavy, and I had the general sensation that I'd slept both too long and not enough. To compound the injuries to my person, it was raining.

I groaned.

Snow appeared in the doorway as if conjured, with a glass in one hand and a bottle in the other.

"Alka-Seltzer, Mother," she said in a neutral-nurse tone, and popped the things into the water, swirling the glass to make them dissolve faster.

"Don't! They're noisy."

"Hmm ... that bad, huh?"

She sat on the bed, and I protested.

"They didn't slip you any poteen, did they?" she asked, suddenly suspicious. "Nevil said they might try it."

"Who's Nevil?"

"A cousin, what else?" She made a face and then giggled. "He's cute. He drove me home pillion. It was tough, Mom."

"Pillion?" I roused myself, regretted it, sank into the pillow. "Oh, that's dangerous."

"Naw! Simon warned Nevil, and they followed us to pick up any pieces." Again the giggle.

"How did Simon get home?"

"He went pillion with Tommy."

"Tommy? Another cousin?"

"A*nother* cousin. *Zzzhish*, Mom, I thought we had cousins by the dozens in the States, but here it's by the gross." She let out a whistle, but I clutched her arm to stop that frightful noise. "Ooops. Sorry! Poor Mommy," and she disappeared, returning a moment later on elephantine feet. With loving concern, she placed a cool cloth on my forehead.

"Where's Simon? It's raining."

"He's talking up a storm with Tommy and Jimmy Kerrigan and Mark Howard. Now you go back to sleep!"

The seltzer made me burp, and my stomach was pacified. The rain was soporific, and I lay there, listening to the soft sound and feeling the cool on my head, and went to sleep again.

When I awoke, I felt a lot better. I heard laughter below me in the kitchen, and the sounds of pots and pans being battered about. So naturally I felt guilty about lying in bed and got up.

The kitchen was not very big, and looked much smaller with the thousand and five youngsters crowded in it, sitting on the cupboards, the woodbox, the chairs. One was perched on the fridge. They were all watching Snow make hamburgers and chips. They were all on their feet with a *thud-thud* when I entered.

"Coffee, Mother?"

"Yes, of course, darling. Did I meet all of you yesterday, or is my memory really going?"

I was introduced to Jimmy and Mark Howard, and Simon (with a laugh) and Tommy, and the long dark-haired one was a girl cousin named Betty. I'd met all except Mark Howard, who was seeing Betty.

Lunch was good fun, and by the time I'd had a hamburger and french fries I felt considerably "more better than," as Snow used to say with ungrammatical expressiveness. Snow also tipped me the news that we'd very little left to eat in the house. Betty had to get home, as she was minding her small brothers and sisters; Tommy and Jimmy wanted to take Simon with them, and it appeared the whole group had a date that evening to listen to Tommy's latest record buys. It was rather breathless, but I was relieved to think that the twins would have friends — relatives, even — with whom to enjoy their vacation.

The kitchen was all tidied before the visitors left with Simon. That's when Snow remembered the mail which had been forwarded to us from the hotel.

One was a letter from Mother, the other from Hank van Vliet. Both held basically the same tidings: Teddie was having fits about my taking the children away. He'd phoned Mother and then visited her, demanding to be told where his children were and what sort of a low bitch did she have a for a daughter.

"I took a great delight in telling my ex-son-in-law where to go, Rene," my mother wrote, her sweeping pen strokes embellished by ballpoint smears, emphasizing her annoyance, "something I've wanted to do for some time, I assure you. I phoned Hank after Teddie got off my line. I'm having no more of that kind of nonsense, I assure you. Hank is writing you, but my advice is to stay on in Ireland no matter what else you intended — at least for the summer and/or until his rage has subsided. But don't worry, you've done nothing wrong or illegal. If you have a phone number there, send it to me and Hank but give it out to none of your other friends. You know how Teddie can extract info if he wants it."

Apprehensively now, with hands shaking because the itch had (damn it) been accurate, I opened Hank's letter, and learned why Mother had enjoined me not to worry. Teddie had had an injunction issued to prevent me from "surreptitiously and without his knowledge" removing his children from the continental U.S.A. I'd left before it could be served on me.

Hank assured me that I was completely within my rights, and he was taking steps to have the injunction canceled, since both he and my mother could vouch for the fact that I had informed Teddie of my intentions. (I wished people would stop telling me not to worry, because it made me worry more.) Hank went on to tell me not to worry about any moves Teddie might make locally to try to coerce me to return to the States with the children. (Oh, good Lord, what on earth could Teddie do locally? Well, if he met up with Auntie Alice or Auntie Imelda . . . That made me laugh, because Teddie would have met his match and retired from the field with that pair.) Teddie had threatened all kinds of imprudent and impulsive actions—Hank couldn't leave me ignorant on that score—but my legal position was secure. After all, Hank could easily prove that Teddie had many times chosen not to exert his legal rights of visitation (particularly when there was a golf tournament or a weekend wingding).

I sighed as I finished this worrying don't-worry letter. "Oh dear!"

"Daddy being a dastard again, Mother?" asked Snow, peering over my shoulder at Hank's concluding paragraphs. "Hmmm. Thought as much."

"What do you mean, 'thought as much'?"

Snow shrugged. "Well, he put on such a heavy father routine that time on the phone . . ."

"What time on the phone? I didn't know your father had called you."

Again that insufferably diffident shrug. "Oh, we knew it would unnerve you, Mommy. Besides, you know how Dad can carry on, and it's only talk."

"*What* did he say?"

"Oh, some drivel about your dragging us some place completely unsuitable for *his* children, and you'd probably make us go to Mass, and oh . . . you know how Daddy goes on!"

"Why didn't you tell me?"

She gave me that round-eyed innocent look. "Because you'd've worried and worried, and we wouldn't have come to Ireland. And we wanted to come with you!"

"Is that why you two organized me out of the country so fast?"

"You said it!" Then she hugged me. "We told Hank about the call, and Gammy, and that's why—"

"Why I was on that plane before I had time to think what Ted might do."

"You got it, Mommy," she said in that I-know-best tone of voice which reminds me so much of my own mother that I tend to overlook how impudent it is in my daughter. Besides, she was correct.

"Why all of you think I'm not capable of managing my own life . . ." This protectiveness only underscored my private opinion that I *was* ineffectual.

She threw her arms about me, her lovely eyes full of remorse and repentance. "Ah, Mommy, don't look like that. You do just great as long as Daddy isn't involved. But when he is, you go all to pieces."

She took me firmly by the arm, handed me my bag and raincoat, and propelled me toward the door. "We've more important things to do right now, like get the shopping done and buy paint. Because if we're going to stay here until Dad cools off, we're not going to flip our wigs looking at this revolting decor!"

The paint cost a small fortune, what with brushes, rollers, paint cleaners, and sandpaper. But Snow took the bite out of the bill by informing me that we'd save a lot by doing the work ourselves. When I countered that it would take all summer, she pooh-poohed the notion, demanding to know how long I thought it'd take with half a dozen brush wielders.

"Which half dozen?" I asked, but knew the answer, because Snow invariably operated on the Tom Sawyer principle. A born executive, my daughter.

"Never mind, Mommy, the task is well in hand."

"That's why the sweet talk and all the hamburgers?"

She gave me a tolerant look and then smiled in her sweetest fashion. "That's how to manage a queendom. Only, Irene was her own prime minister and I just appointed myself yours. She recruited a labor force when necessary. Why not you?"

"Oh?"

"Yes, oh." Snow gave an admiring sort of snort. "She might have been philanthropic, but she was smart too. D'ya know that Ann Purdee qualifies as a lady tailor? She whipped up Irene's clothes. We know that Kieron is a first-rate carpenter. Mary Cuniff is a bookkeeper, she only cashiers because the hours are better while Molly is young, and old Mrs. Slaney was chief cook and bottle washer until she got so crippled with arthritis. Oh, Aunt Irene had her queendom, but her courtiers were carefully selected."

"What about Sally Hanahoe?"

"Typist, but she has better hours as a supermarket clerk."

So our next stop was Sally's supermarket, where I wished she could have got a commission on the tremendous total we ran up. After that large outlay of cash, a visit to the bank was necessary, to cash more travelers' checks. The bank manager was so charming and helpful (he'd known my great-aunt, of course) that I ended up opening an account—much more sensible than carrying around large amounts of cash.

As we drove back to the house, Snow let out a satisfied sigh. "Now tomorrow we should turn this heap in. It's costing us a fortune."

"Not as much as all this paint."

"Paint's an investment, Mommy, and the Mercedes runs, so why *waste* money running this?"

A very good point.

"But we have to tax the car and transfer your insurance. I don't think the American policy is good here."

"How do you know so much?" I asked my daughter.

"Oh, I asked Nevil and Mark. Your best bet for insurance is—"

"Snow?"

"Yes, Mommy?"

"Are you managing your mother?"

She gave me her most charming smile. "Me? Whatever gave you that idea?"

"You!"

The phone was ringing as we entered the house, so I couldn't continue the argument.

"Mrs. Teasey, Michael Noonan here. Would it be inconvenient for me to stop by with some papers that require your signature?"

"Not more bad news?"

"More?" There was, thank goodness, a ripple of laughter in his voice, so his tidings couldn't be all that devastating. "I don't think so. Would half seven be too late . . . or too early?"

"No, no. You do know where I am?"

Again that ripple of amusement. "I'll see you then, so."

Snow was carrying in all the paint gear, muttering under her breath about Simon never being around when you needed him, the rain, and how heavy paint was. The next thing I knew, she was all set to start work immediately in the dining room.

"Not to worry, Mommy." How quickly my daughter got acclimated in language differences. "All the paint's latex, and there's no smell. Says so on the label."

"We have to strip the wallpaper off first . . ." I hadn't the words out of my mouth before Snow had seized a loose edge and *zip*, a whole panel came flying off in her hand.

"No problem at all."

If one is going to undertake a major task like painting a large room, there are certain preliminary steps that the careful workman takes: covering furniture, moving it away from the wall, putting cloths down to protect the carpeting. We did none of those things, but somehow or other, three and a half hours later, we had a Wedgwood-green dining room, with ceiling in matching color, most of the easier-to-reach trim had been done, and we had got the groceries put away too.

"There! Now doesn't that make you feel better, Mommy?"

"I'm not so sure about ivory draperies, though . . ."

"Hey, Mom!" Simon returning from any absence manages to inquire after me in the roar of a bull calf, a summons guaranteed to pierce the unwary eardrum. "What have you gals been up to—Like, hey! Wow!" He whistled admiringly, absently giving me his customary hug and kiss. "You didn't waste much time, did you, Snow? Why didn't you wait for me? And that trim's not done."

"We left something for you, dearest brother of them all," she said, rubbing green paint into her nose. "I'm starving of the hunger."

I was too, and we had just finished when the doorbell wheezed.

"You could fix that if you felt constructive," Snow told Simon as I made for the front door.

Mr. Noonan, looking far too clean and dapper, smiled at me expectantly.

"I forgot all about you!" Not the most tactful remark to make, however honest, and I groaned. (Destroy the Image!)

He laughed and told me not to worry and what had we painted and could he see, and Snow took over while I washed paint off my arms so I wouldn't Wedgwood-green important documents. I returned to find that she had initiated an inquiry about the Mercedes, and Michael Noonan confirmed that I could apply for insurance.

"Now, as to these." He rustled papers and eyed my daughter in such a way that she took quick steps in another direction. "This is for the Trust Fund, now standing at five thousand four hundred thirty-two point thirty-four pounds. The estimated death duties are four thousand two hundred thirty pounds, give or take the odd pound and pence. As soon as probate is accomplished, you will have these funds unfrozen," and he passed me statements from the same bank I had dealt with that morning, one for a savings account, the other for the checking: a total of another nine hundred forty-five point sixty pounds.

"I can't use that until after probate?"

"That's right, but you can use the trust fund."

"And all the just debts are paid?"

He slipped another sheet in front of me. "These small accounts were settled, and of course your aunt had paid for her funeral before the event."

"Pay now, go later?" I couldn't have stopped the words had I smothered saying them, and the pair of us burst out laughing. "Oh, forgive me. It's just that—"

"Don't apologize," said Michael Noonan. "You've the same humor as your great-aunt, too. She'd've loved that. Pay now, go later. Seriously, though, Mrs. Teasey, it is an established custom here to pay for your funeral ahead of time."

Well, with £800 in a savings account and another £145-plus in a checking account, my aunt had not been hungry.

"Mr. Noonan, there's one thing that has puzzled me. There was nothing left in the cupboards when we got here . . ."

"Great Scott, Mrs. Teasey, I told Ann Purdee to clear everything out of the larder, to keep rats and suchlike out of the house."

"Oh, thank heavens."

"No, Irene Teasey never wanted for food, not with Ann and Mary Cuniff and Kieron about." His eyes screwed up with some humorous recollection. " 'Sides, she had a sort of sideline, I guess you Yanks would call it, that always guaranteed her petty cash."

"She did? What?"

He grinned but refused to answer. "Later. Now let's look at that Mercedes."

We all went out to examine our vehicle. Michael peered thoughtfully under the hood. I always suppose that men instinctively understand automobiles but apparently Michael Noonan knew doodly-squat about motors. Just then someone called from the front of the house.

"Sounds like Shay Kerrigan," said Snow, and I could have choked her. "I'll go bring him around. *He* knows from cars."

"Snow!"

"Well, she's the right of it," Michael said with a grin. "I don't. And Kerrigan does."

"You know him well?"

Michael grinned at the squeak in my voice. "You'll find that Dublin is a very small town, Mrs. Teasey, and everyone knows everyone else."

Shay greeted the solicitor as affably as if they were longtime friends. And then Kieron Thornton joined the board of experts. Some may say that the Irish will talk a thing to death before they lift a finger. Not so, or maybe it was the Mercedes. I don't care. What matters is that before I could protest, Shay and Michael were taking the tires to the nearest gas station to be filled, and had said they'd get me a proper battery until the existing one could be charged. They brought back filled tires, petrol, and a battery, and spent the next hour happily setting the car to rights, and off its blocks. And even helped me "sort out" the insurance and tax thing.

There were striking anomalies in the way Irish men treated their women, I thought, with the examples of Sally, Mary, and Ann, the blackmail tactics used against young Maureen. Yet here were three very attractive men worrying and arranging to take care of my very minor problems. Or was it just another case of minor problems being fun and the long-term monotony of marital bliss unendurable? Gerry *had* told me never to marry an Irishman. Then I found myself contrasting these men with Teddie. Depending on his mood, Teddie would have 1) assumed that I was too stupid to handle the insurance/tax/negotiations, 2) complained bitterly as he assumed the burden, or 3) sneered so at my ineptitude that, out of spite, I'd've done the job — and quaked with nervousness that I'd somehow goofed. These men made no assumption of ignorance; they were being courteous and helpful. It would have been churlish on my part to refuse their aid.

Once all the necessary documents were assembled and placed on the small hall table under the shotgun (Had I got my license for that? No? Well, that could be done when I got the Garda to sign the taxation form . . . ), Shay turned to the others and suggested that now a few jars were definitely in order.

"You lot," he said to Snow and Simon, "are all right on your own, aren't you?"

"We've our own engagement this evening," replied my daughter haughtily. Then giggled. "You get my mother in early. She's had a tiring day."

I was told to go wash the rest of the paint off my face and be quick about it. Anomalies all considered, this was a much nicer brand of male superiority than I was accustomed to, and I flew obediently up the steps to wash and change.

Mother would have been ecstatic, and Betty would have remarked drolly that that was the sort of singles club she preferred for me.

We went to a nearby pub where a blind pianist held forth ably, often singing songs of his own composition. Not that I had much time to listen to him with the good-natured teasing and talking that went on. I was ensconced on a bar stool, and the three men loomed about me. Heady stuff, and very, very good for my ego. For the first time, no Shadow-Teddie lurked in the background, casting poisonous looks if I appeared to be enjoying myself in another male's company. And this trio was outrageous. I laughed until my eyes teared and my ribs ached.

I had such a lovely evening that I actually let out a cry of disappointment when the barman called time. My three musketeers saw me home, none of them (they all declared) trusting the others to do so. It was fun until I passed the dark cottages where Ann, Sally, and Mary lived. All-that-glitters evening, I sternly reminded myself.

As I lay in bed, very tired, my mind churning with the evening's good fun, I had only a brief wakeful moment to wrestle with another anomaly: All three men appeared to like each other, so why had my aunt turned so against Shay Kerrigan?

Shamus Kerrigan was also well known, and seemingly well regarded, by the Gardai at the Cabinteely station. I was told not to worry when Shay explained about the Mercedes, the necessary yellow form was instantly produced, and the matter of the gun license would also be attended to immediately.

Shay had dropped Jimmy off at the house to help the twins prepare the living room for painting, so we chatted affably about the redecoration all the way into town.

"If you need to pick up the odd piece of furniture, the auctions here are excellent for that," said Shay.

"Oh, I'll go to a secondhand furniture dealer."

"That's what I was suggesting. They call them auction rooms here. Much more dignified."

Indeed it was. And we talked about the differences in terms and my struggle with the car-registration forms, and then he mentioned that he'd been in the States the previous year. He'd been particularly interested in building methods and restrictions. He'd been amazed to find out how much timber is used in America for building; American lumber is much better, whereas it would be horribly expensive in the States to build so exclusively out of brick and cinderblock. We talked about city planning and had a real laugh, since Dublin's appeal for me was its lack of planning, with awkward turns in the city-center streets and one-ways where they were the most inconvenient (so Shay said), I found Dublin more and more charming, so un-big-city-ish.

The insurance company occupied an old barn of a building on Wolfe Tone Street. There I ran into an unexpected difficulty in giving the proper information to the poor young clerk. About the only thing I had in order were the car's papers. Mine were all in my married name, and when I filled in the form I had to explain about now using my maiden name.

Then came the question of my husband. The clerk insisted on knowing his name, and I insisted that he didn't need it.

"Why, he doesn't even live in this country, so what good will his name do you?"

Utter confusion, and he went away to consult with a superior.

"Well, it doesn't do him any good," I told Shay. "Teddie wouldn't pay for a postage stamp I used now, much less car insurance. Though he's had the accidents, and I've never scraped a fender."

The clerk was back. "Any accidents, miss . . . oh, missus?"

"Never!"

I was so positive that he didn't belabor the point. I paid him my thirty-odd pounds, and then we had to wait about while they typed up a certificate.

"You know," Shay said as we waited, "I don't think you answered a single question according to his not-so-distant training. Obviously," and he gave an exaggerated sigh, "you Yanks exist to bemuse, confuse, and confound us poor peat farmers."

Thirty-three pounds made eighty dollars, reasonable in the light of New Jersey fees, but Shay tsked-tsked all the way to the tax bureau over the atrocious rate. To my relief, getting the car taxed was nowhere near as much of a problem, nor as expensive as I'd thought, the way he carried on.

So we drove back in triumph, taxed and insured. The Mercedes had been washed, polished, and shined in our absence, an accomplishment which brought lavish praises from us both. I insisted that Shay drive the kids in the Merc while I took the Renault back. I was glad I had listened to Snow, for the bill put a substantial dent in my dwindling cash reserves. We tried to persuade Shay to stay for lunch, but he had an engagement. Jimmy was going to help us paint.

"I don't know why you should help us," I said to him over the sandwiches we hurriedly fixed.

He flushed a little, and became engrossed in the texture of the bread.

"I'd just like to, Mrs. Teasey."

"Every free hand is gratefully accepted," said Simon, giving me the "leave it there" look.

Jimmy proved to be a slow but exceedingly careful worker. Almost too slow. As if . . . the notion crystallized in my mind . . . as if he was afraid of doing something wrong. Fortunately, Simon was also a methodical worker, while Snow tended to slapdash through things, good for the over-all effect but not for details. As Simon was quick to tell her.

"Well, I don't take all day to do a square inch," she said, flaring at her brother.

"The inch I do doesn't have to be done over," replied Simon, indicating the fireplace he was trimming.

"Well!" and I could see that Snow was taking umbrage.

"Do you help your father, Jimmy?" I asked, trying to find a neutral topic.

"My father? Oh, yes, in the garden. My dad's a keen gardener."

"You should see the greenhouses they have," Simon said. "All kinds of crazy plants and flowers—and grapes."

"Do you like gardening?" I asked Jimmy.

He finished a delicate stroke. "Well, yes."

I laughed. "The 'well yes' that means 'no.'"

"No," he said defensively. "I do. It's just that . . ."

"Just that sometimes you don't do things exactly the way your father thinks they should be done?"

Jimmy sighed with relief that I'd said it, and nodded.

"The same old story," said Snow, drawling her words out. "I guess dads are alike the world over."

They took up the comparisons game. I listened because I was hearing what Jimmy wasn't saying, and that was a situation that repeated itself all over the world too. He had three sisters and three brothers, and his father was a very busy barrister.

I began to see why Jimmy found us so fascinating: I was far more available to my children than his parents were to him, although there wasn't a hint of criticism in his comments, merely resignation to the-way-things-are. He was a fair ways toward substituting Shay as an active father-figure in place of his own. I wondered if Shay was aware of this. According to Jimmy, Uncle Shay was brilliant, always ready to listen, and quite pleased when Jimmy'd drop in unexpectedly. Uncle Shay had the keenest flat in Blackrock, with a super view of the harbor and all modern conveniences.

"Yes, but what does your uncle *do*?" Snow asked. I'd wanted to ask, so I had to stifle my surprise when Jimmy replied without reticence.

"He buys up land for development, and he's got an auctioneer's license, and he owns a pub in Monkstown and a garage in Glasthule. My father says that Uncle Shamus ought to get married and settle down." Jimmy laughed at such an outrageous future. "Uncle Shay says he'd rather stay single and act married than be married and act single, like some guys he knows."

There was rather a lot of wisdom in that statement.

"Irish men marry late," Jimmy went on. "Or they used to. My father was thirty-two before he married." Obviously that advanced age bordered decrepitude.

"How old's Uncle Shay, then?" asked Simon.

"He's thirty-five—I think. He never says, but he's the youngest in my father's family, and my next oldest uncle is thirty-eight. Mother says she wishes Shay would marry. Then her friends would leave her alone with their matchmaking." Jimmy snickered.

"I have the feeling that Irishmen don't make reliable husbands," I said, thinking of the women in the queendom.

"That's what my mother says," replied Jimmy, and then frowned, painting a few thoughtful strokes. "Though she doesn't mean my father."

We finished the living room by evening, although now the tiles around the fireplace looked dirty. Jimmy declined to stay for dinner, explaining that he ought to get home so his mother wouldn't say he was overstaying his welcome here and prevent his returning the next day.

I was frankly pretty tired by then and took a bath—not quite as hot as I liked, but we'd used some of the hot water for the dinner dishes. Snow dragged Simon off to watch her ride Horseface.

Judging by the sounds I heard as I drifted off to sleep, she'd managed to get Simon aboard the horse too.

 13

I WASN'T ALL THAT HAPPY the next morning, though. I woke early, refreshed, and lay listening to the birds warbling away, half my mind trying to match bird and sound, the other half feeling miserable about Shay Kerrigan and the access.

I didn't abuse myself with the notion that he had been so courteous because he liked my big blue eyes, or that he had fallen hopelessly in love with me at first sight. He was being attentive and helpful so that I'd weaken and give him the access. And yet . . . he was going about the process with such subtle courtliness and charm that . . .

What *had* Aunt Irene against him? Why did she rescind it? Did Michael Noonan really know and wouldn't tell? "It involves someone else's good name" had been Aunt Irene's words. Well, maybe no one except Aunt Irene and that "someone" really knew.

Did Ann Purdee know? But wouldn't tell so as not to cast any of her stones? Now maybe Mary Cuniff wasn't as reticent. She'd been fairly outspoken on Sunday. Ann had too, come to think of it. While I hated to put the kids up to doing my dirty work, Snow could weasel out a lot of information without seeming to. No! I'd best try Mary.

Just then my right hand began to itch, inconveniently in the palm. Oh Lord, what now? That was the trouble spot. I tried valiantly to keep from scratching, as if thus to ward off the foretold trouble. To divert myself, I resolutely rose. But when I was washing my face, I found myself scrubbing the facecloth into my itching palm. Oh, that would never do!

To create a diversion, I sat myself down with a cup of coffee in the living room, the un-paint-smelling, clean living room, planning how to redecorate it around the existing pieces of furniture. By the time I realized that it was getting late and dashed down to Mary's house, it was locked up tightly.

"Mary's away by half eight, you know," Ann Purdee said. She had come up from the direction of the main road, leading a sleepy-eyed, yawning little girl.

"Is that one of your daytime charges?"

" 'Tis indeed. She was asleep upstairs t'other day," and Ann smiled reassuringly down at the pretty thing, who wasn't at all sure about me. "Say hello, Meggie."

" 'Lo" came out in a whisper. Eyes cast down, the small person locked herself against Mary's leg.

"She doesn't see many people." Ann swung the girl up into her arms, at which point Meggie buried her head against Ann's neck rather than be gazed at by a stranger. "Now, now, love, that's bold. You remember Auntie Irene, don't you?"

There was a frantic denying motion of the head.

"Sure and you do, pet."

"Don't bother, Ann. She's half asleep."

Ann craned her neck toward the Slaneys' house. "You know, I've not seen the old lady in two days now."

"Is that unusual?"

"Yes, when it's as sunny as it's been. She likes to sit out in the sun."

"You don't suppose it's because I frightened her?"

"Sure now and Mary and I told her how it was on Friday, and she seemed to understand and all."

Ann went to the nearest of the dirty windows and peered in. Without a word she handed me the child, who struggled only briefly. Ann pushed at the front door, but it was locked.

"What's wrong, Ann?"

"She's there, sitting on the bed. Just staring straight on." Ann's voice had a frozen sound, and when she turned toward me her face had gone white. "I'm going for Kieron." And she was away like the wind.

Kieron came back with her, at a run. He pushed at the window frame, and the wood disintegrated around the catch with very little pressure. He took one good look inside, and we didn't need to see his face to know the answer.

"Oh no!" murmured Ann, both hands to her mouth. She began to wring her hands, tears welling in her eyes. She was one of those fortunate women who can cry without turning all red and blotchy. Kieron gathered her into his arms, and I had a sudden revelation about Mr. Kieron Thornton and Mrs. Ann Purdee. His face, when he looked toward me, reflected none of the tenderness he directed toward Ann.

"Rene, I think you'd better call the Gardai."

"Not a doctor? Or a priest?"

"It's too late for either of them."

"Oh dear!"

"No," said Ann in a muffled voice, "she'd want Father O'Rourke."

When I got to the house I discovered that I still had Meggie in my arms. Snow was coming down the stairs, so I thrust the bewildered little girl at my daughter and told her to cope.

"What's the matter? What's happened?"

My hands were shaking so that I couldn't turn the thin telephone-directory pages.

"What has happened?" demanded Snow, but she was also jigging Meggie on her knees to keep the child's pout from becoming a full-blown howling session.

"Listen and you'll learn," I said, finally finding the page with GA. "Oh God, there're so many stations . . . ah, yes . . ." I dialed the number, my fingers shaking. Why were they shaking over the death of a woman I hadn't even met? They were shaking because I felt a sense of guilt that her fear of me had been the cause of her death.

I did manage to tell the Garda what had happened, and had enough presence of mind to ask him to give me the priest's phone number. There'd be so many O'Rourke's in the phone book that, in my state, I'd never find the right one.

"Good Lord! The poor old thing," Snow said when she'd heard the salient points, and trotted herself and Meggie upstairs.

Father O'Rourke was saying Mass, but his housekeeper promised to give him the message directly he had finished and I wasn't to worry, the poor old soul had gone to the peace of the grave, thanks be to the Virgin Mary. She'd had the last rites during her bad spell in May, and Father would do the necessary, sure and he would.

That done, I stood indecisively in the hall, holding the receiver, wondering if there was anyone else one had to call in Ireland. I suppose that's why I didn't think it odd of Kieron to ask me to phone the police first. Simon came thudding down the steps, buttoning his shirt. Snow may take an inordinate delight in relieving you of all depressing details, but the bare facts were enough for my son. He went to the kitchen and returned with two glasses. He handed me one and told me to drink as he began dialing another number.

"Uncle Shay? I think you'd better get here on the double, if you can manage it. There's been some trouble." Then he put the phone down and sat me on the first step. "Now drink it, Mother. Won't do you any good in the glass."

I took a good mouthful, and the whiskey burned all the way down.

"Ann'll need one too," said Simon.

I watched the tall, broad-shouldered back of my dearly beloved son retreating from the house and mused that the young could have a lot of common sense. Or maybe at his age he still had enough sanity to act on instinct rather than conditioned social reflexes.

My stomach had stopped fluttering and there seemed to be bones in my legs again when Snow appeared, chattering away to the enchanted Meggie.

" 'Scuse me, Mom, but I think I'd better volunteer as baby-sitter." And she exited, rear door.

I didn't want to be alone, so I followed her and found Simon and Kieron standing over Ann, who was making very slow work of the whiskey. Then we heard the awful noise that emergency sirens make in this country.

"Simon, take Ann to the cottage, will you?" said Kieron. His face was bleak as he turned to me. "*You* wanted to speak to the old lady. You couldn't get an answer and asked me to investigate. Right?"

"Well, yes, but does it matter?"

"Kieron," said Simon, stepping beside me, "I'm not sure Mother's up to—"

"Your mother's a foreigner, Simon," said Kieron in a flat cold tone, "and she's the landlady, and there're other reasons. Just take Ann up to her house, and she wasn't here this morning."

Simon didn't argue and I couldn't, because the police car came up the lane as Kieron assured me he'd explain later.

I should have insisted that Kieron could very easily have played the role he was scripting for me, but there I was. Simon and Ann had disappeared into her house. However, the Gardai were so very courteous, sympathetic with my distress and confusion, eager to make all easy for me, that I didn't think beyond the immediate problem. I hadn't a clue why Ann mustn't be involved in the death of an old woman, but Kieron scotched an attempt at honesty when the Garda asked if any of the other neighbors were about.

"Mrs. Cuniff, who lives next door, is at work and her daughter at school. There's no one in the house on the other side," said Kieron.

"And what about that cottage?" the Sergeant asked, pointing his pen toward Ann's.

"Haven't seen them abroad this morning. The tenants have small children and keep very much to themselves."

Just then the Garda's partner came out of the Slaney house.

"You just opened the window, Mr. Thornton?" he asked.

"That's all."

And I knew then that Kieron knew why the police had to be called.

"She's got a hole in the side of her head you could plant your fist in."

I let out a gasp and, I think, a shriek, because Kieron and the Garda were both quick to support me to the nearest of the dilapidated car seats in front of the Faheys'.

"Now, now, not to worry, Mrs. Teasey."

"Not to worry?" I glared at the Garda. "When that poor old woman's been murdered? Why didn't you tell me that's what you saw?" I demanded of Kieron. But I could see why he didn't want Ann involved, and I wondered if she had seen that dreadful sight too.

"Now, now, no one's said that she's been murdered, missus," said the Garda rather firmly.

"With a hole in her head?" I grabbed at Kieron's hands. "I thought she'd just died of . . ." I nearly said "fright." "... Old age."

The other fellow was using the radio in the patrol car. I began having visions of my queendom jampacked with reporters and homicide people and sensation seekers. AMERICAN INVOLVED IN GHASTLY MURDER: That'd be the headline. All I had to do was inherit Aunt Irene's queendom, and instead of applying American common sense, I got it embroiled in a murder case.

"Have you seen Tom Slaney about?" Kieron was asking, in a very conversational tone, I thought, for the circumstances.

"He's back, is he?" and the Garda was very alert.

"I turfed him onto the road the other night," said Kieron.

The Garda turned to the man on the car radio. "Find out if Tom Slaney's in the nick," and then he moved off toward the car.

"If it is murder, we can't keep Ann out of the picture," I said softly to Kieron. "They'll be on to just everyone."

"We can try," said Kieron back to me, softly but fiercely. "Her husband's in town, looking for her. He can't find her. He mustn't find her."

"Can't you explain?"

"I—Now what the hell is he doing here?" exclaimed Kieron, and I saw Shay's blue Jag careening up the lane. It slithered to a tire-slicing stop right by the black Gardai car.

"Simon called him."

"Simon is being—" and Kieron shut his mouth.

"If you please, sir," the first Garda said, stepping in front of Shay Kerrigan.

"And if I don't please, Sean? Now that's a rich one. Mrs.

Teasey phoned me to come by. She said there was some trouble."

Garda Sean began to clear his throat, but that hesitation was sufficient for Shay to slip by him and come to me.

"Old Mrs. Slaney's dead," Kieron began.

"With a hole in her head," I finished, and then dissolved in horror at the rhyme.

"Kerrigan, take Rene up to the house. This is too much of a shock for her."

"Ann?" asked Shay very quietly. He and Kieron stared at each other for a long moment.

"Rene found her," Kieron said in measured tones, and Shay inclined his head understandingly.

"Paddy's back in town, I'd heard," he said. "And this is where I can help, Thornton. Won't be a minute, Rene," he went on, as if a snap of the fingers was all he, Shamus Kerrigan, needed to set things right. He went over to Sean the Garda and began talking in a low voice. The policeman nodded, seemingly acquiescing. Shay wasn't a moment when he came back to say, "If they have to take a statement, they'll diddle the name. But likely it's Tom hit his mum once too often. He's been up for that before now, you know. Irene didn't let him get away with anything."

"Reporters?" I asked.

Shay grinned as if I were missing the obvious. "And this a private lane and all? Thornton, do you have something we can put across the entrance? And you can mount guard, once the Gardai leave." Then Shay pulled me gently to my feet and started me toward the house.

"Where're your children?"

"With Ann. Oh, we'll have to warn Sally."

"Sally?"

"Yes, Sally Hanahoe. She lives with Ann, and Ann takes care of her baby while she works."

"What?" Shay began to laugh. "Not another one in the queendom."

"What do you mean?"

"You might say that Irene made a specialty of deserted mothers and children." He wasn't mocking.

"Aren't there any agencies to help unwed mothers?"

"Sally's unwed to boot? Poor kid. Yes, there are nursing homes that take such girls," and his face and eyes were hard. "And make them feel like pariahs. Has anyone told Mary?"

"I don't think—"

"Call the Hotel Montrose. But first I want to give Michael Noonan a shout." He steered me in through the kitchen, pausing to plug in the electric kettle, and then marched me through to the telephone.

"Why Michael?"

"He's the one Simon ought to have called. Not me."

"Oh dear, I am sorry, Shay. Involving you in my problems when I can't . . ."

"Not to worry, Rene. Promise? Actually, I'm flattered that Simon thought of me." He dialed as he spoke. "I like that boy very much. They're both good youngsters. Hello, there, Noonan, there's been some trouble . . ."

Michael said he'd be out as soon as possible and I wasn't to say anything more until he got there.

Just as Shay started to dial another number, Sean the Garda appeared, very courteously, at the front door. "Here, Rene," said Shay, handing me the phone, "tell Mary . . ."

Mary was shocked and very upset.

"They think it was her son," I told her.

"I shouldn't wonder."

"Did you hear anything, Mary?"

"No. The walls are very thick between the two houses, thanks be to God. Oh, I ought to have called in. I knew he'd been drinking . . . on her bit of pension money, like as not. If only I'd gone over when I hadn't seen her out in the sun . . ."

"I think, perhaps, Mary, it's as well that I found her."

Mary's sharp intake of breath was confirmation enough. "They'll be on to me, I suppose, living next door."

"Michael Noonan's coming out. I'll ask what we should do and say."

"Rene, Ann's name mustn't get into the papers."

"We're doing something about that, Mary. Shay spoke to Sean the Garda."

She had to ring off. I phoned the supermarket to warn Sally.

Like Mary, she was horrified at the idea of Paddy Purdee's being able to find Ann. I explained that Michael Noonan would soon be around to advise us, and that Kieron and Simon would be watchdogs. But as I hung up the phone, I realized that I was by no means as reassured as I sounded, and fervently wished that somehow they could get Tom Slaney to admit he'd done it . . . horrible though it was to think . . . so that there'd be no fuss at all over the poor woman's death. I heard the kettle imperiously rattling its lid, and absently made coffee for myself.

Simon had snuck back in through the kitchen door.

"Ann's in hysterics, Mom," he said.

"Then go back and tell her that *I*, Queen Irene the Second, have admitted to finding the body. Shay Kerrigan's dealt with Sean the Garda, Michael Noonan will know how to protect her, I've told both Mary and Sally, *and* we're barricading the road against intruders."

"Not that I think it'll be necessary," said Shay, stepping into the kitchen with Michael Noonan.

"Hardly likely," said Michael, smiling reassuringly at me. "Not if Slaney's been drinking. As soon as the Garda have had a word with him, we'll know more." He looked wistfully toward the cup in my hand, so I asked who wanted coffee.

Simon said he'd get back before Ann had a stroke.

"Tell her I'll look in as soon as I can," Michael told him. "I can keep her name out of it." But he was thoughtful after Simon left, and spent a long time stirring the sugar into his coffee. "You know, closing off the lane is a very good idea right now. Not that Paddy has a chance of discovering Ann here in the south. She used to live in Santry."

"But what good would it do him to find her?"

Shay and Michael exchanged looks. "He is legally her husband. He could force his way in on her."

"How?"

"He's got the law on his side."

"Well, then, it's a damned foolish law." I stared at them. "You mean, she has *no* protection from him? That he can just walk back in on her?" I was sputtering with indignation. "Why, that's outrageous. Why, in the States, a woman has some protection . . ."

"I told you things were different here in Ireland," Shay began.

"Different? They're archaic. Why, it's inhuman, it's—" I broke off because they were looking at me with the oddest expressions. "Well, what's the matter with you two grinning apes?"

"You sound exactly like your Aunt Irene," said Michael mildly. "She felt the same way, and so, I'll add, do I."

"Myself as well," said Shay.

"Then what are you going to do about it?"

Michael was looking at Shay rather strangely.

"Well?" I demanded again, because I was very, very upset. Bad as Teddie had been, I'd had sure legal redress once I'd made the decision to terminate the marriage. It hadn't ever really occurred to me how extremely fortunate I was.

"I'm doing what I can right now," said Michael. "Admittedly, it's only one isolated incident."

"What about making new laws? You're a solicitor. Or do barristers do that here in Ireland?"

"No, T.D.s—senators you'd call 'em."

"And why don't they?"

"It's not as easy as all that. You're in Ireland now, you know."

"Too well I know, and I thank my lucky stars that I can leave it."

"Now, now, Rene"—Shay's diffidence changed to alarm—"this is all very upsetting—"

"Wow! Understatement of the year!"

"Rene, did you warn Sally, and Mary Cuniff?" asked Michael, taking firm command of the situation.

I took his unspoken reprimand, because this wasn't the time to belabor the point, however morally unfair the situation was.

"They're both upset, but it's all for Ann's sake. Although I don't see that Sally's in a much better position. Or did the guy ever own up to paternity?"

Michael Noonan dropped his coffee cup. Had it been

deliberate? He started making all the right noises, so I had to make light of the matter as I mopped it up.

Another siren heralded the arrival of some new official vehicle, and that gave Shay and Michael the excuse to leave. The next thing I knew, George Boardman was charging in, terribly upset, his silvery hair blown all over his face.

"Mary called me. What's this about old Mrs. Slaney being killed? And your finding her?"

At least my fable was becoming accepted as fact.

I gave George reassurances and a cup of coffee, and by the time he'd smoothed his wind-blown hair down, the front doorbell gave one of its asthmatic wheezes. The caller was the priest.

"Oh, but I've been here some little time now," he told me in a gentle voice, his eyes blinking so constantly that I wondered if he suffered from nerves or just an eye ailment. He started asking about requiem Masses. Fortunately, George not only knew Father O'Rourke but knew what to say about Masses, and the dear blinking Father went off in a gentle daze.

The Inspector arrived before Shay or Michael had a chance to warn me he was coming. They followed close behind, but even if I hadn't three large male friends, and one of them a solicitor, I don't think I would have regarded this necessary formality with any dread—once it was over. The Inspector couldn't have been more courteous, and, after all, the facts, barring my fable, were so straightforward that the questioning didn't amount to much. He did say that he'd have to be back in the evening to take statements from Mrs. Cuniff and any of the other tenants who might have noticed something out of the ordinary. And he was gone.

"There's not much news, Rene," Michael said, "in an old woman found dead in her own home, not with Belfast claiming headlines and everyone's sympathy. However, I'll slip up and have a word with Ann Purdee." And he was away.

"Michael's right, you know," George said, combing his hair again with his fingers. "But I think I'll just collect Mary from the Montrose and give her some moral support. 'Bye now, and God bless."

I was getting messages rather loud and clear.

"I wonder, should I offer him Mrs. Slaney's cottage instead of Fahey's? Of course, maybe he's superstitious or something . . ." Then I caught Shay's expression. "Yes, I guess it isn't the time to make such a suggestion, is it?"

"My dear Rene, you amaze me more and more."

"Why? He certainly wasn't breaking his neck for worry over me. Though now I understand why an architect would be willing to live in a three-room cottage not big enough to house a drawing board. And Kieron Thornton's mad-crazy for Ann Purdee, and it wouldn't surprise me if Sally Hanahoe is still wildly in love with the guy what done her wrong."

"Sally who?"

"Sally Hanahoe, Ann's housemate, the unwed mother."

"Oh, yes. I haven't met that one. She must have arrived after I got in Irene's bad books." He slid into the chair at the small kitchen table, looking tired. I knew how he felt, and sat down opposite him. Then he gave a thoughtful snort, and gazed at me admiringly. At least, I preferred to take that interpretation.

"If you *knew* how much you sounded like Irene then, standing up for the poor, down-trodden Irish female . . ."

"Don't you mock—"

"I'm not, pet," he said, most seriously, and caught the hand I was brandishing. "I'm very much aware of how unjust the current laws are. But it's as much their own making."

"How? When a guy can beat up a little thing like Ann, leave her without a penny to live on, and three kids, and then take up where he left off if he so chooses—"

"Wait a minute. You haven't been in Ireland—"

"Don't give me that old—"

He had both my hands and squeezed them hard. "Listen! I'm not defending the status quo, I'm explaining it, and you don't know it. Now, that's better, listen a minute.

"Simplifying the situation to absurdity, gay young lad sees pretty young colleen, falls madly in love with her wit and light feet, marries with pomp and circumstance and the fear of God from the local priest. All is still lightness and love. But gay young lad knows flipping little about the arts of love, and his pretty colleen even less, because they're good Catholics. So they fumble about, and before you know it she's pregnant, and sick, and he's tired of his pretty wife turned useless. He goes off to the pub for a few jars, where all his old buddies are drinking, and it's a big gas, and lots of fun down in the pub, with the peat fire and the Guinness and the telly and the dart board. And then the bahbee's born and he's a happy man and he's got a wife again, and whaddya know, she's pregnant again in next to no time. And he's off to the pub because her mother's with her, complaining that he's a lecher and a no good layabout and why doesn't he go off to the pub and leave the poor girl to rest. And so the poor girl, pregnant and exhausted, lavishes all her affection on her son, and pampers and spoils him as she'd like, perhaps, to pamper and spoil the man she keeps driving into the pub, and his friends, who are driven there for the same reasons. And then, guess what, the boy grows up, pampered and spoiled and used to seeing his old man go out every night to the pub with his friends, while his mother makes his sisters wait on them hand and foot because it's a man's world, pet, and the men get the best of the stick, and whaddya know. The boy grows up and marries the pretty colleen and gets her all preggers . . ."

"That wasn't the vicious circle for Mary Cuniff. And Ann's busted it."

"Ever seen how Ann treats her young son?"

I looked at Shay, because I hadn't seen Ann with the boy, but I could see that the pattern he projected could be terribly accurate. And it wasn't limited to Ireland.

"Is that why you don't marry?"

He gave my hands a final squeeze, winked one of his very brilliant blue eyes, and sat back. "It could happen, and I'd hate it. I don't want a shrew and I don't want an innocent. I also don't want a woman who's gone too far in the opposite direction."

"You don't approve of women's lib?"

He snorted. "I'd prefer a woman who could speak out for herself. But I'd rather stay single and give joy to untold numbers of lonely females." He pulled himself up off the base of his spine.

"Aren't there *any* happy marriages in Ireland?"

"Law of averages says there have to be. No, seriously, Irene, Jimmy's father and mother are devoted to each other. Sheila's a wonderful person, but Dave got her." He sounded sincerely rueful. "You have been exposed to more of the exceptions than the average visitor."

"It's all so grossly unfair. These girls—Mary for instance—caught in the most ridiculous set of legalities! Can't anything be done for them, Shay?"

"Yes, Rene, they can stay on in the queendom and make their own way. They wouldn't be here otherwise. Irene wasn't impractical in her philanthropies. Which reminds me, Sheila told me of a candidate for Fahey's, once you can get that sorted out."

"Oh?"

Shay got slowly to his feet. "If I can make a humble recommendation?" When I assured him that he could, he went on. "You could even have her in on a caretaker basis. You can check with Michael about the mechanics."

"Who is she?"

"Another unwed mother. She was living with her sister, but the girl got married. Her son's three, so there's not so much work for Ann."

"She's practically got a playschool there."

"With Snow to help, it's no big thing."

"Hey, Mom," said my darling daughter, right on cue, but Shay gave me a quick sign to say nothing. With Snow's exuberant entry came the smell of freshly baked bread.

"Oh, heavenly!" I cried, reaching for the warm loaves. "However did Ann find time to bake . . . today?"

Snow shrugged. "No problem." She was eyeing Shay Kerrigan oddly. "Ann feels that industry is the best cure for panic—and, Mom, she's panicky. No matter what Georgie-porgie and Mihall—"

"I wish you wouldn't, Snow."

"Huh, George doesn't mind!" My daughter gave me a grin, but her smile faded as her eyes swept past Shay.

"Maybe I could . . ." Shay began.

"No!" Snow's reply was emphatic enough to be downright rude.

I remonstrated with my daughter, but Shay smiled. "I don't know *what* turned young Ann against me, but I know where I'm not wanted." I could hear his bafflement as well as the hurt. "Anyway, I'd best be on my way. Look now, don't hesitate to phone if anything else occurs that worries you, or even if you just want moral support. Promise?"

I did, because Shay did reassure me in spite of all these unwelcome undercurrents and curious nuances. I must try to figure it all out one of these days.

## 14

FRESHLY BAKED brown bread, good butter, and honey made one of the most satisfying meals I've had. We ate completely through the loaf, even to wetting fingertips to lift the last remaining crumbs from the table.

"Why did you give Shay Kerrigan such a cold 'no'?" I asked my daughter.

She frowned. "I like Shay, but he was going to Ann's, and she said he'd never set foot in her house again."

"I've been given the impression that they've known each other a long time."

Snow gave one of her indifferent shrugs. "She was pretty positive, Mom. And she wouldn't say doodly-squat more than that."

"Doubtless you attempted to ascertain more details?"

"Sure did, and she warn't ascertaining nothing more. And when Ann Purdee has clammed up, Mom, the clamshell is shut." Snow frowned more deeply, because reticence is a challenge.

"Now, Sara, don't you go antagonizing Ann."

"Naw, I wouldn't do a thing like that," and she glared at Simon for his massive snort of disbelief. "I'm more subtle."

"I bet I find out more than you, and sooner," said Simon. "Man to man."

Abruptly Snow came out with the startling notion that we should forthwith tackle the hall's redecoration, idle gossip being an unconstructive way of spending time. Simon sourly remarked that we hadn't done the finishing in the living room yet. A wrangle developed, which I ended by suggesting that Simon finish the living room and we slop up the hallway. Snow took exception to my phraseology, and I had to put my foot down.

We did the kitchen. It was smaller. Ann came over as we were putting on the last of the contact paper.

"Oh! How lovely it looks!" she said, but she was panting with exertion. She had a child on one hip, Meggie, her Tom, and Fiona holding on to her skirts. I'd thought she wore skirts so much to flatter a thin figure. Now I could see the practical aspect of many handholds for nervous children.

"What's the matter?" I asked her, because her worry was apparent. "Not that husband?"

"I saw Kieron holding back someone at the lane . . ." She was still breathless from hurrying. "And I just thought . . . that if no one was in my house . . ."

Snow was already hauling her into the room and smartly closing the door behind her.

"Well then, since you've a spare minute," said my daughter, "come see the rest of the first floor."

Ann was truly an encouraging person to show through a half-redecorated house. She was overwhelmed by the changes. Snow was urging her up the steps to the second story just as the doorbell wheezed.

Simon waved me back and advanced on the door. Not that Aunt Alice waited for him to open it. She barged past my astonished son.

"Why did you have to kill old Mrs. Slaney? Why couldn't you have stayed in America where you belong?"

I stared at her, unable to credit my ears.

"Now just a living minute," said my son. I'd never seen Simon so angry. "Where did you hear that nonsense? And how dare you accuse my mother of anything so vile?"

"I knew, I just knew, there'd be nothing but trouble and disgrace the moment I learned a foreigner had Irene's property. This never would have happened if Irene'd listened to me."

"Alice Hegarty, get the hell out of this house." Kieron came striding in. He took hold of my great-aunt by the elbows and bodily lifted her out the door, heedless of her enraged sputterings. "Rene no more killed Mrs. Slaney than you did. Tom bashed her once too often."

Alice Hegarty had grabbed the door frame. Her face was contorted with a variety of emotions as she stared at me, but the hatred she emanated made me so ill that I sank to the steps, clutching at the banister for support.

"He said she did it."

"Jasus!" cried Kieron. "And you're the gobshaw who'd believe him!" He laid a large hand on hers and pried her fingers from the wood, spun her around, and shoved her down the walk.

"You'll see, Irene Teasey, you'll just see!" Alice kept ranting as Kieron manhandled her into her car. He had no sooner slammed that door than another car came to a squealing halt.

"Merciful heavens, Alice, are you out of your mind?" It was Winnie, her voice fluting with distress. "Oh, Alice, how could you? Whatever will Rene think of us?"

"Winnie Teasey, you get that woman off this property."

"Who are you to give orders, Kieron Thornton?" said Alice in a penetrating shriek. "You're no better than any of the other floozies and strumpets on the place. Just you wait . . ."

"So help me, Alice, I'll thump you. And there's no one here who won't say you were hysterical and needed a clip on the jaw!"

Alice shut up in mid-vituperation, but the force with which she drove off set Kieron spinning to the side of the road.

"Oh, Kieron," Winnie was crying, wringing her hands in distress, "you wouldn't, you couldn't . . ."

"I didn't have to," said Kieron with a mirthless laugh, dusting his hands off, "but, oh Jasus, wouldn't I have liked to!"

The black Morris was bucking, stalling, starting, and jackrabbiting toward the main road. By the time it had paused there, I realized I'd been holding my breath and that I was trembling with reaction. I wished I'd never come to Ireland. I wished I'd never had an Aunt Irene. I just wanted to go up those stairs, pack my bags, and get the hell back to Westfield, New Jersey.

"Oh, Rene, I am so terribly, terribly sorry," Winnie was babbling, peering up at me through the railing. "The moment she rang off I *knew* she'd do something outrageous! But I never . . . I mean I drove as fast as I could to get here and stop her. I don't know *what* can have possessed Alice . . ."

"Greed," said Ann Purdee in a hard voice. "Covetousness. She had her plans for this property, and well you know it, Winnie."

"Oh dear, but I thought she'd forgotten. Tom spoke to her about it." Winnie's face twisted, and she began to cry.

"Oh, do stop weeping, Winnie," Ann said contemptuously. "You'll start all the children."

"You're not responsible for your sister-in-law, Winnie," I said, because I couldn't stand her distressful bleating either. "It was good of you to come over."

"Where," demanded Simon, "did she get that garbled version?"

Winnie looked startled. "I couldn't tell you."

"The truth of the matter is," said Kieron, coming back into the hall, "that Rene went down to introduce herself to Mrs. Slaney and saw her sitting up in the bed just staring at the window. She was frightened and called me. The door was locked, so I opened the window and saw enough to realize the old lady was dead. So I asked Rene to call the Gardai."

"Then no one entered the house before the Gardai?" asked Winnie, her eyes round.

"Why?" asked Ann. "Because Alice had it that Rene was discovered throwing the poor old soul out of her house so she could let in some other floozy or strumpet?"

In Winnie's startled gasp we heard the truth, which she tried frantically to deny. I felt sicker than ever, and hugged myself against the venom of such a perversion. That settled it. I was in no way required to take this sort of slander. I would appoint a caretaker for the place. We'd make it a home for unwed mothers.

"Winnie, if you don't mind . . ." Kieron said, indicating the door.

"Oh dear, oh dear. I didn't mean to upset you, Rene," she said, coming toward me instead, but Ann firmly guided her out the door.

Suddenly Snow began to laugh. She wasn't hysterical, and I resented her capacity to find anything remotely funny about the past few minutes.

"Well?" I asked.

"But Mother . . . No one . . . would believe it. This scene . . . is . . . like wow!"

Simon's grim expression began to echo his twin's interpretation. By the time Ann and Kieron had returned, the two of them were rolling with laughter and the small children were giggling uncertainly.

"Will you two ghouls stop it?"

"My mother—the Irish murderess!" Snow made a dramatic pose. "A week in Ireland and she done Dublin dirty. Foul American Murders Ancient Crone She's Never Met!" Snow made banner gestures with her hands. "Westfield will never believe it of you, Mommy!"

It was nothing to mock at, and yet Kieron was grinning and Ann Purdee looked considerably less grim as the twins went on, falling into Batmanese. "Westfield Widow Witch! Will This Dastardly Deed Defy Dublin's Dauntless Detectives?"

"Look," Kieron said to me when the kids had somewhat subsided, "you get in that car and take yourself off for a nice long drive . . . away from here . . ."

"Go see the Lady Twins," said Snow.

"I don't want to see anybody."

I started up the stairs, but Simon blocked my way and Kieron marched me to the door, grabbing my handbag and keys from the hall table.

"Go down to the Silver Tassie and have a few quick jars. Go down to the Strand at Killiney and observe the shining sea!"

Getting away from it all did appeal strongly to me. I drove down the lane, each wheel revolution increasing the intense relief. I turned right and put my foot down on the accelerator. I took the next left-hand turn and got lost, naturally. I emerged at a signpost somewhere near Powerscourt, but stately homes were not soothing. Still, the drive was pretty, and I went on and on and on, and there were lovely mountains around me, with richly green growing things.

Power of suggestion and all that, I was at the bend in the Kilternan Road before the Brandel cottage when I recognized my whereabouts. I was determined not to stop, not to inflict myself on anyone or be forced to consider anyone else's troubles—and found myself flicking the turn signal.

Lady Maud was in the garden, in much the same spot as we had first seen her, and Lady Mary appeared in the doorway as I closed the garden gate. It was such a repetition of the first encounter that I momentarily wondered if they might not really be dolls, timeless and immobile, until opening the front gate started the action.

They'd already heard about Mrs. Slaney's death. They wouldn't, however, talk about it until I was ensconced on the love seat, sipping tea and eating dainty sandwiches which appeared magically, I *was* hungry!

"The one facet of today's episode which is completely reprehensible," said Lady Maud when I'd related the day's events, "is Alice's intrusion. I cannot, Mary, like the woman."

Lady Mary sighed. "Maudie love, you are a *very* astute judge of *character*."

I said it without thinking: "Do you know Shamus Kerrigan well?"

Their smiles told me the answer. "He is *such* a charming gentleman. *Always* punctual, and such a *good* heart."

"Then would you know why my aunt turned against him?"

Lady Maud's brows creased in the tiniest of frowns, and she looked down at her shoe tips as she reflected on my question. Lady Mary sighed.

"*Truly* we *don't* know."

"Though we had been aware of Irene's sudden and inexplicable dislike of dear Mr. Kerrigan."

"It seemed to *begin* after her *first* stroke, didn't it, Maudie?"

"Yes, I believe that's correct, Mary."

"But he *kindly* drove us to *visit* her in hospital, and *brought flowers* and candy, and did *all* that was to be *expected* ..."

"I hate to press you, Lady Maud, Lady Mary," and both Ladies nodded acceptance of my reluctance, "but you see, he does want to use the lane to get into the land he owns. Only, in her letter to me, Aunt Irene forbade it. And he's been so charming to me and the twins ... But I can't go against Aunt Irene's specific instructions unless I know."

"Mr. Kerrigan comes from a *very* good *family*," was Lady Mary's contribution. "County Meath."

"Irene could be very harsh with those who disappointed her. But she was fair," said Lady Maud slowly.

"He says he doesn't have an inkling of what he did."

The two Ladies smiled at each other and then at me.

"Men often don't, my dear," said Lady Maud, her blue eyes twinkling.

"He's *so* charming" — Lady Mary took up the narrative — "that one would feel *obliged* to *forgive* him almost *anything*." Then they beamed at me again.

"I expect it will all come out right in the end," Lady Maud added, in such a brisk manner that I realized this subject of conversation was now closed.

"Could you tell me how you heard about Mrs. Slaney, Lady Maud?"

"Actually, it was John the postman who told Mary."

"The postman?"

"In *Ireland* the *postmen* are usually the *worst* gossips of all," and Lady Mary tittered.

"Did he say where he'd heard it?"

"No, I don't recollect that he did."

I think Lady Maud would have been more surprised if he'd acknowledged his source.

"However, Pat the butcher knew it. But then, his wife has a cousin in the Gardai at Cabinteely, so naturally he'd know. And James would tell us, because he knows we're acquainted with Hillside Lodge."

I sighed in surrender, and the conversation turned to other things. They were delighted to learn that I had sung at the tea, exultant at the reactions. They learned that I had met George Boardman. (Oh, a charming young man . . . such a jolly right Pirate King, too . . . ) And wouldn't I consider staying on and doing an audition for next year's show?

I started my usual disclaimer.

"Tell me, dear Rene," asked Lady Maud, "what sort of a life would you be leading in the States next fall?"

"Well, I . . . I mean . . . I'd be . . ." My voice trailed off as I reviewed my probable activities, dull indeed compared to what was already in progress here. There are certain advantages to being dull — safety from slander is one of them. But how much did I really want to feel safe? And how much more stimulating, if irritating, life seemed to be here!

Lady Maud smiled back at me, nodding, her eyes twinkling more merrily than ever, as if she realized the impact of that casual but shrewd question. I evaded any further answer by rising and suggesting that I'd taken quite enough of their time and I'd better get back to my twins before they listed me as missing.

I was never more sincere when I told them that tea had revived me: tea and these irrepressible, valiant, and sensible ladies.

As I drove into my lane (a sense of possession did a great deal to abet the restoration of my equilibrium), I saw that the roadblock had been drawn to the side. Then I was struck by the quiet. Horseface was grazing at the far side of his field, as if he wished to be dissociated from the goings-on in the houses, and there wasn't the least sign of activity. Not even the cheerful chimney plumes of smoke.

I was getting concerned when I saw the tail end of the blue Jaguar in my driveway. I parked hurriedly and almost ran into the house. Now what?

Shay Kerrigan was seated on the steps, looking quite at home, chatting on the telephone.

"Here she is now. Told you not to worry, Simon. Now go enjoy yourselves!"

He hung up, grinning so broadly that my half-formed suspicions of worse to come dissipated.

"We've cleared the whole lot off. Kieron and George have absconded with a veritable gaggle of females." From his expression, one was led to suppose an act of incredible heroism on the men's part. "Simon and Snow have been carried off by Jim-lad, Betty, and Mark Howard, and *I* am taking you away from all this."

He grabbed me around the waist and spun me about in such a vigorous fashion that I had to grab his arms to keep from falling.

"*Were* you at the Brandels'?" he asked, still whirling me despite my protests. "Simon said you'd likely end up there."

"Yes, yes. Now unhand me, villain!"

He stopped suddenly, and I clutched to keep my balance. "Why should I?" he demanded in theatrical manner. "For the first time, I have you alone! In my power!"

His extravagant lightheartedness was an antidote to the morning's grimness—but then he kissed me! All part of the act—but I kissed him back! (Those reflexes—those yearnings—don't die easily.) And he kissed most satisfactorily. How long had it been since a man—an attractive-to-me man—had kissed me? The end effect, however, put my feet squarely under me, and I felt obliged to push firmly free of that embrace. I also felt obliged to laugh—no, giggle—as if I were a fair maiden alone and in his power.

"Sir James, your queen must garb herself afresh." I caught the look in his eyes and made myself whirl away in the best romantic Hollywood tradition. "Adieu, and for a little while adieu . . ."

I dashed up the stairs as if Alice Hegarty were behind me. I was rather surprised at the way my pulse was pounding as I flung open the wardrobe door to find something suitable to wear.

How could I have forgotten that kisses burn on the lips in afterglow? Yes, and how could I have forgotten that something turned my level-headed, fair-minded, friendly great-aunt against the charming Sir Shamus-James Kerrigan?

My composure restored, my make-up repaired, and my knees only a trifle jellyish, I minced back downstairs. Shay came out of the living room, smiling in appreciation at my quick-changery.

"My, my," and he meant the linen sheath I was wearing, "you certainly have wrought changes in the house. What next?"

"Today the kitchen! Tomorrow the hallway!" I made the appropriate grand gestures. "And then," I added, suitably prosaic, "the bedrooms!"

"That green in the dining room certainly sets it off. Were you an interior decorator in the States?"

"No, but I like doing houses up. The nest-building instinct."

"I thought you were a women's libber."

Before I'd thought to control the impulse, I turned to him. "Please don't label me. Please don't generalize like that!"

He raised his eyebrow at my fierce tone, and I relented. "I'm sorry. Teddie, the twins' father, used to do that."

"Well, I am sorry if I offended you, pet," he said.

"I know *you* didn't mean anything by it, I'm very sorry I took your head off. It's just that it seemed so like the beginnings of other evenings that I . . ."

He ushered me out the front door, still reassuring me — or was I reassuring him?

"Fair enough, Rene. All Americans are not rich, all women who have minds of their own are not women's libbers, all cats are not gray — "

"Don't be outrageous!"

"Why not? The night is young and you're so glamorous . . ." He opened the Jag's door with a series of complicated flourishes and a bow worthy of the Palladium on Royal night. "Seriously, though, Rene, you are doing wonders with the house. Have you ever considered doing it professionally?"

"No, I think I'd hate it then. It'd be a job. Take all the fun out of it."

"And you wouldn't do it just for fun, would you?"

"That wouldn't be wise. An artisan is worthy of his . . . or her . . . hire. I suppose it would be challenging to do a house or two, but I'd prefer to know the house and the people so the decoration would be *them*, not me or what the current 'thing' was in some magazine."

He looked slightly puzzled, so I explained the American magazine scene and how to decorate at little cost from old attic remnants and be clever, and laughingly quoted the Flanders and Swann song: "There's no place safe to dress!"

"I didn't think you Americans knew Flanders and Swann."

So we entered the dual carriageway to Bray singing a rousing chorus of "Mud, mud, glorious mud."

## 15

WE'D HAD OUR DRINKS in an old hotel in Bray, gone for a walk on the seaside, oblivious to others about us, had a delicious dinner—supper, Shay called it—at a seafood restaurant. We talked about nothing that mattered, and yet it seemed that we understood each other rather well.

As Shay drove me home, we were both silent, a tranquility born of a very companionable evening. A tranquility pierced by the fact that every light was burning in the occupied cottages and my house.

"Jasus, what's happened now?" Shay asked under his breath as we drove cautiously up the lane.

A figure came out of the gloom, brandishing a flashlight and the shotgun.

"Kieron?" I cried, sticking my head out the window.

"Not to worry, Rene," he said, stepping up to the car.

"Not to worry? With every light on in the place, and you running around waving that damned thing?"

"Someone's been lurking about the place. Snow saw him when she was getting to bed. Simon routed him out of the stable, he ran toward Ann's and then doubled back. You didn't see anyone running down the road, did you? Or a parked car?"

I hadn't been aware of anything but my peaceful feelings, the more fool me. Nor did Shay remember anything unusual.

"Well, so there we are!" Kieron shrugged. "Lock up everything well tonight, Rene. I'll go tell Ann the scare is over."

"Her husband?" I asked Shay as Kieron trotted off.

Shay shook his head. "He's not supposed to know where she is."

"That doesn't mean much, judging by the way news gets about in this town."

Shay laughed. "Don't sound so sour. Sure and *you're* news . . . ah . . . the rich American grass widow!" He was deft at teasing, all right. "Oh, you're news, Rene."

"I just hope it'll be as much news when I leave. Which

I've a mind to do!" I'm appalled to admit that I flounced out of the car in a very bad humor. It just wasn't fair that our lovely time had been spoiled so quickly. It just wasn't fair!

Shay caught up with me at the front door, and kept me from opening it.

"Rene! Rene!" There was real concern in his voice. He took me by the shoulders and gave me a little shake, to make me look him in the eyes. "You can't abdicate." Another shake. "Not at the first sign of hostility. Not strong-backed Irish-American queens!"

"Why can't I? I only came here to get—"

"Away from what you were leaving behind?" He cocked his head to one side, giving me a long searching look. There was a slight smile on his lips, a cynical smile. "No one runs from trouble without it follows them, Rene. And you've a good defendable spot here, with loyal subjects." Another squeeze on my arms. "Who need *you* as much as you need them. Irene had great hopes for your succeeding her here."

"How would you know?"

The twilight was bright enough for me to see the hurt in his eyes, the earnest smile disappearing from his mouth, and I was instantly remorseful.

"Shay, I didn't mean that."

"Why should you mean other?"

"Shay, please, I really didn't mean that. You've been so wonderful, so considerate . . ."

"Having you on, my dear." I didn't blame him for sounding so bitter.

"Oh, Shay, I just don't trust anyone or anything, including myself."

"Including yourself?" He gave a funny little laugh and then pulled me to him, bending his head to kiss me before I could struggle free.

It wasn't fair of him to kiss me that way. It wasn't fair because I had to kiss him back, wanted to go on being kissed and all that followed kissing . . . and loving . . .

"Especially myself," I said, ruthlessly pushing him away. "And thank you for a lovely evening," I added, shoving out my hand formally, because the door got yanked open behind me. By Simon.

"Hey, Mom, we had a prowler! Ann's scared it was her husband."

"Did you have fun this evening, Sim? How would *he* know where Ann is? Did you get a good look at him? And where are your manners? Say good evening to Shay. It was really a lovely evening, Shamus, thank you."

Shay had taken my extended hand in both his, fingers caressing it. And Simon was giving me his "what are you blathering about?" look.

"I said good evening to Shay earlier. We had a smashing time, Mom, and may we go swimming tomorrow with the group?"

"I see no reason why not."

"You'd better phone the Gardai and tell them about the prowler, Rene," Shay said, and then, bidding Simon good night, he disappeared into the dark shadows.

Simon gave a snort. "We did that already."

"Well, I don't know what else we can do, except go to bed." Which is what we did.

The Garda came up the next morning and took full particulars from us and Kieron. When I tried to find out what had happened about Tom Slaney, I got a very polite and embarrassed evasion and Sean the Garda beat a strategic retreat.

"You don't suppose they think I had something to do with her death, the way Alice says?" I asked the twins.

"Ah, fer carrying out loud, Mom." Simon was disgusted.

The mailman came, quite willing to have a chat with me. I had about got used to the Dublin accent, but his, with flat broad A's and a curious nasal quality, had me so fascinated that I really didn't hear what he was saying—at first.

"She what?"

" 'Tis thought, missus, that the poor old thing died from her heart."

"Her heart? With that hole in her head?"

He dismissed that with a *"bosh!"* "I heard that the coroner himself said that 'twas her heart give out, missus, not her head."

"Then her son didn't kill her?"

"Now I'm not saying that, missus. I'm only telling you what I heard."

"She hit her head against something when she fell?"

Again he claimed ignorance. "Did you not get a good look at your prowler last night?" he asked.

"How did you hear that?"

He cocked his head at me, his bright brown eyes twinkling at my amazement. He patted his canvas postbag. "Not all the news that gets about is written, missus."

"Evidently!"

He had, however, a stack of mail for me. "All from Ameriky, I see. All airmail. Desperate the cost of stamps, isn't it?"

We discussed the weather then, and despite the innocent subject, I found I enjoyed the chat. As the twins had discovered their first time out, people took time to talk in Ireland, and they really seemed to be interested in what you were saying. The observation now had a double edge. I shook myself sternly as I watched the little postman amble back down my lane. Was I becoming paranoid? As Shay had said, the American was news.

I riffled through the letters. Most of them were for the children. I had letters from Betty, Mother, my sister Jen, and two bills. I'd a lot to tell Betty and Mother, certainly.

They had a lot to tell me first, however.

"What's the matter, Mother?" asked Snow, briefly interrupting her stream of "oh nos," giggles, and assorted monosyllables.

"Guess," asked Simon sarcastically, waving his own letter, his expression one of deep disgust. "Or maybe he hasn't bothered any of your friends yet?"

"Oh that!"

"What do you mean, Simon?" I asked, alarmed enough on my own account.

"Just that Dad's been to Pete Snyder, Doug Nevins, Popper Tracey, and—"

"Whatever for?"

"Ahhh, had they heard from me in Ireland, where was I, what were we doing there, and—"

"Oh, Mom, don't worry!" Then Snow made a face as she gave me a second, longer look. "Okay, what's Aunt Betty saying?"

"That your father has been phoning constantly, wanting to know what we were doing, what I was up to, taking his children away from him."

"I'll bet I know what Aunt Betty told him," said Simon, chuckling. He was very fond of Betty and her droll manner of speech.

"More or less," I said by way of agreement but without elaborating. I reread Betty's disturbing news:

Teddie-boy seems positive that you have a) gone off with another man, totally unsuitable as a stepfather for *his* children, b) inherited a fortune, which is amusing when you consider that he had categorized the Irish as a shiftless lot of do-nothings, ignorant, stupid, and lazy. Between you and me, I hope you did inherit a fortune. Frankly, you may need it. Teddie was raving about withdrawing support money until you capitulated. So I took the liberty of phoning Hank. Then if Teddie is day-one late, Hank can leap on him. I won't tell you not to worry, because you will and do. But I want you to know that if there isn't a pot of gold, and Teddie-boy cuts off the support money, you need only wire Charlie and me for moral and financial assistance. I mean it, honey.

It was so like Betty to offer help. But Teddie couldn't . . . or would he? I didn't have all that much left in my checking account. I *knew* we shouldn't have spent so much on paint!

Being a glutton for punishment, I hurriedly opened Mother's letter. She had much the same news and suspicions as Betty, and had conveyed the same to Hank. I began to get angrier and angrier. Mother closed her letter by saying that I could always count on her for any financial help I needed to tide me over. And if I trotted obediently back to the States to placate Teddie-boy, I was no daughter of hers.

I was wondering where Ted had got his notion that I had inherited a lot of money when I opened Jen's letter and found out. Of course, she had known all along that I was to be Irene's principal beneficiary, and now I learned that Aunt Irene had even consulted Jen's lawyer-husband about American tax laws. Unfortunately, Jen had taken great pleasure in informing Teddie of my good fortune: "I told Teddie that Aunt Irene had left you enough to buy and sell his agency if you chose."

My dear elder sister occasionally gets carried away!

"I'd have Hank write him a letter, Rene, threatening him with a court injunction before he alienates all your friends. He's calling everyone, saying the most outrageous things about you and your reasons for going to Ireland. I used to think you exaggerated about that man. Now I know you didn't tell the half. So I owe you an apology."

I could just wish that she owed me the allegiance of silence, too. Jen always meant well.

When I lowered the last page of her letter, I saw that both my children were waiting.

"Your father doesn't seem to approve of our sojourn in Ireland."

"So . . . what else is new?" asked Simon.

"Has your father—"

"Missed anyone?" asked Snow sarcastically. "I doubt it. According to him, Ireland is the bog of iniquity, the cesspit of humanity, the modern Sodom and Gomorrah—gold-plated and shamrock-trimmed, of course. I mean, like, what is with the man, Mommy?" A hint of desperation had crept into her final question.

"When we were home," Simon said, "he only saw us if it rained and he couldn't play golf. Or if he was throwing"— Simon's expression turned very adult and hard—"one of his bashes and needed free butling and a . . . a cook."

"What did you start to say, Simon?"

"We *know* Snow can't cook that well!"

*I* knew that *he* knew that he hadn't fooled me. But I also realized that I wouldn't get him to explain . . . not yet, at any rate.

"Not to change the subject," Simon said, doing precisely that as he stood up, "I gotta answer some of these. With the expurgated truth. I don't have much time before our taxi arrives. You ready, Snow?"

"Will be. Now, Mother, you write Hank—if Gammy hasn't

already talked his ear off. There must be something you can do to shut Daddy up." She rose, frowning at me. "And don't stand there wringing your hands. Take positive action. Write!"

I got my writing case, located a ballpoint that wasn't clogged with grease (other people's ballpoints always write better for me than my own), and settled myself at the little table in the living room. I'd a view of the front garden of my queen-dom, the rolling field beyond, and to the left up the hill . . . the hill that Shay Kerrigan wished to populate with . . . no, he'd definitely said they wouldn't be ticky-tacky boxes. And if he positioned them judiciously . . .

I forced myself away from the subject of Shamus Kerrigan. I was spending far too much time thinking about that charmer.

My hand had got a cramp by the time Mark Howard came up the lane to collect my pair.

"Now, don't worry about us if we're not back for supper, Mom," Snow said, kissing me. "You'll be all right, won't you?"

"If someone doesn't try to murder me, yes, of course." I meant to be funny but Snow's eyes got very wide. "For Pete's sake, Snow, go along. I'll be perfectly all right."

I was, and then again, I wasn't. I finished my letters and made myself some lunch, feeling a little lonely. Ah, well, I was truly delighted that the twins had met such an amiable group and were getting about.

I was drying my lunch dishes when I thought of it. If old Mrs. Slaney had died of a heart attack, then Tom would have been released from jail. And he might come back here.

Michael Noonan's line was busy, so I hopped down to Kieron's house, but he was out. Then I recalled that Shay Kerrigan was very friendly with Sean the Garda.

Shay Kerrigan told me not to worry—he was highly amused by the fact that I was worried, but he'd phone Sean the Garda right away and give me a shout back.

I was sitting on the steps, waiting for that reassurance, when I heard a car stopping in the lane. One thing certain, Tom Slaney had no car. I peered cautiously out through the glassed porch, because I also didn't wish to encounter any of those aunts of mine. From the angle of the window and the front porch, I could catch only a glimpse of masculine shoulders and trouser legs.

Never in my right mind would I have voluntarily opened the door for Brian Kelley, but it was he, smiling pleasantly, an exercise that only reminded me of Porky Pig in a winning mood.

"Yes, Mr. Kelley?"

"My client has requested that I approach you again, as he is willing to increase his original offer to you."

"Mr. Kelley, I can do nothing until probate is accomplished."

"Then you do intend to sell?" His eagerness was palpable.

I developed a case of the "smarts," as Snow would call it.

"I'm not at all sure I can abide remaining here," I said, and shuddered as I glanced toward Mrs. Slaney's cottage. Of course, he might not have . . . ah, but from the expression in his eyes, that leaping of porcine hope, I could see that he had.

"Most regrettable, most regrettable."

"Well, you can appreciate my position. Even if the coroner's verdict *was* heart failure . . ." He didn't know that. "However, if you could *assist* in speeding up the probate, and, of course, the price is right, I'd be most happy to see the last of this place."

"Oh, I'm sure that matters can be speeded up most satisfactorily," and he was rubbing his sausage hands together with anticipation. "Oh, that won't be a problem at all."

"Ah . . ." I stopped him as he turned to go. "You didn't mention how much higher your client was willing to go?"

"Well, I've managed to get him to offer thirty-five thousand pounds," he said, with the smug satisfaction of the wily entrepreneur.

"Yes, that would be a lot of money, wouldn't it?" I managed to sound impressed and wistful, although I knew the property was worth double that.

"And I can have a word with the odd man and see that there's no delay in probate." He leaned toward me with the conspiratorial subtlety of a sea lion.

"You would? I mean, I don't want to be stuck here in Ireland any longer than necessary."

"Nothing could be easier, my dear Mrs. Teasey. Particularly once my client is assured of your acceptance. Of course, it wouldn't be wise to mention the fact that you'd accepted. I mightn't be able to speed matters up if word got about."

"Oh, of course, naturally. Mum's the word," and I started to ease the door shut.

He'd his hand raised to keep it open when the phone saved me.

"Oh, I am sorry," I said, "you'll have to excuse me. And do let me know if you're able to secure probate." I gave him my most beatific smile and all but slammed the door in his face.

Shay was chuckling as he told me that Sean the Garda said that Tom Slaney was still very much in the nick, "so as not to be an embarrassment to the nice American lady."

"He's not being accused or anything?"

"Well, I believe the fiction is that he is assisting the Gardai with their inquiries. In short, they're not quite satisfied with his varied interpretations of the last interview he had with his mother. But the cause of death was definitely heart failure. The head wound hadn't bled sufficiently for it to have happened before her death. Sorry about the details, Rene," he said, for I'd given an audible gasp. "Still, Tom wasn't your prowler, so Sean the Garda said they'd be keeping a tactful surveillance on the lane for you. Could have been a tinker for all of that."

We chatted a few more moments about the latest Kelley encounter, and then he excused himself. I was a little disappointed that he hadn't asked if he could drop by that evening. Then I chided myself that he'd given up a good deal of his time already to sorting out my problems. And further, I oughtn't to put myself under too great an obligation to him.

*Why* had Aunt Irene turned against him? Or had he just come on sweet enough to her to get access up the lane? No—from what George and the Ladies had said, the friendship had been of long standing.

To take my mind off such dilemmas, I began to commune with the house. Since I was now obliged to stay here for the summer, I intended to make this house into *my* home. We would need additional pieces of furniture. Simon couldn't continue living out of a suitcase, and Snow wouldn't stay happy long in her sparsely furnished room. There was no reason why

Hillside Lodge couldn't be turned into a very elegant Georgian farmhouse.

I found the previous evening's newspaper and scanned the announcements of furniture sales and auctions. I had seen auction room signs on my travels. Recently . . . I thought hard and remembered where, in Dun Laoghaire. So to Dun Laoghaire I repaired, notions of what to look for bouncing about in my mind.

The people in Buckley-the-Auctioneers were delightful and explained the whole thing to me: that you viewed the furniture on a Wednesday and up till 2:30 on a Thursday, and then waited until the lot number came up and put in your bid. If you were successful, you collected your new possession on the Friday. There were a few beautiful pieces on display in this section of Buckley's, but suitable only for rooms four times the size of my farmhouse. Still, I could see that I'd be spending a lot of time haunting auction rooms, looking for what the Buckley's people described as the "odd piece." I was beginning to appreciate the unique flavor of the Irish "odd."

The weather hadn't exactly settled out into a clear day, but it was bright, with tremendous clouds skittering across the sky, and black thunderheads that went innocently about their business despite omnipresent threats of deluge. And with such clear air, the views were superb—of sea on the one hand, a brilliant blue-green in the sun, and the hills, equally green and worthy of description, on the other.

I followed the "scenic route" until it fed into the main Bray road and then took an inspired right just before the town, toward Wicklow. When I was about convinced that there was nothing spectacular in this direction, I came to a dual car-riageway, and the urge to try the Mercedes at speed was un-bearable. Away I went, and the car could really travel. After a lunch at the Glenview Hotel, I found my way back via a dif-ferent route.

Dublin summer evenings are blessed with a golden light, a clarity which lifts all out of the commonplace. The effect of so many rainbows? The leakages from a commensurate num-ber of pots of gold?

I drove up my own lane, enjoying an unusually euphoric

sense of well-being. Mary and Molly were gardening in the golden light, the scene positively idyllic. Mary beckoned me to join her. Trying not to behave like lady-of-the-manor, I parked my car in my drive and went back to join them. The only flaw in the scene was the closed door of Ann's cottage.

"Kieron took them all on a picnic up Ballycorus Hill," Mary said, smiling to relieve my anxiety.

The sense of tranquility returned, and I sat on the grass, plucking the odd (I was getting obsessed with the word) weed from the border.

"Ann was that worried, I know she didn't sleep last night," Mary told me. "For all of that, neither did Kieron." She laughed a little. "He'd've done better to sleep across her threshold instead of sitting up all night at the gate."

"Do you think it was her husband last night?"

Mary shrugged. "Who can say? I'd guess no, for surely, as I remember the man, he'd've been back as soon as all was quiet again, trying to sneak in the window."

"He'd be that persistent?"

She gave me a piercing look, as if I were a trifle lacking in wit. Then she gave a little sigh. "Of course, you've never met him, so you'd not know."

I shook my head vigorously and was restored to her good opinion.

"I suppose because this is a Catholic country, divorce is out of the question?" Mary nodded. "But isn't there *something* she can do?"

Mary yanked fiercely at a small innocent buttercup. "Stay out of his reach!"

"Not even if she can prove . . . what do they call it . . . oh, 'irreconcilable differences and breakdown of the marriage'?"

Mary shook her head again.

"Well, at least she has Kieron to help her." My observation may have been casual, but it had the effect of a casual bomb on Mary.

"She wants no part of Kieron Thornton! Or any man!" Mary's savage tone didn't apply to just Ann.

"You feel that way about George Boardman?" It just popped out.

Poor Mary. I seemed to be saying all the wrong things and distressing her no end. She looked frantically about her as if the fuchsia hedge had sprouted transistorized "bugs."

"You just got here last week!" she exclaimed, which confirmed my suspicions about Mary and George.

"My ex-husband used to say that I was magnetic for disasters and secrets. The rule of Rene—anything that can possibly go wrong will."

She touched my hand with quick remorse. "I didn't mean it that way, Rene."

"I know. And I'm generally the last person to see subtleties of any kind. It's just that I saw the look on Kieron's face when Ann discovered . . ." and I gestured toward Mrs. Slaney's empty house, noticing that someone had boarded up the window Kieron'd broken. "And then George comes haring in here wild-eyed and bushy-haired for you and Molly, so it was obvious to me. Why are you worried that others would see it? I think George is a doll . . . and . . . oh, but you're not married and not divorced. What the hell, what difference dies it make?"

"I know what you're thinking, Rene," said Mary with a sad smile. "You don't understand Ireland."

"You're certainly right there. So I'll be bluntly American. George Boardman wants to buy one of those two cottages. He plans to enlarge it and live there. I assume it's for proximity to you and Molly. Do I refuse him for the sake of Ireland? Or do I remind you that you have a right to some happiness, and that I'm quite willing to sell him Mrs. Slaney's place and I won't ever ask to know which walls he knocked out? And, since I'm blowing off steam, do *you* know what Aunt Irene had against Shay Kerrigan?"

She did. I saw it in her eyes.

"You might just as well tell me, because I'll find out." Please, God, just once let my bluff work! "In the meantime, it's just possible that there's another stupid impasse. Oh, blast! I don't mean that you and Ann are being stupid . . ."

"I do know what you mean," and there was a terrible undertone of sadness in her voice.

"This is my queendom now. I've the ordering of it in some respects. Oh, I know Shay's been buttering me up something shameful, all to get access up that lane. He won't get it if I feel my aunt's reasons for denying it were valid. If she had good cause, then I'll just forget about him entirely. But he's been damned sweet and helpful these last few days . . ."

Mary looked me squarely in the eyes. "Do you mean you would turf him out?"

"I do." I wasn't really that sure, but . . .

"I shouldn't be saying it, but you *have* the right to know. He's the father of Sally Hanahoe's baby."

That was not what I expected to hear. I know that she had to repeat it because I stared at her with such blank astonishment.

"Who says so?"

"Sally!"

Well, it's true that Sally ought to know the father of her baby.

"But Shay doesn't know Sally!" Of that I was positive.

"Did you ask him?" Mary was aghast.

"No, but he doesn't. Not unless he goes about getting girls whose names he doesn't know pregnant. You see, I've mentioned Sally to him, and he didn't recognize the name."

"Are you *sure*?" asked Mary with bitter cynicism.

I thought back. And I was certain. I would have distinctly heard an evasion or studied ignorance.

"I'm sure. I'm as sure as I'm sitting here pulling weeds with you that Shamus Kerrigan doesn't know Sally Hanahoe."

"But she described him! Big blue car, sandy hair, smooth talker, beautiful dresser."

That could describe quite a lot of other men I'd seen, even in the brief time I've been in Ireland, and I told Mary so. A look of disbelief and distrust passed over her face.

"No, Mary, I'm not saying it because I believe what Shay Kerrigan says. I believe what I haven't heard him say. But now I know what he's supposed to have done—I'm sorry, Mary, the irresponsible-lecher role doesn't suit Shay Kerrigan. Well, maybe I can find out. But that's why Ann Purdee won't let Shay in her house? She's afraid Sally will see him?"

Mary nodded.

The rest of Sally's pathetic story, which I got from Mary, only reinforced my belief in Shamus's innocence.

Sally's Shay K. had given her a lift one miserable rainy evening; he'd asked to meet her the following Friday at the Hotel Wicklow. Mary told me the place was rather well known for "casual encounters" (a fact which strengthened my belief, because Shay Kerrigan would not operate in such a fashion), and he'd wined and dined her frequently, leading up to a seduction one night when he'd got her very drunk. She'd gone with him until she discovered her pregnancy, three months later. She'd been living in a bedsitter in Rathmines. She'd no idea where he lived; he'd always contacted her at her office. The man hadn't talked about his origins or background, never mentioned family (considering how often Shay spoke of his nieces and nephews, another point in his favor). He had mentioned deals in land, and that he owned a garage.

When Sally had confessed her state to him, he'd flatly told her that marriage was out of the question, because he *was* married. He'd railed at her for being too stupid to be on the Pill. She'd threatened him with the Gardai, and he'd only laughed, taunting her with the fact that he was already married and she'd have to prove it was his baby. What good would that do her? Then he'd left her.

She'd tried to find him, revisiting the places where they'd gone, pubs they'd frequented, but she was unsuccessful. Abortion was repugnant to Sally, morally and religiously, and impossible financially. She took a cheaper bedsitter, a closet, Mary described it, and saved every penny she could to support herself when she was no longer able to work.

"What about her family?" I asked Mary, who snorted with scorn.

"Down-country farmers, like mine. Her father would have beaten her to death for the shame she'd brought his name." Mary scowled bleakly. "So Sally never told them."

"Brothers and sisters?"

Mary shook her head. "By the galore, but no help. You don't know how it is in Ireland."

"So . . . she had her baby?"

"Yes. First she went to a house for unwed mothers, but she

said it was so awful with all that repentance that she felt twice as bad as ever before. She wasn't a criminal, after all," and the look on Mary's face made it obvious that Sally had given her a lot more detail than I was getting. "She left in her seventh month and got a summer job minding a baby for a woman having her eighth. She had a bed in the room with the four younger children, she ate as well as anyone in the family, and the woman was very kind. She put Sally in touch with the Deserted Wives and Unmarried Mothers' Association. That's how she met Ann, and they got on like sisters." Mary smiled at that.

Molly had finished her chore of weeding on the other side of the garden, and came over to sit inside the crook of her mother's arm.

"And you? How did you meet Aunt Irene?" I nodded toward Molly in case Mary didn't feel like answering at that moment.

"Oh, I came through a regular channel. This house had fallen vacant and Irene had advertised it. 'Low rent'" — Mary laughed — "which I had to have, 'in exchange for services.' I phoned to inquire what services" — again the cynicism in Mary's voice — "and found out that Irene wanted someone with bookkeeping experience. Did you know that your aunt made a lot of money on pools and horses?"

"No! How marvelous of her! A racetrack tout!"

"Well, hardly." Mary's disclaimer was amused. "No great amounts at any time, but the odd tenner here and there. What I didn't know until later was that she'd had answers by the galore but she was looking for the right tenants, someone like Molly and me." She broke off. "Would you like a cup of coffee?"

"I always like a cup of coffee."

The rooms inside their very neat little cottage were larger and more cheerful than you'd think from the outside, and I was sure Kieron had been busy in Mary's kitchen too.

Pretty though the house was, the evening beckoned us out again to the small front garden. We sat on the grass and compared our respective countries — in superficial terms. I'd guessed that Mary's time for confidences was over. Molly was yawning fit to pop her jaw when we realized with astonishment that it was half past ten, with the sky still bright.

"I wonder where my children are," I said as we rose.

"Enjoying themselves, I'm sure. Not to worry, Rene."

For once, I didn't. I went home and got ready for bed. Bright skies made it difficult to think of sleeping, so I read for a while until I heard a car pulling up and the cheerful courtesies of the twins, the responses of their friends.

They'd had a ball, Snow assured me, and a grinning Simon began to relate the details, but I soon sent them off to bed. Such energy at the end of a long, hectic day is so enervating!

 16

DESPITE A RELUCTANCE generated by ignorance of the protocol and a malaise in any funereal circumstances, I attended Mrs. Slaney's requiem Mass and burial. Fortunately, the Irish are very sensible about such matters, and the ceremonies were conducted without unseemly dispatch or excessive emotion.

Tom Slaney was there, accompanied by a burly plainclothesman. The Ladies Brandel arrived and took their places beside me along with Shay Kerrigan, who had chauffeured them. Ann and Mary came with Kieron Thornton, since Snow and Simon had volunteered to keep all the children. Ann was so bundled up in a huge coat and head scarf that I barely recognized her, which I suppose was what she'd intended. There was also a handful of bent head scarves, and two men sitting at the back of the church, obviously not there for the proceedings.

Slaney kept, or was kept, well away from me, and disappeared with his escort as soon as the brief graveside service was completed. Ann was very nervous too, and couldn't wait to get home. But I didn't really want to be alone, so I was glad when Shay asked me to deliver the Ladies back to their cottage. He'd a business deal that was requiring a good bit of time right now, he explained. I wondered how truthful he was, because Ann had been giving him very cold glances.

The Ladies were delighted to accept my invitation and

were effusive in their thanks to Shay, as if to offset Ann's manner. So we all drove back to my house. The Ladies couldn't have been more flattering in their comments over what we had already done, and they had the most charming way of making suggestions: They'd remind each other of the decor in houses of the same period. Their knowledge of antique and period furniture was far more secure and exhaustive than mine; they'd grown up with the real items firmly ensconced in appropriate settings for several generations.

Snow appeared with Ann's flock, and much was made of the children. Meggie responded shyly, without much coaxing, as if she'd finally found someone her own size.

I'd noticed that Ann had begun to relax the moment that Shay had left. I believed I could now understand her distaste for his company, but if she'd known him so well, how could she believe that Shay Kerrigan—no matter what Sally had said—would do such a shabby thing? He was not the sort of moral coward to take refuge in the obvious lie about being married. And I felt that if he had got a girl pregnant, he'd at least be gentlemanly enough to see her through the ordeal. I resolved to achieve a confrontation between Sally and Shamus at the earliest possible moment.

Of course, Rene's Law instantly came into effect. I should have counted on that, but I forgot to.

The Ladies Brandel looked fatigued, and I suggested that perhaps I'd better drive them home, as it had been a trying morning. I took a quick look into the fridge and decided I could use some more food from Sally's supermarket *and* start my plan.

I delivered Lady Mary and Lady Maud to their cottage, promising faithfully that we'd all drop by for tea in the very near future. They overthanked me and again praised what I'd accomplished in the house.

"Much as we *loved* Irene, she'd a better eye for a *horse* than a *house*" was Lady Mary's succinct remark.

They were such old dears, and I sensed that they had attended the funeral as much to support me as to add to Mrs. Slaney's few mourners.

I had to cash a large check, but the bank manager; no doubt thinking with black-ink visions of my incredible balance, was charm itself. But he'd been equally obliging before the trust-fund money appeared in my account, and I can't honestly resent such charm when it makes life so pleasant.

Sally was on one of the registers, so I patiently waited on her line to speak with her and discover her work schedule. I had planned to invite Shay Kerrigan for dinner on a Thursday, when she worked late. I would discover that I'd forgot an important ingredient that could be got only at her store, and so confront him with Sally. But it was a bit awkward, I decided. I ought to be able to contrive something better. Maybe if I asked Snow . . . except that I couldn't very well do that without disclosing the whole game. Snow knew all about illegitimate children and affairs and that sort of thing—she could hardly remain ignorant in this day and in the society in which she had moved—but my scruples prevented me from enlisting the aid of a fourteen-year-old girl.

Well, something would occur.

I got as far as calling Shay to issue the dinner invitation. His voice answered the phone, but before I could plunge into my carefully rehearsed invitation, his voice continued in an inexorable way to inform any listener that he was away on business and if the caller would leave a message after the beep, he would attend to the matter on his return.

I let the silly recording repeat itself because I was so astonished. He hadn't said anything to me about going away. I tried not to be hurt. After all, he had a legitimate grievance with me for holding up the development of his property.

I got busy in the kitchen, putting away groceries and sternly directing my mind away from Shamus Kerrigan. (Charming rogue? No, Shay Kerrigan *wasn't* a rogue!)

Simon came in with Jimmy, both predicting imminent death due to starvation. I made lunch and then realized that it was nearly two and I would have to rush to make the auction at Buckley's at half past.

"Auctions are fun," Jimmy told me. "Mom loves to go even if she's not in a buying mood."

"Are they worth it, though?"

"Sure, if you know what you want and don't pay more than it's worth," he replied, shrugging. He gave me a mischievous grin. "Sometimes Mom says people go out of their minds bidding against each other when they wouldn't buy the thing brand-new at a shop for the price they end up paying."

The items for auction were all numbered, and after a look in the back room, where the auction had started with depraved lawn mowers, disabled washing machines, kitchen chairs, and the like, I toured the main floor and the balcony. One delightful wardrobey thing, called a compactum, fascinated me. It would solve Snow's closetless-room problem. If it took my fancy, it would probably take others' as well, but still . . .

The mob from the back room surged in, led by a man in a violent-purple shirt. He was followed by a youngish man with sandy sideburns (*he* answered Sally's description of her seducer, too), who was carrying a clipboard. A couple, about my age, smilingly edged in beside me. The woman, in an elegant tweed skirt and cotton blouse, eased herself onto the bureau against which I was leaning, then gave me the nod to follow her example, indicating it would be easier on the feet. I then noticed that other people were casually making themselves comfortable on auctionables. So I did. My friend had a list in her hand and now turned to show it to her husband. I was, in view of my fairly jaundiced experience with Irish married folk, rather astonished at the overt affection in the look he gave her, and the sweetness of his smile as he bent his head to review her list.

Then the bidding began.

I might not have noticed the couple had I not been beside them, but I could only be forcibly struck by his courtesy and her deference. He did the actual bidding; she anxiously followed the rise of price and, with an almost imperceptible shake of her head, indicated when the cost had gone too high on the chest she had wanted. His moue of regret for her disappointment was humorous and good-natured. I couldn't help but contrast them with Teddie and myself in a similar situation. He'd have bid until he got the item, no matter how outrageous the final sum, and would have been furious with me had I suggested an overbid.

I did fancy a little velvet-covered Victorian dining chair. But it reached £11 before I could even raise my hand. And sold for £15.

"That's overpriced," said the man beside me to his wife.

"Dreadfully. Why, we got our four for twenty pounds, didn't we?"

He nodded and caught my eye as he did so, giving me such a pleasant smile that I had the nerve to ask them why a chair would bring such a price.

"Sometimes the owner's here pushing the bid up," he said in a low voice. "Sometimes it's dealers who see a chance to finish a set, or maybe it simply strikes some party's fancy. Is this your first auction?"

I nodded, and was suddenly conscious that the man just beyond the couple was leaning in as if to catch the conversation. I'd remarked to myself on his utter boredom with the auction proceedings, his silence through all the bidding, which now made his sudden attention to our conversation the more obvious. The moment he saw me looking at him, he straightened up and looked away. I had the feeling that I'd seen the fellow before, although I couldn't place the circumstance.

Then the auctioneer called loudly for silence and a bid of £5 on the next item. Once again I became intent on the proceedings. The nosy character had eased away, so I thought no more about him.

Suddenly the auctionables had all had their chance, and people began to file out the front door.

"Better luck next week," the friendly woman said to me as she and her husband moved off.

I half wished that I could have become acquainted, but I didn't want to be considered pushy. Maybe they'd be here next week, too. Still, they had worked their magic on me and given me some perspective. I really had tumbled into an exceptional scene with Ann, Sally, and Mary. Then there was the fact that my great-aunt had been a confirmed-by-choice spinster. She would hardly have attracted the happily-marrieds as company. Certainly she'd performed a much-needed service in succoring girls in real distress, who'd been *done* by rascals. And, I reminded myself as I unlocked the Mercedes, I wasn't exactly the most unprejudiced observer on that count.

Besides which, there was George, dying to marry Mary; Kieron, gone on Ann, despite her not admitting it; and give Sally a chance and she'd probably fall in love with someone a

good bit more reliable than the wayward Shamus Kerrigan—
*her* Shamus, not mine. (*Mine?*)

I nearly braked at the subconscious use of the pronoun.
Shay Kerrigan was not mine, nor was I his, nor did I . . . or did
I? His kissing . . . had been *so* satisfactory, his presence so
reassuring. His—great heavens above, Irene Teasey! You only
met him two weeks ago, he's under a cloud, he's after something, and you're . . .

I turned off the main road up my lane and glanced into
my rear-view mirror as I slowed. The car behind me was driven
by Nosy! Well! That was a coincidence. Or was it? Was he
following me? Ridiculous notion! Supported by the evidence
that, as I turned up Swann's Lane, his car continued on.

"That for your fancies, my girl," I told myself sternly.

Mr. Corrig, the postman, was pushing his bike up the hill
toward my house, so I pulled over. I could save him a few steps.

"And a good evening to you, missus," he said, all af-
fability, touching his cap brim: a salute which made me feel so
very lady of the manor . . . and awkward. "Did your man ever
find you?"

"My man?" I had a second's horrible terror that Teddie
had arrived in Ireland.

"Yiss, missus. He was after asking me who owned the
field there, so I told him 'twas yourself, and he wanted to know
where you lived, and your name, so I gave him your direction.
He seemed desperate anxious to see you."

"No one came, but then, you see, it was Mrs. Slaney's
funeral today, and then I was out this afternoon."

"Poor old body," said the postman, shaking his head and
clicking his tongue. "Many there? Not that I suppose she'd
many friends left living, asides from yourselves."

"Why, yes . . ." and then I stopped. Nosy had been one of
the men sitting way back at the service! "Yes, the Ladies
Brandel came, Mr. Kerrigan drove them over. And, of course,
all of us here. Mr. Corrig, the man who wanted to buy my
land—what did he look like? I mean, I think he's been by
before . . . when I wasn't at home. My son mentioned something . . ." Not the best of prevarications, but Mr. Corrig didn't
seem to notice.

He wasn't very reassuring, either, because it was Nosy he described. And if Nosy *had* wanted to buy my property and had seen me turning into the lane, why didn't he "find me"?

"So maybe he'll call on you later. Here's your mail, missus." He passed over rather a staggering bundle. "The most I've delivered up Swann's Lane in many a year."

"I'm very sorry, but we've had so much to write home about."

"Not to worry, not to worry. Used to enjoy the odd chat with herself, I did, when she was still about."

I murmured something appropriate, and Mr. Corrig beamed at me.

"Good evening, missus, and God bless." He turned his bike around and whizzed off down the slope.

I riffled through the letters — more from my mother, and, oh no, another from Hank, some forwarded from my apartment, several for Simon, and two for Snow. Quite a clutch. Suddenly, I didn't want to open Hank's letter or Mother's all on my own. What bad news they might have to tell me was fortunately three thousand miles away. I could ignore it — for a while. I couldn't ignore Nosy, who was right on my doorstep, so to speak, and I didn't want him any farther in. Whoever he was! So I wanted very much to have a few words with Kieron . . . and I could give Simon his mail at the same time.

Simon wasn't with Kieron: He and Jimmy had gone off to Blackrock, Kieron told me. He invited me into his house to explain.

"I'd an old bike in the shed, just needed some adjusting and two new tires, so the lads went off to get them."

"Good Lord, did Simon have enough money?"

"Sure and they did, between them and me. You take milk and sugar, don't you?" he asked, for his kettle was just boiling.

"As Snow would say, constantly."

"Well," said Kieron, sitting himself down opposite me in the rocking chair, "what's troubling you?"

I groaned, distressed that I was so transparent.

"You forget how much like Irene you really are."

"Forget? I only wish I knew . . ."

Kieron frowned blackly at me. "Now don't you start

greeting over what you couldn't help," he said, then sighed. "I've had enough of that from Ann."

"Did the funeral upset her?"

"No, but the *going* did." He was much annoyed.

"She can't honestly be that afraid of her husband finding her?"

"Oh, I fault your aunt on that score, Rene. She drummed it into Ann's head that she was safe here, that she should never leave, but by God, I know Irene didn't mean never set foot out of the place. How the hell would Paddy Purdee know Ann was here in Kilternan? When he married her, he'd two rooms in Finglas. They lived there" — he gave a short bark of mirthless laughter — "until he deserted her the first time."

"The first time?"

"Forgot you haven't had all the whole sorry story of it."

"True," I replied, a bit stiffly, "it's not something even the brashest American just blurts out and asks . . . particularly not of someone like Ann." I sighed with real regret. "She's such a wonderful person, coping . . . Oh, I know . . ." I had noticed his apprehension. "The Anns of the world prefer to do it their way and the hell with the helping hand."

Kieron nodded, the sorrow in his eyes adding to my sense of impotence.

"You do love her, don't you?" I asked.

Kieron glanced sharply at me for a long, almost uncomfortable minute before his face relaxed and his very charming smile parted the moustache around his lips.

"Yes, I do love her — not that it does me any good," he said with resignation, and stirred his coffee into sloppy turbulence.

"You mean, because of Ann or because she's married and Ireland doesn't have divorce?"

His head came up in surprise. "Sure now, you can get a divorce in Ireland . . . of a kind," he amended, pleased by my astonishment. "No, my problem is Ann. Because one man's been a bastard to her, she'll have nothing to do with any other. She won't believe that men come in different sizes, shapes, and temperaments." Kieron was very bitter. "And it's such a flaming waste!" He propelled himself so forcibly out of the rocker that it nearly overtilted. "And that's no thanks to Irene, sure it's not. Much as I loved the woman, she did me no favors with Ann. And she could have done."

"But I thought Aunt Irene liked you! You're *here*!"

"Oh, she liked me well enough, she did. I had my uses," and his gesture took in the furniture, the kitchen cabinets. "And I'd come back to take care of the old mother when I found my sisters had turfed her out. She was too old to help with the housekeeping," he explained, noting my horror. His laugh was bitter. "The mother, you see, favored the boys in the family, now hadn't she, said the sisters. So let the boys care for her when she couldn't work for her keep. The men aren't the only bastards in Ireland, Rene. Not that I really blame the girls: tiny houses, bad husbands, no money. They really couldn't keep her, even with the old-age money to help out. Mrs. Slaney found her tottering along Kilternan Road late one November evening, and cold it was. Irene took over, of course. There was a letter in Mam's handbag from me. Irene cabled. I was doing a tour of cabarets in the States. I decided that I'd better come back myself to see all was well. Although Mary and Ann *were* very kind to her."

"Doesn't that prove to Ann what sort of person you are? You gave up everything . . ."

Kieron's laugh was amused now. "I gave up nothing, Rene, but it was good publicity. It's best to leave when you're on top. I do as well here, all things equaled."

"But Ann isn't convinced?"

"Not at all. It only serves to show her how unreliable I am, without a regular job, working as it pleases me. Sure and I make more in one night's work than Paddy Purdee did in a week when the trawling was good."

"Surely Ann—"

"Ann doesn't, Ann won't, Ann can't. She's as hidebound as her mother before her, and that bugger hurt her, like her dad did her mother, and he's beat her and bred her and bollixed her so badly that she doesn't know what she wants . . . except never another man in *her* house or in her life. Not that she ever *had* a man anyhow . . ." He glared defiantly at me for what he implied in that phrase. "No pleasure. She was never *married* to that bastard!"

I held my reaction to a sympathetic nod, but I could see why he felt Ann was wasted. She was so lovely, and there was so much more to loving than bedding. Ann didn't even know what she'd missed. I did, and . . .

"You said the first time he left her?" I asked Kieron, grasping for a subject to distract my own line of thought.

He glared at me ferociously, equally distracted by my abrupt backtracking. "Yes. A fortnight after the wedding he left her to go fishing. He got a chance at a berth on an English codder and took off for three months. He'd got her pregnant, and she was poorly when he got back, so he took off again for another three months. When he got back from that trip, she was in hospital with a threatened miscarriage, so he disappeared. He returned a week after Fiona was born . . . he must have had her in the hospital, because Tom was born nine months later. That's when she moved, but he tracked her down, beat her up every night he was home, and by the time he'd signed on another boat she was pregnant with Michael!"

My appalled expression seemed to mollify Kieron, for his fierceness lessened as he shoved his hair back from his forehead with impatient fingers.

"I can't imagine Paddy Purdee roughed her up before she married him," I said, "so Ann must think the change in the man is related to marriage. Why *should* she want it? But, Kieron, you said he deserted her, and yet you said he was . . ."

"Deserted her, yes, in the true sense of the word. He gave her no money to live on, she didn't know what ship he'd sailed with, how long he'd be gone or anything."

"No money? Even when they were first married?"

"The first time he went off, she thought he'd be back on the weekend, and she waited. She'd some money of her own, left over from wedding presents. She managed. Then one of his mates told her he'd signed on the codder, and she got her old job back. Once Fiona was born, of course, she couldn't work. As far as I ever heard, Paddy never gave her any money the whole time he was married to her."

This was much worse than anything I'd imagined for Ann. "But that's a psychological nonconsummation, isn't it? Or a lie, entering marriage under false pretenses? I mean, you're supposed to endow your wife with your worldly goods, cherish, honor, and support, and if he did none of those things . . . why, he never married her! But, Kieron, why can't she get an annulment or a divorce or something, so that at least she doesn't have to live in dread of his forcing himself on her again?"

He cocked an eyebrow at me, and I more or less answered my own question.

"No money!"

Kieron nodded. "Nor wish. So long's Paddy can't find her here, she's content enough."

He was obviously not. "Oh, really, Kieron, surely there's a Legal Aid Society which helps the . . . no? Good Lord. We are in the Dark Ages. I mean, when she's too scared to attend . . ." A sudden thought struck me. "You know, if he lived with her so little, would he even remember what she looked like?"

Kieron did a double take and then chuckled. "*You* tell Ann."

"Which reminds me, Kieron, have you seen a man around here, saying he's looking to buy my field?"

"There was a man nosing about yesterday."

His choice of phrase was a bit unsettling.

"You know," Kieron went on, staring off in a middle distance for a moment, "I've seen that lot before . . . in the church . . . today!"

"I went to the auction today, and I saw him *there*. He followed my car. If he really wanted to buy that property, as he told the postman, why didn't he turn in after me? Do the police really believe what we told them? Or do they think I bashed Mrs. Slaney in the head?"

"Jasus, no, Rene."

"Well, that man is obviously shadowing me."

"I'll give Sean the Garda a shout, just to clear it up."

Any clearing up got postponed then by the return of Simon and Jimmy, festooned with bike parts. I'd only time to beg Kieron not to mention Nosy when the boys were in the door. Nothing then would do but that they get the bike set to rights. "So I've got transport of my own, Mom. Isn't Kieron the greatest?"

I handed Simon his mail, concurring with his opinion

while Kieron grinned sardonically. We all went out to Kieron's workshop. I still didn't want to open my mail alone, so I perched on a convenient surface and stoutheartedly slit Mother's envelope.

Mother had received my news, dismissed the sisters with a choice qualifying remark, and advised me to enjoy the male companionship with a free heart (I thought that "free" had been penned in a broader, admonitory line) and to look into the matter of a good school for the twins in Ireland. She'd heard rumors that Teddie-boy was still acting the fool.

Hank's letter was brief: Teddie-boy had not paid this month's support money, and a telephone conference with his lawyer disclosed that the omission was deliberate, so Hank was taking instant action.

I wasn't as depressed by these newses as I'd thought I'd be. I supposed that I'd half expected Teddie to stop the support money out of pique. The joke was on him, however, if he thought that action would force me back to the States. Sometimes Teddie had a hard time recognizing the Empty Gesture.

I stuffed the letters into my handbag, and was then asked to admire the newly refitted bike.

# 17

AS I COOKED DINNER, I found my mind doing some "what-ifs," mainly financial ones. The days when I could cheerfully or reluctantly refer the matter to the man of the house were long gone. Like Harry Truman, the buck now stopped with me. And the loss of this month's support money disorganized my careful plans. I had, fortuitously, it now appeared, paid the July rent on the apartment before I left, but I'd be down to a nervous-making $10.75 in the checking account. I did have my half of the sale money of the "matrimonial" home, but that was in mutual funds sacred to college for the twins.

Although Hank had already set in motion the legal machinery to force Teddie to pay the support money, better best I not count on that money. Which left me nibbling away at the trust fund. I didn't like that sort of pilfering any better, because if Rene's Law came into effect the death duties might well turn out to be more than the trust fund. Still, for Teddie's benefit, I was finally ahead of the game. I chuckled to myself.

"What's so funny, Mom?" asked Snow, busily writing letters at the dining table, which I was setting.

"I'm winning."

"Huh?"

I was, but I didn't explain it out loud. Yes, I was really overcoming Teddie's latest machination. Stopping the support money was only going to land him in trouble. After all, I *could* work the caretaker routine.

I'd better contact George Boardman in the morning for a firm answer. Michael, too, because I wanted to know what to do about Mrs. Slaney's house. And the place should be cleared of her belongings — not a task I relished, but it had to be done before I could arrange something for George. I should also find out what could be done about bribing Fahey out of his place and leaving the way clear for Shay's candidate for . . . what could I call it? investiture . . . into the queendom.

"How much should I bribe Fahey to leave?"

Simon looked up from his letter-writing and exchanged a meaningful twinnish glance with his sister. I wish I could interpret those cryptic exchanges: I'd know what was going on in their little minds.

"Well, Mom, I'd ask Shay or Michael or Kieron. Not us. But I'm really glad to hear it."

"Why?"

Simon had that "I won't answer you now" look on his face.

"Why?" I repeated, coming back into the room with our dinner plates. I was a little irritated with my obtuseness and their subtlety.

"Oh, because . . ." Snow began, paused, and then added "it's good you're involved enough here to get him out. *He* drank. Almost as much as—" Then she did shut up.

"As Daddy?" I finished for her. I didn't miss the look, which needed no interpretation, between Simon and his sister. (SHUT UP, SIS.) "Both of you used to love your father." They were eating at a rate guaranteed to fill their mouths too full for answers. "You used to love doing things with him. What happened?"

They ate in deafening silence.

"All right, kids, something happened at the Harrisons' party . . ." Not even a look passed between them. "I know your father got stoned drunk that night. Did he embarrass you?"

"You can say that again," muttered Snow.

"Mom," began Simon in that "let's be reasonable" tone, "do you really need chapter and verse on Dad drunk?"

I caught the shudder Snow gave, and the revulsion on her face. I knew that something very deep and disturbing had happened.

"Let's just say, Mom," Simon continued, "that he was the worst he'd ever been."

"I'm your mother. I have certain rights. I can't protect you . . ."

"You did," said Snow in an implacable voice. "You divorced him. If you hadn't . . ."

What I heard then shocked me: *They* would have left. I knew that they couldn't have maneuvered me into divorce; that distressing solution had been in my thoughts long before the Harrisons' party. But it was after that night that I'd noticed a distinct reluctance in the children to do anything, go anywhere, even chat with their father. And he had become almost defensively insistent on their company, lavish with his gifts and affectionate demonstrations. I suppose their attitude toward him had been a subconscious factor pushing me toward divorce.

"Well, I did divorce him, and that's that." Even a clod could have felt the relief in the room, and I decided not to press the subject further. We finished our dinner in a less awkward mood.

"Say, Mom," Snow asked in a more normal voice, "has Daddy stopped the support money?"

"However did you guess?" There wasn't much point in hiding that fact, although I wouldn't have been so frank half an hour ago.

Snow giggled. "It figgers."

"Will it matter much, Mom?" asked Simon, worried.

"Not in terms of eating . . ."

"Don't you dare knuckle under to that kind of black-mail," said Snow, hard-voiced again, scowling at me.

"Hank's already applying pressure."

"That'll annoy Dad," said Snow cheerfully.

I couldn't reprimand her—that would have been sheer hypocrisy—but I sighed. I had refused to have it on my con-science that I had turned Teddie's children against him. (Try to Preserve the Image!) However, I didn't have to worry: He had done the job all by himself.

"Mommy, what if Hank doesn't get Daddy to pay?"

"*If* that should happen, there is more than enough in the trust fund to get us home and maintain us come September. You do have to be back in time for school, you know."

"What? And let Daddy think you caved in?"

Humph! I hadn't thought of that aspect.

"Yeah, we know," said Simon, grinning. "And there are good schools here in Dublin."

"You've been checking?"

"Sure." Simon's grin got broader. "Why not? Plan ahead!"

I leaned back in my chair, as if the inanimate wood could give me moral support.

"Now look, you two . . ." Even as I framed it, my argu-ment about continuity in education/friends/homes seemed weak . . . opposed as it was to the fact that Teddie-boy would think he'd won the game.

"Yes?" drawled my children encouragingly.

"*You* may like Ireland but *you* haven't been accused of murder, or gaining an inheritance under false pretenses. *You* don't have to bear the brunt of outraged elderly aunts and—"

The doorbell wheezed.

"Speaking of outraged elderly aunts," said Snow mali-ciously, "what odds will you give me on our caller?"

"I wouldn't," and I listened fervently for a friendly voice.

The male mutters I heard were encouraging. Shay? I half rose in expectation, berating myself soundly for that notion. I was both pleased and disappointed to see Michael Noonan, tall and very attractive, striding into the dining room.

"I was hoping to find you home, Rene. Can I persuade

you to have a few jars with me this evening? I couldn't reach you by phone this afternoon."

I heard that Michael wanted to talk to me, away from the ears of my adoring children.

"I'll change and be right with you. Snow, show Mr. Noonan what we've done with the living room and the kitchen."

You know, it was really fun at my age to dress up for an unexpected date, without resorting to the pretenses of indifference or keeping him waiting, so as not to appear unpopular.

I slipped quickly into the lemon-yellow sheath with the matching sandals that Snow had bludgeoned me into buying, found the strand of wooden beads that Snow said "made" the ensemble, pulled a brush through my hair, dabbed on scent, eschewed the eye shadow despite what Snow said about the absolute necessity of that, and was back down the stairs in seven minutes flat. Wishing it were Shamus Kerrigan who awaited me.

"Mom, practice makes perfect," said my daughter, casting an appraising eye on my costume.

Michael's expression told me he agreed. Then Simon stepped forward with an exaggerated swagger.

"Now, Mr. Noonan, I don't want any fast driving, she's our only mother, and you're to be home directly after the pubs close. Otherwise we'll worry. Now have a good time, dear."

Michael was at first nonplussed, until he recognized the reversal of roles. He made conventional responses in a mock-solemn tone of voice.

"What a pair!" he said as he guided me to his car, a dark blue Spitfire.

"I'm sorry to let you in for that."

"I'm not," he replied, with laughter in his voice.

"I guess they'd be considered bold here in Ireland. Or cheeky!"

He gave me a sidelong look as he started the car. "They're not disrespectful for all they're vocal, Rene. Then, of course, knowing they're Yanks changes one's perspective." He was not above needling me.

Michael had turned his car toward Dublin as we stopped

at the dual highway. He was glancing in his rear-view mirror, waiting to get out into the traffic, which was fairly steady on the main road.

"Any favorite pubs?"

"I haven't done much searching yet, but I rather had the notion you wanted to *talk*."

He took off down the highway, easing in between two rather fast-moving vehicles with what I thought was a dangerous want of driving discretion. He appeared pleased with his maneuver, but I hoped he didn't continue to drive like this. But he did. At the lights in Cabinteely he took an unexpected—though he signaled—right and then almost immediately a left into the parking area for the Bank of Ireland Computer Building. He pulled on the brakes, doused the lights, and glanced back over his shoulder at the road. A car came tearing past the entrance, and almost immediately we heard it braking. I cringed for a crash-bang-shriek.

"Kieron was right. You *are* being tailed. C'mon."

"Tailed?" I said it to his closed door as he came round the Spitfire to help me out. "Was that what that wild driving was about?"

"I don't normally scramble, Rene."

Just as we got to the roadway, a car backed up past us, braked again, and then angled into the one free roadside parking space, its lights briefly full on our faces.

"Is that the man?" I asked, but Michael told me not to look, and hurried me across the street to the pub.

Unexpectedly, the pub was luxuriously appointed, with thick carpets, paneled walls, deep armchairs, and a cheerful fire on the hearth.

"D'you mind sitting here?" Michael asked, gesturing to a table whose chairs had a discreet view of the door.

"Under the circumstances, no."

We were giving our order when the door opened and in came . . . Nosy.

"He just arrived," I told Michael, leaning forward as if to flick my ash, then nonchalantly glancing up.

Michael sat back, rubbing his chin reflectively. Then he

adjusted his glasses. "You do have a tail: one of our good private detectives."

"Does he know you?"

"He might." Michael sounded doubtful, although he gave me a cheerful grin. "Much of our work deals with estate management, wills, sales . . ."

"But wasn't he hired by my relatives?" Even as I said it, the notion didn't sound plausible. How could a private detective's checking my movements help to contest the will?

"It couldn't be about old Mrs. Slaney?" He shook his head. "My ex-husband?"

He nodded.

"But why? Why now? I've divorced him. What I do is not his business any more—" I broke off because Michael had that anticipatory look, like someone waiting for the players to hit on the right syllables in charades. "He's trying to revoke my custody of the children? Trying to prove me immoral or something? He's out of his ever-loving mind! Just because I came to Ireland for the summer?"

Michael had kept nodding agreement with my various points. "I don't know the man, of course, but I understand that he was not in favor of your holidaying here. In fact, if I may be candid, I've heard from your American solicitor, Mr. van Vliet, asking my advice on custody laws here."

*"What?"*

Michael patted my hand soothingly. "The Irish courts would uphold your custody unless wilful and excessive neglect of the children could be proved." I was sputtering with indignation. "And that would mean you'd have to stop feeding them completely, keep them locked up in substandard rooms without toilet facilities, et cetera, et cetera. Or if you were proved guilty of some felony."

"Good God! How could Teddie have heard of Mrs. Slaney?"

Michael merely nodded in Nosy's direction.

"You mean, you think I've been followed since I got here?"

Our drinks arrived then, and I took a long, long pull. Michael, noticing, indicated to the barboy to bring two more.

"That impossible, incredible man! How could he do such a thing?" Very easily, I realized, remembering the unserved injunction to keep us from even leaving the States. What maggot was possessing Ted Stanford now? "Well, I'm glad you didn't mention this in front of the twins. They'll be livid."

Michael's eyebrows went up. "You're going to tell them?"

I sighed, thinking back to that earlier conversation. "Neither of them is stupid. Sooner or later they'll see Nosy, and it doesn't take them long to put facts together."

"You Yanks!"

"Yeah," I said, with no enthusiasm. "But what *can* he do?" I asked, in a fine state of agitation.

"Legally," Michael said in a forceful way, "nothing. I understand from van Vliet that at their ages your children have some say in the choice of parent." He shrugged as if that solved my problem entirely. "I'd hazard the guess that the man is merely trying to ruin your holiday."

"He's got company."

"I beg your pardon?"

"I was thinking of the aunts," I said, with a heavy sigh.

"Now, now, Rene, cheer up. After all, you *haven't* murdered anyone." He said it to shock me out of my depression, and he did.

"Speaking of Mrs. Slaney," I began brightly, "how much would it cost me to get Fahey out *now*? I really don't need any more unsavory characters on my queendom."

"I'll sound him out. How high would you go?"

"Well, I refuse to be milked, but I don't want anything to do with a man like that. More important: Does Tom Slaney have any legal right to squat in that cottage now that his mother's dead?"

"Tom Slaney's legal rights are nil as far as the cottage goes."

"Is there an inquest coming?" I asked.

"As it happened, her physician had seen her the previous week, and her heart failure was no surprise."

"What about the hole in her head?" I'm not a vindictive

person, but the appalling nature of her final injury made me wish that her son would suffer something in the way of justice.

"Ah, yes, well, she *died* from the heart attack. Slaney admitted to her collapse, said she struck her head on the hearth—I understand there's corroborative evidence—and he put her in the bed. He was, on his own admission, drink-taken. It's been proved that he came back to her cottage Friday night to get money from her, since her pension had just been paid. At any rate, according to the barman, when he returned to the pub he had money enough to drink himself stocious. He did end up spending the night in the nick."

"While his poor mother lay dead . . ."

"Legally one could split hairs on this, and I don't know yet if there will be a prosecution. She died first, you see."

"Of fright, terror, disappointment . . . And where is that creature"—I preferred to call him "murderer"—"now?"

"He's still in custody. He won't bother you, and as far as the cottage is concerned, it has reverted to the landlord—you." Michael patted my hand reassuringly. He had such nice hands.

He started to recount a case he'd been briefed with which was so outrageous and improbable that I had to keep my mind on it. Then he regaled me with several more highly amusing incidents so that "Time, ladies and gentlemen" caught me completely by surprise, and with some dismay.

"Hungry, Rene?" asked Michael as we left the pub.

I naturally glanced over my shoulder to see if Nosy was there. Michael gave me a little shake.

"All aboveboard," he said. "If we can make it to Stepaside by half eleven, we can eat *and* drink. Might as well spend your ex-husband's money on Nosy's expenses . . . huh?"

"Hey, great!" I laughed. Michael was giving me the proper perspective.

As he drove off this time, it was at a circumspect speed.

"Speaking of ex-husbands, Michael, couldn't Mary Cuniff get an annulment and then be free?"

"Of course."

"How much does an annulment cost, then?"

"More than Mary can manage to save."

"Not more than George would be willing to spend, though?"

"Hmmm. My dear girl, you are remarkable. But are you so certain Mary would jump out of one fire into another?"

"George is different! I know she really thinks so."

"Does she?" His question hinted at others unasked.

"Why?"

"Irene . . ." and then he stopped, and took a rather sharp curve carefully.

"I've a suspicion," I began, to relieve his conscience, "that my Great-aunt Irene had some blind spots in her philanthropy. I feel that George is right for Mary. Why must she be condemned to this sort of half life, this sense of being trapped, or Molly, for that matter? It just perpetuates the problems in the next generation."

"And you a divorced woman?"

I sighed. "My marriage to Teddie failed for very understandable reasons. But that doesn't mean that I couldn't and wouldn't make a second marriage work. In fact, I'd be better at it. I know so many of the pitfalls."

"Oh?"

Michael's reply was too bland, and I realized how my attitude had suddenly polarized. In spite of what I'd seen of Irish marriages, and in spite of what I knew about the high divorce rate of American marriages, I was essentially a romantic, cock-eyed optimist. And I really did like having a man about the house. Domestic by temperament, I liked to "do" for a man. I'd missed that these past eighteen months. While it was enthralling to have a queendom of my own, while I was enjoying the redecoration, I was also more and more aware that a good bit of such industry is doing it for a particular man: to please him, to give him a reason to boast to his friends about his home and his wife, and to give him a valid reason for coming home at all.

"Yes, 'oh,'" I said tartly, in answer to Michael. "There are some areas in which the resemblance between my great-aunt and me fails completely. Another thing: How can Ann Purdee get a legal separation? I'm willing to finance it. I can *always* say it was Aunt Irene's wish."

Michael gave a snort. "Irene did not like her protégés . . ."

"Succumbing?" I asked testily, when he couldn't find an appropriate verb. "Will or will not a legal separation give her protection against that husband of hers?"

"Yes, it would," Michael said. "I have suggested it. But the separation has to be made by mutual consent."

"And you don't see Paddy Purdee consenting?"

"Consenting, no. But he'd do anything for a price."

"You know him?"

"Yes. Irene tried to put the fear of the law and the Lord into him."

"Then why is Ann Purdee scared?"

"Irene Teasey is dead. He was afraid of *her*."

I thought of my aunt's diminutive stature. "Good heavens."

"Irene in an angry mood was . . . formidable, Rene." Michael was both amused and respectful. "She tore strips out of him."

"She met him?"

"In my office. I arranged the meeting."

"Then he'd know who and where . . ."

"I doubt it. For starters, your aunt's name was never mentioned. And the interview was attended by one of Irene's very good friends in the Gardai. Unfortunately, that gentleman has also passed on. We'll just hope that Purdee is still fishing a long trip and hasn't heard."

Undoubtedly Rene's Law applied to Ann, and Paddy Purdee would run into some person who knew about Irene Teasey, where she lived, and Ann's situation.

As we turned into the parking lot of the Stepaside Inn, Nosy wasn't far behind us, and I sighed deeply. I too did *not* like being followed. Once more I was visited by the irresistible desire to cut stakes here instantly and go back to my own country. But that would be cowardly, and worse, Teddie would think he had won.

We were lucky to find a table, for the Inn was rather full. As Michael pointed out, it was one excuse to keep on drinking past licensed hours and to get a solid base of food for more drinking at home.

"There's one more business," I said after we'd given the waitress our order.

"Yes?" he said encouragingly when I faltered.

"Do you know why my aunt turned against Shay Kerrigan? I mean, exactly why?"

Michael gave me the blank look which I suspected he found useful in courtrooms.

"Oh, c'mon, Michael, *I* know even if Aunt Irene shoved it under the convenient heading of protecting someone innocent. *Was* she explicit to you? The thing is, I don't think she got the right man. And it would alter matters considerably if I could prove it."

"Oh?" Again that horribly bland response.

"Really, Michael. You're infuriating. And it's not betraying a professional confidence to tell me if she was explicit. You have only to say that much and I'll reveal what I've found out."

Michael took ages to make up his mind. "She said, as nearly as I can remember her exact words, that she had been bitterly disappointed in Shay, that he had abused her confidence and lost her respect; he deserved no assistance from her."

"Then she never confronted him?"

"She absolutely refused to see him."

"That wasn't fair."

"Does 'fair' enter into it?"

"I think so. He's supposed to have fathered Sally Hanahoe's baby."

This was as much a shock to Michael as it had been to me. He blinked and stared at me as if he doubted his ears, strengthening my own belief in Shamus.

"Yes, and furthermore he's supposed to have told Sally that he was married and covered his tracks so well that she couldn't find him. She had to have the baby on her own."

Michael had begun to shake his head from side to side.

"I don't believe it either," I went on. "And for good reasons. One, Shamus made no secret to me of the fact that he's not married, nor likely to marry. Two, he has a keen sense of family responsibility. Look at his kindnesses to his nephew, his courtesies to the Ladies Brandel. They're damned good judges of character. But it fits in with what I'm beginning to understand about Aunt Irene. She would think the worst of a man, any man, without bothering to ask yes, no, or maybe. Furthermore, when I mentioned Sally Hanahoe's name to him it didn't, absolutely didn't, ring a bell. I'd stake my life on it." Michael gave me a knowing glance, which I dismissed angrily. "I hear things when people are dissembling."

"He's got a good barrister in you. Too good!"

"Oh, nonsense, Michael. I simply can't stand injustice and . . . and . . ."

"You're feeling guilty about the access?"

"Well . . . Oh, I *know* he was making nice-nice when he thought he could wheedle the right of way out of me but . . . he's gone on being . . ." The waitress fortuitously arrived with our suppers, and when we spoke again, the subject of Shay Kerrigan did not come up. I heard that somehow Michael preferred not to discuss him any more.

The lights were on at my house when Michael turned up the lane. (My lane.) We were halfway to the door when it was flung open and my children stalked out to intercept us.

"Where have you been, Mommy?" demanded Snow, worried and angry.

"Oh, good Lord, I'm so sorry. We went on for a bit to eat and—"

"It's my fault, Simon, Snow," Michael interrupted, with suspicious meekness. "I know I promised to have her back after closing time . . . but we're only forty-five minutes late."

Snow began to giggle, and Simon's frown disappeared.

"Aw, Mom, we're not that way," he said.

"No, it was inconsiderate of us," Michael said. "It won't happen again."

"Ah, fer Pete's sake . . ."

Then I sensed Snow's unspoken anxiety.

"What's happened, honey?"

Beside me I could see Michael tense, and we exchanged glances. But Nosy had been following me . . .

"Gerry . . . you know, your cousin . . . Alice's son . . . was here with the motorcycle girl . . ."

"And . . . ?" I prompted, silently complimenting Simon on his diplomacy.

"They wouldn't *tell* us." Snow was miffed. "But they're very anxious to see you. Like then!"

"Gerry said he'd give you a shout tomorrow morning."

"Well, that's that, then." I turned to Michael, extending my hand. He held it in such a way that, for some obscure reason, I was very glad of my children's presence. Oh dear, what was wrong with me? Michael was so nice, and yet . . . I thanked him profusely for the lovely evening and the business we'd done in the pubs, and he said that he'd check into matters and ring me later next week.

 18

I DID NOT sleep well, which was surprising with all I'd had to drink: anxiety over Teddie's next ploy, I supposed. But at five thirty, I finally admitted to myself that I was in the thralls of sexual frustration.

I missed Shamus Kerrigan! I missed him for himself, his easy charm, the warmth of his rather boyish smile, the reassurance of his presence in my vicinity, visible or invisible. Not that Michael wasn't charming too; he did have an easy way about him, a nice smile, good hands, but I *relied* on Michael, and I most certainly hadn't wanted to be kissed by him. Which had been very much on his mind during the later part of our evening together.

I was thwarted, too. Michael didn't believe Shay Kerrigan would be irresponsible toward a girl he'd got pregnant but it was Ann Purdee I had to prove that to. Because if I didn't, I lost any chance of influencing Ann. She wouldn't trust me, and I had to be in her confidence to deal with Paddy Purdee for her sake.

But clearing Shay would serve several purposes: One, I'd get in good with him by being able, with a clear conscience, to give him access up the lane; two, it would show Ann that Irene could be wrong about a man or men; three, it would put me in a damned good light. (Preserve the Image!)

I snorted at my conceit. I'd done such a good job of managing my own life that I should give someone else pointers? C'mon, Rene, be honest. The only point of the three is that you'll ingratiate yourself with Shamus Kerrigan. But what if he really is only buttering you up to get that access? You give it, he goes off his merry way, and then where will you be in Ann's and Sally's eyes?

Well, if *that* should happen, I'm wrong about Shamus Kerrigan's character, even if I do prove him innocent about Sally, and I'm well rid of him.

Now there's a dilemma for you to ponder, Rene!

I pondered . . . and woke, disgustingly refreshed, at eight o'clock, the clean fresh air blowing in my window like an intoxicant. There wasn't another sound in the house, but out-of-doors was as busy as could be. Birds, bees, other talking things . . . and loud clanking noisy things . . .

I sat bolt upright as I identified the noise. Bulldozers? I ran to the window, but I couldn't see up the hill past the screening tress. I threw my spring coat around my shoulders and dashed down the steps and out the door. I had to get into the lane before I had any view. A huge yellow bulldozer was on the hill, charging and roaring like its namesake, pawing pieces out of the meadow.

I glanced down my lane: no tracks.

So the dilemma had dissolved last night. I felt defeated. Shay must have bought the access rights in from Glenamuck. Was that the business deal which he'd been busy with? Had he really been away from his office these last few days? Or avoiding any calls from me?

Be fair! How can you blame him, with your shillyshallying?

Despondently I made myself coffee. I didn't even get a chance to mope in solitude. Snow came charging down the steps at such a pace that I yelled at her not to break her neck.

"There's a bulldozer in the field?" Her words were half query, half accusation. "Did you give —"

"No, I didn't." I didn't add that I wished I had. "And there isn't a mark on the lane."

Snow flounced into the other chair. "Then how? Levitation?"

"There was a possible way in from the other side."

"Hey, Mom," and Simon joined us. "What's with the—"

"He came the other way," said Snow.

"Oh!" Simon was also disappointed and uneasy. Oh dear, if Shay's action disillusioned them too, I'd have more than Ann, Sally, and Mary to worry about.

A more somber trio never ate without tasting. It occurred to me as I put limp eggs and soggy toast into my face that the twins were even more upset about this revolting development than I was.

"It's Friday," said Simon for no reason.

"Yeah!" his sister agreed.

"Why?" I asked, to prove I was listening.

"Gotta come sometime, I guess," said Simon logically.

"Okay, Mom, like you always tell us," said Snow, "when you're down in the dumps, look up. There's a lot of work to be done about this place. Let's do it."

That's how we came to sort out Mrs. Slaney's cottage that Friday. I couldn't get more depressed than I already was.

I was, naturally, wrong, but at least I had company. The tired, tattered bits and pieces that had furnished the poor lady's home ought to have been interred too. Nothing seemed worth saving.

Ann concurred when she came over to see what we were doing. "But you've got to remember that Tom Slaney's entitled to it, rag, bag, and bucket. And he's the sort would create trouble if any's missing."

"What'll we do with it, then?" I asked.

"You've a world of space in the barn," Ann suggested.

"We can make a list, Mom," Snow said, "itemizing everything and having Ann sign it."

"Would he accept that?"

"And Mr. Corrig, the postman."

"I'll get some cartons from Sally's store," I said, relieved at an excuse to leave for a few moments.

By the time I returned with the largest cartons that Sally's obliging store manager could find me, Jimmy had arrived and

Molly was abroad. Snow, with a clipboard and lists (two carbons), was organizing everyone, even Meggie, Tom, and Fiona. Before noon we had all but a wardrobe cleared out and stored in the hay barn.

"Eat now, scour later" was Snow's dictum, and we four repaired to my kitchen.

I had managed not to look up the lane at the bulldozer, but my resolve weakened when I passed the phone. While the kids were bickering over who used the john first, boys or girls, I dialed Shay's number. My ridiculous heart gave a leap at the sound of his rich voice on the other end, but sank as the recorded message idiotically reported back. I hung up quickly as Simon came thudding down the stairs with Jimmy.

We tackled the cleaning problem after lunch, and I tried to keep firmly in mind that the poor old lady mustn't have been able for many years. We used a big box of Flash, three cans of Ajax, wore out I don't know how many rags, sponges, and Brillo pads, but the fusty odor of decay had definitely been blown out of the cottage—had she ever opened the windows?—by late afternoon.

"Slaney's may be clean," Snow said as we drooped on the grass, "but it only makes Fahey's look worse."

As one, we glanced to the left. Jimmy sighed audibly.

"Not today," I said, touching his shoulder. "And you are in no way obliged to join our madness."

"No honest, Aunt Rene, I *like* working with you and the twins. It's fun!"

Tired as he was, he meant it, and I was about to elaborate on my appreciation when Mary returned home in George Boardman's car. Soon Kieron put in an appearance, and while the men were occupied with storing the heavy wardrobe, I hemmed and hawed with Mary Cuniff, trying to find an adroit way of suggesting my plan. My progress was nil, because Mary was feeling conscience-stricken about not having looked in on old Mrs. Slaney over that fatal weekend, and not having offered to do any of the household tasks.

"It's a mercy the poor old thing's in her grave, Mary Cuniff," said Ann bluntly. "She'd've been long gone and welcomed it if that doctor hadn't been such a sanctimonious twit.

My, the place looks nice now." Then Ann's gaze fastened on Fahey's, and her mouth tightened.

"Michael's going to buy him out as soon as possible," I said brightly, as a lead-in to my ploy. "Did Michael, by any chance, phone you today?" I turned to George.

"No, he didn't." George looked surprised and, curiously, uncomfortable. "I wasn't in the office, you see."

I wondered fleetingly if his ardor for Mary had cooled, but I had my opportunity. "Well, I'd like to have a man in that cottage, with Tom Slaney floating around."

"He's not likely to come back," said George firmly.

"Michael said something about your applying for planning permission, so if you still want to buy it . . ."

That touched off the reaction. No, it wasn't indifference on his part, or Mary's. I heaved an internal sigh of relief. This playing the lady bountiful/arch meddler can lead to temptation: just one little shove in the right direction . . . Only how was I so sure that my direction was right?

I was tired.

That's what Kieron and Mary said, and Ann and George dutifully agreed.

"I'll cook dinner, Mom," Snow said, "and Simon and Jimmy can help." She flashed them warning glances.

Jimmy said he *had* to be home for tea tonight: His mom was getting narked. He put himself out of temptation's way by flinging himself on his bike and beetling off.

"I'll have a word with you, Ann-girl," Kieron said, taking her so firmly by the arm that she was too surprised to break away.

The rest of us were rather amazed at his masterfulness, but Ann, instead of an outburst of independence, meekly let herself be led toward her cottage.

Mary and I broke into a series of nervous inanities before we all dispersed. I wondered why George kept looking so worried. Did he know what Kieron was up to?

"Hey," said Snow as we walked toward the house, "what's with the strong-arm Kieron's using?"

"I haven't a clue," and I wished I had. Something was up.

The phone's ringing interrupted Snow's supposition. We

all ran to catch the call, with me hoping fervently that it might be Shay Kerrigan.

It was Gerry Hegarty, sounding very relieved to hear my voice.

"I've been phoning and phoning, Coz," he said.

"Oh Lord!" I'd forgotten the twins' message about him.

"We've been housecleaning down below . . ."

"Where? Oh, old Mrs. Slaney's?"

"Yes." Why did that interest Gerry Hegarty?

"Rene, are you free this evening? Maureen and I'd very much like a chat with you."

I couldn't come out and bluntly ask him if it was about the free cottage. So I said he'd be welcome and I'd love a chance to talk with Maureen again.

I worried all through supper about how to let them down gently. It wasn't that *I* didn't want to oblige Gerry (he couldn't help having Auntie Alice as a mother—maybe that's why he was so nice) or Maureen. It was just that . . .

Gerry and Maureen had both been in the house before. They seized on the subject of our redecorations as though I'd done something incredible. At least, Gerry did more of the talking; Maureen just looked apprehensive. The second time the conversation strangled to death, I rediscovered blunt speech.

"Now that I know you approve of my redecorating," I told them, "what is *your* problem?"

Gerry glanced at Maureen, and she, all but squirming, passed the buck back to him.

"Has Brian Kelley been at you again to sell?"

"The figure's gone up to thirty-five-thousand pounds. And if I agree to sell he'll use his influence to assure probate."

Gerry cleared his throat. "I've reason to believe that it's my mother trying to buy the property."

I couldn't help it. I let out a whoop. "But she objected to Aunt Irene buying it!"

"According to the latest," Gerry told me with a sardonic grin, "it was on my mother's advice that Irene purchased the land. Because land south of the city was sure to appreciate."

"The old—! So now, of course, that's why she should be

left the land?" Gerry nodded. "Okay, would she have that kind of money?" Again Gerry nodded, and I whistled.

"Mother's rather shrewd with property."

"City property," Maureen corrected him.

"Then why the subterfuge? I mean, working through a clown like that Kelley character? And forcing Maureen to let him know when I arrived? And his besieging me?"

"For starters," Gerry said, still slightly embarrassed, "she assumed that you only came over here to sell the property . . ."

"And if she could get to me first, I'd sell and disappear forever? And then she could say that Irene *had* left her the property after all? That another will had been discovered?"

Maureen stared at me. Gerry gave a short laugh.

"I thought you'd only just met my mother!"

"I can't blame it on genetics, because it's from Mother's side of the family, but I've got an aunt in the States . . ." I didn't elaborate, because she *was* his mother.

"Do you *have* to sell?" Gerry asked. He glanced at Maureen. "Because if you *have* to . . ."

I scored a large plus for Maureen: She had not betrayed any confidential information about the trust fund.

"As it happens, Gerry, I don't. At least not precipitously. And, well, my affairs have taken such a turn that I'll probably stay on longer than I'd originally intended."

The news pleased them. Maureen actually smiled, with an air of relief that finally permitted her to relax on the chair.

"Say, mind my asking, but how *did* you find out your mother was bidding for the queendom?"

"Something I overheard at the house the other day matched what Maureen had told me about Brian Kelley," said Gerry, with an affectionate and amused glance at his young niece. "You're sure you're all right, as far as death duties are concerned? What I'm saying is, I personally would like to see Irene's queendom remain as she wished it. So for want of the few odd pounds, don't feel you have to sell it."

"That's extraordinarily nice of you, Gerry . . ."

"The least we can be, with my mother carrying on the way she has."

"And the first thing she'd do, did she own it, would be to

turf Ann, Sally, and Mary out," Maureen said bitterly. "And the only one who's paid her any heed is Maeve. It's all very embarrassing," she finished, in a muffled voice.

Gerry leaned over and patted her hand. "I told you Rene would understand, pet."

"I truly didn't know it was Auntie Alice that Mr. Kelley was representing. And Ann and Sally and Mary have had such a desperate time—you don't *know* what can happen to women in Ireland . . ."

"Yes, well, I'm beginning to. I'm arranging a caretaker tenant for Thrush cottage . . . and then, bluntly, I'm bribing Fahey to vacate completely." Ah yes, there was a reaction there. "I'll look for suitable clients in the best traditions of the queendom. Did you by any chance know of someone?"

Gerry saw through that bland question with a chuckle, but Maureen looked surprised, hopeful, and apprehensive.

"I told you she was a downy one, Maureen. And, yes, Rene, we do."

"So does Shamus Kerrigan." What imp made me come out with that?

"Shamus?" Gerry frowned, confounding me. "Which Shamus Kerrigan?"

"She means Shay Kerrigan," said Maureen, "the one who was such a good friend of Auntie Irene's."

"How many Shamus Kerrigans do you know?" I asked Gerry.

He gave a chuckle. "Several, two of whom I hope you never meet. Two of 'em live in Dublin, as well."

I cut through the beginning of his next remark with an urgent question of my own. "Would your mother know Shay Kerrigan, the one who was friends with Irene?"

Gerry glanced at Maureen for confirmation. "Sure and she would. He developed property Dad owned in Ballybrack."

Well, that sort of tied in with another great unanswered question about Shamus: Which relative had given him that bogus permission to use my lane? So my dear Great-aunt Alice had been *that* positive she'd own the queendom? I wondered if she'd socked him a bundle for that one transit. And if he'd got his money back.

"Would you really consider helping someone, Rene?" asked Maureen, almost timidly.

"I sure would. Is she deserted, abused, or unwed? Oh dear, and I'm *not* being snide."

"She's married, been deserted, and has a small boy. Her name's Sheevaun Donnelly, and her man took the boat, which is just as well, as he'd been a bit too free with his employer's money," Maureen said in a rush. "She runs a hairdressing business in Rathfarnham, but the person who's been taking care of her little boy is altogether unreliable."

"We could get our hair done free?" That imp of misplaced humor made me say it.

"Oh, I'm certain Sheevaun wouldn't mind at all," Maureen said, a little stiffly.

"Honest, I'm pulling your leg."

Gerry's laugh was more reassuring than my words, and Maureen began to grin slowly, her eyes still on mine, and hopeful. However, now I could see their strategy in confessing Aunt Alice's abortive attempt to secure the queendom. Ah, well, theirs was the nicer axe to be ground.

"Sure now, Maureen, you know how Irene was in acquiring useful tenants. She liked the old gratitude bit, noblesse oblige," Gerry was saying.

"To be frank, however, I'd prefer less personal service and a bit more rent," I said. "Several pounds a month is—"

"Oh, Sheevaun would be able to pay more than that, Rene," her sponsor said quickly. "She's paying twelve pounds a week for two horrid little rooms now."

"Look, I have to get the cottage back first. But, yes, if I get it back, I'll definitely consider your Mrs. Donnelly. I hadn't actually committed myself to Shay's candidate."

Such a decision called for coffee, at the least, and then we ambled down to watch Snow riding Horseface. As nearly as I could tell, my darling daughter was improving. Ann shouted instructions from the center of the pasture's improvised ring, but she came over to the fence to greet Maureen and Gerry. Maybe she was on very friendly terms with them anyhow, but Ann was unusually expansive. I wondered what on earth

Kieron had said to her. The girl was practically beaming at me with goodwill when she suddenly frowned and tensed.

Following her anxious gaze, we all observed a Mini Minor cautiously drawing up the lane. Ann ducked under the rail, about to fly toward the house, when a woman poked her head out of the window.

"Could you tell me if the Stanford children are still here?"

"Yes, they are," I told her.

Her head vanished as she turned off the ignition and got out.

"Are you taking care of them?" she asked pleasantly. "I'm Mrs. Melton of the ISPCC."

She extended her hand, so of course I shook it.

"I'm Irene Teasey," I said, since that information seemed proper. What was the ISPCC?

"It's very good of you to take on such a responsibility," she went on, mystifying me more.

"No responsibility, really. I am their mother."

"Their mother?" The cordiality died in her eyes, and her whole attitude became wary. More than that I couldn't hear.

"Yes, I'm Irene Teasey Stanford, but I resumed my maiden name when I got my divorce."

"Divorce?" For the amount of information she was getting from me, she was giving poor return.

I looked about, toward Gerry, Maureen, and Ann. Gerry obligingly stepped up beside me.

"Yes, Mrs. Melton, I divorced Teddie Stanford. It was final about seven months ago now."

"Oh!"

"What is this all about, Mrs. Melton?"

"I told you. I'm from the Irish Society for the Prevention of Cruelty to Children."

"You've come for a donation?" An odd sales pitch.

She brushed that aside irritably. "Was there a death here recently?" She looked past me to Gerry.

"My great-aunt, who was also Irene Teasey, died in March," I told her. Or didn't she trust anything I said?

"No, no. Within the past few days?"

"If you mean old Mrs. Slaney," said Gerry as he pointed to the now clean cottage, "she died of a heart seizure this week."

"Heart?"

Mrs. Melton's habit could get on your nerves.

"Yes, sure now and the old dear'd been hanging on to life as if it was worth living," said Gerry, very smooth. I guess he had come to the same horrid conclusion I had. "Rene, here, my cousin," and his emphasis was slight, comforting to me, and noted by Mrs. Melton, "made the sad discovery. Quite a shock it was for her, seeing as how Rene had never laid eyes on the old dear before."

"Oh."

It must have been as plain to Gerry as it was to me: Auntie Alice had spread her "murder" bit about me with a lavish hand. But why on earth she'd bothered the ISPCC . . .

"May I see your children, Mrs. . . ."

"I'm legally Mrs. Teasey."

"Mrs. Teasey. They *are* here?"

"Yes, you may, since you're here. But I think someone has grossly misinformed you and your agency, Mrs. Melton."

She looked sternly at me. "Such a serious complaint has to be investigated, Mrs. Teasey."

"What complaint? As their mother and legal guardian, I have the right to ask."

"I am required to verify their whereabouts, the care they're receiving, and their mental and physical well-being." Her glance passed over the three cottages, settling too long on the mess in front of Fahey's.

"There's my daughter, Mrs. Melton," I said, and waved toward Snow, who was bouncing about on Horseface's back with what seemed like bruising efficiency.

"The girl? The one on the horse?"

"Yes, if you'd like to speak to her while I call my son. *He's* helping a neighbor with his motorcycle."

Her stunned expression told me that she had expected babes in swaddling, or at least toddlers. So it couldn't have been Auntie Alice. It had to be Teddie-boy.

"Simon!" I roared to release some of my spleen. And

bless him, the bullcalf roared back in a matter of seconds. "Yeah, Mom?" He came running at an admirable sprint.

"Mrs. Melton, this is my son, Simon Stanford."

"How do you do, young man?"

"A bit greasy, thank you ma'am," he said, "so I'd better not shake your hand." He gave me a "What's up?" quirk of his eyebrow, which I countered with a mute warning of my own.

"The girl on horseback is this lad's twin sister?"

"Yes, she is. I agree, they don't look much alike, but I didn't have any say in the matter."

My levity went down badly with her, but it cheered me!

"They also don't look fourteen," said Mrs. Melton, as if that *were* my fault. She was very put out. "Since I'm here, perhaps I'd better see where you are all living." She turned toward the cottages, with reluctant distaste.

"If you'll step this way, Mrs. Melton," and I couldn't help making a grand gesture as I indicated the house.

"I'd like a few words with your son and daughter, if I may."

I told Snow to give Horseface to Ann and come up to the house immediately. Simon must have given her the private sign, because she too turned very dutiful, sliding off Horseface. Ann, Maureen, and Gerry gave me a "Help you?" look, which I appreciated but dismissed with a grin behind Mrs. Melton's stiff back.

She sat, rigidly erect, on the little settee as the twins ranged themselves close to me.

"Mrs. Teasey, my office received urgent communications from the American Red Cross, the American SPCC, followed by a request from the Embassy to trace your children. We were given the distinct impression that *infants* had been illegally removed by you from the continental U.S.A. and were being kept in substandard conditions by, I will not mince words, a dangerously unstable woman unfit to have the care of small children, and under suspicion of committing a felony."

"Daddy couldn't have!" Snow's explosive denial blended insult, indignation, embarrassment, and fury. "Mrs. Melton, I'm so sorry. I could die! Why, you must be livid, being dragged out on a fool's errand on such a lovely evening. Oh, Mother, can't Mr. van Vliet do *something* about Daddy? I mean, this is the end!"

"Sara!"

"Mrs. Melton," Simon began, and he was so incensed that his voice cracked a little, "our *mother* has done nothing illegal. She has the custody of us. Dad knew where we were going and when. Because Snow and I told him. He's just—"

"Simon!" I felt I'd better call the children to order or some of Teddie's ridiculous accusations might bear weight. "I too apologize most profusely, Mrs. Melton. I can't think what has possessed the children's father. You see, I'd inherited my great-aunt's estate . . ."

"Twelve acres, four cottages, and this lovely old house," said Snow at her most guileless, "and that lovely old horse— would you believe that he's twenty years old?"

The frost receded a bit more from Mrs. Melton's attitude.

"It seemed a good idea," I went on, "to inspect the inheritance and for the children to meet our Irish relatives."

"We love Ireland," Snow said enthusiastically, "and I'd never get a chance to ride horseback where we lived in the States." My darling daughter made it sound as if we'd come up considerably in the world to inherit an Irish Georgian farmhouse. "We're just started with redecorating—would you like to see what we've done?"

Mrs. Melton rose. "Thank you, my dear, but I have seen all that I need to."

"Then you won't have to send us back to Daddy, will you?" The fear on Snow's face was not sham.

"No, my dear. There's no need to. The facts of the situation were grossly misrepresented to my agency."

I would have escorted her back to her car, but at the front door she turned to me and held out her hand.

"Thank you, Mrs. Teasey, and I apologize for intruding."

"Oh, no, the apologies are all on our side, Mrs. Melton."

"It is scarcely your place to make any apologies, Mrs. Teasey," and when Mrs. Melton smiled, she was a very different, totally likable person. Then she shook her head, stern once more, and walked briskly away.

What had been fulminating within my savage breast

during the interview had now reached boiling point. How I had been able to keep my cool while Mrs. Melton was in the house, I don't know. I suppose I must have realized how important it was for me to be pleasant and conciliatory, and give the appearance of being well-balanced.

"What time would it be in America right now, Simon?" Not that it made any difference, because I was picking up the phone and dialing for the overseas operator.

"You're calling Dad?" And the anger on his face turned to gleeful anticipation.

"No, I'm calling Hank. I couldn't hear your father's voice right now without foaming at the mouth. Hank's got to start proceedings or whatever to keep that man from harassing us. First he has me watched—" Whooops!

"Watched?" Both kids leaped on that one.

"You can call Hank if you want to," Simon said through clenched teeth, "but I'm calling my father. And I'm telling my father—"

"Not if I get the phone first, Brother," said Snow, in every bit as quiet a tone. "Watching *you* or us, Mommy?" she asked.

"Me." I suddenly wanted them to go easy on their father, but my answer didn't please them.

"Why? To open a custody case or something?" asked Snow and there was a sort of look on my daughter's face that was going to haunt me: It was too remorseless, too adult, too cruel.

"Well, he hasn't a hope in heaven," she went on. "You tell Hank that, and we'll tell our doting daddy."

For a wonder, Hank was actually in his office. Feeling my veins bubble again, I gave him a rundown of the recent indignities of surveillance, harassment of the children's friends in the States, plus the nice lady from the ISPCC. Hank blew his cool all the way across the Atlantic. At an inverse ratio, I began to calm down. I even began to see the amusing side of this.

"When I get through with Theodore Teddie-boy Preserve-the-Image Stanford, there won't be anything left in the mirror of his narcissism to reflect an image. He'll—" Hank broke off, inarticulate for once. "What time is it there, Rene? I'll phone back as soon as I have something in train."

I told him, thanked him, and rang off. Simon took the phone out of my hand. And I walked out of the room. I wanted to hear what they said so badly that I couldn't listen. I kept right on walking, as much to work off the energy of that excessive spleen as to quit the scene of combat. To my surprise, because I'd forgotten all about them, Gerry and Maureen were still at the pasture fence, chatting with Ann. Horseface was grazing contentedly, reins looped about his neck.

"It seems," I said as I joined them, "that my ex-husband said his children were being lodged in substandard conditions, cared for by a murderess. The only agency he doesn't seem to have called on to find his poor lost infants is the U.S. Marines."

"Infants?" Gerry and Ann had exclaimed as the words were out of my mouth. Gerry grinned more and more broadly as I went on with my explanation. Maureen just stared, but Ann's face got darker and darker.

"It never stops, does it?" asked Ann when I finished. "Whether you're American or Irish, the man persecutes whenever he feels like it and gets away with it."

"Oh, no he doesn't," I said firmly. "And not all men. Just certain thoroughly spoiled immature temperaments who've never got it through their thick heads that you can't win 'em all with charm and a sweet smile." Some of my own anger cooled before the hopeless look on Ann Purdee's face. "Besides which, I can't really uphold the theory that says all men are bad, or all women nice. Look at Auntie Alice for a bad example — Oh Gerry, I'm sorry. Kieron's sisters, too." That comparison was hardly better chosen.

"But there's no way of knowing, is there?"

I blinked at her vehemence, ruing the disappearance of that happy, relaxed Ann of a scant half-hour before.

"Not one hundred percent sure, but you do have clues," and I thought of the kids' theory about hands. "Ann, how old were you when you got married?"

"I was nineteen."

"I was only nineteen when I married, too," I told her. "Just took me a little longer to realize what a mistake I'd made."

"Your case is different," Ann began, almost belligerently, her eyes sparking.

"I know," I said, with all the rue I could put into my voice. "In my country, there are legal mechanics to solve the problem."

"Can you do something about *that*?" asked Ann skeptically, jerking her head to mean the recent visitation.

"My solicitor is handling the matter with due legal process."

"Then, girls," Gerry said, spreading his hands wide, "you should always marry Americans." A wide grin kept the remark from being snide. Nonetheless, I sensed that the tone of conversation did not please him, wherever his sympathies might lie with the present company, or whatever he had told me about never marrying an Irishman.

"Good old Yankee know-how," I said with a self-deprecating grin, and heaved an exaggerated sigh. "Well, my sense of proportion is operating again, and I fervently hope that the twins are putting their paternal parent straight."

"The twins? Their father?" Ann was astonished.

On cue, the "infants" appeared among us. Their father had not been in his office and was not expected in, and they were mightily disappointed.

I also felt let-down and cheated. And yet, funnily enough, I was relieved. Some inner scruple in me wanted a good relationship (if not the image) preserved between the twins and their father: Children should love and be able to respect both parents, if possible.

"I know three gals who stand in the need of a jar or two," said Gerry.

"Oh, I couldn't . . ." Ann physically stepped away from the invitation.

"Nonsense," said Snow, who had started to unsaddle Horseface. "You *never* go anywhere—except to funerals! And the kids are all asleep, so don't weasel out because they'd cry if you weren't there."

"There's safety in numbers," Gerry said, teasing. Maureen added her urgings.

"He can't have spies in every pub in Dublin, now, can

he?" I argued. "And when was the last time you went anywhere? Without kids ... without ..."

Ann muttered something dark about Kieron, stopped, and glanced apprehensively at his cottage.

"He's free to come too, you know, though it cuts the odds for me a bit." Gerry's grin was calculated to egg her on.

Ann found one last, feeble evasion — her clothes — but Maureen asked since when had one had to dress formally to drink a jar with friends?

"I've a pair of huge dark glasses you could wear," said Snow, all enthusiasm, "and that floppy hat. You'd look just like any other Yankee tourist."

"Oh, what will Sally —"

"Sally's got a date tonight, and you know it," said Snow, with disgust at her protestations. "What're you aiming for? Sainthood?"

For some reason, that taunt decided Ann, and we all linked arms to march over to Kieron's cottage. He gave Ann one long searching look after his initial astonishment.

"I'll just wash my hands," he said, and did so.

Then we all clambered into Gerry's blue Humber and jackrabbited away in a cloud of dust.

"You know, we should have got Mary and made it a residents' association meeting," I said, suddenly in the best of good spirits.

"She and Molly've gone out with George," Ann said, nervously peering out the car window before scrunching down in the back seat.

Did she really think that that husband of hers would pop out of the hedges to waylay her? Speaking of popping out of hedges, I noticed when Nosy's car edged into sight behind us. I opened my mouth to comment on that, then decided against it. Ann might see Paddy Purdee's hand in that too.

I don't remember what we talked about that evening, since so much happened later of more importance, but I remember what a fine time we all had — even Ann, once she got used to the notion of enjoying herself out in public. Not that she was public in the back of the dark booth with her hat and glasses on.

As usual, time was called all too soon. The jars we had poured into Ann Purdee gave her sufficient Dutch courage to sit straight up by the window in the back seat—well, as straight as she could with Kieron's arm about her. Maureen adroitly joined Gerry and me in the front seat. I was feeling good too, and for some reason or other which I can't now remember, we kept singing the unexpurgated version of the Colonel Bogey song. Kieron knew the most scandalous variations! A very merry carload pulled up the lane, right to Ann's doorsteps. My two were deep in books, and there hadn't been a sound upstairs, they told Ann.

I felt very good about the world and the future of mankind as I undressed for bed. Surely Ann would emerge a little from her man-hater's view of the world. As I drifted off to sleep, it occurred to me that my Great-Aunt Irene *hadn't* really been *all* that liberal in her views.

 19

I WASN'T DEEPLY ASLEEP—I'd had a shade too much, or too little, to drink—when a sudden sharp noise woke me. I lay there in a sort of rosy doze with my mind idly bouncing from one topic to another, like those word-cuers in a sing-along film. But I couldn't identify the noise in my dozy state. I suppose that's why I roused further. And *thought* I heard a man swearing softly. It was that sort of a still night, clear, breezeless, on which sound can carry.

My first thought was, *good Lord, doesn't Nosy ever sleep?* And then, *is he making sure where* I'm *sleeping?* It amused me to think that he'd have to break and enter this house to be certain. And then I wasn't amused. After what Teddie-boy had already done, he was capable of doing anything.

With that notion rankling in my no longer sleep-soothed breast, I went to the window. And *thought* I saw a shadow pass in the lane.

Well, if Nosy or anyone was now prowling my purlieu, I was going to give him a rude surprise. I'd had it with this nonsense. And who but Nosy had told Teddie about Mrs. Slaney? I slipped on my loafers, grabbed up my top coat, since navy blue is *the* color for skulking after skulkers (Preserve the Image), and padded downstairs. I removed my trusty fouling piece and proceeded in search of a target. I giggled a bit at the notion of actually firing the shotgun, although the thought of creating some mayhem of my own did have a certain shining appeal. I even checked to make sure the damned thing was loaded. Because if it wasn't Nosy, and was Tom Slaney, or even that Fahey creep . . .

If I was to skulk properly, I'd have a less impeded vision if I came up the lane from Ann's. I'd meet him head on, since he was proceeding down it. So I scooted along the back path to Ann's and came around her house by the kitchen door.

He was there! Trying to get in. Trying to force the door. And it wasn't Nosy. It was, I realized, in a blaze of outraged perception, Paddy Purdee! Next to Teddie-boy, he was the man I most wanted to meet on a dark night with a loaded shotgun in my hands.

"What are *you* doing here?" I cried in a stage whisper. If Ann found out he knew where she was . . .

"Huh?"

He whirled at the sound of my voice, and in the clearness of the night his white eyes stared at me in fright. His jaw dropped and his hands—they were nasty big porkfingered paws—went up in an automatic defensive gesture.

"Who-who's that?"

I was surprised but very pleased at the real fear in his voice.

"How did you find Ann? Who told you where she was?" I demanded, still in my hoarse whisper. If I could just scare him away . . .

His hands were raised now to his eyes, and he started to step backward, away from me.

"No! No! Go away! Go away! You're dead! She said you were dead. She *told* me you were dead."

Wow! Hey, I'd better preserve that image! He thought I was Aunt Irene.

"Didn't I tell you once that you were never to bother Ann

again? Didn't you promise me? Did you think I wouldn't remember that promise?"

I advanced, keeping in the shadows of the house, backing him up the lane as I spoke, trying to sound as sepulchral as possible. I hoped he wouldn't realize that, though I sounded like my great-aunt, I was five inches taller. Or that ghosts don't generally carry shotguns.

I shrugged off the topcoat, because my nightgown was long and filmy and shroudlike.

"Paddy Purdee, you have sinned. You have sinned against Ann. You have broken your sworn oath. Your soul is in grave mortal danger. And I, Irene Teasey, will not rest until you have paid for your faithlessness."

He'd stopped stepping backward, and was running, trying to put distance between us. Although wife-beaters are usually bullies, I wouldn't have thought him such an arrant coward.

"No, she *is* dead. The old woman wouldn't lie."

"Irene Teasey is not dead . . ."

"It's a trick. That's what it is. It's a trick!" He started for me, his voice getting firmer as his confidence returned.

There's nothing like having your bluff called when you're playing ghost. How the hell could I disappear convincingly?

"A trick is it? You fool! This is Irene Teasey. But Irene Teasey is dead. Whose voice is speaking to you if not Irene Teasey's?" Ghosts use cryptic language, don't they? To confuse the people they're haunting?

"Rene? Irene, is that *you*?" cried a woman's voice in the night. It came from Mary Cuniff's cottage. "Oh, Rene, what are *you* doing here?"

The real panic in Mary's voice was sufficient to loosen Mr. Purdee's tenuous grip on common sense. He turned on his heels and sped down the lane as fast as his legs could pump, yelling at the top of his lungs.

"But she's dead! The old woman told me she was dead! She's got to be dead!"

The light went on in Mary's cottage, and her front door sprang wide.

I ran toward her, trying to keep her from rousing everyone, particularly Ann, when I tripped over the nightgown.

I went down, and the last thing I heard was a huge *bang!* right by my head.

Suddenly, there seemed to be an awful lot of light in my face. And someone was weeping bitterly in the background. I heard several male mutters and Snow's chirp. When I opened my eyes, only Mary was in my room, busily wringing out a cloth in a basin of water. My head hurt.

"I'm here again," I said, with what I felt was some originality. I did know where I was. "And I shot off that damned gun, didn't I? I hope no one was hurt."

Laughter and concern warred in Mary's face.

"Yes and no."

"Oh? You mean that I hit the right person but not fatally?"

Her laughter bubbled up. "That was buckshot, you know, and it has a wide range."

"Right persons?"

She nodded encouragingly.

"I must've got Paddy Purdee." She nodded again, egging me on. "*And* Nosy?"

She agreed with considerable enthusiasm and then, rising, went to the door.

"She's conscious. I told you she'd only knocked herself out."

Ann Purdee, her face streaked with tears, rushed into the room. Kieron was right behind her, with Simon and Snow a poor third and fourth but looking righteously smug. Sally Hanahoe hovered tentatively by the door. And I could see a blue hulk and the shadow of a hat that suggested a Garda in abeyance.

"Oh God, not the police again!" I groaned, before I caught his smiling face.

"Well, sure now and you can't go around shooting everyone in sight without the Gardai taking some sort of notice," said Kieron. He too looked immensely pleased.

"Oh, Rene, you *are* all right, aren't you?" cried Ann.

I grabbed her hands, which were ice cold and shaking. "Of course I am."

"But he might have hurt you. He might have—"

"Him? That lousy coward? Running from a ghoulie-ghostie . . ."

"Who went bang in the night!" finished Simon with a loud crow.

"Well, if you've been afraid of that poor excuse of a man all this time, Ann Purdee, you ought to be ashamed."

The Garda tactfully cleared his throat and rocked on his feet in and out of the doorway.

"Please come in. I am decent and well chaperoned," I told him. "Besides, if I tell you the story in their presence, then everyone will know and I can get some sleep. My head is splitting." It wasn't, not badly, but my ear hurt. And my left arm and knee!

"Well, now, missus," the Garda began, taking out his notepad.

So I told him that I had spotted an intruder, that we'd had other intruders, that I knew I was under surveillance by a private investigator sicced on me by my former husband, and about the ISPCC, and Paddy Purdee deserting his wife for the last few years (I could see the Garda knew all about that), and my voice being like my aunt's (he recognized it too), and so I thought I'd put the fear of God in Paddy Purdee, and I'd about chased him away with Mary's inadvertent assist when I tripped on my nightgown and the silly gun had gone off. And had I killed anyone?

His eyes were twinkling as he gravely assured me that both men had taken only minor injuries. "Not where a *man* would wish them, missus," which figured if the two were hightailing it.

My intervention had been timely, because Purdee had jimmied open the lock on Ann's door and had been about to enter.

At that point there was a wheeze from my front doorbell, and Simon went clattering down, muttering something about the doctor.

"Good Lord, I don't need a doctor for a lump on the head."

"And a few lacerations," said Snow.

"If it's the doctor," said Kieron, beginning to steer Ann out, "we'd best be off." Sally, grinning mischievously at me for my evening's work, started to follow them.

Ann got no farther than the door and stopped dead, all color draining from her face. She shot such an apprehensive glance behind her that I thought for a moment that some idiot was making her confront her husband. But Shamus Kerrigan walked through the door.

"Are you really all right, Rene?" he asked, brushing past Kieron, Ann, and Sally. He reached my bedside in a swift stride and took my good hand in his warm, firm, and very comforting grip.

I was so terribly, terribly glad to see him that I nearly burst into tears. I was trying to reassure him and not disgrace myself, or count too much on the unnervingly anxious expression on his face, so that I didn't really see the byplay until Kieron spoke.

"Sally, have you ever seen that man before?"

Kieron was pointing at Shay even while Ann was trying to lug Sally out of the room.

Sally peered obediently at Shay, who looked around, mystified. I recovered my wits.

"This is Shay Kerrigan, Sally. Shamus Kerrigan."

Sally's hand flew to her mouth, but there was no recognition in her eyes as she and Shay looked at each other.

"Well," said Sally after a very taut pause, "he's not the Shamus Kerrigan *I'd* like to meet in a dark lane with a shotgun."

There was a little moan from Ann.

"Thanks, Sally," I told her, but I felt no triumph now. In fact I felt sick because of the terribly sad look in Shay's eyes as he turned back to me.

"Is that why Irene turned against me so?"

"It wasn't fair!" I cried. "I knew it couldn't have been you. I only just *heard* what it was, but you'd gone away and I couldn't *tell* you and . . ." I started to cry. Reaction set in: some pain, intense relief, and that sick feeling in the pit of my stomach for the injustice.

I was being held against a comfortable masculine chest which smelled reassuringly of fresh linen and ironing and soap and shaving lotion, with gentle hands stroking my hair and patting my shoulder, and a vibrant male voice muttering soothing-nesses in my ear, so that it was scarcely surprising that I wept up a storm. And mumbled all kinds of inanities in between sobs.

"She should have *known*. And you've lost so much money, and I ought to have given you permission, because the twins said you had hands and they liked you and *they're* smart enough to know. Only you didn't come back and I was—"

"There, there, Rene. Don't distress yourself so, pet. Now, do be a good love and stop crying. There, there!" My sore hand and arm were being gently kissed, and then he had the inspiration to put his hand on the nape of my neck, and, like a kitten, I sort of shook myself and sagged into silence.

"Oh, my God, my face. I look such a sight when I've been crying," I said, sort of knowing it wouldn't matter to Shay at this juncture, and caring all the more because it didn't.

A cool facecloth was tenderly pressed against my eyes and hot cheeks while suitable reassurances were conveyed in that heavenly voice.

"Oh, Shay," I had such a budget of things to tell him.

"I don't know why I have to time my entrances like this," said a man from the doorway.

It was some minor comfort that, with this gross interruption, Shamus seemed as reluctant to release me as I was to be released.

"You don't *act* concussed, Mrs. Teasey," the doctor continued, swinging his heavy bag to the bedside table. He looked tired and disgruntled. I couldn't blame him. I felt the same way.

He gave my injuries a quick glance, grunted, made with the light in the eyes, remarked on the sites of probable contusions for the morrow, and complimented me on my markswomanship. He then forced me to take some little white pills "because you look as if you would benefit from a good night's sleep," and glared at Shamus, who had been hovering in the hall. Then the doctor turned out my light and firmly closed the door behind him. Leaving me alone. I could hear Shamus protesting, and then the doctor's firm "Come along now, it'll all keep till morning!" And two heavy treads going down the steps.

I lay there, appalled, annoyed, and aching. Wondering if Shay had meant all those comforting, lovely things, and being finally able to relax in his innocence. Honestly, how *could* Aunt Irene have ever suspected him?

Whatever the doctor had given me was working with extraordinary speed . . . my legs were numb and my hands and arms. I must really ask him for a few more . . . less potent . . . Shay's voice and Snow's and Simon's . . . damned birds outside heralding a dawn that came at 3:30 in the morning in Ireland . . .

 20

I WOKE SLOWLY, aware of the sweet scents of sun-warmed air, the myriad little muted sounds which meant that ordinary events hadn't waited for me to wake. I moved, found myself stiff, and . . . remembered.

I did not shoot bolt upright in bed. First I had to struggle to get up on an elbow, then move myself around carefully before a judicious shove raised me somewhat. My head didn't ache, but my ear (had I hit the ground ear-first?) felt bigger than it should, hot and pulsing. So did my elbow, hand, and knee.

I did make it to the loo, and fearfully inspected my face. Which looked just as it ought to: sleepy. Washed, it looked perfectly normal, which was reassuring.

I peered out the bathroom window and saw Shay's blue car parked in front. Ridiculous waves of relief coursed down my spine and into my tummy.

"Good Lord, glad Nosy isn't about! That would have been provocative . . ."

"Mom? You conscious?" Snow's dulcet tones floated up the staircase. She sounded anxious.

"Yes indeed." I leaned down the railing and grinned at her. "Any coffee?"

"Sure thing. You just pop right back into bed, Mommy."

I had that precise intention, because breakfast on a tray,

when Snow is in a good helpful mood, is a real treat. But if Shay's car were outside my door, I didn't want to miss another opportunity.

I shucked my nightgown, slipped into panties, and was fastening my bra when there was a knock at the door. I said "Come in," even as I thought that it was odd of Snow to knock. I turned, and there was Shay, balancing a tray on one hand. We stared at each other for a moment, me horrified, him just . . . just taking me all in.

He said, "Don't please," as I reached wildly for my discarded nightgown. He put the tray on the bed, kicked the door shut, and came toward me with both arms outstretched and a look on his face which rearranged a lot of my resolutions instantaneously.

His hands closed most proprietarily about the bare skin at my waist, and slid up around to my shoulders to hold me sensually against him. At the same time, he was kissing me in such a devastating way! And bare skin, compromising situation, and impropriety notwithstanding, I was kissing him back with all the longing that had been building up in me, with all the conflicting emotions that had dominated our relationship since the bulldozing day we'd met.

We both sort of had too much at the same time. He released me, his hands still caressing my bare back, but holding me slightly from him so that we could look into each other's eyes.

"You'd better put that thing on, Rene," he said unsteadily, and dropped his hands to his side. "I'm sorry," he went on, turning about, one hand jammed in his pocket, the other nervously combing his hair back. "Snow said you'd gone back to bed . . . Hell, I am not sorry!" He circled abruptly back to me, his eyes dark with an expression I knew I reciprocated.

But I'd managed to get the gown around me while I rummaged in my closet for the dressing gown. He let me put that on and then reached for my hands, drawing me back into his arms.

"God, you're pretty," he said, smiling down at me, and he didn't mean my face. "Long and slender." His fingers walked down my back to my waist. Then he took a deep breath and spun me toward the bed. "Get in there, safely, get that tray on your lap. Your darling daughter sent me up with your breakfast, but she'll be up in a minute or two or my name isn't Shamus Kerrigan."

"Wasn't that a bit of luck last night?" I said, seizing on any topic to divert my torrid thoughts.

"Huh?"

"Sally being here and all, so we could prove to Ann that you really weren't *that* Shamus Kerrigan."

Shay gave me a long keen look. "And *that* was what Irene—and Ann—had against me?" His tone was bitter and resigned. "I can credit Irene, but not Ann. I thought she trusted me."

"It may be that she felt Irene had the right of it, and I gather my great-aunt was a trifle difficult to argue with . . ."

"But for Ann to think that I'd abandon a pregnant girl to the mercies of Ireland? Jasus!"

"I don't fault Ann, considering her experiences with Paddy Purdee, as much as I fault my aunt. She was older, wiser, and presumably a far better judge of character than Ann. *She* should have known that you—"

"No, Irene had no use for men at all."

"Oh yes she did." I contradicted him, because it was pointless for us to be arguing on the particular sides we'd chosen. "Look at George and Kieron and even Fahey . . . Oh, as long as a man was *useful* . . ."

"And the Queen's courtiers had to be without flaw, sin, or blot on their escutcheons." And Shay smiled in a bitter nostalgic fashion. "She was such a fascinating woman . . ." His gaze went beyond me and the room to some memory. "She was the most charming woman I've ever met . . . she could get you to do the most tiresome jobs for her . . . while you'd wonder how you got yourself talked into it . . . Oh, Irene Teasey knew how to manage people."

"Well, then, she had no right, if she was so smart, to accuse and find you guilty without ever letting you speak in your own defense."

"Not to worry, pet."

"And if you think I'll let you blame Ann—"

"I said not to worry, pet," he repeated, capturing my

gesturing hand and smoothing the skin across the back, his fingers lightly caressing.

"That's enough to make me. However, now I know she was wrong, and Ann won't have a conniption fit, I can—" I broke off. "It was Auntie Alice who gave you that bogus permission to use the lane, wasn't it?"

Shamus let out an embarrassed "Whuff."

"Wasn't it?" I persisted. "Because she thought all she had to do was wave twenty-five thousand pounds under the nose of the usurping American and I'd grab it and leave! Why didn't you tell me? It worried me so. Oh, well, that doesn't matter now," I added before he could speak, "because now you *can* have the access."

"Hold it, Rene. *I* have something to say."

"But—"

His fingers stopped my lips. "I don't need the access any more."

I thought of the bulldozer cheerfully working away on the tract, and I thought of the sort of man I knew Shamus Kerrigan to be, and I thought . . .

"You've sold it!"

He looked sheepish. "Well, I considered that solution, I can tell you. I'd a lot of money tied up and—"

"Oh, Shay, will you ever forgive me?"

"Pet, not to worry." And he laughed at me. "As I said, I seriously considered that possibility. Then I realized that the next owner might just build those ticky-tacky boxes you were so narked about. So I swallowed my pride and bought access in from Glenamuck."

"At five thousand pounds?" I was aghast at what I, and Irene, had cost him over that hideous farce of names.

"I'm mortgaged to the hilt, all right." He didn't seem depressed.

"Can't you renege or something? I can give you free access now."

"And always wonder if I married you for that?"

"Oh, Shamus . . ."

"You will marry me, won't you?" He was dead serious

and dead worried. "I know I'm rushing you. I'll wait — we only just met, but I've waited for some miracle like you."

"Oh, Shay . . ."

"Look." His grip on my hands was painful, he was so intent on persuading me. "I know you've seen horrible examples of Irish marriage and husbands, and I've no way of proving that I can be any better, but honestly, Rene, I'd do — "

"Will you let me talk?"

He paused, mid-word, his blue eyes darker by several shades, and the expression on his face making it rather difficult for me to breathe, much less think or talk.

"I'm not nineteen, Shay, and neither are you. And I think horrible examples are necessary, to know the pitfalls to avoid. Anyway, we've as good a chance at making a marriage work as anyone. I think I'd like to try. I try very hard if given any encouragement."

"I'll encourage you constantly," he said, and his lips slid over mine with exactly the kind of encouragement that was liable to lead to . . .

"We can't do that now. Snow . . ." and then I groaned and my pretty bright bubble of hope burst all around me.

"What's the matter, pet?"

"There's Simon and Snow . . ."

"But I like your kids. I really do, and they seem to like me."

"They do, Shay, or why would Simon phone you the minute the least thing goes wrong? No, it's Teddie."

"Teddie? Who's he?"

"Their father. My ex-husband."

"Oh, him! Well, he certainly doesn't have to approve your second husband. Oh, I see — he might not approve of me as stepfather?"

"No, no . . ." I couldn't articulate my nebulous worry.

"I didn't think his approval would be required."

"No, but look at what he's done already, with Nosy, and — "

"Pet," and Shamus put his strong and compelling hand on the back of my neck to hold my head straight because I was bouncing around on the bed, I was so agitated. "If you have custody of those kids and they wish *you* to be custodian, there's nothing that ex of yours can do about it. Now, I've already been on to Mihall this morning about that clown—the twins told me about the ISPCC—and I do believe that between us we can sort him out. Now, if you've no other objections to me of any significance . . ."

Our glances locked, and I heard so much that he wasn't saying, felt so deeply the beautiful bond growing so swiftly between us now, that more words were redundant.

"Rene?" His rough whisper was exciting. "Thank you, pet." He leaned down to kiss me, and my urgings got the better of common sense. I reached up to unbalance him when his hands grabbed my wrists. "My dear girl, you know what could happen . . ."

"Uh huh." I returned the challenge candidly.

Just then Snow raised her voice in argument with Simon in the kitchen below, and all my sensuality drained out of me. Shamus saw the change and laughed.

"Will you be less the mother when you're my wife?" he asked in a soft, teasing voice. He picked up the tray. "I'll get you some hot coffee. And this time . . . be dressed?"

I was, but for insurance's sake he brought Snow and Simon with him, both beaming from ear to ear. Snow embraced me, muttering happy things, and Simon gave me a suddenly awkward boy-kiss.

"What a relief, Mom," he said, flopping onto the stool. "It'll be nice to have moral support. You don't realize what you're letting yourself in for, Shay. I mean, I had to grow up with it so I'm used to it—"

"Huh!" said Snow with a contemptuous snort. "You poor abused child. Say," she added, in a complete change of pace, "you can give Mommy away, can't you? And I can be maid of honor, can't I?"

"Now, just a living minute . . ." and I cast a worried eye at Shay. Many's the man who's fled before the too-eager bride.

Shamus only laughed. "Not so fast, you two. I want to give your mother plenty of time to change her mind—" He couldn't go on because of their protests. "Well, women do, don't they? And repersuading her can be so much fun."

"Shamus Kerrigan! You're shameless!"

"Shameless Shay-mus." Snow went off into one of her giggling fits, which was, as usual, mainly relief.

"Anyway, you two," Shay went on, "how could you tots know I'm the proper husband of her and stepfather of you?"

"Ha! We knew right off," Snow said with a toss of her head, her eyes twinkling. And I thought to myself that Shamus Kerrigan would at least have the handsomest pair of stepchildren in the Island. "You've got hands!"

"Hands?" Shamus looked at them, mystified. "Most people do."

"Naw, you don't know what we mean," and Snow was tolerant of his ignorance and quite willing to enlighten him at length.

"Look, children, that can wait."

"What?" Snow obviously felt the topic was of vital importance.

"Right," said Shay firmly. "We do have more urgent . . . if not as fascinating . . . business to attend to this morning. Mihall Noonan's coming over. He needs the details about this visitation from the ISPCC, and also what you plan to do about Purdee."

"What do you mean, what I plan to do? Like prosecute?" Shamus nodded. He was serious.

"What about the buckshot? Couldn't they prosecute me?"

He shook his head. "You have every right to protect your property from unlawful intruders."

"Invaders, you mean," put in Snow.

"And Nosy?" I wondered what sort of ammunition his report would give Teddie.

Shay drew his face into a lugubrious expression. "You had no notion you were under surveillance . . . which will be removed, I can promise . . . so if you shot at one intruder and got two . . ." He shrugged.

"Nosy's removed anyhow . . . with a rear full of buckshot," said Snow, chortling. "Do you think he gets double pay for risk?"

"But what about Purdee?" I said. "Ann won't have a

restful moment now that he knows where she is—" I broke off. "And it was Auntie Alice who told him where she is."

"By Jasus, you may be right," said Shamus, blinking his eyes at my suspicion. "Winnie's in the fish business, after all, and while she may babble like a brook, she doesn't say much. But if Alice were interested, she'd know where to look and who to ask about Paddy Purdee, sure and she would."

"Great!" I said sarcastically. "Then as soon as he's well, we can expect a return engagement."

"Oh, I don't know about that," replied Shay in the slow way that I was beginning to realize meant he had a trick unplayed. "Between ghosts and buckshot, and by the time Mihall gets through with him . . . If you'll go along with our strategy, he won't be likely to show himself."

"Yes, but will Ann believe that?"

"Sure and she will . . . if you say that you'll threaten to prosecute him for breaking and entering *unless* he agrees to sign a legal separation agreement for Ann."

"Oh, Shay, would that work?"

"Mihall suggested it. She can have legal custody of the children and legal protection from his . . . physical presence. That's all she wants right now."

Snow cocked a sophisticated eyebrow and jerked her head toward Kieron's cottage. Shamus saw her.

"Make haste slowly, young Sara," he advised kindly. "You lot have upset quite a few barrows in the short time you've been in Ireland. Let the mud settle a while."

"Say, Mom, now that we know Shamus didn't father Sally's baby," Snow began, and I stared at my precocious daughter. She grinned knowingly.

"Snow, if you and I are to have a congenial relationship," Shamus began.

"This is for *your* good," she replied archly.

"I've got access to the property, Sara Virginia," he said, and took the wind right out of her sails. For one split second.

"Evidently, but does it have to be right in front of our house? Mom owns *that* field, doesn't she?" Snow gestured out the window to the meadow beyond Kieron's cottage. "Be smart, wouldn't it, to carve a hunk off the far side of that and have two routes into the development . . . all well away from us?"

It boded well for that same congenial relationship that Shamus took the time to consider that proposal, and the look he then turned on Snow was approving.

"I think I'd better listen to you, pet, when you come up with sensible notions like that."

"And it would make me feel a whole lot better about the Glenamuck thingie," I said.

"Oh, I'll make that outlay up in the purchase price of the houses," Shamus assured me blandly.

"Speaking of purchases, Mom," Simon said, "you forgot to get more coffee . . . and someone" — he looked at his sister — "ate the whole box of cookies and . . ."

"I'll spot you all to dinner at Lamb Doyle's tonight," said Shamus, and the offer was cheered.

"Could Jimmy come, too? I mean, like we are celebrating, aren't we," said Simon, eagerly, "and he's been in it from the first, so to speak."

"Speaking of whom, guess who just turned in the lane?" said Snow, and the twins nearly got jammed going out the door together, each vociferously claiming the right to tell Jimmy first.

"Oh, good Lord, Shay, should we broadcast it so soon?"

"Trying to back out on me already?"

There was that sort of a grin on his face as he folded his arms around me that made me want to see what would happen if I did.

"Think what a relief it will be to his mother and father," Shay went on in that low, deliciously teasing voice.

"And how distressing to half the female population of Dublin!"

"Each with a bastard under her arm?" he asked, his eyes glinting.

"You *know* I never believed that." I hadn't meant him to take that interpretation.

"Why not?" He wasn't about to let me get away with it.

"Because . . . because . . . because you've got hands! And *they* don't lie!"

Those same hands were arousing rather dangerous sensations in my body, so I grabbed one of them, to give him as good as I'd got, and dragged Shay out to the safety of the great outdoors.

There was no questioning Jimmy's reaction: all systems green and go. When the shouting died, Simon reminded me about "coffee, Mom, you'll die," so Shamus masterfully popped me into his car and took me off, muttering about falling into uxorious ways before the banns could be published.

We went to Sally's store and waited in Sally's register line-up, and Shay kept up the most ridiculous stream of patter with me, then Sally, nodding now and then to people he knew. He seemed to know rather a lot of people. Teddie had, too, but faces didn't light up when Teddie hailed them: They sort of closed up, like defensive clams.

"Good thing we're making it formal, Rene," said Shay with the devil in his eyes as we left the shop. "Or Nosy could really play hare and hounds with your reputation."

"What? Being seen grocery shopping with you?"

"Do American husbands go grocery shopping with their pretty wives?"

"Great American pastime." Of course, Teddie never had. "But we don't have to do it the American way, you know."

His left hand covered mine, and he shot me a brief amused look. "Not going to reform my feckless ways?"

"Good Lord, no. You're just the way I like a man to be."

"And from the back bench a vote of confidence!"

"I am not a reforming woman."

He chuckled. "Oh no?" And I heard his opinion of all I'd got myself into already in Ireland.

"Oh dear."

"Rene, love," and his voice was tender, "not to worry."

And for the first time, I didn't.

## 21

AS SOON AS we pulled up behind my Mercedes, the kids piled out of the house for the groceries and a message for Shamus.

"Shay, the guy up the road, Mick somethingerother," said Simon, "needs you on the site."

"I'll leave the car here, if I may." Shamus grinned. "Now I've got a handy field office too. You see what a conniver I am?"

He didn't kiss me, but the pressure of his hands on mine was a promise.

"I thought you only went for coffee and cookies," said Snow as each of them hauled in a large sack.

"I was talking," I said haughtily, and suggested that she had better do the beds, as I was much too stiff to bend down. I made pointed comments to Simon about the length of the front-garden grass and wasn't there a lawn mower somewhere in this queendom? Actually, I wanted a few moments of silence so I could assemble my scattered wits. I also wanted to savor the elation of Shamus's proposal. I hadn't been so absolutely euphoric since . . . since the twins were born? Good Lord, fourteen years ago? Oh, no, I'd had some brief spells of happiness. Into each rain some life must fall?

I was, at this precious moment, happy, and I would wallow in the experience, knowing it might have to last me a bit. Disenchantment has a way of creeping up on you. I thought back to the day Teddie had proposed. Good God, I'd had to shop that day too. And he couldn't find the brand of tomato ketchup he preferred. You'd've thought the shop had not ordered it to spite Teddie. Of course, I agreed with him that day.

I shook myself. I was not superstitious. I said it out loud. I also told myself that Shay was a much more stable personality. I couldn't imagine Teddie patiently enduring Aunt Irene's ostracism of him. No, Shay was a man.

I'd thought Teddie was a man too, hadn't I? At nineteen who knows what's a man?

Maybe I *was* rushing into marriage again. I'd been

separated two years, true, but my divorce was barely seven months old. The twins liked Shamus, but as a permanent fixture? But he did seem to know how to cope with Snow without steamrollering her the way her father had started doing.

And it's lovely to get swept off your feet in a romantic fashion, but . . .

Dully I found places for cans of beans and tins of fruit.

Shay really could be marrying me for the land. I'd have to be very cautious and keep the queendom in my name. Surely a wife could hold property in her own right in Ireland — and if Shamus Kerrigan was marrying me for me, he wouldn't object.

I heard a car driving up the lane: Michael coming to extricate me from my latest escapade. And he wouldn't be all that happy about the latest development with Shamus, now, would he?

I sighed and straightened my shoulders. Thinking pleasant thoughts, I went to admit my caller.

Teddie's angry face glowered down at me.

"What the hell are you still doing here?" demanded Teddie, his eyes popping from his skull and his face flushing violently, as it did when he was upset.

"Where else would I be?"

He rallied quickly, more quickly than his second wife did. Florence stared as if I were the last person she had expected to see. She also looked slightly embarrassed.

"Is this hovel where you've stashed my children?" he demanded.

"As it's an excellent example of Georgian farmhouse architecture, and I've already been offered seventy-five thousand dollars for it, it can't be classed as a hovel."

"Seventy-five thousand bucks for this?"

In the shock of seeing Ted Stanford on my once-safe Irish doorstep, I had responded with the first things that came into my head. By instinct, I had chosen the one effective stopper: snobbery. Teddie instantly reassessed the place, as did Number Two. She wasn't a bad thing, after all.

"So . . . where the hell are they?"

"The children?"

"I sure as hell didn't come three thousand miles to see your face again, Irene."

I didn't flinch under that old twisting sneer of his. I couldn't. I was frozen solid. He'd come to see the twins? That made as little sense as his coming three thousand miles to see me.

"I've got a legal right to see my own kids," Teddie went on. "Only don't try shooting at me, Annie Oakley, or you'll be in more trouble than you already are. They deport undesirable aliens, you know. And it is Saturday, the legally agreed-upon visiting day."

Because I was clutching the door frame, I remained upright, and my mind parroted, *It is legal. He does have the legal right . . . but I don't want* them *to see* him. *It'll upset them terribly.*

"They've made other plans for the day."

"They can damned well unmake them. *I'm* here."

"*Quod erat demonstrandum!*"

An angry flush reddened his cheeks still more. "Quit the stalling, Rene. Where are they? And I'm warning you, I'm looking into this business of your firing a shotgun irresponsibly around minors."

"Speaking of firing, that Mayday you gave the ISPCC has backfired. They were looking for kids in their diapers."

"Oh?" Teddie affected smug innocence. "My secretary must have mistranscribed her dictation." He took a step closer to the door. "Simon! Your dad's here," he yelled. "Ready and waiting. Sara? Where are you, dollface? Your daddy's come to see you."

His yell was superfluous.

"I'm here," Snow's voice came from behind me. She was crouched on the stairs, her fingers gripping the banister so hard that the knuckles were white.

"Dad." Simon's voice announced his presence right beside me. And I wanted to burst into tears at the sound of defeat in their subdued voices.

"Snow, honey, I can't see you. Come give your old daddy a big smacker." Teddie had executed one of those lightning changes of his. Now he was Ye Affable Sire, Doting Daddy, Popular Papa. He peered over my head toward the stairs, Eager

Smile #3 splitting his face in two. He took another step, but I blocked his way. I did not want Teddie's aura to contaminate my house. As he moved to push me aside, Simon stepped into the breach, his hand formally extended to his father. Teddie shook hands absently, then frowned as he realized he was being prevented from entering the house.

"Simon! What a formal way to greet your old man after all this time!"

"I saw you three weeks ago, sir." Simon took a deep breath. "Sara and I resent the way you've been persecuting Mother."

"Persecuting her? Ah, now, Simon boy, I didn't persecute her." Teddie displayed incredulous, jocular denial.

"With a private detective watching us? With that nonsense of the ISPCC? You only thought that up to embarrass Mother."

I stared at Simon, as astonished as his father. Then I felt Snow's hand fiercely latching on to mine. She edged close between me and Simon, her young mouth taut and her face very pale.

"Not to mention embarrassing us with all our friends," she said, "with stupid questions they couldn't have answered. And what excuse do you have for hanging on to the support money? Mother didn't fleece you, as she should've. You're getting off easy and you know it. You laugh about it often enough with those precious friends of yours—"

"Snow!" I couldn't believe the way she was addressing her father.

Teddie gawked, speechless for once, at his daughter. His wife had eased herself away from the doorway, hoping not to become the next target.

"Why, you filthy bitch," Teddie said to me, his eyes blazing, his chest swelling with inhaled anger, "turning my own kids against me . . . What kind of—why, I'll—" His clenched fist lifted.

"I wouldn't do that!" said Simon, stepping in front of me.

I gasped at the unnatural sight of my son raising a fist to his father.

"My son!" exclaimed Teddie in a muted whisper. "My

only son, ready to strike his dad! What have you done to my children? I'll have you in court for this! You can't corrupt two nice — "

"You're a fine one to talk about corrupting. Daddy-dear." Snow's strident voice was almost unrecognizable. She'd stepped up beside Simon, but she still held my hand in that bone-crushing grip. "Oh, you've got a nerve! Corrupting? Nothing's too good for the client, is it, Daddy-dear? Including your own — "

"SNOW!" Simon's shout was a warning and a command for silence, but I'd heard what she hadn't said. And Teddie knew. His face turned white, and he staggered back, away from the revulsion in his daughter's face and voice.

I clutched at the door frame, because everything was whirling about me. Of all the things I'd imagined might have happened that night at the Harrisons', this . . . this . . . was appalling. No wonder the twins had turned against their father! When I thought of all the platitudes I'd uttered . . . of how often I'd tried to build their father's image in their eyes . . . And then he'd pandered to preserve an account . . .

"I think you'd better leave, Mr. Stanford." Shay's calm voice broke the tableau. "It should be obvious, even to you, that your children do not wish for your company."

"But they've got to. I mean, I'm their father!" Teddie had a very curious notion about rights and prerogatives. "I mean, I've got to have a chance to talk to them. There's been a terrible misunderstanding. They got it all wrong. She's brainwashed them — "

"Simon, Sara." This time it was Michael speaking.

The shock which had engulfed me cleared enough for me to realize that we were scarcely alone in the front yard. Shamus and Michael stood on the left, with George and Kieron by the gate and Mary and Ann at the driveway: the loyal courtiers come to relieve the beleaguered queen.

"I'm Mrs. Teasey's solicitor, Mr. Stanford. I've been in touch with Mr. van Vliet."

"Good man, now we can settle this all legally." Teddie turned with smug self-assurance to Michael, his hand out-stretched. Michael evaded that issue by reaching into his jacket pocket for some papers. Teddie redirected his hand to his forehead in an exaggerated gesture of relief. "I came here to avail myself of the visiting privilege granted me by the court. I have the right to see my children every Saturday during the year and to have them for a two-week vacation in the summer. I have decided to take them on a European trip, since they're halfway there already" — Teddie's attempt at a jocular laugh met with no responsive echo — "and this morning we're going to discuss where they'd like to go."

"No, Mommy, no," said Snow, clinging to me, once more a child needing her mother's protection. Oh, God, how I hoped that spitting demon of a few moments ago had disappeared . . . forever.

A hopelessness had settled on Simon's face at Michael's words, but now he was glaring intently at the solicitor. Hearing something?

"Yes, sir, those are your legal rights," Michael said agreeably. I felt as cold as Simon looked.

"However, your children are now over fourteen, aren't they?"

"Well, yes, of course they are. Don't they look it?" asked Teddie smugly, as if he were solely responsible.

"Under American law, and indeed under Irish law, they do have certain rights at that age, which I believe Mr. van Vliet explained fully to them."

All at once the taut spring in Simon's back relaxed, and he turned to his father.

"Thank you very much for the invitation, Father, but we decline," he said, quietly but decisively.

"You . . . you *what*?" Teddie's head jutted forward from his body in utter astonishment.

"We don't want to go with you," Simon said, gathering courage from the expressions of support on the faces of our friends.

"Nothing would get us to go with you again, anywhere, Daddy," said Snow, with a resurgence of that bitterness.

"But — but —"

"I think that's plain enough, Mr. Stanford," said

Michael. "Your children do not wish to accompany you. I'd suggest you leave."

"Leave?" Teddie's eyes popped out again, his chest swelled, and his face reddened alarmingly.

It was a sight which had often reduced me to ineffectual tears and pleas for forgiveness. Now he only looked ridiculous. He was drinking too much again, I thought with utter detachment. He'd put on a lot of flab. She really ought to get him on a high-protein diet. He doesn't resist that.

"Yes," Michael was saying, "leave." He stepped up to Teddie with a gesture of dismissal.

"Now just a living minute!"

Teddie solidly planted his feet, and I knew he was capable of slugging everyone in sight.

"Where the hell did all of you come from?" he demanded, just then aware of the full audience.

"Sure and we're friends of the children and Mrs. Teasey," said Kieron in a dangerously soft voice. "Come to speed you on your way, since you're leaving."

"Why you little sawed-off Irish bastard—"

Kieron assumed a semi-crouch, which would have warned anyone not blind that the "little sawed-off Irish bastard" was prime for a rough-house.

"Oh, for God's sake, Ted, John Wayne you are not," said the second Mrs. Stanford in utter disgust. "And there are four of them! Let's clear out. If your two kids don't want to go, who needs 'em? I don't. They'll be sorry soon enough."

If she hadn't added that last remark, she might not have succeeded.

"It'll be too late then," said Teddie, drawing himself up with massive and sorrowful dignity. "I've missed our weekly get-togethers, kids. I've worried about you a great deal. One day you were safely in Westfield, where I could keep a good watch over you . . ." Even Teddie saw the inappropriateness of that line, because Simon's head jerked up and Snow's laugh reminded him of the kind of watch he had been keeping. "Well," and Teddie half turned, head bowed, "you always know where to reach me. You've my telephone number in case of emergencies. You're still my children . . . Good-bye."

I think the catch of his breath was sincere, but he spoiled it with a sideways glance to see how effective he'd been. We all held our positions until we heard his car start up.

Snow's eyes still flashed with anger and anxiety. "He'll think of some other ploy. He always does!"

"Perhaps," said Shamus with gentle amusement. Snow gave him a dark look, but his attitude evidently reassured her. Then he began to unhook my fingers from the door frame, and smoothed them out on one palm. "Holding the house up, Rene?"

"Vice versa," I managed to reply through a dry mouth. Would my legs work if I asked them to move me? Shamus now took my arm as if he heard. I leaned into him gratefully. "Thank God you appeared. If you hadn't . . . And Michael, you scared me to death for a moment. But how'd you know?"

"I sent Jimmy for the Marines," said Simon, with a ghost of a grin on his anxious face, "the moment I saw Dad coming up the walk."

Michael took my other arm and led me into the living room. "I thought Henry van Vliet had explained your rights to refuse," Michael said to Simon and Snow. "He told me that you'd both asked about that on several occasions."

"What?" I stared at the twins. "You never told me . . ."

"We don't tell all," said Snow facetiously.

"But you always went . . . you made no protest . . ."

"Because he'd've made things tough on you, Mom," said Simon, at his most conciliatory, "if we hadn't gone."

"But we *never* went with him in the *evening*," said Snow, her blue eyes blazing again, "not *ever* again!"

"Oh, my darlings, if you'd only told me!" My chest was constricted in anguish for what they had endured.

Snow took my hands in hers and, sitting beside me, kissed me sweetly, reversing our roles for a moment.

"Mommy, it's all right. It's all over, and nothing actually happened. Simon made like big brother."

I decided not to think more about *that* right now . . . or I'd be actively ill. I felt Shay's hand sliding comfortingly around my shoulder, and I was mightily relieved by the thought that he'd now be able to protect Snow.

"What I don't understand is why Hank didn't warn us . . ."

"Actually," Michael said, clearing his throat, "I had a cable from van Vliet this morning . . . came in late last night, in fact . . . warning me that Stanford was on his way with the avowed intent of taking the children. Ostensibly on a European tour, citing the vacation clause of the custody agreement, but van Vliet was convinced that Stanford would fly them to the States and let you battle to get them back."

"That fiend! He can't do that! He can't!" My last vestige of control slipped.

Very calmly, my daughter fetched me a sharp little slap across my cheek. "If there's anything more revolting than a dramatic dad, it's a moaning mom."

I thanked her profusely, tears streaming down my face, but the incipient hysteria didn't overwhelm me, as my children comforted me.

"We can prevent him, Rene," Michael said firmly.

"We bloody well already have," Shay said, laughing.

"But Snow's right," Simon told them. "He'll try."

Shay was looking steadily at Michael, who nodded slowly. "Then, I think, Rene, we'll just sort him out right now," Shay said.

"Jasus, yes," said Kieron. "We've only just lifted the siege on one lady's demesne." He handed me a glass and told me to drink it, not to spill a drop, mind.

Whatever it was burned all the way down, but the quivering of leftover nerves subsided instantly and the pressure of tears behind my eyes eased.

"All right, then," I said, getting more of a grip on myself. "I really do not wish to box myself or the twins up on this queendom like" — I glanced hastily around for fear Ann was in the room — "but I shamefully confess that's my intense desire."

"Nonsense, Rene," said Kieron sharply and with startled concern. "You've shown Ann a thing or two."

"Me?" A poorer example I couldn't imagine just then.

Shay grinned. "You're quite an antidote to Irene, pet, though you start at the same point."

That was too devious for me right then, but at least they

approved, and I didn't want to lose their approval. Shay gave me another squeeze on the shoulders and moved away from the couch. My instant courage dissolved as fast.

"Don't leave ..."

"Sure now, Rene, that ex of yours can't regroup his forces that fast. Most of your bodyguard will stay."

"But where are *you* going?"

"For reinforcements, love."

With that I had to be content.

"Two to one Teddie knows somebody who's buddy-buddy with the Ambassador," I said, determined to be pessimistic.

"All we need," said Snow in an oddly muffled tone, "is for Daddy to meet up with Auntie Alice."

"Oh, for Pete's sake," I exclaimed in sharp disgust, "you come up with the most extraordinary ideas."

"You might say I've had practice, Mommy," Snow replied, propelling herself off the settee and out of the room.

I started to tell her not to leave the house, then realized how silly that was, but Simon, gesturing to Jimmy, went after her. As long as the three were together, they were safe. Jimmy knew who the Marines were in this battle.

"I think if you'll review the situation carefully, Rene, you'll realize that you may be unnecessarily anxious," said Michael.

I heard him thinking that Snow's weren't the only ridiculous ideas. "Humph." I had to get my wits together. "*You* didn't live with that man for fourteen years. His pride has been bruised ... badly. He'll feel he *has* to reinstate himself with his children, if only to prove they were wrong about ..."

"What can he do?" demanded Kieron with irritable sarcasm. "Kidnap 'em? Your daughter's got the lungs of a pig-farmer, and Simon's no way weak."

"I suppose you're right." I began to believe them. And what on earth was that heavenly smell?

Ann walked briskly into the room with a tray, and the three musketeers were right behind her, falling over themselves to keep up with that tantalizing odor.

"You've had a shock and all, Rene, and Snow said you'd no breakfast. So, as the bread was just baked ..."

Kieron and Michael were quite as willing to be fed as I, and once that lovely, still-warm-from-the-oven, violently fattening, delicious brown bread found my stomach, I did indeed feel considerably more like facing whatever other challenges the day presented. We all did.

"Stop fussing with things now, Ann," said Michael, pointing authoritatively for her to be seated by me. He gave me a look, and I suggested to Snow and the boys that they'd better clear the empty bread tray.

"I stopped by to see both Rene and you, Ann. As you know," said Michael, flicking a look at Kieron, "you can get a legal and binding separation from Paddy."

Ann opened her mouth to protest.

"It's no more than the cost of my time in drawing up the proper agreement." Ann kept opening her mouth, and Michael kept waving her silent. Then Kieron grabbed her hand, and she subsided to a low fume. "This is the first time we've had Purdee where we could catch him for a signature. This is the only way in which you can achieve any legal protection against him for just the sort of thing he attempted last night. You can also have sole and legal custody of the children. You can also require him to pay support money—"

"I don't want his money!" cried Ann fiercely.

"Sure and you don't think he'd pay it?" said Kieron with a laugh. "It's only another way of insuring he stays away altogether."

"If he'd sign at all." Ann held no hope for that occurrence.

"Oh, that's no problem now," said Michael, his eyes twinkling at me. "I'm sure Paddy'll sign if Rene is willing to drop charges of trespass."

"Oh!" Clearly Ann hadn't considered that possibility.

"You'd be free to come and go as you please then, Ann," Michael assured her. "He'd need your written permission to enter the house or see the children. And if he so much as grabs your arm, you can have him up for assault."

"Sure and it would cost the earth," she said in a flat voice.

"Oh, for Pete's sake, Ann, don't worry about money," I began. Kieron and Michael flashed me warning glances. "I mean, you've the fees for taking care of another child. I doubt

Michael'll starve in the meantime and—oh hell, after what you've been through, this is what you need . . ." I kept fighting with myself not to play Lady Bountiful.

"Are you certain, Rene?"

Then I heard the root of her anxiety: Was it *right* for *her* to achieve this freedom?

Right in whose eyes, I wondered. Hers, Irish society's, Aunt Irene's? *Had* Aunt Irene suggested a legal separation before? And had Ann refused? Or had Ann not been pushed to the breaking point? Divorce, even among Irish Protestants, was not yet totally accepted, so perhaps divorce had been "dirty" in Aunt Irene's lexicon. But if reassurance was all Ann needed, I could give her that courtesy and be quite honest about it.

"Yes, Ann, I'm positive the separation is right for you. It'd be far better, of course, if you could get a full divorce. You've got nothing to lose, certainly. And you've been existing under . . . under . . . what amounts to a house arrest!" I became exasperated with and furious for her. "You're so young! Live a little! Enjoy." Then, because I felt I was getting too intense, I added with a laugh, "They always say that in the States, 'Enjoy!', but never what."

The quip rated a laugh from the men and a slight, worried smile from Ann.

"Look, you've even forgotten how to smile! Say," and I turned to Michael, "does Paddy Purdee still think it was Aunt Irene's ghost after him?"

Michael ducked his head to hide a broad grin, and Kieron chuckled openly.

"Well, he's not all that certain," said Michael. "The Garda told him Miss Teasey's niece shot off the gun at intruders, but no one's told him that you're an Irene Teasey too, or that you sound exactly like your aunt."

"I like it. I like it," I said. "Do him good. Might even give him some religion."

"It won't do that," Ann said, but, for a wonder, there was a gleam of amusement in her eyes.

"That must be Shay back," said Michael as we all heard the sound of a car braking in the drive.

I hurried to the door, eager to see whom Shamus had brought. The last people in the world whom I would have anticipated! Shay carefully handed out first one, then the other, Lady Brandel.

I was given lavender-scented, silken cheeks to kiss, and soft little hands seized mine while I was beamed upon.

"We were so overjoyed to see dear Shamus, Rene," said Lady Mary, tucking her hand under my right arm while Lady Maud claimed my left. "He's *told* us *all* the happenings. My dear Rene . . ."

"He's also told us how we can help with a few words to the right person," said Lady Maud, "so if we may have permission to use your telephone, Rene . . ." She hesitated before the phone just long enough to receive my dazed acquiescence.

"There are *moments* when a *telephone* is so very *useful*," said Lady Mary, folding her hands in front of her as she took a place beside her sister.

"Whom do *they* know?" I whispered to Shamus as Lady Maud unfolded a tiny notebook and carefully found the page she wanted. She pressed it flat on the table, ran her fingers down the entries, paused, peered, frowned at the number, and then, picking up the receiver, dialed very carefully, silently enunciating each numeral.

"Oh." Her face, serious from the delicate business of dealing with the unfamiliar instrument, brightened. "And good afternoon to you too. Is it at all possible for the Colonel to have a few words with Lady Maud Brandel? The matter is rather urgent . . . Yes, thank you, I'll wait." She turned her head to smile pleasantly at me, all cool, composed Grande Dame. She ignored Lady Mary, who was hovering rather breathlessly.

"Colonel who?" I hissed at Shamus. He signaled me to be patient and listen.

"Oh, Dermot, how good of you! Yes, thank you, I'm quite well. Yes, so is Mary. I trust that Derval and the children are well? Oh? Another grandson? How pleased you must be! Well, I'll come to the point if I may, for I know you're a very busy man. But one of my dearest friends" — she acknowledged that accolade to me with a courtly bow of her head — "is being harassed by an American in the most unpleasant way. Totally unnecessary. Her solicitor is standing by me, and I'm sure he can explain the pertinent details. You will then be able to judge the merits of the case. Yes . . . She's Irene Teasey's niece. You remember Irene, of course. Rene, that's the niece, has inherited Irene's property, you see, no problem that way, but you must know Michael Noonan? Well, let me just put him on to you . . . But I'm sure you'll see that something must be done directly. I know you won't disappoint me." She rose and handed the phone to Michael.

"Noonan here." A stunned look came over Michael's face, and unconsciously he stood straight, all attention. "Yes, *sir!*"

"I'm positive that Dermot can oblige," said Lady Maud as she and Mary drew me into the living room. Shamus gave me a push from behind.

"That *dreadful* man!" Lady Mary was saying. "When Shamus *told* us, we were *appalled* to think of the *ordeal* you've been through . . . How distressing for our twins!"

"Shay, did you tell them *everything*?"

"Oh, Rene, we'd've *heard* it *soon enough* anyway, you know," said Lady Mary reassuringly, and she peered across me at her sister for confirmation.

"Pleasant to have the truth of a matter from a competent source" was Lady Maud's reply as she smoothed her skirts out on the couch.

"You see, *we* know *just* the person to *assist* you."

"Who?" I asked bluntly.

"Let's just say, a high-ranking official at the Castle," said Shamus. "I don't think he'll care for official thanks."

"Well? What's going to happen, then?"

"Oh," and Shay's eyes got wide and devilish. "I would suspect that shortly several officials will call on your ex-husband at his hotel and suggest, very politely, that his presence is unacceptable to the Irish Republic. He will be politely escorted to the airport and put on the first available flight out. And I don't think he will ever get back in again."

"But—but—" That was more than I'd counted on. "Can they *do* that?"

"You're in Ireland."

"But—but—"

"It's such a relief," said Lady Maud at her most placid, "to know that we could perform a little service for you . . . and Irene . . . after all you've done for us."

Her expression was guileless — like Snow's — but I wondered then, as I've wondered often since, if Lady Maud and Lady Mary were quite as ignorant of the origin of their trust fund as everyone assumed.

"Now, what is this that Shamus has been telling us about you two, dear Rene?"

I could not deny it in the face of their obvious delight and pleasure.

"And *how* could dear Irene have *so* misjudged Shamus? *You* barely *knew* him and yet *you* realized that he was *incapable* of *so* ungentlemanly a *deed*."

I stared at Shay, who grinned and shrugged. "They *are* over eighteen, pet."

"As I've had occasion to remark to you before, Rene," said Lady Maud, putting a conciliatory hand on my arm, "we are aware of the ways of the world, whether we chose to follow them or not."

Simon, Snow and Jimmy came traipsing delicately in at that point, tray-laden. Before I knew it, I was eating again, drinking tea with the good Ladies. Michael joined us rather absently, and soon rose abruptly. "I have some legal tying up to do," he said. "If anything develops, I'll ring you this evening, Rene. Lady Maud, Lady Mary," and he bent with graceful dignity over each daintily extended hand. "My respects!" His grin indicated that he'd recovered his composure.

One day, I'd find out who had impressed him so!

"Don't panic, Mihall, if we don't answer here between seven and midnight," Shamus was saying as he and I escorted Michael to the door. "We've some celebrating to do, if Rene feels up to it."

"Of course Mommy'll feel up to it," said Snow emphatically. "She's going right upstairs now and rest."

"I'm being bossed."

The Ladies Brandel said that they would have been prostrate with exhaustion and wasn't I clever, and it was so nice to know that my lovely children and I were staying on in

Ireland. They'd really get to know us. And I was going to sing with the Rathmines group now, wasn't I? Carrying on in Irene's tradition?

Michael then offered to drive them home, as it was on his way. Which seemed a neat ending to the day's activities.

As usual, Irene Teasey spoke too soon. No sooner had Michael's car pulled out into the main road than another came slithering over the loose gravel at the entrance.

"Good God, now what?" I complained, moving closer to Shamus in alarm. "I've seen that car before. It's Aunt Alice!"

"Good!" said Shay. "I've a crow to pluck with the old cow."

As well he was primed, because Auntie Alice Hegarty came charging out of her car, her face suffused with the blood of angry vengeance. It was me she headed for. Shay's hand was strong and warm against the small of my back. Not that I would have retreated. I was (Preserve the Image!) too proud.

"You'll sell now, won't you? You promised!"

"Sell?"

"And you!" She wheeled on Shamus, brandishing her rather heavy handbag. "Your check was stopped. You had no right to stop it!"

"All the right in the world, you old phony. You had no right to sell me access up the lane. Then or now. I think I'd better have a word with Tom."

"Tom doesn't enter into this matter at all!" She was defiant, and scared.

Oh, Tom was her husband, Gerry's father. The big-bear man who played accordion. But *he* scared Alice, even if he appeared innocuous to me.

"Perhaps not, Alice Hegarty. I could of course prosecute you for illegally selling rights you did not possess."

"Prosecute me?" She took another backward step. "I won't go to court. No Hegarty has ever been dragged into court." She got her second wind too quickly for my liking. "*You!*" The purse swung round to me. "You! You said you'd sell once the will was probated."

"I said I couldn't sell until the will was probated, Mrs.

Hegarty." I took a deep breath. "And I certainly wouldn't sell to you."

"You'll be glad enough to be quit of Ireland when that fancy man of yours finds you and takes your brats away."

"He's been and gone," Shay said, his voice treacherous as silk, because I was bereft of speech. "And I'd say it was yourself told Paddy Purdee where to find Ann?"

"Of course it was," and the angry red returned to Auntie Alice's face. "I'll have the whole lot cleared out of here . . ."

Two more cars came tearing up the lane. Winnie Teasey popped out of the first one, in such a state that the car stalled with a buck. The other driver was Gerry, his usually affable face set in hard, angry lines.

It became a Donnybrook of words: Alice raging with frustration, Winnie wringing her hands. Shamus was adding some trenchant remarks about illegal permissions. Winnie said that he shouldn't upset poor Alice this way with talk of courts and suing. Shamus wanted to know what else could he do. Alice raved about his stopping checks when he'd made a strictly business arrangement . . .

"What check?" asked Gerry, in such a roar that everyone shut up.

"Why," said Shay, completely at ease, "the money I paid her for the use of this lane, which she didn't have the legal right to lease."

Gerry turned slowly to his mother. She drew her small stout self up against his scrutiny.

"This property is mine, Gerard. You *know* Irene meant to leave it all to me . . ."

"I know nothing of the kind, Mother. Now get in that car and drive home. Unless you want me to tell Dad that you've been meddling again?"

She didn't want to go. She opened her mouth to protest, but Gerry took her firmly by the elbow and marched her to her car. Winnie had been reduced to sobbing, wringing her hands and murmuring. "How could Alice? How can she be this way?"

When his mother's car swung on to the main road, just missing a truck, which honked a loud, continuous blast, Gerry turned to his aunt.

"Now, you calm down too, Winnie. Get along home, and we'll say no more about this."

She was being deftly inserted into her car by Gerry. Bucking and stalling it, she did manage to turn it around and leave.

"I *will* have to tell my father, I think," Gerry said to us. "I can't even say she means well, Rene," and Gerry sighed. "But we'll sort her out. Not to worry. I'd better go after her, if you'll excuse me. And forgive?"

I hastily assured him I did, and then he was away, leaving a cloud of dust to settle on the well-used lane.

"Well, will he?"

"Will he what, pet?" asked Shay guiding me back to the house.

"Contain her."

Shamus chuckled. "Sure enough. Once Tom hears of this, Alice will be mild for months. There are, you know," and he smiled affectionately at me, "some good reasons for Irish men to beat their wives. Now and then only, of course — for the good of their souls and the peace of the neighborhood." His hand gently pushed me into my house. "Now, you're to go upstairs, alone, and get some rest. You've had enough on your plate."

"The twins?" I knew it was silly, but I was apprehensive.

"I won't take my eyes off them," he said, capturing my waving hands and drawing me close to him for a very satisfactory kiss. Very satisfactory because I was thinking that the twins were big enough to keep an eye on themselves, and I wanted his on me.

"Oh!"

We broke away, or rather I tried to, at the soft exclamation of dismay.

Ann was in the doorway to the dining room, looking flustered and utterly dismayed at our carrying-on. Blankness came over Shamus's face.

"We'd better all be friends," I said to neither in particular, "and let bygones be. You'll be seeing a lot of Shay again, Ann."

"A lot?" Shamus challenged my qualifier.

Ann's lips met in a firm line of disapproval.

"Yes, Ann, a lot. In fact, you might say a continuous

performance, if he hasn't changed his mind after all the tumult and shouting today."

Shay's hand crept up my shoulders to rest on the back of my neck in the most caressing and possessive of gestures. I felt feline enough to want to wiggle with delight at that touch. But Ann was there, and I should Preserve the Image.

The hell with that! I'd preserved, destroyed, tried on enough Images for one person for the rest of her lifetime. From now on I was going to be me, Irene Teasey Stanford . . . God willing . . . Kerrigan.

"I've discovered that *I* can't function properly without a man in my life, Ann," I said, looking at her unapologetically as I pressed closer to Shay. "I like having a man to take care of, who'll return the courtesy by taking care of me. And yes, I made a mistake, and I may make many more."

"Not with me, pet," murmured Shay, so fervently that Ann stared at him in a startled fashion.

"But I'm not about to close the book of my life for one mistake, and you shouldn't either, Ann Purdee."

She looked so stricken at my attack that I relented and reached out to her.

"Ann, honey, it's right for me, for the way I am. I know it is now. I wouldn't have thought so even three weeks ago, believe me. I'd finished with men. But I'm not too proud or too stubborn or too stupid to change my mind for a good reason. And now that Paddy Purdee's off your back, you can look around a bit too."

She shuddered at a notion still abhorrent to her. I now appreciated my friend Betty's wry smile.

"That's what this is all about, Ann, your being here. It's probably what Aunt Irene really wanted for you, in good time. It's what women's lib is all about—you, me, Mary, Sally, the Ladies Brandel, everyone having a chance to find their own way to . . . Oooops, I'm sorry. I'm the last one who should sermonize anyone! Enjoy! Enjoy, Ann, let yourself enjoy even a little!" I broke free from Shay's insidious proximity and rushed halfway up the stairs in my embarrassment at having spouted so intensely. "If you want to pick up the pieces about seven,

Shay dear, I'll be ready. But right now I have to regroup my energies, as Snow used to say."

"At seven, then, your courtier will await thee, Queen Irene!" Shamus swept another of those ridiculously involved, flourishing bows. "She makes a bloody good queen, doesn't she, Ann?" I heard him say as I clattered up the rest of the steps.

"Sure and she does!" replied Ann, so firmly that I knew I *could* rest awhile. My queendom, for the moment at least, was in good hands!

# BESTSELLERS
## FROM TOR

| | | | |
|---|---|---|---|
| ☐ ☐ | 50570-0 | ALL ABOUT WOMEN<br>*Andrew M. Greeley* | $4.95<br>Canada $5.95 |
| ☐ ☐ | 58341-8<br>58342-6 | ANGEL FIRE<br>*Andrew M. Greeley* | $4.95<br>Canada $5.95 |
| ☐ ☐ | 52725-9<br>52726-7 | BLACK WIND<br>*F. Paul Wilson* | $4.95<br>Canada $5.95 |
| ☐ ☐ | 51392-4 | LONG RIDE HOME<br>*W. Michael Gear* | $4.95<br>Canada $5.95 |
| ☐ ☐ | 50350-3 | OKTOBER<br>*Stephen Gallagher* | $4.95<br>Canada $5.95 |
| ☐ ☐ | 50857-2 | THE RANSOM OF BLACK STEALTH One<br>*Dean Ing* | $5.95<br>Canada $6.95 |
| ☐ ☐ | 50088-1 | SAND IN THE WIND<br>*Kathleen O'Neal Gear* | $4.50<br>Canada $5.50 |
| ☐ ☐ | 51878-0 | SANDMAN<br>*Linda Crockett* | $4.95<br>Canada $5.95 |
| ☐ ☐ | 50214-0<br>50215-9 | THE SCHOLARS OF NIGHT<br>*John M. Ford* | $4.95<br>Canada $5.95 |
| ☐ ☐ | 51826-8 | TENDER PREY<br>*Julia Grice* | $4.95<br>Canada $5.95 |
| ☐ ☐ | 52188-4 | TIME AND CHANCE<br>*Alan Brennert* | $4.95<br>Canada $5.95 |

Buy them at your local bookstore or use this handy coupon:
Clip and mail this page with your order.

Publishers Book and Audio Mailing Service
P.O. Box 120159, Staten Island, NY 10312-0004

Please send me the book(s) I have checked above. I am enclosing $ _____
(please add $1.25 for the first book, and $.25 for each additional book to cover postage and handling.
Send check or money order only—no CODs).

Name _____

Address _____

City _____ State/Zip _____

Please allow six weeks for delivery. Prices subject to change without notice.

# SUSPENSE FROM
# ELIZABETH PETERS

| | | | |
|---|---|---|---|
| ☐ | 50752-5 | BORROWER OF THE NIGHT | $3.95 |
| ☐ | 50753-3 | | Canada $4.95 |
| ☐ | 50770-3 | THE CAMELOT CAPER | $4.50 |
| ☐ | 51241-3 | | Canada $5.50 |
| ☐ | 50756-8 | THE DEAD SEA CIPHER | $3.95 |
| ☐ | 50757-6 | | Canada $4.95 |
| ☐ | 50789-4 | DEVIL-MAY-CARE | $4.50 |
| ☐ | 50790-8 | | Canada $5.50 |
| ☐ | 50791-6 | DIE FOR LOVE | $3.95 |
| ☐ | 50792-4 | | Canada $4.95 |
| ☐ | 50002-4 | JACKAL'S HEAD | $3.95 |
| ☐ | 50003-2 | | Canada $4.95 |
| ☐ | 50750-9 | LEGEND IN GREEN VELVET | $3.95 |
| ☐ | 50751-7 | | Canada $4.95 |
| ☐ | 51242-1 | LION IN THE VALLEY | $4.50 |
| ☐ | | | Canada $5.50 |
| ☐ | 50727-4 | THE LOVE TALKER | $3.95 |
| ☐ | | | Canada $4.95 |
| ☐ | 50793-2 | THE MUMMY CASE | $3.95 |
| ☐ | 50794-0 | | Canada $4.95 |
| ☐ | 50773-8 | THE NIGHT OF FOUR HUNDRED RABBITS | $4.50 |
| ☐ | 50774-6 | | Canada $5.50 |

Buy them at your local bookstore or use this handy coupon:
Clip and mail this page with your order.

Publishers Book and Audio Mailing Service
P.O. Box 120159, Staten Island, NY 10312-0004

Please send me the book(s) I have checked above. I am enclosing $ _____
(Please add $1.25 for the first book, and $.25 for each additional book to cover postage and handling.
Send check or money order only—no CODs.)

Name _____
Address _____
City _____ State/Zip _____
Please allow six weeks for delivery. Prices subject to change without notice.

# FANTASY BESTSELLERS
# FROM TOR